W9-BZF-014

"TARGETS features intelligence operations in Saigon in 1969. Major Charles Taylor, tough and professional, but given to following his conscience, joins an undercover unit whose seemingly impossible task is to locate a certain Binh, an important VC agent. . . . Information gathered in sleazy bars, ambush, murder, brutal 'interrogations,' and the tracking of targets hard to identify and harder to kill. . . . Taylor finds his search complicated by a GI drug trafficking operation, a hostile American journalist, and his love for a beautiful Vietnamese. . . .Excitement aplenty!"
—*Publishers Weekly*

"Enough action, tension, and good writing to keep the reader pinned down to the couch for a weekend."
—*Lone Star Book Review*

TARGETS

a novel by
DONALD E. McQUINN

TOR

A TOM DOHERTY ASSOCIATES BOOK

TARGETS

Copyright © 1980 by Donald E. McQuinn

A Tor Book

Published by Tom Doherty Associates, 8-10 W. 36th St., New York City, N.Y. 10018

First printing, March 1983

ISBN: 0-523-48060-1

Printed in the United States of America

Distributed by Pinnacle Books, 1430 Broadway, New York, N.Y. 10018

To CAROL,
for all things

The jets went to full power, heat-shimmering thunder heaving the plane into the air with a suddenness that sent stewardesses lurching down the aisles. The lights of Travis Air Force Base still glittered behind and below when the voice came over the intercom.

"This is the pilot speaking. Sorry about the hurried takeoff, everyone, but you'll be happy to know we went wheels-up at eleven-fifty-nine. Your tour in Vietnam starts as of the eleventh. Remember that when you get there, because it'll cut your tour by one day."

Everyone cheered.

BOOK ONE

1

THE APPROACH TO SAIGON was delusive, the August masses of seasonal rain clouds permitting only glimpses of static green mountains, fields, and paddies. The stewardesses, however, were in constant motion, almost running up and down the aisles, their tension growing as if in relationship to the terrain detail as the 707 lowered.

The constant hum of conversation across the South China Sea after the stop at Clark Field in the Philippines had ebbed to infrequent comment as the coastline of Vietnam crawled across the horizon. An even more infrequent laugh hung in the air like an unpleasant remark.

Taylor noticed the stewardesses invariably fretted and turned to mark the source, young schoolteachers unsure of their classroom discipline. He wondered if any of them had seen breakdowns on the entry flight and decided it was unlikely. The whole business was such a mess of hurry-up-and-wait that no one had much time to brood.

He looked out the window again, forcing himself to the realization that he was back and there was a war going on down there. It was a different picture this far south. When he'd flown out of Chu Lai a few years ago, he'd gone by chopper to Da Nang—they'd seen two fire fights on the trip. And here he was returning with a bellyful of steak served by a lovely woman.

Everything was going to be different. Seventeen years in the business and for the first time he'd be on a staff too big for him to know everyone. It was at once a blessing and a curse. He'd always enjoyed the closeness of the people he'd worked with before. Now he was a passed-over Marine officer, failed of selection to Lieutenant Colonel. It was a peculiar position. He compared it to a falling from grace. It had still been an unpleasant shock to find that some old friends tended to avoid him.

They were settling faster now, banking sharply. As they pierced the swirling whiteness of clouds the city appeared suddenly as a sprawling mass of muted colors. The filtered light palled even the vigor of the paddies. He was thinking it was a singularly unimpressive welcome when they made a hard turn and he knew this was the approach leg. Pressing his face to the window to look ahead, he noted the incredible clutter of aircraft parked around the airport. He recognized insignia from the US, Korea, and Vietnam instantly, but some others escaped him. Observation planes taxied around lumbering cargo and passenger craft like small herd dogs. Helicopters flitted on bee-like errands. Everything stayed well clear of the runway as the 707 touched down.

It was an obeisance. This was the entry of a queen, the arrival of a superstar. As long as the Deltas, the Pan Ams, the Braniffs, the TWAs continued to appear, the exiles would know that The World was still out there somewhere. The 707 carried in her belly a commitment. Rested, she would take on the responsibility of transporting those who had made their contribution to that commitment, survived, and were going home. It was no simple safety precaution that cleared the way for her. She was the Freedom Bird, now that she was on the ground, and protecting her was as elemental as the possessiveness of a prisoner toward a barred patch of sunlight.

The doors swung open as a voice tumbled out of the intercom. After eighteen hours of voices and instructions, Taylor mentally sifted out key words.

"—copies of orders—board buses from the front of the aircraft—directly into the terminal—entry briefing—"

He picked up the manila envelope holding his records and shuffled down the aisle. Looking back, he saw a blonde stewardess crying. One of her partners held her, stroking the golden hair as the trim body jerked with sobs.

It seemed out of place to Taylor. He hadn't expected brass bands to signify his personal entry to Saigon, but it vaguely irritated him that his last contact with home should be the sight of an unknown girl crying goodbye to strangers.

8

He continued the herdlike debarkation, dredging his mind to determine why the girl should disturb him. Then he realized it reminded him of similar scenes with his former wife. She never understood, either. Memories flooded his consciousness instantly at the sudden collapse of a dam of denials carefully constructed brick by brick over the years. He willed his attention to a study of the neck in front of him.

Saigon's late afternoon drizzle caressed his face as he exited. There was a moment of surprise at the faint cloud of steam rising from the runway, followed by resignation to its inevitability. A first deep breath was a greeting, the thick air burdened with the unmistakable odor of the Orient. The rain didn't wash it from the atmosphere nor could time and distance scrub it from the memory. In a few days it would be part of his clothing. In a week it would go unnoticed. In a month the lack of it would have him sniffing and pivoting like an old blind dog.

For now, however, Taylor wanted to absorb every detail available to his senses. The airline flags over the Tan Son Nhut terminal building twisted and snarled in the light breeze, bright against the overcast. To the right, passengers disembarked from an Air Viet Nam craft. He decided it must be Caravelle. He'd assumed he'd be seeing a lot of French influence around Saigon and made a mental note to insure he wasn't simply leaping to a conclusion.

His attention was drawn back to the debarking civilians. Old women carried bundles that could be lunch or jewels, men in suits carried briefcases. One tall blond Caucasian hurried to the front of the crowd. An Oriental trotted behind him, looped and packsaddled in a melange of photographic equipment.

Two Vietnamese girls in shimmering blue *ao dais* flanked the group while a third preceded it, the three of them conjuring their flock toward an exit gate with unobtrusive charm. The off-loading men saw them and a general murmur of approval hummed from the line. Taylor remembered reading that the *ao dai* enjoyed the reputation of being the most beautiful of national dresses. He also remembered that the pronunciation was ow-zigh. No matter what they called it, the sheath from neck to ankle, slit up to the knee so the black-trousered legs could move freely, was both simple and attractive.

Then he was down the ladder and entering the waiting bus. The bored Vietnamese driver watched an Army MP in pressed fatigues checking names off a roster. The trooper looked up as Taylor boarded.

"Major Taylor, Charles Alfred?"

Taylor nodded shortly, turning to find a seat. The MP interrupted him.

"Are you going to the Marine Advisory Group, Major, or to MACV?"

"MACV. Why?"

"Wanted to save some hassle if you were headed for the MAG, sir." He gestured toward the terminal. "They pick up their own people here and I could direct you to them. Checking in's a big enough problem without going to all the wrong places." The MP smiled, the old hand enjoying knowing all the ropes. It was a familiar game.

"Thanks. I appreciate it. Do I just ride along with the crowd, then?"

"Yes, sir. Just have a seat and we'll get everyone committed to this loony-bin right on schedule."

They both laughed and Taylor moved along, pleased to find the bus was air-conditioned, a Japanese Isuzu. He wondered what the difference in price would be between this one and an equivalent US model and fervently hoped the subject would never come up back home. The American model would cost more, even without the air-conditioner. Let some politician get his teeth into that one and that'd be the last of the Japanese buses.

An additional touch was the security fence mesh over the windows to prevent grenades being thrown through the glass. A friend of Taylor's had described such an incident.

"You never saw anything like it, Tay. I never saw naked panic before and, by God, I hope I never do again. That thing came—crash!—through the window and thirty men went apeshit. Guys were trying to grab it, trying to get out, screaming, hollering—everything. Then it went off. The goddam bus went up on the sidewalk and Viets went in all directions. One of those motorized rickshaw things—a cyclo—flew right by the window like a fucking bird—the engine was still running. I was standing outside before I found out I had a chunk in my butt."

The man telling the story had grinned. "How's that for a war story to tell your grandchildren? 'What'd you do during the war, Grampa?' 'I got fragged in the ass riding a bus in beautiful downtown Saigon.' I'll spend the rest of my life hoping no one asks how I got my second Purple Heart."

They'd laughed then, drinking to honorable wounds honorably received.

Now Taylor studied the wire with the feeling that if he knew where to look he'd see his own mortality reluctantly exposed like the quivering muscle tissue in a deep wound. He noted the location of the emergency door.

The bus slid into motion and he stared past a seatmate, watching the crowd flow around the terminal. In spite of the abounding uniformed personnel, it was hard to conceive of Tan Son Nhut as a combat zone. The majority of the people were civilians. He amused himself wondering which were VC, a harmless occupation on a par with crossword puzzles. The rest of the day would be a loss, "checking in," the process of being properly fed into the hopper. In keeping with that drab prospect, the bus stopped. The trip had covered approximately two hundred yards.

Out of the bus. Into the terminal. MP briefing. Drone, drone, drone. Back on the bus. Around the side of the terminal, through the parking lot. Full of cars, an amazing number of cars. Few American models. International road signs. The yellow bulk of MACV Headquarters—past it. The MP, roting his Grayline guide bit, so incongruous Taylor thought it'd drive him mad.

"That's MACV Headquarters on your right. For any of you who haven't read your orders, that's Military Assistance Command, Vietnam." A pause for laughter passed in silence.

"Most of you'll be assigned here. Those going up-country won't have to go inside, but you'll draw your gear here tomorrow before you leave to join your outfits."

Taylor stared at a large brick building on the left, obviously left over from some previous use of the land. It was actually two buildings about thirty yards apart with a lattice roof joining them. In disrepair, it was splattered with the signs of squatter occupancy—children raced around it, ranging from half-dressed to naked, rickety tables defied stacks of cookware, laundry hung on bushes in the rain, waiting for sunshine. A small herd of goats browsed on tethers, safely distant from the clothes.

Another bend in the road and the MP said, "On your left is the famous Rainbow Room, men. Please don't hesitate to wave back at the ladies trying to attract your attention. If you're billeted here, you'll find them totally hospitable."

Lending action to his own words, he leaned past the driver and waved at the half-dozen girls standing outside the bar. Young and remarkably pretty, they squealed and laughed and waved at the bus. Amid a chorus of whistles and masculine cheers a wildly waggling mass of fingers poked through the grenade screen.

Above the uproar, the MP resumed his chatter. "Directly in front of us is the famous MACV annex. As soon as the bus stops, please follow me directly into the building on the right." With the girls left behind, he quickly had his audience back. "Once inside, we'll start your in-processing. You'll be assigned bunks for tonight—tomorrow you'll receive briefings on Vietnam, draw weapons, clothing, and equipment."

They were on the base. Two-storied, white-painted buildings faced onto a muddy street in geometrical precision. Attempts had been made to individualize some with picket fences and tropical plants, but a being from another world would have known on sight that this place was designed to feed, clothe, and house a regimented population. Signs pointing to a gym, hobby shop, library, theatre, club, and so forth proved that these were cared-for regimented people. Even so, an aura of enforcement reached through the eyes and into the mind.

Everyone stood up to get off and Taylor smiled inwardly at the types. The experienced merely functioned, proceeding to the next stop. The new men's self-consciousness glared as they walked carefully, peeking, not wanting to appear too interested. Forming another line, everyone filed into the building where, in his turn, Taylor was given a building and bunk number. His assignment to report to the Personnel Section of J3 for further assignment was verified. He asked for and was given the number to call for transportation. Forms were issued, filled out, whisked away.

The precision was phenomenal. There was practically no confusion and the people in charge seemed positively bored with their own capability, like workers supervising cans in a brewery. The thought of being stamped "Black Label" and packaged off to a desk provided a moment's fancy. It also reminded him how good a cold beer would taste.

The MP's voice cut through the hubbub. "All of you can go to your assigned buildings now. You're through for the day. Enlisted men will be assigned quarters at tomorrow's briefings. There are many Bachelor Officers Quarters and all officers will be allowed to state a BOQ preference, but please remember that all preferences can not—repeat, not—be honored."

Taylor wondered how to find out which was the best BOQ. On learning he was going to Saigon instead of I Corps a friend had counseled, "If they're going to force you to live with your butt in the feathers, don't screw it up. Plenty of people haven't earned it and you have. Don't go all noble on us."

For now, however, he wanted to stretch out and rest, preferably after that beer. As he started from the building, men were hauling luggage inside, and he spotted both his seabag and clothes bag.

Gesturing with his baggage checks, he asked the MP, "OK to move my gear down to my bunk?"

"Sure. Which building you in, Major?"

"Christ, who knows? Let me look."

He pulled a form from his pocket. The MP reached for it, nodded, and jerked his thumb down the line of white buildings. "Second one down, sir. Can you handle your gear by yourself? I can get one of these guys to give you a hand."

"No, thanks." Taylor hoisted his bags. "I'm traveling pretty light."

Ten minutes later he was stripped down to his skivvies, sprawled on a lumpy mattress stretched over springs that sang like the crickets of the world. He watched the old-fashioned ceiling fan spin, listening to the moving-in sounds of others. The thought of the cold beer was still nudging around in his mind when he fell asleep.

2

SOMEONE CALLED HIS NAME.

He chose to ignore it and rolled over. The call persisted. He sat up and glared at the young Lieutenant.

"I'm Major Taylor. What the hell do you want?"

The Lieutenant saluted. "Sir, Colonel Winter sent me to invite you to his quarters."

Taylor waved at him. "I can't return that salute, so get your hand down."

The man lowered it warily.

"I'm sorry to wake you, Major, but the Colonel said—."

"I don't really give a damn what he said. I'm tired. I just—." He checked his watch. "Um. Dark. Been asleep. Anyhow, who's Colonel Winter? What's he to me?"

The young face remained impassive. "Sir, all I know is, Colonel Winter said for me to find you and invite you to his quarters."

As he tried to recollect anyone named Winter, Taylor stared at the intruder. A hard stare and silence usually forced an attempt at communication. The Lieutenant, visibly uneasy, clamped his jaws and Taylor understood he was equally determined to wait him out. The congealed features said he'd be good at it—square face, firm without being sullen, the eyes straight ahead, the chin up. Silent—the inviolate refuge of the subordinate.

"I never heard of any Colonel Winter. You've got the wrong man." He flopped back on the chorusing springs.

"Major, he told me to find you—name, service number, Social Security number, and physical description. The Colonel said I was to be tactful but persuasive." He displayed a notebook as he spoke and replaced it. "Sir, I've worked for him a long time. I've learned not to screw up."

"Give me his phone number. I'll call and make my own apologies. That gets you off the hook."

"Major, it doesn't make any difference about the phone." The stolid expression threatened to break, the eyes widening slightly. "He said if you asked questions or didn't want to come, I was to remember I was addressing a senior officer of

14

another service and to make you understand that he strongly desired you come with me."

The recitation was so stilted there could be no question that it had been memorized.

"Who the hell does he think he is?" Taylor swore, getting out of bed. "What the hell kind of game is this? 'Make me understand,' my ass." He jerked open the metal wall locker, angrily grabbing soap and towel.

"You seem to carry messages well. Hear this. Get on the phone and tell your goddam Colonel that Major Taylor sends his respects and regrets he'll be delayed because he was asleep when you got here and needs a shave and shower. You got it?"

"Yessir."

"Well, by God, you tell him exactly what I told you. Tactfully. I want him to know, tactfully, I think he's a fucking idiot. And don't forget persuasive."

He stalked away to the shower room at the end of the barracks. The Lieutenant watched him, grinning, then left to find the telephone.

After a furious shower, Taylor shaved with swooping strokes. A slick of moisture still covered him and standing under the large fan cooled him mentally and physically. He finished dressing, brushed a hand across the black crewcut stubble, and walked to the front entrance. The Lieutenant was already waiting in a jeep and Taylor swung into the passenger's seat.

"Before we get rolling, suppose you tell me your name. I know it's on that tape over your pocket but I was too angry to notice it before and it's too dark to read it now." Taylor extended his hand.

The Lieutenant took it, straight-faced. "I'm Bill Harker, Major. I'd have said so before, but—." He checked Taylor's expression, debating a full smile.

Taylor grinned. "I guess we didn't exchange much social chat, did we? Get this thing moving and let me know what's going on, OK?"

The return smile that had brightened Harker's face was immediately pushed aside by a frown. "I can't tell you much, Major, I really can't. The Colonel didn't say what he wanted."

Harker watched to see how his passenger would take that.

He was pleased that things hadn't gone too badly yet, and the quick muscle bulge of the Major's jaws made him apprehensive. Then the older man relaxed and Harker blew a satisfied sigh. He knew he'd never get used to these errands, especially the ones where he had to bug some senior officer.

This one sure doesn't look like anyone special, he thought. Maybe a tad over six foot—no moose for size. Average looks, unless his eyes are always that hard. He looked like he was measuring me in there. Winter'll find out what's in him if he decides he can fit in. I wonder if he can imagine what the Colonel has planned?

As the jeep pulled through a tight U-turn the headlights revealed a surprising number of men brought out by the relative cool of the evening. The scene was a surrealist's Main Street—no women, no children, just men standing or sitting in pairs and groups, most wearing shorts and undershirts.

Taylor said, "Look at those people. This is a combat zone?"

Harker laughed. "You'll find it a lot different from I Corps, for sure, but if Charlie decides to lob in a few one-twenty mortar rounds or chuck a grenade at you, you won't be missing the old days."

"That's another thing I worry about. It's going to be a strain wandering around wondering who are the hostiles."

"You get used to it." The grim prospect conveyed by Harker's easy answer drove Taylor to concentrate on the pleasure of the ride. He recognized the general outline of the Tan Son Nhut terminal to the right and the angular mass of MACV Headquarters to his left. Squat cement bunkers crouched immediately behind a high chain link fence, black embrasures staring outward. He hoped their primary function was artillery cover—that close to the wire they were absurdly vulnerable to grenades or planted charges. Then they were past and Harker was pointing out other things.

"That chopper coming in over there in that big vacant lot on the left is headed for the Third Field Hospital landing pad. You can tell when there's a heavy fight somewhere—it gets really busy. At other times it's mostly courier stuff coming in. And on the right is the VNAF club—that's Vietnamese Air Force—and they've got a bar, and the restaurant serves really good Chinese food."

The club loomed against the glare from the air base, its sweeping pagoda-style roof an exotic presence. The outline was accentuated by a string of colored lights. The attempted festive appearance fell flat, reminding Taylor of a honky-tonk.

They leaned to the right at a fork in the road and Harker continued his commentary.

"Over here on the left is Two Hundred P Alley. The name's out of date, 'cause you can't buy any woman around here for that much anymore, but that's what it's called. You can get anything you want, though—no sweat. It's off-limits but nobody does much about it." He gestured to the right. "We just passed the main gate to Tan Son Nhut Air Force Base. The military and civilian field are the same, just different terminals. I've watched a few times, and I don't know how they handle it all."

Taylor agreed. "I noticed all the planes when we came in. Do they have many accidents on the field?"

"None I can think of, but just a few months ago a chopper headed for Third Field fell in the street right in front of the Massachusetts BOQ. Wasted the pilot and co-pilot, but the gunner got out. Funny thing is, it plowed through all that traffic on Cach Mang and no one else got hurt, if you don't count a couple hundred cases of diarrhea."

Harker turned off the main road as he finished speaking, stopping at the gate of a walled compound. An MP stepped out of his sentry box to identify them. Taylor was puzzled by the shape and size of the thing and was amused to recognize it as a concrete sewer pipe with a section cut out of the back. Positioned just a foot from the cement wall behind it, it was good cover. A poncho on poles formed an inadequate roof.

Harker interrupted the inspection. "You may have heard of this place back in the world. It's BOQ 1, for Colonels and Light Colonels. All the rooms are air-conditioned, they've got refrigerators in most of the Colonels' rooms—maybe in all of them, I don't know—and there's a swimming pool, and—."

"Hold it! A swimming pool? Like a motel?"

"Just like. Got a couple of nice bars and a great steak restaurant, too."

"Sonofabitch," Taylor marveled, "that's too much. Does the pool work? Can anyone use it?"

Harker laughed. "Only if you're the guest of a resident or a

17

female. But they're building another bigger one for us peons over at MACV."

He pulled the jeep into a parking slot and grinned at Taylor's expression. "The bit about the females get to you? You'll find out this's the most feminized war anyone ever saw. We've got Red Cross dollies, State Department types, WAFs, WACs AID girls—God knows what all. Hell, I forgot the nurses."

During his litany, he carefully strung a heavy chain through the steering wheel and locked it before setting off toward a wing of the building. Taylor fell in and Harker chattered on.

"Usually on Sunday afternoon there's broads all over the pool. A lot of these old jerks plop out there soaking up sunshine and booze and when a couple of good looking chicks show up they pant 'til it sounds like the surf's up."

Taylor shook his head.

Inside, the building smelled of fresh floor wax, disinfectant, and humanity. Carrying through all of it was the electrical taste of mechanically cooled air, although the dun hallway wasn't appreciably cooler than outdoors. Harker knocked on one of the doors.

"Come in! It's not locked."

Holding the door for Taylor, Harker spoke past him to the man sitting in a rattan easy chair. "Colonel Winter, this is Major Taylor."

The Colonel smiled broadly as he stood and walked across the room, thrusting out his hand. In spite of the lower temperature in the room, he wore only shorts.

Taylor had been prepared for some drawn look of contemptuous authority. Instead, the man suggested a friendly doctor, with his warm brown eyes over the welcoming smile. Taylor felt himself disarmed, embarrassed by his preconceptions.

The Colonel's body belonged to a wrestler—torso and thighs blocky, the long arms heavily muscled. The strength of his handshake implied more available on call. His hair was thick and black, a fact that made the small stark white irregular patch in the middle of the thatch on his chest even more incongruous. In spite of the Colonel's near nudity and his own recent shower and shave, Taylor felt grubby in his wrinkled wash-khaki.

18

"I'm pleased you could come on short notice," Winter said. He put his hand on Taylor's shoulder. "It was rude to roust you this way, but it was important that I see you before too many other things get started." He steered Taylor toward a second rattan chair. "Sit down and have a drink while I unfold a tale of the mysterious Orient." He took the other chair himself and turned to Harker. "Slide that coffee table over here and find something to sit on. I'll want you to talk to Major Taylor, too." Turning back to Taylor, he produced a packet of cigars. "You use these?"

"No, sir." Taylor reached into his sock for his cigarettes. "These are my problem."

Harker leaned over with a lighter, first to Taylor, then to Winter. He replaced the lighter and Taylor said, "Want to try one of mine?"

Harker said, "I don't smoke, sir."

It was apparent he carried the lighter for the Colonel. Taylor looked away quickly.

"I figure it'll be a nice souvenir when I get out of the Army." There was a note in Harker's voice Taylor couldn't identify. Winter snorted and plunked ice cubes in glasses. The Lieutenant displayed the lighter for Taylor. The decoration was an eagle clutching a streaming banner with ornate lettering that read "Fuck Communism." "The other thing," Harker went on, "is some people get forgetful, you know?"

Winter poured whiskey without looking up. "Young pup," he growled. "They don't make Lieutenants like they did when I was a shavetail." He glared mock anger at Harker. "Someday I'll take offense at your insubordinate mouth and send you to Laos on a one-man patrol."

The younger man enjoyed what was transparently a running joke.

Handing a glass to Taylor, Winter said, "Add water as your taste dictates, Major—it's in the pitcher. Incidentally, my apologies for the lack of variety. All I've got in the place is Scotch. I hope you like it."

The glass jerked to a stop half-way to Taylor's mouth, the suddenness spilling some. "Colonel, it's just fine. I'm only worried about the Red Queen running through here. After all, swimming pools. O clubs. 'I'm sorry we've only Scotch'—I still don't even know why I'm here in your quarters. Quarters, yet!"

"It's a shocker, isn't it?" Winter leaned back. "And you're getting it all in one lump." He took a long swallow of his drink, looking at Taylor over the rim. When he lowered it the smile was gone and the eyes had become speculative.

"Let's get right to cases, Major. You know I had a reason for asking you here. Harker, get me that bio."

Harker picked up a single sheet from the desk in the background. He extended it to Winter who waved it away.

"I want the Major to read it and comment."

In the upper right-hand corner was his name: Taylor, Charles Alfred. Under that was rank, service number, Social Security number, and security clearance. The narrative section was single-spaced, wide-margined.

Subject white male is 6'1", 190 pounds, eyes blue, hair black. SUBJECT stays in excellent physical condition, but considers himself slightly overweight. SUBJECT is divorced. Separation reasonably amicable; no re-contact established. No children. Former wife remarried. Parents of SUBJECT native-born citizens, deceased. SUBJECT is infantry officer with field experience in Korea and Vietnam (see Summary of Duty Assignments, Tab A) and has been assigned duties in intelligence field on three occasions. Only two are applicable, as per data requested, forwarded under separate cover. SUBJECT is terminal in grade of Major. Failed of selection to LTC as result of fitness report submitted during previous tour in RVN. No derogatory information in previous or subsequent reports. Investigation and evaluation of SUBJECT indicates high degree of probable capability *re* potential mission. SUBJECT has proven adaptable to unusual circumstances. SUBJECT is considered an adequate choice.

The other men watched Taylor closely as he put the paper on the coffee table. He reached for a fresh cigarette, the only sound in the room the mechanical click of Harker's lighter. Then Taylor shoved the report gently away with one finger.

"Colonel, this is bullshit. You've already read a detailed bio on me and those other assignments. You're running a spook operation. Why try to snow me?"

Winter grunted. "Wanted to see what you'd do, more than anything. Not one of my better ideas. Still, I think I could use you. You've been under consideration for a long time." The ice in his glass made a thin clatter.

"I don't think I want in. I'm flattered to be considered. My

20

ego'll never recover from the pass-over. But all I want is to do my share and go home.''

"Your ego doesn't mean shit to me.'' Winter grinned as he said it, but Taylor knew there was enough truth behind the smile to make the statement stick. "I'm in the market for people who can do the sort of work I have in mind. I think you're one of them. I've bought you your first drink in-country. I think you owe it to me to hear me out, give me a little more consideration than an immediate negative.''

Taylor spread his hands in a defensive gesture. "I'm not trying to be inconsiderate. The less I know about your operation, the less I have to worry about my mouth.''

Winter nodded. "You won't learn anything but generalities, don't worry. But you might find the prospect more interesting than drawing blue arrows on a map.''

There was a stirring in Taylor's guts that angered him, resentment that Winter could so nearly describe his own attitude toward the faceless job he expected.

"I'd be pleased to talk it over with the Colonel, but I don't believe I can help, sir.''

"Possibly.'' Winter shrugged. "If I come to that conclusion, you'll know it.'' He looked to Harker. "Get us some of that squid and some cheese, why don't you? We'll snack while we talk.'' He faced Taylor again. "You like dried squid? Friend of mine brought some back from Japan. Number one.''

Taylor nodded.

"Thought you would,'' Winter continued. "But let's set some stage for what I want to tell you. In the first place, this war's the most screwed-up property on the books. Here it is August '69 and we're still fighting a war that should've been over in '65. In fact, a war that shouldn't have gotten off the ground. It goes on because we don't fight the right way.''

" 'Separate the people from the guerrilla?' '' Taylor interjected with a touch of boredom.

One of the brown eyes winked approvingly. "Exactly. Everyone knows it, but it lacks glamor. No serried ranks advancing in the sun. The mentality that caused the French to lose here isn't exclusively Gallic. Until we eliminate the Viet Cong, as well as the reasons for it, we're swatting flies with a sledgehammer.''

"Colonel, I've watched people try to generate data on the VC. When the intelligence snuffies in the 2 shack get any they can't give it away unless it's an excuse to fall in a battalion. If you're interested in going for the heart of the VC, I might be interested, but if it's just dicking around with statistics and charts, I'd rather do something that won't confuse me into thinking we're making progress."

He noticed the disapproval on Harker's face and wondered if it was because of his attitude or his behavior toward the Colonel, then continued.

"Even if you do hope to go after Charlie, I don't see how I could help. I've just barely started to study the language, and I sure as hell won't pass for one of the locals."

Winter tipped his glass and peered over the rim again. Lowering it, he said, "The genuine report on you made quite a point of the fact that you value your own judgment. It's a good quality, but try not to let it get the best of you. Would you seriously want to try for Charlie's heart, as you put it?"

The question followed the rebuke so smoothly Taylor didn't know which to address. He ignored the sharp comment, hoping it would die more quickly that way.

"I'm not afraid of work, if that's your point, sir. I just don't see how a round-eye can get into their machinery. The last Viet I saw try it was up around Chu Lai and they sent us his head in one of those little rice baskets." He imitated a man carrying a small, unpleasant bundle.

"Charlie can be pretty blunt when he's of a mind." Winter worked his cigar from one side of his mouth to the other, studying Taylor. Abruptly, he asked, "You think we're going to win this war, Major?"

Taylor said, "I don't know. Charlie can't win it from us, militarily, but I don't think that makes much difference. We're losing it in Berkeley and New York and D.C."

Winter closed his eyes in thought. Taylor helped himself to the cheese, musing he might as well enjoy it. If the Colonel didn't appreciate the last answer, he'd get no more.

"You mean that little speech about not being afraid of work?" Winter finally asked.

"Yes, sir."

Jerking out the cigar, Winter jabbed with it at Taylor. "I

mean dry, dusty work. Dull. While you learn enough to be valuable."

After being awakened to attend this ridiculous party, he was being interrogated. Taylor knew better than to lash out, but was too stung to stay with the simple answer the situation required.

"I've been told I already have a dull job, Colonel, and it must be worthwhile, or it wouldn't exist, would it?"

"You spoke of Charlie's heart." Winter ignored Taylor's irritation. "I asked if you thought it was a worthwhile target and you told me a war story. Now, I want to know, clearly, if your cherished ego's completely crushed or if you still have enough professional pride to carry out a mission that would put demands on you."

Taylor felt his throat tighten even as he willed calmness into his voice.

"Yes, sir, Colonel. I still have my pride. Sir."

The full face broke into the same bright smile it wore when Taylor entered the room. "I can see you do. Thought you would. A man without pride's a waste. A soldier without it's a menace. I'm pleased I didn't misjudge you." He laughed out loud. "That's good for *my* ego."

He stood up, moving past Taylor toward a small bathroom. "I'm hungry," he said over his shoulder. "Let me get a quick shower and I'll buy you a steak. Have another drink. If you use the last of the ice, be sure you fill the tray with water. We wouldn't want to find ourselves out of ice when we come back." He closed the door behind him, then opened it again to stick his head out.

"Life's hell in the combat zone, ain't it?" His laughter rang until the rush of the shower obscured it.

3

TAYLOR POURED HIMSELF ANOTHER DRINK, replacing the ice tray.

"I don't suppose you want to elaborate on anything," he said dryly, cocking his head at the bathroom door.

Harker's grin was eloquent.

"I thought so." He'd merely accepted Harker as another Lieutenant before, but now he looked at him.

He'd seen the same bland face with its clear blue eyes and thick, fair hair a million times in catalogs or twinkling a smile ten feet wide on highway billboards. It was an apple-pie-and-mother face. The floppy tropical uniform effectively disguised the six-foot body inside it, but if the rest measured up to the arms, he'd be strong as a bull. The muscle on top of his forearm was a long wedge that bunched with every move. Rolled-up sleeves constricted his biceps. The knuckles and outer edges of the palms were calloused and hardened, a contradiction of the ingenuous face.

"I've been studying you," Taylor said. "How long have you been working at karate?"

Harker responded with pleased shyness. "I got started in college, about five years ago. I got some good instruction at Fort Benning and when I was sent to Japan I was lucky enough to get in a really great class."

"Get much opportunity to work out around here?"

"The Colonel insists on it."

Taylor looked questioning and Harker continued. "He says if the Army can spare a man for traffic safety lectures, moral guidance, and VD movies, it can spare him long enough to practice his trade."

Laughter bubbled from Taylor in spite of himself. He waved to dismiss any offense.

"Jesus, do you memorize everything he says? You've even got the voice pattern down."

The younger man's expression intensified, with the odd effect of making him look even more boyish. "I do admire him. He's a helluva soldier. He doesn't belong in this rear area mess. He's a leader."

Taylor made no comment and Harker continued almost defensively. "I'm no brown-nose, Major. I've met so few men like him I just consider myself lucky to serve with him, that's all."

"I can understand," Taylor said. "You stay in this business long enough, you'll find out it's a constant race to escape the horse's asses and find the real soldiers."

Not caring to continue the course of the conversation, Taylor pointedly turned his attention to the room.

It looked like a seedy motel straining toward oblivion. The paint, whatever its original color, had long since altered to a tan-white. Great patches of plaster had ruptured outward and for some reason they were faintly darker than the surrounding areas, like pimples not quite ready to come to a head. The single window, in the wall directly opposite the door, was completely boarded over save for the cut-out left open to receive the wearily buzzing air-conditioner. The Colonel's desk squatted directly in front of the machine, flanked by a wooden clothes closet to the left and the bed to the right. The room had obviously been occupied by a football fan at one time—the four closet doors each wore a Dallas Cowboy decal, discolored with age and starting to peel.

Winter had made some decorative additions of his own. Three Thai temple rubbings hung framed on the right wall, one a warrior in a chariot, flourishing his bow. The others were of female musicians, dreamy-eyed and languorous, sleek and proud-breasted. The bedspread was no more than a length of Thai silk, its bold colors violently opposed to the relentless doughy texture of the room. The remaining furnishings were the three rattan chairs, the refrigerator, the coffee table, and a scabrous dresser. An olive-drab towel was spread across the latter, providing a padded surface for glasses, bottles, a wallet, and a shoulder holster enfolding a .38 revolver.

If these are Colonel's quarters, thought Taylor, the rest of us must live in toilets.

"What's your job?" he asked Harker.

The Lieutenant blinked before answering. The simple gesture seemed to actuate a switch that made his face a plastic mask.

"We keep tabs on as many known VC as we can find," he said.

"Sounds fascinating." Taylor made the sarcasm heavy.

Harker's chin jutted. "We think we do a little good. It's not always easy and it's not always fun but we feel like we make a contribution."

Neither had noticed the shower was silent and now Winter stepped back into the room.

"A pretty speech, young tiger," he boomed. "Clarity and brevity. Soldierly modesty. Idealistic, but not maudlin." He advanced on Harker as he spoke, one hand securing the wrap-around towel. When he reached the younger man he clapped the free hand on his shoulder. Drops of water sprayed onto the open-weave material where they spread rapidly.

Winter faced Taylor. "Speaking purely socially, this has to be the dullest bastard in Vietnam." He shook the shoulder and the grinning head bobbed loosely. "Operationally, however, he's as warped as a Chinese smuggler. I swear he has two channels in that pea-like brain." He dropped his hand and walked to the closet, pulling out his uniform. "One channel works in cadence, causing him to pour forth military clichés like swine before pearls. I'm told if he makes love within fifteen minutes of removing his uniform he hums martial airs during the ensuing entire performance."

He grunted as he pulled on a boot and continued his commentary while lacing it.

"Give him a mission, though, and he changes channels. You can practically hear the click."

Taylor thought back to the effect of the blink of Harker's eyes.

Winter's voice shifted to an excellent imitation of W. C. Fields. "Without even stepping into a phone booth he becomes Horrible Harker, right before your eyes. VC have been known to swear allegiance to Mary Poppins at the mere mention of his name."

He rose and ushered his guests into the hall. Both were laughing as he swung in between them, swaggering and enjoying himself.

Harker stepped ahead, holding open the door to the outside, and Taylor was impressed again by the almost physical impact of the moist heat. In addition, the belching traffic outside the BOQ compound offended his ears. He glanced irritably in that direction and Winter smiled sourly.

"Get used to it," he said. "If you don't, the noise of this city'll drive you nuts in a month. Do what we do, deep breathing exercises. Get enough of this filth in your lungs and the rest of your senses shut down."

"You know, it's funny," Harker said, "the one thing I never thought about in connection with Nam was pollution. I mean, you think of humidity and muddy rivers, not rivers that're open sewers and air blue with exhaust smoke."

"I guess we're pretty much to blame for the air," Taylor

said. "You can hear those damned trucks blowing and bellowing even in the Colonel's room."

"Maybe so," Harker said angrily, "but we didn't fill the rivers with junk and those greasy goddam cyclos aren't our fault."

Taylor smiled. "I didn't mean to step on your nerves."

Harker flashed his own sheepish smile. "I know—sorry 'bout that. It seems like anything that goes wrong is our fault. Snapping back at people gets to be a reflex."

" 'People?' Who else is there, but us?"

"The whole fucking world," Winter spat, then laughed, a harsh bark like nothing Taylor had heard from him before. "Major Taylor, you're at MACV. Welcome to the world's only war under glass. There's a different gaggle of bastards out here to tell us what we're doing wrong every other day. I don't see how the Generals stand it. If you could hear some of the inane idiots they have to deal with—respectfully, yet—." He stopped. "The hell with it. Let's get some dinner."

They turned a corner of the building and he pushed open a screen door. Immediately inside he opened another door to the right.

A gush of noise poured out, a susurration of voices carried on cold air like the draft at the very surface of a mountain stream. The decorative colors of the room revealed to Taylor's astounded eyes were predominantly red and black. Candles gleamed on small tables, complementing discreet indirect lighting. A U-shaped bar protruded from the wall on the right and customers stood three deep. The waitresses were Vietnamese in black skirts, white blouses, and red vests. Dwarfed by even the smallest Americans, they seemed to flit from place to place like small, brilliant birds. Their voices pierced the dominant baritone and alto murmuration, high-pitched tonal Vietnamese trilling counterpoint. When they dealt with a customer, he enjoyed their complete attention, but as soon as that contact was broken they shouted and laughed among themselves as if they were alone.

Winter moved through the crowd with the certainty of the well-established citizen on home ground. A quick handshake for one man, a smile for one too distant to grasp, a conspiratorial whisper for yet a third. He left a clear trail of smiles and nods behind him.

The bar was well stocked. Taylor remembered back to Chu Lai, where a Bottle of Tiger beer was a treasure, illegal because the word was that the VC had poisoned it. This created considerable apprehension but no lack of business for the children who packed the stuff up to the Marine positions.

Winter ordered martinis, paying for them himself while assuring Harker and Taylor he'd collect from them in the future. When Harker asked a question about a proposed trip to Long Binh, Taylor took the opportunity to inspect the crowd.

It was a mixture of uniforms, races, and most surprising, sexes. The only Oriental women were the waitresses and cashier. American women far outnumbered them. They were dressed in civilian clothes, the blotch-on-blotch camouflage of tiger suits, or Army fatigues. Regardless of apparel, they each had an entourage of males.

Winter broke off his conversation with Harker to watch Taylor with amusement.

"It's something, isn't it?" he asked rhetorically. "This place is busy all the time. But wait 'til you see some of the places in the city. They threw out the French, but they remembered the cooking." He paused. "I wonder if anyone will say even that much about us when we're gone."

In his own mind, Taylor was wondering how many French troops had sat at tables like this, watching the crowd, trying to adjust to the idea that in this room, right now, the war was ugly gossip. Maybe none. The French never created the elaborate compounds of the Americans that divorced them from the environment.

Their waitress materialized, greeting Winter with obvious pleasure, acknowledging the other two men with a short nod.

"Ahhh, Miss Oanh," Winter beamed. "The prettiest girl in Vietnam."

She blushed and turned her head. Typically, she hid her laughter behind the menu.

Winter said, "Miss Oanh, this is Major Taylor. He just arrived today."

She favored him with a measured portion of a charming smile. "Your first time come Vietnam?"

"Second time," he said. "Before, I was in Chu Lai."

She looked blank and Taylor sat dumb.

Winter said, "Up north, in I Corps. Major Taylor is a Marine."

Her face twisted as she tried to understand. "I know I Corps, but not other thing you say."

Winter said something that sounded like *Tooey Kong Look Chin* and Miss Oanh's expression went through several rapid alterations, eventually settling on alert neutrality. She pointed at Taylor, repeating Winter's phrase, questioning.

Taylor looked helplessly to Winter, who said, "That's Vietnamese for their Marine Corps."

Taylor turned back to the woman. "That's what I am. Whatever he said."

"They kill many VC." She said it the same way she might say the salad had lettuce in it, yet somehow conveyed more than conversational intensity. Taylor couldn't tell if he'd been challenged or identified.

"We fight the VC. Yes, many die. We fight North Vietnamese, too. Maybe North Vietnamese go home, no more war."

Relaxation softened Miss Oanh's entire stance. "Be good for war stop. Too much people die. I hope you kill many-many VC. VC kill my father, one brother."

"I hope we can even the score for you. I'm sorry."

She turned to Winter again, who spoke rapidly in Vietnamese. She listened intently, then touched Taylor's shoulder.

"I understand now 'even score.' More important you be careful." Her eyes probed his for an instant, but when she returned her attention to Winter, she was laughing.

"Better you order or boss give me bad time."

Winter ordered, checking with Taylor only to ask how he preferred his steak and choice of salad dressing.

As soon as Miss Oanh was gone, Taylor said, "I hope they're not all that good looking. There's enough distraction around here."

"Don't worry about it," Winter said. "Not many are as pretty as she is, and she's not available. I think every GI to hit Saigon's tried to get into her knickers. You can kid around with her, but that's it."

"Maybe she's anti-American," Taylor suggested lightly.

"God knows. I guess she's too smart to get mixed up with some sonofabitch who'll leave her with a kid when he rotates

29

home to Momma." A sly smile creased his face. "She's determined about her virtue, too. Some stud Captain got all liquored up here one night and ambushed her over by the bicycle rack when she quit work."

He leaned over the table, warming to his story. "I was on the rack, reading, just about to go to sleep, and I hear this scream—raised the hair all over my body. I grabbed my .38 and tore outside. I should've stood in bed—she needed help like Custer needed more Indians. I couldn't have been more than thirty seconds getting here, but by the time I made it, our Captain is on his face, her bike bent over his back, and she's trying to kick his lungs out. I'm making the best time I can, running barefoot in the goddam gravel, and I was afraid she'd kill him before I could reach her. She'd ra'ar back and holler 'You son bitch!' and drive her little pointy-toed shoe into his guts like a knife. Every shot he's going 'Ugh!' and puking like a geyser. I wrestled her off to one side—made my whole day—and calmed her down."

"She wasn't hurt?" Taylor asked.

"Only the bicycle. Someone convinced the Legal people she'd press no charges if she got a solatium that'd pay for one of those Lambretta putt-putts."

Taylor said, "That's a decent swap—a motorscooter for a bicycle."

Winter's smile turned brittle. "One of the few times one of the little people ever made a profit, Major."

Before the silence could grow too heavy, she was back, bearing a tray loaded with their dinner. It appeared too heavy for her, but she dodged between the tables with a grace that was almost dancing. While she positioned the plates, Taylor asked, "Don't you ever drop something in a crowd like this?"

She shook her head. "No can do. I drop tray, boss get very angry." She grinned. "Anyhow, easy for Vietnamese girl. Get *beaucoup* practice carry many things in market, more people than this." She put down the last plate, then paused as though considering. Suddenly she looked back at Taylor, pure mischief in her eyes.

"Oanh same-same VC. Americans big, move too slow. Before can touch me, I quick run past."

Taylor's lips pulled into a tight line and she giggled and

30

tapped him on the shoulder. "I joke you. You not angry with Oanh?"

"Very angry." Taylor twisted his face into a ferocious scowl. Miss Oanh's smile trembled. He went on, "Angry because you don't understand. Look, I want to show you something. Give me your pen."

"No have time," she protested. "I got work."

"Give me the pen. This'll only take a minute."

She extended it reluctantly. In swift lines Taylor sketched a large crane peering down a sword-like bill at a frog.

"The crane is large and slow, Miss Oanh, and the frog is small and quick. You never see the frog eat the crane." He jabbed at the crouching frog with the pen, making a misshapen blot on its side. "The crane is patient. And, in time, always wins."

She studied the sketch for a moment before looking at Winter. "This man work for you, Colonel?"

"Maybe."

She nodded approval. "Good. You take care of him, he hurt VC. He think like us."

With no word or further glance further, she resumed her dance through the crowd.

Winter smiled at her back.

Right you are, pretty Miss Oanh, he thought. More than either of you know. I need this stiff-necked bastard for just that reason.

The actual eating passed quickly and Winter led them back to his room for more Scotch. He stripped off his jacket and threw it on the bed, settling into his chair.

"I can use you," he said bluntly.

"I'm flattered, Colonel—."

"Bullshit." Winter jammed the word into Taylor's response like a pole into spokes.

"No, I'm serious," Taylor protested. "I'm proud of having done my job well. The thing is, in spite of the intelligence training, I'm an infantryman inside. If I can't be where the action is, I'd just as soon sit at MACV and count days. I'll be damned if I'll get mixed up in some schmear where I bust my ass filling out 3x5 cards on Viet schoolteachers."

The speech made no visible impression on Winter, who

leaned forward with deliberation, carefully sipping from his drink before answering. "I've been wrong about people before. You may turn out to be worthless to me."

Out on the street a car horn hooted derisive agreement.

"I run the American half of a joint unit." He straightened in the chair, apparently resolved to give Taylor a deeper view. "My counterpart is Colonel Do Van Loc. We go back a long way. I've got more time in this country than any American I'm aware of. I won't tell you how long it took to get our unit—the Records Research Unit—established. I certainly won't tell you how many asses we had to kiss."

His right hand moved almost involuntarily, as though turning off someone else's conversation. When he continued he was less contemplative.

"We're a small group—twelve Americans, including clerks and drivers. Viet counterparts are another ten men, officers and enlisted. We've existed a little over a year. If you come in, you'll indeed be busting your ass filling out cards. And computer cards. And charts and graphs. The paper work justifies our existence and you'll know every scrap of it before you're operational. We've tried our wings on a few jobs and been successful. We've worked too long and too hard to let anyone screw up what we've accomplished."

He stopped for another drink.

"What I'm telling you is that I hold power, Major. Tons of it. I've worked like a sonofabitch for it and I intend to keep it and use it. If you come in, I'll want you to learn this city—the alleys, the markets, the neighborhoods. When something starts to boil, I'll expect you to be able to find out who built the fire and what's in the pot."

"You must have access to a million sources. You want me to act as some sort of coordinator?"

"Initially. You'll set up your own contacts, as possible. Counterpart people will help. Later, when you know your way around, you'll exploit your own contacts."

Taylor squinted dubiously. "I'll have to learn the language. I don't want to deal with people who can talk around me."

"I've considered that. Your bio says you speak, read, and write Cantonese."

"Not much anymore. I was told not to—the bio should have said that, too."

"It did, and it still holds. Stay away from it. The bio goes on to say you have what amounts to a genius for language assimilation. We'll provide you with an excellent teacher. Understand, I expect—no, I *will* have—very fast results. If you think a long-haired dictionary will help, feel free, but let me know first, so we can run a check on her."

Taylor had to grin. Shacking up had come up in the past, but always behind a thicket of euphemisms and official disavowals.

Winter caught his expression and grunted. "Goddam Marine. I knew that'd catch your attention."

"Everybody should have a hobby," Taylor said. "Listen, if I find two of those dictionaries, do I have to turn one in?"

Shaking his head, Winter said, "Be serious, goddamit. You're being recruited. Show a little respect." He let the moment pass, then continued seriously.

"Your language instructor will be a woman, the widow of a Vietnamese officer. She lives with her mother and father. He's a wheel in government—used to be a big businessman. The mother's from down in the delta. Her family rents out a lot of land down there."

"The family knows about the unit?"

"Christ, no. See that you keep it that way. We've run several people through her classes and you better not be the first to make a mistake."

"You're running along like I was already aboard. Am I allowed to ask what our primary mission is?"

Winter hoped Taylor couldn't see his pleasure at the word "our." He studied Taylor before answering, establishing exactly what he wanted to say.

"We're on both sides of the street. We're targeted against certain VC activities, but sometimes we slop over into other areas. Colonel Loc answers to one man, me to another. We get approval, or at least tacit approval, for operations from them. They're very understanding."

"You make it sound pretty spooky, Colonel."

"It is. It's a rotten job in the middle of a rotten war. You come aboard, you'll find out."

The studied dramatic pause that followed amused and aggravated Taylor. Eyes locked to Winter's, he waited.

"Think you can handle it?"

What the hell, Taylor thought, Change One. Just like a damned dog. Ol' Master kicks you dizzy, but let him break out the gun and boots and you jump through your ass to fetch his fucking birds.

"Deal me in."

"Fine." He clapped his hands together, turning to Harker. "It's already past curfew. Get him back to the Annex. Pick him up at 0630, get his ID card, PX ration card, and all that crap out of the way. Get him a driver's license. Collect his gear and move him into the villa."

The word "villa" rang in Taylor's mind. He decided against asking questions.

Harker stood up to leave and Taylor drained his glass and joined him. Winter continued to stare at his table top. Taylor wondered if they were expected to go or stay. As he was about to ask, Winter looked up.

"I've been thinking," he said. "Maybe I ought to explain something to you." He paused again, clearly organizing his words. "Not everything we do is what you'd call sanctioned, Major. You'll be forced to face up to some very harsh realities. Maybe you'd best sleep on this."

"I think I know what the Colonel's driving at. I said I was in, and I'm in." Taylor smiled easily.

"No, that won't cut it." Winter pressed forward heavily, hands splayed out across his kneecaps. "You'll *know* what I'm driving at. I'm telling you you could be called on to kill."

Taylor's sharp laugh surprised Winter.

"Colonel, what the hell else could you have been getting at? I've got no family to speak of and I took my finger off my number on the lineal list years ago. I won't have any second thoughts."

"If you're going to, now's the time," Winter said. "I don't want to hear about it when it's time to squeeze the trigger. It happens, you know."

"Not to me," Taylor answered flatly.

Winter stood up. "Glad to have you aboard." He shook Taylor's hand and as he did, Harker opened the door, turned, and saluted. Winter returned it with a half-smile as they left.

He stood that way for a few moments, then walked slowly back to his desk and got comfortable in the chair, sipping at the icewater remains of his drink and nibbling absently at twisted white strands of squid. He reached for the bottle to pour more whiskey, looked at the level, and replaced the cork.

Damn a war that runs on a one-year cycle, he thought. It may be that long before he gets something rolling and then I'll have to bring along a new man. He's professional—that may help. God knows he's cold enough.

He looked at the bottle again and pulled the cork, pouring a bare finger in the glass. Holding it to the light, he rotated it slowly back and forth, watching crystalline sparks spring from the ice chips.

He'll work out, he decided.

He tossed down the drink, draining ice and all.

"Just fine," he said to the empty room. "Poor bastard."

4

ONCE THE JEEP WAS CLEAR of the BOQ parking lot, Harker turned to Taylor. "What're they saying about the war back home, sir?"

As soon as he'd asked, he aimed his attention back to the nearly deserted street. The fumbled attempt at unconcern almost forced a laugh from Taylor.

"In terms of popularity, it's somewhere below syphilis. No one seems to understand it. It's killing our people and hardly anyone's willing, or able, to believe it's worthwhile."

"What's the attitude toward the guys who ran off to Canada or Sweden? What do people say about them?"

This time Taylor did laugh. "Anything you want to hear. They're the greatest propaganda goldmine the doves could hope for. Then the hawks are busy proving they're all born losers, anyhow. They're heroes or bastards. Depends on who's talking."

"You're a professional, Major—what do you think?"

"Me?" Taylor was surprised. "I don't think about them much at all."

He caught the unguarded glance of disapproval and added, "Don't misunderstand. I didn't say I didn't care. I don't worry about what anyone does as long as it doesn't affect me, and those people don't. For that matter, I keep thinking how

35

our country was founded by people who were considered deserters, protesters, and so on. We see them as men of immense vision. The Indians saw them as the most rapacious sons of bitches outside hell's front gate. No, let 'em go, and Godspeed, says I.''

"You think they ought to get amnesty when this is all over?" Harker was rigidly deferential.

Taylor was silent for a moment while he phrased his answer. "Personally, no. Not out of vindictiveness—or justice, for that matter. I just feel I could never trust one of them, you know? Right or wrong, I'd always believe that when the heat came on, he'd find a reason to skip. Anyhow, what I think doesn't matter. They'll likely get their amnesty. It's the time of the anti-hero and us reactionaries might as well learn to love it.''

Harker was frowning steadily now. "You don't seem too enthusiastic for a man who was willing to come back here for a second tour, sir.''

"Enthusiasm?" Taylor said it musingly. "I guess it's nice, if you need it. I'm a professional. I also believe I'm in the right. If you expect a cheerleader, you're in for a disappointment. I've looked at the information available to me and decided what I think is right and what's wrong. If that means I have to fight, that's that. And thus endeth the lecture. What's this mess in front of us?''

The road was blocked by wooden barriers, bright lights behind them, barbed wire in front. The glare obscured vision beyond, although a massive object hulking in the road was barely discernible.

"This is the MACV-Tan Son Nhut checkpoint. We have to snake around through it." Harker slewed the jeep to the left, where Vietnamese and American MPs checked ID cards. The Vietnamese watched the process with idle curiosity, smaller replicas of the Americans, except for the letters QC replacing MP. One of the Americans said something about curfew and Harker displayed another small card. The MP read it and waved them on.

"After-curfew pass," Harker explained. The headlights exposed the thing Taylor had dimly perceived blocking the road. It was a six-by, the standard two-and-a-half-ton truck. The jeep barely passed between it and the ditch.

"This whole works is a left-over from Tet," Harker explained, once more. Taylor was beginning to feel very ignorant.

"That's one I'm glad I missed," he said, wishing he could simply ride and look.

"It was a bitch," Harker said, squashing the hope. "I couldn't get into MACV for three days and I was two more getting back out."

"You were here then?"

"Yes, sir. I'm finishing my first one year extension. I've been approved for another one."

"Jesus, no wonder you're asking about attitudes back home. You'll have to apply for immigrant papers."

In the dim light spilling from the MACV headquarters compound, Taylor saw pride in Harker's eyes.

"A lot of people think I'm a nut, but I'm putting away some money. Besides, it's an interesting life. I've even made a few decisions. Like you."

"Winter was right about you," Taylor said. "You're a brash young man, putting down your elders."

Harker grinned as they slowed, passing the Rainbow Room, now dark and deserted.

Taylor asked, "Will I be having one of those counterparts Winter mentioned?"

Harker chuckled. "I've been thinking about that. You'll be working with Major Duc. Nguyen Ngoc Duc. He's barely five feet tall and built like a beach ball, but don't let that fool you. He's got the stamina of a truck."

"Swell," Taylor said dryly. "Seventeen years building dignity and prestige so I can be half of a Mutt and Jeff act. How about you? Who's your counterpart and what's your job?"

"His name's Le Duc Hon. He's a Lieutenant. Most of our operations are with SOG—that's Special Operations Group. We like it 'cause it gets us out in the field a lot."

Taylor grunted his disgust. "You say nothing very nicely."

The answering low laugh blended with the crunch of gravel on the road shoulder as they came to a stop outside Taylor's barracks.

"I'm glad you're with us, Major."

Taylor lit another cigarette, knowing he was smoking far

more than usual. He traced it to an insistent sensation he'd committed himself to something he couldn't escape. In the glare of the flame, Harker's face was taut in study of his passenger. Taylor let him stare, watching the smoke spiral to the roof of the jeep. It coiled there, hesitant tendrils doubling back on themselves.

The hell with you. The hell with any more explanations and reasons. I don't owe you. Stay out of my brain.

"Glad to be aboard. See you in the morning." He heaved himself out. Harker's hand flashed in the dark and Taylor returned the half-seen salute.

The growl of the departing jeep faded as he entered the building. Even before he opened the screen door its occupancy laved over him. Someone muttered unintelligibly, muted as though in conscious consideration for the rest of the inhabitants so neatly arranged along both walls. The light from the head at the end of the long room provided ample illumination and he was spared having to pick his way in complete darkness. The heavy breathing of the massed bodies created an irregular, solid welling of sound, a constant asthmatic exhalation. He considered the odor of damp cloth, sweat, and a hothouse thickness of toiletries and decided it smelled like a flower show in a locker room.

The ceiling fans paddled through the cloyed air, whispering and snickering, one to the other. As he settled himself on the bunk someone down the line rolled over with a loud sigh and began a racking snore.

"Beautiful," he muttered softly. "Saved it just for me." He stubbed the cigarette.

After folding his blanket toward the foot of the bed he hung his clothes in the wall locker. Hangers clattered, but no one stirred. Finally he stretched out on the marvelously cool sheet. When his head hit the pillow the stuffing flowed outwards like liquid. Swearing, he transferred the blanket to the head, put the pillow on that, and lay back down. This time the sheet was warm and he was already slick with a damp film of perspiration.

He stared at the fan, listening to a chopper chuffing importantly overhead. Before it was out of earshot, he heard a distant burst of automatic weapons fire. A lull of a few seconds and then another, shorter burst stuttered. The sound pleased him. It was reality.

His last thought as he closed his eyes was a formless pity for the snorer down the way who continued to rumble, unenlightened.

5

COLONEL DO VAN LOC DELICATELY FLICKED HIS LIPS with the napkin and snapped his fingers. The orderly poised in the hall trotted in silently, removed the lacquered tray from the desk and trotted back out. Loc smiled at the soldier's back and permitted himself a flourish as he lit his after-breakfast cigarette.

Breakfast was always a pleasure, an unfailing routine that started his day. A bowl of the rich beef broth, *pho*, a croissant, and coffee—Vietnamese, French, and American influences, all in one sitting. It gave him a sense of history, of the progress of things. More, it was cosmopolitan.

The facet of this particular morning that glittered most attractively, however, was his monumental self-control. He exhaled smoothly, congratulating himself on completely hiding a fury that actually caused physical pain.

Loc equably reflected that today was the first time in years he wished he could kill a man. The matter of arranging the death was a simple matter and it would provide some pleasure. Still, it would be meager compensation for the insult to the Unit.

His lip curled, unbidden, as he thought of his counterpart, Winter. Setting his mask, he snapped his fingers once more. The orderly entered with a quilted tea caddy, placed it on the desk and left.

Winter would be equally angry, and Loc hoped he'd conduct himself well, because the American's unrestrained emotions frequently taxed Loc's admiration, if not his friendship. They had discussed this failing and now it was almost as painful to watch Winter try to control himself as to be exposed to the raving.

Lighting a cigarette from the previous one, Loc poured a glass of tea and stood, facing up to the inevitable. Carrying tea and cigarette, he opened the door to the adjacent office.

"Good morning, Win," he said, buoyed by the sound of his own precise English. "Do you have a minute?"

Winter answered in Vietnamese, gesturing toward the sofa against the far wall. *"Chac vay, Anh Hai."* His general tone and the use of *Anh Hai*, meaning Brother Two, assured Loc he was relaxed and untroubled. Further, Loc allowed himself to hope that the language would put Winter in a Vietnamese frame of mind.

"You have a spot on your blouse," Winter added.

"You lie," Loc replied easily. He sipped his tea, not deigning to look. Among a people who considered neatness and cleanliness primary virtues, Loc's fastidiousness was remarkable.

Winter examined him as he settled onto the sofa, smiling with reminiscence. When they'd both been Majors in the field, grimy as Pigs in a pit, Loc would manage to bathe, produce a clean uniform from somewhere, and be ready for inspection before anyone else had caught his breath. He was tall for a Vietnamese, a shade over 5'9'', and Winter suspected his elegance reflected an awareness that he stood out in a crowd.

He's aged well, Winter went on mentally. The face has grown a little sharper. It's tight-skinned and there's bitterness now. The eyes a bit quicker, not as open. It would be a fanatic's face quickly.

The last was a disturbing notion and he was glad to have it interrupted. Loc put his tea glass on the coffee table, asking, "Your evening went well?"

"Very satisfactory. He's making remarkable progress. We spoke nothing but Vietnamese. He bargained with the taxi-driver, ordered dinner, and talked with the waiter. He's all we could ask."

"He shows more promise than a Major I remember from my past." Loc's narrow lips arced in a faint smile.

Winter snorted. "Taylor's teacher is prettier than mine was. And not devoted to bad jokes."

"It was not a bad joke. Merely a prank."

"It is no prank to give an innocent American a phrase to greet an attractive bar girl when the phrase means 'Good evening, Miss Bird-dropping.' I could have been killed.''

"I paid for the damages. I explained your ignorance."

"Truly, you were of great help."

Loc moved them to another subject. "How long will you keep Taylor at his present assignment?"

Winter recognized a loaded question. Loc was being too casual.

"He should be about ready to become operational. He's worked well in the Compilation Section. He hates it, but he's worked hard. Major Duc tells me he knows the city very well. And I told you how much Vietnamese he's learned in these four months."

Loc nodded slowly. "Most foreigners have a terrible time with the tones. He learned them almost as if he'd practiced before."

You bastard, Winter thought ruefully. I wonder how much you know? And I wonder what you're going to drop?

He continued to speak Vietnamese. "I am sure. Duc is anxious to be on assignment. Compilation has been dull for him, as well. Do you think he and Taylor could work on the problem of Nguyen Binh?"

The quick blink of Loc's eyes were gratifying, telling him he'd placed his shot well.

Loc said, "Do you think they are ready? He is very clever. It could be dangerous."

"They have learned something," Winter said. "Would you like to hear it with me? I can call them now."

Loc considered. If Duc and his American counterpart had found a weakness in Binh's operation, it would be a tremendous step. And it would be good news for Winter, hopefully enough to offset the unpleasantness that writhed in his own mind. He decided his own news could wait. He nodded. Winter turned to the gray intercom mounted on the wall next to the air-conditioner and called Taylor and Duc to report on the Nguyen Binh matter.

The intercom rasped a quick answer.

Winter leaned back and massaged his neck. "It will be a miracle if they have something worthwhile. What do you think?"

"You know how I feel about that bastard." Loc's grin was a snarl. "He has supplied the VC with our ammunition and sup-

41

plies for years. How many of his contact people have we picked up? How many times have we tried to infiltrate his operation? We never get close!" He shook his head and pursed his lips, an extravagant show. Then he took another cigarette from his case and lit it with studied deliberation.

Winter punched another button on the intercom. "Carl?"

The answer rapped back immediately. "Yessir."

Loc's upper lip twitched.

Keeping his voice serious, despite the smile brought about by Loc's reaction, Winter said, "I'm having Majors Taylor and Duc in. They've got some information they want to discuss. I'd like you to sit in."

"On the way, Colonel." The box crackled to silence.

Winter said, "You really ought to make more of an effort to like my exec, Loc. He keeps me out of trouble."

Loc made a noise in the back of his throat. "How can such a man be tolerated? He is an old woman. And he hates us."

Winter tried to lighten Loc's mood. "Well, maybe he knows you better than I do."

Loc ignored the attempted humor. "He knows no one. His life is rules, regulations. He needs them for his own in—inse—" His fist tightened on his thigh as he strained for the word.

"Insecurity," Winter supplied.

Loc repeated it. "Exactly. He must have a rule to permit anything."

"On the other hand, if he can't find a rule that permits us to do something, he'll find a rule that says we aren't absolutely forbidden. And sometimes he finds ways to hide things."

"How well I know. If he feared you before, it's worse ever since you made him risk his comfortable existence."

A careless wave dismissed the indictment. "Denby never feared me and he doesn't now."

"Perhaps fear is the wrong word. You know his life is a search for the perfect way to do nothing. He is an excellent administrator because he can do it without moving. You endanger that. You have involved him with us, which could even endanger his career."

"So he'll be all the more careful. He's up for Colonel in two years. He'd cover for Hitler to make full bird."

Loc swallowed his retort at the knock. With Winter's invitation to come in, the door swung open slowly and a round face peered past the edge. The roundness was emphasized by a receding hairline of cropped brown stubble and circular rimless glasses glinting above a pug nose and a rosebud mouth. The eyes flickered from Winter to Loc and back again before the red lips bent in a smile and the man nodded himself into the room. The hang of the tropical fatigue uniform spoke of additional roundnesses hidden from view. The man paused, still wearing the tiny smile.

"Have a seat, Carl," Winter greeted him. "Taylor and Duc are on the way."

"Yessir." He settled on the opposite end of the sofa and turned to Loc. "How are you this morning, Sir?"

Loc faced him, his eyes penetrating the unkempt figure to focus on something beyond before turning to the front again.

"I am fine, thank you."

At the chilly refusal to make conversation, Denby looked to Winter, only to find him busy shuffling papers. He eased back against the sofa cushions and froze the smile to his lips.

Snotty little prick, he fumed inwardly. And Winter—letting a goddam zip snub an American Lieutenant Colonel. I'm as important as anyone in this outfit.

He stared at Loc's immobile precision, then at the placid Winter, asking himself why Winter always treated him with faint reserve, no matter how friendly he sounded. Loc wasn't that hard to understand. If there was anything snottier than a dirty little zipper-head, it was a clean one, and this one always looked like a squeaky doll fresh out of the package. Prissy. Probably queer. At least a latent.

The thought lifted his spirits and he resolved to weasel some information out of the Unit's contact at the Military Security Service. If there was anything at all worth knowing about Loc, the Vietnamese MSS would have it. He should have done it long ago.

There was another knock at Winter's door, this time Taylor and Duc. The latter carried a bundle of 5 x 8 cards.

"Good morning, gentlemen," Winter greeted them. Loc confined himself to a smiling nod. Winter said, "Please sit down. We'll continue this discussion in Vietnamese. It's good practice for Major Taylor and I expect Major Duc will do most of the talking, anyhow. Carl, you'll have trouble following, so

43

just holler if we go too fast."

Major Duc twitched.

How could this happen? he asked himself. The idea is Taylor's, not mine. I only made small suggestions. I don't want to speak in front of Colonel Loc. I have done nothing to deserve this.

Loc was immediately aware of Duc's discomfort. It amused him, because he actually had a great liking for the Major. For all his fat, Duc had a mind as thin and edged as a knife. If the tall, exceedingly American-looking Taylor was half as competent, they would make an interesting team. He decided to be helpful. He continued Winter's lead, using the Vietnamese word for Major as he inclined his head toward the nervous Duc. *"Thieu Ta,* I am pleased you have been able to help *Thieu Ta* Taylor learn the duties of the Compilation Section. I see you have been there long enough to refresh yourself. I understand you feel you have learned something important of that piece of pigshit, Nguyen Binh. Enough for someone to act on the information?"

Duc leaned forward eagerly. "Yes, *Dai Ta,* we think so." He held up the cards. "May I use the small table to display these?"

Loc nodded and Duc arranged them on the table. Winter came from behind his desk to look. Three were singles with photographs attached. The fourth item was three cards stapled together. There was no picture.

"The cards with no photograph concern Nguyen Binh," Duc said apologetically. He tapped the next card. "This man is Do Chi Trung. He is known by sight to me, Major Taylor and Captain Allen."

"Do we need Allen?" Winter interrupted.

"No," Duc said. "All he knows of Trung is that he has seen him delivering whiskey and other contraband."

Winter nodded and Duc moved to the next card. "This is Nguyen Van Tu. He has been arrested for black market, twice. Small crimes. They are both partners in a place called the Friendly Bar. It is used by Americans." He tapped the final card. "The last man is named Sam An. He is Chinese."

Taylor had to stifle a smile. Duc had consistently used the correct Vietnamese word for "he" or "him" when referring to

44

the first three men. He used the contemptuous *thang* when he spoke of An.

"You have pertinent information of these men?" Loc asked pleasantly.

Duc plucked at his collar and when he spoke he started to use the American rank, Colonel, before correcting himself and calling Loc by the Vietnamese equivalent. *"Dai Ta*, it is very complex. The bar is registered as the property of a woman, the cousin of Trung. He is closely associated with the Chinese, An. Taylor and myself have seen the three men in conversation many times."

"So?" Loc asked quietly. "You feel these conversations deserve the attention of Special Branch, or the American CID?"

A wince danced across Duc's face. "I know a person in that place. We stopped there one evening for refreshment. My contact mentioned Trung and Tu. That same evening, we saw all three talking. Taylor has been there several times since."

Duc stopped, hoping he had cut himself out of the remainder of the discussion.

Loc persisted. "How long have you known the contact?"

"About two years, *Dai Ta*."

"You have received information before?"

"Yes, *Dai Ta*."

"Was the information accurate?"

"Yes, *Dai Ta*."

"Did the informant tell you anything about these men?"

"Only that they have business in the black market, *Dai Ta*."

"Why have you not gone back to this place with *Thieu Ta* Taylor?"

"Because no one there knows he speaks Vietnamese, *Dai Ta*. We thought he should go alone, like any other American, and possibly overhear something."

Loc pivoted slowly to face Taylor. "Do you approve of *Thieu Ta* Duc's taste?"

Taylor stared blankly. "Taste, *Dai Ta?* I do not understand."

Loc's smile was a shadow. "You lie with the charm and ineffectiveness of certain senior officers."

Taylor blinked confusion in Winter's direction, receiving an unhelpful faint shrug in return.

The quiet voice came for him again. "The acquaintance of Duc—what is her name?"

Duc hissed as if in pain. Taylor ignored it, watching Loc, twisting in his mind for a way to cover Duc, and finding none. "Her name is Tuyet, *Dai Ta*," he said, and felt like an informer.

Loc's expression seemed to brighten. "Does she speak well of Duc? Specifically, does she find him an acceptable sleeping partner?"

Duc hissed again.

"We haven't discussed it, *Dai Ta*, but I can tell you she calls him the Round Tiger."

Loc's laughter carried like a loud whisper, overriding Duc's groan. "Then we have reason to believe she may tell us an occasional truth," the Colonel said with an elegantly ironic bow toward Duc. "Women are untrustworthy, but a satisfied one may speak from a sense of gratitude. You agree, *Thieu Ta* Duc?"

Duc managed a strangled answer.

Loc readdressed himself to Taylor. "What has your—outpost—in this bar taught you? Restrict yourself to professional matters, please. My esteemed elder brother, *Dai Ta* Winter will require the other lurid details later."

Taylor relaxed. His palms were damp and a quick glance showed Duc was practically in shock. The trouble with Loc was you never knew if he was joking until he got ready to let you know. Meanwhile, you sweated.

"I've spent a fortune in there," Taylor said, "for Saigon tea for her. She's part of the operation. I've spoken to Trung. I told him I was in Supply, scheduling ammo to Long Binh, Binh Hoa, and so on. He discussed my 'job' with Tu and Sam An."

Loc exhaled a thin smoke plume. "The woman told you this?"

Taylor smiled. "They discussed it at the table next to me while I bought tea for Miss Tuyet."

Winter made a harsh sound. "They just talked it over while you listened?"

"They enjoyed doing it," Taylor said in English, then went back to Vietnamese. "They talked about my mother for a

46

while. Then they discussed my sisters and what they'd like to do to them, if I had any. When that bored them they debated my manhood. Miss Tuyet and I spoke English about the price of food, the possibility of me getting her some things from the PX, and other matters. She tried very hard to laugh only when I said something amusing."

"You gave no sign you understood any of that?" Loc inquired softly.

Taylor shrugged. "They would not have discussed bribing me if they thought I understood them."

"Good work," Winter said. He cocked his head to the side, examining both Taylor and Duc. "Now that we know they're willing to bribe someone, we can turn the information over to Special Branch. They'll set something up."

"Please, there is more," Duc said. He shot a look at Loc before continuing. "Taylor heard Trung say that the man to handle such an opportunity would be Nguyen Binh. It was Tu who suggested blackmail. They believe Taylor is such a fool a bribe is unnecessary."

"They used the name Nguyen Binh? You're absolutely certain?" Winter pressed.

"Yes, sir. The name meant nothing to me, but I thought it might to Duc, so I asked him. That's why we reported right away."

"You have a plan, Duc?" Winter asked.

Duc ran a hand through his thick, gleaming hair, his eyes jumping back and forth between the two Colonels. He stammered, finally managing a miserable, "We brought the information as duty requires. We have no plan."

"Then you'll have to make one."

It took a moment for the implication to sink in and then the moon face broke into a baby's smile.

Winter rocked in his chair, enjoying the effect. "Taylor, I'm bringing you up to op status, if Colonel Loc has no objection. We'll turn you and Duc loose on this contact." Loc met his questioning look and nodded.

"I understand that last bit!" Denby's smile apologized for the interruption. "Major Taylor's just learning his way around. I'd like to put him to work detailing VC Security Sections. We'll be losing Major Krause in a couple of months—." The sentence died in mid-air.

"They've started something. We'll see where it leads." Winter looked back to the two Majors, concentrating on the American. "You're aware that most of the information we generate through our cover operation—the business with the records—is handed over to CID, Special Branch, the Counterintelligence Directorate, the MSS, or whatever."

Taylor waited.

"Colonel Loc and I decide what's processed onward. Our sources and operations are completely independent. You report to us—only—and you put nothing on paper unless told to. Understood?"

He nodded, still unspeaking.

Winter went on. "There are perhaps five Americans in the country who actually know what we do, and maybe ten times that many South Vietnamese. Some of the latter are more dangerous than all the VC together. The last man who tried to kill Colonel Loc was hired by a Vietnamese General. As for the VC, God only knows how many of them know all of us on sight."

Loc inclined forward slowly, resting one hand on the coffee table. "Allow me to interrupt for one moment, please."

Winter waved acknowledgement. Loc faced them and Taylor wondered what he was reading in the spare man's piercing brown eyes. It could have been embarrassment, resignation, irritation—he realized he'd never be certain.

"What Colonel Winter hesitates to speak of is the corruption. Much of it is Vietnamese." Taylor shut out the sound of Duc's nervous shifting. "It has become a way of life. The temptations and reasons are too many to discuss—I merely state a fact. I am not interested in a democratic Vietnam, Major Taylor, nor in communism. I fight for a free Vietnam, self-governed by honest men loyal to this country."

Taylor said, "I already know how loyal your officers and men are, Colonel."

"That is one of the ironies of the situation. I must insist they be loyal to me. Personally. It is a tragic necessity. You must take my word we ten plan no coup. I tell you these things so you will not be painfully surprised when you find us targeted against our own, and *your* own, people."

"I understand. Thank you."

Loc settled back, pleased that Taylor had accepted the message with no visible surprise or polite protests.

"OK," Winter resumed in a quieter voice. "That's settled. Now we'll deal with some specifics. When you leave here, you and Duc write up an op plan to exploit the lead on Nguyen Binh. Do you have any ideas?"

Taylor grinned at Duc. "I know he has, even if he hasn't told me about it."

Duc bobbed his head, too excited to be nervous.

"I think we should let them blackmail him. It should be an easy thing. Then we arrange for them to receive a shipment of ammunition. As soon as they get it, we arrest them and question them."

Winter said, "Work on it, put it together, and we'll check it out."

As they shuffled their cards into a neat stack, Winter tented his fingers and dropped his chin onto the crown of the triangle formed. The gesture gave him the appearance of an aged missionary contemplating acolytes departing into a sinful world. He raised his head to speak.

"Your idea is fine, as far as it goes, but I—we—want Binh. If this is the best you can come up with, we'll have to brainstorm it some more."

Taylor faced him, his hand tentatively stroking his lips. He almost appeared to be erasing a smile, but the eyes above the hand were appraising.

"Want him what, Colonel?"

"Alive. At all costs."

"We'll try to come up with something clever."

"Do."

The frigid response was a surprise. Taylor knew he'd been warned. He slurred his departing "Yessir" into one word, easing the door shut behind him.

Winter's unexpected show of tension disturbed Loc, putting a brusque edge to his own voice when he spoke to Denby. "I must ask you to excuse us. There is something I must discuss with Colonel Winter."

Denby smiled and nodded his way out, his anger at the ultimatum in Loc's manner visible in the color of his cheeks.

Once the door was closed, Loc said, "You act as if this Taylor may be able to do something for us."

"I think his luck is good," Winter said. "If it is, we may get our chance at Binh. I *want* him, Loc."

Loc sighed at the returned intensity, resigning himself to the fact that he had no choice but to get his own problem exposed.

"We need some luck, Win. We may need Binh as much as we want him."

The larger man herded his coffee cup around on the desk top with an index finger. "I knew damned well you had something on your mind when you came in here. You'll tell me what it is now, I imagine."

"Am I so obvious to you?" Loc groaned mock dismay. "I've succeeded too well. First comes understanding—soon you'll aspire to culture. I'll be responsible for a new race of whites."

The intercom buzzed before Winter could respond. He flipped the switch and a voice said, "Corporal Ordway, sir?" Winter answered and the voice crackled again. "There's a Lieutenant Colonel Earl to see the Colonel?"

Winter smiled, listening to the Southern lilt that made a question of statements and the punctilious use of the third person that identified his enlisted Marine. It further amused him that this and other niceties coincided with Taylor's arrival.

"Have him come up," Winter said, his smile changing to a grimace as he looked to Loc.

Loc clamped his teeth, aching to tell Winter of the problem facing them and his disgust for the man approaching. First Denby and now this one—it was too much! He lit another cigarette, refilled his tea glass, and was seated again when Earl knocked. He forced himself to respond with civility but pointedly omitted any reference to welcome.

"How are things over at MACV?" Winter asked affably. "Keeping you busy?"

Earl grinned, an expression that suited him. It brought highlights to the electric-blue eyes and the perfect teeth: Blond hair, barely long enough to comb, lay in correct order on a well-shaped head.

"Always busy," Earl said, and the grin faded to a smaller smile that made him a bit less overpowering. "Sometimes I think we should just take all the paper out of MACV and build a wall with it. We could encase the whole country in a few months. And that's why I'm here."

"Because of paperwork?" Winter frowned. "Our required

reports have been right on schedule. I checked.''

Earl included both men in a look that said he knew he was being evaded. "Not routine reports. I have to know about operations. I have to make my own report back to the world and we both know your unit's been sneaking around doing things off the record. And I get it in the ass every time something comes up."

Winter looked puzzled. "I don't understand. If these things we're supposed to be doing are so sneaky, how does anyone know who's doing it? And why would you be in trouble?"

Some of Earl's friendliness melted. "We've been over this before, sir. When the Senator reads that a black market operator or a drug connection or a VC honcho's gone down, he wants to know how it happened. When my office can't tell him, he goes apeshit."

"We don't have anything to do with combat operations," Winter said. "We gather information for others to process. Our sources are very sensitive. The people you want to talk to are in the Phoenix program."

"The Phoenix office is a short walk from mine, Colonel. I talk to them the way you talk to Colonel Loc. They deny any connection with the murder of those men and we have a ton of reports from your unit concerning each of them, right up until they died."

"'Until they died.'" Winter repeated it softly. "Not 'until you murdered them?' And how'd the word murder come up, in the first place?"

Earl set his jaw. "Someone blew one up on a street corner, another one died when a grenade went off in his bedroom, and one disappeared. No one's ever been arrested."

Winter made a face. "The VC?"

"When the VC eliminate someone, they publicize it, get all the propaganda from it they can."

Placing his elbows on the table, Winter balled a fist in the opposite hand. "Now, there's another interesting semantic exercise. The VC 'eliminate' their victims, but if someone nails one of *them*, that's murder. Is that one of your unofficial instructions from your Senator? Everyone in Nam knows that sonofabitch has been trying to castrate the Phoenix program since—."

"Because it's wrong!" Furious, Earl hunched forward in his

chair. "They're no different than the VC! They're worse! They kill civilians, torture prisoners, anything you can name!"

"As you said, we've been over this before. Frankly, I wish you were as anxious to prosecute the war as you are the people fighting it."

Calming himself, Earl said, "The prosecuting's being done, Colonel. Other countries have held war crimes trials and convicted the accused. The United States can't take that kind of international pressure."

"Why?"

"Because we're in the wrong here. We're defending a government shot through with corruption—."

Loc interrupted. "Two of the dead men you spoke of were the ultimate in corruption. If we bring them to trial, your newspapers accuse us of rigging the trial. Worse, the criminals take advantage of other corrupt officials and buy their freedom. Is it any wonder honest men break? If those men were murdered, how can you blame the killers?"

Earl shook his head stubbornly. "If you don't have a decent government, a clean government, then it's obvious it has to be replaced."

Rising to his full height, Loc glared at Earl until, as a junior officer, he reluctantly stood. The Vietnamese had to tilt his chin to meet the American's eyes once Earl was on his feet. If the height disparity bothered the shorter man, he hid the fact. When he spoke his voice crackled with emotion, but it never rose above conversational level.

"You imply that this goodness flows from the north. If it is such a paradise, why do the refugees always run south? If we lose, they will see a functional government, exactly as in a prison. And you will be back in the United States. What a pity we are all evil and there are no Christ-figures among us. You will be cheated of the opportunity to wash your hands of us!"

With a sharp nod for Winter, Loc stalked from the room.

Earl sat back down. "Now I'll have to apologize. I can't make him, or you, understand I really care about what happens to these people."

"That's not enough."

Earl threw his hands wide. "Not enough? I'm here, aren't I? I'm trying to help!"

"A rationale to gladden the heart of Torquemada. We bring

the heathens the true faith and if they don't accept it, with proper gratitude, why, they deserve to burn. You're so blinded by your own goodness you can't find your way into the gutter with those of us fighting this goddam war."

"That's the point. If we have to sink to the level of the terrorists, we've proven nothing."

Winter gestured shortly and got to his feet. "I've heard all these arguments, yours and mine. They bore me."

Earl stood up again, features tightly controlled. His breathing was quickened, as after light exercise. "I'm sorry if you find my objections to this war and to murder out of line. Fortunately, the Senator doesn't. For the past two months my office has been preparing a weekly briefing for him and we've been ordered to continue. He's told the Army he's working to have the Phoenix program terminated. He'd like to go further and see anyone involved thoroughly investigated."

Winter opened a desk drawer and withdrew a tattered manila folder. He let it fall to the desk.

"Don't ever think I take you lightly. Dangerous fools scare me more than clever enemies." He tapped the folder with a thick finger. "If you ever lose your copy of one of your reports, feel free to borrow mine. Or the official return correspondence from Washington, if you'd like."

Earl blanched. "You don't! You can't! Who—?"

"I have it," Winter interjected coldly. "You've been indiscreet in some of your off-the-record comments, you know. There're Generals who'd be unhappy over your analysis of their characters, despite your accuracy. But don't worry about it. I'll deny I have this trash as long as I can. You follow me?"

"It's come to this, then? You'd blackmail a fellow officer?"

Winter clapped his hands and laughed. "You're fucking priceless. You walk in here, accuse me of murder, suggest I'm likely to be tried for it—you'd sell your sister on Tu Do for evidence this unit's responsible for something illegal—and you're shocked because I'm blackmailing a 'fellow officer.' Go back to your politicians. And don't give me a reason to step on you."

Earl moved to the doorway rigidly, his normal erect bearing transformed to stiff geometry. He paused before leaving. "Don't think I take you lightly either, Colonel. My only questions about you are if you personally had those men killed and how far you'd go to protect yourself. You may be a greater menace than the VC. I intend to be very careful about you."

The door closed behind him and Winter spun, frowning through the window into the heat at bay outside, his thoughts disorganized as wind-driven sparks. Earl had been an irritant before, a believer in the anti-war point of view, but no less dependable for that. No one else understood what the hell was going on, so why should he? But this was different. Everything was changing. Generals had always scuffled for political influence, but to see a Lieutenant Colonel blatantly allied with a Senator was a new experience. And dangerous. The war had become a power struggle among the ambitious of all political stripes. The killers and the killed were simply statistics to determine the progress and direction of the machine.

Loc knocked softly and admitted himself. "Does he want to make trouble?"

"*Beaucoup*. We may get political influence, Loc. From our Senate."

"If it happens, it happens. I think Earl will stumble soon. He runs too fast for his head to keep up."

"I hope you're right."

Loc drew a deep breath and opened the new problem.

"One of our people has broken our trust." The words came smeared with hurt. "I cannot be certain he has broken our security. He is involved in money exchange, black market, and I suspect drug sales."

He watched in fascination as the muscles in Winter's jaws began to pump in and out, in and out, like small bellows.

"You have proof?"

Loc shook his head. "Only a report, so far. I want to discuss it with you."

"If the report is correct, there is nothing to discuss. The man has become an enemy."

Contentment quenched some of the heat of anger and apprehension in Loc's mind. Things were going to proceed in a correct manner. From their first meeting, years ago, they had agreed on how to deal with the enemy. Still, it always chagrined him that this grim moré was the only area where no cultural difference had ever intruded.

"How did the information come to you?" Winter asked. "Are any of our people in danger?"

Loc waved a languid hand, as though dispersing smoke. "I think there's no danger at present. My concern is for the future."

Winter nodded, waiting for Loc to continue. It was a long wait and he became uncomfortably aware of the hum of the air-conditioner, nagging at his patience.

At last Loc said, "The young Lieutenant, Le Duc Hon, the one you do not trust, brought me the report."

"I don't distrust him. I don't like him always arguing politics. We're not a debating team."

"We're off the subject." Loc smiled. "I will start at the beginning. Lieutenant Hon has been keeping me informed, through his CID contacts, concerning the Major at MACV suspected of money manipulation."

"I know of him."

"Then you know he hasn't been caught. He has a way to get money out of country through some neutral source, or some such." Winter remained mute and Loc continued, "They are certain the Major is the source of funding for a bar on Plantation Road. Lieutenant Hon was privileged to see some pictures taken during surveillance of the Major. He recognized a familiar face in two."

"One of us?"

"Sergeant Nguyen Van Hai."

Winter pursed his lips and pinched them between his thumb and knuckle. Dropping the hand, he turned to the window. "What've you learned?"

"The details are tedious, Win. Basically, the Major and Sergeant Hai meet. They exchange a few words and part."

"And?"

"The CID has made no effort to follow Hai. The contacts have been too brief to excite their interest. But Hon was interested. He watched the Sergeant leave the Major and go to a small restaurant. Hon could not go in, but when the Sergeant came out, he carried a package. Hon followed him to the vicinity of the vice area of Plantation Road and lost him. We also have learned that Sergeant Hai's brother recently bought property and two fishing boats in Da Nang. A few months ago he was a poor fisherman."

"What do you want to do next?"

"The man who manages the bar on Plantation Road has an

office above the place. There are two doors, one onto the hall leading to the bar, another leading to stairs outside. Late tonight some Vietnamese civilians will ask the manager questions. He will answer reluctantly at first, but with greater enthusiasm as time passes.''

Winter made a face. ''For a man who prides himself on subtlety, you have a knack for the direct approach.''

The ghost-smile flicked on and off as Loc bowed.

Winter said, ''Is there any chance the manager will complain about this interview?''

''No,'' Loc said thoughtfully. ''The men will advise against that. He will understand.''

''Do we have any idea who these men might be?''

Loc turned his palms up. ''Who can say what men prowl such a disgraceful place at night? In my mind, I could envision two who resembled Sergeant Le Minh Chi and Lieutenant Colonel Tho.''

Winter whistled. ''You're really pulling the plug, aren't you?'' He sat behind the desk again. ''Tho and Chi? You're sure the manager'll survive the discussion?''

''It's necessary. We may want to talk to him again. And now I go to discuss matters with Tho.''

''OK. I have to sign off on some papers. You want to sit in on Duc and Taylor's rough op plan when it's done?''

Loc tugged an ear, thinking, then, ''Yes, I would. I'm curious about Taylor. I want to know why you have such high hopes for him. He has not impressed me yet.''

''I'll call you.''

Loc waved, a graceful, almost feminine gesture, and left.

6

THE LAST EFFORTS OF THE SINKING SUN were turning the clouds to molten copper as Taylor settled into the back seat of the tiny Renault. Like all the other Bluebird taxis, it was battered and weary, floor scarred by innumerable cigarette butts, upholstery threadbare. The interior had the gentle greasy feel of a properly oiled weapon. Unfortunately, in this case it was an accumulation of grime. The trick to riding a Bluebird and emerging in reasonable condition was to touch as little as possible. It wasn't accomplished often, because the average American found his head jammed against the ceiling, his knees against the front seat, and his body jerked about unpredictably in the maelstrom of Saigon traffic.

The driver turned a wary face to his passenger.

"BEQ One," Taylor said.

"One hundred P." The voice was demanding.

Taylor answered wearily, "Aw, bullshit. Forty P, or I take other taxi."

The driver was adamant. "BEQ One one hundred P. All taxi same-same."

Every night the same thing, Taylor thought. We both know it's a twenty P ride for a Vietnamese and a fifty P ride for an American and we always have to start at a hundred and haggle. He stripped fifty piasters from his wallet and extended them to the driver. Muttering, the man grabbed the money and shoved it in his pocket, simultaneously lurching into the traffic on Cach Mang. He whipped into an immediate U-turn. Motorcycles and motorbikes shoaled gracefully past and a huge six-by trumpeted as it dodged clumsily to avoid them.

The quitting-time crush from MACV and Tan Son Nhut reminded Taylor of the Mixing Bowl at the D.C.-Springfield interchange on an August evening. The scale was smaller, but the performance made up in lunacy what it lacked in size. No one kept to prescribed lanes, smaller vehicles crowded in between larger ones, engines and tempers overheated in tandem, and the lightning of multilingual cursing arced through the smother of exhaust. Buses and trucks roamed with the arrogance of small-town bullies. Smaller cars and motorcycles got out of the way or were shoved aside.

At his first exposure, Taylor marveled that no one did anything about it. Since then, he'd decided the larger miracle was that there was no shooting.

The driver executed a suicidal left across traffic onto Truong Ming Giang and picked up some speed. The faint, humid breeze, stirred by their progress, was a blessing, cooling the civilian shirt that already clasped Taylor like damp plastic. He perked up, observing his surroundings instead of anticipating a crash.

The market on the near bank of the Rach Thi Nghe was always active. The creek itself, noisome as the pits of hell, glistened like rancid chocolate. In the shade of the bridge it was black. Shacks made of any material imaginable backed away from the paralleling streets and crowded into the space above the water, some precarious, on thin, awkward pilings made of debranched saplings. He always wondered what really held it all up.

Once across the bridge, a roofed alley opened to the left, the tunnel-like entrance to the Chantareansay Pagoda. There were rumors of militant monks struggling for leadership of the Pagoda and the city shuddered at every hint of trouble from the saffron robes.

A few blocks further on, the Bluebird pulled to the curb. Taylor got out quickly, urged by the honking behind him. The driver listened for the sound of the door closing, then jerked away into the torrent. At no time did he look to see if his passenger was safely out.

Taylor walked around the corner and set off toward his appointment. He could as easily have taken the cab to Mrs. Ly's, but at the outset of his lessons he'd walked the streets convinced that unseen eyes noted every step. Now he winced inwardly at his conceit.

Once off the main streets, the traffic thinned. Although hardly a suburban environment, it was possible to walk the shaded sidewalks and imagine the Saigon of quiet beauty that was presently submerged by a flood of refugees.

His destination was a large home set back from the street and surrounded by a high wall, crowned with teeth of broken glass that glittered in the light from the windows in a fierce corona. He knocked at the wall's massive door and waited for the guard's eye to come to the spyhole for recognition. The wooden mass swung away with the complaint of hinges never designed to accept the weight of the additional steel plates bolted to the interior side. The thud of its closure behind him cut off the world.

The house was a sanctuary, shaded by huge trees, surrounded by exuberant tropical plants constrained by discipline as effective as it was apparently artless. The house itself was a balanced arrangement of rectangles and squares, functional and beautiful. Inside this citadel the Pham family fought a graceful battle to continue an existence they could barely remember.

The maid, wrinkled age in contrast to her pressed white jacket and black pajama-trousers, opened the door at his knock, bobbing and smiling.

"*Chao, Trung Ta,*" she greeted him, then, proudly, "How you are?"

Surprise lifted Taylor's eyebrows and she took a deep breath, adding, "*Toi hoc tieng Anh*—I am study English."

He answered in Vietnamese. "Ah, *Chi* Hong, if you learn English, how can Americans have secrets?"

She laughed. "Americans have no secrets."

"Only hair," he said, making a sad face.

She clapped her hands over her mouth and ran from the room with a gait like skater's strides, shrieking with laughter. He watched her, remembering how upset *Ba* Ly was at the end of their first lesson when he'd shown off and called the maid *Ba* Hong. Servants were *Chi*, he'd been told—the word for sister—and he was to remember it. It was fairly easy to remember to use the given name instead of the family name. The word *Ba* didn't mean exactly the same thing as Mrs., but it was sufficiently approximate that both cultures understood the intent of the translation. *Ba* Ly would be Mrs. Nguyen Thi Ly in America. In Vietnam she was *Ba* Ly and her husband's family name was practically unused.

He stayed just inside the entry, hesitant to enter further without invitation. The peacefulness of the place gave the eye a chance to study, to coordinate things. *Ba* Ly had already told him the flowing modern furniture was locally built, rosewood and teak. The upholstery was a rich tan and felt as good to the touch as the sensuous wood. Beside him towered a huge vase, shoulder high, its surface a mass of intertwined dragons, clouds, mountains, blossoming trees and frothing streams. Aside from the vase, the only other bright colors in the room came from the Oriental rug and two smaller vases full of flowers. It came to him that he'd never seen any part of the house when it didn't look as if the Phams were expecting the photographers from "House Beautiful." It also occurred to him that with two full-time maids, a cook, and a yard man, the place ought to look pretty squared away.

Ba Ly entered from the dining room. As with many Oriental women, she wore eastern or western clothes with complete ease. Today she'd chosen the *ao dai*, the outer sheath daffodil

59

yellow. As she passed a window the reflected light from the panes lanced across the material in shining swaths. The muscles at the small of Taylor's back bunched.

Her usual placid beauty was disturbed by a puzzled frown. "What did you do to *Chi* Hong?" She motioned him toward the sofa. "She is laughing so hard she can barely speak."

Taylor grinned as he sat down. "I confessed that Americans have no secrets, being only hairy foreigners."

The frown was swept away in laughter and then she shook a finger at him with mock severity. "You shouldn't give her excuses to laugh at you. You will lose face."

"Maybe. I doubt it. And I'm not that worried about my dignity. Not with her. We know each other."

She leaned to one side. "She likes you, you know. You have made a conquest. Now she says there are good as well as bad things to say about the Americans."

"She disliked us before?"

"No, not disliked. Before, there were bad things to say, but that was offset by the fact that you meant well. Still, there were no *good* things. Now she tells her friends there are Americans trying to understand us. She knows one, and if there is one, there are others."

Taylor's grin skewed to a rueful expression. "I should go home. I've won a heart and a mind. I've made my quota."

She refused to be amused. "I know you joke, but there is much truth in it. This war will be won with words."

Meanly, Taylor wanted to say, a little land reform wouldn't hurt. I've heard about your mother's family's holdings. Instead, he tried to explain his actions, rather than his beliefs.

"I have to make jokes. As confused as I am, if I don't keep laughing, I'll go crazy."

She looked at him with sympathy. "It is very difficult for you. There are things we don't understand and it is our culture that is involved. It must be terrible for you."

He held up his hands in surrender. "Uncle Ho's the best example. We came here prepared to hate him because he started this mess. Can you imagine what a shock it is to find South Vietnamese fighting his army and loving him?"

"Almost all of us respect him greatly. Those who understand what the communists really are can't accept his politics, but he's the man who gave us independence. We can't forget that."

"But now you have the Americans."

Her eyes flew wide open. "Never say that, Major. Never. Too many Vietnamese already believe it and the rest would take it as a very bad joke."

"So bad as that?"

She leaned toward him, her hand settling on his arm with butterfly nervousness. "Any hint from an American, especially an officer, that you think of South Vietnam as a colony is worth a battalion to the VC."

He was as aware of her confiding hand as he would have been of a branding iron. Blunt pictures of his monastic existence popped into mind.

"I'll remember," he assured her. "I have enough trouble without Colonel Winter accusing me of recruiting for the VC."

"Not even he would be so harsh," she said, laughing easily again. She withdrew her hand and folded both in her lap. "Anyone who watches you knows you are a professional soldier."

"Oh?"

"Of course. Even here, you do not study, you attack the words. You learn our customs one by one, as if each piece of knowledge is a fort to be captured. You start with a puzzled expression," she mimed his face, "and then, when you do not see the answer immediately, you scowl." She drew arched brows together and stuck out her lower lip. "Finally, you make words deep in your throat, like growling. I never hear the words, but I know you say very bad things."

He defended himself. "Any man would be angry, trying to learn a language that has tones like a song. I'm allowed to growl."

"Oh, there's more than that. I have seen you walk down the street. Your back is straight but you look at everything like a forest animal, always ready to move in any direction. When you come to my door you look at the maid, then right away you look past her into the house searching."

"But I feel so relaxed here," he protested. "I may look cautious out on the street, but I'm comfortable in your home."

61

"That is what made me certain. If I leave you, sometimes when I come back you look at something far away. It is the face of a small boy, dreaming of adventures. The first time I saw that, I knew you were not just another man in a uniform."

"You said I was the one who looked at everything," he chided her.

She clasped her hands around her knees and rocked back on the sofa, a childlike expression of pleasure.

"But you made a mistake," he continued seriously, and she looked confused. "When you come back, I have no dreams of adventures. In English, we would say my expression is wistful. When you go, my thought is, 'How sad the garden, when the flowers have gone.'"

For a full second she stared at him in shocked surprise. Then she blushed. Her hands reached to cover it and she laughed.

"Now see what you've done! My face is burning! I will be afraid to leave you to get tea for you!"

"Then we both have a problem." He feigned sadness. "You will be afraid to go and I will be afraid you will not come back."

She stood up. "We must both be good soldiers then, and attack. Would you like tea?"

Taylor also rose, looking down at her upturned face. The move brought them within inches of each other.

"Please," he said, disturbed to feel the single word force its way out like a bubble through viscous liquid.

Her eyes flicked away and she took a step backward, covering the movement with a quick half-smile. Swiftly bending to pick up the language text from the coffee table, she handed it to him and stepped back further.

"It'll be a minute, only. Study the section on predicative elements."

He opened the book to the proper chapter and tried to concentrate. He was finally able to dismiss her but his mind perversely brought up the meeting arranged for that evening with the people at the Friendly Bar. He'd have to be as attentive as ever to Tuyet and after what had just happened, that would be difficult.

He squeezed his head to force the problem away and *Ba* Ly's image returned.

The situation would be impossible. If he asked her out and

she accepted, most of her friends would ostracize her. And he knew the reaction of most Americans toward Vietnamese women who were seen with other Americans. It would take a peculiar combination of determination and compromise to submit a woman to all that.

When she returned with the tea she was the teacher and he the student. The conversation was over and the hours trudged by.

Suddenly he was aware of time. His momentary preoccupation was enough to catch *Ba* Ly's eye. She closed the book.

"Enough for this evening," she said. "Is it becoming clearer for you?"

"Slowly, slowly." He massaged his temples.

She patted his hand. "That is not so. You are the quickest student I have ever seen. And you work harder. You are my prize pupil."

"Is that why you let me stop early?"

"A few minutes. It won't hurt you."

The thought of the meeting at the bar made his smile more rueful than he intended. He looked at her and the thought of the ardently avaricious Tuyet intruded.

He got to his feet. "I don't know what my appetite will think, being attended to so early in the evening. It's not quite eight o'clock—still the hour of the cat, right?"

She was pleased. "In a few minutes it will be the hour of the dragon. Do you know what comes next?"

Wryly, he said, "The hour of the MP, who enforces the curfew."

"You are terrible!" She clapped her hands together, laughing at him. "Now, be serious, what comes after the dragon?"

"The two hour period of the day known as the hour of the dragon is followed by the sixth two hour period of the day, the hour of the serpent, followed by the hour of the horse." He stopped the monotoned recital, grinning at her. "Want more?"

She wrinkled her nose at him. "You show off." She tossed her head, causing the long black wings of her hair to flutter from her shoulders and settle on her back. "I said you were like a small boy."

He bowed gravely. "At my age, dear lady, a statement like

that can only be a compliment."

A sound of rustling cloth interrupted them and they turned together as *Ba* Ly's mother, *Ba* Lien entered the room. She, too, wore the *ao dai*, a rich maroon, and could easily have been her daughter's older sister. Her face was unaware of the march of years, her figure trim and firm. There was about her, though, an aura that pressed on imperiousness. Her dealings with Taylor always left him with the impression that he was welcome, not as a guest or student, but as an intruder who was oddly entitled to all the rites of hospitality.

Taylor half-bowed. "It's good to see you, *Ba* Lien. You and your husband are well?"

She smiled. "We are well, thank you, *Trung Ta*. And you?"

"Your daughter makes me work too hard, but I am still healthy."

Ba Ly made a face.

"And our friends, Colonel Winter and *Dai Ta* Loc?"

"They are well. They will be honored that you asked about them. I hope our talking didn't disturb you this evening?"

"No, I was reading in the library while my husband works on some of his constant paperwork." Her expression turned to disdain. "The government thinks enough paper will solve any problem. But it is I who must apologize. I have interrupted your lesson."

"We were just finishing, Mother."

Taylor said, "I'm glad you came in. It gives me a chance to tell you again how I appreciate your kindness, allowing me to study here with *Ba* Ly."

"We are happy to be able to help. In these times, everyone must do whatever possible."

He nodded gravely, wondering why she didn't just go ahead and add, "no matter how painful." It was a good cue to exit on.

"Well, ladies, if you'll excuse me, I'll go now. I'm staying too long."

"*Chao, Trung Ta.*" *Ba* Lien's sibilant *ao dai* whispered her departure.

"Same time tomorrow?" *Ba* Ly asked.

"Same time. See you then." He stepped out and she stood in the doorway.

"Be careful, Charles."

He waved over his shoulder, walking past the guard and onto the sidewalk. It wasn't until the sound of the closing gate was in his ears that he realized she had used his first name.

Ly was aware of what she had said as soon as the word was spoken and the impact of the situation dazed her. She shut the door hastily, staring at the paneling.

Never in my life have I used the first name of a foreigner, she thought, the memory ringing in her ears.

Her mind raced on. He is a good man. I like him. I look forward to his visits. There could never be anything more than those visits. I must make that very clear to him when he comes tomorrow evening. It would be rude to mention this incident, so I will simply not mention it. I will call him by his rank, only—even one of them will understand what I am doing.

She turned from the door just as Hong entered.

"He has gone?" the maid asked.

Ly walked to the table and picked up the textbook. "Yes, he just left. Did you wish to speak to him?"

"No," Hong said guilelessly, "I wanted to see how he said goodnight to you."

"What do you mean?"

Hong shrugged. "I am an old woman, and poor. There is no excitement in my life. The movies cost too much. I thought it would be good for my heart to see some romance. Is he as clumsy as the Americans we see on the TV?"

"It will do you no good to spy," Ly said sharply, "unless you hope to improve your language."

Hong picked up the tea glasses and the ashtray, turning eyes that were at once challenging and sad on the younger woman.

"A pity. Of course, he *is* as hairy as the rest of them, but he doesn't smell too bad and he looks strong."

"I'm sure he's very healthy."

Hong scratched an arm while she considered. "No, he cannot be. You are a beautiful woman, still young. You are alone with him every evening for hours, side by side. He only studies." She shook her head. "He is not healthy."

Ly tossed her head. "There have been many Americans come here as my students. They mean nothing to me."

"That is so." Hong puffed the sofa cushions and Ly resumed her course toward the stairs.

"On the other hand," Hong's voice checked her, "with the

others you sat at the table in the dining room. The student sat at one end and you at the other. One heard words clearly. Now you sit here on the sofa and there is only buzz-buzz-buzz.''

Ly felt her face warm again. Twice in one evening! It was insufferable!

She rounded on Hong. ''You have been spying!''

''I do not spy.'' Hong oozed dignity. ''Sometimes I look in to see if an old woman may be of some help, but I never look long. There is never anything to see, anyhow. And all I ever hear is his great, deep voice,'' she lowered her own as far as she could, *''toi kheong biet!''* she burlesqued, horribly mispronouncing the Vietnamese for ''I don't understand.''

''That is not true! He speaks very well! In another month he will speak better Vietnamese than you!''

Hong cocked her head to the side, her expression suddenly as sharp as a market haggler's. ''Does the teacher defend her pupil, or the woman defend an exciting man?''

''Don't be silly!'' Ly hacked at the air angrily. ''I am twenty-seven years old, not some silly village maiden!''

Hong cackled happily. ''When I was only twenty-seven I considered every man I could see! My husband never knew a full night's sleep!''

They faced each other for a long moment, one frowning and the other smiling, until both expressions began to alter, the younger afraid and the older sympathetic.

''I know how old you are,'' Hong said. ''I was with your mother when you were born and I have been here since. I have not seen you happy for a long time. The American amuses you. I have seen it. A woman your age—.''

''A woman my age is fortunate to have the affection of one so wise,'' Ly interrupted. She walked to Hong and took her hand in her own. ''I am grateful. But you must understand. He is not a toy I can play games with.''

Hong nodded and disengaged her hand. She walked away, her gaze on the rug, weariness blotting its bright colors from her sight.

''That is what I feared,'' she said under her breath.

7

IN THE CROWDED OFF-WHITE CUBICLE that was their office space, Taylor and Duc relaxed, sipping jasmine tea the American had brewed for the occasion.

"To the first morning of our own operation." Taylor raised his glass in a toast. "I'm grateful to you. You'd have been doing something all this time if you hadn't been my nurse."

Duc nodded, answering in his own language. "It is necessary. There are many things you must know. If you did not learn Vietnamese so quickly—." He grimaced.

As he spoke, he watched Taylor. Colonel Loc always said a white man's face was a map of his mind. It was true. In Taylor's he could see embarrassment at the compliment, pride, and anticipation. Duc wondered if he liked Taylor. It was difficult to dislike the Americans. They were so earnest. A quick shudder ran up his back as he remembered the first weeks with Taylor, his insistence they speak only Vietnamese. It seemed they spent half their time silent while his huge hands thumbed an English-Vietnamese dictionary to tatters. Then, suddenly, he began to speak with authority.

Colonel Loc had smiled when Duc reported the rapid improvement, the tight-lipped expression that could mean anything and always made Duc's armpits trickle.

"It is not a trick," Loc had said. "I have spoken to *Dai Ta* Winter about this man. He has a mind that grasps languages. It is curious he never mentions other instruction, and our tones come quickly to his tongue. You will learn what other language he speaks."

Duc masked distaste with a vigorous nod. The Americans reported on him and all the other Vietnamese in the Unit, just as the Vietnamese reported on them, but it was unpleasant.

The memory of the conversation jogged his mind. He was also supposed to speak to Taylor about staying in Vietnam longer than his normal one year.

He decided to be direct, as the Americans were. "Will you extend to stay in Vietnam?"

Taylor pulled up from his glass in surprise. "Me? No fucking way, buddy. I have to get back to the States and start making contacts for a job when I retire."

"I understand." Duc carefully stifled boiling resentment. The one thing all Americans did that truly angered him was to treat the war as an unpleasant incident.

My earliest memories are the sounds of war and the sight of armed men. To me, peace is an incident.

He retreated to the present. "Do you have any thoughts on the plan we must present tomorrow?"

Taylor smiled, untouched by complications. "I haven't thought about much else. Let's really sell them the truckload of ammunition."

"You joke?" Duc sputtered.

"I hope to Christ I can get a reaction like that from your ice-cube up topside. I'd give plenty for that."

Duc frowned. "You better hope he laughs."

"I'm not kidding. I mean it."

"Crazy," Duc muttered. "Some small thing, OK. Fool them and arrest them, OK. But trucks? Real ammos?" In his anxiety to be clear, he switched to English.

Taylor said, "I think we can make it work. I haven't done all my homework. Let's get the morning moving and go talk to Kimble."

Shrugging, Duc reached for his hat and followed, the irritable clump of his stride inaudible over the untroubled steps of his partner.

Despite the things on his mind, Taylor found himself remembering the morning Harker drove up to this place with him. It had been General Officers' quarters at one time and stood isolated from the other buildings in the ARVN compound, its singularity emphasized by a seven-foot-high cement wall surrounding the acre it stood on. The wall was painted a dusty pale rose, the building a tepid yellow—colors that struggled to lift moderation into an environment of tropical vitality.

The building was regularly pierced by tall narrow windows every few feet. In another time they would have been thrown wide open, the lower ones protected by the overhang of the second floor balcony and those upstairs by awnings that would jut beyond the roof line. Jalousied shutters would have been hooked back and a breeze would have caressed the people and things inside with humid smells hammered from the ground by the sun. Now most of the shutters were closed. Metal-rumped air-conditioners poked through carefully cut holes.

Geometrically centered in the area allowed, the building was like a handsome woman grown old and denied grace, eyes shut to the world, constantly exhaling a breath tainted by smoke and aging insides.

All American personnel had living spaces on the second floor of the main building, where Loc and Winter had their offices. The first floor was used for working spaces. One large room, set aside for relaxation, contained a television, movie facilities, and reading material ranging from *Playboy* to two Bibles and a hymnbook.

A series of three identical small houses squatted a few feet inside the east wall, quarters for the Vietnamese enlisted personnel. Arranged by Colonel Loc, they were an unheard-of privilege.

Taylor and Duc turned the other way, toward a single cement block building. It was called, simply, the shop.

As they entered it, a tall, thin Lieutenant turned from a workbench. His sandy hair, cut short, was a furry crown on an otherwise angular set of features. The lips were thin, the eyes intensely bright despite their pale color, a washed-out blue. He blinked rapidly behind steel-rimmed glasses, vision adjusting from staring at the small electronic device in his hand. The walls were all given over to shelf space, full of a jumble of technological bits and pieces. A solitary desk filled a hole between some of them, its surface matted with paperwork. A huge calendar hung from a tack in one of the boards, convenient to the swivel chair. The smell of burnt ozone completed the picture of a scientific monk's cell.

"Hi," the Lieutenant said. "You gentlemen come over to hide out for a while?" He gestured at two straight-backed chairs. "It's always quiet in here. Everybody's afraid I'll electrocute 'em. Want some coffee?"

Taylor said, "No, thanks, and we're not on the run. We've got a chore and I think you can help."

Lieutenant Kimble said, "We aim to please. Kimble's Toy Shop. Beepers, blasters, and other odd shit, made to order. Warren Kimble, at your service—Supply Officer, technician, and general good fellow. Name your poison, gents."

The angular body folded into the swivel chair and he grinned at the two visitors sitting across from him.

He hoped his welcome hid the apprehension settling in his bowels.

Don't let them want anything explosive. But it will be, I know it. I've listened to you, Taylor—you and your rice-burning shadow. You've been pawing the ground. I can smell death on you.

Lenore's face flashed into his mind, her tears salty on his lips as he kissed her. Lenore, who cried when he left for Fort Benning.

And when she discovered she was pregnant five hundred miles from her mother in Philadelphia.

And who cried alone nights when he had the duty.

And when he left to go overseas.

So many reasons for so many tears.

She wrote every day and sent a tape at least once a week in her desperate loneliness. On the tapes she tried to stop the recorder before the sobs broke through. Sometimes she was slow, though, and he heard her first sniffles. His throat constricted as he fought the urge to shout at the two men before him and tell them, make them understand that war was pain, longing, fear.

"—a small, powerful transmitter," Taylor was saying.

Embarrassment stung Kimble. "I'm sorry, Major. I was thinking about this thing." He gestured with the equipment in his hand. "What was it you had in mind?"

"I want to know if you can build me a transmitter, battery powered, that'll fit inside an 81mm mortar round, and what sort of range you can give me."

Kimble smiled. "How much range do you need?"

"Like everything else—all I can get. The dummy round'll be in a case, and the case'll be inside a stack of cases. Sooner or later, they'll all end up underground. I want to be able to follow them wherever they go."

Duc squinted at Taylor, understanding.

Kimble concentrated, eyes shut. "Let me use an interrupted signal and I think I can give you a safe guess of a thousand meters while they're above ground. I can't promise anything once they're buried. Too many unknowns."

"How long to make ten? Different frequencies."

"Ten?" He opened his eyes, surprised.

Taylor nodded.

"A couple of weeks, give or take."

"Good enough."

Kimble's joints felt as though they'd been frozen and were pleasantly warming.

"I'll need some rigged rounds, too, and some grenades," Taylor added.

The joints began to ache again.

"I want some grenades with instantaneous pull fuses. I want others with delay fuses that'll pop, say, two weeks after they're put in the grenades. On the mortar rounds, I want some that go off when the round drops on the firing pin and some of the self-destruct fuses for them, too. I'll need at least twenty doctored 81mm rounds—ten with one fuse and ten with the other. Same deal on the grenades. Can you handle that in the same two weeks?"

The joints were throbbing now. "I'll need help."

"Duc and I can help." Taylor turned to the Vietnamese. "You see what I'm building up to?"

Duc said, "Maybe work. What about M-16 ammo? Very valuable."

"Is that so? Then we'll fix some." He faced Kimble again. "You can get C-3, can't you?"

Kimble nodded, wanting to deny the question and not knowing how.

Taylor spoke to Duc, pantomiming in his intensity. "We'll need about five pounds. We pull the bullets, empty the powder and reload with C-3. Then we mix the bad rounds with the good ones. No one can tell the difference until he squeezes the trigger. He knows something's wrong when he sees the bolt coming at his eye."

Duc laughed and shook Taylor's bicep. "You got some good ideas. Very dirty. Maybe we make VC glad you only live here one year."

They stood up to leave. "I've got to get this scam approved. If they buy it, I'll let you know, so you can get started," Taylor said to Kimble.

Kimble mumbled at their departing backs. Duc's remark about one year reminded him he hadn't marked off the day on his calendar. Picking up a felt-tip pen, he started to fill in the square before noticing he was using black. He'd used black yesterday. He rummaged until he found a green pen—it'd been several days since he used green—and colored the box before looking hungrily at the next date. The small handwritten number under it said tomorrow he'd have two-hundred-seven left. He underlined the numbers.

He should have been anticipating his R&R in Hawaii by this time. Lenore's folks said they'd take care of Debbie. Mrs. Hocker had folded her flabby arms and sighed the way she always did and said, "Well, if it means so much to Warren he's willing to spend all your money just to sit on the beach, we'll baby-sit. We can get a cab to the doctor's or the hospital if anything goes wrong. It won't be no worse than taking care of her when you was 'way down there in Carolina and Lenore was working. At least the poor little thing's older now."

Lenore had killed the R&R, insisting they'd need the money when he got out. It'd really pissed him.

"I'll be going to work as soon as I get home," he'd explained. "You'll be working while I'm gone. We'll have plenty of money. What's the sense of having money if you don't use it?"

Shouting. "I can't just take off whenever I feel like it. If I tell them I want time off they might fire me. And what if there's a raise coming? You think they'll give it to me if they think I might just take off any old time?" He could still see her determined little face, the chin jutting out so defiantly.

His love for her then had wrenched his heart. She was willing to fight even him to make theirs a solid marriage. Despite knowing her practicality was right, the thought of a year's separation had driven him to further argument.

"No bank can be that narrow-minded. It's not a goddam jail, after all. Even bankers take vacations."

Mrs. Hocker had snuffled disgust and clumped her coffee cup on the table.

"Warren," she'd said, "when Lenore asked to live here so's you two could save money, I worried about it. I don't mind her being here when you're away. Glad to help. So's her father." She paused momentarily, as if a wandering memory had surfaced and drawn back again.

"I worry about how the Army'll change you. We try to understand you young people, but we can't change our ways overnight. I've been worried you'd bring back bad language," her eyes sneaking to Lenore and back again, "and other things. I won't put up with it in the house."

Before he could apologize, Lenore defended him.

"It was a slip, Mama." She'd patted Mama's hand. "We know you try to understand. It's not like he wanted to be in the Army, anyway."

Mrs. Hocker had peered at Warren suspiciously. "He never even tried that conscientious objection thing. If he'd worked harder in school he could have stayed longer, like the Morgan boy is doing. And those boys going to Canada aren't risking their lives or leaving their families."

Both women had poised for an answer, their eyes reminding Kimble of birds'. It had made him uncomfortable.

"I'm doing what I think's best," he'd said lamely. "I don't like it. I think it's best."

Lenore had been disappointed. Mrs. Hocker smiled.

He'd lost both arguments and couldn't even remember how the second one had started. He said he'd be leaving early in the morning to get back to the base. Lenore left with him to go upstairs, her mother scowling as she cleared off the table. The stairs were old and they sighed under the burden of each step. The thought of the unimaginable year away from her pounded in Kimble's head and in the darkness of their room the warm woman-scented night settled in his loins and expanded. He took her in his arms.

She buried her face in his chest. "Oh, Warren, I've been so upset I forgot to take my pill. I just couldn't, anyway. My head is spinning."

Kimble jerked himself away from the past and the calendar in the same movement. There'd be plenty of time to think about that sort of thing tonight. All it could get him now would be a hard-on and it'd be just his luck someone would come in and see it.

He looked to the notes on his conversation with Taylor and Duc. The smile slowly returned to his face. It was simple stuff, really. With luck, he'd farm the ammunition out to some engineers or an ordnance outfit. He'd handle the transmitters. It'd pass the time. Besides, they didn't explode. His stomach rumbled at the thought of explosives. It was bad enough putting together charges for that idiot Harker, but rigging ammo —ugh!

His hands and eyes automatically continued the work of

73

constructing the electronic timer on his workbench. His mind refused to consider anything but the explosives and he cursed the companion who'd sold him on ordnance school.

It had tied in so well with his knowledge of electronics and the immediate follow-up request for the Defense Against Sound Equipment course at Fort Holabird had been an inspiration. It meant more time in the States and it was only a couple of hours from Philly.

Lenore was fascinated by the cloak-and-dagger hints that surrounded the classes. When he confided he hoped to be assigned to a security unit in the States, she was ecstatic.

"You won't have to go to Vietnam?"

"I hope not."

"What'll you be doing? Where'll you go?"

"We run sweeps and stuff to make sure our phones and offices aren't bugged, that's all."

"But what if you find something? Then what?"

"We report it. Someone else decides what to do about it."

"You don't put any bugs anywhere, do you?"

"No, all I do is look for other people's."

"But the papers and TV always say the Army is spying on the protesters and the black-power niggers and all. Don't you do that?"

"Not me."

"Would they keep you near home?"

"I hope so."

"Oh, me too."

Then came the orders for Vietnam. The next weeks had been a nightmare of applications for other schools and trying to comfort Lenore.

He thought again of the stupid sonofabitch with his ideas about an ordnance course. His finger brushed the hot soldering iron and he cursed it and his former friend simultaneously.

That was what happened when you didn't think things through, when you listened to other people.

He sucked on the burned finger, almost sickened by the already hard patch of skin against his tongue.

That's exactly the way it goes, damn it. You start taking advice or let yourself get distracted and you end up burned every goddam time. Make your own decisions, like about

Lenore. If I'd listened to the rest of them about that, I'd have missed out on the only true beauty in my life.

Lenore.

His groin began to ache again.

8

THE SHARP KNOCK JERKED TAYLOR UPRIGHT from his paperwork. Corporal Ordway met his questioning stare impassively, confident that pressed utilities and freshly barbered hair were talismans against aggravated officers. His short, heavy legs spread in a sharp parade rest stance, supporting a thick torso that tapered from wide shoulders to a narrow waist. The face was blunt, pug-nosed, tough.

"Does the Major have a few minutes?"

"What's the problem?" Taylor put down his pen, hoping Ordway would make his point quickly, then almost smiled, thinking how Ordway's drawl made any oral message a long-term project.

"No problem, sir. I just wanted to talk to another Marine for a bit."

Taylor winced. "Congress called the wrong one of us the gentleman. Have a seat. Coffee?"

"No, sir, thank you kindly." Ordway settled into the chair beside Taylor's desk. "I got used to chicory in mine and this GI stuff all tastes like hog piss."

"I've tasted your chicory coffee. Liked it. But I thought that was New Orleans and you're from up north."

Ordway's careful expression shifted, and he was a very young blond man in a uniform, remembering.

"Gantry," he said. "Gantry, Louisiana. We like the chicory, no matter. You'd like it there, Major. Good people. Peaceful, if you don't fuck over 'em, you know?"

Taylor grinned. "You could say as much about Saigon."

They laughed at that and Ordway talked of home, of the family tensions when his sister married a staunch Catholic boy, and the great making-up when the first grandson was born. Then they got onto football, followed by hunting stories, memories of winter walks and warm fires. At that point Ordway sobered.

"Would the Major be upset if I asked a personal question?"

"I doubt it. Ask—we'll see."

"That shotgun the Major carries around—the sawed-off? Where'd the Major get that thing, and what the fuck does apeneck come from?"

Taylor laughed again. "That's two questions. The shotgun's from the Army MI unit. I don't know how I'll turn it in with the barrel cut off, but I'll worry about that come summer. I call it Apeneck after Apeneck Sweeney, a man in a poem."

"A poem? Like real poetry? Apeneck Sweeney?"

Professing scorn, Taylor said, "Certainly, like poetry. Don't they teach anything but football and 'possum skinning in redneck country?"

"I don't believe so," Ordway said. "People only learn what counts." He winked a dark brown eye. "You know, the Viet troopers really dig that thing, Apeneck. I believe they're all hoping Charlie'll jump you one day, so they can brag it up later."

"Thanks a lot, for Christ's sake. What if I lose?"

"They ain't hearing that shit. Neither am I."

"That's dumb, man. I can't see out the back of my head and I can't tell a VC from anyone else out there. Listen, I carry that thing 'cause it gives me a better first-round chance, that's all."

Moving his gaze to the right of Taylor's ear, Ordway said, "At least the Major's seen enough action to know about that kind of thing."

The look on the young face was too familiar to Taylor. Men wore it the day before their first battle. It had no sense of horror. Taylor looked at the eyes, as he had done so many times before, knowing the one thing he would never find there was understanding. That came later.

"Are you telling me you want a transfer to I Corps?"

The brown eyes blinked, still not meeting Taylor's. "It's not personal, Major. I mean, I like working with you all here, sir, and the doggies ain't all that bad, but I come in this outfit for three things, and I don't figure to get but two of them here."

"Three?"

"I want my ass back in Gantry in one piece. I want to see

76

some action. And I want a Good Conduct Medal.''

"A what?''

"I'm going to walk into my high school principal's office and jam it up his ass.''

"That ought to impress him. I'll tell you what—I'll talk to Winter. But remember, you've only got a few months to do. You'd have to extend. And what if you get greased?''

"Not your problem, Major.''

"Shit.'' He cut the air with the edge of his hand. "Let me get back to work. I'll see what I can do. But don't bug me.''

Ordway thanked him and barely got his face beyond the door jamb before the grin split it.

Sergeant Miller watched from the end of the hall, disapproval honing his sharp black features to a series of angles. When Ordway was close enough, he spoke softly.

"You gung-ho asshole. You get your transfer?''

Sergeant Wilton Miller, escapee from the Pittsburgh ghetto, lounged against the wall, one foot on the floor, the other cocked against the paneling. It was an out-of-place posture in the quiet hall, better suited to concrete while a man surveyed a crowded city street. It suited a pimp or a thief or a lookout, all of which Willy Miller had been before his twelfth birthday. Now, at twenty-six, a professional soldier, he still emanated the same sense of unresting awareness even in repose.

In answer to his question, Ordway said, "He's going to work on it. He ain't the Commandant, you know. He can't just ship people around.''

"What you want to go there for anyhow?'' Miller moved from the wall, suddenly a full head taller than Ordway. "What's so fuckin' wonderful about livin' in a fuckin' hole and eating cold chow and walking on mines and all that shit?''

"We talked about it plenty of times. I have to find out what I'm made of, man—that's all.''

"And I told you, Charlie's gonna drop an artillery shell in that hole with you and everybody's gonna know what you *used* to be made of.'' Miller walked out into the sunlight and Ordway followed.

"Willy, I got in the Corps to fight, not mess with drug pushers and black market and all that. It's the communists—.''

"Fuck the communists!'' Miller's arm flailed in a furious

77

arc. "That's all politics and people like you and me are going to get it in the ass from politicians no matter who's in charge. But we're allowed to kill them fuckin' dope pushers, man, and that's the only good thing about the whole motherfuckin' war."

"Shoot!" It was Ordway's turn to be scornful. "You ever heard of a pusher getting killed? They bust some PFC for holding once in a while. The big dealers are the old lifers and officers and Viets and blacks—don't look funny at me, you said it yourself—and you know nobody's fucking with them."

Miller looked away. "Well, don't it make more sense then to try to get one? Just one, Tony—Jesus, one of them'll screw up more people—! Don't it make more sense to try and get one of them?"

"Forget it. If you even got a good case, he'd buy his way out. They got the clout."

"Yeah, yeah. I know." Miller sagged momentarily, then started walking again. "But I won't quit. And you shouldn't neither. Not to run off and die in the jungle."

Ordway was apologetic. "I'm tired of this stuff. All you and me do is hang around in town and keep the Old Man posted on what we can find out about people pushing shit. What good's that do? Nobody does nothing."

Miller gave him a sly smile. "How'd you like it if I told you there's something going down that might change that?"

"If I believed it."

Miller's eyes went around the compound in an automatic scan. "Listen, Loc's turning loose Lieutenant Colonel Tho and Sergeant Chi on some dude down on Plantation Road. Remember the Major they think's sending home so much money? You know the joint called the Princess Bar? Well, they think the Major owns it."

Ordway's interest showed in his quickened words. "That's the place a couple of buys went down. You think the Major's in on it?"

"Got to be." Miller laughed sharply. "The money market's a hassle, now they got so many controls. But the woods is full of heroin, man. The sonofabitch has to be dealing." Despite their distance from anything, he slid closer to Ordway. "I talked to Chi. He owes me a couple favors. We can go with them, but Tho says it's off the record. If Winter hears—." He drew a finger across his throat.

"I'm in." Ordway punched Miller's arm. "You may turn out to be more'n pain in the ass yet, Willy."

"Just wear some dark civvies tonight. We'll leave here about 1930. Chi said to be in that alley-like that runs behind all those bars at 2145, exactly."

"What do we do between 1930 and 2145?"

"Check inside and memorize faces, every round-eye in the place. I'm going to make something out of this."

"I hope so." Ordway left, Miller's grim stare worrying his mind. He wished his friend could take a more reasonable view of drugs. A man who was always angry wasn't the most dependable soul in the world.

9

THE TWO VIETNAMESE and their Chinese partner huddled at a table in the far corner of the Friendly Bar in their PX sport shirts and slacks, sipping beer, trying to ignore the loud prattle of the Americans and the bar girls. A particularly ringing laugh grated on An's nerves and he broke his silence.

"How can one army produce so many fools? Every night is the same. They spend money on these worthless whores as though they were princesses."

An was the smaller of the three. His movements, as when he lifted his glass or dragged on his cigarette, were marionette gestures, exaggerated and imprecise. His right hand, holding the cigarette, constantly darted at the overflowing ash tray. He glanced down each time to verify he'd gone past it or was off to one side, corrected, then rapid taps dislodged a few flakes to flit erratically down toward the container. Whatever missed was swept away with infinite patience by the taller of the two Vietnamese.

While he cleaned up An's latest miss, Nguyen Van Trung turned to look over his shoulder toward the rest of the bar. "The Americans need love," he said, "or the illusion of it. The women who make the most money are the ones who convince them they are not buying sex, but helping a poor girl support a family. You may be right to call them fools. But they

79

have money. As long as they spend it to our advantage, I do not care if they drool."

An's head snapped back and forth in staccato nods. "On that we can agree." He turned to the second Vietnamese. "If we can keep our angry friend under control, we should make a fortune."

The subject of his criticism scorned it as a sulking bass will ignore a badly placed cast. After a moment, he rolled his eyes toward An.

"It would please me to poison them all." He resumed the study of the triangle of marred tabletop framed by his forearms.

"That would be a mistake," Trung chided. "We get better information from the ones who return frequently and our responsibility is to acquire information."

Do Chi Tu raised his head to look Trung full in the eyes. Where Trung's face was sleekly mobile and An's sharp and distinctly featured, Tu's was compressed, as though the parts were unified in a struggle to resist seething internal stresses. His lower jaw tapered to a sharp point at the chin, thrusting ahead of him like a belligerent prow, and the flesh of his nose gullied in above his nostrils. The effect was not unlike a dog on the verge of a snarl.

"I know my responsibility as well as you, Trung," he said. "You are happy here, playing at war and counting your money. I do not like play, and money only interests me because it helps our cause."

Trung blinked. Tu was testing his response. If it was incorrect, he would be forced into more tedious self-criticism at the next meeting.

"I must disagree with you," he said. "It pains me as much as you to cater to these buffaloes. We all have our assigned tasks and we must perform them unquestioningly. When we question assignments, we question our leaders."

Tu straightened in his chair. "I question no one. I only wish to strike harder blows, blows that give a man some pride."

"A proper spirit." Trung nodded sagely. "Still, there are those who would be disturbed to think you are not proud of your work, although we know that is a wrong interpretation of what you have said."

Trung sipped his beer, pleased to force Tu into a position

where he would worry about explaining his own thoughts to their mutal superiors instead of making trouble for others. "Furthermore," he continued, "if our plan for using the man Taylor is effective, you will be in position to ask for other assignments."

Tu grunted a reply, returning to his slumped-over examination of the table. Trung found the rejoinder intellectually unsatisfying but acceptable. Tu never outwardly agreed with anything, saving his breath to argue when he disagreed.

An understood, too. Realizing their conversation was ended, he asked Trung, "Are you certain we can blackmail this American? Tuyet says she has the hook in his mouth but sometimes he makes me think he is not as foolish as we would like. He makes me nervous."

"Everything makes you nervous," Trung said, almost concealing his contempt. "The smell of money seems to reinforce your courage, however, so think about that. You will be paid well to supply the transport when the time comes. We will take care of everything else."

"It is not all profit for me," An complained. "I pay a fortune in bribes. My expenses are terrible."

"The perils of commerce," Trung observed mildly.

An forgot his retort when he saw Taylor enter the bar.

"He's here!" he whispered.

"Why so secretive?" Trung laughed. "You could scream in his ear. He cannot understand." He waved at the American.

Taylor acknowledged the greeting while he searched for Tuyet, wanting to speak to her first. From her he'd gauge the attitude of the three men.

The Friendly Bar was easily inspected, once his eyes adjusted to the dark after the glaring lights of the streets. A rectangular room, approximately twenty by thirty feet, it featured a bar than ran the length of the right wall and ten randomly scattered tables. A patch of bare wood six feet square gleamed at the base of the stereo components shelved on the left front wall. It was a concession to the undeniable urge of the young Americans to stand up and work off some energy. Dancing was illegal, but one couple leaped about, tempting fate. The sole attempt at atmosphere consisted of a few dim yellow lights on the walls and a half-dozen artificial palm trees propped up in wooden tubs. The trees sagged as if decayed, burlap bark streaming in ragged hanks toward the floor, plastic leaves palled with dust.

The girls, both at the bar and the tables, were aware of the new entrant the moment the door opened and the unclaimed ones flashed mechanical smiles. They returned to their chatter when they recognized him. There were some bars where all the girls were pleasant. The Friendly Bar was geared for a selective approach. Taylor had noticed that men who talked a lot seemed to get better treatment. There was an obese Air Force Sergeant who was practically a member of the family. Taylor had watched him spend several evenings downing an endless succession of beers, finally leaving with one of the girls on each arm. He'd never seemed to pay anyone and Taylor had made a mental note to check out his popularity at some future date.

Tuyet's head craned from behind one of the phony palm trees. She winked and nodded toward the bar. Picking his way between the tables, Taylor seated himself and ordered a *Ba Muoi Ba*, the Vietnamese-made "33" beer. He took a long, thirsty swallow before turning to watch Tuyet shear the lamb of the evening.

He was Special Forces, one of the green berets propagandized as invincibles. Taylor felt sorry for them. Superbly trained and led, many of them came to Vietnam and found themselves holed up in static fortified villages on mountaintops where the war was nothing more than anticipation of the supply chopper and the daily certainty that this was the night Charlie was coming.

This one, red-headed and freckled, was obviously on an R&R turn. His boots were scraped and marred under their shine. His fatigues had the listless drape that came with rough washing and exposure to sunlight. Sometimes a rear-echelon type managed to keep a set long enough for them to acquire a similar color, even to the whitened knees and elbows. They never had the small frays where a sleeve had hooked a thorn or the brush-rubbed circle at the trouser's blouse just above the boots.

The soldier lifted his drink and drained it. Tuyet finished her tea.

"Give me money," she commanded. "I get more drinks."

The soldier waggled a finger at her. "I only got a little bit left. I'm saving it for you. I drank—drunk—." He scowled, only to break into loud giggles. The sound embarrassed him and he stared around the room owlishly until he was satisfied no one had heard.

"I drunk enough," he said.

Tuyet leaned on him, rubbing her breasts back and forth across his upper arm. At every stroke, the low-cut red satin of her evening gown pulled downward. The soldier's head wobbled in time with her motion. His eyes bulged with the strain of trying to see inside the top, despite the bad lighting and bad whiskey.

"Buy one more time," she coaxed. "I not ready go yet. This time I get real drink, not tea. Whiskey make me horny."

Licking his lips, he reached into a baggy pocket for his wallet. Tuyet pressed against him harder.

"I like feel your hand there." She slid her chair closer. "Leave hand in pocket little bit." She gyrated her hips. The trooper squirmed to turn his hand toward the movement and furtively checked the room. Taylor ducked before he was caught watching. When he looked again, the soldier was staring at Tuyet with the crystalline deliberation of a pigeon stalking popcorn. The hand in the pocket writhed like a small animal trapped under a blanket. Every time it made contact with Tuyet's thigh the bunched cloth formed a ravening mouth that opened and closed frantically.

Through it all, Tuyet's eyes remained closed in artistically simulated ecstasy. She made crooning noises when the hand closed on her leg, gleaming pink tongue sliding across her lips while she wrinkled her forehead in an impassioned frown.

Taylor was impressed. He knew those kneading fingers had to feel like tongs.

She placed both hands on the man's waist and pushed herself a few inches away.

"How much money you have?" she asked, staring into unfocused eyes.

The hand in the pocket swiveled on the wrist and came out holding a wallet. The trooper tore his gaze from Tuyet and started to open the wallet under the protective overhang of the table.

"Oh, I hope you got enough! I want make love you too much." She put her head on his shoulder. Her right hand snaked under his forearm and clutched at his crotch.

His eyes leaped in their sockets as though they would leave him. He started to rise from his chair, but her grip sharply arrested his progress. His mouth formed an amazed circle and issued an "Oooh!" composed equally of surprised delight and agony. The wallet flew from his hand onto the table. He sat down quickly and covered it with trembling fingers. A trickle of sweat ran past his ear.

"I got enough," he croaked. "I know I got enough. Let's go!" He reached to unclench her hand.

"How much?"

He whispered in her ear and her eyes gleamed. She shouted to the bartender in Vietnamese.

"Bring me a bottle of whiskey and the bill. I am taking this one home."

She turned back to her soldier, stroking his cheek. "I tell him you buy whiskey. I get my purse. You not leave before I come back?"

He giggled again and she spun around, discovering Taylor with a great show of surprise. "I not see you!"

She whirled back to the instantly suspicious soldier. "This man my friend. His girl friend not here tonight. I be just minute." Her smile placated him and his frown faded until he read the check. "Jesus," he muttered and began counting out bills.

Tuyet put her hand on Taylor's arm. "Good deal you come tonight." She indicated the three men in the back. "They talk about have party, go Mr. Trung apartment. Have *beaucoup* food, whiskey." She gave his arm a squeeze. "Girls be there, too. Play cards, maybe something else. They think maybe ask you but they afraid 'cause you officer, they not speak good English."

Taylor looked dubious. "I don't have much money with me. I might lose all I've got."

She laughed. "You not worry. I come later, give you good luck. You want talk them?" She tugged gently on the arm.

"I thought you were taking him home?" Taylor gestured covertly at the fidgeting soldier.

"Pretty soon he sleep good. No trouble. You want talk Mr. Trung?"

"Yeah, I guess so." He slipped from the barstool, bumping into the soldier. He excused himself.

"'S all right." A gentle sway contrasted with the challenging scowl. "I come over for Tuyet." His head swiveled to fix on her, the eyes seemingly locked directly forward. "You ready, honey?"

"I get purse." She rustled off, hips pumping under the red material.

"She's takin' me to her pad," the soldier confided. "Really hot, y' know?" He grinned hungrily, hostility forgotten. "I'm really lucky, man. This the first bar I come in and right off I find a broad really likes me, y' know? Some guys spend hunnerds o' dollars here in Saigon and they never find no broad really likes 'em, man. They end up with some whoor just wanted their money." He leered toward the darkness where Tuyet had disappeared. "She's just a cheap bar girl, but she likes me. 'S different, like." He executed another turning movement to look at Taylor again. "She does this for money for her mother and sisters."

His eyes went out of focus again, boring through Taylor. His mouth bowed downward. "Y'know, 't's a fuckin' shame, man."

"It certainly is," Taylor sympathized. "It's a total fucking and a shame."

Tuyet popped out of the darkness wearing a miniskirt and blouse. She had scrubbed off most of her makeup. It wasn't the first time Taylor had seen the metamorphosis from hooker to demure miss, but the transformation took the young trooper by storm. His jaw sagged.

"Hey, man! Shit! That's *cool!*" he whispered.

Taylor stepped away. Cool's not the word, kid, he thought. Try polar. Or absolute zero. I hope she leaves you enough money to buy that souvenir you promised someone back home.

He dismissed them from his mind as he came abreast of the table where the three men sat. Trung and An smiled greetings. Tu, glancing up, moved his head in a minute nod. Trung gestured at the vacant chair and as Taylor sat down, he asked, "Miss Tuyet speak you?"

Taylor said she had. "I thank you for the invitation." He spoke slowly and clearly. "I have little money to play cards. Very small money." He held his hand out, miming something small between thumb and forefinger.

Trung smiled. "No sweat. Play poker. American game. We pay." He indicated shoving something across the table at Taylor and laughed.

Taylor joined in. "I hope so. We play poker in BOQ. I lose *beaucoup*. Be good I win."

Trung and An exchanged glances, ferrets on the same scent. Tu noticed.

"What did he say?" he demanded.

"He's already in debt," Trung explained.

"The fool is perfect," An gloated. "We will get anything we want from him, and at no cost." He rubbed his palm across the knuckles of his opposite hand in nervous rhythm.

Tu twisted his head to smile at Taylor, who returned it with the bland American expression that tells the world that a friend is at hand. Then he looked to Trung.

"Mr. Tu ask if you come. He glad," Trung said.

Continuing to smile idiotically, Taylor thought, I know how glad the little sonofabitch is. Wait until he sees how glad I am to get my hands on his throat.

Trung stood up and gestured toward the door. The four of them moved through the tables. Taylor dropped to the last in line where he could shed the aching false smile.

10

THE SOUND OF VIOLENT RETCHING boiled out of the darkness behind Ordway and Miller. It irritated the shorter man, standing further into the alley than his partner.

"If that sumbitch don't die in the next minute, we're gonna all have to walk past him to get to those back stairs."

Miller nodded, the movement barely discernible against the night. "You're right. Get rid of him."

"I don't want him puking on me!"

"I don't want him puking on nobody, but if he does, it's going to be on the Corporal, not the Seregeant. Get rid of him."

A moment later Ordway passed, supporting a shambling figure at arm's length. When he returned, he tilted his head back toward the side street.

"They're coming. Chi on this side, Tho over yonder."

Miller straightened. Chi came first, identifying them as he passed. Tho followed shortly, stopping in front of them.

"The street has been empty?"

"There was a drunk, sick. Ordway moved him."

Tho's eyes swept the alley again before resting on Ordway's blondness. "He was drunk? You are certain?"

"Yes, sir."

"We careful, all same. I go now. You wait two minutes, follow."

He faded into the darkness. When the time was up, they moved after him, staying close to the walls across the alley until they were opposite the foot of a long flight of stairs where Tho watched a door at the top. Light flashed into the night as it opened and closed. They crossed quickly and he led the way upward.

Chi greeted them from a comfortable chair, an automatic pointed at the prone figure of a man on the floor. Another chair blocked the door opposite the one they had just entered. Ordway immediately blocked that one with the remaining chair in the room. Tho smiled approval, then moved to Chi's side. Incongruous music, loud and insistent, throbbed into the room from the bar downstairs. Laughter, so frenetic it suggested dementia, soared and died. Tho grimaced at it before speaking to the man on the floor.

"We must ask you some questions. We wish no trouble, nor do we wish to disturb you more than necessary."

The man moved to look at his interrogator and Tho quickly blocked him with a foot. "It is best if you not see me," he said conversationally, the very normality of it sinister. The man on the floor began to tremble.

Tho said, "You have been investigated. You are an honest man, yet you work with this filth. Why is that?"

"I must work somewhere. I am not involved with them. I am only the manager. I—."

"I have said you are honest. You are in no danger yet. But I must know more about the American Major who owns this place and what he does with the money it makes for him."

The man's head rocked from side to side. Ordway could see his nose wrinkle and fold and wondered if it hurt. An unexpected chill gripped him and passed. He wished he could understand what they were talking about.

"They will kill me," the man said, almost comically shrill. "They are cruel. I am afraid."

"We are all afraid," Tho said. "And we are all the victims of such men while they live among us. No one will ever know we were here. Help me and I promise your name will never be mentioned."

Suddenly the tremors ended. The man went limp and Ordway tensed in unconscious imitation of Tho's reaction. Then the words started.

"The money the Americans call MPC—the Military Payment Certificates—are delivered to the Major. He pays other men to spend them for PX merchandise to resell, but he is looking for a better way. The Thai and Korean units have their own informants in the PX and they take whole platoons to buy up the stereo sets or televisions when they come in."

"I know about the black market," Tho interrupted gently. "What I must know is how the profits are banked and where they are invested and how the money goes from our country to another."

A new shudder made the man's clothes stir as though a breeze had entered the room. "The bar is part of a company," he said. "The American is a small part of it. The money goes from here to the company account in the bank. I do not know who owns the company. I do not want to know. All I can tell you is that the company buys supplies for the government and builds roads and other things of great size. Because it is international, the government lets them bank in other countries and do business there. I have heard them say that certain politicians have an interest in the company."

"Perhaps," Tho commented dryly. "Now, let us speak of details. How much money does this place make in a month?"

Ordway watched Tho relax as the questioning fell into form, the questions short and infrequent, letting the story unwind of itself. He turned to Miller.

"Is he asking about the dope yet?"

Miller frowned. "I don't think so. Tho talks so damned fast and the other cat's got his face buried in the rug. I ain't up to this shit. Tho knows what I'm after, though."

"That's another thing—why you reckon he's doing this? The Old Man'll bust our nuts if he finds out we're looking in on the Viet side of an operation. And can you feature what Tho's boss'd do to him?''

"Don't sweat it. Nobody'll rat on anybody. I'll write up a report that says I got my information from some other source. Winter'll never know any different and we'll both be happy.''

"And then what?''

"And then, goddamit, we'll see some asses stacked in the slammer.''

"Shee-it.'' Ordway drawled the word out to a tune of disbelief.

Miller glared back. "You watch. I'll put together a case nobody can argue with. And once we get some of these motherfuckers, you know they'll blow the whistle on everybody else to save their own ass. One good case, that's all we need.''

Stifling further argument, Ordway concentrated on the interrogation, catching one word in twenty. His mind wandered. He marveled at the singlemindedness of his buddy and at his own increasing involvement in his cause. Sometimes it amused him—it was pretty far out for a redneck to team up with a black, much less become buddies, but heroin? Heroin had always been something they talked about on TV or in the movies. Right up until the whisper about the Assistant DI ran through the boot platoon at Parris Island. For the real country boys, like himself, it was unimaginable that a Corporal who owned a Bronze Star could be an addict. Then one day he was gone and the DI answered the first man to ask about him with a belt in the mouth that sent the silly bastard spinning right through the window. The Corporal's name was never mentioned out loud again, and when the platoon had a routine drug lecture the DI stood behind them and afterwards they told each other how they could *feel* that mean fucker's eyes.

And Miller had lived in a world full of drugs. Ordway had tried to imagine what it must have been like, but he gave up. He remembered Willy, drunk, crying, talking about his sister cursing him, begging him to find a trick for her so she could buy a fix. Thinking about it made Ordway's stomach tingle, like standing on the edge of a cliff. His sister! Jesus, if you said something funny about somebody's sister in Gantry, her brothers or cousins or daddy or somebody would kick your ass. He'd wondered once if maybe blacks didn't care about family the way whites did, but dropped the notion. That was

Daddy talking, that's all. Well, Daddy was right about most things, but if he got to know Willy, he'd find out he was wrong about blacks.

"What you want ask him?"

Ordway jerked out of his reverie at Tho's question.

Miller said, "Ask him if this Major's into the dope business, and if he is, how it works, where's it come from, who buys it."

Tho nodded and stepped back in front of the prostrate form.

"A few more questions," he said, "and then we shall leave as quietly as we came. I want to know about the American's connection with drugs."

The man's head moved convulsively. "I know nothing of any drugs. I am only the man—."

Tho tapped him with a foot. "Please, do not lie. You are an honest man living in evil times. Anyhow, drugs are an American problem. What do we care for their foolishness?"

"I agree, I agree completely." The man squirmed his anxiety. "But I truly know nothing. I can only tell you he is interested. He has made contact with a large distributor. I know only that the distributor is black and he is large. That helps?"

"A little. Now I will speak to my friends. Please do not move."

The man tried to nod in a prone position. "I will not look, I swear."

Tho walked to Ordway and Miller, summarizing what had been said. Miller listened intently and thanked him. Tho returned to the prisoner.

A sudden welling mix of shouts and screams erupted from below, freezing each of them momentarily. Chi appeared to fly to the side of the prone man, pressing his automatic firmly against the base of the shaking skull. From Ordway's position he could see the prisoner staring at the floor as if he would see through it and by sheer force of will put an end to the disturbance that was draining his life away.

The shouting changed from anger to complaint to discussion. In less than a minute, the only sound in the small room was heavy breathing and the pulse of the music. Tho gestured Chi away and resumed speaking to the prisoner, who began to shake more violently than before.

Ordway bent to Miller's ear. "You didn't get much. You reckon the Major's clean?"

Miller shook his head, then cupped a hand to Ordway's ear. "I'm afraid to push it. If he thinks I made him lose face, I'm done. Gotta be patient. I got enough."

Tho straightened, pointing at the door. As Chi removed the chair, Ordway hurried to darken the room and a sudden view of stars was the only way he knew Chi had opened the door and was out on the landing.

A moment later the chunky body of the Vietnamese Sergeant loomed in the frame, a darker form against the night. He grunted softly and Tho touched the Americans, indicating they should leave.

The prisoner's voice startled them. "Remember," he said, "you promised silence. My life is on your hands."

Tho closed the door softly.

At the foot of the stairs they split, the Americans moving to the right, the Vietnamese to the left. In seconds they were around the opposite corners and the alley was empty, only muffled music from the bars rupturing its stillness.

After a few minutes, however, something stirred in the shadow of one of the ramshackle buildings opposite the Plantation Road businesses. These smaller buildings were actually houses, mean places, existing in the lee of the neon-spangled moneymakers whose back ends they faced.

The thing stirring at the side of one of them could have been a dog, but it rose, man-high, and when it moved out into the alley, resolved itself into a short man who rolled his shoulders and deliberately stretched his legs, one at a time, before moving off.

11

WHEN TAYLOR AND DUC ENTERED WINTER'S OFFICE they found him flanked by Loc and both executive officers.

Taylor faked surprise. "Is everyone so interested in our plan, or does the Colonel want enough people here to beat up on us if it's a bad one?"

Winter chuckled. "I hadn't thought of it, but it's a good

idea." His smile hardened. "You'd understand, if you knew how badly Colonel Loc and I want this Binh."

Taylor decided to go directly to the point of the meeting. "Duc has the written plan. I can brief you on the way we've set it up."

"That's what we're here for," Winter said.

Denby added, "We'll review the written plan later."

Awareness of that painful truth brought quick color to Duc's cheeks. Taylor kept his head bent over his papers.

When he was ready, he began, "The most likely prospect is to go with their idea and let them run their blackmail scheme. They know I gamble. We've played some penny-ante and there've been some hints about higher stakes. They're thinking it over and sniffing around."

"These high stakes, *Thieu Ta,*" Tho interrupted, "has any figure been mentioned?"

"No, *Trung Ta.*"

Tho smiled thinly, writing in his notebook. Taylor knew the matter of the stakes would come up again. Tho was meticulous in the interest of effectiveness. Denby would scrub the operation because an appendix was mislettered. When Tho looked up from his pad, Taylor continued.

"They believe I have access to ammunition. Basically, we want to give them some."

Denby lowered his chin to peer at Taylor over the rims of his glasses. "Which will be used against us at the first opportunity."

"That's a possibility. We'll doctor the stuff, though." He explained the arrangements. "They'll test some rounds, so everything else has to be straight. If they pull one of the funny rounds, we lose. On the other hand, if they spread the stuff around as we expect, we trace it to each way stop and a final destination. And in two weeks those grenades and mortar rounds start going off wherever they are."

Loc sipped his tea before breaking the silence. "If everything works, I see no reason why we should think we are any closer to Binh. It's a good plan to harass the VC, but I see no danger to Binh. He will have been tricked and he will lose face. *He* is the important target."

Taylor said, *"Bat ca hai tay."*

His listeners looked up sharply.

"'Catch fish with both hands,'" he translated. "It's a sound principle, like most proverbs."

He directed the comment to Winter, managing a surreptitious glance at Loc. The smaller man's eyes were just recovering from widening in surprise and Taylor hurried on.

"The rest of our plan is soft, admittedly, but it's an attempt to strike at Binh from two directions. We feel it's time to get the VC after him, too."

Denby snorted scorn. "You think the VC will execute him for getting cheated?"

"No, *Trung Ta,*" Duc blurted in protest. "We are not so fools as that." In his haste, he slipped into Vietnamese, "If the plan goes well—." He stopped abruptly at Loc's partially raised hand.

"In English, please."

Duc's relieved exhalation was almost a whistle. He nodded with sufficient vehemence to make his cheeks bounce.

"If plan go well, we send men to start rumor. Binh have sudden big bank account in Bangkok. Other three—Trung, Tu, Sam An—disappear. Other rumor say they guests of government. We have them stay in hotel."

Loc's gaze wandered as Duc paused to dab at a moist upper lip. Denby was hunched forward, intent on Duc's face, his own forehead bunched in a frown. Loc signalled to Duc.

"Thieu Ta," he said, "I would like to hear Major Taylor continue. It is good for us to listen to English."

Denby immediately leaned back in his chair and Loc chided himself for seizing on the incident as another reason to dislike him.

Taylor said, "After the bad ammunition explodes, similar large bank accounts will be discovered in Hong Kong, naming our three so-called guests. They will be seen getting on a plane to go there. The plane will leave here and land in Da Lat to pick up casualties. It will land again in Da Nang. Our three will be carried off on stretchers, ostensibly more casualties being unloaded. The plane will continue on to Hong Kong and in a short while, there will be a message saying they're settled, have their new identities, and everything's OK. The message will be official, but there'll be an administrative foul-up and it'll come in uncoded. It'll also mention similar arrangements await the fourth man, on completion of his work for us."

"Jesus Christ." A pink wash spread across Denby's normally pale face. His ears turned bright red, making it look as though they were leaking the unusual tint into his system. He looked at Winter before returning a disbelieving stare to Taylor and Duc. "What the devil do you think we are, something out of James Bond? Bank accounts! Smuggling prisoners around! Radio messages! If one link fails, it all fails, and we've got nothing!"

Taylor kept his voice calm. "Not entirely, sir. At the absolute worst, we've got the three guys we already know about and we hand off a nasty problem to the VC with the ammunition. For all we know, one of those three can give us a solid lead on Binh. The only risk is in passing out the good ammunition and I feel the possible gain warrants that."

Denby said, "I don't like it, Colonel. It's too tenuous. We haven't a single guarantee."

Winter chose to speak to Loc. "It's weak."

Loc concentrated on Duc, one finger idly stroking his chin. "I lean toward Colonel Denby—we have no guarantees."

"True, *Dai Ta,*" Taylor said, "but it's a chance. If we try, we may succeed. If we don't try, we can't win."

Loc's smile slit across his face. "The only part of your plan that attracts me." He turned to Winter. "If we fail, Binh will at least know we have not forgotten him. And I am certain *Trung Ta* Tho will convince the three fish in the net that they should tell us anything they know. There will be gain, however small."

Tho smiled broadly at Taylor and Duc at the mention of his name. Taylor smiled back, unsure if it was the right response. He had never seen Tho in action. Winter made it explicit that none of the Americans be involved in the more rigorous Vietnamese interrogations. Still, the word got around, and it was sufficient to discourage most of the Americans from exercising any curiosity. If they discussed Tho's work at all, it was to debate the necessity for his technique and the actual value of his findings. There were stories of prisoners confessing anything to simply get away from him. On the other hand, it was estimated that at least a third of the verified information on the 5 x 8 cards in the files originated from Tho, garnered in small dark rooms. There was another story that Winter had raised unholy hell about the matter once, a long time ago, and had been pointedly told to keep his nose out of the way the Vietnamese chose to run their part of the war.

Winter's decisive voice banished the problem for the moment.

"Leave the paperwork with Colonel Denby and Colonel Tho. We'll give this thing a run."

Duc scrambled to rid himself of the folders, one in Vietnamese, the other in English.

Winter added, "Now if you gentlemen will excuse us, Colonel Loc and I have some business to discuss."

Tho and Denby followed the Majors into the hall, the former merely stepping across into his own office. Denby called Taylor.

"Major, I want to go over this thing with you. In my office, please. Now."

Taylor started toward him and Duc moved to follow.

Denby put out a hand. "Major Duc, you keep yourself available for a call from Colonel Tho. He'll have some questions for you about this, too." He extended the manila folder out to his side and flicked it with a finger. In the quiet hallway the paper made a crack like wood breaking.

Duc said, "Yes, sir," and when Denby turned to enter his office, smiled sad sympathy at Taylor.

The XO's office differed radically from Winter's. Smaller, it looked more like a consultation room than a soldier's working area. Behind his chair, wooden shelves held a wide selection of books ranging from novels to technical manuals. The wall separating the office from Tho's had been turned into a gallery. A lacquered tray depicting a proud rooster glowed from its place directly above the connecting door, muted gold and silver shimmering iridescence that imbued the bird with an eerie lifelike quality. Eight examples of Chinese embroidery, the pieces called mandarin sleeves, hung with mathematical precision between the same door and the window, their ornate intricacy clashing with black and white photographs of a grinning Denby shaking hands with Generals, being decorated with medals, and drinking with dignitaries.

The desk was relatively clear of clutter, holding only a monkey-pod mug full of pens and pencils, the inevitable In and Out baskets, and a carved representation of two elephants mating. The elephants were a present from Loc. Denby's disgust for them was well known, as was his fear of even trying to rid himself of them, due to their origin. What was also known to all the Vietnamese and most of the Americans—but a secret from Denby—was that Colonel Loc had told Tho, "It is the only thing I have ever seen which can suggest what a huge fuck I think he really is." The statuette had been presented and accepted with gracious smiles and rested, ever since, front and center on the desk. It was the first thing Denby saw when he came to work every morning and it never failed to draw a wince.

He swept around the desk and seated himself, making no indication Taylor should take a seat. He jabbed a short finger at the operation plan.

"You don't even mention how these signal-emitting rounds of yours are to be constructed."

"I don't know all the correct terminology, sir. Kimble says he can do it and I'll include the technical data as a separate appendix."

Denby grunted. "Here's another thing—you say five pounds of C-3 to booby trap 'some' M-16 rounds. How many is some, Major? How do you know this stunt will even work?"

Taylor felt his fists clench and willed the fingers limp again. "I'm assuming it'll work as planned, sir." He was delighted to see Denby brighten, seizing on the assumption. Taylor added, "I've done it before, with .45 rounds."

Disappointment dragged through Denby's next question.

"You experimented with this idea?"

"Yes, sir, in I Corps. We got two grease gunners and three pistol shooters. One of the grease gunners was wearing the whole bolt assembly in his bellybutton when we found him. It works, Colonel."

Denby sneered. "I'm sure you're quite adept at your concept of your trade. My responsibility is to see that we conduct feasible operations—practical, sound operations, not cunning contrivances. That requires plans, as opposed to schemes. That's what this is—an undocumented, badly written, poorly conceived scheme." He shoved the folder away as if it was offending his nose, then leaned back in the swivel chair and watched for Taylor's reaction.

"I'll rewrite it, sir."

He was thinking, Poor Denby. He knows the operation's a

go. He can complain and bitch, but he can't override Winter.

"You certainly will rewrite it," Denby said. "Tho may accept something like this. I won't. I'll have it in my hands, properly written before you start, or I'll fight to kill it."

"Yes, sir."

Denby extended the document to Taylor, who accepted it with exaggerated solemnity.

In the adjoining office, Winter and Loc were discussing the details of the interrogation on Plantation Road.

"The manager was a disappointment," Loc said with a bland smile. "He cooperated rather readily."

Winter nodded. "Give him an unsat mark for loyalty and outstanding for judgement."

The customary cigarette bobbed as Loc drew on it, then spoke. The smoke provided his punctuation.

"The Major is involved in everything but dope and he is negotiating for that."

Inflamed patches appeared to lift out from the flesh of Winter's neck. Loc had difficulty understanding his almost inarticulate question.

"Are you sure?"

"We have it on good authority," Loc said dryly.

"Does Tho know who's involved in the drug thing?"

"Only a large black man. It is a new lead, Win."

"There's more!" Winter erupted from his chair and stalked the room as if he would attack one of the walls. "What else could our Sergeant have been working with?"

Searching for a soothing approach, Loc said, "Your view is too dark, my friend. Consider—we have established that our suspect is on the edges of the drug problem. We have information we can turn over to other intelligence organizations, since we have no resources to investigate an operation of the size our informant described. I will see to our traitorous Sergeant. We pursue Binh."

The unreasoning emotion drained from Winter's stride and his whole body shivered in the move back to a normal attitude. Still, his voice remained defensive.

"There's millions of dollars in drugs, Loc, millions. It'd be a great source of income for Binh. And it destroys our people better than bullets."

"I know." Loc purposely waited to continue until Winter faced him, hoping the sight of his own deliberate behavior would influence the larger man. To his pleasure, it seemed to, but the question remained if he was convincing his friend of the wisdom of his course or merely distracting him by bringing up Binh. Either way was right, he decided.

"There is actually little money involved in drugs here, Win. You know that. It is too cheap. I agree the communists use it as a weapon against you, but Binh deals in the logistics of combat, not politics."

Winter resumed his seat, practically falling into the chair.

"You're right. One thing at a time. I have this foolish urge to spread us too thin. Have you learned anything further about Sergeant Hai?"

Loc moved to the door before answering. "He has betrayed us all. He is already morally dead. Only the formalities remain. They are my responsibility."

Immediately on the door closing behind Loc, Winter let his head sag forward and massaged the aching muscles in the back of his neck.

Straightening, he drummed fingertips on the chair arms, surveying his office. A GI metal desk, a sofa, three chairs, a coffee table, and three filing cabinets—an unimpressive inventory for a room where a man's life could be decided.

His vision trailed listlessly across the bare walls, coming to rest on the sole decoration, a large chart. He knew it by heart, a detailed breakdown of the Central Office for South Vietnam. COSVN. A difficult acronym. The communists showed little imagination in their titles.

He wondered if they could approach the Major, let him know he was a priority suspect. If he retreated entirely—dropped the bar and everything connected with it—. There'd be no justice in that. His profits would be safe. He'd rotate home with his routine Bronze Star to prove he was a hero. Screw that. Good men died in this goddam place with no medals, no songs, nothing.

Opening his eyes again, he was aware of pain in his forearms. The muscles were bunched and his knuckles gleamed white against his tan from squeezing the arms of the chair. He folded his arms across his chest and rubbed the hurt, sharper bites of pain gave a brief respite from mental misery.

It reminded him of sitting all cramped up in a goose blind on the Maryland eastern shore.

He closed his eyes again and the smell of the bitter autumn wind was suddenly so strong he could analyze its parts—salt tang of the bay, rich loam of the pit, musty odor of camouflaging cattails. There was the touch of strong coffee-and-whiskey from his own breath and the animal scent of the black Labrador that panted with excitement in spite of cold that razored through to the guts.

Then the geese came, high and wary, and the crackling stiffness of the muscles was gone. Faint gabbling wavered down and the birds scanned the decoys. You lifted your call slowly, slowly, and lured the flight to you. Reassured, they banked and began their approach.

Jesus God, they were beautiful. You could see the contrasting stark white and black markings now and hear the powerful wings whistle, stroking the sleek bodies through the air. The polished silver of dawn's sun pinioned them against the distant clouds and dark waters of the bay. The Lab whined and trembled. You stood up, throwing the 12-gauge to your shoulder, jamming the butt hard, ignoring the shock of the frigid walnut against outraged cheek. Cursing the wind that teared your eyes, you blinked, lined up the black ball, squeezed the trigger. The lead bird huge—.

The sound of the shot was so real Winter lunged bolt upright, slapping splayed hands down on his desk as though trying to keep his balance. He remained immobile for a long moment, orienting himself.

"And now it's men." He spoke aloud, tasting bile.

Had it always been men? No, that wasn't the answer, that was sophomoric psychology. The world war and Korea had been killing on a grand scale but the massive unhumanness of it made it impersonal. The enemy was almost always unseen, some machine hidden on the next hill that kept throwing death until you destroyed it. Then the enemy was a ripped-up bundle of bloody cloth or something charred and stinking or a dazed animal staring a dual prayer at its captors, thankful for continued life and pleading to be allowed to retain it. Sometimes you looked at them with the screams of your own men flaming in your skull and you wanted very much to kill them. But you didn't, for some reason.

There were executions. In Europe, during the peacetime tours and after the transfer to Intelligence, he'd seen one. It was a simple thing, mundane in its crudity. A trusted agent—and a double. Something had warned the man and he skipped. It was luck that let them capture his handler, and with the capture, the double was a dead man. His only value alive would have been to tell what he'd given the handler and now that information would be recovered. The handler described the double's escape route. Winter was assigned back-up to the man responsible for running him down. Like hounds, they tracked. Too late at the first stop, they continued. At last, in a depressing greasy port town where the fog smelled like cold garbage, they walked in on him. The double opened his mouth —Winter often wondered if he meant to scream or bargain— and the partner shot him. The only sounds had been the muffled thumping of the silencer, the crash of the body, and the insistent drumming of the double's right heel. One last bullet put a stop to that. The partner inspected the body and they left. The thing had taken about a minute.

For years afterward, Winter believed he'd seen war reduced to its common denominator. Then he'd been sent to Vietnam for the first time. He'd learned of a different kind of war, where the ingredient wasn't violence, but cruelty. All of Southeast Asia had been a battlefield for so long that death wasn't so much a visitor as a constant companion. The people fought for freedom or to enslave someone else, for plunder or to hold what they had, for riches or to avoid starvation. With the end of World War Two had come the twin panaceas of democracy and communism. The common people, beset by legions of messiahs, understood neither the unfettered freedom of the one or the closely structured organization of the other. Still, they were lovingly herded into one of the faiths, baptized by immersion in propaganda and promises, and set at each other. Centuries of struggle had prepared them well. The result was to provide a unity, a sense of over-all purpose to what had heretofore been a disorganized series of skirmishes. Since 1945 the haphazard taradiddle of the snare drum had been replaced by the world-satisfying roll of tympani.

He rolled the idea of a religious confrontation around in his mind and decided he was one of the earlier prophets. He, his contemporaries, and their mutual adversaries had come on the people with The Word as spoken in .30 caliber and 7.62mm. They had scourged with fire and sword and they were being replaced by latter-day prophets who spoke of a return to peaceful times they didn't know never existed. In the South they exulted at their cunning in the overturn of the false idol, Diem. In the North they eliminated dissidents with the beatitude of self-castration.

The ultimate cruelty of people dying for unfathomed ideals was being replaced by a return to the prosaic business of people dying in order that the strong should retain their strength.

Perhaps that was progress.

After my first year in Vietnam I hated the VC and distrusted the press. In fourteen years the greatest change in myself is that I've learned to distrust the VC and hate the press. Surely if God sees me and my enemy as simple animals killing each other in the dust, He must see them as the dispassionate vultures jostling to be the first to peck at our dead eyes?

12

THE ROUGH BRICK WAS COOL and relieved the pounding in Taylor's head. There had been no way to refuse the constantly refilled glass. Hours earlier Trung had contemptuously abandoned his amateurish cheating and simply handed out cards. One of the women would provide a clumsy distraction and Taylor was assured of an excellent hand—second-best at the table. Now, standing outside with his host, he was having no trouble pretending to be drunk. On the contrary, he'd have trouble pretending to be sober. The idea amused him. Steadying himself with a hand, he levered himself away from the wall and laughed.

The sound filled him with doubt. Was it all right to laugh? He decided it was. He was drunk, wasn't he? And he'd left chits for thousands of dollars in Trung's apartment. It was a hell of a way to fight a war. He allowed himself to fold gently back against the wall, laughing harder.

"You OK?"

Trung's nervousness reminded him he'd have to make his way through the curfew-blackened city. It was a disturbing prospect. He brushed away the other man's stabilizing grasp and lurched a few feet toward the main street where a light gleamed. A beacon. Someone he knew had a smile like a beacon. He tried to remember who it was.

No time for smiles. Long frigging walk ahead—nothing to smile about.

"I'm awright." He brushed irritably at the hand reaching for his shoulder and thrust his own into his pocket, coming out with a wallet.

"What I owe you? Goin' home now, gotta pay. How much? Take MPC?" He felt for the wall and leaned back again, waving a finger at Trung. "You want green dollars, go piss up a rope. MPC's illegal, green dollars illegaler. No got green." He stood erect, dignity marred by imbalance. "I always pay debts. Honor."

"I have car. I take home. Maybe someone thief you. Maybe MP pick up. You drunk. Big trouble." Trung continued to pluck at Taylor's sleeve.

A swing of the larger man's arm sent Trung away and up against the other wall. "Want MPs," Taylor declared. "They won't 'rest me. I'm Supply. They all want something. I got the keys. No sweat." He stuffed the wallet back in his pocket. "See you in a couple days. You add up what I owe you, OK?"

Trung stood away, absently rubbing the shoulder that had scraped the wall. In a way, he hoped someone would smash the drunken imbecile weaving into the light at the end of the alley. As long as he didn't get damaged too badly, he amended. If the American died a lot of whiskey had been wasted. A broken arm would be satisfactory.

On the main street, Taylor braced and began taking deep breaths, arching his back and stretching his shoulders to pull more air into his lungs. Then he began the trek home.

For the first couple of blocks the only sound was the echoing crack of his boot heels on the sidewalk. Then, in the distance, a truck crescendoed through its gears. It complained its way into the distance. The rhythm of his pace was alone again.

At the turn onto Cong Ly he heard the new sound. Without

changing stride he looked back as he turned the corner. A car with no lights on eased out of a side street, coming his way. While his mind assured him it was nothing, the accumulated tension of the night seemed to snap in him all at once and he felt the surge of adrenalin. He quickened his pace, covering a block with no sign of the car coming after him. In the middle of the next one he looked over his shoulder once more, ridiculing himself.

The car slid around the corner and the headlights flashed on, the twin spears of light preceding the turning machine like the lowered horns of a bull.

The distance between them made it unlikely that the driver could see him. He increased his pace to reach a doorway and ducked into it, squatting on one knee, cursing the liquor as his fingers seemed to fumble eternally with the Beretta holstered to his ankle.

The gun had the stopping power of a gnat. He cursed it too. All he could hope for was to spoil someone's aim. The headlights built shadows that grew more distinct as the car hummed down the street. Taylor desperately wanted not to die in a stinking, saliva-spotted doorway.

The car stopped, the unconcerned clattering of the engine obscene. Taylor tried to squeeze lower just as the beam of a flashlight struck the opposite wall, reflected light pinning him like a specimen on a tray. He drew back into the corner, the pistol aimed out and slightly upward. A moth danced across the doorway, heading for the light source.

"Taylor?"

Relief shivered through his whole body. "Who's that? Is that you, Denby?"

"Denby? Hell, no, not Denby. Is me, Duc. You OK?"

Taylor rose slowly, hand trembling as he re-holstered the automatic. He stepped into the glare, one hand shielding his eyes.

"Turn that thing off, man, you're blinding me."

He slid in beside Duc.

"Why you ask Denby?" Duc was indignant. "I not sound like that clown."

Taylor leaned back luxuriously. "I thought it was your voice. I was sure it was Vietnamese, and I knew it wasn't

Denby's. I figured if it was a Vietnamese who said he was Denby, I had to get in the first shot. All you guys sound alike, man."

"All Americans look alike, man."

"Viets are sneaky."

"Americans are rich."

Taylor reached out in the dark and shoved Duc's shoulder and they both began to laugh uproariously. Taylor finally coughed to a stop.

"Buddy, you scared me spitless! How'd you know where to find me? And why the tail? I thought I was a fucking statistic, for sure. What's going on?"

Duc started the engine. His answer came in Vietnamese. "Loc has been worrying about no guarantees, as Denby put it." He whipped the car through a U-turn on the deserted street, starting back toward the city. "He decided we need someone inside the club. Winter finally agreed with him. It was decided to approach Tuyet."

"He's wasting time," Taylor said scornfully. "She's one hard bitch. What's all that got to do with scaring me out of my mind?"

"Colonel Tho is still talking to her. He wishes to avoid telling her you are involved with us. She is to think her information is for Tho's use, not for your protection. He thinks you may be able to help him with some knowledge of her, and I knew you were with Trung."

The whiskey crept back into Taylor's blood. He rolled his head from side to side and sucked at the cool rush of night air.

"I've heard some hard things about Tho, Duc. He's not working her over, is he?"

Duc twisted his face and pursed his lips. In the half-light it made him look like a chubby child exposed to long division for the first time.

"I do not know. Maybe not. Loc and Winter told him he could pay her any reasonable amount." He nodded to himself. "I do not think she will make trouble."

They sped along the deserted streets with no more conversation until they pulled into a driveway where an armed Vietnamese trooper blocked their way. As he checked identification a second man came out of the darkness carrying a bomb detection mirror attached to a long pole. He passed it along the bottom of the car on both sides, waved to the armed sentry, and retreated to the shadows. The sentry saluted them through.

"Where are we, Duc?"

"An interrogation center." There was something in the answer that made Taylor turn to look at him. Duc concentrated on parking. The pressure of the silence finally forced him to continue. "It is used for special prisoners, not connected with Special Branch or MSS."

He turned off the ignition and got out, proceeding into the square building without waiting for Taylor to catch up. As he crossed the threshold he lit a cigarette and Taylor overtook him.

"What's eating you, Duc? We're here, man—you might as well tell me."

Duc dropped the cigarette. "Maybe nothing. I do not like this place."

A sleepy duty clerk got to his feet at their approach.

"We are here to see *Trung Ta* Tho," Duc said.

The clerk said, "He is in the room at the end of the hall, *Thieu Ta*. He said you were to knock and wait in the hall."

The mismatched strides of the two men pounded an unsyncopated drumbeat in the dim passageway. An undersized bulb dangled from a ceiling cord ahead of them, its tremulous light seized by the darkness and dissipated before it could do more than call attention to the dull gray of the walls. Taylor realized they were walking a cell block, the evenly spaced doors solid except for a barred spyhole four inches square in the center of each. He approached the small, lighted area impatiently, trying to determine what lay beyond it, trying to analyze the smell that clawed his nostrils. A few steps breached the weary pool of light. One last door faced them at the base of the hall. As Duc rapped on it, Taylor was able to identify part of the stink as a mixture of sweat and disinfectant. It was a heavy smell that seemed to coagulate as it hit the throat. The door swung open quickly and Tho slipped into the hall. In that instant Taylor damned himself for not recognizing the other odor. It was fear.

Tho closed the door, leaning on it as he extracted a cigarette and offered the pack. Taylor took one.

"Your affair with Trung went well?" Tho asked.

"Perfectly. I understand you have Tuyet."

Tho indicated the door.

"Why?"

"It is necessary. If you are being tricked, we have no way of knowing. We do not want you lost."

"I do not think they suspect me."

Tho smiled as he flicked ashes. "You do not know it. We are trying to establish an informant who can find out before it is too late. If they ever suspect you and you are not fore-warned, it could be very unfortunate."

"I go armed, *Trung Ta*."

"I know." Tho was sober. "I think it would be a mistake for them to challenge you. That is the truth. You are a brave man, but you are only a man, nevertheless, and they would never give you an opportunity to defend yourself. It is not your courage or your life that concerns us the most. It is the Unit. You would tell them too much."

Taylor felt heat building in his body. Tho pressed on.

"The woman sits in the far right corner of the room. There are strong lights in her face. She will not know you have entered. You must not speak. She must never suspect you are connected with us. She believes we only came about Trung, Tu, and An because we suspect them of black market activity. We have not mentioned you, nor has she. We have learned interesting things from her, but she refuses to work for us. Is there anything you can think of that might help us convince her that cooperation is safe and wise?"

Taylor massaged his scalp. The first faint pressure of a head-ache was building. It would be hammering in a little while. "I can't think of a thing. We speak only of money, the PX, Trung—I know almost nothing about her."

A grimace squeezed one of Tho's eyes shut. "What a mercenary bitch she is! How can anyone speak on so many occasions and never mention home, friends, family? No in-terest in anything but money!"

"She mentioned once that she has always lived in Saigon. She was gossiping about some of the other girls and she said something about her sisters. I cannot say if she meant the other girls in the bar or real sisters."

A short gesture dismissed the matter. "No worry, no worry. We shall see if she has reconsidered."

They stepped into the room quickly, Duc and Taylor immediately side-stepping to the left, where they backed against the wall. A dull glow filled the large room, the backblast from four massive pole-mounted lamps aimed directly into the corner. In their glare, Tuyet squinted uncomfortably in an attempt to see beyond them. She sat in a large, cumbersome chair, her slight figure minimized and refined by its bulk. She raised a hand to shield her eyes.

"Stop!"

Taylor recognized the voice as Sergeant Chi detached from the far wall, seeming to materialize. Tuyet's hand dropped quickly back to her lap.

Tho settled into a smaller chair, just outside the stark bulbs. The chair squeaked.

"Trung Ta?" Her voice was rough with exhaustion, her eyes red-rimmed, and puffy. "It is you?"

Tho's silence disturbed Taylor more than any answer. He caught himself rubbing his hand on the opposite sleeve, drying the palm. He looked at it and his eye was caught by the rapid movement of Duc's lower jaw as he chewed his lip.

"Please, may I go home now?" The tired plaintiveness was totally different from the coarse wheedling Taylor was used to. "I have helped you. I have told you everything I know. If they knew what I have said, they would kill me. Please let me leave this place."

"I am tired, too," Tho answered. "Soon it will be dawn." He put a match to a fresh cigarette and Tuyet's eyes leaped to focus on the flame as a sign of life outside her enclosure.

"You have told us much, and that is to your credit," Tho went on. "However, I have offered you a generous salary for continued cooperation and you have refused. I have no wish to repeat this type of tiresome effort when I wish to know something of the dogs who employ you. Do you wish to go through this every time I have need of information?"

Tuyet's eyes remained fixed on the spot where the match had flared. "It is too dangerous. They will kill me. I am afraid." Twin tears puddled down her cheeks.

Oppressive silence amplified the darkness. When Tho spoke, his voice was softer, giving it a disembodied quality.

"Life is full of fear. And danger. You are so afraid of these men that you will refuse to help your government? Even for the money I have offered?''

She leaned forward to bury her face in her hands, her voice muffled as she sobbed, ''Yes, yes! I am sorry!''

''These are painful times,'' Tho said, and the silence followed the words until broken again by Tuyet's sobs. She peered at the darkness, fearful hope lifting her brows.

Tho sighed heavily. ''You may stand now,'' he said.

With pained agility, Tuyet raised herself from the chair, pushing against it with both hands. As soon as she was able, she brushed the tears from her face, continuing to stare where she thought Tho to be. She took a graceless step forward.

''I can go home now?''

''Remove your clothes.'' Tho's voice was no louder than before. Still, it raised the hair on Taylor's neck. He spun to face Duc.

''What's—?'' He got no further as Duc, anticipating, grabbed his bicep and squeezed. He put his finger to his lips and shook his head violently. Taylor jerked his arm free and fell heavily against the wall.

''Clothes?'' Tuyet's mouth formed the word and then slacked open foolishly.

''Now!'' Tho shouted and the shattering volume of the harsh command caused both men against the wall to start and they bumped together hard enough to stagger Duc. He caught himself, never taking his eyes from the back of Tho's neck. As the echo died, a single sleep-ridden moan drifted into the room from one of the cells down the hall. Taylor had to try twice to swallow.

The woman's startled reaction flung her backwards. She caught herself, avoiding a fall by clutching at the arms of the chair. Her face grew vacant as she unbuttoned the blouse and dropped it to the floor. Only after she looked down at the soft mound of color on the floor did the impact of her situation appear to penetrate her mind. Her eyes widened slowly, her whole body trembled, and a gleaming layer of perspiration silvered her flesh. She folded her arms across her breasts.

''What are you going to do?''

The boredom in Tho's answer frightened her almost as terribly as his earlier shout. ''Your virtue is in no danger, little whore. Do as I have told you or my assistant will help you.''

Her eyes darted around the walling light, seeking, and at the sound of a scraping boot, she hastily fumbled at the buttons of her skirt and stepped out of it. She stood, crouched over, in black bra and panties of yellow with two red valentine hearts embroidered on the hip. The incongruity screamed in Taylor's mind and nervous laughter scrambled in his throat. He reached for the door to escape. Again, Duc's hand clamped on his bicep. When Taylor turned to curse him, the pained sternness of the smaller man stopped him. The American wiped a sweaty cheek with an equally wet hand and waited.

"The rest," Tho said, and Tuyet mechanically stripped herself naked.

"Sit down."

She eased into the chair, elbows in her lap, hiding her face in her hands. Long silken hair hung almost to her thighs, cloaking her in a mourning shawl.

Sergeant Chi stepped into the light, kicking the clothes into the darkness. From his pocket he pulled rolled athletic bandages. In a matter of seconds, Tuyet was bound, arms and legs firmly lashed to the corresponding parts of the chair. A separate lashing held her firmly against the back. The unnaturally erect position vividly outlined the musculature of her stomach and her breasts pointed tautly upward, the nipples in constant tremor from her ragged breathing and shivering.

Chi left, then re-entered the circle. He bent quickly in front of her, then left again. Her bulging eyes stared wildly at two wired clips attached to her index fingers.

"Those are attached to a small telephone generator," Tho lectured clinically. Another match flared and died. A jet of smoke boiled into the circle to join Tuyet, where the heat from the lights whisked it up and out of sight. "When I turn this handle, it creates electricity."

There was a grating whir and Tuyet jerked in the chair, wincing her eyes shut. A shrill squeak forced its way through her twisted lips.

"The faster I turn it, the more electricity it produces." The whir repeated, louder.

The slight body strained rigidly against the bandages and an amazing low-pitched growl rushed through the wide open mouth aimed at the ceiling and suddenly she was limp, chin on chest. Taylor listened in shocked stupor to her gasping inhalations, each matching exhalation marked by a sighing grunt.

"Why do you force me to do this?" By now the reasonable, controlled voice from Tho made Taylor's skin crawl.

"I have—told you—every—thing." The tonal words came disconnectedly, a broken song of hurt and fear. "They would —learn. Kill me."

"But you will learn other things as time passes. I will want to know what you have learned. I can always find you. One way or another, you will always tell me what I want to know."

Chi stepped into the light again, his body between the men at the wall and the woman. When he stepped away, Taylor first noticed Tuyet's head turned up and to the side, her face locked in an expression of dreadful anticipation. Then he saw the wired clips attached to her nipples.

At the first shock her eyes flew wide open, staring into space. Taylor's nails bit his palms, waiting for her scream. There was none.

"Only a delicate touch," Tho said. "It will help you consider."

Taylor could barely discern the slight flicking motion of Tho's finger as he gently manipulated the crank. Tuyet twitched in harmony with each movement. Madness frosted her staring eyes and runnels of perspiration traced the contours of her body. Her back arched as far as she could manage, and in contrast to the defined muscles writhing under her skin, her face went limp, lips loosely parted. A long, erotic moan slid through the darkness, then another. Her head slumped and she watched her breasts dance with each measured surge. A detached smile curved her lips and the lower one disappeared between her teeth. Her fingers clutched at the arms of the chair. Her hips twisted.

There was a meaty thump as her lower body slammed viciously against the back of the chair. The languid idiocy altered to reality and agony and she threw her head back and ululated. A pause, and she slid forward against the bindings, and then she was rigid again, the scream thinner and higher. Another pause, another cracking leap, and a dog's short yip of pain, to be repeated again and again and again.

Taylor's vision fogged. His knees tried to buckle and he shoved hard against the wall, concentrating on the burning at the back of his throat, swallowing it back. He heard himself saying, "Oh, Jesus, no," over and over and had to bite his cheek on the inside to stop.

Then it was quiet.

Tho's voice profaned the blessing.

"I believe you have a sister. It would be wise to think of her for a moment. And, please, do not pretend to be unconscious. You will only waste my time. I have no wish to cause you more pain. Look at me."

Her head rose slowly, the hair tugging straight as it trailed through sweat on the arms and body. Eyes as featureless as mud-slimed rocks aimed at nothing.

"You will do as you are instructed?"

"Yes. Please, yes. Yes."

"Good. My assistant will release you. You may wash before you leave. A taxi will take you home. I will contact you soon."

The woman remained motionless as Chi unwrapped the bandages. Tho approached the men at the wall and Chi gave an angry exclamation. At the same time, Taylor's nose was assailed by a new smell. He had no trouble identifying it. He looked to see Chi angrily ridding himself of the urine-soaked wrapping from one of the legs. The sight pleased him.

Tho motioned for them to leave. Taylor willed his legs to propel him to an outdoors that beckoned like paradise. The expectant silence behind the cell doors as they passed was broken as they neared the end of the passage. Sobbing eased through the portal in the last door. The sound seemed to float upward from hell's bedrock. Taylor hurried through the lobby and into the dawn-light courtyard, where he spun to await Tho.

"You inhuman bastard!"

Tho's hand brushed across his forehead and he locked eyes with Taylor.

"Yes," he said.

"You didn't have to torture her!"

"Yes, I did." His eyes refused to waver. Duc took a step toward the American and Tho waved him back without breaking his gaze. "Her absolute cooperation is necessary. We have it. It was my job to get it. She feared for her life before. Now she will fear for the quality of life. I use the weapons I can find, Major Taylor."

111

"I think—," Taylor said, and Duc launched his body into him, knocking him stumbling. When he regained his balance, Duc was looking at him with nervous concern. They remained unmoving.

Tho's head jerked toward the building. "You do not have to tell me what you think. Come now—Chi brings the woman shortly. She must not see you. This way."

They moved to the side of the building, watching as the Sergeant came out, one hand under Tuyet's elbow. She walked in a mincing shuffle, testing her legs at each step. She wavered once, and only Chi's solicitous grip kept her upright. A taxi pulled up and he gently helped her be seated. It was the finishing touch for Taylor.

"Excuse me," he said thickly. The inanity of the apology enraged him further as he stalked off behind a thick-boled tree and began to heave spectacularly.

Between efforts, he heard Tho say, "He is shocked. I understand. It is natural. I will explain that he will not be at work until late today. Take care of him."

"Thank you, *Trung Ta*," Duc said.

Taylor forced himself erect and tried to curse at both of them. Another spasm bent him double again. He collapsed against the tree to avoid falling to the ground and continued to gag, hating everything that entered his mind.

13

"SOMETHING ON YOUR MIND?"

Winter looked at Taylor without raising his head from its bent position over the papers on his desk. He registered no apparent response to the dirty, haggard, civilian-clad appearance of one of his officers.

"You wanted to see me," he prompted.

"I want out," Taylor said.

Winter leaned back in his chair. A staring match ensued, neither man breaking contact until Winter spoke. "I can fix it. Where do you want to go?"

Taylor dropped his eyes to the papers. "Can you get me to Third MAF?"

The flat expression behind the desk creased. "I don't know about that. I can keep you in MACV easily enough. Your people are awfully hard-assed about assignments. As you probably know."

"I'll take anything I can get. Just get me the fuck out of this."

"It'll take a few days. I'll ask you to do two things before you leave—help Duc and Kimble set up the transmitters and ammunition and give me your word you won't discuss the Unit, ever."

Gesturing erratically, Taylor said, "You know I won't say anything. What good's the other stuff? I was the contact. Trung won't deal with anyone else."

"We'll have to try to work someone else in. If it works, it works. If it doesn't, we'll pick up the three live ones, or something."

The passive acceptance was making Taylor nervous. He wondered if that was the purpose. A burst of anger burned his stomach. He didn't care what motives were involved, the important thing was to insure he'd never go through another session like the interrogation. Never again. The anger metamorphosed into another wave of nausea.

"I hope the operation doesn't come apart." The words were distant in his ears, felt odd in his mouth. "I feel like I'm ditching you all. I know how much you want Binh. I just can't take that stuff." He moved his head to indicate the other side of the hall.

"Tho?" Winter smiled wearily. "Don't be too hard on Tho. He does what he has to do. I won't tell you he doesn't enjoy his work from time to time. It'd be an easy lie to see through and I hate to be caught lying."

"And that's what you sent me into? Thanks."

"Don't wet yourself. I hate to tarnish my image, but the dull fact is, I had no idea what was eating you when you came in here. I guessed what happened. I honestly had no idea the young woman would give him any trouble. I wish she hadn't."

"Give him trouble? Jesus H. Christ, man, he nearly broke her fucking mind!"

"How?" Winter leaned forward.

"He hooked her up to a double-E eight." Thinking about it aloud broke a sweat on him and his voice rose. "He kept turning that handle and talking in that voice and I watched a human being turn into a goddam animal, a—a—a bunch of meat, only the nerves were still working. How'd you like to watch that?"

"Shit, Major." The expletive was drawn out, pitying. "What you saw was nothing. You understand that? Nothing!" His face mottled irregularly, sunbursts of scarlet against a paled tan. "I've watched things that still wake me in the night, goddam you! Stood there with puke in my throat—yes, by Christ, with a mouthful of it, praying I could get rid of it before I passed out—and you come in here and lecture me because you've seen someone get flipped around on the end of a fucking telephone generator. What do you expect from me, sympathy? You think I haven't tried to stop it?"

"You haven't stopped it, though. I was there, Colonel."

The colored spots on Winter's face and neck darkened, then faded.

"You're right about that. And I don't want you leaving us with the notion that I haven't tried. I even went back to the States, trying to convince people we had to get it stopped. I talked to the Pentagon. I even talked to a Congressman." He laughed harshly. "I still can't believe the sonofabitch. He's making speeches about the immorality of this whole war today, and I talked to him in '66. I put the wood to him about helping the honest Viets and hanging the crooked ones and insisting on proper treatment of POWs and all that shit. He showed me a newspaper clipping. Some Buddhist monk was touring the country, setting up sympathy for their own parochial objectives. The article said—I can still quote it— 'What happens to the Vietnamese when they are dealing with one another is not your business.' The Congressman liked that. Sat there licking his chops over it."

"So then what?"

"So I told him I hoped the only homicides in his constituency were committed by locals. That way it wouldn't matter to the rest of us."

Taylor winced.

Winter smiled. "I never figured to make General anyhow.

But that's all immaterial. I just wanted you to know, before you leave. I'd have kept you out of there if I'd known what was going down. And I want you to know I oppose it and can't do a damned thing about it.''

"I shouldn't have sounded off, Colonel. I mean, I knew it went on, but I never saw it, you know? It tore hell out of me.''

A knock on the connecting door interrupted them.

"Come in, Loc,'' Winter said.

Loc stopped short when he saw Taylor. The surprised twitch of his eyebrows was gone quickly and he was as expressionless as ever. He crossed between the two Americans and sat down. At his gesture, Tho followed, closing the door behind him, and turning to give Taylor a quick smile that could have been sardonic or mocking.

"I thought you would be asleep,'' he said. The menace of the soft voice slipped through the words, even in these surroundings. The sound of it poked around in Taylor's mind like a loathsome thing looking for a place to nest.

Loc spoke to Winter. "Major Taylor has told you of last night's happening?''

Winter was grim. "He hasn't slept. He's asked for a transfer.''

After studying Taylor silently for a long minute, Loc asked, "You won't reconsider?''

Taylor realized he'd been holding his breath. He had to inhale in order to answer. "No, sir.''

Loc intertwined his fingers, elbows on his knees. "That is unfortunate. I had believed you would be of help to us. I knew you wouldn't engage in the harsher interrogations. I hoped you would understand the necessity for them. They are unpleasant for everyone.''

Tho's eyes weighed heavily on him and Taylor turned to return the stare coldly.

"It's not my style,'' he said, facing Loc only after the statement was made.

"I understand,'' Loc said. *"Trung Ta* Tho said you were very disturbed by what you saw.''

The remark struck Taylor as artful understatement. He waited for Loc to continue.

"Since you are leaving us, it is unimportant—as you will

115

probably be in the basement of MACV—but I think you should know that what you have seen is not exactly what you think you have seen."

Taylor felt his lip curling in a sneer, and after an instant's hesitation, let it develop of itself.

Loc ignored it. "There is psychology involved, Major. The woman's fears are well-founded. If she is uncovered as an informant, she will likely die. Very unpleasantly." Taylor thought he saw a flash of irony in Loc's eyes, but it was gone too quickly. "There is more than that, however. Perhaps it is part of the Oriental culture you westerners have come to call 'face.' You see, the woman knew she would work for us. She knew she would betray her employer as soon as Tho made the proposition. Unfortunately for her, she felt money alone does not excuse betrayal. Now if she is uncovered she can explain that she was tortured and that fact may save her life. Furthermore, she did not do it merely for the money, in her own eyes. She has been overpowered. She can live with that."

"What you say may be true, *Dai Ta*," Taylor said. "If it's not universally true, I'm sure Colonel Tho felt it was true in Tuyet's case. I don't claim to know everything. I know me, though. It's not my style, this other thing." He shook his head vehemently.

"What, then, is your style?" Locs features intensified. "If the woman were to betray us, let us say, and Colonel Tho was interrogated as she was, what would be your reaction?"

Taylor knew he was being led. His face heated. "I'd grease her as soon as I could catch her."

Instantly, Loc's eyes flew to Tho. "And you?"

"Capture her, *Dai Ta*, to learn what she could tell us of others."

"There is the difference." Loc closed his argument with a flitting gesture. "Your enemies are potential corpses. Ours are potential weapons, even potential allies. Your judgement of Colonel Tho is premature and excessive." A sulky tone surfaced in his words, a startling sound from him. "You should know that, in spite of the level of your work in the Unit to this point, my men respect you. They have already nicknamed you. They are men who have been at war all their lives and they think they see something in you. They call you the Cobra Who Laughs. They will be sorry to see you leave us."

Loc rose in the uncomfortable silence.

Winter said, "Perhaps the Major would like to think about his decision."

Taylor stood mute, meeting their noncommittal inspection with his own tightly controlled reaction. Behind the fixed look, his mind leaped like a hooked fish. He saw Tuyet's face shifting before him, changing from a terrified mask to a sub-human horror responding to nerve signals. If he stayed, he'd be part of that. If he left, it would continue, regardless. If he stayed, could he influence it, perhaps stop some of it? And the Binh operation, so important to Winter? And a chance to have something to do with the war?

Incredibly, a half-joking lecture from his father came to his mind, forgotten all these years.

"Never be an innocent bystander," he'd said. "If a brawl starts and you can't do the intelligent thing and run away, for Christ's sake, pile in hard. Every time you pick up a newspaper you read about a fight in a bar—'Three men in bar fight hurt,' it says. 'Innocent bystander hit with a brick and knocked dead.' The innocent bystander is an unnatural thing and an invitation to disaster. Either run or fight, and if you have to fight, fight like hell. After all, you may be on the right side."

Taylor forced words. "I'll stay. But there's no way I can work on anything like last night. No way."

"Agreed," Winter said.

"I agree, also," Loc said, moving to leave. He reached up to put a hand on Taylor's shoulder as he drew abreast. "I will keep your delicacy in mind, and not call on you unless we need someone killed."

"The Colonel is most considerate."

Loc's laughter hissed through a thin smile. He squeezed Taylor's shoulder and left. Tho followed, passing an oblique smile at Taylor as he pulled the door closed. Taylor couldn't find it in himself to smile back.

"Don't be too harsh on Tho," Winter said.

"I won't make any trouble. Duc deals with him more than I do. He'll deal with him all the time, from now on." He paused and Winter waited patiently, understanding, letting Taylor burn it all out.

"I've been in the Corps a long time," he said. "Seen pain and heard screaming. I don't like it. I can't understand how a man can do that to another human."

Winter said, "Let me tell you about Tho. I'm not apologizing for him, I want you to have a better basis for understanding him. He's a northerner, a Catholic. When he joined the Army, back in the days of the French, the Viet Minh butchered his mother. They meant to teach him a lesson, and he learned it. It was their bad luck the lesson he learned was to play their rules."

Taylor shook his head. "It won't cut it. They do it, so it's OK if we do it. You know that's a copout."

"I said I wasn't apologizing for him." Winter stood and stretched. A joint cracked authoritatively and he frowned absently as he continued. "He doesn't like us much, you know. He knows if he's ever tagged for some of the things he's done, he'll have half the world calling him a war criminal, with Americans leading the pack. It bothers him that no one applies the same standards to the other side. We're still digging up bodies in Hue—hundreds of executed civilians. Have you ever heard of anyone asking who the North Vietnamese General was who's responsible for the units that pulled that? My Lai's an atrocity and someone deserves to be racked for it. Hue's just unfortunate, I guess. We know who was in charge. I keep waiting for one of our unbiased journalists to print it." He laughed, the same hard sound Taylor heard the first night they met. "I also buy a sweepstakes ticket every year."

Taylor managed a thin smile. "Don't get me started on the media. I'll end up defending Tho."

Winter laughed aloud again, mocking. "Well, there's nothing we can do about any of it. Why don't you go clean up and get some sleep? You're a disgrace. You Marines attract dirt."

"Yessir!" Taylor opened the door and turned. "You know, that's odd. That's exactly what they told me at Headquarters Marine Corps when they said I was being assigned to work with the Army."

The quickly slammed door muffled an outraged roar.

14

TAYLOR CONCEDED THE SIN OF PRIDE. He sipped his beer, scanning the Friendly Bar, and mused that he had a perfect right to gloat.

The operation was working.

More, he'd never have to visit this place again. That alone made the evening great.

The ammunition was delivered. The transmitters were a marvel, working like little charms. For almost two weeks they'd all been holding their collective breaths, but there'd been no sign their work had been discovered.

Perhaps this meeting would tell them otherwise. A pulse hammered in Taylor's temples as he thought about that possibility. His eyes took in the club once again.

Harker sat at the bar, sipping beer. Just another customer. Captain Allen was at one of the tables. The thought of that urbane Ivy Leaguer in a dump like the Friendly made him smile to himself while he drew a neat chain of linked circles with the bottom of his sweating glass. Allen was so well-connected back in the States he'd been snatched up by Winter to drift through society in Saigon. As tall as Taylor and darkly handsome, his job was to seine useful information from the constant flow of rumor and gossip. He complained constantly about what he called his "booze and bullshit" circuit and begged to be part of this operation. Taylor hardly dared look his way. The picture of that muscularly elegant and graceful figure matching fake passions with the ugly whore sharing his table was too much to bear without laughing.

Taylor decided he was still unsuspected. Tuyet's greeting had been warm as ever, an obsequious taint noticeable only if you knew what to look for. The bartender's smile was still that of a scornful conspirator. Taylor idly wondered how much the bartender actually knew, quickly dismissing the question. It was something that'd come out later. And not that much later, he corrected himself. This was the crunch, redeeming the IOUs. He imagined the expressions on the faces of the three when the whole scam unrolled in front of them. The realization that he was grinning made him jerk the glass to his mouth again, spilling beer on his blouse. It splashed into a large stain directly over the transmitter taped to his chest. He dabbed at it with his handkerchief, his nose practically touching the spot.

"Duc, can you hear me? If you can, give me three quick beeps on the horn!"

An answering triple blàt penetrated the murmur in the bar and Taylor blessed the unknown soul who'd forgotten to turn on the stereo. The thought of losing contact when it was time to bust Trung, Tu, and An was unpleasant. And if he shorted the radio with a lousy spilled beer, Winter'd crucify him.

Tuyet stepped from the dark end of the room into the lighted area by the barstools, showing him a smile. She indicated the trio following her, then rejoined the chattering covey of bar girls. From the corner of his eye, Taylor saw Allen swivel in his booth, the woman turning with him like a thorny branch.

"You have the—papers?" Taylor tried to sound like a frightened victim.

Trung shook his head, smiling gently. "Have in my apartment. You want now?"

Eagerly, Taylor said, "Yes, yes. I must have. Now. Quick. Please." He wondered if he was overdoing it.

Trung seemed to think not. "No sweat. All OK. We go now." He turned to the other two. "We will go to the apartment to finish this, as planned."

Tu nodded, not bothering to look at Taylor. His eyes swept the room.

An grinned. "The frightened fool." The words were conversational, carrying no warning for anyone unfamiliar with the language. He nodded pleasantly at Taylor. "How did such stupid people become so wealthy?"

Taylor half-smiled in return, facing Trung. "Is he saying we go now?"

Trung guided him toward the door, his hand light on Taylor's elbow. "Yes, deal *fini*. Go get papers."

They rode to Trung's apartment in pregnant silence.

Trung lived on the top floor of a three-story building set flush against a narrow alley. Cars, motorcycles, and bicycles stood parked in solid order in the front, or street side, with each available millimeter accounted for, save one car-sized gap directly in front of Trung's entryway. The blank space always waited for Trung's car.

They stepped from the street into a hallway leading to the central core of the building. The whole had been designed as a square around an open shaft, permitting a maximum flow of air through the rooms. The lower level acted as a courtyard. As they climbed the stairs that zigzagged up each inner wall, the lingering smells of cooking swirled around them. A tiny face, child-curious eyes shuttering in fascination at the sight of an American, peered from behind a curtain. Instantly, it was gone, the billowing cloth filtering muttered mother sounds.

The face was the first inhabitant Taylor had seen. There were other family evening sounds, like the nervous mother—an occasional raised voice, someone hawking and spitting, music, laughter—but never a glimpse of another human. The group's footsteps on the stairs could have been the coughing of tigers, sending the lesser creatures scurrying. Waiting for Trung to unlock his door, Taylor looked down into the shaft and watched lights going out, one here, another there, a third across the way on the next level down. It was like seeing people in a crowd close their eyes to something disturbing. A radio in one of the apartments flowed melody, a girl's clear voice singing of love and happiness.

A perfunctory tap on his shoulder moved Taylor into the sparsely furnished living room, maneuvering to insure he had first option on the chair closest to the door.

He held his hand out toward Trung. "The paper. Give paper. I go."

Trung denied him with a gracious host's gesture. "Have drink. I see movies, business in America do with drink. We same-same business, OK?" He lifted a bottle of Scotch and four glasses from the bookshelf, pouring without waiting for an answer.

Taylor eased himself into the chair.

"Why waste time?" An complained. "I want to see him squirm." He turned to smile at Taylor. "You ugly white worm."

Tu's laugh was scornful. "How fierce you are! If he frowned and farted, your heart would stop!"

An's voice rose, "You cannot insult me!"

"Be careful, little miser." Tu's laugh quieted to a lopsided smile as he took his drink from Trung.

"Both of you be careful," Trung said, handing the next drink to Taylor. "The shock of what I tell him will be greater if you do not make him nervous. It will be much more entertaining."

"What's going on?" Taylor protested. "What they say?"

Trung made himself comfortable on the sofa next to An, handing over the remaining drink and tasting his own before answering.

"Not important. They just talk. We talk business."

The cords in Taylor's neck strained and he remembered to look puzzled, maintaining his facade. A sense of apprehension lent veracity to signs of nervousness. There were no sounds of footsteps on the stairs or on the access balcony outside.

"Business?" he repeated. "No business. I get ammunition, you give paper. No more business." He cut across his body with a flat hand.

Tu interrupted. "Enough. Tell him he will cooperate or we will expose him. If his conscience bothers him I will kill him now and we will be through." He bit at a fingernail. "We should kill him anyhow. He is a traitor. How can we trust him?"

Taylor looked from one to the other as Trung took up the argument. "There is no trust. He will cooperate to protect himself. We will let him make a little money. I will conduct this matter because I speak the barbarian language and I amuse myself as I choose."

When he turned his attention back to Taylor, his face was no longer that of the merchant. There was a hard dedication there, a change as surprising as a shout in the night.

"No paper. You work us now."

An was laughing happily at the American's stunned fear when the door exploded inward. Harker bounced into the room, crouching in a wide-footed stance, the shotgun in his hands a malignant blue-black magnet for the eyes of the three Orientals. For the space of three heartbeats it swung across them, daring motion. An's laughter died, his face a study in disbelief. Trung sat rigid, only his eyes moving with the barrel of the shotgun. Tu leaned forward, watching, timing.

"Tu!" Taylor shouted. "If you move, you die!"

Hearing Taylor speak in Vietnamese seemed to deflate him.

122

He spat a wordless hate at the Marine and slumped backwards.

Captain Allen stepped through the doorway, sidling behind the other Americans until he could bring his own shotgun to bear on the three prisoners. He moved with an assurance that surprised Taylor. Arched dark brows over the blue-green eyes showed his controlled excitement and his nostrils flared with each breath. Long-fingered hands grasped the ugliness of the weapon with firm competence. Even in that pressurized moment, Taylor saw him as an underweight linebacker determined to make a game-saving tackle.

Taylor got to his feet. "An! Get up slowly, hands on your head. Walk to that man." He pointed to Harker, saying "Shake him down." An glared and moved.

"You are very clever," Trung spoke up. He rolled his eyes to concentrate on Allen's shotgun. "We never suspected you understood our language." He shrugged, raising his palms almost level with his shoulders.

As Taylor turned to check on Harker, Trung lunged from his chair and dove at Allen. The Captain's eyes flew wide open. He slid his left foot back, swinging his weight to the right and forward. The butt of the shotgun snapped upward between Trung's outstretched arms. There was a squashing sound, like over-ripe fruit dropping from the tree, and Trung stopped immediately. The follow-through of the butt-stroke threw his head back until the column of his throat stretched smooth. He collapsed backwards, eyes rolled to expose only whites, and Allen whipped the muzzle of the shotgun down to hover within inches of Tu's face.

At the same time Taylor heard Harker's surprised grunt and whirled to see him sagging downward, his face wadded with pain. He clung to the shotgun desperately while An wrestled for it. The smaller man sensed Taylor's approach and darted through the door. Harker fell forward, blood staining his left side. He groaned as Taylor raced in pursuit of An.

He was headed for the stairwell and suddenly broke, running past it. As he did, Duc charged up onto the landing. He turned and aimed carefully at An's fleeing back.

Knocking the automatic aside, Taylor whispered hoarsely, "No! He's going for the roof. I'll get him. Help Harker and Allen!"

Taylor ran to the stairs leading to the roof, checked the

narrow passage closely, then began a slow climb, clinging to the wall. He wondered if An would find anything heavy to throw down at him. Or jump down himself. He sprinted the last few steps and threw himself out onto the flat roof, rolling to his right, then scrambled straight ahead until he crouched against the retaining wall at the roof's perimeter. He held his breath and listened for movement. There was only the traffic and the thudding in his chest.

He stood up and shouted into the darkness. "An! There is no other way down! It is finished!"

A car door slammed on the street, strangely mocking. Taylor's vision adjusted to the dimness on the roof. On the far end of the building, directly over what would be Trung's apartment, there was a three-sided shelter, the kind the women used for shade while hanging and sorting laundry. It was the only break in the featureless surface. He approached it cautiously, feeling like a man advancing on a cornered animal.

An had surprised Harker during the scramble between Trung and Allen—that alone was enough to make a man think. The little bastard was more than he'd anticipated, Taylor admitted to himself. So was Trung. And now things were screwed up, but good.

He stopped and listened again.

Nothing.

Approaching the shelter, he circled it slowly, occasionally dropping to the roof to look upward, hoping to silhouette his quarry against the luminosity of the clouds.

The shelter was empty. Taylor squatted with his back to the retaining wall, confused and angry.

On impulse, he looked over the wall at the sheer drop to the alley. There was no place to hide and it was too far to jump. He checked the other walls, and they were identical. All that was left was the courtyard side.

He looked over, and there was a small ledge, no more than a foot wide, running parallel to the wall. Slowly, he stalked it, straining to see the humped irregularity that would be An.

It didn't take long. He saw the figure from a distance, back toward the rooftop shelter. It was stretched out face down, wedged into the cement intersection, trying to be invisible. Taylor stepped away from the wall and hurried forward until he was immediately adjacent to the spot. Then he inched forward on all fours until only the wall separated them. He waited and was finally rewarded by a faint scratching as An shifted position. Standing, Taylor looked directly down on An's back.

"Come up!"

An twitched and his left hand clawed frantically at the outside edge of the shelf. Steadying himself, he twisted his head to stare, one-eyed, over his shoulder at Taylor.

"I will never surrender!" The ragged voice reinforced Taylor's earlier thought of searching for a cornered animal. An went on, "If you move toward me, I will jump!"

Taylor lifted a foot onto the parapet. "Jump, then, motherfucker."

An twisted further to insure his one eye was looking at the right person. Taylor said, "You are useless. I can get no information from you. All you are good for is finding drivers and I know who they are. You are nothing. You know nothing. Jump. It will be interesting to see."

An's voice skated on the rim of hysteria. "If I go to prison they will torture me! They will ask me questions I cannot answer and they will not believe me and they will torture me more!"

"If you tell me the truth, there will be no torture. You have my word. But I do not care if you surrender. If you do not, you will not have to jump." He bent over An. "I am going to push you."

The glinting spot of An's eye winked as he closed it. A shiver ran through his body and when he opened his eye to look at Taylor again, its luster seemed to have dimmed. His voice was defeated.

"If I had not dropped my knife crawling out here, I would fight you. I could have killed you while you crashed about out there." He pushed tentatively against the ledge and inhaled noisily. "You will have to help me. I think your man broke my arm. The left is all right, but I must hold onto the roof with that hand."

Taylor reached to wrap his fingers around the small man's belt. His fist showed against the shirt as a blob that spanned most of the other's back. The wall was just high enough for Taylor to brace his knees against it and crane An backwards onto his feet. He reached with his right hand to steady An as he came erect.

His hand contacted An's shoulder as his eyes told him the smaller man was thrusting at his exposed stomach with a knife. His ears registered the shrill wheeze forced out of the man by the effort. Instinctively, he thrust away with the hand on An's shoulder. Unbalanced, An spun, the blade stabbing harmlessly at the sky. The slight body pivoted outward and Taylor bent quickly, letting his knees jam against the wall again, taking the jar of An's weight with his thighs and back muscles. His arm strained less than he'd expected and the belt held. An hung over the void, scrabbling to keep his feet on the ledge, his arms waving.

For a moment there was only the sound of rapid breathing and the scrape of leather on the cement. Then, from the balcony under them, the air was full of Harker's rattling moan. The knife in An's hand gleamed and Taylor saw it rip Harker's belly and felt the searing rip of muscles severing and peeling back on themselves. A harsh cry left an even greater following silence and Taylor's imaginings stopped.

Pulling his thumb from under the belt, he opened his hand, imparting a gentle forward motion to the angled body. It appeared to dangle momentarily as the arms whirled in frenzied circles. An said, "Uh?" with infinite incredulity as he fluttered toward the courtyard.

At the hollow impact of his body, the broken blade of the knife went tinkling across a lone gush of light from a lower floor window. Before the echoes stopped whispering in the corners of the shaft, the light disappeared and the courtyard was a black pit.

Taylor hurried from the roof to the balcony where Harker lay against the wall. He rounded on Duc. "Is he alive? Has anyone called the ambulance?"

Duc said, "He said it would make noise. He asked me to call for a jeep from the Unit. It will be here in minutes."

"He's bleeding like a bastard. Call the goddam ambulance."

Harker drew a shuddering breath as he reached for Taylor. "No ambulance." His speech was more controlled aspiration than words. "Duc checked—cut's not bad—not deep. Keep things quiet." He sucked in air again. "Kicked me, Major. Hurts. Own fault." An attempt at a sheepish grin turned into a spasm and he turned his head and retched.

Gently, Taylor disengaged himself from Harker's grip and entered the apartment. Trung was conscious again, seated on the sofa next to Tu. The latter looked his hatred, then resumed the study of his shoes. Trung watched Taylor coldly, his sleek grooming shattered by blood and disarray, the eyes above the battered mouth alert through their pain.

"Ready to move 'em out?" Taylor asked.

"Yes, sir." Allen jerked the gun barrel a fraction of an inch toward Trung. "He's OK now. Is Harker—?"

"He's bleeding and hurt. I think he'll be all right. Did this one spit out any teeth?"

Allen was puzzled. "No, sir. He may have swallowed some, but he didn't spit any out."

Taylor said, "These two may be our showpieces. I can't use them if they look like they've been run through a cement mixer. If Trung's only bruised up, he'll heal quicker."

Allen looked away. In profile, Taylor could see the tip of his tongue working to moisten his lips. After a moment, he said, "I've been looking at him, the one you call Trung. I never struck a man that way before. I find myself hoping I didn't damage him permanently and then I hear Harker outside and I want to hit him again. I guess I really want to smash the one that hurt Bill. That's transference, or something, isn't it?"

"Maybe. I'm not sure. Whatever you call it, you did a damned good job. We'd have lost the whole works if you hadn't been cool."

Allen's head moved in a minimal nod. "Thanks, Major. You're sure Harker's going to be all right?"

As if responding, a babble of quiet voices and the rustle of steps on the stairs drifted through the open door.

"That'll be the back-up people from the Unit," Taylor said. "He'll be in the hospital in a few minutes. I'm sure he's OK." He moved toward the door, pointing at the prisoners. "Don't let 'em blink."

Allen signalled by raising the thumb of his left hand. Sweat sparkled on the metal of the barrel where it had rested. "One more thing, Major. The one who hurt Bill—he didn't get away, did he?"

Speaking in Vietnamese, Taylor said, "An is free."

The eyes of the three men in the room fastened on him. He ignored Allen's disappointment to savor the contempt of Tu

127

and the pleasure of Trung.

Taylor extended his right arm, the hand balled in a fist, then splayed the fingers, palm down.

"I dropped him from the roof."

He spun on his heel in the awed silence and stepped onto the balcony, wishing he could bring himself to pour a shot of Trung's Scotch to wash away the greasy taste he blamed on the frying-oil smell in Trung's apartment.

15

WINTER SAT BEHIND THE DESK in his quarters, a dead cigar crushed between his teeth. He rolled it from one side of his mouth to the other, muscles in his jaws bunching. He wore no shirt and he leaned forward across the plastic surface, his fingers grasping the opposite overhang. Agitated squeezes lifted his elbows and contracted his pectorals.

Taylor watched and waited, not daring to look at his watch, sure the silence had lasted at least a quarter of an hour. Winter had not even acknowledged his greeting, save to tell him to sit down. Since then, the frown had not altered and the pinched brown eyes squinted.

Taylor steeled himself as Winter's hands relaxed.

"You fucking blew it!" Winter sprang erect in the chair and pounded a fist on the desk. The top bowed under the impact and the desk bounced. A paperback skipped off the edge to land on its flared pages and skitter under the bed like a frightened bird. The two men locked eyes again.

"No, sir."

"Don't 'no, sir' me, goddam you! Is Harker in the fucking hospital or isn't he? Did you kill the fucking Chinaman or didn't you? Is the other one—what's his fucking name? Trung!—beat lopsided or isn't he? I depend on you to make a simple pick-up with all the goddam back-up in the world, and you end up with one of my best people possibly maimed and one of the prisoners a stiff!" He thrust the cigar at Taylor. "Why weren't you in the villa when I sent for you? Where were you?"

128

"At the hospital, sir, with Harker."

"And?"

"The cut is long, but not too deep. No serious damage, but bloody. One of his testicles was driven up inside the muscular ring in the groin, or something like that. The doctor says he'll be all right in a couple of weeks or so. No permanent damage."

"You better hope so. Why'd you kill An? From what I hear, it was deliberate."

Taylor dropped his gaze. "It was." When he looked up again, there was anger in his face to match Winter's. "I didn't know if Harker was dying, or what. I heard his throat rattle and I had that little prick hanging there and I wanted him to die so I pulled the string on him. I told myself, 'It won't matter. Ol' Colonel Winter'll still have two playpretties for ol' Colonel Tho to diddle around with. This man don't know much, and he just put a knife in a fine young man'—I didn't know he'd stove in his nuts then—and I decided I didn't like him very much anymore."

The sound of the air-conditioner underscored the silence.

Winter took the cigar out of his mouth. "You lip off at me like that again, Major, and you'll learn more about sorrow than anyone you ever heard of." He delayed to let the message sink in. "Now, let me tell you how things are. I let Allen go along on this thing because he's been wanting to do something besides socialize. Those three men were supposed to end up in Da Nang so they couldn't blow his cover. Everything was going to go so quietly the neighbors wouldn't pay attention. How many eyes do you think took in all of you after you turned the whole deal into a war? I can't quit using Allen and I don't know if anyone there can, or will, identify him. That's one problem. I've lost Harker for at least a couple of weeks. That's another. The worst one is, the shot at Binh is gone. Everyone in that building knows there was an arrest made. They know who was arrested. Binh'll hear about it by daybreak if he hasn't heard already. You won't find him in the same grid square with anyone who even knows any of our three. He'll know they didn't sell him out and so will the VC. I trusted you and you bitched things up completely. Either your references were a lot of bullshit or you've lost your touch. I don't know and I don't care. You're going back into Compila-

129

tion." He indicated the door with a tired wave. "I should have let you go when Tho shook you. We'd all be better off for it."

Taylor got to his feet, favoring his knees. "Will the Colonel answer one question?"

"Possibly."

"You got your information on tonight's exercise fast. Where'd you get it, sir?"

"That's immaterial." Winter moved to leave his chair.

Taylor raised his voice a fraction. "Not to me, it's not, sir. The Colonel hasn't asked me how any of this happened and the Colonel hasn't asked me what steps we took to try to square things away after the trouble. If I'm going to get screwed, I'd like to know who's doing the screwing."

Winter backed into the chair. "I run my outfit, Major."

"Does the Colonel want to know what happened?"

"I know enough."

"Will the Colonel hear me out?"

With a brief grunt, Winter heaved himself out of his chair and walked around the room. Taylor talked from his seat, swiveling to keep Winter in view.

"As soon as the back-up showed, I had An and Harker hustled off. After that, Allen, Duc, and some of the others hung around in Trung's place for a while. We made lots of noise—laughs and songs."

Winter stopped, looking back at Taylor thoughtfully before continuing on his march. Taylor rushed ahead.

"I had Lieutenant Hon, Sergeant Duc, and Sergeant Chi go to every other unit in the building. They explained to everyone there'd been a killing—."

"Good God!" Winter's unbelieving exclamation brought a heated flush to Taylor's face. He continued to talk.

"They explained that Trung and Tu were VC who'd been partners with An. Trung and Tu had been cooperating with the government. An found out and tried to take them—and me—prisoner. There was a fight and An went off the roof. Everyone was asked to tell what they'd seen. One man saw An fall. He couldn't identify who was fighting with him."

"How'd the neighbors react?" Winter interrupted.

Some of Taylor's tension melted. "Lieutenant Hon has the complete information. He told me most of them seemed pleased Trung wouldn't be around anymore. A couple were sure he was VC and they all knew he was bad news. They were afraid of him."

Winter nodded for Taylor to continue.

"We got Trung and Tu out without any fuss. They're in the ARVN compound, as planned." Taylor got to his feet. "Colonel, nothing's been lost. I figure we're even ahead. Everyone in Trung's building'll be talking up the story we gave them. We can even release the news of Trung and Tu defecting. An'll be a big VC hero and Binh can't have time enough to move all that ammo. Jesus, it's in fourteen different dumps, Colonel! If we drop a hint in the news item that there was heavy money involved, and those dumps start to blow, Nguyen Binh'll be running for his life before the last one goes off."

Loud laughter erupted in the hallway. Winter's head snapped up from his concentration in irritated surprise. Turning his back on the door, he fiddled with his coffeepot, clearly going over Taylor's report in his mind. He measured out coffee and water meticulously and Taylor thought of a shaman mixing a potion, auguring the future.

Focusing on Taylor, Winter said, "I've been thinking you've got to be the luckiest sonofabitch I ever saw, Taylor."

Taylor opened his mouth and Winter cut him off with a curt hand movement.

"Then I decided you're a throwback, an anachronism. You know the etymology of the word? It comes from the Greek and it means something happening out of its time. You killed a man tonight. You were angry and you had the chance and you did it. No remorse. Then, when it's done, you salvage things by figuring out how to use the death to advantage."

The coffeepot burbled applause. Winter looked at it as if it could be criticized for bad manners, and the dissatisfaction on the older man's face dismayed Taylor. He'd begun to hope Winter was changing his mind, but now it didn't look that way. While he waited for the hammer to fall, Taylor tried to understand how this assignment had become so important to him. A feeling of futility smoked in his brain, obscuring thought. He waited dully for Winter to get on with it.

Winter said, "I'm glad you salvaged something out of tonight's catastrophe. It's what I thought I saw in you originally. It's what I have in Harker and a couple of the Viets. For a while I was afraid I'd been wrong. I was afraid you were a panic case, or worse, a simple mechanic, responding without remembering the end objective. You did remember. But nothing like this had better happen again.''

Instead of seizing the opportunity to escape, Taylor made up his mind to see the entire problem opened for cleaning. "If I tell you who I think tried to make me look like an asshole tonight, will you tell me if I'm right?"

"I see no reason to go into that. I know what happened and why. That's sufficient."

"But I ought to be sure I'm not suspecting the wrong party. Denby had the duty. He raced right over here with the scoop, right?"

Winter nodded reluctantly.

"OK. Now I know for sure. Why's he so anxious to put it to me?"

"Carl's a good man. He's not as good as he thinks he is, but no one is, are they? I need him to keep the system happy. He dislikes you for the same reason he dislikes me. The Army's a business career for him. There's none of the warrior in him. That's all right. He's very intellectual, Taylor. In his mind, my operation is base savagery." He smiled sadly and began to doodle on a desk pad. "He has a point. Anyhow, I need him."

"He's going to hurt someone someday. He was tickled to try to zap me—how do you know he won't take a shot at you?"

The unconcerned laugh irritated Taylor.

"He knows better," Winter said. "I'm the guy who writes his efficiency report. That's the overriding factor in his life. The only time he'd dream of not doing exactly what I tell him is if he thinks it might affect his chances for promotion. He knows he'll get the best marks I can give, so he's content to lay back and bitch and do his routine excellent job. You think I don't know he hates my guts? Give me credit for some insight."

Taylor remained dubious. "I hope you're right. He wasn't bashful about blowing the whistle on me."

"You're not a Colonel. But you're more experienced than he is. He's uncomfortable around you, too unsure of his authority. Don't let it bug you."

"Are you shitting me? After tonight? If I hadn't had a chance to explain to you, I'd be on the awkward squad forever."

Winter grimaced. "That was as much my fault as his. I shouldn't have paid so much attention to him. But you did ball it up."

"Admitted. But the man I went for was an enemy. He tried to kill both Harker and me. I didn't screw up because I got confused about who's on my side. I'm going to find out if Denby knows the difference."

"Don't push," Winter warned. "I don't care if you two don't get along, but don't rock my boat."

"OK, Colonel, I leave him alone. But will he leave us alone? If he gets scared, he's got a lot to talk about."

Winter rubbed his nose with a fist before answering. "What's going to frighten him?"

"If he thinks something like tonight's trouble's going to break open—." Taylor's shrug finished the thought.

"He knows he'd be right there in the crapper with the rest of us."

"All the same, I'll be watching him."

Shaking his head, Winter said, "That's amazing. Everyone else in the Unit'll know by 0630 what happened and applaud, but you've zeroed in on the real key—can we kill our enemies the way they kill us—and get away with it?"

Taylor's head snapped up, his chin forward aggressively. "You expect an investigation?"

"There may be some questions. I think I can hold the pass."

"Sonofabitch!" Taylor pounded a fist in his palm. "Can't we just squash it?"

"I hope so. You've met Colonel Earl?" Taylor nodded and Winter continued. "He'll run with this if he can. I think we can get the people upstairs to buy our version. If so, they'll go the other mile and classify the whole show. There'll be a press release and so forth, and that should be the last of it."

"It better be." Taylor relaxed enough to shake his head. "I don't want to have to dance around with some goddam investigation board over a worthless bastard like An. I don't want to go to the brig. Not for that."

"I know how you feel. I'll cover you, don't worry. And don't think you're taking needless chances. I told you you'd learn how rotten a war it is. Who'll worry about people like our three tonight if we don't?"

Taylor laughed and walked to the now quiet coffeepot and

133

poured himself a cup. He sipped before answering. "I'm not sure dropping people off roofs is the right way to go about things, even if there's some rough justice involved. Not that it makes any difference what I think."

"I'm curious." Winter was serious. "I honest-to-God don't know what goes on in that head."

Saluting with the coffee cup, Taylor said, "I don't know what to think. It seems like every time we try to support someone here, a scandal turns up and our press screams for us to dump him. I can't believe they're out to get us. I think they believe in democracy and all that. And that puzzles me, 'cause they sympathize with any law-breaking that obstructs national policy here."

He returned to his chair and sat, bent slightly at the waist, his attention apparently fixed on where the far wall joined the floor. Winter thought it odd how very vulnerable the man looked, particularly in view of the fact he'd killed a man a few hours prior.

Then Taylor said, "I went to Korea a shiny-bright Lieutenant to protect Syngman Rhee's democracy. I got into Seoul once. A six-by passed me. I heard it stop, and when I turned around, about a half-dozen troops tumbled out the back. They jumped on some poor civilian and clubbed the cheerful shit out of him and dumped him in the truck. I saw a bunch more like him in there. I asked an MP Major about it and he told me it was a Korean draft board. And it's worse here. At least in Korea the news people only reported what they wanted the people back home to know. Here the fuckers sit in judgement and slant the news to fit. Well, I believe in what we're trying to do, no matter how screwed up we are. We may not be allowed to win, but I'm going to do my damndest to make sure some people won't be around to celebrate my whipping."

Winter swung his complaining chair around and threw his feet up on the desk. "Jesus," he said, "I suspected you had a couple of thoughts on the subject. I misjudged you. You've never said much about it before."

"It's not one of the things that fills my heart with song, Colonel."

"And what do you suggest?" The tone was insinuating.

"Hey, Colonel!" Taylor waved both hands in front of him-

134

self. "It's been a rough night and I've bared my soul. I haven't lost my mind. I despise the people tearing at what I believe in —I still can't imagine sending them to Siberia. The military could take over in twenty-four hours. We know that. But it wouldn't be America any longer, would it?"

With a hunter's gliding steps, Winter moved across the room to his dresser. He pulled out a fresh cigar, dampening it well, insuring it was perfectly to his taste before lighting it.

He said, "Will it still be America if those other people have their way?"

"That's not about to happen." Taylor was emphatic. Winter's face was mystic, wreathed in heavy smoke, and the effect of the day began to trouble Taylor's vision. He looked away to speak. "There's not enough support for radical take-over. Anyhow, they'd never agree on who was the leader and they haven't got the sort of mind that kills the opposition, the way Charlie does it. They want to remake the world cosmetically. I don't think the place is ready to be run by the Avon lady." He waved his hands in the dismissing gesture again. "They'll generate some changes—probably good ones, and ain't that a laugh?—but in the main, we'll just outlive the stupid bastards, clean up the mess they leave behind, and get on about the business of surviving."

"Tell me something." Winter moved from behind the swirl of smoke, staring hard at the younger man. "Did any of this reasonability course through your mind while you dangled An over eternity?"

A frown rutted Taylor's forehead and he consciously eliminated it. "An wanted to play war. That wasn't a manifesto he stuck in Harker. When he pulled the knife, he stepped on my turf. Even so, if I hadn't believed Harker was dying, An'd be our guest now. Those noises though—." He twisted his face painfully. "That's when it all became academic."

"You fascinate me. You really do. It's going to be exceptional, watching you while you're here. Which reminds me, when're you going to put in your request for extension?"

"I'm not extending, Colonel." The flatness of his answer pleased his own ears. "I'm not involved in any crusade and I need time back home to find a job before I'm retired."

"I'm not going to try to talk you into it, so relax." Winter

135

hoisted his feet off the desk and dropped them to the floor with a thump. "I was hoping you'd want to see the Binh thing through to a conclusion."

"What's that mean? We're doing all we can. Don't you think this plan's going to work?"

"Oh, I think it'll work. I don't think it'll work quickly. Binh has no reason to think we'll treat him gently." He flicked a probing glance at Taylor and continued. "It's my bet he'll crawl in a hole somewhere and pull it in after him."

"That wouldn't be too bright. He'll have Charlie and us both after him, and Charlie must know all his rat-holes."

"Don't you believe it!" Winter snorted derision. "He's lived this long knowing we may get our hands on someone who'll make him for us. He's taken steps to insure a place to run where no one knows to look. He deals with thieves and profiteers all the time and I'll bet there're plenty of comrades only too anxious to believe he's on the take. He'll run and hide and we'll be in a footrace to find him first. When we get him, we'll be rolling up VC all over the country."

Taylor said, "If that's supposed to whet my appetite, forget it. I'll read about it in the papers."

"Summer soldier. No perseverance."

"Don't give me that shit. You've gone Asiatic."

Winter smiled. "You may be right."

"Why do you hang in here? Is this place all that important to you?"

A cold stare marred the atmosphere momentarily, but Winter blinked once and it was gone. When he answered, his voice was as even as ever.

"It's what I do." There was a hint of resignation in the words. "A long time ago I decided I had to throw in with the Vietnamese. I simply love the country and the people. Oh, I know—a psychiatrist would trace it all to my father or potty training, or something. I'm not good at that sort of self-analysis, and to tell you the truth, I don't think many people are. All I know is I've never been able to get my reasons for leaving to match my reasons for staying."

The definition in Winter's facial planes faded, the subtle change of a cragged coast muted by an incoming tide. Taylor realized that, for the moment, he no longer existed for the other man. Time and distance had dissipated in his mind and he was living entirely within himself.

On Plantation Road a piece of heavy equipment raced its engine, an unintentional prelude to Winter's next words.

"You've probably heard that my wife died in '57. Cancer. I don't think losing her is the reason I've continued to extend here, but it gives me a reasonable excuse. I miss the kids, our daughters, but hell, they're grown up, gone, married, kids of their own, the whole bit. I can't stand to visit Joan. Her husband gives me the pukes." He growled in his throat at some recollection. An expression of mild surprise brushed away the burgeoning frown and he looked at Taylor directly once again. "This is where I belong," he finished simply.

Taylor half-saluted. "Good days, Colonel."

Winter repeated the gesture. "And quiet nights, my friend."

Taylor rose. "Sir, if I hurry, I can manage some sleep before breakfast. Duc and I have a lot of things to police up today. Anything you want us to pay special attention to?"

"No." The answer was drawn out. "I think you're handling this well, in spite of everything. Check with me about 1600 and let me know what's happening. Keep a low profile for a while and stay away from Denby. You sure you're OK?"

"A little pumped up, still. Hope I didn't talk your arm off."

"Not quite. If the bounce is too hard when the excitement runs down, stay in the sack."

"Thanks. I'll be OK."

Taylor pulled the door shut and headed down the hall. One of the other BOQ residents, returning to his own room from a card game, didn't trouble to look twice at the unkempt Marine Major repeating, "It'll be OK. It'll be OK," as he walked past.

They were all strange, one way or another.

16

Ba LY TURNED FROM THE GARDEN as Taylor entered the yard and gave him a warm smile, one hand brushing a stray plume of hair. He approached thinking how she could make any chore seem bright and pleasant. The glint from the cutting edge of her shears emphasized the muted blue satin of the *ao dai* and the robust colors of the flowers cradled in her arm contrasted with calm ivory skin. His footsteps pounded in his ears as he grew closer, wanting to hold the soft curve of her jaw in his hands and kiss her, a lover's kiss of tender implication. Her eyes would well with surprise before the lids would slowly fall. She would return the kiss. He would break the contact and raise his head and she would laugh, content.

"Good evening, *Ba* Ly," he said.

"Good evening, Major. You are a few minutes early?"

"I had some administrative matters to clean up, and when they were done, the Colonel said I could leave early. I visited a friend in the hospital."

Harker's face surged into his memory, looking up from the stark sheets, the tropical tan dirty, like undusted furniture. The minute change in Taylor's expression failed to escape her attention.

"He is badly hurt? Is it someone I know?" The plea in the questions was offset by an aggressive forward movement, as though closer physical proximity would force denials from him.

"The young Lieutenant, Harker—a student of yours some time ago. He was in a brawl, a fight. His injuries are painful but not serious. He was lucky. It could have been worse."

"A fight?" Her concern gave way to tentative disapproval. "How did it happen? How was he hurt?"

Taylor squelched a mad urge to say Harker had been kicked in the nuts. Lying about the circumstances was second nature. Still, she might learn about the nature of the injuries eventually, so it would be unwise to try to cover that up.

"He was cut with a knife." She gasped and hugged the flowers tighter to her breast and Taylor hurried to explain. "It isn't a dangerous wound. The other injury is more painful,

138

and it's not serious either.'' He smiled wryly. ''Let's say it's an indelicate injury and the Lieutenant's social life will be very dull for a while. He's also going to walk funny until he recovers.''

Her eyes mirrored her efforts to grasp the American speech pattern and terminology. When the import registered, she pulled the flowers across her body and buried her face in them, laughter shaking her shoulders. Taylor ignored the sound of embarrassed amusement, studying the effect of the blossoms against the black hair.

''You are cruel,'' she scolded, straightening. ''The Lieutenant suffers and you make me laugh about it. I am ashamed of myself. There is no sympathy in your heart.''

The sound of An's question as he felt the release of his link with life was suddenly in Taylor's ears. He clenched a fist and, too late, saw her notice the movement.

''There is more,'' she said. ''It is something that involves you.''

He tried to disguise the reaction with a quick smile. ''You read minds as well as English?''

''Do not joke with me. There is something. I know. I do not want to know, but I do.''

''I was with him. We'll have to make official statements and the Colonel is angry because we got into a situation like that. It's nothing.''

''I see.'' She stepped past him toward the front door. ''We can go inside. We will work hard today and push these troubles from your mind.'' She turned to insure he followed, her look appraising.

He passed her on the steps, reaching to open the door. She swept into the room, talking over her shoulder. ''*Chi* Hong is away this afternoon. She is going to the *cai luong* with her sister. I will get a vase for these flowers and be back in a minute. I have marked the section in the text for our study.''

He said, ''Wait—you said *cai luong?*''

She laughed lightly. ''I have been neglecting you. You can never understand Vietnam until you understand two things, *cai luong* and the novel of Kim Van Kieu. *Cai luong* is our opera. I think you call it 'folk opera' because it is for the people. It speaks to all of us, rich or poor, educated or illiterate.''

She walked back into the room, the vase forgotten. "It is our version of *hat boi*, the ancient Chinese opera. The costumes, the makeup, the scenery—everything is bright, bright!" She stamped a foot and postured, holding the flowers by their long stems and pointing at him as with a sword. "The actors gesture fiercely and the women are totally female, sometimes cruel and haughty, other times soft and tender."

Posing and gesturing, she whirled around the room, her expressive face keeping pace through constantly changing masks of emotion.

"They speak and sing of all things. Even if you do not understand what is being said, the gestures and the music tell you the story. It is all very symbolic, very sophisticated, and still it is plain enough to attract all of us. Because it is colorful, we can forget the mist of sadness in our own lives. Because it is only a play, we can lose ourselves in it. It is not real, so we can laugh or cry and not think of things already too heavy to think about, things that have been thought about too much."

As she finished, the false expressions were discarded and she spoke into the flowers babied in her arm. With the hand holding the shears she reached across her body to them and stroked petals with a finger. He watched, not wanting to speak, content to assimilate a new picture of her, marveling at the vivacity that had shone before him.

When she looked up, he was startled to see the face of a furious child, spiteful and wanting to hurt.

"Westerners do not understand. Our music is different, so you say it is unpleasant, 'like someone killing cats.' You do not know the significance of the symbolic gestures so you laugh at the strange movements. You look at our opera, this thing that is at the center of our culture, and you mock."

Without waiting for a reply, she stalked out of sight around the corner.

Heat washed up and down the back of Taylor's neck. He rose, fidgeting while he waited for her to return. When she did, she placed the vase on the coffee table without looking at him. He waited until she turned.

"Now it's my turn." The harshness of his voice was greater than he intended, the English blunt and coarse. "I've never seen or heard your opera. Maybe I never will. If I do, I may not like it, but I won't laugh at it, and I won't laugh at the people who enjoy it. But, by God, I don't have to like it! And I don't have to be responsible for the people who don't like it, or make fun of it, or anything else. I won't be blamed for something I haven't done. I can't run all over the goddam world feeling sorry because someone I don't even know had done something to someone I never heard of. I make my own mistakes. They're sufficient.''

"Truly, they are." Her eyes burned again. "You are in my home, Major. I will not be spoken to this way."

"I know where we are. As a guest in your home, I didn't expect to be accused of bigotry. That's not part of *my* culture."

Her laugh rang like steel. "You are not a guest, Major. You assume too much. You are a customer, a student who pays well. I never asked you to come here. You never asked to come here. Colonel Winter arranged for me to teach you our language. The mistake was in trying to discuss culture with you."

He stared silently, knowing that a single word more would push them to a point that allowed no retreat. The phrases of anger swelled in his throat and he dropped onto the sofa with his fists against his temples, refusing argument. He scorned himself for a fool, panting at a woman who couldn't see him even when she was trapped with him. He remembered the fantasy in the courtyard and swallowed sour embarrassment, asking himself if leaving might not be the only smart thing to do. Even as the idea entered his mind, admission crept to the surface of his denials and he realized he'd want to come back here under any circumstances. My God, he thought, with a shock of fear, I'd be lying if I said I wouldn't come back.

He picked up the textbook, flipping to the page she'd marked, and willed himself into study. After a while, he became aware of a distraction, a sound outside her normal murmur that accompanied his reading. He'd learned to ignore that, as he shut out anything else that interfered. This was different.

She was calling his name. "Charles—are you listening?" There was both plea and demand in the words. *"Xin ong nghe toi!"*

"'Please listen to me!'" Taylor translated automatically. He essayed a smile. "I'm listening. You know how I am when I concentrate. I'm sorry."

141

Her answering smile appealed. "The argument?"

He nodded.

"The things I said about Westerners and our culture were true, Charles." She traced a series of spirals on the sofa cushion with a finger. "I had no reason to be rude to you. Many Westerners are not like that, but the ones who are insult us terribly. You understand?"

"None of it ever happened. I have forgotten it." He hoped she couldn't hear the extent of his relief. His lungs ached with pleasure at a deep breath.

She watched herself continue to draw invisible figures. "You shame me. It is difficult to be wrong and be forgiven so easily."

"I said nothing about forgiving, I said I'd forgotten. If you remind me, I'll be angry again."

She tilted her head just enough to look at him through heavy lashes. "I don't know what to think about you. You have cruel eyes, Charles. When I look at them and you are upset, you make me afraid. But you are kind. Until today, you have always spoken to me softly." She stopped drawing on the sofa, transferring the patterns to the back of her hand. "Do you know why I attacked you?"

He frowned involuntarily at the peculiar choice of words, then had to smother a smile.

"A bad day," he said easily. "Something bothered you and I happened to be available. It's natural."

"No!" She shook her head and stood up. A coil of hair, flung awry, draped down the front of the *ao dai*, curling over her right breast.

"I told you I saw that something is bothering you. It is not some small fight. I look at you, I hear your voice, and I *feel* you are not the same." She tossed her head and the hair flicked back over her shoulder. "It is too hard to say. I know you are very troubled and I want to help. I have no right to feel that way about you. I must not—care for you. My mind burns from too many things."

He was afraid to move. The muscles in his jaw tightened and he clinched his tongue between his molars, enjoying the slight pain that gave him something identifiable to focus on. Finally, he rose to his feet.

"Would the sky fall if you were to—care for me?" He

mimicked her phrase gently. "You seem to be aware of almost everything in my mind, Ly. You never wondered how I feel about you?"

She smiled, a wan look. "You feel the same as the others." Her hand came up defensively as he opened his mouth to protest. "No, Charles, don't argue. If you say anything, you will speak of love and that will be a lie. You don't love me and I don't love you. If I did, I don't think I could live. It would be hopeless." She turned completely around, her back to him, and lowered her head to upraised hands.

His eyes traversed the rounded slope of her shoulders, following the delicate inward-thrusting lines of her back, balancing the tiny waist on the foundation of rounded buttocks. He stepped forward until he was nearly touching her.

"Are you so afraid?" He placed his hands on her waist. With the thumbs extended and touching, his fingers curved around in front of her and he felt the entire girdle of muscle draw tight.

A mute nod, then, "Yes, I am afraid. You are not so blind that you have not seen the way others look at one of us with an American. You have heard what people say of her. And they are right. You will leave here—forget the war, forget Vietnam, forget me. I am not afraid of you, Charles. It is life that frightens me."

He moved his hands upward, caressing. "I only know one thing about life." He dropped his head even with her ear. "It is uncontrolled. Sometimes you use it and sometimes it uses you."

Her elbows blocked his hands. He felt the rest of her body grow rigid as he forced them outwards, the resistance giving way with the sensation of a net unraveling. He cupped a breast in each hand and she drew a long breath that came in a shuddering series.

Uncoordinated thoughts crackled through his brain, red and flaming. He wondered at flesh so soft and still unyielding, wondered if he should take her now, as she was, unresponsive. He knew he had no choice. Short of rape, he was going to take her and to hell with everything.

At that point she suddenly whirled and was facing him, her eyes probing his. The anguish he saw checked him as physically as any wall. He felt his arms grow slack even as his

143

loins raged need. Then her eyes seemed to deepen in color, almost to suffuse within their sockets. Her lips pulsed as she stretched up to kiss him. Her fingernails dug into his neck. There was a barely perceptible hesitation, and then she pressed her body to him. As quickly as she had reached to kiss him, she pulled away. He held her, and she buried her face in his chest.

He tried to speak and the words jammed in his throat. He tried again, managing a guttural whisper.

"God, Ly, we've got to get out of here! Now!"

"No. We are alone in the house." The small voice against his chest was a carnival of vibrations. "You wait. I will call you." Lithely, she was out of his grasp and gone up the stairs.

After a few seconds of agitated pacing, he threw himself on the sofa and drew out a cigarette. On his first attempt to light it, the match flew from his fingers and he leaped to stamp on it, cursing and laughing. The second attempt was successful, except for regenerated amusement at the sight of his trembling hands. There was time for a few jerky drags before she called.

"Charles?"

He ground out the cigarette and paced himself to walk the stairs. At the top, her voice came down the hall.

"The second door, on the right."

His only impression of the room was inchoate colors and smells. The single thing that registered clearly in his vision was her face, framed by her fanned black hair on the pillow. She had the sheet pulled to her chin, breasts thrust against the white cloth, the nipples crowning them with smaller peaks. The material clung to the contours of her slightly spread legs.

He sat on the edge of the bed and stripped his clothes off, flipped the sheet away, and rolled to take her in his arms. There was no time for preliminaries in his desire, nor did she require any, reaching to embrace him, gasping once, clawing her nails at his back, and then they were both writhing.

Afterwards, lying in overwhelming lassitude, he held up his free hand and turned it to and fro. A wry smile played across his features as he noted the lack of tremor and he laughed softly.

Ly stirred at the sound, rolling a sleepy leg across his own, her thigh smooth and caressing. She pulled her head back from where it had rested on his shoulder.

"You spoke?"

"I laughed." He bent his arm to stroke her hair and she snuggled back onto his shoulder, rolling the thigh suggestively.

"You have a strange sense of humor."

"Do you think I should be sad?"

She pinched him. "Animal! You know what I am saying! There is a difference between happy-satisfied and happy-ha-ha. You cannot lie in my bed and laugh at your own secrets!" She pinched him again and he squirmed.

"Stop it, goddamit! I wasn't laughing at any secrets! I was only thinking how good I feel now and how bad I felt earlier and it made me happy and I laughed. Big deal!"

She moved against him. "Good. I don't want you to have too many secrets. I want you to be mine." She raised up to look into his face, her long black hair draping in protective folds, shielding their meeting eyes. "Did your people ever tell you that here in the south it is traditional for the women to dominate the men? In the north it is the men who are boss, but in the south, the woman is the strong one in the house."

"I've heard it. I don't know if I believe it, and if it's true, I don't care. I'm not Vietnamese and I'm from a helluva lot further north than *any* Vietnamese, so you can imagine how dominating I can be, if that's the game you want to play."

Her laughter cascaded across his chest before she dropped back beside him. "See, you twist our customs to suit yourself. What pleases you, you adopt, and what does not please you, you ignore. You are the worst of the colonialists."

He stroked her hair again. "You may be right."

She tensed and her voice came to him muffled, distant. "Now you want to speak of serious things. You are relaxed and pleased and you will say foolish things about you and me. Please, Charles, do not. Right now we are children stealing fruit the farmer will not miss. It is exciting and it is harmless. That is all it is. Like children, we must someday become adults and live in a world where stealing—even fruit—is a crime." She stretched to kiss the hollow at the base of his throat. "I do not want to grow up again, Charles. When you leave, I will become an old woman. You must promise you will never talk of things that can never be for us."

A coldness swept through him, a sense of waking to find himself naked before a killing wind.

"I'll promise not to speak now. We've no right to build a

wall around each other or around ourselves together. We'll wait and see what time does for us."

Once again she rose on her elbow. "You haggle like a fish peddler." She twisted her face in mock ferocity.

He pulled her down and kissed her. Her thigh slid upward between his legs like warm oiled silk. When they broke the kiss, she smiled mischievously.

"What a warrior we have here! So soon after one battle and seeking another!"

He grinned back at her. "You know how it is. Winning isn't everything, it's how you play the game."

She giggled as he rolled her over and there was no more laughter for a while.

Later, she insisted that he dress first and wait for her to join him in the living room. Once on the sofa, he sprawled and hoped no one would come home soon so he would have to try to act alert.

When she entered the room, immaculate in her *ao dai* again, a faint tinge in her cheeks was the only thing to betray her. She kissed him lightly, then sat on the opposite end of the sofa. When she addressed him, it was with her prim teacher's voice.

"It would be a mistake for you to call me *Ba* any longer, I think. You would forget and your embarrassment would be too clear. I cannot call you Major any more, either. My parents and that sly Hong will suspect, but they will not know. Sooner or later they will learn the truth. By then they will have suspected for so long the knowledge will be a relief to their curiosity instead of a shock to their feelings. We must be very discreet."

"You said yourself you're no child, Ly. Maybe it won't shake them up as much as you think."

She looked at him pityingly and he felt like a small boy who's blurted a dirty word in front of company.

"I have made myself your woman. There has been no talk of marriage or love. Even if there had been, my parents are not the sort of Vietnamese who would welcome a white son-in-law. They have known too many lies from white men, they have known colonialism, they have known what it is to be barely tolerated tenants in the land of their ancestors. When they learn I have made love to you, they will accept it calmly only

146

because they won't know what else to do. Then, in time, they will find a reason for me to live somewhere else. When more time has passed, they will find it inconvenient to visit me or ask me to visit them. One day they will simply forget I was ever here. It will be very civilized.''

Looking at her, he wanted to shout at the controlled serenity, storm at the carefully modulated voice. In his need, his mind sought reference points, and he was thinking of a jade princess in a museum, beautiful, precious, and eternally resigned. He went to her and took her shoulders in his hands, his eyes straining to see through hers.

''You should have told me! You expect me to live with something like that? You know you're destroying your life and you make me a party to it? I won't, Ly! I can't do that!''

''You must,'' she said, still calm. ''It is what you want and it is my life and it is what I want. I am the one who will pay, and it is worth it to me. My life with my husband was short. It was good. He made me learn what a woman can be. Since he died, I have lived with memories. Now there is you. When you are gone, I will have that memory. When I let myself want to make love with you, it was weakness. Now that I have done it, I feel strength, more than I ever knew I had. I hope you will come back to me, Charles. It is shameless to say so, I know. But I want you. And if you do not—.'' She paused, then, ''It is not written anywhere that life is always what one wants.''

''I'll be back.'' He looked away, exasperated. ''I've never understood any woman, but you're impossible. You only give. There's no taking. And you give too much, risk too much. You are a strange woman.'' He took her hand in his.

She laughed at him, untroubled. ''There is no give or take, Charles. It is all fate. Anyhow, you are the strange one.''

''Me? I'm the one who benefits. I'd really be strange— hell, I'd be crazy—if I didn't make the most of the situation.''

She drew her brows together. ''That's not what I mean. You are strange because you think you can lie to me.''

''I haven't lied!''

''Of course you have.'' The teacher's voice was back. ''You, the students before you, and especially the clever Colonel Loc and Colonel Winter. Do you think I am a fool, that I cannot see the type of men who come here for lessons?

147

Grim, hard-mouthed men, full of determination. These are men who scribble on paper, who draw charts? I have looked at soldiers all my life."

"You are mistaken. We are soldiers, true, but our work's exactly what you've been told. It's dull, but it needs to be done, so we do it."

She moved to place the palms of her hands on his cheeks and rubbed her fingers across his ears, studying them tactilely. "Poor darling. You are such a loyal liar. And it was you who convinced me."

"There's nothing to convince you of. You're imagining things. You watch too much television." A tickling sensation told him a glaze of sweat was forming on his upper lip. He clenched a fist to avoid reaching to wipe at it.

"Of course I watch television. I watch people, too." Her fingers curved from his ears and the index finger of each hand drifted back and forth along the bone ridges under his eyes. "I told you you have cruel eyes. Tonight, when you arrived you laughed and talked and there was something there that would not go away. Only when we were in my bed did they change, and now they are the same as they were when you came here. Death swims in your eyes like a soul in the yellow springs."

"Yellow springs? What kind of poetry is that?"

"It is poetry. An old expression for the land of death. I saw that when you first came and it made my heart weak. I fought with you because I knew you needed me as terribly as I needed you."

He stepped back. "I did need you. I will again. But you're wrong about me and wrong about the Unit. I'm glad you were, because I wanted you—want you—more than I can tell you, but your reasons were wrong."

She nodded slowly. "Then it will not trouble you if I tell you I'll pray for your safety."

"Everyone should have someone praying for him, if he has to fight Saigon traffic." The dull humor clacked in his ears. Still, she responded in kind.

"Men who tease need prayers to protect them from knives in their sleep, too."

The tension in the room ebbed, an emotional tide retreating with unpleasant driftage. They both heard the heavy door of the fence thud home outside and he brushed her lips in a final kiss.

Her father was just reaching for the front door with his key when Taylor pulled it open. The small Vietnamese looked up and started at the appearance of the Marine in his doorway. When he steadied, he stammered a question.

"Y-you are l-late tonight, Major. You had trouble with the lesson?" He glanced at his watch. "It is almost nine-thirty." A veneer of anger and suspicion colored his belated awareness of the hour.

"We practiced conversation instead of grammar," Taylor explained. "Like so many conversations, this one lasted much longer than we realized."

The parents entered and the father turned to pointedly stare Taylor on his way. "I understand, Major, although I am sure you understand you must be careful in the future. There are people who live for gossip."

"I apologize, sir. I would not want to be responsible for idle gossip. I will be very careful."

Ly waved goodbye hurriedly, turning away. Her mother watched her, then looked at Taylor's retreating back. Her left eyelid made tics as though a particularly hardshelled insect had intruded there.

BOOK TWO

17

"GENTLEMEN! A TOAST!"

Winter raised his glass and his companions at the long table quieted and waited. He began with grave pomposity.

"You're all probably wondering why I've called you together here." He openly reveled in the laughter and applause from the assembled men of the Unit.

"We've kept the good tidings from you all day, and we scheduled this last-minute dinner to celebrate. Colonel Loc and I received a report at 1000 this morning concerning a disaster that has befallen our enemies." He raised his glass a notch higher and placed his other hand on Loc's shoulder, who flinched minutely, although the tiny smile remained fixed to his lips.

"From 1000, and as of 1600, our foe has seen eight of his clandestine ordnance storage areas disappear in smoke and flame."

Duc turned a baffled frown on Taylor. "I do not understand," he whispered.

Winter noticed his confusion, as well as the blank stares from some of the other Vietnamese at the gathering. He leaned forward.

"What I'm telling you, Major Duc, is that eight of the ammo dumps we booby trapped have blown to shit. OK?"

Duc leaped to his feet, waving his arms dangerously. *"Khong biet,* OK for sure!" he shouted. "Number-fucking-one, you bet!" He weaved and the whiskey-ruddied features wobbled as he structured his next phrase. A quick glance at Colonel Loc, however, and he flowed back into his chair, despite the latter's obvious amusement.

The laughter quieted and Winter proposed his toast. "To continued success! To the destruction of Nguyen Binh and his entire organization!"

A bilingual murmur of assent rolled, each man agreeing in his own manner. Glasses thumped around the table. During the self-congratulatory babble, Taylor inventoried the spartan banquet room of BOQ One and its twelve occupants. They sat in cafe chairs at a long table that jiggled on uneven legs. It sat at the mathematical center of a room painted a bright yellow as false as a pimp's smile. An occasional glad shout from the swimmers in the pool wavered through the night and washed across the more subdued laughter of the party.

Taylor had been detailed to make the arrangements for the dinner. He'd asked Winter why he was so insistent on the austere room instead of one of the fine restaurants in the city and been told, "Because it's one place I can be reasonably sure isn't bugged and I want everyone free to talk. What's the sense of a party if everyone has to sit around and count every goddam word he says?"

Looking around again, Taylor thought, give us each a tin cup and we could do a Jimmy Cagney prison messhall scene, except for the colored shirts. Still, the locale seemed to be having no ill effect on the others. Tomorrow was going to be Hangover City.

He amused himself watching the others, sparing little time for Winter, Loc, or Duc.

Kimble was interesting. He drank with everyone else, measure for measure, but managed to give the impression he was observing a ritual. There was no depth to the smile on his face, like oil on water. To his left, Lieutenant Colonel Tho was a complete contrast, keeping involved with several conversations at once. He was pleasantly serious with Denby, to his own left, and openly interested in any statement from Kimble. When either of those conversations lulled, he'd lean forward and direct a comment past Denby to either Loc or Winter. Taylor wondered idly if Tho used interrogation technique to keep discussion flowing.

On Taylor's own left, Captain Allen nursed his martini, the only one at the table. Taylor caught Allen's eye and grimaced at the funnel-shaped glass.

"You just can't let any of us forget you're Ivy League, can

151

you? Everyone else sits here banging back booze, but not you. Oh, no! You have to stoke up on before-dinner martinis. Where the hell d'you think you are? The Four Seasons?''

Allen was arch. "I certainly should be. My association with you plebeians is simply a burdensome exigency of war. I drink martinis while you swill," he sipped to emphasize his point, "because it's incumbent on me to uphold the mores of the better element. A form of *noblesse oblige,* if you will. You may wish to write down that phrase, although I can't imagine you having need of it. It's French, of course. Perhaps you noticed? French is the language of diplomacy, you know. You've heard of both things, surely."

Taylor laughed. *"Du ma,* Ivy league. There's a phrase a lot handier around here than your fruity *noblesse oblige.''*

"It's something I've heard." Allen yawned his ennui. "I suppose I should ask what it means. Learning is never to be scorned, regardless of the source."

"It means mother-fucker. Where'd you ever hear such talk?"

Allen choked on his drink and scrambled for his handkerchief. After a series of strangled barks, he dabbed tears from his eyes and blew his nose.

"That was a dirty trick," he said, voice rough from coughing. "I just bought a brass tray from a guy down on Tu Do this afternoon. When he gave me my change he was smiling and the last thing he said was, 'Thank you, Captain. Have good day, *du ma.'"* He mimed the peddler's bobbing head and sing-song English, then laughed at himself. "Zapped again. I ought to go back tomorrow and pound the tray around his skull like a helmet."

"Gracious goodness!" Taylor cupped his chin in a limp-wristed motion. "A violent emotional outburst? Whatever would your embassy chum-buddies say?"

"You'd be surprised. Some of those people may act like ultimately urbane citizens, but inside? Some of them were born with a bellyful of snakes. When they talk about soul food, they mean eating real souls."

He turned in his chair, warming to his subject. "Some of them are forever pumping to learn something, anything, about American intentions here. I was wondering what they'd look like if they could have seen me rearrange Trung's face with the butt of that shotgun. They might not be so anxious to ask questions. It can get to be an awful drag, talking to people whose main interest in the war is how it's going to affect investments or trade agreements. Or if Charlie may drop a rocket on the power plant and knock out the air-conditioner."

Taylor nodded, aware no comment was wanted, knowing Allen was talking out half-understood personal problems.

"They're not all like that," he rushed on. "A lot of the women work in hospitals and orphanages and so on. Still, you begin to feel like a parasite, knowing guys like you and Harker and Duc are doing things, and I'm milling around sucking up cocktails, wondering which hors d'oeuvre is the one that's going to have me racing for the crapper all the next day." He paused to make a face. "Can you get a Purple Heart for diarrhea? I mean, is there a percentage figure, like, 'Captain X, during his tour in Vietnam, did suffer explosions in his lower intestine approximately 87.3 percent of the time, causing him intense physical discomfort and psychological trauma as a result of breaking off an average of 12.7 conversations daily in order to sprint for the shitter, occasionally with an absolutely horrid lack of success?'"

Allen's mock gravity made Taylor laugh until he hurt. "You're plain crazy, you know that?"

The Captain sniffed. "You spend the best part of a year staring at bathroom walls and you'll grow a little kinky, too. You ever read Milton's 'On His Blindness'?"

"You're not going to give me, 'They also serve who only stand and wait,' are you?"

Allen effected exaggerated surprise. "Oh ho! Literary pretensions from the mercenaries!"

Taylor gave him the finger.

Denby injected his precise voice into their laughter. "Run out of conversation, Marine?" His teeth were displayed in a disarming smile that shadowed none of his malice. Behind the glasses his eyes challenged and he licked his lips as if anticipating.

Even as he rose, Taylor knew it was the whiskey making him respond. Reason pulled at his mind and anger overwhelmed it easily. Under the table, Allen's boot cracked against his shin hard enough to pain. He swung that way, ready to deal with that injury first.

Allen's eyes never left Denby. "We were discussing language, as a matter of fact, sir." He spoke with underling's caution. "I was saying how English is becoming almost a universal tongue, much as Arabic was the trade language of the Muslim empire and beyond, during their expansion. The irony is that the language is spread by sailors and soldiers and entrepreneurs, rather than teachers. Grammar and scholarship suffer. Obscenities become common currency. Major Taylor was demonstrating that speech isn't the only way to display crude behavior. It's certainly not philology, but it's communication, isn't it?"

Denby's smile drew in on itself. "The sort you expect from some, yes."

Allen extended his own finger upward, peering at it as it unfolded, twisting his head to inspect it from varying angles. "I'm not sure I can agree completely, Colonel. A thing like that, there's no way of knowing where it'll turn up. Pardon the pun. I'll bet I could take that nimble creature anywhere in the world, whip it on the populace, and every one of them'd know exactly what I was telling them. Isn't that amazing?"

"You two go ahead and amuse yourselves." Denby's smile thinned, degenerating to frustration as he stared at Allen's finger before returning to his conversation with Tho.

Relaxing his hand, Allen said, "That's one you owe me, Major."

From the other side, Duc leaned to speak past Taylor. "I thank you, *Dai Uy*, even if this one not. I not know how you make him sit. If you not, be *beaucoup* trouble, for sure. And you got that Denby good. Thank you for two things."

"My pleasure," Allen said, "especially fucking over Denby's mind. As for the Major, I made him sit down by kicking his shin. Come to think of it, that was a pleasure, too."

Duc's face warped into a drunken frown. He pursed his lips so hard they protruded in front of him like a fleshy bud.

"Not good *Dai Uy* kick *Thieu Ta*. Bad morale thing. And he more big than you, too." Duc hoisted an elbow onto the table, planting it firmly in the saucer holding it up so that when he tried to speak the taut skin between his septum and upper lip caused the words to flutter incomprehensibly. Pulling the hand away, he glared accusation at it, then said, "Next time, you pass word me. *I* kick him." Pleased by his solution, he

154

sagged back against his chair.

"What a relief to know my future is in such good hands," Taylor observed dryly. "Kinda gets you right under the old emblem." He patted the sport shirt on the left breast pocket, where his Marine insignia would be on his utility jacket.

Allen's answering smile was perfunctory. "Watch Denby, Major. He won't mess with me 'cause he keeps hoping I'll get him in on parties. I take him just enough to keep his appetite sharp. He really digs that crap. But he's got a hard-on for you. You ought to know about it."

"What makes you think that?"

"Everybody knows it. And he may have more free time to let you know about it from now on."

"Are we playing riddles?" Something in Allen's attitude warned Taylor and his own question was clipped. Allen averted his eyes.

"There's talk—." He stopped and shrugged. "It's not just talk, it's fact. The Unit's a goner, Major. No replacements. We're going to disappear through 'normal attrition.' The Old Man doesn't even know it yet. Denby's been told, but he's afraid to tell him."

"How could Denby know a thing like that without Winter knowing?"

"He got the word in a letter from a guy in D.A. back in D.C."

"Shit!" Taylor tipped his drink and took a long swallow. "What that tells you is Department of the Army's buckling in the heat. We must be doing something right. Does Denby know where the trouble's coming from?"

Allen surveyed the room furtively and the reaction angered Taylor further. "What're you looking for, spies?"

To his surprise, Allen grinned. "Them is us, Major, remember?" Then, soberly, "Look, I don't want to be around when the Old Man gets the word, and I sure don't want him getting it from me. Denby doesn't know any more than I told you, except the guy who wrote is sure of what he said and scared shitless of whoever pushed the decision through."

Taylor drank again. "That figures. A month's pay against a dime it's one of the assholes who wants to see us get whipped."

Allen clamped his lips together, unsure of himself, worried

155

by the taller man's bitterness. He thought, he's pretty cool most of the time, but right now he's looking off into space. He sounded like an old-fashioned fascist when he let himself open up.

As though aware of the thought, Taylor threw a glance at Allen that noted his continued presence and passed on, noncommittal. Allen felt an involuntary tension in his shoulders that passed quickly. He took the opportunity afforded by the continued silence to further analyze his feelings toward this man who could close himself off so quickly.

He didn't really like him, he decided, puzzled, because he had no firm reason for it. It wasn't as if he actively disliked him. The man was friendly enough and if he was always aware of his rank, he was scrupulously aware of everyone else's, too. Was it that thing he did to make himself seem to draw away from others?

His mind divorced itself from Taylor's silent frustration and the boisterousness of the others.

He was years away from all of them.

He sat on the ground, tears burning his face, watching the chestnut hunter prance delight at dumping its twelve-year-old rider. The stirrups glittered uselessly in the bright spring sun as the animal frisked out of sight behind a thicket. He got up from the ground slowly, building courage to feel his right arm and see if it was broken. It felt wrong and hurt and he was afraid. Anger and embarrassment forced more tears. A rumble of hoofbeats from behind stopped in a flurry of ripped turf and his uncle was looking down at him.

Uncle Paul the surgeon. To everyone, Unclepaulthesurgeon, one word, as if surgery and the man were born of a piece. He sometimes wondered if Uncle Paul really needed a scalpel when his eyes cut better than razors. He looked into them now, slick like the almost-black agate bookends on the library fireplace mantel. His crying turned to sobs.

You're not hurt, Uncle Paul ordered.

He fought the sobs, lost, talked between them. *My—arm—won't—work—right.*

Stop that infantile whining. The agates searched the thicket where the horse continued to snort and thrash, unseen.

You have to control the horse, not let it control you. Raise your arm. The voice was a dull knife, unlike the eyes. It tore instead of slicing.

I can't. It hurts. It feels like it may be broken.

The eyes came again, into his own, opening his brain, halving it like a head of lettuce, exposing the hidden wrinkles and folds. Then the movement, too swift to avoid. The sure grip on the wrist and the smooth lift until only his toes scraped the grass and his nose was mashed against the bristling flank of the horse and he was too shocked to scream before realizing the pain was no worse than it had been. He was dropped, staggering backward before collecting himself.

Fists so tight his fingernails gouged palms.

You big, mean sonofabitch!

Cool out your horse properly. He's a valuable animal.

The memory fell apart, disappearing as a mass of elusive colors and scents.

No, Taylor wasn't as distant as Uncle Paul. The eyes sometimes brought Uncle Paul to mind, but Taylor's lacked the chill vacancy. It was truly a puzzle, the lack of liking. He gestured unconsciously, telling himself he'd always be glad to have Taylor around, even if he wasn't one of his favorite people.

"What was that for?"

Taylor's question snapped Allen out of his musing. "What was what for?"

"You moved your hand, like you were saying something, or going to say something."

"Thinking. Guess I did it from habit."

"What kind of heavy thinking makes you wave at nothing?" Taylor smiled as though the earlier anger had never surfaced.

"About Winter," Allen lied quickly. "Every once in a while I wonder what he'd have been in a different time. Elizabethan England, for instance, or maybe right here, say, around the turn of the century. He'd be a romantic figure in any era, wouldn't he?"

The pressure of Taylor's stare turned him to face the other man. "I think I'm getting a little drunk, aren't I?" He laughed self-consciously.

Taylor shook his head. "No drunker than me. I think all of

157

us play that game, but there won't be much romance in the air if this scuttlebutt of Denby's is true."

Suddenly Allen had to know more about Taylor's earlier statement. "Do you really believe whoever set up the policy for the Unit wants to see us beaten?"

"I don't know what else to think, sometimes. I think it, but I can't believe it. Not in the sense of a fifth column, or anything. I don't know. I'd like to take an NVA division into Berkeley and turn them loose to establish peace and a liberated zone." He grimaced and threw down the last of his drink, holding his head back to let the last drops drain through the ice.

"Fuck it," he added, wiping his lips. "Fuck 'em all."

A loud knock at the door stopped all conversation immediately, and Miss Oanh pushed a loaded serving cart into the room. She grinned at the welcoming chorus, directing her chattering crew, the red-and-black costumed girls bringing a freer, innocent laughter with them. When the steak dinners were distributed she shooed them all out.

"If want more wine or anything, I bring, OK?" She smiled back from the doorway.

Loc answered. Taylor had the impression he had no need to raise his voice. When he spoke, no matter the distance, people heard.

"That is thoughtful, Miss Oanh. We will have six bottles of the Mateus now, please. After you have brought it, you will please see that we are not disturbed unless we ring for service."

"I understand, *Dai Ta*." The casual bantering manner used with the Americans was missing.

The dinner proceeded quietly. Allen embarked on a detailed discussion of Vietnamese cooking with Sergeant Chi. Taylor looked past the American once and Chi flashed a cheerful smile. Taylor managed to produce his own, fighting the image of Chi's bulk manifesting from darkness to strap Tuyet to the chair. He stared at his food and wondered if Chi ever thought of screams and blood and urine in the middle of a meal. He looked for help from Duc, something to talk about to clear away the fogged pictures.

Duc was attacking his steak with the fervor of a man who knows he eats too much and wants to finish his meal before his conscience catches up.

Taylor sliced his meat mechanically, spearing the morsels and chewing without relish. He determined to concentrate on the enlisted men at the party. They were the ones who had monitored the radio signals from the doctored rounds and Winter had sworn they would attend the celebration in BOQ 1. Taylor had no idea what sort of weight he'd thrown around to accomplish it, and he'd given up conjecture about Winter's off-the-cuff accomplishments. Being around him was the same as watching a magician—nothing was as it appeared, and finding out how it was done took all the fun out of it.

The man to attract Taylor's scrutiny was Corporal Tranh Minh, probably as typical an Oriental soldier as could be found. It was impossible to give him an order he would question, he worked as hard as he could at any job assigned him, and he wanted but one thing in the world, and that was to go home to his farm and raise his family in peace. Right now he watched Miss Oanh pour his glass of wine, too interested in the swirling color to attach any significance to the fact that he was the last one being served. Taylor suspected that, had it been pointed out to him, Minh would have still been more interested in the wine than the order of its serving.

With Miss Oanh's second departure, the men all fell to serious eating, and it was a short while before she was back. She brought another serving cart, this one equipped as a bar, and while she arranged it, her crew cleared the remains of the dinner. She looked to Loc as the last of her girls left, noticeably relieved at his bird-like nod of approval. She hurried after the others.

The two Colonels strode to the bar and fixed themselves drinks and the rush was on.

Backing away with his whiskey and water, Taylor leaned against a wall and realized he was standing next to the man he'd been thinking about a few minutes earlier. He raised his glass in greeting and Minh grinned, repeating the gesture with his glass of beer.

"No whiskey?" Taylor asked. "The Colonel is paying and we do not get many chances to get drunk on his money."

Minh's grin expanded and Taylor noticed each of the dark eyes seemed to be focusing on different objects.

"I think of that, *Thieu Ta*. I drank before very fast. I afraid he change mind. Already I pleasing drunk, thank you much.

159

Colonel Winter be angry I thank him for make so good drunk?"

Taylor delayed, giving the question grave thought. "No, I am sure he would not be angry. However, I think it would be more thoughtful if you did not say anything to him about it."

Minh rolled on his heels, an inner ground swell causing him to yaw slightly. He scratched his head to indicate confusion.

In Vietnamese, Taylor said, "We must consider his face, Corporal. It would embarrass him to hear praise of his generosity. He can look at you and see you enjoy the party. To speak of it would be too much, would it not?"

Minh heaved a breathy, "Ahh!" of understanding and drew himself erect. "I must speak in my language. My English will not say what I want you to hear. Sometimes I think you could be Vietnamese, Major. You see things with our eyes and our hearts. Why do you not find a good woman and stay with us?"

"You are truly very drunk," Taylor said quietly.

Gesturing, Minh said, "Would I, a Corporal from a small village, speak so to an American Major if I were sober? Tomorrow when I see you at the villa, I will run and hide like a chicken from the cook and I will hope that tonight you are too drunk to remember the things I have said. So tonight I talk too much."

Taylor laughed. "Very well. Tomorrow we will question your future. Tonight we will talk. But we will not talk about finding me a woman. We will talk about you. Where is your home, Minh?" Saying it, he shifted against the wall, getting comfortable so the Corporal would feel free to speak in detail. He continued to watch Minh and saw something like the luminous trail of a shooting star hurtle across the depths of his eyes, gone so quickly there was no clue to identify it. When Minh spoke, it was in the soft tones that can turn Vietnamese speech into distant music.

"My home is north of here. My ancestors have lived there always. Our small farm is at the base of a tall mountain, facing east. In the morning the sun comes fresh from the sea to our crops. We fish, saving most of the remains for the vegetable garden. Fish parts are very good for the soil, Major. If you ever farm, you should remember that. Crushed shells are good, too. The sea can be a great help to a farmer."

160

Taylor agreed silently, acknowledging the importance of such knowledge.

Enunciating carefully, Minh said, "Farming is a good life. A man knows his land and it supports him. We were happy." His vision left Taylor, the room, the party, resting on scenes for him alone. "The trouble came unexpectedly. Strangers said we must fight the government. I did not like the government, but I did not want to fight anyone. I walked away and they called me names, but they did nothing. Then the government men came. A soldier stole some of my ducks. I did not like that and I considered that the men who called me names took nothing from our village without paying for it. After some weeks, the government soldiers came back. They had men with large containers on their backs, with hoses that sprayed a liquid that smelled. They said they would return until they killed all the mosquitoes that bring the disease you call malaria. The whole village cheered then."

He stopped and for an instant he smiled, an expression of self-contempt for a long-dead weakness.

"When the soldiers and the others left, we heard a loud explosion down the road. We all ran to see. The VC propaganda team was waiting. The government soldiers and the other men were all dead. The ones who lived through the explosion were shot. The propaganda team said a government that cannot defend itself against a few VC could never kill a valley full of mosquitoes. They said the spray would poison the water and we would die. It was days before we tried our wells. No one got sick. The spray people never came again. That year my only son got the malaria. The next time a VC came to our village, he came alone. He said if we had a doctor we would have no malaria and promised us a doctor. I asked him why they killed the men who tried to help us. He laughed at me and said I was a tool of the government."

Minh stopped again, and his eyes were clear once more.

"No one should laugh at a man who has watched his son die, Major."

"What did he say after that?"

A muscular movement that was almost a smile moved Minh's lips. "Nothing. My axe was in his head. I took my wife and we hid in the forest while I tried to think. I did not like the government, especially the soldier who stole my ducks, but even if they stole them all, they tried to do something to protect my son. I told my wife it is not necessary to steal ducks to be a soldier and it is not necessary to kill men who wish to help other men. If I must be a soldier I would rather be on the side that steals ducks than the side that steals life from children." He drained his glass with a steady hand. "I would be permitted one more glass of beer?"

"I'll go with you."

With fresh drinks, they walked away from the cart and Minh turned to Taylor once more.

"Why do you never use Ordway, Major? He is a Marine, the same as you. Do you dislike him?"

"No. There has been nothing for him to do."

Minh sighed. "He is ashamed." He scratched his head again and this time it irritated Taylor. It suggested Minh was doing a mime from an old Stepin Fetchit movie.

Unnoticing, Minh continued. "He has always done his job well. It is in his heart that he should fight. I have seen this with other Marines and when I was a small boy, there were men of the Foreign Legion near our village. You and Ordway remind me of them. I think it is a very strange way for men to be."

"Go get him. We'll sit and talk."

When the two Corporals were seated across the table from him, Taylor opened the conversation by saying to Ordway, "We haven't had many chances to talk. Has the Colonel told you how well you did on the radio job?"

"Yes, sir. Wasn't much to it. Nowhere near as exciting as driving through traffic."

There was just enough expression to let Taylor know exactly how Ordway felt about his work. If he hadn't seen him drinking, Taylor realized, the Corporal's minor slurring of his sibilants would have gone unremarked.

"Everyone knows the job was long and boring. The operation wouldn't have meant shit without you doing your part. You should be proud."

"'Boring.'" Ordway made the word an indictment.

"That's the business—tons of boredom so we can recover from the ounces of terror."

"I wouldn't know, Major. I've never been terrified. Just fucking bored."

"You feel cheated?"

Ordway took the question as a challenge and his face flamed. From the corner of his eye, Taylor saw Minh flinch.

"Yes, sir, I do." Discipline, pride, and alcohol warred in his voice. "I'm as good a Marine as any sonofabitch in Three MAF, Major. I didn't ask for this shit—this candy-ass typing and driving and running fucking errands. I come in the Corps to be a Marine!"

"You ever been shot at?"

The Corporal leaned back in the chair and sneered openly. "C'mon, Major, don't psych me." He gestured around the room. "You got a good reputation. Don't come down with a lot of happy horseshit about how we all got our job. I'm as good a Marine as anybody. I may not be as smart and I ain't no officer, but I'm good. You don't have to worry about me, I won't get in no trouble. Don't ever talk about re-enlistment, though."

It made Taylor feel incredibly old, made him feel age in his body like heat applied to a sand statue, driving off the sustaining moisture, letting individual grains crumble away faster and faster.

"You're a lucky bastard," he said. "If I was a Gunny Sergeant, I'd knock you out of that fucking chair and we'd find out just how tough you are. If I was some officers, I'd bust you back to Private. What I am, though, is full of enough booze to listen to your shit and try to understand. I'll tell you a story. Then maybe *you'll* understand. When I was a platoon leader in Korea, we went into reserve and we all got loaded. I got in an argument with the battalion CO. He was worried about some day making a tactical error and I was saying our job was to insure his plans worked, good or bad. We had a fun argument right up until my company commander and the battalion exec carried me outside and shoved me into a snowdrift to sober up."

Ordway's face softened in a faint smile. "Did it work, Major?"

Ruefully, Taylor said, "I got sober, but I don't think I got smarter. There isn't that much snow anywhere. My point is, we really do have our jobs to do and we all envy the other guy, one time or another. This Binh op is our whole war, right now. I've spoken to the Old Man about I Corps for you. It's in the hopper. And I'll promise you if anything comes up around here, I'll get you in on it if I can."

The young man leaned forward. "I'll do anything. I'd really appreciate it, sir."

Rising, Taylor said, "I told you before—or I think I did—if you get opened up, don't remind me I spoke up for you."

"Deal, sir."

"Yeah, sure. You two have a good time. I'm going to have another drink." Both Corporals stood to see him leave. He walked away without looking back, still able to hear the sound of Ordway's voice. For a moment he was curious as to what he might be saying, then decided it would probably depress him further.

Winter, laughing hugely, spotted him and waved for him to join them. Taylor smiled carefully, pointing at the bar cart with his empty glass. Winter gave him a thumbs up.

"Draw one for me while you're there. We don't get many chances to celebrate, so let's make the most of it."

18

ORDWAY SIPPED AT HIS CLEAR DRINK, hoping everyone would assume it was something made with gin, and wished he'd learn to keep his mouth shut. Miller, resplendent in black slacks and green dashiki, waved and headed his way. Ordway watched him approach with an apprehension that had him locking and unlocking his knees.

Miller's greeting was, "Make a lot of points with your iron-jawed buddy?" and the knees locked firmly and stayed that way.

"We were just talking."

"Shee-it!" Miller looked away. "You stroking me again? Even if I wasn't watchin' you turn red, I could see Minh. He was so nervous he was jumping."

Ordway looked sheepish. "It got a little warm. I said a couple things."

"Dumb. You determined to get your ass ruined, shot off or chewed off, one."

The glass in his hand was too small for Ordway to hide behind, but he tried, raising it to his lips and pretending to take a long drink. When he noticed Miller's easy manner change to a charged intensity, Ordway lowered the glass, its purpose now completely forgotten. He was troubled, unsure if Miller's earlier behavior had hidden tension or if the new posture and ceaseless sweep of the bright eyes had been started by something in the room. Without preamble, Miller faced him and said, "I been thinking. We're going out tonight."

"Out? Out where? For what?"

"To talk to a man."

"What man? What you up to?"

Miller grinned and Ordway half-turned from it, keeping his eyes glued to the shining teeth. "You got a load and you want help carrying it. What's going down?"

Indicating the door with a sharp head motion, Miller led the way out. "Tho did some asking around about the black guy our crooked Major's trying to get with, you know? He hangs out mostly around Tu Do."

"Everybody hangs out mostly around Tu Do," Ordway sneered. "Some hot lead. You're goin' down there and find one black?"

They were at the door and, ignoring Ordway's pessimism, Miller pressed ahead. The sudden silence in the hallway, once the door closed off the party noise, drove Miller's voice to a harsh whisper.

"I'm gonna make him come to me, dummy. If he's looking for some people to put together a junk-running deal between here and the States, why not us?"

"Us? What do we know about smuggling?"

"Everything." Miller shoved open the door to the courtyard and they stepped into heat, the liquid noises of the swimmers, and sunset's first colors. Miller said, "We got files on every smuggling dodge ever tried in this country, and a couple others. You want smugglers? A couple hours in those files and we're it, baby."

Ordway levered into the jeep, waiting until Miller was behind the wheel before answering. "You know, for such a smart guy, sometimes you talk like an asshole. All those smugglers? You know why we got files on them? 'Cause we caught ever' damn one of them, that's why."

"I know that. What difference does it make? We ain't gonna *do* it, we're gonna make him *think* we're gonna do it. Then we go to the Old man and get the whole thing busted."

"Do the whole thing by ourselves? The two of us? Not tell him? You ain't talking like an asshole, you are an asshole. He'll find out, man, and when he does, your ass has had it."

"Our asses, buddy. Yours and mine. I need help."

"You need a fucking doctor."

"Look, let's do it this way." Miller raced across one lane of the traffic ripping up and down the street in front of the BOQ and melded in between two trucks in the other. He resumed the conversation as if there had been no break. "We'll bait this dude. Drop a few hints, you know? No big thing. If anything happens, we'll see what we got. If it's enough to bother the Colonel with, we'll do it."

They approached a traffic light and Miller joined everyone else in jockeying for position, each driver determined to keep his place in the order of things. Miller pulled within inches of the bumper ahead. Any deviation from a straight line invited another car to slide a fender into the gap, trying to shoehorn forward a few inches. Slack between vehicles was seen by motorcyclists as license to crowd in, secure that no one would deliberately crush another person.

While Ordway considered this last, most aggravating stunt, two young men did it. They were Saigon cowboys, the driver in oversized belled trousers and white shirt, his passenger in jeans, boots, and a scarlet western-cut shirt. Taking advantage of Miller's momentary distraction when the car ahead crept forward, the motorcycle whipped a front wheel into the vacancy. Miller was infuriated.

"What the hell do you think you're doing?" he shouted. "You're crowding! Get out of there!"

The driver glanced over his shoulder and away without expression. The passenger looked back and smiled, reflective sunglasses making him look like an impudent bug. He was close enough for Ordway to see himself in the twin mirrors.

Miller fumed helplessly and Ordway sympathized. "They're nuts. And they make us nuts. What do you care if he gets in front of you?"

"It ain't just him! It's the whole fucking country, man! Why ain't that sonofabitch in the Army? It's his fucking country, man! Why am I sittin' here in a jeep and that little prick is riding around on his Honda?''

The motorcycle passenger's smile drew tight and he spoke to the driver from the corner of his mouth. The driver raced his engine and smiled at nothing. When the light changed the motorcycle leaped to wedge in and Miller let him move forward before gunning the jeep. The fender brushed the passenger's leg as he was giving the Americans the finger and his grin blew away in a howl of anger. He yelled over his shoulder at them while they sat stonefaced, flowing inexorably with the traffic.

Others looked in their direction. Ordway noticed there were no other Americans in sight and his hands felt wet.

"We're in it now, shithead," he said, watching the other drivers. "If you see a way out of here, you better by God grab it. There's some ugly shit coming down."

They slowed to another stop, a smoking river of machinery temporarily damned. The rider in front continued to shout complaint, rubbing his calf. He got off the motorcycle and limped in a tight circle, making faces of accusatory pain. Horns blew from other cars and motorcycles. Voices rose with the scorching exhaust fumes. A second motorcycle growled up on Miller's left and a Vietnamese soldier spoke to the aggrieved civilian. He listened, nodding at intervals, then walked his own motorcycle backwards until he was abreast of Miller.

"You hurt this man," he declared in careful English. "He very injured."

"He very full of shit," Miller retorted, unconsciously imitating the soldier's speech at first. "I'm not even sure I touched him. I just brushed his pants. Tell him to show you a mark."

"No time mark. Come later."

"There won't ever be one. I didn't hit him."

The soldier shook his head. "Very hard hit. Leg hurt. Big hurt."

"Big bullshit," Miller snorted. "He's another cowboy trying to rip somebody off. Fuck him."·

"Easy buddy," Ordway cautioned. "There's a lot of people watching."

The two cowboys wandered to where the soldier argued their case, the injured one limping dramatically. Ordway got out of the jeep to stand in front of the soldier's motorcycle where he offered to shake hands with the driver. It was refused with a blunt move back and a sharp phrase. The passenger smiled at the action before pointedly staring at Ordway's hand and looking past to the soldier.

The latter leaned closer to Miller. "Accident you trouble. Police come, make big trouble you."

Miller shifted in the seat. "There's no need for police. I didn't hit him. I might have brushed his leg, but I didn't hit him hard enough to hurt."

The soldier said, "Police come soon. Make trouble. Maybe man forget hurt, you pay something."

"Hear that?" Miller called to Ordway. "They want money."

Ordway looked at the civilians, who seemed to have understood Miller's last word. They smiled. Ordway looked back to his partner.

"Tell them to shit in their hats. Tell that doggie we're going to make them pay for the damage to the jeep." He went to the right side of the vehicle. The cowboys watched him go, listening to the soldier's translation with growing fury. They began to shout again.

Miller looked at the crowded scene around them, wishing that whatever had traffic held up would break so he could get away. A few drivers and riders from other vehicles were on the street now, and none of them looked neutral. He told himself they weren't necessarily hostile—it was hot enough to make a statue frown—but the logic failed to stop the electric sensations in his knees and elbows.

The soldier's confiding tone gave way to outright threat. "Many Vietnam people here. Not like American hurt other Vietnam people. You pay."

"Screw you." Miller gripped the wheel. "We'll wait for your goddam cops."

"Police too late, maybe. Maybe come, you hurt."

"What's he saying?" Ordway called from his position by the fender.

Before answering, Miller sized up the crowd again. There were more people standing outside vehicles now, and horns were blowing. The heat seemed to have gone up twenty degrees since they'd jammed up. Even the lowering daylight contributed to his feeling of being separated from all things familiar.

"He's saying they might go for us."

To Miller's surprise, Ordway raised both hands, waving them across his body and shaking his head. "Don't do that," he said to the soldier. "We can fix." He pointed to Miller and himself, repeating, "We fix, we fix." Pointing again, he indicated the soldier, then the fender, saying, "You look. Come see."

The soldier laughed at Miller and spoke to the cowboys. They laughed with him and fell in behind as he moved to Ordway.

The Corporal smiled at them, offering his hand to the soldier, who took it and spoke rapidly in Vietnamese. The cowboys laughed some more and he smiled his appreciation.

"You have to look over here," Ordway said, penitent. "See where the threads stuck. From trousers." He gestured them down further. Bending to touch the fender, he said, "How's the traffic look, buddy?"

"You can see it, same as me."

"The oncoming traffic, you dumb shit." At the hard sound, the soldier grew suspicious. Ordway immediately patted the fender again. "Mistake. We make mistake."

Miller said, "I can get out as soon as this truck passes."

"Stand by." Ordway nodded and smiled for the soldier. "Tell them we sorry make trouble. We want be friends. How much we pay?"

"OK," Miller said, urgency lifting his voice. The soldier was turning to speak to the cowboys. Ordway put his left hand on the back of the cropped head and rammed it in the face of the driver, sending them tumbling to the ground with the motorcycle in a thrashing mass of limbs and wheels. The passenger grabbed at him and Ordway ducked, driving his fist into the unprotected stomach stretched in front of him. The man's breath whooshed and he doubled over, limp fingers trailing down Ordway's arm as he jumped for the already moving jeep.

Miller let the clutch out and pounded the gas pedal to the floor, sending the jeep lurching into a squealing U-turn that sent them bouncing off the opposite curb. At the first corner, he cut in front of a bus, forced his way through some miscellaneous traffic, and dodged around the next corner before slowing. He glanced over his shoulder. "Anyone coming?"

Ordway had been watching behind. "Nobody."

A half-block further Miller's relief boiled out in nervous laughter and remembrance. "I didn't know what the hell had happened to you, man!" He pounded the steering wheel. "'We fix, we fix'" he imitated. "You sure did fix. You hear that kiss when you pushed that soldier? Ponk! Sounded like somebody cleanin' used bricks, man. Ponk!"

Less enthusiastic, Ordway said, "I figured we had to get out of there, you know? If that sucker hadn't started a riot, we'd still have ended up in a sling for getting in a hassle. I'd just as soon get court-martialed for thumping some sonofabitch like that as for some phony shit about hurting one of 'em's leg."

"Ponk!" Miller shouted. "Blackmailing little bastards. Be a long time before they try that again."

Leaning back in the seat, Ordway edged his right hand under his thigh, still able to feel the tremor, despite the weight pressing on it. It had stopped by the time Miller spotted a parking place and braked. Ordway hopped out, waiting on the sidewalk until Miller was done. They walked Tu Do Street together, ignoring the whores and vendors. Miller pointed down a side street. "There's where we lay out the bait."

In the rhythmic flare of a blinking yellow neon sign, three black soldiers lounged against the wall of a bar grandly titled The Golden Lotus. Two more blacks stood at the curb, arguing in heavy voices with a tiny Vietnamese woman who waited politely for them to finish before spitting a stream of obscenities at them. The men against the wall laughed at the entertainment. The woman tossed her head, playing to them, and one offered her a drag on a cigarette. She took it, pulling hard enough to make the coal glow, holding the smoke deep while the two men picked up the argument again.

"That's a black joint, Willy," Ordway hissed. "You want to get my head busted?"

"You're with me. Nothing's going to happen."

"Sure. Me and my accent in a slopchute full of juiced spades. Shit."

"Keep your mouth shut, then. Do everybody a favor." They were abreast of the door and Miller nodded to the three against the wall. The middle one stepped in front of him, looking past to Ordway.

"No whites," he said. The other two stirred, but remained in place.

"It's OK, brother," Miller said, laughing. "He's with me. No problem, man."

"No whites. A-tall." The man's eyes rolled, having trouble focusing.

"Forget it," Ordway said. "You go in if you want to. I don't need any more trouble, you know? I'll wait in the jeep."

"Fuck that." Miller glared at all three men. The skin tightened over hardened muscles in his jaw. "I got a right to go anywhere I want with anyone I want."

"Not here, you don't." The voice came from behind, and Ordway turned to see the two men who'd been at the curb had moved closer. The woman watched, a hand pulling anxiously at the hem of her blouse.

The man in the doorway said, "It don't make a shit if you Martin Luther King and this here's your honky lawyer, no whites goes in here."

Ordway stepped back so he could see all of them, moving smoothly, hands loose. "I told you all, I don't need any more trouble. I'm leaving."

Miller listened to the retreating footsteps without turning, the anger in them as clear to him as speech. He stared into the eyes in front of him until the other man's gaze broke. Slowly, he inspected the others.

"You holdin' inspection?" one sneered, and the rest laughed.

"I don't want to forget none of you," Miller said, putting a hand to the shoulder of the man blocking his way. The man allowed himself to be moved.

"Be sure and bring some more o' your honky friends," he called, and Miller's stomach wadded up. He was surprised at how his knees hurt when he sat down at one of the small tables in the dark room.

A girl joined him immediately, her age smothered in makeup. He looked into her eyes, lifeless as the used-up yellow blouse exposing the top half of her breasts. One of them was bruised, the discoloration showing through powder she'd used to cover the mark. He bought her a Saigon tea without waiting to be asked, ignoring her instant sales pitch, letting her chatter while he examined the customers. He found what he wanted in a matter of seconds and leaned toward the girl, one hand covering hers.

"Over in the corner," he said, barely moving his head that way. "Will that man sell me some stuff?"

Understanding flashed in the dull eyes even as she shook her head. "I not know. What you want buy?"

"You know what I mean. Does he sell it?"

"I not know. You want take me home?"

"Never mind. I'll find out for myself." He walked to the corner table where a small man in a spangled shirt and wide-brimmed hat held court. The man watched him come. The two hangers-on failed to notice until he was only a table away. They glowered and looked especially menacing, like watch-dogs caught napping. Miller paid no attention to them and the small man smiled a greeting that brightened his whole being.

"Good evening, my man, good evening." He moved a hand across the table top. "Find a chair and pull up."

The warmth of the reception startled Miller and he sat care-fully, watching the other two at the table. The small man noticed and laughed, a sharp sound.

"Don't worry about them. They OK. How you keepin', man? Ain't seen you around lately."

Miller said, "You got the right man? My name's Miller, Willy Miller. I never met you."

The small man laughed again, enjoying himself. "I know it. But I know you. Make it my business to know who hangs out, like. Seen you out on Plant Road a lot. You a Sergeant, work in some research deal in that ARVN compound. What you all do in there?"

Miller made himself look amused and said, "Push paper, like everybody else in the Nam. What about you? And what do I call you?"

One of the watchdogs laughed. "He wants to know where you work." He looked to the small man and sound died in his throat. Miller looked at the small man's face and felt sorry for the watchdog. Then the small man was friends again.

"That's all right, Otis, forget it. Just don't let your alligator mouth overload your hummin'bird brain once too often, you dig?" To Miller, he said, "Otis a good man, but sometime he

talk too much. But I ain't introduce myself. Bobby Mantell."
He extended a hand and they gave each other power.

"I come in with an idea," Miller said, shooting a significant glance at each of the other two. Mantell raised his eyebrows in mocking surprise. After a hesitation, he said, "You all go get us something to drink. I'll let you know when we want it."

Waiting until they'd reached the bar, Miller then turned back to Mantell. He leaned forward, hands flat on the table. "You don't know much about me, and I don't know nothin' about you, but I got to start somewhere, and you look like the kind of man I need."

"You want a stereo? Want to sell an air-conditioner? Find a woman? You name it, Willy, I can handle it."

Miller's attitude challenged. "I can handle that much by myself." He turned his hands over on the table, resting them palms up. "Look. No marks. You want to check anything else, let me know."

Mantell's smile was replaced by the hard look he'd shown Otis. Miller ignored the swift rush of fear, knowing this was only the first of many blind leaps and there was no jump back. He remained unmoving until Mantell broke eye contact to scan the room. He pushed at Miller's hands.

"All right, goddamit, no tracks! So what! People lookin', man!"

"I want you to know you ain't talkin' to no user. I want you to know I take care of business."

"You?" Mantell snorted. "You ain't got no business. You just another brother with a soft job."

Miller continued as if uninterrupted. "You might know somebody can deal. I mean deal, man. No dime bag shit. 'Cause I can move it. You know anyone wants to talk about the States, I know how to get the stuff in. No risk, you dig?" He pushed the chair away and stood up, hands still on the table. "I can move it."

Mantell laughed. "You been readin' them comic books, Willy. I know you ain't no narc, but you must be workin' for one, so you and him go find a corner and suck each other. You runnin' with whites, I hear. Man do that, somethin' wrong with him. You sure you ain't a little—?" He finished the sentence by holding out a hand and letting it slowly droop at the wrist. A large diamond glittered in a gold ring, dew on ebony. Laughter from the bar distracted Miller and he realized all eyes were on him. He straightened and deliberately looked around the entire room. The sound level dropped appreciably. He looked back to Mantell.

"That's country, man." The angry vibration in his voice made it difficult for him to speak softly. "I'm giving you a chance to make more money than your small-time ass can understand, giving you a chance to be somebody, not just a fuckin' do-rag nigger scuffling for clothes money. You don't want it, fuck you. I'll find me a man who does. Somebody with more sense than to get smart with a good deal. You think about it. I'll be back. You sure as shit ain't movin' up in the world. I know where to find you."

He walked for the door, picking his way through the jumbled tables, feeling the eyes and the unnatural silence pushing against his skin like plastic sliding across the muscles. He itched all over by the time he stepped into the humid night and walked toward the jeep. After a block with no one following, his step loosened and he felt good, free.

"Sure took you long enough," Ordway grumbled as his partner swung into the driver's seat. "I figured they'd cut you up and fed you to the fishes by now. What happened?"

"Pussycats, my man, pussycats." Miller dropped the jeep into gear and shot it out into the street. Ordway rocked in the seat, grabbing for a handhold and swearing his surprise.

"When they deal with ol' Willy, baby, they all pussycats." He warped the vehicle around a corner and began to sing. Ordway improved his handhold and cursed in a steady monotone.

19

ALLEN HAD WATCHED ORDWAY and Miller leave with a rueful malediction for both of them. Now, an hour later, he looked at his watch for the eighth time in fifteen minutes and made his move. He moved quickly through the passageway into the courtyard and hurried toward the gate.

"Captain Allen!" The call stopped him so abruptly his foot dug in and gravel bounced away. He turned to Lieutenant Colonel Earl and composed his best smile.

" 'Evening, Colonel. How are you?"

Earl, casual in slacks and Hawaiian shirt, came closer. "Same as ever, Captain, same as ever. What you doing around here?" His eyes were wider than normal, rearranging the fine features to a look of surprise, as though the slight weaving of his body was constantly catching him unprepared.

"Just having a few drinks with the Colonel and some friends," Allen said, watching Earl and wondering if anyone in Saigon was not drinking on this particular night. He pointed at the gate. "I'm on my way home, as a matter of fact."

Earl moved to drape an arm across Allen's shoulder. "Leaving early? Got something special lined up, huh? One of the embassy chicks? Has she got a friend? Must be something to drag you away from your buddies."

"It's not that. Some of the Unit—."

"Oh, the *Unit!*" Earl stepped back. "That sounds like a party! Celebrating? Celebrating what? Everybody still enjoying the way that jarhead Major threw that poor little bastard off the roof? I'll bet Winter's pissed he wasn't there to see that!"

"No one threw him, Colonel. There was an arrest in progress, he struggled to escape, and he went over. You've seen the report."

"Report!" Earl flung out an arm and staggered. "What

175

fucking whitewash! You were there! You know that sonofa-bitch killed him in cold blood. Why isn't anyone allowed to interview the other two, the two that fucking brush ape wasn't allowed to get his hands on?''

"They're prisoners of the South Vietnamese. You know what they're like about sovereignty."

Rocking, Earl glared while Allen silently urged him to go away. The Colonel failed to leave, but at least the anger drained from his face and he looked at Allen in sadness.

"What are we doing to you young people?" he said, looking away into the night sky. The question was so soft it could have been entirely self-directed. "How did all this happen? Are we really going to destroy everything in order to protect it? Is that what we've come to?"

"Colonel, I'm running a little late." Allen indicated the gate again. "If you don't mind, sir—?"

Instantly the knowing grin flashed back on. "I know where you're going. Got something hot lined up, right? Hey, you remember the party we went to a couple months ago, that ARVN Colonel's wife? Beautiful thing—'way too young for the old bastard. Him in Da Nang, her all alone down here. Remember?"

"Not too well, sir." Allen looked at his watch.

"I remember. Name was Dao. You ever see her? I think she liked me." He winked.

"I see her from time to time. I'll mention your name. But I have to go, Colonel."

"Well, go, then." He spun to leave, dignity marred by another unfortunate stagger. He tried to salvage it with minor bluster. "Don't forget, you see that Dao, you tell her I'd like to talk to her."

"Right." Allen threw the word behind him, trotting out the gate. Outside, he got lucky, walking less than a block before he spotted the Bluebird and flagged it. He gave the address and closed his eyes, not stirring until he felt the vehicle stop and heard the driver's mumble. He paid without haggling, nodded briefly at the apartment-house guard, and stepped into the lobby. After a moment's indecision, he chose the stairs, assuming the self-service elevator was out of order again. It was only one flight and the exercise was less bother than the aggravation of waiting for a machine that worked on whimsy.

At the top of the stairs he turned right, stopping at the apartment fronting the building. He fitted his key to the lock and let himself in.

Across the width of the room a figure stirred in an overstuffed chair in front of drapes that shielded the window from the street below. A flowing pink nightgown identified the person as female. The only illumination in the room came from the narrow beam of a reading lamp aimed at a book in her hand. She dropped the book beside the chair and the light, deprived of anything to reflect from, drew in on itself. The thump of the book combined with the dimming effect to provide a sense of threat.

Allen laid apology over explanation. "I said I'd be late."

"Not late." Anger slurred the vowels, emphasizing the lilting Vietnamese accent. "Very late. I fix good dinner. Not special, good, same-same. You come home too late. All gone cold. I gone cold, too. You piss me off, for sure."

Waves of weariness assaulted Allen and he massaged his temples. "How many times do I have to tell you 'pissed off' is bad? And don't say 'same-same,' either. It sounds like one of the street girls."

"What!"

His hands ceased their work to fly to a defensive position. "I mean that's the way they talk, that's all. You don't want to sound like that, do you?"

"I never sound like street creep!" She rose quickly, stepping between him and the light. The nightgown was suddenly luminescent and she was a dark silhouette against a rose-pink glow. Allen felt his whole body respond.

"God, Dao, you're so beautiful," he breathed.

She was scornful. "You come home late, drunk, think all you have do is say sweet? You *do* think I street creep!"

"No." He dropped his hands. "I don't blame you for being angry. I'm sorry I'm late. But I'll never stop telling you you're beautiful."

"You just want go bed!"

His face lit up. "You better believe! You think I'm too drunk? Never!" He reached for her and she scooted under his grasp and past him. When he straightened and turned, she was giggling at him from behind another chair.

"You big liar," she said, interrupting herself with more

177

giggling. "You come here from other woman, try fool me!"

Stalking, feinting from side to side, he said, "There's no other woman. I need all my strength for you. And you're going to need all of yours, tonight." He lunged and missed again, laughing at how clumsy she made him look. Like a cat, he thought. Everything about her is catlike.

She danced away, giving little yelps of delighted fright until she had the other chair between them again. "Big talk," she huffed from safety. "Anyhow, I not interested. I told you, I already got cold, same-same dinner."

Another futile grab and he said, "Dammit, stop saying 'same-same!'" He held up a hand. "Look, let's get this settled. Peace. Now, the phrase is 'just like your dinner.' You say it."

She grimaced. "'Just like you dinner.'"

"No, no. 'Just like *your* dinner.'" He stepped to the light and turned it on her face. Even frowning at the sudden light, she excited him. "Now say it again," he commanded.

Tiring of the game, Dao glared. "Just like *your*—."

He grabbed her before she could react, vaulting across the chair to scoop her up in his arms. She squealed and pretended to bite his neck before arching to stare up at his face.

"You make me too much afraid when you late. I worry all time."

"I told you we all had to go to BOQ 1. I didn't think I'd be this late. I came as soon as I could." He walked toward the bedroom door. She lowered her face against his chest.

"I fix good dinner. You not come. I worry."

"I'm here now." Feeling very sober and very tender, he lowered her to the bed, sat next to her and started undressing.

"You stay tonight?" The question was hopeful.

"I can't, honey. I've got to see Winter first thing in the morning."

"How you get back villa? You bring jeep?"

"I'll have to walk."

"No!" She put her arms around him and pressed against his bare back. The nightgown wasn't between them and his heart pounded.

"I want you stay. Walk at night dangerous."

Pulling free, he stepped out of his shorts and lay down next to her. "We'll argue later," he said.

178

"Wake up!"

He rolled toward the sound, delighting in her laughter as she fended off his hands.

"Too much, you want," she pretended to scold. "I got breakfast for you. Come on, you be late, be mad me."

He got out of bed and stood up with a muzzy smile for her as she looked up at him, already dressed in jeans and one of his shirts.

"What time is it?"

"One-half past five."

He nodded. "Good."

She sniffed. "Good? You crazy? Terrible. Get up in dark morning never be good."

"I didn't mean I like it. I mean it gives me time to tell you something."

"What?" She stepped back, preparing herself. Her eyes widened almost imperceptibly and her full lips thinned. When he reached a hand for her, she retreated another step. "What? What you want tell me?"

He stood with the hand outstretched. "Dao, it's no big thing. I only wanted to tell you I saw Colonel Earl on the way over here."

The fear continued to play across her features, diminishing like a heavy mist. "That's all? No other thing?"

"No other thing." He stepped forward to cup her chin. "He wanted me to tell you he'd like to talk to you."

Deviltry replaced the previous light in her eyes. "He hot for me, yeah?"

"He too much hot for you. I don't like it."

She took his hand and kissed the palm. "I like for you be jealous."

"That's the damndest part of this whole thing. I'm jealous of another man's wife."

"I tol' you many-many times, not same-same wife. He got number-one wife. I minor wife."

He removed his hand from hers to continue dressing. "Goddamit, Dao, that's medieval! I don't care what he promised your parents, he can't—."

"Yes. Can." She walked out of the bedroom. "Not talk anymore. I put breakfast on plate."

He was still muttering when he sat at the small kitchen table.

179

She slid scrambled eggs and toast in front of him and sat opposite, sipping coffee, looking at him almost pityingly.

"You never understand Vietnam, Hal. Here, man with power do anything. All men work get power. Not use, why have? Man get rich so get things. Young wife always nice thing have, no?"

"You're not a thing. Don't say that. Don't ever—."

"Never mind. I not unhappy be minor wife. He help my father, get my brother school in France."

Allen rolled his eyes and looked skyward. "Jesus, don't I know it! You're given to an old man so your brother can go to medical school in France and I'm here to fight for the country for him and you and the old man. What's going on?"

"If you not come, we never see each other. If I have real husband, I never speak you. Old basserd husband idea work pretty good, huh?"

"You're incorrigible." He grinned, getting to his feet. "I can't argue with you."

She walked beside him to the door, trying to hold him inside an arm stretched across his waist. "What that word mean— that incor—in—?"

"Incorrigible." He kissed the top of her head. "It means you're a naughty girl. Bad. *Xo lam.*"

He waited for her to look up, scolding or pouting, to participate in the joke, but when she turned her face to him, tears smeared her cheeks. She grabbed his shirt in both hands and pulled him down, kissing him with a desperate longing.

"I *am* bad," she cried, and broke away. "I not want be bad. You make joke. I make joke. Not funny. I love you too much."

Holding her to him, shaken mentally by the violent change in her and physically by the sobs against his body, he gently rocked her and dropped his head to hers, the mass of him almost enfolding the delicate woman.

"Don't cry, sweetheart, don't cry. I love you. You know that. I'll think of something. We'll work it out."

She sniffled, checking the sobs. "I want belong you. I want be yours, only yours. I not want—."

He pressed her head to his chest, quieting her. "We want the same things, Dao. Leave it to me. We'll get married, I

180

promise.''

She brushed away tears and managed a smile. "We be happy now. I crazy for cry. OK now. You go! Hurry!" She shoved him out the door, turning up the streaked face for a dutiful housewife's kiss. Allen obliged, taking her face in both hands.

"I promise," he said, looking deep into her eyes.

Nothing stirred there and he left wondering if a man could tell himself a lie so well he believed it.

Taylor was waking under different circumstances.

The alarm clock jack-hammered at his hangover. He'd gone to sleep knowing the pain would be waiting for him when he awakened. It depressed him that his foresight had alleviated nothing.

He jerked aside the camouflaged poncho liner that was the standard Vietnam blanket and swatted at the clock.

The single room guaranteed him privacy of vision only. Sound penetrated the plywood walls unhampered. At this time of day, when all the rest of the world seemed still, each scuffle, yawn, flatulence, or dropped boot resonated. In his present state, it was like being caged in a drum.

Dressing with studiousness, he considered each movement, wincing at any that disturbed the position of his head. Blousing his trousers evoked a series of self-pitying groans. He shuffled out of the tiny room and down the hall to the community head. Allen, cinching his belt, followed him in.

"Morning, Major. You surely look terrible."

Taylor grunted and turned on a water tap that afforded a bare trickle of water, yet managed to roar like Niagara. A deep breath to strengthen his resolve, and he sloshed cold water over his head and neck, snorting like a mule. It helped. When he straightened, colors were no longer pastel blurs and the headache was a mere battalion of artillery. He decided he'd live.

Allen whistled while he shaved. When it became necessary to alter the shape of his mouth, he broke the tune, picking it up as soon as the affected area was free again. The stuttering irregularity of it curdled in Taylor's brain.

"Will you, for the love of Christ, either whistle or shut up?"

Allen turned half-lathered innocence to him. "Hung over

181

that bad?"

"It's not the noise." Taylor squirted shaving cream into his hand and smeared it on. "It's the goddam tweet-tweet, pause, tweet-tweet." He drew the razor down the side of his face with exquisite care.

"I can't do it any other way, Major. If I don't unpucker, I'll cut myself. I don't think the sight of blood'd do you much good right now, you know?"

Taylor leaned his head against the mirror and gripped the edges of the sink with both hands. "The thought of you bleeding is the single prospect of delight on my horizon, Allen. Only my iron will keeps me alive to clean up and gain enough strength to die with dignity." He pivoted, keeping his head pressed against the cool glass. "I've earned that. 'I have fought our country's battles on the land and on the sea. First to fight for right and freedom and—.'"

Allen pushed a fist to his mouth and backed away in a parody of horror. "I quit! No more whistling, I swear!"

"You're an honorable man." Taylor resumed shaving. "You also whistle well, when you're not mucking it up. A talent you developed while idling about with the other rich folk, I guess."

"Some cats got it, some cats ain't."

"Too true. On the other hand, I've always considered myself blessed to have been born good looking instead of rich. They're not going to give you a new face, come payday."

Allen's snort blasted shaving cream onto the mirror. "Hung over and still raving drunk! A marvel!"

"It's called a tolerance level. Us poor people learn a lot about tolerance. We learn it along with agility, dodging polo pony turds."

"You're just jealous."

"Bet your ass."

"Anyhow, if it wasn't for rich dudes like me, what would you sturdy peasants have to aim for? The fact that we exist keeps you hustling. It's good for you."

A bitter taint crept into Allen's speech, sharp enough to make Taylor glance his way, puzzled. He discounted the feeling and splashed his face some more, coming up making derogatory noises.

"When I think of how I'm over here fighting a war so you

capitalist bloodsuckers can get richer—. You ought to be ashamed of yourself."

"It's all for the best," Allen said.

Once more, something about the tone and manner was out of place and Taylor would have sworn he stopped, as if he'd checked himself before continuing.

"Play your cards right," he went on, "and when this is all over I'll get Dad to put you on as a groom. Then you can walk in front of the ponies."

Taylor stopped in mid-squeeze with his toothpaste. "You honest-to-God have polo ponies?"

"No! We own a couple of riding horses, that's all."

"Humphh!" Taylor mumbled through a mouthful of suds. *"Nouveaux riche.* I should have known."

"With all due respect, Major, sir, fuck you."

"Not now. I have a headache."

Allen gargled and choked, finally asking, "Going to chow?"

Taylor said, "Absolutely. Let me get my blouse on and a couple of aspirin down. I'll meet you on the porch."

A few minutes later, stepping out into the dawn walk to the messhall, Taylor reflected that it was something he enjoyed, rain or shine. The one thing that intruded, that galled him daily, was passing the neighboring ARVN enlisted married quarters. His first view of them had been in a pre-dawn like this one and revulsion had surged in his stomach.

Separated from the Unit's own ARVN compound and a similar American facility by an eight-foot high chain link fence, the barracks-like buildings stood in the half light in precise rows, as if strict geometry could offset the shabby construction. He had continued toward them of necessity, having to pass in order to reach the messhall. Abreast of the first building, seeing children at the mesh fence, a memory from a shrouded corner of his mind surfaced. It was of transient worker's camps, carrying the same air of disinterested squalor and a smell that affected the mind more than the nose, because it was the odor of rotting dreams that lay unclaimed for fear of the derision of the confirmed losers.

Here, the children cadged apples and oranges with a challenging boldness that took what they did out of the realm of begging and turned it into a game. The more aggressive and fortunate invariably shared. The mothers stood in the background, embarrassed, smiling. Taylor had seen only two Vietnamese soldiers ever acknowledge what was happening at the fence. They had glared and turned away. The others ignored it with stiff backs.

The Americans handing out the fruit behaved much like the women. Some spoke to the children. Most simply forced their offering through the wire or pitched it over and hurried on. There was one man who was there frequently. Always carrying several items under his blouse, he distributed them with no favoritism, no conversation, and a steady, bumptious friendliness. He was a favorite of both the kids and the mothers. When he'd finished, he always waved to the wives. They waved back at him, the only American who cleansed the tension from their smiles.

Taylor knew he'd wonder all his life why the man had bothered to establish that rapport. Perversely, he knew he would also cherish not knowing.

This morning was no different, with the children calling to the passersby. Taylor shouted a greeting, generating a chorus of brash demands. He continued on, avoiding looking at the housing. The initial loathing had long ago given way to rage at the thought that good men lived like that while his own government pimped for the men who arranged their deaths. And grew rich.

Allen's gesture in the direction of the houses caught Taylor's eye, interrupting his contemplation.

The younger man said, "Every time I walk past here I want to turn around and run back to the office and thank the Old Man for letting me in on this Nguyen Binh deal."

"I know what you mean. He's linked with someone on our side of the barb-wire, that's for sure. I doubt if he'll tell us who. If we catch him."

"Tho'll get it out of him. Sometimes I think he's the only man in Nam who knows how to treat the badasses. I could name a couple for him."

Even in the half light, Taylor could see the belligerent thrust of Allen's jaw and the taut line of his lips. He recognized the statement as a cue and realized the other man was thinking of something far removed from Binh. He determined to keep the conversation firmly centered on the known.

184

"Tho's system doesn't always work. He's not having too much luck with Trung or Tu."

Allen appeared to relax a little before answering. "He hasn't unloaded on them yet. You know Loc's holding him off because he'd like to use them for interviews or something."

"I know. And I think he's nuts."

"He must think he can get away with it." Allen gave a bitter laugh. "Can you picture the swoons at one of my mother's liberal conclaves if they're watching TV and Trung comes on and says, '—and that fascist beast, Captain Harold Allen, smacked me across my peaceable chops with his capitalist shotgun?'"

"Your mom's friends are like that?"

They trotted across the street to the messhall. Safe on the other side, Allen resumed. "You can't imagine it. While I was doing my number on Trung, I'd bet anything Mom was packing a placard somewhere denouncing the war."

Taylor said, "I've heard of people getting a 'Dear John' from their mother."

"Don't laugh. You know what she sent in my last Care package? A Swedish travel brochure! Is that subtle?"

Taylor was still chuckling when he paid the cashier in her booth. He waved a greeting at the waitresses across the large, crowded room and turned back to Allen.

"You all must have a lot of fun conversations at the old dinner table. How's your father take all this?"

One waitress, bolder than the rest, waved them toward her table. They moved toward it.

"He's like us, I guess," Allen said. "Confused. Angry. Worries about me more than he needs to. I keep telling him my greatest danger is a tainted canape. He's trying to equate this mess with Korea or World War Two. It doesn't work."

They sat down. Taylor ordered his normal huge breakfast and the waitress strained to control her giggling while she scribbled on her pad. Allen watched the unvarying routine before ordering only coffee.

Taylor invariably ordered practically everything on the menu as well as taking quantities of fruit from the self-service rack in the middle of the room. The tiny women initially refused to believe his orders. Once they realized he was serious, they watched eagerly for him to sit in their sector. As soon as the chosen one had everything on paper, she scurried to the galley door where the other waitresses waited. Every morning they went over the list, item by item, glancing at Taylor, whispering, and occasionally shrieking amusement. It was the highlight of the morning shift.

Taylor tried to explain he ate no lunch and a light dinner. It made no difference. The fact that he ate that much in a day, much less a single meal, delighted them.

Allen said, "If you ever go on a diet, you'll break their hearts. What kills me is, you were sick with a hangover not thirty minutes ago and now you're about to shovel in a ton of rations."

Taylor dug into a cantaloupe. "Germ theory," he said.

"Pardon?"

"Simple." Taylor waved the spoon. "Down there in my tum-tum are all these bad guy germs, jumping around, making my head hurt. I drop all this chow on them," he spooned another chunk of cantaloupe and swallowed it, "and it mashes the bastards. Can't beat medical science."

"The girls know about this?"

Taylor paused in his attack on the fruit. "Naw. They just get a kick out of a man who enjoys. Funny thing, with all the misery in Asia, there's a streak in all them that lets them enjoy seeing another person enjoy. When they get envious enough and mad enough, they'll kill you. Nature's way of redistributing the wealth, I guess. The difference is, here, when they're done burying you, they'll all smile, and someone'll say, 'He sure knew how to have a good time, didn't he?' and everyone'll nod and go home hoping to be next on the good times roster."

Allen's face was frozen into determined neutrality. "You think it's a built-in response, a reflex? You think because they're Orientals they're supposed to accept abuse until they break one way or another?"

"You think I'm bigoted." Taylor said it easily, making light of the younger man's masked hostility. "My comment was an observation, not a comparison, and it was a generality." He returned to his meal, watching Allen stir his coffee.

The Captain said, "I keep trying to understand the attitudes here, and they keep getting away from me. I mean, how do they stand for some of the things that go on?''

"If you have to ask, you're right, you don't understand. Give it some time. You, too, can go bamboo like the rest of us old farts. For now, quit pestering me so I can get to work. My girls and my stomach are waiting." He bobbed his head at the approaching waitress.

"God forbid!" Allen leaned back. "I'd get between Momma Bear and her cubs before I'd stand between you and your hotcakes."

He recovered some of his normal manner as he said it, and Taylor was glad of the familiar openness of the face across from him. Yet, it wasn't exactly the same. There was a difference and he couldn't define it.

Eating provided something to do while he puzzled over it.

He told himself Allen was probably only suffering the same whiskey malaise. The idea died aborning. No, he decided, there was something else and the man was having trouble expressing it.

A grim smile flicked on and off as he considered that Allen was possibly looking for help and afraid of losing face. He could be closer to understanding the East than either of them realized.

20

THE AFTERNOON SUN pressed against the window of Winter's office, shouldering through in an oblique slash of energy that added the only touch of color to the self-conscious spartan arrangement. Loc watched the slow retreat of the shaft, wishing he knew a way to point out to his friend that, as the powerful sun moved slowly, they, too must exercise patience.

Winter stirred irritably at his desk, and a whirl of dust motes escaped from the rug into the path of light.

He said, "It's been a month, Loc. We should have him by now."

"Everything has gone well," Loc said. "All infiltrated dumps have blown up. We have Trung and Tu in the interrogation house. Binh has done nothing unanticipated. He is hiding. Trung has given us the name of most of his contacts, I am sure. It is a question of time."

"And Tu has told us nothing." Winter refused to be mollified. "He could give us the names of Special Section people —the hit men, the sappers. All we've really gotten from Trung is black market operators and low-level VC sympathizers."

"It has been your choice, Win. I now believe we may never get anything from Tu if you will not agree to Tho's interrogation methods. Tu is a fanatic, a true believer. Trung is an opportunist. You knew I have received pressure to release him?"

"I knew. And still no idea where the heat comes from?"

Loc tapped ash from his cigarette. "When has it ever been different? A person of importance suspects Trung is not safely in Hong Kong. We should be grateful the person is not powerful enough to create more trouble and that Trung is not important enough to be worth more attention. To use your barbarian's jargon, a little more horsepower and we would be doing some tall explaining."

"I'll see that sonofabitch dead before I'll turn him loose."

"No you won't. If the pressure becomes too great, we will release him to the proper agency. He is not worth the death of the Unit. If that much pressure builds, he will be an issue. He will no longer simply be someone of whom we may say, '*Chu ay qua song,*' and that is the last of it. Our only hope, if you think he has other information, is Tho."

"I disagree. We can turn him around if we use the proper psychology. We've got to outwait him."

"As you wish. I am the one who suggested patience originally. I think we presently waste time, but you appear to suffer the most."

"Time moves slowly for an old man."

Loc permitted himself a small sound of disbelief. "You are not even old enough to claim wisdom. Anyhow, there are other things I wish to speak of. There are rumors in our headquarters, rumors from people who have been well-informed in the past, that people in your government are opposed to this Unit and what it has done."

"That's no rumor. We've known it since we started and we've lived with the pressure since our first covered operation proved that District Chief was crooked. I told you then we were in for a rough ride."

"Your memory fails you. Perhaps you are growing old. It was I who said we should act on our evidence that time and simply tell the government, again, *Chu ay qua song.*' You were the one who insisted we arrest him. When he was killed after that farce, that was when the pressure began."

Winter repeated Loc's Vietnamese phrase as if tasting it, ruminating. "'He crossed the river,'" he translated. "God, how many ways we have of describing killing. He had to die. He was evil, involved in forced prostitution, usury, spying. What we did was justice."

"Justice?" Loc's eyebrows twitched in mock amazement. "Your people have no interest in justice here. Even in your own country, they replace justice with legality. Here, where the white man's burden is so heavy for your liberals, they must be even more stringent."

"I don't want to argue." The larger man's voice was almost pleading and he stared at the restless hands on his desk. "Not today. Let's stay with business. What's on your mind?"

Brushing at a non-existent speck on his blouse, Loc said, "The rumor is that people in your government will arrange the end of American work with this Unit, that you will be 'phased out.'"

"No," Winter said firmly. "We have friends, the same as we have enemies."

"You expected a replacement for the Major who rotated last month. Where is he?"

Uncomfortably, Winter said, "Personnel problems. It doesn't mean anything."

"Perhaps. It is certainly no problem now, because we have only one operation in progress. Do you realize that, Win? On the American side, the entire covert effort consists of catching Binh. And you can do nothing but wait."

Winter lunged out of his chair, thrusting it away with a sweep of his arm. He turned to the window and stared down into the courtyard. The wind from the air-conditioner pushed at his midsection, working inside the shirt. The air coursed around his body, billowing the material in back and seeking outlet through the arm holes.

He found himself having difficulty addressing his mind to

Loc's assertion, distracted and yet gratified by the sensations of the breeze. An image pestered at the corner of his mind's eye. He resisted it half-heartedly, then let it dominate his consciousness and was remembering a young man clad only in tattered shorts on a gaffrigged ketch in Puget Sound. The youth was in sharp focus now, wide-stanced on the foredeck, a warrior, eyes clear as he shaded them against the setting sun and admired the Olympic peaks. The evening air, cool enough to bring a chill, played sensuously across his body hair. There was no white patch on his chest and Winter observed sadly that the man was too naive to concern himself with misfortunes such as Montagnard arrows and ambushes and betrayals. The young man had learned to accommodate war and believed it was the ultimate evil.

He was a fool.

Loc's voice pulled him into the present. A blink and the mountains were gone, their place taken by the sterility of the compound wall. The sunstruck grass absorbed the vision of the cool waters. He turned back to the office.

"Sorry. Mind's not functioning today. You're right about Binh. I admit it. But I firmly believe he's worth the trouble. He can lead us to VC cadre, Loc—people we've never heard of or suspected! He knows who they are and where they are and he's the only man of that importance we have any chance at! We have to concentrate on him!"

"I can only tell you of the rumors. However, there is the matter of the Major and his illegal activity and the possible drug connection. We have done nothing about him, and your CID—." He dismissed them with a flick of his hand. "Our General Staff is glad to have you pursue Binh so hard, but some people question why an American criminal is not even being investigated."

Winter's face flamed and Loc tensed, prepared for the uproar. To his surprise, the answer was low-pitched.

"You tell those people your American counterpart said they can kiss his ass. It's been months since a drunken ARVN light Colonel murdered one of our MPs, right down on Tran Hung Dao, remember? We can't even get the sonofabitch arrested. You tell your fucking General Staff I'll give them the Major if they'll give me the Colonel."

The silence that followed seemed to emanate with Loc, an

outflowing of angry pain that cloaked both men.

"You tell them that." There was a petulance in the voice, the result of denying the knowledge he should apologize. "I'll call Denby in here and see what kind of manpower we can spare. Maybe we can push a little harder."

He turned to the intercom. When he was done, they avoided conversation or eye contact, waiting for Denby's knock.

He entered as he always did, the round face and its thick glasses appearing around the door at a forty-five degree angle. As usual, he paused at that point, eyebrows up. "Something up, Colonel?"

Winter gestured him into the office, denying himself the pleasure of telling Denby that nothing was up, he'd merely been called in to dust the furniture.

"We've been slacking off," he began, with a sharp glance at Loc. "I've been slacking off, not requiring enough production from our people."

Behind the professionally respectful attitude, Denby's mind stormed with activity. Overriding everything was the anger. It pulled his eyes toward the diminutive Loc and he strained against that, fearing the hatred would boil out through them.

Miserable little zip bastards—the words burned in his mind. This bullshit about increasing activity has to come from Loc— that look from Winter said so. And who'll run the risks? The Americans, you bet your ass. The fucking zips could kill each other by the gross and no one'd miss them. That's where Winter's crazy, bad as his gook buddies. On the other side he'd be a hero, but he'd never understand this war was their property. If he'd just do his time and go home like everybody else, we wouldn't have to wake up every fucking night in a sweat from dreaming about a court-martial.

Go home like everybody else.

Even as one part of his mind supplied his tongue with answers concerning the unit's personnel rotation dates, another part was twisting that phrase, figuring a way to use it. Still, he feared it, feared Winter's reaction when he learned the replacement problem wasn't a problem but a policy to eliminate the Unit. The thought that Winter might learn he had the word and said nothing was constantly snapping at him and now the image of the scene that would transpire burst across his thinking like a rocket.

He decided to capitalize on the existing situation, not loose animals like Harker and Taylor to make more trouble. He didn't have all that long left to do, himself. It would be a gamble, but he should be able to stall his way through to his RTD. Survive, he reminded himself. A dead soldier is an ineffective soldier.

"Colonel, if we want to investigate a matter of importance, I suggest we concentrate on something we already know about and something that'll be good PR for us. I mean that Major and his bar. Even if the cover gets blown off, people will see we've been going after our own corrupt people. Not even CBS can complain about that."

He was pleased to see the significant look that went, this time, from Loc to Winter. That's right, he told himself, that's just like the cold-blooded little bastard. He'll crucify an American while his precious zips get away with anything. Turns your stomach.

"I agree," Winter was saying and Loc looked as if he might smile. "Until this personnel thing straightens out, I don't want to start any projects that may mushroom and catch us short. I think we'll have Sergeant Miller try to penetrate the operation. The Marine, Ordway, can help him. Can you provide someone to work with them, Colonel Loc?"

"Corporal Minh, for surveillance or anything else he can do. He can also report to Lieutenant Hai on Vietnamese involvement."

Denby tried to keep the sneer from his voice. "Even one of our own people will have trouble approaching this Major. He's shrewd, Colonel. I admire Corporal Minh, but I don't think he'll be much help. And what if we find drugs showing up? Minh doesn't know heroin from cocaine, does he?"

Winter interceded for Loc. "Not to worry. Miller could teach most pharmacists a few things. But is Minh smooth enough to avoid being burned? These are careful people."

"My little farmer?" Loc was assured. "He hides in a group of three so well most people remember only the other two. Because he behaves like an ignorant farmer, Minh will listen and learn more than Miller may discover with all his cunning."

Winter looked back to Denby. "You'll have to be in charge. Put together the op plan and maintain the paperwork. The troops'll handle the field work, but we'll have to have an officer signing off on the paperwork as the responsible party. Supervisory authority.''

Denby smiled and excused himself. Wooden legs carried him to his own office and he slumped in his chair, asking himself where everything had gone wrong.

After all this time! The injustice of it burned like a brand. So much care, avoiding any direct connection with even the most innocuous operations and now he was to be control officer on a deal that could reach to Christ-only-knew where. Winter was supposed to put one of the others in charge, but oh, no, he had to get sucked in by that little snake. Put good old Carl in charge! Show 'em you mean business! Give the little shit a light Colonel! And what did they give good old Carl to work with? A Sergeant and a Corporal. Two Corporals, if you counted the zip, and who the fuck would? It was a guaranteed disaster, and his name'd be all over it.

He closed his eyes and imagined Ordway telling Taylor what was going on and Taylor, the senior wolf, leading the cub. He saw them grow impatient because his superior intelligence rejected their flimsy evidence, saw them slip into an alley and blow away the Major.

Jesus, could it really happen? Or what if the people behind the Major got their hands on Minh? He'd finger everybody in a minute, especially a white officer.

He sighed and twisted his chair around to face the typewriter, mechanically inserting a fresh sheet of paper. For a long minute he looked at the intimidating blankness of it and then his fingers hopped among the keys, grinding out the comfortingly familiar phrases of the standard operations plan. There was no way out of the situation, so he would build a paper wall to hold off the hard-chargers and in the meantime, he could delay and delay. With luck, the whole thing would decay under the paper and no one would ever even find the bones.

There was more than one way to skin a cat, he told himself, feeling somewhat better. The formal, tortured phrases patterned onto the paper, further restoring his confidence.

The conversation in Winter's office continued, Loc saying, "I am puzzled by Taylor. He has been busy, but it is not the kind of work you brought him here to perform. He seems undisturbed by that now, and at first he was very impatient to be active. He only became alive when we gave him a job away from the office. Now the operation is still and all he does is hang pictures of Special Sections, run errands. It's the same administrative work he hated before. And he makes no complaints."

"Not every man could do what he does. Finding out he doesn't have to do it every week lets him relax."

"No." Loc's disagreement was quick. "What you say is partly true, but he killed An because he wanted to, not because he had to. I think you could send him out as often as you wished and it wouldn't bother him. There is a feeling around him, a violence. And he is a hunter. But that is not what bothers me. I have spoken to *Ba* Ly's parents a few times in the past month and I see a change in their attitude. The mother's, in particular. She makes a great point of how well Taylor speaks the language, how hard he studies, how quickly he learns our customs and about Saigon. She praises him greatly."

"So? You're the one always bitching because Americans don't try to learn about your country. I'm glad she's pleased. Should think you'd be, too."

Loc's hands twitched. "You break my heart. Every time I dare hope you are acquiring some genuine culture, you show yourself to be only another big-nosed foreigner. She hates his guts."

Winter rolled his eyes. "Oh, God, we're going into our deep Oriental number."

"I'm sure he's sleeping with *Ba* Ly," Loc said with offended dignity. "At least that is what I think *Ba* Lien is telling me."

"You think? The perceptions honed by two thousand years of civilization aren't certain? Surely, *Ba* Lien spoke from under a load of hay? Or it was too dark for a glance at her eyes, a view of the tell-tale pulse in her throat. There must have been something, O Wise One."

Loc muttered, "Savages, savages," then, louder, "I am trying to make you understand we may lose the services of *Ba* Ly."

"I'll speak to him."

"Thank you. The parents are friends. And *Ba* Ly is a good,

194

safe teacher. It would be unfortunate to lose her. Or see her hurt."

"Even the savages understand some things, my friend."

Loc sighed as he rose. "Ah, progress, I may save you yet."

Winter flicked the button on the intercom and Taylor entered moments behind Loc's departure.

"The Colonel wanted me?"

"Not as much as some, apparently," Winter said with some asperity. "Sit you down. We have to talk."

Taylor settled on the sofa and looked into the frank appraisal, seeing a certain understanding and an unmistakable challenge. Caution prodded him forward to the edge of the cushion.

"You called me, sir. That's all I know."

"How're the language lessons?"

"Great. Ly's showing me around, teaching me history—." Stopped by Winter's expression, he felt his own twist into a rueful smile. "And you've heard there's more to it than that."

"A helluva sight more. Straight?"

"Straight. No one planned it. I know your rules on checking out women, but I knew she'd been cleared. And having people mess around in her past stuck in my craw."

"You still should've told me."

Taylor bridled. "This isn't a shack job, Colonel."

Winter's eyebrows climbed comically. "You're in love?"

"It could be. The whole works sort of blew up in our faces. Neither of us really understands what's happened. " He looked away suddenly. "I don't like this, Colonel. I feel like I'm sitting here without any skin on."

Winter came around the desk and dropped a hand on his shoulder. "Don't sweat it. You're a pain in the ass, though."

"Yeah, I know. I don't like having this sneak up on you, but—."

"Oh, shut up! You sound like Andy Hardy, for Christ's sake! If it was some bar girl, it'd be a lot different. If Ly's fool enough to put up with you, that's her problem. One of your problems is to keep her parents cooled off."

"Oh?"

"I don't want them making a stink. He's got some influential friends and her people are important. I've got enough to do without skidding around town stomping on sparks generated by your inflamed passions."

"No problem. We've been pretty careful."

Winter smacked his forehead with a palm. "You think a fucking bird flew in here and chirped in my ear? Her parents know or suspect what's going on, dummy. The old broad's down on you."

"She's down on everyone. Screw her."

"Don't be greedy. And don't be stupid. No more than necessary, anyhow. You're in the middle of what could be a bitch for you, Ly, me, the Unit. Either you find a way to keep a lid on it or I will."

"Thanks. I have to tell you, you've got to be the piss-poorest Cupid in the world."

Winter ambled back to his chair. "Doesn't it embarrass you that a middle-aged Marine needs a Cupid?"

"Middle-aged?"

"Temper, temper. Save your emotions for when it counts. I doubt if you have enough to afford to waste any." He leaned forward, arms on the desk. "And now to business. Real business. I've been letting you pull Ordway to race around with you. So, how's he coming along?"

"Pretty good, sir. He's still not happy with his lot, but he's busy, and that helps."

Winter meshed his fingers, an almost devotional pose. "He's one of these young studs looking for a crack at a medal. He still believes in glory."

"You can't criticize that."

"Don't you start up with me. I get enough culture shock messing with the Viets. I don't need you running around here hollering 'Semper Fidelis!' all day."

"It's the way it is. Nobody joins the Corps who doesn't have something to prove."

"You're telling me you're going to get him shot at."

"I'm not going to set him up, for Christ's sake. He wants to ride to the sound of the guns. There are people like that. Goddamit, I'm like that, and under all the wise old Colonel bullshit, so're you. Let the kid see the elephant. Maybe he's smart enough to be afraid of it after one look."

"You know, they're right, you people are crazy."

"It's an enlistment requirement. After that, you go downhill."

"You better be kidding." Winter shook a finger at him. "I've just detailed him to work with Miller on the Plantation Road problem. It's to be an information gathering operation, not a cavalry charge. You make that clear to him." His expression slid to a sly grin. "Denby's in charge, and I wouldn't want him to think of the Corporal the way he thinks of you."

Taylor remained unsmiling. "I don't sweat Denby."

"You may have to. I'm giving you a detail he'd love to have."

"Thanks a million. What's the deal?"

"There's a communications outfit down in Vung Tau. They've got some electronics experts. I'm sending Kimble to bullshit with them. This last stunt with the transmitters worked so well I think we can improve on it. I want you to go along to pick their technical little brains about possible applications. Learn how small we can get, ranges, shapes. Can we get a long, thin one to fit in a hoe handle, for instance? Can we use it to transmit on demand, or does it have to be continuous? Stuff like that."

"They won't know us. You've made arrangements?"

"They expect you tomorrow morning."

Taylor threw up his hands. "You're better than Santa Claus. You come down the chimney any time you please. Why the rush? And why should me going piss off Denby?"

"The chance came up unexpectedly at the mess last night and I grabbed it. Denby's going to be upset because Vung Tau's an in-country R&R town. I'm surprised you didn't know. Silvery tropical beaches. Pleasant BOQ. He'd think of a way to spend the night and come back late the next afternoon."

"All *right!* Establish a good, solid rapport. Oh, my, yes! This'll take all of tomorrow and most of the next day, easy."

"I thought it might." Winter fumbled in his desk drawer and came out with a memo sheet for Taylor. "You're booked on Air America at 0800 tomorrow. Make your own return arrangements. There's a phone number on the memo. Call it and they'll send a jeep to the airport for you. Ask for Major Martin. And make damned sure you get back here day after

197

tomorrow, at the latest."

Folding the paper into his wallet, Taylor said, "Let me take Ordway."

Winter looked dubious. "There's this other thing just starting—."

"It'll be a break for the kid. He might even come in handy. And I promised I'd keep him busy."

"If you can get him on the plane, OK, but that's it. A boon-doggle's one thing, but you're setting up an office party."

"My naturally sociable disposition." He grew serious. "Any new word on Binh?"

The helpless gesture said it all, but Winter added, "He's crawled in a hole and pulled it in after him. I had a hunch he'd have one. I sure didn't think it'd be such a good one."

"No leads?"

"He's flat disappeared."

"Nothing from Trung or Tu?"

Winter made a spitting sound. "Somebody's building a fire to get Trung out. Loc's getting heat. I'll be next. And Tu won't talk. He's hard. Tho hasn't gone to work on him, but I know for a fact some of the boys at that interrogation house have kicked the shit out of him a couple of times and he takes it. I wish he'd open up, because if we lose Trung, Tu's all we've got. The worst thing is, if we do lose Trung and we don't have Tu turned around, they'll verify each other's story about us. And the odds on turning Tu are pretty poor."

"We've met."

Winter acknowledged the understatement with a crooked smile and Taylor continued. "How come the strain about Trung? We've had a good run in the Viet papers about how the two of them came over to our side. Is there a leak some-where?"

"Not in the Unit. Probably a relative or a connection who suspects we've grabbed him and wants to find out how much we've learned."

"Well, there's nothing I can do, I guess." Taylor stood. "OK if I start checking with Air America?"

"Sure. And while you're in Vung Tau, watch Kimble. He knows his hardware, but he might talk too much."

Later, having insured Ordway's seat on the plane, Taylor

walked into the clerical office to give him the news. He interrupted an argument over the merits of the Vikings and the Chiefs.

Miller said, "Oh-oh. Two Marines in the same room. Somebody must be planning a counterattack."

Taylor scowled. "And guess who's leading, Willy."

"No-o-o." Miller swayed his whole torso in a negative. "Cold day, Major. No way are you blue-eyed devils making a martyr out of this innocent black youth. Genocide. That's the new word, Major. You trying to get us all killed off over here, but you ain't getting me."

Taylor dropped into one of the empty desk chairs and flung his feet up on the desk. His boots landed with a thud.

"Now, goddamit, Sergeant Miller, that's the kind of black militant crap that stirs up unrest and hate. It's not that genocide'd be immoral. Forget that there's more white guys on the line than blacks. Never mind any of that. Look at it as economics. If we get all you soul brothers zapped here in Nam, who's going to run the car washes? How the hell will the Pullmans work if all the Georges are holding up headstones in Arlington? And what about all those Klan sheets, with the holes already cut in them? Naw, Willy, we need you folks. Good help's already hard to find."

Miller turned sadly to Ordway. "You see how it is? You see what the world's come to? No, you don't see, you hillbilly. What you're lookin' at is cultural piracy. Don't ever forget you saw this man do it to me. This officer and gentleman is doin' the dozens on me, and that is a black man's game. He is stealing my culture!"

"The dozens?" Ordway asked blankly.

Miller sighed. "He's hopeless, Major. No shit. The man knows nothing." He threw his head back to stare at the ceiling. "Gantry, Louisiana. Sweet jumpin' Jesus! Gantry, Loo-si-anna. If my momma knew I was gonna be cooped up with a redneck Cajun in this Army, she'd have strangled me. With my luck, she'd probably have strangled one of my brothers, by mistake." He rolled his eyes back to Taylor. "You should'a seen me back on the Hill in Pittsburgh. Sharp? I was *the* sharpest. Then come the draft. Then come the Nam. Then come this outfit and these funky threads look like hand-wove horseshit and the best friend I got is a goddam honky sits around listenin' to shit-kicking music. How come all them people sing like they got a icicle jammed up their ass?"

"At least you can understand them," Ordway said, his interest in the forthcoming trip sidetracked by Miller's assault. "Beats them tub-thumpers and yay-yay'ers you listen to."

"See what I mean?" Miller shrugged his helplessness. "No soul whatsoever. Zero." He closed his eyes as though dropping off to sleep. "Gantry, Loo-si-anna. What the fuck *is* that?"

"Miller?"

He opened his eyes and fixed Ordway with a cold stare. "Yes, my man."

"Screw you."

The dark lids slid shut again, the features still expressionless. For the first time, Taylor noticed the eyes had an almost Oriental tilt. He forgot his amusement, wishing he knew more about African heritage, wondering what ancestry might account for the knife-edged bone formation and corded muscu-lature.

Ordway's curiosity concerning the trip reappeared, in-terrupting Taylor's thoughts. "You said we were going on a trip, Major? Anyplace special?"

"Yeah, as a matter of fact. Vung Tau. You know the Air America ops shack? We leave from here at 0800 and come back sometime the next evening."

"I knew it!" Miller was instantly alert, his outburst over-riding Ordway's whoop of excitement. "I stay here in this stinkin' city, prowling in bars and alleys, risking my life, surviving on natural wit and smarts, and the whiteys are going to the beach!"

Quietly, Ordway asked, "What's wrong, your tan fading?"

"Oh, that's a hard remark, jarhead."

Taylor interrupted. "I'm sorry. I thought I heard a word I can't believe I heard."

Miller's expression was virginal innocence. "I said, 'It's far to the head.' I believe that's what you all call the latrine, isn't it? I was going to offer to flip to see who walks past it to the fridge for Cokes."

"You slick bastard," Ordway muttered.

"Sergeant slick bastard," Taylor corrected. "I'll have no

disrespect toward senior NCOs.''

They fished in their pockets for MPC small change notes, each sandwiching his between his hands.

"What a lousy war this is," Ordway griped. "Can't even flip a coin. Goddam monkey money. Odd last number buys?"

They lifted hands simultaneously. Miller and Ordway stared at Taylor's with naked delight.

"Hot damn!" Ordway cheered. "We got us some field grade money, buddy!"

Taylor dug two more ten-cent notes from his pocket. "Dump mine in the kitty for me. I'll get my drink later. I've got more to do than sit around guzzling soda pop with hustlers."

"Thank you kindly for dropping by, sir," Ordway gloated. "I'll be waiting for the Major at the op shack at 0730." He waggled the bills. "We surely do look forward to the Major coming by."

Taylor growled over his shoulder from the doorway. "That's the third time in a row you fuckers have nailed me. I'm beginning to smell a con."

He moved into the hall quickly to let his face relax into the grin tugging at it, responding to the strangled hilarity behind him.

21

AN HOUR LATER Miller stepped into the hall, crushing his Coke can in his hand. He closed his eyes and set the scene. Four seconds on the clock? No, two. Two seconds and the Knicks down by a point. The Celtics closing on him, knowing there was no time for a pass, knowing Willy Miller had to unleash the famous fall-away jumper and make it or the championship was theirs. Twenty-five feet, easy, and Cowens—damn Cowens!—hanging in front of him, defying gravity, desperate to block the shot. Miller opened his eyes, rose, lofted the container toward the GI can.

It rattled a victory knell. He closed his eyes again.

Shouting! Screaming! World Champions!

"Sergeant?" The voice was just short of incredulous.

After the icy shock of recognizing Denby's voice, Miller was in command of himself again. He turned around smoothly, unruffled.

"Yes, sir?" His level gaze acknowledged only bored normalcy. Denby was the first to blink.

"Come up to my office for a few minutes. I have to talk to you." Without waiting for an answer, he turned away and moved toward the stairs.

Miller considered making a face at the retreating back and squelched the impulse, telling himself it was childish and, anyhow, Denby was the kind of cheap prick who'd irritate a man and then turn around to see if he was making a face about it. They still hadn't spoken further when Denby settled into his chair. Miller pointedly stared at the copulating elephants before raising his eyes to the other man's.

Ignoring the by-play, but unable to keep the edge from his voice, Denby said, "The Colonel has decided to push this case with the Major and his bar. You're familiar with the situation?"

"Yes, sir, I know a little about it."

"Well, the Old Man wants to know all about it. I'm to write up an operation plan for infiltrating it."

Miller remembered the manager's attempts at describing the size and complexity of the apparatus. "What's my job to be? What d'you want from me?"

"Find out where their supplies come from. Find out who handles the money. See if you can learn how it gets out of the country."

"Just like that?" Miller was disbelieving. "I'm supposed to go down there and sort of ask around?"

Denby shrugged. "Your cover's good. You probably already have a few ideas about what's going on there."

The tone was suggestive and Miller decided to probe further. "You think they're doing dope."

"You were as close to Sergeant Hai as anyone on the American side of the Unit. Maybe some of the people you both knew—?" He ended the sentence with a quick hand gesture.

"I'd have to think about that. Incidentally, what's the story on Hai? What'd he do? Where's he now?"

It was Denby's turn to grow apprehensive and Miller hoped his own eyes never betrayed him so readily.

"He's up in IV Corps, I think. Yes. Transferred." He affected great impatience. "He's not our concern. We can't be responsible for—. Look, I've told you what your basic responsibility'll be. Do you have any ideas?"

Miller said, "I got questions. First off, why haven't we moved on this creep before? He's short, now. Been making his scam almost a year. What I want to know, what're we into? I don't want to fuck around and then find he's got enough clout to stop the machine. Or have me snuffed."

Coloring, Denby said, "The Colonel wants it done."

The silence grew long enough to become an embarrassment before Miller said, "That does it, I guess. OK." He relaxed, growing thoughtful. One leg cocked out to the side and he stood hipshot, unaware of Denby's disapproval. "Might be I can come up with something. Who's running the show, Colonel? You in charge of this one?"

Denby nodded, determined to cover his irritation at Miller's clear surprise. "And this one's by the book, believe me. I don't like surprises. We'll take everything one step at a time and each step exactly in sequence. I'll want to know *before* you make any moves. You'll have Ordway working for you and the Viet Corporal named Minh, if you can use him for anything. I'm not sure he's all there, myself."

Miller ignored the routine slur. His attention had fastened onto Denby's vehemence concerning style. His knowledge of the speaker combined with his understanding of the words and clearly illuminated the actual message. The mission was a loser.

Why? The single word grew to a barrage.

Was the Major protected that well? Who was in the bag? If they thought he was doing drugs—and it was sure as hell he was trying—why the delays? What hold could somebody have over Winter to make him let his own people die like poisoned cockroaches?

Miller watched the round face before him, buttery with sweat despite the cool gush of the air-conditioner. The rimless glasses blinked back at a foundering fluorescent tube, disguising the eyes and making the entire man a mechanical piece.

Denby broke the spell by pursing his lips and starting his outline of the operation. Miller listened patiently, glad he'd held back the Mantell contact and wondering what his next move should be. He heard all of Denby's pronouncements and dismissed them. As that list grew, so did his determination to exclude everyone from his own efforts. He would move in secrecy, trust only Ordway, use Minh infrequently. Compartmentalize himself, that was it.

Resentment caused him to blunt his own resolution almost immediately. "What's this sudden interest, Colonel? We've known about drugs for years and this Major's place for months. Why haven't we busted more people? Why push now?"

Denby appeared to expand in his chair and he let his arms dangle over the sides. "We're not on a drug hunt. Don't forget that. But to answer your question, you know the big operators aren't Americans and we don't have any jurisdiction over the foreigners."

Miller said, "Even so, the Viets could bust them."

"If the Viets hassle them, the foreign government squeals. Meanwhile, we're so anxious to have somebody recognize this government, we underwrite the Korean racketeers and the Filipino gunrunners, and so on. Their troops die and their politicians profit and we cover all bets. We pay for their troops. The only ones I don't think are on the take are the Aussies, and everyone knows they're crazy."

The view wasn't new to Miller, but hearing it from those wet pink lips was a goad. It wasn't that Denby wasn't affected by the damage, it was that he simply didn't care if someone else was. To him, it was all an exercise.

"Goddamit, Colonel, can't somebody at least complain, just once? Aren't our GIs worth that much?"

Denby reacted with amused self-assurance. "Complain? To whom, Sergeant? State? They set up the deal. The UN? They're delighted to see our people die. We're enjoying a new kind of war, courtesy of Kennedy and his wizards. We're proving a powerful nation can go to the defense of a small nation invaded by a small neighbor, make itself look like the aggressor in both countries, and buy its own defeat at the hands of a bunch of ignorant monkeys."

"And the ones who get hurt? What about the dudes whose minds are used up or who get crippled?"

"Breaks of the game." A flicker of emotion altered his features, as a movement below the surface of a pond will sometimes create a visible suggestion of hidden activity.

"The people getting hurt in this war are natural victims, Miller, people who either hunt for dangerous situations or are too dumb to avoid them. Look, I know I'm not a popular man around here. I don't care. This is my career, and I don't take chances with it or my life. And that's the way we're going to run things."

He finished with a flourish, leaning forward. Miller recognized the move as one of Winter's and the repressed laughter in the back of his throat was bitter enough to burn.

Wigwagging a hand in irritable dismissal, Denby turned back to his typewriter. Miller left quietly.

Walking down the hall, he told himself the hell with it. I got Mantell. I'll get past that nothing. I'll put together so much stuff they'll have to do something.

He passed Taylor's office when he got downstairs, considered confiding in him and thought better of it. He was an officer and white. He'd never understand about dope. Like this shit now—worry about the money market, with the dope incidental. Whites had trouble with it, but blacks had it in their lives. Even Ordway couldn't understand, and he was a buddy.

Black and white brought Denby's anti-Viet bigotry to mind and he asked himself how much was left over for blacks. He couldn't remember a hint of it and finally conceded the man seemed biased exclusively against non-Americans and thought how that must hurt when he had to deal with Americans who looked Oriental.

The image of Denby struggling with that dilemma brought back the first ray of his normal good spirits.

Screw all of them. It's a black man's problem and it's blacks bringing down a world of hurt on other blacks and it's right a black should put a stop to it. No Denby's going to stop me, and when I reach the top of the ladder, whoever I find there is going to fall. No shit.

Passing the refrigerator, he stopped, crouching, whipping left jabs at the handle.

A crossing right caught the befuddled Ali squarely on the point of the chin. Sadness flooded Miller as he watched the calculating eyes snap shut and struggle back open to reveal only the dregs of awareness to acknowledge defeat. Rather than punish the man, Miller stepped back, letting him fall.

When he stepped outside onto the porch the sunlight poured over him like applause rolling down from the arena seats.

22

RAIN FELL IN GREAT SHATTERING DROPS as Taylor watched from the shelter of the villa porch, listening to the frequency and intensity of the individual strikes increase and finally coalesce, turning the air into a constant hiss. He concentrated on one parched blade of grass, noting it flattening to the ground at each direct impact and springing back up. In fact, it seemed to have increased its vertical angle after a few moments and he wondered if the plant regarded this trial as a necessary part of existence and laughed at himself. He looked around nervously to see if he'd been observed.

Stepping into the downpour, he broke into a run for a few paces before slowing to a normal walk, reflecting that the attitude was the influence of the country. The Vietnamese rarely ran through the rain, usually strolling along and accepting the wetness. It had taken a while for him to accept the wisdom of that. In the first place, one usually got wet from sweat, racing along, and in the second place, getting caught in the rain here wasn't like the same experience in the states. Here, the sun came out and you dried off without any bone-cracking chill. And the rain felt good. He tried to whistle as he walked. Drops slid off his lip and the tune exploded in a spluttering trill.

He thought about his destination, the shop, and the meeting with Captain Kimble. He hoped the subject of the promotion wouldn't come up, because he didn't want to listen to any more dreary excuses for discouraging the normal celebration that went with it. If the silly bastard didn't want a party, he told himself, that was certainly his privilege. But he'd said his piece and he ought to keep his face shut about it.

As soon as he stepped into the shop Taylor damned his personal Vietnamization. He'd forgotten about the air-conditioner. From something cool and natural, his utilities turned into a dank encumbrance that grabbed at every point of contact. He jerked off his cover and hung it on a nail.

"Yuk! These clothes are freezing!"

"It's because they're wet. The rain."

The inanity brought sarcasm to his lips, but a look at Kimble made him swallow it.

He'd still not gotten to know the man. Even when he was loose and talking freely, there was a reticence about him, as though he said what he knew he ought to be saying but was thinking something else, thinking *about* something else. None of the others seemed to notice, making Taylor doubly unsure of himself and even more uncomfortable. Today the feeling of psychic distance was even stronger.

Taylor stripped to his waist and draped his clothes over chairs. "The rain feels good when you're outside."

"Did you know we have a lot of pneumonia patients here? They've had some deaths."

Taylor rubbed his torso briskly. "Is that my cheery thought for the day? I wade over here to bring you good news and all you've got for me is a possible diagnosis of pneumonia."

"You bring my mail?" Kimble's increased attentiveness was palpable.

"Better. We're going on a boondoggle down to Vung Tau." He explained the purpose of the trip, adding, "Two fun-filled days of sun, sand, and surf."

Watching Kimble's apologetic smile, Taylor had the eerie sensation he could see the required muscles being willed to position.

"Does it have to be me? I've got a lot of work backed up—." He waved distractedly with both hands.

"The war'll survive without us. The break'll do you good. There's even an official reason for it. Your conscience bothering you?"

"It's not that—." His hands fluttered again, ineffective as before.

Taylor cleared a space on the work bench and hitched himself up. Rainwater dripped from the toes of his dangling boots. For a moment the plops and the electric hum of equipment were the only sounds in the room.

"Look, Skipper, let me put it to you this way. We're going. I'm going to have a good time. Corporal Ordway's going to have a good time. You're not going to spoil the trip for us, so feel free to be as miserable as you want. If it'll help, though,

207

I'm a pretty good listener.''

With no answer forthcoming, his eyes wandered around the shop, coming to rest on the multi-colored calendar.

"C'mon, Kimble," he coaxed, "you're too short to be so down. You've only got—what is it?" He studied the calendar more closely. "Jesus, not even three months! I can't imagine double digits and you've got less than three months?"

"Never mind my calendar!" Harshness crackled in the rising voice.

"Sure." Taylor lowered himself from the workbench and started wringing out his skivvy shirt.

Kimble averted his gaze. "You weren't prying, I know that. You wouldn't understand, that's all. It's a personal thing."

This is your day to spotlight the apparent, thought Taylor, regretting the entire conversation. He twisted into the damp clothes as quickly as possible and was reaching for his cover when Kimble spoke again.

"I haven't had a letter for six days, Major."

"From your wife, you mean?"

Kimble nodded, his attitude more like an admission than an explanation.

"That's not such a long time, man. She's probably got a cold or the kid's got one. She's got a right to some problems of her own. You'll probably get six letters in a bunch today and feel like a jerk."

"I'd sure like to hope so. When I first got here she'd write twice the same day. I always got a tape at least twice a week. Now I get a letter every couple days or so and sometimes it's a week or ten days between tapes."

"Are you shitting me? I know what her trouble is. She's run out of words. Corresponded herself to exhaustion."

Kimble's smile was slightly less pained. "You're probably right. I notice everybody gets uptight when they start to get short."

Taylor snorted. "First you tell me I've got pneumonia and now you're reminding me how long I've got to do. Disgusting. I'll see you at 0730."

Laughter followed him out, but as Taylor turned to wave, there was that same armoring of Kimble's features. The picture hung in his mind as he sloshed back toward the villa. He hunched his shoulders irritably, pushing back at the rain, and suddenly found himself thinking of Ly. What was he going to do about that?

He was in a foul mood when he stomped into his office and stripped for the second time. Duc was gone, having left without leaving a note, and that added to his frustration. As a result, he met Allen's appearance with a grim stare and a flat, "Well?"

The Captain's exaggerated apology helped. Taylor said, "All right, you caught me at a bad time. It doesn't have anything to do with you. Yet. What've you got?"

"Are you sure you want to talk? You look more like a man praying for a fight."

"You're nattering. I can't stand nattering."

"Nattering? That's a British expression. Were you in England?"

Taylor took a deep breath and exhaled slowly. "Hal, you're a tonic, you really are. You know, I'm crowding forty. Sometimes that depresses me. And then you show up, youthful, virile, swift of foot, stupid as a load of bricks. It really helps my perspective."

"Ah, that's the crusty curmudgeon we've all grown to love and respect. For one fleeting moment I had the ridiculous notion your heart had turned to muscle." He sat in Duc's chair and helped himself to one of Duc's Salems and casually extended the pack to Taylor, who shook his head in disbelief but took one anyway. Allen lit them both. "Actually, I dropped by to extend an invitation and ask you a favor. I thought by adding the one I'd improve my chances for the other."

"You've found a good expensive restaurant and you want me to accept your hospitality."

"No, not exactly. But I'll keep you in mind. My membership in the Cercle Sportif has been approved."

"Go away, Allen."

"Please don't try to be blasé." He exhaled a huge smoke ring. "It's not your style, at all. You were kind enough to prevail on Winter to let me into your sewer in the matter of the Friendly Bar and I'm reciprocating."

"I ought to reciprocate my fist and your nose."

"The Uniform Code of Military Justice forbids it. Anyhow,

Harker'd never forgive you for spoiling his evening.''

"Harker?"

"They say he can have a night out in a couple of days. He's still confined to the hospital but he's taken to chasing the nurses, so they assume he's well enough to move around town a little. We're celebrating.''

"That's different. I'll be needing someone to talk to about then.''

Allen looked puzzled. "Something wrong?"

"Nothing special." He paused, considering. "What do you know about Kimble?''

Allen's relieved expression preceded an easy answer. "He's pleasant enough. I don't think he has any outside interests. His life revolves around his electrons and his wife, in that order. Why?''

"He bugs me. I try to talk to him and get the impression he's not there.''

"Really? How fortunate for him. I'll have to find out how he manages it.''

"Ever read up on what the UCMJ says about insubordination?''

"I'll assume that's not an academic question and take my leave, sir." He got to his feet, mashing the cigarette butt. "Can we figure on midafternoon on Sunday for Harker's coming-out?''

"Yeah, I'll have had time to report on this trip to Vung Tau and all I'm doing around here is matching names and aliases on some Security Section people." He flung an angry arm out across the papers on his desk. "You know we've got one Section that doesn't even know each other except by alias? 'Brother Nguyen,' 'Brother Do!' What a pain! See that dude in that picture? That's 'Brother Do.' Special Branch nailed him. Out of a team of six, he's only seen three. He doesn't know anything about them except their aliases and what they look like. He thinks the one he calls 'Brother Nguyen' is nearsighted. How's that for a live-wire lead?''

"Surely he knows who recruited him?''

"A guy in a bunker in the Parrot's Beak in Cambodia. And you should see his back-up. His ARVN discharge papers aren't forgeries, they're real. Ol' Loc's been kicking ass and taking names all over the city, trying to find out how many more like him we've got running loose." He held up the photograph and shook his head with rueful admiration. "When these jokers talk security, they mean it."

Allen took the picture from him. "The amazing thing is that we catch any of them. How'd he get picked up?"

"Pure accident. Got in a hassle with a neighbor and the neighbor snooped around and saw him oiling a pistol. He blew the whistle on him, Special Branch came on, and he sang us a lousy two bars."

"You enjoy hunting these people, don't you?" The younger man stared with frank curiosity.

Taylor laughed, letting the sound trail off at the sight of Allen's reaction of embarrassed irritation.

"Look, Hal, I'm not a butcher and I'm not a robot. Sure, I enjoy the excitement. I could live without it if I thought the other side would let me live in peace. *My* kind of peace, not on their terms. And I don't like the killing, I don't care what you've heard."

"How unfortunate."

Taylor's head jerked in surprise and then he saw the light in Allen's eyes. He played it straight. "What's so unfortunate?"

"I'd like to see you become famous, Maj—a General, maybe, or a politician. But you don't have the scope. Can't you see us high-and-mighties can't abide the idea that you lower-income folk should live in peace with your neighbors? Without a war, you're merely unemployed, whereas the real decision makers must put up with this rending boredom. What's the use of money and power if—."

The banter stopped abruptly and he reached for the door jamb as if unsure of his balance. He paled and he looked past Taylor.

"Hey, you all right? What's wrong?"

The features struggled to present a smile. "I just thought of something."

Taylor said, "Listen, if you rich guys are so far above my simple soldier level, what the hell are you doing here?"

Edging out the door, Allen continued to work at presenting a carefree manner. He was still rough-looking, but found a line. "Keeping an eye on the help, Major."

Regardless of his appearance, he was nimble enough to dodge the book Taylor heaved at him.

23

THE HIGH WING of the Porter provided a degree of shelter from the early morning drizzle. Taylor centered himself under it, watching the moisture collect in rivulets and craze downward. He shifted the getaway bag, half-smiling at the incompatibility of Apeneck wrapped in beach gear, then checked his watch again.

"Mornin', Major." Ordway saluted briskly as he approached.

Taylor returned it. "How you doing? See Captain Kimble or our pilot in the shack?"

"No, sir, I didn't. What kind of plane is this, sir?" His enthusiasm bubbled as he paced and bobbed, examining the plane from all angles.

"A Porter. Got one helluva nose on her, doesn't she?"

"That's for sure, and I'm damn glad of it. I hope it's all engine and strong as a mule."

"Don't you like flying?"

"I ain't sure yet. Only plane I was ever in was coming here, and I was too nervous about Nam to worry about much else. This thing looks like you could knock it down with a handful of rice hulls."

"Rice hulls! Only a Cajun would think of that."

"Like I told you, sir, I'm a redneck. Big difference." Ordway grinned. "Can't make Willy believe it."

From the direction of the ops shack, they heard Kimble's greeting. He threw a combination wave and salute as he came toward them with another man. From the corner of his eye, Taylor saw Ordway check his right hand halfway up, taking his cue from himself, refusing to acknowledge a salute that wasn't really there.

"Our pilot, Sam Kolchak," Kimble said. The two Marines introduced themselves.

Kolchak shook hands, mumbling around a cigar that whisked back and forth under a heavy black moustache. Taylor fell in behind him as he walked through his preflight check. While Kolchak wiggled the rudder, Taylor said, "Listen, Skipper, you could do me a favor."

Kolchak groaned, aiming a finger at Taylor's blouse. "When I saw that globe-and-anchor, I knew I was going to be conned for something."

"This's a little thing." He ignored the raised eyebrows. "The Corporal's only been up in a 707. Can he ride up front with you?"

"Is that all? Sure! I'll have him flying the thing by the time we get there."

"That's not necessary," Taylor said, swallowing.

Kolchak climbed into the plane. "C'mon up front, Corporal," he called. "If a Navy Captain rates an orderly, so do I. You'll be co-pilot, steward, and all the rest."

Ordway stared at the pilot, then at Taylor.

"You better git," Taylor said. "He could change his mind."

Ordway practically shoved Kolchak ahead of him.

The roar of the engine put the passengers into the hallowed pre-flight silence of groundlings. Taylor was surprised by Kimble's serenity. He dismissed it and concentrated on Kolchak's handling of the plane. They taxied past revetted cargo aircraft and lined up for their opportunity at the runway behind a huge C-130. The prop blast from her blades buffeted the lighter plane. Kolchak rode it out with the aplomb of a bronc buster on a merry-go-round. Ordway's eyes remained locked on the aluminum bulk in front of them and only when it pulled out onto the runway did he settle back against his seat.

A few seconds later they followed. The little plane seemed to poise—the impression was more of vaulting into the air than racing to take off—and they were climbing. Kolchak indicated it was all right to smoke, waggling his cigar stub. Taylor lit up and turned to Kimble.

"You look pretty cheerful today. Mailman finally do right by you?"

The Captain indicated his overnight bag. "Got a letter yesterday afternoon."

"You brought it with you?"

"I haven't even opened it yet." He looked boyish and shy. "It's a fat one. She must have been saving up all the news. I want to wait until I'm on that nice sandy beach and read it in peace and quiet."

"For Christ's sake. Listen, everybody knows how you hang on mail call. You mean you've been mooning around for days and now—?"

"Like they say, the anticipation is half of it."

"Maybe so. I never tried to balance it out, myself."

"You would if you knew Lenore." Emotion glazed his features and he propped himself on one shoulder to face Taylor. "I know what the rest of you think of me. I've seen you smile when I get my mail and how you look at each other now that there's not as much of it. I must look pretty funny. Well, I don't care what any of you think. My wife and kid are what count with me."

"Don't get all over me, man. I don't care if you all use the same toothbrush. But you do sight in hard on whoever's handling the mail."

The cold edge of Kimble's hostility blunted a bit. "You bet I do. Those letters are my lifeline."

Taylor shuddered at the jutting jaw, sensing it was determined to flap its message. Fervor pitched Kimble closer, raised his voice so no pearl of wisdom could be crushed by the drum of the engine.

"I was a man without any goals when I met Lenore, I really was. Things happened and I went along. If it wasn't for her, I'd probably have headed for Canada."

Taylor's shocked reaction hurried Kimble along.

"Oh, she didn't want me to come to Nam, but she's the one who showed me I had to compete, get a commission, plan ahead. It was a big disappointment when I got orders here, but when I get back we've got my GI Bill benefits. I'll get a Bus. Ad. degree and we'll set ourselves up an electronics place."

Carefully noncommittal, Taylor said, "Sounds like a good program. Can you raise the money to start up?"

"Mrs. Folker—Lenore's mother—says she'll help. Trouble is, they don't have much. She raised hell when we found out I was coming here. Carried on about how I was likely leaving Lenore to be a widow with a baby."

"I know the type." Memories layered a chill on his voice that was more apparent than he intended. Misinterpreted by Kimble, it fueled the earlier hostility to full heat again.

"You don't know her. She's a good woman. She takes some understanding, that's all." He took a new tack, became confiding. "It's the old man who's the problem. He doesn't say ten words a day, you know? She's always after him to get a raise, or something, but he just shrugs his shoulders and smiles and that's it. When I was stationed at Bragg and Lenore had to go home 'cause she was pregnant with Teri, Mom hassled every politician she could write to to get me sent to Fort Holabird. We'd argue about what to say and Lenore'd cry. Man, it was tough. And that old fart'd sit there and watch the Eagles like we were on another planet. It's no wonder Mom's so tough about goals, you know?"

Vung Tau slid into view below them and Taylor pointed silently, feeling reprieved.

The reason for the trip and the name of Nguyen Binh tugged at his thoughts and he brushed them away, including the stern image of Winter for good measure. At the same time a grinning Ordway gestured down and forward where a protective arm of land thrust into the white-capped green sea, holding multi-colored fishing boats in the curve like a woman cradling a basket of fruit to her breast. Shadows cast by cloud bolls drifted across tiled roofs, dusty streets, and a myriad plant colors reaching for the sun. The plane dropped sharply and Taylor craned to look past Kimble for a fleeting glimpse of rolling combers north of the headland, gleaming foam-crowned pyramids discolored to slate gray by the roiled bottom.

After landing and taxiing to a stop, Kolchak pointed them at the ramshackle terminal.

The three new arrivals bought coffee at a small lunch counter after phoning for transportation and barely finished it before their jeep arrived. The driver identified himself, saw his passengers aboard, and uncommunicatively drove them through a semi-deserted area of warehouses and administration buildings. They turned through a gate past a disinterested MP.

"Where the hell is everyone?" Taylor asked. "The place is like a ghost town."

"Part of the draw-down," the driver said. "Pretty soon there won't be nobody here. There's some kind of intelligence school off that way and the slopes have a school over there, rural development stuff. They dress up in black pajamas like Charlie. Supposed to go out in the country and teach the farmers.'' He made a hissing noise. "Bunch of fucking draft dodgers.''

He stopped in front of a building shedding white paint like matted hair and got out of the jeep. "The Major had bunks set up for you here. It used to be an office or something. It's got its own latrine and all. He thought you might want to stay here instead of the BOQ. It's up to you. That's our building, just down the street. The jeep's yours 'til you get ready to leave. The Major says to come on down whenever you're ready.''

Inside, the building exuded the smell of abandonment like sweat. Three bunks crowded against the walls as if trying to avoid attention, two to the left, one to the right. A circulating fan whirred at them from the far corner, swinging back and forth, welcoming with its imbecile drone.

"All the comforts of home.'' Kimble tossed his bag on one of the bunks. "I'll check out the latrine.''

Taylor picked a bunk and dropped his gear. "What I want you to do, Corporal, is scout this place while Kimble and I are busy with this lashup. Recon the R&R beach, a good place to eat, see what you can learn about the bars. And don't get carried away with that last bit. We'll sleep here tonight. You do a number here, it's a short time, and if you come up with a dose you better hope it's fatal, because if you live, your ass belongs to me. Any questions?''

"I wasn't figurin'—.'' Ordway reddened and let the sentence die.

Taylor managed to remain stern. "Good. I've got enough to do without standing tall in front of the Old Man explaining why you squeal when you take a leak.''

Kimble re-entered. "Somebody left a bucket and a mop in the latrine when they cleaned the place.''

Taylor jerked a thumb at Ordway. "That's how you can tell it's the enlisted men's head.''

"Shee-it.'' Ordway grinned.

"Take your bathing suit when you leave,'' Taylor continued. "I want to know if the water's the right temperature for officers. Be back here at, oh, 1500.'' He tossed the keys to Ordway who took them on the move.

Kimble said, "What's all that about?''

"Scouting. He'll enjoy it and we won't have to stumble around looking for things when we go out this evening."

The sun was a liquid pressure forcing Taylor's body into the sand. He tensed and relaxed the muscles in his feet, calves, thighs, working up to his neck, feeling each area swell and melt luxuriously back to repose. Sweat ran darts across his skin and the richness of suntan lotion mingled soporifically with the salt breeze. He inhaled to the limits of his lungs, enough to cause a catch below his ribs, and hoped he wouldn't sleep long enough to burn.

Kimble's voice clattered in his ear. "I still say we have to tell these people exactly what we want this stuff for, Major." He shifted, as he had on the plane, the sand grating under his beach towel. "I've been thinking about it. We can't ask them to work in the dark. We've got to give them the whole picture."

Taylor swallowed to clear the heat clogging his throat. "They're not stupid. They know what we're doing. They know everything they need to know and they'll guess more. What else could we tell them?"

"About the Unit and the kind of people we're after. They're inventive. They'd come up with good ideas."

"They will already. Anyhow, they already know our names."

The conversation stopped and Kimble's disapproval was as physically present as the heat. Finally, he asked, "What were you going to do, give them a phony name?"

"I'd rather." Taylor shook his arm and listened to a dislodged fly hum past his ear.

"We can trust them," Kimble maintained.

"It's not the trust. How do I know one of these clowns isn't going to blow off his mouth to his girl friend about the keen toys he's building? For the dark Marine Major and the thin Captain with the glasses from MACV. All the broad needs is our names and we're burned. You want that running around in your head every time you go downtown? You get made solid enough, Charlie'll put a Security Section on you, personal. You may find that exciting, but it scares the shit out of me. If I had my way the only man in Nam who'd know my name is the Finance Officer."

Kimble was thoughtful. "I guess that comes from working with hardware all the time. I never considered the street work."

"Please do." Taylor opened the eye on Kimble's side, squinting against the searing glare. "There won't be any heroes come out of this war, not our side of it, so don't get anyone nominated, OK?" He closed the eye again.

"That's a roger." Kimble chuckled quietly. "God knows I've worked hard enough to duck it myself. I've always been careful to stay away from anything like that. Getting zapped in Nam would screw up my plans, you know?"

"Unless you're a seance freak."

"The only bumps in the night that interest me come in bed."

"I'm surprised at you. Lenore'd be scandalized. You finally read her letter, huh?"

"Not yet." The vibration from the hand patting the ground was like a gritty heartbeat. "I've got it under my towel. I'll read it here on the beach."

"What are you, some kind of masochist?"

"It's like having her here. I can't explain it. It's like knowing I'm not alone. When I read it, it's only a letter. There won't be anything world-shaking in it, but until I open it and read it, it's a promise, you know? A reassurance, or something."

"It's weird, is what it is. You're gonna go home in one of those funny coats with the long sleeves."

The answering laugh was superior in its contentment. Taylor heard him shift again and hoped the conversation was dead. He tried to turn his mind inward, wanting sleep, but a visual collage of the moods of Ly shimmered through the blackness. Kimble's drivel about his precious Lenore had set off his own longing and highlighted his own problems. Damning Kimble scattered the images and he willed himself to concentrate on the afternoon's discussions of miniaturization, ranges, and frequencies.

A cold hand shook him. He realized he'd dropped off and looked to see Ordway haloed by a lowering sun.

"If you're going swimming, Major, you'd best wake up. You've been makin' z's for a while. It's near 1700."

"No kidding?" Taylor twisted his arm to get the face of his

watch out of the glare. Sitting up, he noted Kimble's absence and the torn open end of the envelope peeking out from under the towel. It was a sight to inspire mixed relief and dread. He wouldn't have to hear any more about its holiness, but he was sure he'd hear every crushing detail of Lenore's activity.

"The Captain swimming?"

"Yes, sir. He walked around picking at seashells for a while. He's in now."

"I'll see if I can find him." He rose slowly, gratified to see he hadn't burned. A few minutes later he was bobbing in the surf next to Kimble. They leaped upward as each wave rolled to them, pushing seaward to avoid being shoved back, then dropping to stand on the bottom and wait for the next one. The crested tops passed to curl and foam ashore, growling as if disappointed.

"Wouldn't it be great if we could just start paddling that way?" Kimble pointed east with his chin as another wave rolled under them.

"No way. With my luck, I'd catch a current and end up in Haiphong. Anyhow, I'm as far from land as I like to get."

Kimble looked at him quizzically, and Taylor added, "I don't like the sea." They lifted up the face of the newest wave and slid down the reverse slope. "It's a kind of fear. It's so big it scares me. It just does what it wants, and that's that."

"Life's like that, too."

They bobbed again. "Naw. Life you can fight. Kick and scream. You've got a chance. This big mother? No slack. You slip one time, your butt's fish bait. It's a nice place to visit, but I wouldn't want to die there." He slackened his paddling and let a wave nudge him toward the beach. "You about ready for some chow?"

"Good idea." Kimble turned on his face and tried to body surf. He missed the crest and coasted to a stop. Taylor caught up and they treaded water, flipping over and stroking furiously as another wave approached. They caught it together, bodies planing, the sense of speed out of all proportion to their actual progress. They were in the boiling froth that spent itself in a last clutch at the sand before tumbling away, and when they stood, the water barely reached their knees.

"Oh, man, that was good." Taylor shook water from his body in a flurry of spray.

"I was in longer than I thought." Kimble held up his hands, laughing. They were pale and wrinkled, ancient things grafted onto the young body.

They walked to their towels, the sun now a benign warmth, the hot sand lively against their feet. Ordway waited for them.

Taylor said, "We've got to get Captain Kimble into town and pump some beer into him. He's all shriveled up."

Kimble displayed the hands again and Ordway said, "Sure hope that's the only place to get drawn up like that. Be hell for a married man if it happened some places."

Kimble's amusement dropped instantly. He opened his mouth as if to speak, flushed, and bent quickly to retrieve his towel and letter.

Ordway, uncertain, turned to Taylor, who frowned at Kimble's back and shook his head. Ordway nodded and picked up his own gear.

Kimble regained his composure by the time they started for the beach house and the three of them talked easily of dinner, weighing Ordway's report. They balanced the high prices of the Vietnamese restaurants against the routine of the cheaper BOQ meal. It was Kimble who summed it up for them.

"Look, if we splurge on a fancy meal we won't have much left over for barhopping after. It doesn't mean all that much to me, of course, but I know you guys want to go out and look over the girls. Let's save money on dinner and spend it on whiskey like reasonable men."

Ordway agreed with an enthusiasm that relieved Taylor because it gave him an excuse to uncap the laughter welling in his throat. A glance at Kimble had revealed a glitter in his eye that seemed to blatantly deny his disavowal of the bar girls.

After showering in the R&R facility they walked to the limit of the compound, where the taxis waited. The ride was uneventful, each man busy registering his own impressions. Taylor found the trip unpleasant.

The area had been beautiful once, cared for. Now it had a musty quality, as though the huge-boled trees and stately homes were cardboard stage props, deserted by the magic that had given them life. The people appeared cheerful enough, and the children laughed and ran as always, their gaiety underscored by the occasional appearance of a wounded Vietnamese soldier sent here to recuperate. At one corner they swung wide to avoid one, legless in a motorized wheelchair, operating the controls with his remaining hand. He looked up, smiled and waved. Taylor returned both until they were away, then let the smile go and closed his eyes.

They changed into civilian clothes in their office-cum-bed-room and drove into the R&R BOQ for dinner. Again, Taylor was taken by the change in Kimble. He plunged into the evening with frenetic vigor, insisting on martinis and making a great show of ordering the wine. The difference between this performance and his normal drinking habits was apparent as they stepped outside.

Ordway led off, pleased to see Taylor beside him and Kimble lagging. He glanced back before speaking.

"Is he all right, Major?"

"Who knows?" Taylor shrugged. "He's wound up because he got a letter from his wife. First one in a few days."

"He's half in the bag. Does he always get so loaded so easy?"

"Not usually. It's mostly relief, I guess."

Ordway tugged an ear. "It looks to be a short evening. We'll be packing him before long."

Kimble caught up. "What the hell's goin' on? We on a hike? Where's the joints, Ordway?"

"We're there, sir." He pointed. "They said this place has the best women in town."

"The Red Rose." Kimble repeated the flaring neon sign. "'A rose by any other name,' right men?" He slapped Taylor's back, staggering slightly. "Let's get in there and mix it up, right?"

"Oooh-whee!" Ordway breathed. "Is he ever ready! What-ever his old lady put in that letter, she should've kept it!"

Inside, the noise of the street was overwhelmed by stereo-phonic bedlam. All three stood uncertain, trying to adjust their eyes to the darkness. Dim figures appeared, tugged insistently at them. A chorus of invitations, some lilting, some raucously obscene, tried to penetrate the music. Ordway caught both officers by the elbows and physically propelled them through the women and toward another door. He opened it to reveal a flight of stairs and pushed them through, slamming it shut behind him. The noise level dropped off immediately, as did their entourage.

"They call the downstairs the Hamburger Stand," he explained. "There's a roof garden upstairs and they said that's where we ought to go."

"The mysterious 'they' strikes again," Kimble said. His face was flushed, muscles working under the skin. "Onward! Upward!" He tried to take the stairs two at a time, stumbled, and eased to a wavering trot. Ordway and Taylor hurried after him.

The contrast between the roof garden and the melee on the first floor was almost as stunning as the blast of music had been. The women marked their arrival with sharp-eyed poise, making no move toward them. Colored lights strung overhead cast suffused light on small tables covered with bright-striped tablecloths. Each table had its own candle mounted in a bottle, the shape barely recognizable under encrusted melted wax. The music was pleasant, marred only by the determined rhythms pumping through the structure from below.

Kimble made for a pair of tables clumped near the back of the building. They were against the retaining wall and as Taylor sat across from the younger man, he was pleasantly surprised to find himself looking down at a small garden and flowered fish pond. The outdoor lighting was tasteful and the scene buoyed him.

"I could sit here and look at that all evening," he said. Ordway stood to peer past Kimble.

"Real pretty," he agreed. "I didn't even know about that."

"Aha!" Kimble was triumphant. " 'They' screwed up!" He swiveled to look back into the garden and broke into a happy chortle. "There's a 'they' now! Two of 'em! Don't scare 'em off!" He gestured for silence as a rotund American came into view clutching one of the girls under a thick arm.

They watched the pair walk the gravel path to the fish pond where she spoke to him. He smiled indulgently, reached into his pocket, then threw a coin that winked once, a silver eye absorbed by the black water.

"Big spender," Kimble sneered. "Probably ten dong."

The man said something to the girl. She looked up at him, laughing, patted his cheek and turned to leave. As she did, he reached out and grabbed a buttock in each hand. She whirled with a speed that left him with both arms still outstretched, the hands curved to the shape of her flesh. He still wore the sly smile of a juggler who has intentionally dropped his oranges when she stepped between his arms and shoved.

It was one short step to the edge of the pond. With histrionic grace, he sought out and back for something to hold onto, then splashed among the softly gleaming water lilies. The girl ran back the way she'd come, her laughter chiming up to her audience even as the water continued to slop out of the pond. The man bounced to his feet, spluttering wildly, and raced after her, mouthing incoherent rage.

Kimble pounded the table and whooped. "That'll teach the sonofabitch! He'll learn! Treat the whores like ladies and the ladies like whores! That'll teach him!"

The noise from the garden and Kimble's racket drew the girls from around the roof garden. Taylor was acutely aware from their expressions that some of them understood enough English to follow Kimble's speech perfectly. They buzzed among themselves. He attempted to salvage the situation.

"Could we buy a drink for three of you ladies?" He directed the question at a slim girl in a red and white blouse and skirt combination. She smiled hesitantly, looking to the others. He guessed her age to be probably twenty, which meant he was literally old enough to be her father. Another woman, older and obviously more at ease in her work, gave the girl a gentle shove toward Taylor and moved in on Kimble. She caught the eye of a third, who slipped into the chair next to Ordway. A waiter materialized.

"Whiskey!" Kimble shouted, overriding Taylor and Ordway, waggling a finger at the waiter. "Real drinking whiskey for the men! And see that you get the girls the best Saigon tea! No hypocrisy at this table!"

The waiter looked warily at the woman with Kimble. She nodded shortly as she dropped a hand to Kimble's thigh and turned to face him.

"First time you come Vung Tau?" she asked.

"Why, yes, it is." Kimble punched his glasses up onto the bridge of his nose. "Do you come here often, my dear?"

She blinked. "I live Vung Tau. Stay here all time. What your name?"

Kimble covered the hand on his thigh with his own. "You may call me Warren, you impetuous creature. And what's your name?"

223

Her smile was wavering now and the blued eyelids shuttered constantly. "My name Suzette." She looked to Taylor and suggested hopefully, *"Beaucoup* drunk, no?"

He nodded. *"Beaucoup* drunk, yes."

Kimble got to his feet with flourish. "I don't have to sit here and take insults from strangers. I'm a married man. Come, precious, we shall dance the night away, far from the sham of false friends."

Suzette swept along with him, alarm giving way to weary confidence that she knew how to deal with an ordinary drunk.

Ordway was deep in conversation with his companion and Taylor turned to the girl beside him.

"And what's your name?"

"Cindy." Her eyes were wide, hopeful and apprehensive.

"You understand English well."

She ducked her head and smiled. "I understand better than speak."

He paid the hovering waiter and tasted his drink, annoyed by its weakness, then faced the girl again. "You do well. You have steady customer here?"

He hoped his amusement was hidden as she tried to calculate her best answer. He could read speculation, concern, and finally resignation.

"Have no steady."

"I believe you. Never mind. Tonight you have steady customer. I have girl friend—Saigon. Tonight you drink, talk with me." He touched his chest with a finger. "My name Charlie. Same-same VC. You talk, I talk—you make money—everybody happy, OK?"

She relaxed, the plain pleasure of her smile so out of place it jarred him, created a clamping sensation in his stomach.

She was remarkably pretty in the manner of all unaffected young girls. He imagined her walking a village street with other girls her age, shy eyes that pretended not to see the young men and the confiding giggle for her companions. He closed his eyes and opened them slowly. The unwanted image was gone. He leaned back in the chair.

"Tell me about Cindy. Where is her home? Where are her brothers and sisters? If I buy tea, you must earn it."

She laughed at that, meshing her fingers and tucking her hands under her chin. Again, it was such a natural gesture it disturbed him. She talked, growing more comfortable with each word, yet when she spoke of schools and family and friends, it was as though she described a previous world.

The first awareness Taylor had of the passage of time was Ordway's announcement that he wanted to take his companion home.

"It'll mean either staying there all night or taking a chance on the curfew, Major."

Taylor checked his watch. "I don't want to carry her in the jeep. Take a cab to the BOQ. We'll get the jeep and follow you from there. I'll find out where the place is, take the Captain home, then come back after you. We won't miss curfew by much and I don't want to have to wonder where the hell you are all night. It'd probably be as safe as our place, but I don't want to risk it. I warned you you'd be in for a short-time."

Ordway winked at the girl. She smiled.

Taylor looked to the dance floor and tried unsuccessfully to catch the eye of the wildly gyrating Kimble. Finally, Cindy waved to Suzette, who nodded and literally hauled her partner toward the table.

"Cindy?"

She turned to Taylor's call, expectant.

"How much does the girl with my friend get?"

Dully, she said, "Ten dollars, short-time."

Taylor dipped into his wallet, watching her face toughen. He handed her a ten dollar MPC. "You can get P?"

She nodded, avoiding his eyes.

He stood up. *"Cam on co* Cindy. You are very nice. Maybe sometime I see you again."

Confusion marred her forehead. She waved the note vaguely. "You say thank me? For why?"

"Because I owe you, that's all."

She was still tucking the money in her blouse when Kimble and Suzette swept into their chairs.

"All time you talk," Suzette chided good-naturedly.

"That's a goddam fact." Kimble's volume drew sidelong looks from some of the other tables. He leaned across at Taylor. "Join in the fun, Charlie! You don't mind if I call you Charlie, do you? Suzette calls me 'sweetheart Warren' and we've never been formally introduced. But you'n me're old buddies, right?"

The multi-colored overhead lights were surrealistic blobs on the intense, sweating face. His head was angled downward, giving Taylor an untinted view of the eyes behind the glasses. He felt compelled to search deeply there, but all he could discover was the flame of the candle captured in each pupil.

He said, "Sure, we're buddies. And I've got to get you back to the rack." He explained Ordway's problem.

Kimble's face contorted. "What about me? What if I want to take Suzette home? It's all right to suck up to one of the troops, but we've got to set an example, right? Morals. Officers and gentlemen. That makes you feel big, doesn't it?"

"If you think so. Now get up. We're leaving."

The women sidled away and Kimble calmed with visible effort. Ordway maneuvered to be between them and the distraught Captain. Kimble ignored that, probing in his pocket. He withdrew his latest letter, wrinkled and frayed, dropping it in the puddles on the table.

"You wouldn't think a little piece of paper'd change your whole life, would you?"

Taylor sat back down. "Dear John?"

"You can read it, if you want." Kimble sagged like a beaten fighter.

"Not me, Warren. I don't want to know."

The quick laugh was startling until its bitterness registered. "I didn't want to know either. She's been going to meetings, you know? Protesting, to get us home. Her mother wouldn't let her go alone because she was afraid she'd get raped." He laughed again, raggedly, and it took a moment for him to subside. "Lenore works in a bank. She started going to the meetings with the sonofabitch that works next to her. I got a fucking Dear John from my wife and my fucking mother-in-law in the same envelope."

The laughter erupted once more, this time pealing from a face drawn into straked pain that threatened to fall into shock. A red bulb over his thrown-back head smudged his tears and for a disconcerting moment Taylor thought how much it looked like fire pouring across his features. He walked around the table and helped the unresisting body to its feet.

They made it down the stairs and back to the BOQ. He settled the sobbing Kimble in the back seat of the jeep and set out to follow Ordway's taxi, thinking there should be some sort of moral in the situation but too weary to dig it out. He noted landmarks, instead, trying to ignore the snuffling noises behind him and an inaudible phrase repeated monotonously. In exasperation, he finally made the effort to decipher it.

Kimble was saying, over and over, "I'm nothing without her."

Taylor wished he'd paid no attention.

24

"OK, WARREN, WE'RE BACK." Taylor squeezed his shoulder. "C'mon, you've got to get some sleep. We'll get you back to Saigon tomorrow."

Kimble remained where he was, head resting on his crossed arms on the back of the front seat. His sobs had quieted on the way back to the base.

"What good will that do? She's not in Saigon." He looked up at Taylor, his face pale in the dark. "I told you you wouldn't understand. You don't know about needing someone, what it is to be alone whenever that person's not with you. You think you're so goddam self-sufficient! You're not! You're afraid! You don't love anyone because you can't admit the need!" He gulped air and lurched out of the jeep, shoving past and into the building. Taylor followed, flipping on the solitary naked overhead bulb. The hard light spiked Kimble's sprawled form to the bunk.

Taylor walked past him to the head. When he returned, Kimble was sitting up, his expression straining for hope.

"You think Winter can get me out of here?"

Taylor thought, soft answers, and said, "I can promise you he'll try. Maybe he can get you emergency leave and a drop. It's not too far out. Try to get some sleep. We'll be quiet when we come back."

"No!" Kimble leaped to his feet. "I don't want to sit here alone! I want to be near someone."

"All right, all right. I understand." Taylor stepped out and Kimble rushed to keep up.

He babbled, scurrying into the passenger's seat. "I don't

usually need people around me. Lenore's not like just having someone around, you know? She gave meaning to my life. Meeting her was like being born, like having another soul."

Taylor dropped the jeep into gear and his mind into neutral and allowed himself to hope Ordway's presence would shut him up. Going through town provided some relief, the sights and sounds enough to mute the continuous chatter. He fed in an occasional grunt to satisfy Kimble's infrequent pauses for response.

Curfew was approaching and the streets filled with Americans headed for their quarters. They looked like workers off shift. Taylor abruptly realized that's exactly what they were. They had labored the entire evening, forging whatever pleasure they could from the raw materials available—colored lights, noise, liquor, whores. Men with hungry eyes above gashed smiles ignored the bronzed boredom of Vietnamese shopkeepers who stood aside to watch them straggle homeward.

Ordway stood at the edge of the small sidestreet, waiting for them. At the approach of the jeep, the blurred shape of the woman moved swiftly to the house. Taylor rolled away while he settled into the back seat.

"Feeling better?"

He heard the smile in the answer. "Yes, sir. Very much. Nothing like it in Gantry, I'll tell you."

"You tried it all in Gantry, did you?"

"Well, not all, but enough to know the difference between an amateur and a pro."

Kimble snorted contempt and the trio lapsed into a prickly silence that lasted until they were through town and on the road approaching the base.

"I'm going to be sick." Kimble's voice was precise.

Taylor stepped on the gas. "Hang on. We'll be home in a few minutes."

"I can't wait." He leaned over the side and retched dryly. "I'm afraid I'll fall out! I'm dizzy! Stop!"

Braking gently, Taylor pulled to the side. Kimble staggered around to the back, making horrible noises.

"The wages of sin," Taylor observed, glaring at Ordway. "You better not have any dues to pay."

The younger man's teeth gleamed. "No sweat. I kept my fingers crossed the whole time."

"I'd be happier if she'd kept her legs that way."

Kimble interrupted them. "Major, I can't—I'm passing out."

Ordway spun to grab his shoulder and Taylor eased out from behind the wheel. In back, he took Kimble's elbow and said, "We'll get you back to the sack. You'll be all right."

Before he knew what was happening he was sitting in the road, listening to Ordway's shocked, "What're you doing?"

Kimble raced to the driver's seat. Taylor scrambled upright, yelling as the gearshift rammed home. Ordway turned, reached back for him, and they linked hands as the machine bolted forward. It bucked once, the split second just enough for Taylor to throw out his other hand and grab the rear of the body. Ordway heaved on his wrist and Taylor vaulted in on top of him, both of them tumbling to the floor in a flailing of arms and legs. Taylor worked his way to the front seat as Kimble careened down the road, speeding away from the town and the base.

"Stop this thing, you crazy sonofabitch!" He shouted without taking his eyes from the road, wincing at the speed with which brush and houses loomed up and shot past.

Kimble's exultance sliced the edge of hysteria. "We're going back to Saigon! You said the Old Man'd try to get me home! We'll be there when he comes in! I'll be on my way!"

"You'll get us killed!" Taylor reached for the wheel and Kimble batted the hand away.

"Only if you try to stop me!"

Taylor grabbed the seat with both hands and struggled to keep his voice calm as they squealed around a curve. "You don't even know the road, Warren. Charlie owns this place at night, man. Even if you don't put us in the ditch, we could get bushwhacked."

Kimble grinned in triumph. "I thought of that. Look under the seat."

A cold spring gushed in Taylor's stomach as he felt the canvas overnight bag wedged under him. He pulled it out and looked at Apeneck and Ordway's .45.

"I slipped them in there while you were in the latrine. Extra ammunition, too. I could've taken the jeep then, but I thought about Charlie, too. If anyone comes at us, you'll have to get us through.''

"For Christ's sake, use your head! I don't know where we are!'' He looked back toward the smudge of light that marked Vung Tau. Ordway's eyes met his, then flashed immediately back forward to concentrate on the road. Taylor rapped him on the knee with the pistol.

"Take this goddam thing and pay attention to what the road looks like behind us. If we ever get this maniac turned around, we're going to have to find our way back. Understand?''

Ordway's stammered answer washed away under the sounds of the jeep.

Taylor cradled the sawed-off in his lap. "Look at this road, will you? Does this look like the road from Saigon to Vung Tau? It's a damned track, Kimble! You're on the wrong road!''

Kimble giggled. "Special providence for fools and drunks, remember? I've got to hit Saigon if I just keep heading north and west.'' A crossroad appeared as he spoke and he whipped onto it in a shuddering turn, gravel spraying into the brush with a sound reminiscent of the surf. The memory of the afternoon on the beach entered Taylor's mind in fogged outline, like some remembrance from childhood.

All at once the brush fell back from the roadside, revealing a stripped, scarred landscape marked by low humps in the ground and a distant tree line hovering on their flanks at the outside limit of the lights. Taylor recognized it as a defoliated area, 'dozed clean for ambush protection. He relaxed slightly, as if the encroaching foliage had been a weight on his back.

A slight knoll rose ahead and to the right, etched sharply against a star-spattered sky. The road bent to the left at its base, potholes and irregularities black in the tunnel of illumination, giving the whole an appearance of primitive cast silver. Electric apprehension crept up his neck. He bent forward, trying to see around that bend. It made him feel foolish but it was an irresistible urge.

Kimble tensed at Taylor's change of attitude. "You see something?'' The headlong pace slowed drastically.

They entered the curve, the knoll now paralleling them about fifty yards away. The ground to the left spanned off into darkness, flat and featureless. A shallow drainage ditch appeared on the right. The curve bent sharper quickly and both men in front saw the mound of fresh dirt across the road at the same instant.

"Cut left! Head back!" Taylor shouted. He tried to keep the knoll and the road-cut in view at the same time, sweeping from one to the other with the shotgun and praying that the killing squad hadn't had time to establish their position on the knoll. From there an enemy could pour fire onto the road and their own weapons would be as effective as spitballs.

Kimble hit the gas and twisted the jeep off the road. The first rut tore the wheel from his hands, throwing him heavily against Taylor. The machine leaped insanely back toward the road and burrowed the front wheels into the shoulder. Unrestrained, they buckled sideways to their limits, the sudden deceleration pitching both officers against the dashboard. The shotgun flew from Taylor's grasp like a released bird, glittering, bouncing toward the mound now only a few yards distant.

Another shape descended into the still-blazing headlights, sprawling soddenly between the gun and the jeep. The clarity of his comprehension amazed Taylor as he instantly recognized Ordway, and then the jeep was rising under him. He felt Kimble's weight increase as the machine rolled ponderously, like an old horse preparing to roll in the dust. It dropped over with a dull thump and Kimble scrambled across him and disappeared behind it. Ordway twitched briefly, the shadows magnifying the slight motion.

Bright pain rocketed up Taylor's leg when he tried to crawl. Again, his mind surprised him as it coolly inventoried the data that his foot was pinned and his chest ached when he breathed. He knew he should get away and he yanked at the obstinate foot, ignoring the pain. As he did, the silence was broken by a scrabbling noise. He sought the source, hoping he would not see what he knew must be there.

At the junction of the trench and the ditch to his left front, a small man rose to his knees. He raised an oversized fist above his head and pointed the other at Taylor. He was just inside the illumination from the lights, his pose and stature an illustration from a temple wall, an imp from hell indicating his victim. Taylor waited helplessly for the raised arm to pitch the grenade. Red spouts exploded toward him from both sides of the kneeling man and the sound of the rounds going overhead was one with the muzzle blast.

There was a lake on the base at Quantico. Sometimes it got this hot and humid there, too, and the night-dwellers hummed around you. Sweat rimmed white arcs under your arms and on your back it sketched a child's map of Africa. You listened to a frog. A fish splashed. If the moon was right, the small waves blinked diamonds as they hurried away from the disturbance. Always a whippoorwill chanted in the forest. Fireflies challenged the stars with cool green-yellow messages to the universe.

Another movement distracted Taylor.

Ordway scrambled forward in the dirt, arms, legs, hands and feet thrashing in a frenzy. His right hand closed on the stock of the shotgun and he extended it toward the man in the same motion. The throaty rumble of the twelve-gauge boomed authoritatively over the sharper crack of the VC weapons. The face of the kneeling figure collapsed in frothing action. For an instant the naked mass of the brain shone exposed, disappearing as the smashed head bent back impossibly, spraying chunks of flesh torn away by buckshot. The body, as though in pursuit, lifted off the ground, the lower legs still neatly folded. The grenade hung in the air before plummeting. A cry of unbelieving terror rose from the ditch to stop short in a surge of flame and the crush of the explosion. For a second or two after that there was a rainpatter that Taylor told himself was earth and metal.

A bubbling moan called from where the grenade had gone off. Ordway rolled to his feet, charged to the edge of the road, and fired. He dropped to the ground again.

Silence came back, trying to heal the night. Ordway, carefully coming erect, failed to disturb it. Taylor basked in it, still alive. A tug at the pinioned foot brought back awareness of that pain as well as the one in his chest. Pain reminded him of Kimble. He twisted to face the rear of the jeep.

"Help me, you worthless bastard!" he hissed. "We've got to get out of here!"

Kimble's head popped out, a caricature of relief and residual fear.

"Are they all dead?"

"Get my foot loose!"

Kimble came around the jeep on his hands and knees. He stopped abruptly and rocked back on his haunches, holding his right hand away from his body. He stared at the ground and grunted. Cautiously, he lowered it again and lifted something.

"I found the .45!"

"Just get me loose!"

"Yes, sir!"

Ordway's shouted report drove home the foolishness of their whispered dialog. "Four of 'em! Dead!"

Taylor shouted back. "Good! Give us a hand! I'm stuck!"

Ordway trotted to them, leaned the shotgun against the hood, and pulled at the seat. Taylor felt the pressure ease and rolled on his back. Planting his hands, he jerked back and was free. He wiggled the foot and winced. "Thank Christ that's over. It's not broken or anything. Let's—."

A burst of fire from behind them sprayed dirt in front of the jeep. Ordway dove for the shotgun as Kimble dug at the automatic under his belt. All three whirled to see one of the VC staggering toward them from the ditch. He carried an M-16 in his left hand, the right dangling in a pulp, funneling a stream of blood down his leg. From the eyebrows down, the face was devoid of features, a wet slab marked by a darker hole that had been a mouth.

He squeezed the trigger again, still aiming by guess and still low to the right. Taylor found himself able to see only the muzzle of the rifle and hear nothing but screams before Ordways return fire plucked ineffectually at the useless right arm and kicked up dirt in the distance. The sightless body swung toward the sound as Kimble stepped in front of Taylor. He held the pistol awkwardly in a classic target-firing position. It bucked only slightly as his bullet took his man just above the black pajama trousers. A small dust cloud puffed from the strike and the man snapped shut like a pocketknife, his feet clearing the ground and his arms flying together. When he landed his hands were still touching in front of him as though he was apologizing for a grave social error.

The man rolled onto his side and forced himself to all fours and clawed at the ground for his rifle. Kimble took two steps forward, positioned himself, and shot him again. The man skidded sideways and lay still. Kimble prodded him with a toe and, satisfied, turned to Ordway with the expression of a librarian hearing whispers.

"Don't you ever make a mistake like that again," he said.

Taylor and Ordway looked at each other. The Corporal smiled, giggled, began to give way to the hysteria Taylor felt expanding in himself.

"That's enough!" He snapped it at Ordway, relieved that his voice didn't crack. "We've got to get the hell out of here!" He limped to the rear of the jeep, Kimble hurrying to help at the front. They leaned into it, grunting and cursing, finally rocking it and dumping it back over on its wheels.

Taylor said, "You drive," to Ordway. The engine grated ominously before coming to life. He backed and filled, grinding gears indifferently in his haste, and then they were roaring back toward Vung Tau. Taylor twisted in the front seat for a look at Kimble and found him looking back when they'd been. Before Taylor could speak, the Captain faced him, features limp in misery.

"I'm sorry, Major. My God, I—."

"Sorry? You don't know anything about sorry, motherfucker, but you will. I'll see to it."

"Sir?" Ordway's voice was conciliatory.

"You'll do yourself a favor if you'll shut your mouth and drive. You hear me?"

"Yessir."

Taylor fumbled in the bag still under the seat until he found three rounds to replace the expended ones. He reloaded, holding each shell with his fingertips, thumbing them into the weapon and scanning the road at the same time. That done, his right arm held the weapon snug against his chest, the other hand stroking away dirt and grit with sensual gentleness. The night chilled and the motion stopped, the hand tightening on the barrel. He shivered, then jammed back against the seat as soon as it passed. There was no talk and little movement until they were almost to the gate.

"Buzz right past the guard," Taylor directed, having trouble getting the words past unaccountably stiff jaw muscles. "He won't bother us. Pull this thing in behind our building.''

Ordway did as instructed, leaving the unapproving sentry behind. As soon as they stopped, Taylor stepped to the ground.

"Nothing happened tonight, you understand? Nothing happened. We're going to wash this thing. If either of you knows any prayers, you better say one for no holes in it. The scratches on this side were there when we came back to the BOQ parking lot from the bar. We picked up the Corporal, got lost, drove around, and finally got back here. That's our story. Is it clear?''

Even as they nodded agreement, he sent Ordway for the bucket and swab in the quarters.

"You're not going to tell the Colonel about this?'' Surprise forced Kimble's voice up, making it almost childlike.

"Of course not. Much as I'd love to see him crucify you, I'm not covering for you, I'm covering for me. I'm senior and he'd have to put me down with you. Sooner or later you may think that's an attractive idea. Don't bet on it. You may embarrass me, but you'll get no joy from it.''

Kimble shook his head. "Major, I don't think you can imagine how ashamed I am. I'm the world's authority on embarrassment. No small accomplishment for someone who's less a man than most, is it?''

Weariness struck through Taylor's body, a scalding solution that ate at his joints and left them reluctant.

"Warren, I've put up with your infantile bullshit since I got here. When that little prick came up with the M-16, you stepped in front of me. You had a golden opportunity to continue being the incapable asshole you think you are, and you blew it. You probably saved all our lives. That doesn't mean I won't make your remaining time here a living hell, because you put me in that spot in the first place, but I believe there's something there you ought to think about.''

Kimble gestured and started to speak and Taylor poked a finger into his chest to stop him. "I'm not done. One more thing. Speaking as one gentleman to another, I'm telling you if I ever hear you mention that insipid bitch Lenore again, I'm going to break your fucking skull.''

Kimble gasped and Ordway showed up with the bucket of

water and swab. Taylor turned away. The Captain stood stiffly alone before stalking heavily to join in sloshing water over the vehicle.

It took two hours to clean the jeep and assure themselves there were no bullet holes in it. Afterwards they showered, no one interested in conversation, and fell onto their bunks.

Taylor smoked a last cigarette, losing himself in the wane and glow of the coal.

Ordway wished he could go to sleep, or at least slow down the rapid drumming of his heart, so hard he was certain the Major had noticed it. When he closed his eyes the exploding face of the first VC traced across his mental vision in a never-ending series of stop-action photographs. His mind persisted in alternating Disneyesque shots of flowers opening. It made everything worse and he had to keep opening his eyes to avoid being sick.

He'd made a mistake, not checking the bodies closer, but there just didn't seem to be any way a man could look like that one did and still be alive, much less be able to move. He'd done what needed done and they'd lived because he got the guy with the grenade. His memory balked at that, leaping to the image of the Captain dropping the VC. That wasn't any good either, the way the VC walked toward them. The hairs raised on his arms, starting at his wrists and moving up, like an advance of fleas.

He tried to think of nothing, nothing, nothing.

Kimble remembered the same VC. He thought of moving to protect Taylor, desperately wishing he didn't have to. He admitted to himself he hadn't reacted instinctively or by moral guidance, but because he didn't know what else to do. That puzzled him and he tried to think it through, but the harder he tried, the more he found his mind calling up the screaming when he shot the man. Why would Ordway, who'd been so coldly efficient at first, yell like that when the other VC came at them?

Taylor wanted only to forget the terrible helplessness of being trapped. He had been so sure of death, not once, but twice. Being able to feel pain, of knowing he was alive, had been incredible. And then had come the shock of more shooting and the blind malice of that rifle, like a dead snake striking in reflex. He shuddered and dropped the cigarette butt in the seashell he'd brought from the beach. His last thought was the hope that his throat wouldn't feel so raw in the morning.

25

SHORTLY AFTER 0900 they stood in front of Winter's desk, watching for any signs of disbelief while Taylor spun an explanation for their premature return. Kimble added nothing, satisfied with nods of punctuation, the rest of his body slumped inside his baggy uniform. Taylor maintained a relaxed parade rest.

By the time it was over, Winter was hunched over the desk, head down, both arms extended parallel. As if in sympathy with Kimble's nods, his fingers tapped the wood like a pulse. For a full minute the room was otherwise silent as he studied the problem, occasionally shifting his cigar from one side of his mouth to the other. When he removed it, he looked at Kimble.

"I'll do everything I can to get you out of here as soon as possible." At Kimble's wild grin he cautioned, "Don't get too enthused. I can't just sit you on a plane. There's administrative stuff. And I won't consider releasing you until I'm assured your relief's on the way."

Kimble's grin melted and he made an attempt to come to attention. "I understand, Colonel. I'll appreciate any help. I have to get home."

"I'll do what I can. I'm truly sorry you have this problem."

"I know, sir."

Winter nodded solemnly, but there was something in the response that caused Taylor to cut his eyes far enough to check Kimble's expression. It was the same forged determination he'd displayed all morning. Still, Taylor was sure he'd caught a flash of apprehension in Winter's manner.

Winter himself put an end to the speculation. "Now I've got another matter to discuss with Major Taylor," he said. "Write me a detailed report of your meeting with the Comm people.

Prepare a separate tab for your impressions and recommendations."

The fatherly concern drained as Kimble approached the door. By the time it closed, Winter was grim.

"You were limping when you came in. What happened?"

Taylor said, "Twisted my ankle running on the beach. No sprain or anything."

"Good." The upper lip curled over the cigar in a sneer. "There was a fire fight of some kind down there last night. No one seems to know what happened, except a jeep ran into a road cut. The VC had rounded up some locals to do the work. Apparently the civilians lit for home when they heard the jeep coming. The cadre stayed and four of them got wasted."

"No one knows who was in the jeep?"

Winter's stare was fixed now. "Nobody can figure it. The best guess from down there is that it was a load of drunks on the back roads. And that doesn't explain why they were armed, unless they're nuts."

"Maybe it was one of their own patrols that got lost and don't want to admit it."

"They don't send out people armed with shotguns."

"Did they find shotguns? Must have belonged to Charlie."

"They didn't find any. They found two VC with enough buckshot in them to build a tombstone." He lolled back in his chair. "If they find a jeep full of bullet holes down there, somebody's ass is candy. If I was the CO, I'd hang 'em."

Taylor grimaced. "Hard to figure what gets into people."

"Sometimes it's harder to figure how people get out of whatever gets into them gets them into."

"You want to try that in English?"

He heaved himself back to his leaning position on the desk. "It's not important. Not right now. I sent Kimble off because I wanted to let you know the Binh thing is falling apart fast."

"How come?"

"Same old shit. Pressure. We can't hold Trung much longer."

"He could have an accident. The VC could find out where we've got him stashed and get to him."

"I thought of that. No good. The pressure source must know we have both Trung and Tu. Nothing's been said about Tu. I figure that means the heat's from a relative of Trung's. If

238

it was VC stuff, it seems like they'd be yelling for both to be released. The story is, the girls who sat in on the poker game are willing to swear that 'someone' threatened to have Trung and Tu locked up because they cheated the 'someone' at cards. And if anything happens to Trung, we'll really catch hell to produce a healthy Tu."

"How about a stall? After all, they're both supposed to be hiding in Hong Kong."

"The concerned party is willing to go to Hong Kong." He rubbed his nose with a forefinger. "That means money and it means enough influence for an exit visa and so on. Trung's friend is no alderman. This is a biggie, my boy."

"This biggie—is he big enough to survive an argument with a truck? Maybe he could have Trung's accident."

Winter chewed on his cigar. "You know," he said at last, "conversation with you has a chilly quality—like talking to a disaster, first hand. Are you sure you weren't the black plague once? Anyhow, I already thought of that, too. We don't know who he is and we don't have the time to set up anything. And it could be legit, a relative seriously concerned about Trung."

"I can't believe you said that. Not even a Vietnamese could be so tied up in family he'd give a damn if Trung died."

"Probably," Winter conceded and sighed. "I'm walking through the swamp blindfolded again, but I think we're being offered a deal. Free Trung and we can keep Tu. Remember, his name's never come up."

"And as soon as Trung hits the bricks, he talks to anyone who'll listen and Binh's back at the stand."

Winter appeared to mull that, unfavorably, and Taylor moved on. "There's another thing. Trung may be able to make Harker and Allen, and he's got me for sure. If he turns us, things'll hot up fast for us. He knows Tho and Chi, too. You let that mother loose, you're liable to end up with a roster full of blank spaces. As acting spokesman for us potential targets, may I say, sir, we don't cotton to that shit."

"You silver-tongued devil." Winter laughed as he checked his watch. "Maybe I can use your oratorical genius. I'm going to make a pitch down at State this morning. Get the jeep and meet me out front."

Taylor started to leave. "This about Trung?"

Winter continued to rummage in his desk until he found his

.38 and had it in the shoulder holster. "Yeah. The waves have reached them, too. I'm seeing a Mr. Carr."

When Taylor went to his own office after the keys he found Duc waiting.

"You hear about prick Binh?"

"Just left Winter. Everything's going to hell fast."

"You better believe. What we do now?"

"How do I know?" Taylor stirred the accumulation of incoming papers on his desk. "Maybe you could immigrate to the states. The Mafia could use a hit man who takes in laundry."

"Honky bassert."

"When'll you learn? There's a 't' in the middle and a 'd' on the end. 'Bastard,' not 'bassert.'"

"Never mind how I say. You know *what* I say."

"Too true. Listen, seriously, I've been talking to Winter. I still think he ought to give Trung to us."

Duc blinked, shifting mental gears. "I tell same thing Colonel Loc. He say too much complicate."

"Well, we tried. I'm going down to the embassy with Winter now. An appointment to talk about Trung. Maybe he'll work something out."

Stretching, Duc said, "Maybe. I don't think so."

"You know something?"

The answering shrug was as lazy as the stretch. "I know too much you not know. Especial I know your embassy. They not help you on thing like this."

"What's this? Today your day to hate Americans?"

"Not hate all Americans. Don't know all Americans. Only know honky bas-tar-dis."

"Sergeant Miller won't be happy if you call him a honky."

In the sing-song English of the streets, Duc said, "Black honky, white honky, all same-same poor Vietnamese."

Taylor made as if to leave, and Duc reached to touch his sleeve. "Now you be serious. You hurt leg Vung Tau. You also act funny. Different. I see Kimble and Corporal—they look *very* different. What happen Vung Tau?"

"Nothing, really. Kimble got bad news from home and made a damned fool of himself and I twisted my ankle on the beach, that's all."

Duc turned his head, ending up looking at Taylor from the

corner of his eyes. "Maybe you, Kimble bullshit Winter. I not think so. You not bullshit Duc. Too much I know you. You not want speak, OK. Remember, you need help, you tell Duc first. You get it?"

Taylor made a great show of stalking out of the office. Duc's voice trailed after him, back into the street rhythms, "Come back, GI! Give me Sa-lem, OK?"

Taylor was still grinning when he got to the jeep where Winter waited.

"What're you grinning about?"

Pulling away from the villa, Taylor said, "Duc's got a new word. Honky. He's working it out on me."

Winter grunted. "Swell. Cultural interchange at work."

They swept through the gate and into the traffic. Winter was suddenly upright, hanging on with both hands, as Taylor switched lanes in a race with a truck. He nipped into a minute gap and immediately braked for a traffic blockage. The driver behind blatted his horn and shouted unintelligible complaint.

"Jesus, you're as bad as the rest of them."

Taylor raced the engine. When the light changed, the jeep leaped into motion. Winter improved his handholds.

"You're pretty wound up, Tay. Now slow down and sort of flow with the tide for a while. You get me killed and the State Department will be absolutely furious."

"Sorry," Taylor said. "I guess the scene with Kimble hit me harder than I thought." He eased off on the gas.

"Harder than I'd have thought, too." There was a crackle in Winter's voice, but when Taylor turned to look, the blunt features were aimed dead ahead, guileless. Unnoticing, or ignoring, Taylor's move, he continued to make conversation.

"This meeting should be an education for you. That's why you're coming along. This Mr. Carr and myself are going to be deciding a man's fate. He's our mutual enemy. And I'll bet you my soul, or what I have left of it, Mr. Carr'll literally be Trung's advocate."

"That's prejudging the man."

"Why not? The message sending for me said, I quote, 'Mr. Trung's continued well-being is a source of concern to the government of the United States.'"

"So what can you hope to accomplish? Why bother?"

"That's where my experience in this war comes in! Instead

241

of telling Mr. Carr how we can develop a proper legal case against Trung, I'm going to lie through my teeth and do what my moral judgment tells me is correct. What half my moral judgement says, anyhow. The other half'll be screaming while I do it."

Taylor headed for the curb across the street from the embassy and Winter altered his position, ready to get out. The jeep continued over the curb and across the sidewalk, groaning to a stop under a huge billboard.

Winter hopped to the ground. "What the hell do you think you're doing?"

"I always park here when I come to the embassy. Nobody cares and the billboard throws some shade on the seats." He ran the chain through the steering wheel and locked it. "Which half of your soul is going to do your suffering in there?"

The question pulled Winter's mind from the parking situation and the disbelief gave way to the returning frown.

"The half that knows both Carr and I should be eliminating people like Trung and whoever's helping him. This isn't my first time down this road, although I've never dealt with anyone as high-up as Carr. What scares me most is that none of our friends from the Agency'll be there. We're cold alone on all of this. I feel like some dumb cop who's ticketed the Mayor's son. Only here we've got people fixing tickets for guys who're killing us."

They waited silently for the traffic light to change and when they were able to move, both men instinctively sought out an interstice in the crowd around them before resuming the talk.

Taylor said, "I told you, Colonel, give me a little time and I'll fix it."

"You may have to." He looked straight ahead and his voice reminded Taylor of bare branches. "I'm about out of ideas."

They paralleled the gleaming white wall surrounding the equally white building, the whole an imperturbable iceberg thrown down into the heat as though by a god with a taste for irony. A bored Marine in a guard tower at the end of the wall watched them pass through the gate. Immediately inside the building another Marine, immaculate in every detail, waited for them. He saluted.

"Good morning, Colonel, Major. Can I help you, sir?"

Taylor kept a straight face. The Sergeant's greeting was better than proper, it was friendly. It also carried the strong suggestion that if the Sergeant couldn't help you, you didn't belong on his turf.

"I have an appointment with Mr. Carr. Major Taylor is accompanying me."

The Sergeant rattled off a room number without referring to a directory and indicated the elevator to their left.

The secretary who welcomed them to Carr's waiting room provided coffee and chatted easily about restaurant prices and her upcoming trip to Hong Kong. Taylor listened, avoiding leaning against the chair and plastering his skivvy shirt against his back. A buzzer sounded and the woman smiled a goodbye for them, pointing at a door next to her.

The first sight of Carr was encouraging. A short, wiry man with a precise moustache, he smiled broadly and stepped from behind his desk, shaking hands with a firm grip. A jacket, shirt, and tie on a hanger behind him gave Taylor hope the casual shirt on his back indicated his true character. He had coffee brought in for himself and Taylor, Winter refusing, and started the conversation with a question for Taylor.

"What's a Marine doing here in the big city? I thought all of you were in I Corps or else protecting us in this building from the VC."

Taylor looked at Winter before answering. "I can't be sure, Mr. Carr. Some of us think we're doing public penance."

He was pleased to see Carr enjoy the dig, and his hope for a compromise with the man took another step. Winter's attitude loosened, too, but the wary shift of his eyes was still there.

Carr wasted no more time on the periphery of their meeting. "I understand we have a problem," he said to Winter.

"We do indeed. You mind if I smoke?"

Carr extended a box of cigars. "Try one of these. Philippine."

Winter hesitated and Carr added, "Please. I'd like your opinion. I think they approximate Havanas."

After a sniff, Winter winked at Taylor. "We're in trouble. We haven't been in the man's office ten minutes, and he's found my price."

Carr chuckled. "I wish it was always that easy. I have a suspicion it may not be today, either."

243

Lighting the cigar, Winter exhaled a rolling cloud. "You may be right. I hope we can work something out." He waved the cigar like a miniature baton. "Very nice."

His approval drew a preoccupied nod as Carr said, "I'm afraid there's not much to work out. We know Trung's a black marketeer. Still, there's someone of importance on the Vietnamese side very anxious to see he's, shall we say, contented?" He looked from one of them to the other, probing for a break. "Exactly where is he, Colonel, and what's his condition?"

"Technically, he's the prisoner of the South Vietnamese, Mr. Carr. Their information puts him in Hong Kong with a large bank account. He should be quite well."

The leather-and-chrome chair squeaked disapproval as Carr swung from side to side, tenting his fingers on his rib cage. "If you don't mind, Colonel, I'd like to ask exactly where you fit in here. You're the contact I was given by the General. Why? How's a Records Research Unit get in on the defection of a low-level VC-slash-crook? What are your sources?"

"I can't do that, Mr. Carr. Our sources would dry up overnight if I started discussing them. All I can tell you is that by virtue of the joint nature of the Unit and long tenure in-country, I hear a lot. I make it a point to know where the skeletons are."

Carr winced dramatically. "An unfortunate metaphor. If Trung's a skeleton, we don't have a problem, we have a catastrophe."

"My mistake. While we're asking things, exactly who is so concerned about Trung?"

"Touché." Carr cocked his head to the side. "If I knew, which of course I don't, I wouldn't tell you."

Without thinking, Taylor laughed. Winter's quick glare was a warning. Carr was curious.

"You wanted to say something, Major?"

"No, sir. I was just thinking how long it's been since I saw a two-handed game of Blind Man's Bluff."

"It does look like that, doesn't it?" Carr's move from taut curiosity to a smile was beautiful to watch, smooth as an acrobat's progression from stunt to pose. The lips parted and the new expression glossed his features, defying interpretation, unselfconsciously a stock item.

"The Major has a point, Colonel. We're sparring. Impasse.

However, I'll take a step your way and tell you frankly I've tried to resist the pressure to produce Trung. I failed."

The decision to trust Carr showed in Winter's attitude. He bent forward slightly, a minimally aggressive move subconsciously intended to increase his bargaining weight.

"Assuming I can prevail on my sources, when would he have to be available?"

"Guarantee the date and I'll guarantee you another three days and try for four. Five is out of the question."

"That's not much time, Mr. Carr. There are complications—." Raised eyebrows suggested a infinity of possibilities.

Carr said, "Call me Pete. I hope you're not telling me he's —injured?"

"I'm sure he's not. And my friends call me Win."

"Win it is. As for our friend, whoever's responsible for him had better insure he's not injured. I have a gut feeling he'll become a cause célèbre if things go too far. I smell a plan, and him a part of it. Ever since Tet, the VC have been withering. The NVA and the politicians back home, that's what's left. I happen to know a major VC figure has dropped out of sight, and my sources," he broke and the polished smile worked its transformation quickly and was gone, "report rumors that he sold out his comrades. If that's so, the opposition'll need a distraction, a media blitz to popularize some abused freedom fighter. It'd generate enough stink to overwhelm any credit we might accrue from the big-time VC's defection or elimination."

Color rose from Winter's neck and his eyes narrowed. The silence fell apart at the peremptory ring of a telephone in the outer office. When a light sprang to life on Carr's phone, he punched at it with a finger that consigned it to another time.

Winter said, "W're not talking about a jaywalker. This bastard buys or steals bullets that kill our men."

"The people who take his side don't care about that. How long since you've been home, Win?"

Cautious at this new tack, Winter's chin tucked back to a defensive posture. He hedged his answer.

"Quite a while. A few years, now. Why?"

"You should take a leave, bring yourself up to date."

"What's your point, Pete?"

Bitterness burst past the modulated speech pattern. "The war's lasted too long. The opposition is organized, the politicians are terrified, the people are confused. We're getting out with all possible haste and as little fuss as possible. There will be no martyr named Trung."

"He can identify some people involved in his capture. It could be sensitive."

They matched stares for a moment. Carr said, "You're a soldier. You've sent men to capture minor pieces of ground knowing damned well it'd cost some of them their lives and in a year's time no one would remember it happened. That's where we are with this. Everyone's going to have to take their chances."

"Not everyone. Just the fools." Winter got to his feet as if his legs troubled him. "I'll see to the arrangements. But I want something from you. Get the word to Trung's friend that silence is all that keeps Trung alive. I promise you, if I ever suspect one of my people's been hurt because we had to turn the sonofabitch free, I'll watch him die for it. And anyone connected with him. No considerations, no exceptions."

"I'll try. No promises."

"I appreciate that. You're not in a position to keep it if you make it. I understand."

Carr tried the smile, and it came up unbalanced. Taylor moved to the door as the civilian extended his hand and was suddenly remembering the events of the previous night, now a thousand years old, and despite the horror of the scenes in his mind, it had an honesty of spirit that made his present surroundings tawdry and demeaning.

He stepped into the next room and turned to see the two men smiling at each other and they looked to be grinning in rictus, like dogs dead on a roadside, struck down by a force they'd never challenged and would never comprehend.

26

TAYLOR WHEELED TO A STOP in the parking lot. Allen helped Harker out, the blond man gingerly probing ahead of himself with a cane.

"Careful," he warned. "Let me down easy, 'cause if you jar my jewels I'll raise raw welts all over you with my trusty walking stick and cry salt tears in the wounds."

"Don't threaten me," Allen said. "I know how vulnerable you are."

"I'm getting better fast. Give me a few days and I'll be ticking along on two like everybody else."

"You're one lucky man." Taylor came around to join them. "The doc says no real damage done?"

Harker's smile was grim. "Depends on what you call damage. Everything's going to be functional as ever. I don't know if I'll ever be able to work at karate again. Every time I even think someone's eyeing the ol' Golden Target I'm afraid I'll curl up in a ball and faint."

"Yeah, yeah. You're justifying your Purple Heart."

"Don't say purple." Harker wrinkled his face histrionically. "I don't want to hear purple. Or green. And damn black-and-blue. Colors bring back bad memories."

"Odd you should mention purple," Allen mused. "I was thinking we could have dinner tonight at the Crab Pot. They serve an excellent eggplant, fried in batter. I love eggplant, the bulbous shape wine-dark, taut-skinned. You test them for ripeness by squeezing." He held out a hand, demonstrating.

Harker groaned. "You sadistic bastard." He stopped and groaned again. "Oh, wow! Steps! I didn't know we had stairs!"

The other two exchanged looks and each grabbed an elbow, shuffling up the few stairs, Harker floating between them on his rigid arms. The need for slow progress gave Taylor a welcome chance to inspect the building.

The Cercle Sportif was another legacy of the French, a white building luminous in the shade of towering trees. The interior was elegant and spacious, with the high ceilings of tropical architecture. Everywhere he looked, lovingly polished hard-woods of intricate grain glowed welcome. Subdued lighting made it manorial.

"I wonder how many guys sat in here and told themselves Giap was going to beat his brains out on the wire at Dien Bien Phu?" Allen said to no one in particular.

"Steer me to a chair." Harker pointed with the cane. "I want to sit down."

They chose a small table near the wall. Taylor helped Allen position a massive armchair for Harker, thinking how they looked exactly as they'd look in the club on a hot Sunday afternoon in Quantico. Harker leaned against the soft leather and sighed.

"It's worth it," he declared. "It hurts to take a deep breath, but it's worth it. The first time in a month I've been able to inhale and not get a lungful of disinfectant."

Allen signalled a waiter. "I'll drink to that."

"You and me, babe." Harker straightened in the chair. "Then I want to go out to the pool and watch the chicks."

"Are you up to it?" Allen asked.

"Don't say up!" Harker jerked his chin downward. "If that devil hears you and takes off, I could die!"

"Good Lord! You've got more proscribed words than the Church! Taking you out of that hospital was the same as a vow of silence."

"Not a bad idea for either of you dirty-minded youngsters," Taylor said, standing. "We've got company."

Following his gaze to the front door, his companions saw Ly enter, spot them, and wave.

"Hey, great!" Allen said. "Maybe she'll join our cele-bration."

"I guarantee it." Taylor continued to watch Ly. "I asked her to meet me here."

Harker said, "Well, I'll be damned," as he rose with Allen to greet her.

Ly said, "Captain Allen. Lieutenant Harker. I haven't seen you for a long time. You both look well. I was terribly sorry to hear you were injured, Lieutenant. Are you feeling better?"

Harker blushed. "I'm—ah—fine, thanks. And thank you for your note, too. I enjoyed it."

She made a gesture of dismissal. "We were concerned," she

said. "Please, sit down." Taylor held a chair for her and she leaned back against his hands for a moment. Then she was all solicitude for Harker.

"Is the food good in the hospital? Is there anything I can get for you?"

Harker inclined at the waist in a careful bow and raised his glass in a toast. "I just want to sit here and enjoy the company. Someone so pretty, and in a blue dress, after a steady diet of nurses in white. We came to celebrate Hal's new membership in the club but I think I'll celebrate your joining us."

Ly turned to Taylor. "He will make me blush."

"Please don't!" Allen protested. "It's the first time he's ever shown good taste and we don't dare destroy the moment."

Her hand fanned, as though to disperse the flattery. When it brushed Taylor's bare arm the warm rush in his veins surprised him. The two reactions fed on each other and created a delicious anticipation.

She rose and they followed suit.

"Would you excuse me? I promised to meet someone else here. She's playing tennis. I'll be back in a few minutes."

"I'll walk with you, if you'd like," Taylor offered.

"No, please. I'll only be a little while." She smiled up at him, waved to the others, and was gone. Taylor sat back down and was pinned by knowing amusement.

Harker winked broadly at Allen. "What's the line about old dogs and new tricks? There's a legend shot in the ass, huh?"

"Feet of clay, feet of clay," Allen murmured, paying for their drinks. "The typical military mind for you. Buy 'em books, send 'em to school, and they put the make on the teacher."

Taylor stared down his nose at each in turn. "I'd actually forgotten what immature whelps you two are."

Allen continued to look at Harker and tilted his head Taylor's way. "Probably feels sorry for him. You know, sees how he's tumbling into middle age, due to retire to a chicken farm somewhere. Sort of fading away."

Harker agreed soberly. "Respect for the aged is a keynote of Oriental culture. Like charity. Probably figures to give him one last chance. She'd gain a lot of merit that way, being a good Buddhist and all. I always admired her mind, and God knows she's lovely, but I'm really impressed by her compassion." He frowned in heavy concentration. "No, not compassion. It's deeper than that. Pity. That's it. Pity."

"Good thinking." They shook hands and Allen continued, "Superb perception. Let me buy you another drink." He gestured for the waiter, who looked at the more-than-half full glasses without a flicker and left for refills.

Taylor said, "You two were born fifty years late. You could have killed vaudeville single-handed."

"Vaudeville." Harker pursed his lips and tapped them gently. "I remember reading about that. Way back in his younger days, I guess. Twenty-three skidoo, Al Capone, all that."

"Wait a goddam minute! That was long before I was born!"

"No kidding?" Allen was taken aback.

"Up yours," Taylor grumped. The waiter lowered the fresh drinks. Harker enjoyed himself so much he spilled some and he replaced the glass clumsily, laughing and groaning simultaneously. He cupped his hands over his stomach.

"Serves you right," Taylor said. "I hope your goddam stitches pop and flog you to death."

Harker managed a wheezing halt. "It only hurts when I laugh. Who said that was funny?"

"We're back to vaudeville," Allen said. "Better ask the Major."

Doubling over further, Harker said, "Shop. Let's talk shop. Tell me what's going on down at the office."

Taylor shrugged. "That ought to kill thirty seconds. Or less." He filled in the highlights of the Binh operation, omitting the talk in Carr's office.

Harker took a long drink when he'd finished. "So we've got nothing, right?"

Before he could answer, Taylor's attention was drawn to Allen's stare aimed at the front entrance, all sign of pleasure drained from his face.

"Oh-oh," he breathed. "Everybody on his toes!"

The others followed his look to a Caucasian signing in, flourishing the pen across the register. He appeared to be in his mid-thirties, about Taylor's own height and build, wearing casually stylish clothes that shouted money. Rich brown hair curled neatly below the line of his collar, offset by slightly darker sideburns and heavy moustache.

Taylor asked Allen, "State Department?"

Allen's eyes widened and he grew sardonic. "Don't let him hear that. That's Mr. Benjamin Barline, celebrated journalist, author, and chronicler of America's misdeeds."

Returning to his drink, Taylor said, "So that's the motherfucker. You said this is a class joint. I liked the crowd at the Friendly better."

"Watch it!" Allen hissed. His broad smile directed itself over Taylor's shoulder. "I know him. He's coming over here."

"Allen! How the fuck are you?" The voice boomed right behind Taylor, filling the room only to die in the echoing hush. "How come you're not at some embassy bash with the fat cats? Run out of bullshit?"

Taylor watched an immaculate hand slide past his ear to shake Allen's.

"How are you, Ben?" Allen said. "Meet my friends."

Barline touched hands with them quickly, noting names with nods and eyes that bored into theirs. "Any friend of Allen's is a natural enemy of mine," he said, and laughed. "He keeps turning up at the same drinking events I go to. We've had some interesting debates. He actually believes in this whore's war. I assume you two agree with him?"

The eyes lanced challenge at them, inferring hidden knowledge. Taylor's professional respect for the man's technique bounded upward. His mind flashed back to an apparently unrelated training film, a cartoon on tactics, showing arrowed armored units racing to blast a defensive position, curling back like waves from a cliff until one forced a breach. Belatedly, he realized his subconscious was telling him that Barline's questions would be on the same order.

"All wars are bad from most points of view," Taylor answered.

"You're a Major?"

"Yes, sir."

"Don't 'sir' me. Meaningless bullshit. Call me Ben."

"No, I don't think I want to do that." Taylor met the eyes and held them. "Your reputation's preceded you, Mr. Barline.

I'd rather keep things formal. I'm not as mentally nimble as the Captain and I could talk myself into a hole very easily."

Barline said, "That's funny. My next question was going to be if you'd do the talking for the junior officers and you already answered that and told them to keep their mouths shut at the same time."

"They can say whatever they want. I wasn't around when you talked to Allen before. God willing, I won't be again. They're officers and responsible adults. I believe they'll speak honestly."

Reaching for his drink, Taylor caught the worried frowns of the others and ignored them.

"Does that mean you'll answer questions honestly, Major?"

"I didn't say anyone would answer questions, Mr. Barline. If I choose to, I'll be as honest as I can."

" 'As I can.' That's an interesting qualification already. Does that mean you'll lie to me only if you think you have to?"

"No, sir, it means I'll stop lying to you when you tell me when you stopped beating your wife."

Barline laughed and signalled the waiter, crooking a finger in the standard western manner, a gesture reserved by the Vietnamese for calling animals. When the waiter arrived, he spoke in his direction, rather than to him. The waiter's eyes met Taylor's and he smiled, the lips underlining sadness and appreciation for someone's understanding. His parting glance for the back of Barline's head was venomous.

Ignorant of the exchange, the writer continued. "Seriously, what do you think of what we're doing? Do you think we should be interfering here?"

Taylor rolled his eyes. "You really believe we're as stupid as you say we are. In the first place, I go where the Congress says I go. I don't like any war. My friends are dying here. I could be next, in this fat-assed chair. And who says we're interfering?"

"The whole world. Don't you think you were interfering at My Lai?"

"You're doing it again. First it was 'we' interfering and now it's 'you' at My Lai. I'm supposed to melt with guilt and pour out through my own ass, defending My Lai, right? Listen, if

—if—there was a massacre at Mv Lai, it's my reputation, my country, that's smeared. I only hope whoever's responsible is caught and tried.''

"And I'm supposed to believe all professional soldiers are so virtuous."

"As virtuous as you people are unbiased."

Barline's keyed-up searching manner had changed to steady determination. His right hand clasped a kneecap, the skin stretched across the bulge of the knuckles. Taylor had the feeling the man was weighing him and it rankled.

Barline said, "Let's forget My Lai—.''

"I wish we could," Harker said. Barline fired a look of annoyance at his presumption and faced Taylor again.

"Let's look at the overall picture. We came here as the world's policeman. Can you justify that?"

"No, not really. On the other hand, I can't justify being taxed to support everyone in the world, or why we're the fat dummy who sends food to every inefficient slob who asks for it. The non-interference thing's two-edged, isn't it? And while we're asking questions, how come you guys never dump on a leftist regime with one of your propaganda barrages?"

"Propaganda? Ridiculous!"

"You bet your ass, ridiculous. And you've convinced a lot of people they don't have a thing left to lose. No American or Vietnamese on our side has gotten even one percent of the ink you spilled over that rice-brokering usurer or that silly little shit who got executed because he only tried to blow up McNamara. I'm tired of seeing my people die for bushwhackers and a government you won't let us deal with."

"In effect, then, you're simply confessing that the military intervention has been a mistake. You're agreeing with me."

"On that, if nothing else." Taylor leaned forward, driving a finger at the table top to make his point. "It won't be long before the Middle East blows up again. If the Arabs ever get their gear in order, they'll waltz across Israel. When they win, they'll throw a party that'll make Dachau look like a garden club meeting. It's horrible to contemplate, but intervention there'd mean confrontation with the Soviets and the whole socialist world. And for what? A bunch of Jews who ran off the Palestinians in the first place and who've got no oil in the second place. If we learn anything here, it better be the complete immorality and impracticality of interference. It'll be hell on the Jews, but those people're never satisfied. They must have four times the territory the UN allowed them."

Barline had grown increasingly rigid as Taylor's monologue continued. At the end, he was taut, perched on the edge of his chair, fists bunched in his lap.

"You bigoted sonofabitch." The cursing wheezed through lips thin as blades.

Taylor raised a placating hand. "I understand how you feel. I've got friends MIA here I thought of as brothers, friends in cemeteries back home. When the Palestinians get done with the Jews, I'll feel the same about them as you feel about my friends. I really mean that, Mr. Barline."

Backing away from the raised hand as if it signalled contaimination, Barline rose, his progress erratic and stressed. He opened his mouth to speak, shut it, and finally pointed to the other two men at the table before getting words out.

"Do you work with them?"

"I'm assigned to MACV." Taylor made it sound like a negative. "Another paper-shuffler."

"That's too bad." Barline was regaining a cold control. "I was hoping you were a real soldier here on R&R. I wish you were getting shot at every minute of your life."

When no one answered in any way, Barline scanned them all once more, then spoke to Taylor again.

"I make a bad enemy, Major."

"You've been my enemy for years."

Unspeaking, Barline spun on his heel and stormed out the door leading to the pool. Allen's heavy exhalation broke the silence at the table, and then he said, "You really put your foot in it, Major. Didn't you know he's Jewish?"

"I knew it a long time ago." He laughed, a silent movement of his shoulders. "He really got steamed, didn't he?"

Harker's quick movement sent a twist of pain across his face, but he pressed his question anyway. "You're really that anti-Semitic? You'd bait him like that?"

"Anti-Semitic? Hell, no. I'm not even anti-Israel or pro-Arab. In fact, I admire the Israelis. If I had to make a choice, I'd probably throw in with them. I just wanted to drop a hot rock in Barline's fucking gizzard. Let him hold my end of the stick for a while."

"I don't know." Concern aged Harker. "He's good with his hatchet."

"Forget it. He hates our guts. Why be nice to him?"

"He's right," Allen said. "Barline's not interested in any facts that don't prove his viewpoint. I can't see what he could do to harm us more than he already has."

"At least he left already." Harker nodded toward the side door. "Here come the girls."

The woman with Ly could have been her younger sister, judging by their similar beauty. Shorter by about an inch, her mini flamed oranges and yellows. Her hair was cropped close, an ebony helmet, and where Ly seemed to drift across the polished floor, the shorter one walked athletically, as though she might break into a dance at each stride. She smiled a welcome at the men who stood waiting their arrival.

"This is Le Thi Dao, Major Taylor. I don't believe you've met?" Ly put her hand on the girl's shoulder, presenting her.

"Never had the pleasure." He took her hand and she smiled with a bold self-assurance. It made her less gamin and more woman.

Allen stepped up with a chair for her. "Dao already knows me and she's met Harker." She nodded at Harker and thanked Allen with a glance.

"The world is full of secrets and surprises," Taylor observed, holding the chair for Ly.

Dao was immediately interested. "Secrets, Major?"

Taylor indicated the younger men. "These two were giving me a bad time because I asked Ly to meet me here without telling them. Now I learn they expected to meet you and they didn't tell me."

"Oh, no! Not planned. I arrange meet my friend, not know Hal and Bill be here."

"You've known them long?"

"I meet Hal when he only one week Vietnam. My husband then with—I think you call Information Ministry? I meet Hal at party. Sometimes now I see here, sometimes other parties. He help me with my bad English."

Allen said, "People continue to invite her to their homes even though her husband's assigned to Da Lat now. She's too pretty to forget."

She smiled again and this time Taylor couldn't fully interpret it, felt he'd missed something. She pointed a flame-tipped finger at Allen. "I know English word for you. I look dictionary, special. You fat—flatterer!"

The group laughed and she threw herself back in her chair with a triumphant smirk. The conversation drifted on then, easy words floating on subjects that meandered across familiar, pleasant experiences. Taylor tended to contribute little, content to savor.

Ly rose reluctantly, showing her watch as apology. "I must go. My mother will worry if I am not home before they leave. There is a reception and they must arrive by seven."

"Wait, I go with you." Dao stood and Taylor used the distraction to move behind Ly and whisper "Seven-thirty?"

She nodded shortly, combining the move with a turn toward Dao. "You must leave also?"

The shorter woman indicated the room with a pugnacious jut of her jaw. "Better to leave. People see me with three Americans, alone, be talk, talk, talk."

"Why don't you walk the ladies to the door?" Harker suggested. "I'll wait here, if no one minds."

The women hurriedly walked back to pat his shoulder and reassure him, then headed for the door. Taylor and Allen fell in beside them, stopping at the door to watch them leave for their respective cars.

Allen said, "As Winter would put it, 'Life's hell in the combat zone.'"

A car hummed through the parking lot, coming toward the front door in order to turn out onto the street. The horn blew as it drew abreast and Barline, eyes bright, leaned past the driver to wave at them. The driver looked quickly and returned to his job.

"He looks a little less furious." Taylor started back to the table.

"I wouldn't bet on it. He'll try like hell to get at you."

"You worry too much."

"Maybe you can get him up on the roof to discuss it." Taylor turned sharply to see Allen's eyes belying the seriousness of his voice.

"I never mix business with pleasure."

Allen feigned a shudder. "My God. You've managed to pervert the entire work ethic with one short sentence."

27

IN THE DARKNESS of Ly's room, Taylor sat in a chair buttoning his shirt. The smell of her body clung to him and he inhaled, luxuriating. She stirred and he let the breath trickle free, sensuousness even in the simple relaxation of his rib cage. He stood, turning for one last look at the mounded sheet.

"I have found an apartment."

Her voice hit like a bright light and he stumbled, moving to the bedside.

"You've found what?"

"I have found an apartment." The sheet rustled as she sat up, bringing the material with her to form a truncated pyramid in the dark. "I am not some prostitute to entertain customers in dark corners. I do not want you sneaking the streets in the night. I am going to live in my own apartment. You may come there when you choose."

He sat beside her and she stroked the line of his jaw with a single finger.

"Your parents will never allow it."

"They will be unhappy. They cannot stop me."

Her hand lingered before sliding gently along his cheekbone. He twisted to kiss the palm.

"There has to be a better way, Ly."

She sighed. "There is no other way. I want you to be able to come to me. I have arranged it."

Wind bells stirred outside and a tendril of his consciousness grasped the distraction, weaving the melancholy night-chiming into a vague symbolism of movement without freedom.

"I don't know what to say, Ly. I want you too much to let you go and I don't want to see you hurt."

"There is no need to say anything. You may come to me or not, that is the only choice now. If we continue this way, there will be greater shame for my parents. They will find out I have dishonored their house. I must leave here."

"Then leave as my wife."

"I would like that."

He bent to kiss her and she warded him off. "No! And do

not speak to me of love!" She turned warily to face him again and he straightened. "I know you need me as I need you," she continued. "My path is to look for love with you, I see that. You cannot know how hard I tried to deny it. You would marry me now for the pleasure I give you. It would be easy because you feel sorry for me, and I for you. Sympathy and need are not love."

"You won't believe me if I tell you I love you?"

"I would die to hear you say it if I believed you. That is why you must not say it. I must believe it before you say it."

He reached up to cover her hand. "What do I have to do to convince you? Are you going to set some task, like a princess in a fairy tale?"

She laughed softly, the sound melding with the wind bells in his ear, and pulled at his hair. "Don't make me laugh when I'm being serious! No, there are no tasks. I pray only that you will be careful." She turned her hand to hold his and squeezed. "I am very selfish. If I ever lose you—."

"Lose me? Try to get rid of me!"

She made a noise, non-verbal, exasperated. "Don't treat me like a fool! You know what I mean! You are changing, you worry. All of you. Something is happening to you."

He disengaged her hand. "Have you said anything about this to anyone else?"

"Of course not!"

"Good. Don't. You're imagining again."

She tossed her head, black hair cascading across her shoulder, an intensified shadow spilling down the covering sheet. "Not as much as you, believing you can lie to me. We will discuss it no more. I only ask that you be careful."

"Sure. How do I find out where this apartment is?"

"I will contact you at your office." She pushed his shoulder. "Now go, before it is too late." The paleness of her face came to him for a last kiss and broke away. "Quickly!"

He did as he knew he must, trailing his hand the length of her leg as he moved away.

"Good night, my Ly."

"And good night to you, my Charles." Urgency replaced tenderness. "And be quiet! The guard is gone from the gate, but if Hong has returned, she has ears that hear every sound."

He moved silently down the stairs and out to the gate, where he turned and searched the grounds. There was no movement, no noise save the working of insects. Easing through the gate and onto the deserted street, he stepped off on the long walk back to MACV. At the corner he moved into the bright daub beneath the lamp post and a streetwalker going home from a wasted evening across the street from BEQ One automatically arched her back and swiveled her hips at him in one last try. A look at his unswerving course told her he hadn't even noticed her and when she saw his thunderous scowl, she was glad, and hurried past him.

Chi Hong had no way of knowing any of the action on the street, as she remained in the shadow of the old tree next to the house, her black clothes making her one with the night. When she was sure the *Thieu Ta* was not returning, she hurried to the house, grumbling to herself.

"The huge fool! They will be home in minutes! Longer than two hours! My bones are broken from standing still so long. But I would bet that he is wearier!"

Abruptly, she giggled, stifling the sound with her hand, then composed herself and padded on bare feet through the house to listen at Ly's door.

Moaning sobs stabbed through the paneling and struck at her. She retreated to the living room as silently as she'd come, where she stole a cigarette from the lacquer box on the table and lit it.

"They will shout with anger when they think they have caught me," she muttered to herself, needing the sound of conversation to steel her for the inevitable scene. "That will give her warning to stop her tears."

She savored another forbidden puff.

"Perhaps they will be late enough for me to have another one. Even two."

The anticipation in her eyes guttered and a frown pained her face.

"My precious blossom!" She rocked back and forth. "What can I do?"

The gate groaned shut with its customary thump. *Chi* Hong dried a tear, cursing herself for wasting time like a foolish old woman, and dragged furiously on the cigarette.

28

TAYLOR SQUATTED IN THE STREET, drawing numbers in the dirt with a fingertip. The old woman in front of him huffed scornfully, erased the number and tripled it. He sighed.

"*Ba*, I want to buy five limes. Only five. You ask more than the tree is worth."

The two women watching giggled. Behind them the market clamored a babble of commerce.

The woman ignored the two watchers. "They are good limes. That is my best price."

"Truly—the best price anyone ever got for five limes. Because I am an American does not mean I am a fool."

The old woman speared him with a look. "Oh?"

Laughter from the other two applauded her point.

"Certainly I am not such a fool as to pay that much. I can buy durians for that price."

She shrugged, again wrinkling the furrowed face in clear disdain. "You do not look old enough to need durians. However—."

Taylor had to grin, knowing he'd been stuck again. Durians were an evil-smelling but delicious fruit, supposed to restore sexual vigor to old men. The listeners leaned on each other and howled while his antagonist affected bored triumph. He tried to regroup.

"All I want is a fair price. I know you will charge me more than you would charge a Vietnamese, but please do not try to charge me as much as an American."

She sniffed. "If you did not speak so well I would ask double." She drew a line under her number.

"If I talk twice as much, will you charge half as much?"

Her tongue clucked aggravation. "You already talk enough, *Thieu Ta!* While we argue I have no other customers. You cost me money!"

He pointed at the numbers. "At this price, you need no other customers."

"Oh, all right! So I can have some peace, I will cut the price in half! You steal both my fruit and my time!"

"You are very kind. I will try to equal your thoughtfulness." He erased her figure with the edge of his hand and wrote another number. "Sell me the limes for that price and I will be gone. I will be happy and you can brag all your life about how you cheated the big American."

She rocked back and grabbed the leg of one of the other women, hand over mouth, laughing until her eyes squeezed shut. Finally, still laughing, she nodded. He counted the money onto the hard callouses and ingrained dirt of a palm that had never known any greater luxury than a new tool. He drew out his cigarettes, shaking free a half-dozen. He extended them to the woman, indicating her friends at the same time.

"Take these. They are payment for the lesson." The woman frowned uncertainly. He gestured with them. "Now I know why the women do the marketing in Vietnam. No man can resist you."

She took the cigarettes quickly, laughing again, waving as he left.

The market was his fascination. The sensory impact of so much variety drove away disciplined appreciation and he simply absorbed. The warning-sharp scent of *ot*, the crimson hot peppers, mingled with the seaside smell of *tom kho* and *ca thu*, dried shrimp and fish. Next to them stood a wicker basket of *chom choms*—orange-red hulls like golfball-sized cockleburs, hiding a succulent fruit that rivaled the best table grapes.

"*Thieu Ta!*" He turned at the call, puzzled, and discovered a boy, perhaps ten years old, arched backward in order to look up into his face. His hair was rough-cut, shaggy over eyes far too wise. Surprisingly, his frayed khaki shirt and shorts were spotless.

"A friend wants to talk to you," the boy said. "Do you really speak our language?"

"A few words. Who is this friend?"

The boy tugged his shorts with one hand and picked his nose with the other. "I do not know. He gave me ten piasters to tell you I would take you to meet him. He said when I bring you there, he will give me another ten."

Taylor fumbled in his pocket. "I will pay you. Tell me where I am to go."

The boy stepped back. "I cannot tell you. I must bring you or he will not pay me."

"If I pay you, it is the same thing."

"No. He said he would have other things for me to do if I do this right."

Possibilities whirled through Taylor's mind. It could be a set-up. It could be an informant with something urgent. The wry prospect that neither of those excluded the other twisted a corner of his mouth in an unconscious smile. The boy noticed it and responded quickly.

"You will come?"

Taylor nodded and the boy immediately darted past him, knifing through the crowd. Taylor struggled to keep pace, handicapped by his bulk. The boy glanced back and slowed, audacious with tolerant amusement. They walked two blocks away from the market and he stopped, pointing.

"Bamboo Palace Bar. You friend waits inside." He trotted ahead, up a narrow staircase. Taylor followed slowly, increasingly glad of the belt-holstered .38 under the utility jacket. It lacked the authority of Apeneck, but it had been a wise choice over the piddling .25 automatic.

At the head of the stairs the boy pushed open the door and waited. Passing him, Taylor entered slowly, scanning the room. Some Koreans at the bar inspected him casually. In the dim distance a man in a white shirt waved. The boy squatted on the top step and Taylor moved toward the table.

"Welcome to the Bamboo Palace, Major." Taylor recognized Trung just as he spoke. "I am honored that you would visit with me. I am already in your debt for so many things." He waved at the chair across from him. "I have already ordered beer for you. A small portion of repayment for all of your hospitality."

"We have been asking about you. We hear you are being very correct, living up to your end of our bargain."

Trung's eyes wandered as if he was having trouble controlling them. "Yes, our bargain. The world is full of bargains. Unfortunately, the one I am supposed to have made, the one for great wealth, seems to have escaped me. And there are people who still believe I earned the money at their expense."

"Life can be cruel."

"Especially when one must live a lie, with the truth but a breath from leaving his mouth."

The waiter came with the beer and both men ignored him,

staring at each other. Trung broke the contact to sip from his glass.

"You sent the boy after me because you want to talk about life?"

Trung put his glass on the table and his eyes floated off on some independent search again. "The people I have offended are not vindictive men. They know I am trustworthy because there have been no arrests. My good friend Tu is another matter."

"He survives."

Trung's face grew thoughtful and the eyes came back to rest on Taylor's hands. "Yes, but at what price? We are very concerned about him."

"Please." Taylor rocked his head back and forth. "We know each other too well to trade hints. You know the agreement. You cooperate by your silence and no one comes looking for you. You are not worried about Tu. If there is a thing in your belly that you must say, then say it."

The strained affability broke down, fractured by anger that froze Trung immobile in his chair. "I am not as helpless as you think! And you are not as safe as you think! Have you thought that we knew exactly where you were, to send the boy for you? He could have had a different purpose."

He stopped and tried to re-establish his calmness with a long drink. When he spoke again, the hatred was a mere undertone. "I have heard suggestions that your death would convince certain people of my loyalty."

"Then those people are mad. You have no loyalty. You are no real Viet Cong. Why speak of my death? You will do nothing about it." Trung tensed and Taylor gestured him back, careful to keep the motion soft, not trusting the fury building in himself, not wanting the hand to turn to a fist. The harsh sound of his own voice warned him further of his dwindling control, paradoxically serving as an additional goad.

"You will not even help a Special Section trap me, Trung. You have friends? I have friends. When they come for you, where will you go? To the north? You would be safe there. Would you like to live in the north? Or spend the rest of your life in the Rung Sat or hiding in alleys? No, you would not like that. And I do not want to worry all the time. Look at me. I will kill you if I have to, do you understand? For fifty U.S. dollars I can have you disappear forever. If I die, you can never find enough money to buy my people. While I live, you live. My life is not in your hands, yours is in mine. Save your threats for your whores.''

His progress to the doorway drew another disinterested glance from the Koreans. At each step he considered which way to leap at the sound of a shot, the choices flipping past his eyes like line sketches. There was a chill in his spine, like being on point, praying the first shot misses, praying to make cover before the second one. The sound of the door closing behind him unleashed a shudder of relief.

The boy was at the foot of the stairs. He looked up at Taylor's approach.

"You got Sa-lem, OK?"

Almost reflexively, he shook out a cigarette for the boy, a part of his mind taking pride in the steadiness of his hand.

"Not Sa-lem," the shrill voice complained.

The picture burned into Taylor's mind, the banality of the childish dissatisfaction contrasting with the threat of violent death moments earlier to shock his mind into suspension.

"Why not Sa-lem?"

The repetition got him moving again. Handing the boy some piasters without bothering to count, he headed back toward the market. It occurred to him he still had the five limes in his pocket. A tense smile brought glances from others on the sidewalk while he wondered what they'd say if they knew he was thinking of Winter's face if five limes had shown up on his personal effects inventory. He continued toward the center of town, calming himself, objectively turning over the ramifications of the meeting.

There was the chance he was already targeted. Trung could've started the wheels the day he got out. He mulled that, facing the prospect.

Trung wouldn't set him up and then call him in to hint at it. But would he call in to let him know he was a future target in order to enjoy watching the fear build? It took another block to discard that possibility.

Again, Trung would consider his own skin before anything else.

By the time he entered the lobby of the Rex BOQ he'd convinced himself it was nothing more than a bluff. That, and a warning that the VC now knew for a fact that Tu was a prisoner. The elevator groaned like an ancient curse all the way to the roof garden, irritating, opening the way for rage at being threatened to surface again. Stepping out, he collected himself once more before moving into the restaurant.

Harker greeted him from one of the tables by the railing. "You look like a man with a problem."

"Amen to that." Taylor sat down, waving off the approaching waitress, and described his day. Through it all, the faint sound of traffic floated up to them as a prosaic backdrop.

Harker waited until Taylor was through. "Stupid bastard," he said. "Winter and Loc'll have him wasted before he knows what hit him. Is he crazy?"

"It's no big thing—he had me puckered, but I don't think he was serious. There'd be nothing in it for him, you know?"

"Maybe. For all you know, he's thought up a way to set you up and turn a profit at the same time."

"Thanks. No, I think he's gloating because he's out and back in business."

"And you better watch yourself. Business would be a lot easier for him if you were dead."

"He knows better. I told him you'd even things up if anything happened to me."

Harker grinned wryly. "Well, shit. Goody. Now he'll be looking for both of us."

"It'll keep you alert."

Harker snapped his fingers. "Speaking of such fun things reminds me of something I forgot and meant to tell you before I got sidetracked. Tho worked over Tu. Want to guess what he learned?"

"Tu's the illegitimate son of Ho Chi Minh?"

"Not even that. Tho gave him some of his best and Tu just kept screaming he'd never talk. He really wants to be a martyr."

"Then Tho's his best friend." Unobtrusively, Taylor moved his head closer to the guardrail, where he could pull the superheated air rising up the cliffside of the building through his nose and drown the smells oozing through his memory.

Harker caught the sudden distance in Taylor's eyes. It disturbed him. The more he thought about it, the more he decided the Major had been behaving differently for quite a while.

He tried to put his finger on it. There wasn't anything physical he could see, no nervous movements or habits. And the eyes were the same as he'd first seen them, volatile, changing all the time. But something was missing. He tossed the notion around for a bit and discarded it. Nothing was gone. Something was added. That was it. That would explain the change.

The man wasn't careful now, he was cautious. For all his professionalism when he first arrived, he seemed to be edging toward a fuller involvement in what was going on around him. It was as though he'd come to Vietnam prepared to do whatever was asked of him to the best of his ability, and in doing it, had learned to care how it turned out.

It was amusing conjecture, but nothing to push. He was still a man to be treated with care. Harker decided to hoard his discovery and indulge in more harmless small talk.

He asked, "When you were down in Vung Tau did you get a chance to drive around?"

Taylor continued to stare down on the squirming mass of traffic. "No, we got out to the beach and that was about it."

"I just wondered."

"Why?"

"I thought you might have been near Allen's ranch."

Taylor's head swung around and his brows drew together in a line. "His ranch? He's shacking with someone in Vung Tau?"

Harker's stomach jumped, the surge that comes with recognizing a stupid error. He worked to be nonchalant.

"Not really in Vung Tau. There's a house they visit sometimes. You met her at the Cercle Sportif, remember? The woman with Mrs. Ly?"

"For Christ's sake, she's married!" He balled a fist on the railing, looking as if he would strike at the city. "What's wrong with him?"

"Old story. Young wife, old husband." He hurried on, nervousness tightening his voice. "They're in love, Major. Really."

"Who gives a damn? Here we're busting our butts to keep as far out of sight as possible and he's making it with a married woman? Does Winter know any of this? He can't know—he'd have fired Allen up-country long ago.''

Silence fell over them, padded by the shuffling and bleating from the streets. Harker turned toward it, letting his eye carry down Nguyen Hue to the heavy brown river. The swamp-smell of it came to him at that moment, carried in on a cooling breeze. He turned back to Taylor.

"I probably shouldn't have told you, but you'd have learned pretty soon, anyhow. Mrs. Ly's apartment's in the same building as hers, Major. The first time you go see her in the new pad, you'll probably hear the whole story from them.''

"How long's it been going on?''

Relief loosened his muscles and Harker took a surprisingly welcome deep breath. The scenario was familiar now—Taylor grim, but trying to understand. When he was angry, he was a little frightening, as though all of his attention wasn't necessarily concerned with a solution, but that part of him was straining to jump directly to the source of the problem and destroy it.

"They've been together almost since Allen got here. She's got it all set up to go to the States as soon as he rotates. Once she's there, they'll get married. She's not a legal wife, Major. Once she's out of here, her Colonel won't be able to do a thing.''

"How do you know she's not another PX lover?''

Harker blanched and struck back. "Is that what Mrs. Ly is?''

Taylor's face froze, then, "I deserved that. You think this deal is straight, do you? Allen and the woman—what's her name?—they're serious?''

"Her name's Dao, Le Thi Dao, and I've never seen two people more in love. Never saw anyone suffer so much for it, either. They're good people. They don't like this slipping around.''

"The Old Man ought to know about it. He could get caught with his ass out.''

"No chance. They're too careful. Allen's only got something over a month to do and then it'll be all over.''

Taylor squeezed the guardrail, making up his mind.

"OK, I'll go along. But it's a mistake. If two people know

267

anything in this place, it's a cinch someone else knows it, too, and they're just laying back waiting to use it for some kind of profit. I just hope Allen gets a drop and gets the hell out of here before the lid flies off.''

Harker recognized the time to end the conversation. "You going back to the villa?"

Taylor nodded, and they left for the elevator. "I've got to tell Winter about this thing with Trung," the older man said, and Harker laughed.

"I'd like to have been there to watch Trung being brave. And I'd like to see what old Winter does when he hears about it."

"You've got some sense of humor." Taylor made himself grin and turned away to punch the elevator button, grateful for something to do that guaranteed Harker couldn't see the anger swelling in him all over again.

29

WILLY AND ORDWAY STOPPED AT THE CORNER, leaning against the wall of the Rex BOQ, watching the activity in the park that divided Nguyen Hue. To their right front, beyond the looming Vietnamese Marine Memorial, the Senate building cowered behind its concertina wire, an anticlimactic dot to the exclamation point of Le Loi Boulevard. Closer, the fountain at the intersection danced in the sun, its splashing a delight to the eye and denied to the ear by the traffic. A tired breeze brought them the smell of sunbaked dirt freshly watered. Miller paid no attention, but Ordway closed his eyes and was overwhelmed by memories of lawn sprinklers and shaded porches. His tension refused to be so easily dissuaded and his eyes popped open.

"You see him?" he asked.

"He said to be here. He's around," Miller answered, filtering apprehension from his voice. He thought of every name he'd ever heard and called them down on Mantell. Where the hell was he?

A black trooper in fatigues approached them, his face half-hidden by huge reflective shades.

"You Miller?"

"Yeah. Who're you?"

"This your honky?"

Ordway leaned away from the wall and half turned to Miller.

"I told you this was a bunch of shit. I knew we'd run into a bunch of heads." He turned back to the stranger. "You just blew it, asshole. The fucker you work for can't move his stuff without Willy and Willy can't do a fucking thing without me, and you piss me off. The deal's a bummer."

Miller's knees trembled. "What?"

"I said fuck it, Willy. I don't have to put up with this asshole, even if you want to. Fuck him!"

"Hey, man, hey, hey. Just be cool, man." The trooper put a careful hand on Ordway's shoulder. "I wasn't thinkin', you know? Like, I didn't mean no harm. I didn't know you was so tight with the brother here, you know? Just be cool."

Naked fear reverberated from the man's manner. Miller had been there himself, known the feeling of looking down a tunnel with a beating waiting at the other end. Ordway had put them in good position.

"It's OK, buddy," he said, playing the game. "He didn't mean nothing. We can go along, see what's on."

Ordway stepped away from the guide's hand. "Keep your fucking hands to yourself."

Miller sidled a few inches closer to him, afraid to interfere and afraid Ordway would push too hard. "Let me handle it, OK?" He got between Ordway and the stranger. "What's the deal?"

"You follow me," the man said, glad to deal with Miller. "Let me get ten, fifteen yards ahead and you follow. Don't make no signals and don't go lookin' around. Anything funny and we got people around to put a stop to it."

"Anything funny?" Miller was contemptuous. "Shee-it. We're here to take care of business, man. Go ahead and take your lead. We'll be behind you."

The man moved off, to any observer no more than another GI enjoying some free time in the city. Miller and Ordway trailed him, wondering how many of the eyes on the street were watching them, wondering which window or vehicle might hide an aimed gun. They tried to make conversation for a block, but by the time they reached the intersection at the end of Nguyen Hue, both were grateful the other had run out of things to say.

They were led in a complete round of the block, turning on Le Thanh Ton toward the towering steeple of the Catholic church in Kennedy Square until they intersected Tu Do. Turning right again, they moved toward the Senate building and the Caravelle Hotel. Right again on Le Loi, they passed the Marine statue. At the Nguyen Hue corner, the trooper waited for them to catch up.

"Everything's cool," he said. "You wait here. Be a van come along in a minute. You get in the back."

"How do we know it?" Miller asked.

"You don't." The man grinned and a gold tooth sang in the sunlight. "We know you. The man'll call you."

Watching him leave, Miller said, "You scared me to death, you crazy hillbilly."

"Us southern boys know how to handle uppity niggers." Ordway buffed his nails on his jacket.

Miller shook his head.

When they heard the voice call out "Miller!" they both jumped. Another black leaned across the front seat of a Navy gray van, gesturing. They trotted across the sidewalk and climbed in the back. The voice from the front shouted "Close it!" and Miller did. They were in darkness immediately, a partition between them and the driver, and the rear windows painted out. Over the sound of impatient honking a key grated in the lock outside. They barely got planted on the benches against the walls when the machine jerked into motion.

The ride seemed interminable. Miller agonized in the hot-metal darkness, afraid for Ordway. Imagining the things that could happen to them if anything went wrong, he looked at his thoughts as objectively as possible and conceded that an unworthy part of his fear was purely for himself. Bouncing and pitching, he kept reminding himself that getting inside a major drug operation was worth any risk. They were into their big step. Without it, their best bust would be Mantell.

He noticed the van was moving differently, with a pattern shaping up. First, a dead stop, then a steady acceleration, a steady deceleration, and another stop. Residential patterns. They were out of the main part of town and moving on a long street with less traffic and regular intersections.

The movement stopped, as though even that slim motion of location was too much. They bounced harder, despite slowing to a bare crawl. Miller was sure it was an alley and congratulated his judgement when the van stopped to make a slow torturous turn. A noise behind them could only be the closing of a gate. The next noise was garage doors slamming. The back of the van opened and the driver was ushering them out. Another man, Vietnamese, watched with eyes as unrevealing as the M-16 leveled across his forearm while the driver checked them for weapons. Satisfied, he indicated a paneled door and shoved them toward it, using just enough force to overcome their inertia.

Taking the lead, Miller pushed through and stepped into the room beyond. He stopped so suddenly Ordway bumped him from behind. Jammed in the doorway, they both goggled at the scene before them.

A naked man, his body polished with sweat, sat on the only furniture in the room, a bed with no legs. The man was black, color and size startling against the sheets. His back was against the wall, legs flat in front of him. The lap formed was occupied by a tiny naked woman, her shining black hair barely even with the man's lips. Twin lamps flanked the bed, providing the only light, enough for the two arrivals to see there were no windows and only one other door. Nor was there paint or wallpaper. Every surface inch except the floor was totally covered with pictures of women, ranging from centerfolds to the clinically obscene.

The girl on the man's lap smiled greeting with a dazed mindlessness. The man laughed throatily, twisting the taut breast nearest Miller and Ordway to aim the nipple at them.

"Don't move, cats. Got you covered."

He threw back his head and bayed amusement at the ceiling. The girl looked slowly back to him and burst into childish laughter with him before looking down at the hand still gripping her. She had difficulty focusing and seemed puzzled by what she saw. Relocating the two men in the doorway proved just as difficult and when she accomplished it, she laughed again, as happily as before.

The unreality of the thing set off a hum in Miller's ears. He inhaled to steady himself and was hammered by the sweet, thick smell, a composite of hash, tobacco, sweat, and sex. He had an almost instant erection and perspiration washed his face as he tried to think away the swelling in his trousers.

The man on the bed boosted the woman to her feet and slapped her rump. She struggled to balance.

"Run along, baby," the man said, never taking his eyes from Miller. "I got business. Go do something."

She wobbled across the mattress, her stability only slightly improved when she reached the harder surface of the floor. She was still smiling as she left.

"Pretty." The word snapped Miller's and Ordway's attention away from her and back to him. "Startin' to run down, though. Oriental chicks can't handle hard shit. Don't take long, and it's all they little heads got left. She be on the street earnin' her keep in a little while. Plenty to take her place."

Miller nodded, totally dumb.

The man took his silence to be impatience. "Not much for small talk, are you? All right. You been sayin' you can get my stuff back to the States. How much?"

With his crotch finally under control, Miller could act more sure of himself. "We got a system. But I don't know your name. I can't say, 'Hey, you,' all the time."

"That's good for now. When I think you need my name, I'll tell you. What's your deal?"

Miller shrugged and started again. "My cousin's an officer on a merchant ship. Ordway's uncle owns a couple gift shops in New Orleans and Miami. He's ready to branch out into import-export and Ordway's gonna handle that part of the business, OK? So the deal is, we pick up the stuff and get it into the States."

"That's what I heard. My man said all you wanted was to be in the middle."

A chill tiptoed on Miller's neck. Carefully, he said, "That's what I told him."

The bulky torso pulled away from the wall. "Say what?"

"I told him we could move it. How you pay for us movin' it is something we got to talk about."

"I knew there'd be fuckin' jive in this."

Miller found a smile. "There's room for everybody."

"Room to do what?"

"Deal a little. See, me and Ordway, we got friends in a

272

couple of towns. We want paid in merchandise."

"I pay you with my stuff so you can deal against me? What the fuck's wrong with you? Think I set myself up like this bein' stupid?" He swept a thick arm in an arc taking in the room.

"We don't want to work your territory." Ordway stepped forward a pace. "We can agree on what's yours and what's ours. You can't sell to the whole country."

The man finally got to his feet. He was taller than either of them and young. Miller guessed him to be no more than twenty-five, but the stomach was beginning to round and the muscles across his chest were acquiring a smoothness that could only be fat. Enough tone remained in the body to give him a certain grace as he stepped off the mattress.

"I'm gonna give it one helluva try," he said, holding up a clenched fist. "I am that tight with the zipper-heads in Thailand and Laos and them Chinese dudes up in Burma. They have all done business with me, face to face, and they knows I pays cash and I pays now and they ain't no shit in my action. They trusts me."

"You trust them?" Miller asked.

"Gooks? Fuck no, man."

"That's what I figured. And that's why I figured you'd want to keep out of the shipping end of the operation. It's the trickiest part. We'll handle it and be happy with a little territory of our own."

Pacing, scratching, the man muttered to himself, shooting baleful glares at Miller and Ordway until he appeared to have come to a decision.

"How much you figure to charge to get the stuff in?"

"Twenty-five percent of the weight."

The man's eyes bulged. "What?" He took a step toward them. "Fool, you think I been lookin' down guns for a fuckin' year so I could get ripped by a couple jive assholes? Get outta here 'fore I have somebody break you an arm. Go on, git!"

Miller turned to Ordway. "I don't think he'll go for twenty-five." Ordway refused to look away from the man, who suddenly flung himself back on the bed, laughing.

"Cool," he said. "Good. OK, let's quit shuckin'. You make me believe you can do it and you can skim two percent off each shipment. And you can sell at my price in Miami or New Orleans."

Ordway said, "Twenty percent. Norfolk south and New Orleans east. Whatever price we can get."

The man looked his way. "Last white I talked to said he was part of an organization. Big deal. You mixed up with them?"

"No. I'm like you. Out for number one."

The phrase generated a flick of the studying eyes from Ordway to Miller and back again. "Best not be one of them. Soon's I get ready, I squash them mother-fuckers."

"I hope so. Less competition." Ordway left to study the walls, leaving the negotiations to Miller.

Knowing everything was going by the numbers, Miller still wanted to call his partner back, but instead he squatted, Vietnamese-style, and haggled. In a moment he was enjoying it. A minute later he was imagining the discussion was real, that he was arguing for first claim on the drug business throughout what had been the Confederate states. Grudgingly, twisting and complaining, he watched his percentage waste away to fifteen, his empire whittled to seven states. When it was done he was tired and yet there was a sense of elation, a feeling of something important going forward. He was just starting to wonder why that should be when the man spoke again.

"Now tell me exactly how this shippin' thing is supposed to work."

Ordway whirled from his study of the pictures. "No fuckin' way, man. We'll pick up the stuff whenever you say and deliver it wherever you want it, but the only two people who know about it when it's in our hands is Miller and me."

The man smiled, the expression clearly false. "You two really somethin'. You think I hand over ten, twenty, fifty kilos and you give me some kind of fuckin' receipt?"

"Money up front," Ordway said, "We put enough money in a bank to cover the purchase price. When we deliver, you give us our percentage. If the shipment gets lost, we're out our end, plus the money."

"That's sweet. And what if you all take the stuff and never show up again?"

"No way. I couldn't skip if I wanted. I'm a businessman, with responsibilities. Miller can't skip and let you grease his cousin. You got hostages, man."

While they continued to argue, Miller concentrated on his own emotions, still puzzled over why he should feel so high

274

over what was nothing more than a simple scam. The idea of so much money and power was exhilarating, but there was something more going on in his head, if he could just grasp it. The man on the bed fumbled beside it for a second and came up with a cigarette. When he lit it, the flame reflected from his eyes and Miller was seeing the glass stare of his dead sister. More than anything in the world he wanted to see the man on the bed wearing the same look.

"Willy?"

Anxiety covered the word and he smiled at Ordway to dissipate it. "Just thinking," he added.

Ordway nodded, failing to dislodge the remnants of a frown. "You hear what he said? He's going to run a check on us. He needs some information."

"Sure." The sense of purpose surged through him so fiercely Miller feared it would show. He studied his boots. "You gonna run a security check, like J-2 does it?"

The man laughed. There was a change in it. Miller analyzed it, wondering if something like the new feeling he'd discovered in himself wasn't being mirrored. When he looked up, the man wore a new smile, as well.

The right corner of his mouth lifted up and the left dropped. It was a cruel, confusing picture, reminding Miller of the two masks they showed at movies and stage plays.

The man was saying, "I surely will run a security check on you. You in the big leagues, dudes. I got a man in Special Branch. In a couple weeks, I know more about you than you momma."

Miller wanted to be sick. Special Branch. Ties to CIA, MIS, the embassy, everywhere. If the man had a rat in the Special Branch files, it was all over.

He answered the questions automatically, each piece of information enlarging the cold hollow in his stomach.

He cursed the inner voice that had cheered for a kill. Why had it forgotten to remind him this prey shot back?

But he had to keep pushing. As long as he could.

30

THE DARK SHADE OF THE QUIET SIDE STREET was soothing and Winter reflected that it was even more welcome than usual. Taylor's report necessitated something to alleviate it. He glanced at him as they strolled, pleased by the other's stoic acceptance of Trung's threat.

"He said nothing about anyone else? The ones who picked him up? Tho? Chi?"

Taylor said, "No. Charlie's probably got a full book on the Vietnamese. He was really out of control for a few seconds. I think if he could identify any other Americans, he'd have let it slip then."

Sunday mornings the streets in the neighborhood of the zoo were almost free of traffic. Winter liked to walk them then, denying the decline that assailed his eyes, enlisting his memory to tell small lies about the present. It was helped by the smells of trees and cooking and masonry warming in the sun and his own Sunday-best cleanliness. As he thought about that, he looked to the right, up a cross street, and caught sight of an armored personnel carrier belching across a distant intersection and harsh truth broke through to his interior view.

He looked away, too late, thinking how, in the early days when the city grew hectic, a man was assured it would drop back to repose. Now the spasms were more and more frequent and the subsidence left the level of ease more and more behind. Still, these were the mornings when an effort could usually remind him of what used to be.

He choked off his reminiscence.

"This could get pretty messy, Tay. The only thing keeping his mouth shut is that he knows I'll have him killed if he opens it. Sooner or later that'll wear off or someone connected with Binh will scare him worse than we have." He stopped abruptly, driving a fist into his palm. "I *know* what Binh's doing. He's hiding out and waiting for this thing to resolve itself. Our sources tell us the VC are all screwed up. Even with Trung free, they don't know if we've turned Tu, or what. They're working overtime to find out. And there's a helluva split over Binh. They don't know if he's gone sour or not, and they can't find him to check."

"And if Tu dies without talking, if he knows anything, everything cools off and we're back to zero."

Winter made a small gesture of helplessness and they turned to walk up a different street.

Taylor said, "Let me take a crack at Tu."

A smile worked across Winter's face, but disappeared when he saw Taylor's seriousness. "You think you can improve on Tho's work?"

"Not the way he does things. But I think I can reach Tu."

The smile broke clear and Winter joked to take the sting out of it. "Thinking about appealing to Tu's better nature?"

Taylor's answering look was defensive. "Harker was saying Tu seems to want to be a martyr. Let me work on that. What can we lose? Tho's going to kill him in a little while, regardless."

The smooth delivery of the statement snapped Winter's head around. Taylor's manner was bland, although a flash of alarm sparked through his eyes at the suddenness of the response. It faded as quickly when no outburst accompanied the movement.

That troubled Winter. He couldn't be sure if Taylor was being satirical or demonstrating a change in his own attitude. He remembered the man's first night in-country, his reluctance to embroil himself in the underside of the situation. What would have happened if he'd been left alone to do his quiet little job? Even at that stage he'd shown a cold acceptance of killing as part of being a soldier and he'd since then amply demonstrated he could kill in anger. This new view, that a man's death should be considered inevitable, a part of the way of things and therefore inconsequential, was deeply disturbing. It was a vast, repugnant difference.

Winter brushed the thought away. The frustration of the Binh thing had him seeing hidden meanings in everything. He told himself some callousness was natural in this business. Hell, it was a necessity.

"What do you have in mind?" He heard the gruffness in his voice and hoped it would be misconstrued as skepticism.

Taylor shook his head. "No sir. I want a free hand and privacy. You'll have to trust me."

"You ask a lot. Tho's going to flip when I ask Loc to deal you in."

"Use your charm."

Winter grunted. "Wise ass. Big deal. Secrets. You better be right."

"Hey, I didn't guarantee anything."

The smile Winter turned on Taylor was meant to cut. "I expect results. I'm feeling the pressure. Now you get some."

Taylor looked blank and Winter explained. "It's part of the drawdown. I haven't even told Loc, although he's heard a rumor, so keep your mouth shut. The General says, unofficially, the Unit gets no replacements from now on."

The husband's always the last to know, Taylor thought, and said, "You're sure?"

"I'm sure." An anger that made him shiver pounded along his muscles. "It's so stupid! Always the goddam maneuvering and the deals!" He stopped, then continued more calmly. "MACV is to 'exercise selectivity' in its attrition. The Phoenix program, the Marine CAP work, the MI effort—all to be allowed to expire of normal rotational attrition, or some such bullshit. The assholes in D.C. say we're too mixed up in the politics of the war, as if it was anything but politics. They say we have to concentrate on military operations until we clear all our forces. Then they wonder why we're taking casualties. That's what makes Binh so important! If we can catch him and some like him, maybe even turn them around—if we could eliminate the terror and have some goddam peace."

Winter broke off at the look on Taylor's face, the polite pretense of interest a veil across preoccupation. Instead of angering him, it made him feel old and afraid. He set about reconstructing his normal mental pattern for this walk. Instead, his eyes sought the grimy windows, his nose burned from the tree-killing haze, and his ears admitted nothing but the hack of helicopters and rumble of trucks.

Taylor said, "We'll be out of business in no time. Kimble—."

Winter cut him off, resenting the younger man's insistence on mundane practicality, his refusal to even consider the larger issue. "We've got one important operation. The other is superfluous. We go for Binh."

"Colonel, we may not have time. Allen leaves in days,

Kimble's right behind, then there's Ordway. You'll be down to a skeleton crew."

"I'm aware of the personnel situation." He sounded pompous and couldn't help it. "It means we work harder. it means I'm depending on you to get something from Tu. Harker'll have to dig up something with his contacts out in the countryside. We push until we get a break."

"Or until we break."

The small joke only added to Winter's growing frustration and he snapped in spite of himself. "I may see the humor in that after we're successful, but not just now."

Taylor's chin moved forward and his shoulders inched upward. "I understand, sir."

"Fine."

Having killed the conversation and ruined the morning, Winter set a course back to the jeep, Taylor acknowledging his lead with studied indifference. He stole a glance at the Major and was startled to see a gray—no, a couple of gray—flecks in the thick black hair. It was an odd awareness. He tended to think of him as a younger man. Today, the civilian clothes heightened the image. Bright colors seemed to suit him. Looking again, trying to be objective, he saw good skin tone and a stride that told of good condition. The lines in the face were the true indicators. Though they were sharpened by a justifiable irritation now, they were so clear he wondered at himself for not paying more attention lately. There was age there. And, yes, by God, cynicism he'd not seen before, layered on the indignation. He'd been far too short with his best man. The only decent lead they had came from him.

Apology swam in his imagination, the words rearranging themselves, seeking a face-saving pattern, until he wearied of them. In the dull silence, he sought reasons for his behavior.

The need to capture Binh wasn't the whole thing. He knew that instinctively and logically. After all, he'd been frustrated before and there'd been no reaction like this. Why did he feel so pressed for time? The question bothered him back to the jeep and even though the conversation came alive again on the ride back to MACV, his attention remained on his inability to read himself. When he was finally alone in the office it bothered him further to realize that this kind of introspection and self-interrogation was becoming more and more a part of his daily life. It would have to stop. It wouldn't have happened today, but for his intentional hiding out the day before, when Taylor wanted to find him and report about Trung. He asked himself if he'd been slowing down, taking off too much or not really committing himself when he was in the office. He resolved to keep a closer watch on his own activities.

Down below in his office, Taylor was surprised to find Duc at his desk, muttering to himself and flipping through a stack of 3 x 5 cards. Several other stacks tottered nearby.

"What's going on?"

"Goddam homeworks," Duc spat. "Colonel Tho say ever sons bitch ever speak Tu, he's want know."

"You shouldn't get so mad. You lose all your English."

"Sorry 'bout that." Duc refused to be cheered. "I need computer." He jabbed at a stack and misjudged. A foot-high pile of cards cascaded to the floor. He stared, then ran through his vocabularly of English obscenities and shifted to Vietnamese until that was exhausted. Taylor helped pick up the cards.

"Winter's going to give me a shot at Tu," he said.

Duc whirled to face him. "You work with Tho?"

"No way. All by myself."

A dark frown twisted the round face and Duc's whole body seemed to check. "Tho be—." He clamped his jaws and returned to picking up cards.

"You too?" Taylor said. "Everybody's more worried about Tho's feelings than Tu's information. I thought we were all on the same side, working together."

"Not that. You embarrass Tho if make Tu speak."

"I don't think Tho's that childish."

Duc's eyes worked in an angry wince. "Not child, not behave like child. His job question Tu, learn what Tu knows. Not your job. You make Tu speak, Tho look bad."

"All I want is to win. What difference if my idea works or Tho's?"

Duc heaved his shoulders in an exaggerated shrug as they got to their feet. "Maybe no difference. Maybe Tho feel same-same you. Also maybe you fall on ass, make him look pretty good."

"You two arguing again?"

They turned to see Denby standing in the doorway.

"No argue," Duc said. "I try explain he crazy but he too crazy unnerstan'."

"Understand this." Taylor gave him the finger and turned from Duc's amusement to Denby's prim disapproval.

"I came by on business." His tone implied that Taylor's behavior had somehow sullied his mission. "I wanted to let you know Kimble's orders are in. He'll be leaving the same day Ordway rotates. I think that means you'll have to arrange any technical assistance we'll be needing."

Taylor glanced at Duc and, seeing his head averted while he rearranged papers, indicated Denby should step into the hallway. Ushering the heavier man toward the front door, Taylor spoke with low-pitched urgency.

"I heard about the non-replacement thing. I don't think we ought to discuss it in front of the Vietnamese for a while, do you?"

Denby's eyelids fluttered furiously, but he said nothing, continuing to walk.

Taylor went on. "I'm not going to bring it up to the Old Man—he's got enough on his mind just now. I think I can get any tech help we need, anyhow. When it seems like the right time, will you tell him that?"

Denby gulped back indignation. *That toady bastard Allen! After all the warnings to keep his mouth shut, he races off to spill his guts to a fucking jarhead. Mealymouthed jarhead, at that. "Will you tell him that?" my ass. Winter's the kind to kill the messenger bringing the bad news. Let him learn some other way.*

"When the opportunity comes up," he said judiciously. "However, if you feel it's important, don't hesitate to talk it over with him. No need for formality, not in a small unit like this." He glanced around conspiratorially. "Let me give you a tip. If you should discuss it, remember, it's all a rumor. That's the best reason for keeping it back from the zips and it's an even better reason for not letting the Old Man know where you got the information."

Taylor blinked and opened his mouth, only to be cut off by Denby. "Just keep the whole thing under your hat," he said, and stumped out into the sunshine. Taylor stood for a few seconds, trying to understand what was going on, then returned to his office, telling himself no one really knew anything. He joined Duc in putting the cards back in order.

Out in the courtyard, the insistent heat added to the emotional fire in Denby's scandalized frame and in seconds he was wet, walking with his arms dangling out from his sides and legs straddled to avoid irritating the heat rash speckling his crotch. He hated heat rash. He escalated that to a package, hating the heat rash as a manifestation of an all-inclusive hatred for Vietnam and all things Vietnamese. He reviewed the scope of it as he walked and broadened it to include bigmouthed bastards who sucked up to people to learn secrets and then blabbed like small-town gossips.

Who could've thought it? Goddam Allen. All polish and smiles and bullshit, laughing behind other people's backs. Rich prick.

A group of Vietnamese troopers straggled past as he left the Unit compound and moved toward the main gate. Each of them looked him over coolly, none offering a smile of recognition, much less a salute. When they were past, he broke wind thunderously, denying the temptation to turn around and enjoy the effect. Incompletely mollified by their imagined responses, he refused to return the salute of the gate guard, satisfying himself with a bored nod. He heard the man hawk and spit as he waited for a break in the traffic.

The question of dealing with the guard's insubordination— should he tell Loc or Winter?—was still tormenting him when a shiny gray Scout stopped in front of him. He looked to the traffic squealing and dodging behind it, shaking his head in mute sympathy with those offended by the Scout driver's rudeness.

The sound of his name being called finally registered and he started, realizing it came from the vehicle. He bent to look in.

"Hurry up and open the door!" Earl commanded and Denby scurried inside. They ripped away from the curb, forcing a bicyclist to maneuver desperately to reach the relative safety of the outermost edge of the street. Curses and a brass section of protesting horns followed them away.

The vehicle's movement stirred a breeze, acrid but welcome, against Denby's wet clothes. He glowered back over his shoulder. "Listen to those people, just because you stopped to give someone a lift. They talk about culture and they're simply coarse."

Earl's laugh was strained. "It seems to be an epidemic. If the city wasn't so crowded, maybe—."

"I don't think so." Denby cut him off with the assurance of almost two full years' seniority. "They're a greedy, rude bunch and they always were and they always will be."

"You ought to be infantry," Earl said. "You could shoot at them."

"Me?" Denby enjoyed the joke. "I'm a lover, not a fighter. Combat's for fools and heroes, if there's any difference. Either way, I'm happy in administration."

Earl grinned knowingly. "It's where the power is, isn't it?"

"You bet. I laugh to myself all the time, watching these macho types swagger around town. One twix back to DOA and they're back out in the woods where they belong. Never know what hit 'em, most of the time." He tapped his forehead and winked.

"You sent someone back to the line?" Earl delicately balanced surprise and skepticism.

"Only one. Two, actually. I finished the paperwork on one just after I got here and the other was a Ranger type that didn't work out for us."

Earl turned into the BOQ One parking lot. While he was going through the routine of locking up the vehicle, he said, "I shouldn't think any Ranger type would work out in a Records Research Unit. What would he do?"

Apprehension bubbled in Denby's mind and the cool clothes suddenly turned clammy.

Goddam questions. Especially from Earl. He had power, real power. He knew Senators and argued with Generals and handled the whole thing with the sureness of an electrician handling killing voltage. That's exactly what it was, too, the kind of shock that could fry a career in a minute.

Denby acknowledged it and wished he could enjoy it from some safe gray area. The best thing in the world would be to have your hand on the switch, though. Let someone else play with the wires. And forget standing around in the light, too. A man with good sense would always be in the background, making sure there was an order covering everything and controlling without being seen, risking nothing, ever.

"We can use almost anyone," he told Earl, easing out of the Scout. "The man spoke the language and had a pretty good knowledge of Communist-bloc weapons. Winter thought he might be able to build up a pattern of shipping routes or depot locations by checking our ammunition lot numbers and so forth. Waste of time. There's so much junk hidden out in the jungle you can't move without tripping over it. Anyhow, he started moaning about his workload, so I told Winter he wasn't worth the trouble he was causing. The Old Man left it up to me, naturally, and I had the man out to Cu Chi with the Tropic Lightning before he could change his tune."

"The Captain—you didn't mention his name. Whatever happened to him?"

"Who knows? I'm sure he had a name, but I've forgotten it. He's probably out there charging the enemy. I hope he charges enough to make expenses." He laughed at the joke and turned to leave.

Distaste drifted across Earl's features as a light breeze will bend a flame and let it go. When the effect had passed, he called to Denby's retreating form.

"Where are you eating tonight?"

Denby turned around. "Here, I guess."

"Why not come on into town with me? Get out of this place for a change. I've been talking shop all day and I've had enough of it. How about you?"

"It costs too much. I don't mind spending money, but I hate to be robbed, and these people charge too much."

Earl laughed, tapering off at Denby's wounded expression. "I agree with you. But I meant at a friend's place."

"Oh, well, then I couldn't. I mean, your friend hardly expects you to bring another guest and—."

"That's the point." Earl overrode the protests. "We've been talking to each other for so long we've heard everything we've got to say. We're looking for people who can talk about something besides the damned office. I can't say I know you all that well, but what I've heard you say on several subjects interests me. It's a chance to get a little better acquainted."

"Boy, I'm tempted. I'm so tired of this place—."

"Good." Earl unfolded from behind the wheel. "I'll shower and change and meet you back here in an hour, OK?"

Denby checked his watch. "An hour. Perfect. See you then." He moved off quickly, and when he was in the shower, he hummed. Dressing, he looked in the mirror and coughed in a humorless laugh, a sound he bit off as if afraid it might expand.

It popped out again at the thought of Earl trying to set him up, to pump him.

The evening was going to be fun. And possibly beneficial. He scowled at his reflection, brushing his hair, remembering the need for caution. It would be good to have Earl think of him as a friend. Sooner or later Winter was going to make a mistake, get caught on one of his sprees, and Earl's influence would be important. The fine point would be to insure Earl never got enough information to move against Winter. That old bastard would figure the source eventually and then God only knew what he'd do.

The thought so bothered Denby he turned from the mirror, replacing the brush on the dresser by touch. Still looking away, he located his cologne and sloshed it on with a deep sigh of approval. He squared his shoulders and sucked in his stomach, heading for the door.

The name of the game was rapidly becoming Cover Your Ass and there was no sense being caught short. There was nothing dishonorable or improper in a bit of political foot-work to protect yourself. It wasn't his fault Winter felt himself above the law and it wasn't his fault he was assigned to Winter's Unit. It wasn't as if he'd be working against Winter in any sense. Hell, the Old Man'd be the first to agree a man had to look out for himself.

Earl was already in the Scout, waiting. He started an easy conversation about Denby's last duty assignment and they chatted idly about that until he suddenly parked and flicked the lights off. Denby winched upright, his head swiveling busily, the eyes questioning the unresponsive house fronts rising into the dusk.

"Where are we?"

"This is where my friend lives. It looks better inside."

"That's OK." The lie had an off-key ring. "It must be a nice neighborhood." He stepped to the ground as if testing for mines. He followed Earl without further comment, telling himself he'd been a fool not to eat at the club and reminding himself that Earl had been here many times in the past and had no more wish to die than any normal person. He crowded through the front door literally on Earl's heels and was turning for a wary look over his shoulder when he realized Earl hadn't bothered to knock. Before he could ask about that, he heard another voice.

"Hey, you made it. Good fucking deal. I was beginning to wonder if dinner'd get cold. This your friend?"

Denby took the greeting hand in trained reaction, his mind devoured by the recognition of his host.

"Hi," the man said, perfect teeth flashing ingenuous welcome. "I'm Ben Barline. Dick says your name is Carl. I've been looking forward to meeting you."

Denby's stomach rolled and he heard his voice make words.

"Ben! Call me Ben." He squeezed Denby's bicep and steered him toward a carved teak bar, opened to display glittering bottles and glasses. Numb, Denby agreed to Scotch and soda, watching with frozen eyes as Barline dumped a good three fingers in a tumbler and splashed it with soda. At the first sip a shock whipped through Denby, almost a voice screaming for him to get himself together, and he sat the drink on an end table and plumped into the overstuffed chair next to it.

He spoke to Earl. "This is the way to live. Look at this furniture—rosewood and teak from Hong Kong, I'll bet. And the lacquer-work pictures! I've only seen a couple like that."

Barline said, "You like them? They're pretty old. Made in happier times. You like Oriental art?"

Denby felt himself relaxing, felt something move in his brain, wanting him to understand he belonged here. These people had depth.

He said, "Art's primarily an investment for me, I'm afraid. I love to own it, but every time I see I can make a profit on what I've bought, I unload. Doesn't do me any good, though. The money just goes into another piece, more expensive than the last. I guess I'm more of a businessman than connoisseur."

"Not necessarily," Earl disagreed, slouching on the sofa across the room. "The important thing's to realize the fact of the art. You're allowed to change your mind and you're not required to like all forms equally."

"Holy shit!" Barline smacked his hand against his forehead in burlesqued astonishment. "Who can believe this? Two dogfaces discussing art and taste! They'll drum you out!"

Earl swore at him easily and Denby felt his control of the

286

situation growing as surely as night follows day. It wasn't a bad metaphor, if trite, he decided, because he certainly had them in the dark. They were going to seduce him. No good-guy/bad-guy act, and no hard sell. It was going to be kindred souls enjoying a stimulating evening and later would come the hints that it'd be nice if he would help them put a knee into Winter's balls. As gentlemen, naturally.

He exhaled in contentment, an apparently careless finger nudging his barely touched whiskey further away. They continued to chatter and a few minutes later a woman appeared in the doorway at the opposite end of the room. Denby had suspected it led to the kitchen and her disheveled appearance convinced him. She shouted over the continuing conversation.

"Deep?"

Barline nodded without looking. Immediately the woman hurried to put down a bowl of cheese dip and some crackers on the coffee table in front of Earl. Denby got up to help himself, enjoying catching Barline's attempts to read the new guest's reactions.

Denby continued to enjoy the evening, manipulating the conversation with a skill that gave him intense pride. Every time Barline brought up the war, he was able to find a phrase to link the statement to art or literature or something of equal innocence. By the time the woman was clearing away the dessert dishes Barline was showing his irritation and Earl was watching him with increasing concern. In fact, Denby noted as Earl turned from Barline once again, he was looking practically desperate.

"What do you hear from Trung since you had to turn him loose?" Earl literally blurted the question and with it, the sociable atmosphere whined with anticipation. Barline's eyes drilled as though they would suck the truth directly through Denby's skull.

Whatever they hoped to achieve, Denby's spirits soared. He was in control. They had brought him here to use him, and he was in position to let them use him, but on his own terms. He wanted to dance.

He said, "You mean since the government freed him. We don't hold anyone. He's not doing much. We wouldn't hear anything from him, at any rate."

"Bullshit." Barline said it quietly. "He hates your guts, you people in your snooper's unit." He laughed at the inadvertent alarm that swept Denby's face and leveled a finger at him. "He won't talk to me—he must be pretty scared—but he doesn't have to say a fucking word to make his meaning clear. All he'd say is that he's turned the whole thing over to his friends and is relying on them to see justice done. That last is a quote, incidentally. Maybe you can tell me exactly what his friends might do."

Anxiety tugged at Denby's grip on the meeting and he fought to maintain himself. "If Trung's going to wait for his friends to do something, he'll wait a long time. He doesn't have any."

Earl said, "I wouldn't bet on it. He got out, didn't he? And a lot of other people are very upset over the high-handedness of what your people did."

"High-handed? This is war, Dick. You want our people reading rights to VC before they can shoot?"

"Oh, stop it," Earl protested wearily. "Trung's a civilian and he does have rights, VC or not, and you haven't proven he is. And that story he was an informer has a bad smell. There was some kind of fast deal, and Trung had a card Winter didn't know about. He'd never let anyone go if he wasn't pushed to it. Someday the real story's going to break and the shit'll really hit the fan."

Barline gestured with a coffee cup in his hand, either unaware of or ignoring the spillage. "Were you there when they busted him? Did one of your people kill the third man?"

"I wasn't present, of course. And you know the third man died by accident. Why must you with the media insist the Army kills for sport?"

Barline jerked a thumb at Earl. "I know some that don't. But most of your people'll kill anything that moves so they can get back to their easy living."

"I'm sure you believe that. And I didn't come here for this kind of argument." He held one hand in the other in his lap, quieting the tremble starting there at the awareness that he had to establish himself concretely now, or the opportunity was gone. He constructed a sneer for Earl. "This is your idea of a pleasant conversation?"

Earl averted his eyes. "You're right. I shouldn't have mentioned Trung. Not to you. Ben and I were talking about him the other day. Ben tried to interview him and got nothing, as he said, and I knew Winter had something to do with the operation. Maybe I'm wrong, but I've had the feeling you don't always approve of everything that Unit does, and I wondered if you knew how terrified Trung really is. And, to be candid, Ben hoped you could help him with an angle on a story. Situations like that involving Trung have to be exposed, but I had no right dragging you into an argument about it."

The sincerity of the apology satisfied Denby. Even Barline accepted the truce, although with a brittle silence that indicated he was ready to start any time. Denby decided a breath of flattery might soothe him.

"I understand your feelings, Ben. Sometimes we—the military—are so interested in winning we lose sight of the things we're actually fighting for. I know you only want the truth. If it wasn't for the press, I'm afraid we'd have some people go completely out of control."

"You fucking well know it. I've seen some who don't need anything but a swastika armband to be right out of the old newsreels."

"Oh, I don't think it's as bad as all that. There's no arguing, though, the press is the single greatest moral influence on both our policy here and our people."

Earl's eyebrows rose. "Moral influence?" There was tentative approval in the question and Denby fastened to it, knowing he had holding ground to anchor the new relationship between himself and Earl. Even as he put his answer together, he realized he should have seen the link long ago.

He cleared his throat. "Everything we've undertaken here has to be evaluated in terms of moral correctness, or the whole effort is simple interference." Barline tapped his fingers on the table and said, "Hear, hear!" the sarcasm not completely obscuring a growing interest.

"I mean that," Denby declared, and Barline interrupted again.

"Look, there's no morality in this thing. No nation should interfere in the internal affairs of any other nation. If you do, you have no right to even discuss morality."

"I'm not talking politics. I'm talking about our behavior as individuals. No matter our reason for being here, we should be required to behave honorably. We've flooded the economy by

289

overpaying for everything, we've undermined the family by hiring children at wages the parents can't earn, made whores of innumerable women—.''

"You constantly surprise me." Barline shook his head, looking to Earl and back to Denby. "One minute you sound like you're getting off on the same old shit and then you're saying something intelligent. I wish I were in a position to do something about your view."

"You are," Denby said, feeling inspiration swell inside him. "Why not write about the errors, the breakdowns in morality? We can't do anything about it. The public is convinced the military wants to destroy the men here. If we try to court-martial anyone for anything, everyone back home screams it's not the poor boy's fault. You're against the war and I'm against corruption. If you prepared a series of stories showing what's happening to our people—drugs, VD, loss of self-respect, and so on—you'd be doing everyone a favor."

Barline slowly leaned back away from the table and lifted his hands up behind his head. "Well, shit. You know, I think you're right. The effect of evil on the ones exposed to it. And the people are right, you know, the kids on drugs and clapped up would never have had those troubles if they hadn't been sent here." He closed his eyes, internalizing his view. "Even better, why not show that and the impact of imperialism on the people? The possessions sold to make expenses, the illegitimate kids, the whores and their drugs. It goes on forever!"

Earl nodded semi-automatic approval with a frown that signalled reservations. Realizing he was being observed, he said, "People're bound to get hurt. If you identify our men, you'll be telling small-town America their sons are junkies or fathering bastards all over South Vietnam, or both."

"Fuck 'em!" Barline snapped. "Without the names the stories have no actuality. We're talking about a rebirth of a sense of individual integrity and you can't have that without pain. I'm going to use names and I'm not restricting myself to the kids, either. I've seen too many of these old-timers and officers whoring it up. It's time somebody blew the whistle on those assholes and made them live up to all the 'good example' shit they throw around."

Earl's face broke into a slow smile. "Now you're losing your audience, right, Carl? Didn't anyone ever tell you you don't pick on officers? We're above reproach."

"Your ass," Barline laughed. "Everybody's fair game."

Denby chuckled. "I guess we'll have to warn all our high-living friends. I feel like someone out of English history, running through the streets shouting, "The Roundheads are coming!'"

"Very apt," Earl agreed, "except you can start by racing through the halls of that palace your unit lives in. I hear you've got a couple of ranchers."

"Only one to worry about. Allen'll be gone in a little while. Our friend here won't have time to get after him. It's a good thing, too."

Barline leaned forward again. "Now you've got my curiosity aroused. I know Allen. Who's he shacking with?"

"Sure," Denby laughed, looking to Earl, enlisting him in his resistance. "I tell you about him and you slaughter him. Forget it."

Earl smiled complicity and Denby was relieved to see some sense of proportion being maintained.

Barline said, "OK, so it's between us. For Christ's sake, who's he screwing? The President?"

"That'd be a switch," Earl observed. "C'mon—who is it?"

"I won't give you any names, but I guess I can tell you she's married. Her husband's stationed out of town so she shares an apartment with Allen. I've often wondered if someone didn't set that up for him. He's got some influential friends, you know."

Barline twisted his face. "You bastard. Look what you've done to me. Sex, intrigue, corruption in high places—the whole fucking bag and I said I wouldn't use it. What a prick!"

Denby said, "Breaks," and felt the lightness of the mood dissolve at the instant he saw Earl's expression. Immediately, he faced Barline again.

"I tried to put a stop to it, of course. Told the Old Man it was a bad situation, a terrible example for the troops. And what would the Viets think, if they knew, a Colonel's wife, and all? Bad business, bad business."

He was jabbering and he knew it. Clamping his jaws together, he determined to say nothing further unless questioned. He'd answer in monosyllables, he promised himself.

Earl saved him.

"It's late," he said to Barline. "I don't want to keep Carl too long because I'm hoping he'll want to join us again." He turned to Denby. "I supply some of the food and wine and add a couple of bucks for the maid's extra trouble. Why don't we make it a threesome in the future?" He accepted Denby's agreement as given, looking to Barline, who nodded approval.

"It's settled then." Even in Earl's hospitality, Denby sensed something out-of-place, a feeling of misdirection. He knew it had something to do with Allen's escapade but couldn't convince himself that Earl could be so upset over what was merely another sordid Saigon incident. He swept the matter from his mind. The important thing was to let the matter die.

Earl pointed at the door. "There's only one latrine," he said. "You want to go first?"

Denby accepted the offer quickly, glad for the opportunity to get away from Earl's peculiar mood. With the door closed behind him and the water splashing, he could hear the other two having a fine argument, although the words were lost in the liquid sounds. From the voices, he could tell Earl was the one speaking urgently and Barline seemed defensive.

He delayed until the commode was quiet in order to eavesdrop a bit and was rewarded by hearing Barline say, "Relax, will you? Even if I did check it out, it's not the way I'd want to start, all right? What else can I tell you?"

That meant Earl had won the argument, whatever it was about. Denby grinned at himself in the mirror. Jesus, what a day! Up and down, up and down. But he'd handled all of it. No harm done the Unit and he was on the inside with both Earl and Barline. The scowl falling across the face in the mirror reminded him that the stakes had been very high and this was but the first pot. From now on, everything would be very close to the chest. No more gambling.

His last look at the mirror repeated congratulations.

31

DUC STOOD AT THE BASE OF THE TREE, turning slowly, inspecting the surrounding sandbag wall with the plump irritation of a child unable to find the soap in the tub. His uniform was already blotched by nervous perspiration. Taylor stood next to him, holding a black briefcase. He was prim in pressed utilities, and they made a strange picture, so different in appearance, and inside a circular wall of new, green sandbags arranged five high.

"What we do now?" Duc spoke with resignation.

"I want all the prisoners but Tu brought out here."

Duc relayed the order to one of the guards. Within minutes six men in shorts and sandals were marched out of the building, squinting in the unaccustomed daylight. As they shuffled along in single file, one twisted his head eagerly and Taylor wondered how long since he'd seen sunshine. When they arrived at the circle he had them seated inside, their backs against the sandbags. From the briefcase he produced a roll of wide adhesive tape and used it to secure each man's wrists to his ankles. They watched him with the vague interest of hens seeing the farmer sharpen a hatchet.

"Now I want Tu and a folding chair," Taylor said. The guard trotted off.

Tu preceded him out of the building, took in the scene at a glance, and swaggered toward Taylor. A livid bruise puffed one eye almost shut. Hatred gleamed from the slit as powerfully as from the undamaged one. At Taylor's gesture, he stepped over the wall almost eagerly. The guard placed the chair where Taylor pointed and left the circle.

"Sit." Tu did as he was told. Taylor wrapped tape around his ankles. "Stand." With Tu on his feet, Taylor circled him, taping the left arm to the body, the wide bands glowing white against the dark skin, circling above and below the elbow. Then he drew another double loop around the body and the tree, leaving approximately a three foot clearance, effectively leashing the man to the trunk.

"Are you afraid I may strike back while you beat me?" Tu sneered. Proud approval discreetly altered the faces of the six men trussed against the sandbags. Taylor said nothing, turning his back and pulling Tu's free right arm straight, pinning it with his own. Then he bent over, still keeping Tu's arm clamped to him, and fished in the briefcase momentarily. One of the prisoners hissed surprise as he caught a glimpse of the object in Taylor's hand and Tu squirmed to see. Taylor leaned back, his weight forcing the smaller Vietnamese against the tree trunk. A few quick wraps of the tape and Taylor faced Tu again. Before the smaller man could react, Taylor lifted him by the waist and boosted him to a standing position on the chair, then stretched on tiptoe to force the taped right hand against an overhanging branch. The reach to the branch was such that Tu could touch it without excessive strain. Folding the hand in his own, Taylor smiled into Tu's face.

"I will wait here with your friends. We will have a holiday, sitting in the shade." He indicated the other prisoners with a move of his head. "These dogs have lived too long. You think I hate them, but that is not true. I do not care about them at all, so you may kill them if you want."

Raising his other hand, Taylor pulled something away from Tu's, against the limb. Tu's eyes widened as he recognized it. Taylor dropped both hands and gazed at his handiwork. A grenade nestled in Tu's upraised palm, irrevocably taped to it, the pin pulled and the spoon pressed against the branch. Tu registered it as if seeing a cancer.

Taylor sat on the wall next to the prisoners. "You tire me," he said. "You will stand with these dogs' death in your hand until you agree to tell me what I want to know. Choose to die instead and they will die with you. That is their misfortune. We will probably have to release them eventually. I would prefer they die in an accident."

"These men are not afraid of death!"

"Not even you are such a fool. Look at their faces. And can you be sure they are not still valuable to your cause?"

The prisoner who had blinked so rapidly in the sunlight licked his lips and turned to stare at the man next to him. Another stared at his kneecaps. The rest watched Tu's hand with the intensity of snakes contemplating an egg in a nest.

Taylor pivoted to the outside of the wall. "Get chairs and

coffee for Major Duc and myself. Bring chairs for any other guards who wish them."

It was more than an hour before Tu moved. He balanced on one foot and rubbed the calf of his leg. In a few minutes he reversed the process. His eyes never left Taylor.

One of the prisoners called out to the guard for a drink of water. The guard told him to be quiet and Taylor countermanded him.

"They may have water or tea." In response to the man's questioning look, Taylor added, "That pile of shit in the chair gets nothing until it talks."

Tu smiled grimly. A prisoner ducked his head forward to wipe sweat from his brow onto a kneecap.

At the end of another hour one of the men declared a need to relieve himself. The tape was cut and he was led away, brought back, and repositioned.

Sweat now drained steadily from Tu's body, rainwater on smoked glass, dying a band at the top of his shorts and creating a triangle in the crotch. When it dripped into his eyes he shook his head violently, always focusing again on Taylor.

The sun edged to directly overhead. Food was brought to the prisoners. One man's hands were freed at a time, the feet remaining bound. Two prisoners took advantage of the general laxity and whispered to each other. The guard casually cuffed them both.

"Let them talk," Taylor said. "I think they will die soon. Their talk now means nothing."

The man on the end of the line looked at the grenade and sucked a grain of rice from some cavity in his teeth. He chewed it contemplatively.

The meal passed uneventfully, the sibilance of rice and broth being ingested replaced by comfortable belching. Duc took it on himself to send the guard for beer, with orders for the rest of the security force to join them, except for two men on the gate. The new arrivals grouped in the shade of a flowering shrub, drank their beer, and gossiped animatedly.

Tu's stomach muscles drew taut. He began shifting his weight with increasing frequency. Suddenly there was a new sound, high-pitched and metallic. All attention rushed to the grenade before everyone recognized the disturbance for what it was. A golden stream gushed from Tu's groin to ring merrily on the metal chair seat. A prisoner's giggle scratched the hot air and for the first time since leaving his cell, Tu tore his eyes from Taylor. He glared at the offending hysteric, who stopped instantly. His laughter was replaced by guffaws from the guards. Taylor sat, cold-eyed, and waited for Tu to come back to him.

Even with his bladder emptied, Tu's muscles were wearing away. A long cord jerked spasmodically in his upraised arm. Veins bulged in his ankles and knees, in the raised arm, across his pectorals, routes carved through a geography of pain. His knees trembled in a delicate vibration, scarcely greater than the stroke of flies' wings.

A beetle stalked off the limb and across the grenade with brainless dignity and picked its way through opals of sweat on the wrist. Tu twitched his arm to dislodge it, his wince generating a muted chorus from the six. He sneered at them. The arm continued to pulsate irregularly. The beetle ignored the peculiarities of his walkway, forging downward and then angling nearer the horizontal to follow the bicep toward the shoulder. Tu watched until it was within range and blew it into the air. It caught itself with wildly beating wings, its departure marked by pendant complaint that hung in the shade of the tree long after it was gone.

The men at Tu's feet resumed normal breathing and the guards went back to their chatter.

By mid-afternoon Tu shivered as though he stood naked in snow.

The prisoners virtually took turns requesting to relieve themselves. The guard had to hurry to keep pace as they left and shove them along as they dawdled on their return.

At four o'clock Lieutenant Colonel Tho called and asked if Tu had started to talk. Taylor replied that he had not, but that he expected him to in another two hours. Tho asked his reasons and Taylor evaded a direct answer. Tho arrived at the interrogation house at four-forty.

Tu had been in the same position nine hours and forty minutes.

Tho took one look at the scene in the courtyard as he stood in the lobby with Taylor and said, "Is that a grenade?"

Taylor explained what he had done and why.

Tho said, "What do you expect to accomplish?"

"He is a man who will die, but I do not think he will kill those other men."

"And if you are mistaken?"

"Seven more men will wait for me in hell."

Tho lapsed to a thoughtful silence and Taylor knew he was evaluating the residue of information that might remain in the six prisoners. Uncertainty picked at his eyes when he looked to Taylor again, but his question was direct.

"You think he is about to break?"

"Yes, *Trung Ta*. I think he might last until six, but I expect him to break sooner." As he spoke, Tu's bicep bulged in a cramp and his face warped with the pain.

Tho raised his arm in a slow arc and examined his watch. "I think he is coming to us on schedule."

Taylor trotted to the front entrance, then strolled casually to the wall. Tu's face remained contorted, sweat seeking the channels in the flesh, coursing over and around the lips to form a rapid dripping stream off the chin. Taylor stepped to the wall and leaned across the heads lined up beneath.

"Drop your hand, Tu," he coaxed. "One man is missing. You will only get five if you drop your hand now. Maybe you will save the most important one. You have demonstrated to everyone that you are a true hero, although I never saw a hero take so long to be heroic. A brave man would have held the grenade to his own chest ours ago. A brave man would have thought to take the explosion himself, cheating me and saving the lives of his friends. Now you cannot control your arm and the chance is gone."

The guard hurried up with the missing prisoner, practically throwing him into place and re-binding him with shaking hands before vaulting over the wall. Another prisoner immediately clamored.

"No more," Taylor said. "You will empty yourselves soon enough."

"Help me!" Tu's plea was a scream crushed to a whisper. "Help me or they die! I can hold it no longer." His head sagged and saliva drooled over his lower lip to mix with the sweat. taylor hopped over the wall as the grenade shifted. The spoon raised slightly. Tu found the strength to raise his head. "Get them out of the circle! Hurry!"

Taylor turned and Duc had already started to work with one

of the guards. They had an efficient system. They flanked a man, grabbed him under the knees and elbows, and rolled him backwards over the top. The first two hit rolling, putting as much distance between themselves and the grenade as possible. The rest bounced against the wall, flattening themselves to the ground. Except for the impact of bodies and the slither of flesh on grass, none uttered a sound.

Taylor reached for the grenade at the same time Tu pitched forward. He screamed, "Death to the imperialists! Long live the People's Government!"

The spoon arced over Taylor's head making a tinny sound that absorbed the world around it and became a carillon peal. Through it, Taylor heard the hoarse shouts and yipping cries of the guards scrambling for cover. He caught the falling man and stared at the victory in the eyes before him.

A hollow silence smothered the panic. Tu blinked and forced his head to turn toward the grenade, his eyes locked with Taylor's until the last possible instant. They flicked to the ugly, ribbed shape and back again. Triumph drowned in the huge tears that plummeted down his cheeks.

"You fool!" Taylor's scorn slashed across the entire courtyard in a lightning-crack. "Did you really believe I would let you go so easily? Of course the grenade is fake!"

One of the distant prisoners timorously peeked over his shoulder at the tableau under the tree. He looked from it to the bush where the guards cowered and met the eye of one of them. The prisoner essayed a smile. The guard returned it with a nervous chuckle. The prisoner giggled and another rose to see over the wall. He laughed. The other prisoner giggled again, higher and louder. In a second they were all shouting laughter and comment. Men insulted each other for their dives for cover, the prisoners laughed at their own displays of fear during the long day. Duc circulated, cutting bonds, and one prisoner rose stiffly, raising an arm and glaring, aping Tu's pose. The laughter rose to a crescendo.

Drawing his knife, Taylor slashed the band of tape holding Tu to the tree, catching the body as if shouldering a rolled rug. He walked quickly to the building, his long strides bouncing the inert form. Sobs wrenched through Tu's slack jaws at each step.

In the cell, Taylor lowered him to the edge of the mattress

and carefully arranged him at full length. After stripping the tape and the inert grenade from the unresisting body, he massaged the arm and shoulder. Tu groaned continually as the bricklike muscles and tendons loosened. When he could manipulate those joints with relative ease, Taylor went to work on the legs. Duc opened the cell door and looked in. Taylor frowned at him, gesturing for silence. Duc nodded and left.

When the legs loosened a bit and the blood vessels looked less likely to burst, Taylor fetched water. He pressed the tin cup against the down-curved lips. They resisted, then loosened, letting the liquid trickle through. Dribbles ran from both sides of the mouth, joined shortly by more tears, the streams dividing the face into sectors.

"I have won," Taylor said softly. "Understand that."

A long sigh broke from the figure on the bed.

Taylor pressed a cigarette to the lips. Again there was a trace of resistance before acceptance and then a deep draw. Tu's eyes remained closed.

'When the pain is fading," Taylor continued, "it will come to you that you have told me nothing. You will think you have one last hope, that you can continue to remain silent and people will know, somehow, that you never talked. After what has happened today, who will believe that? You heard them laugh today. I am the only person in the world who can make you a man again."

He gripped Tu's shoulder and squeezed hard. Tu grunted at the pain and the ash toppled from his cigarette onto his wet chin, turning black and white like a smudged bird-dropping.

Plucking the remains of the cigarette from Tu's lips, Taylor stepped into the hall and signalled a waiting guard to lock the door. He lit a smoke of his own, holding the match, willing the shaking from his hand before the flame reached his fingers. Then he walked to the lobby where Tho waited.

"How long before he can talk?"

"He should be OK by morning. Stiff, not hurt."

Tho said, "What you have done is very clever, *Thieu Ta*. You surprised everyone. We thought you would die."

Duc came in, uncertain of Tho's frame of mind. He looked to Taylor, questioning silently, and at the American's easy smile, returned a delighted grin before hurrying back to the courtyard.

Tho put his hands behind his back and paced, speaking to Taylor. "You are the man who did not want to work with me." The smile he showed detracted nothing from the accusation.

Taylor nodded ruefully. "I know what you are thinking. I have thought the same thing."

"Are you certain? I have been thinking I never saw a man so cruel. You do not take away life, you take away hope for an honest death. It is a terrible thing when all a man has to live for is a purposeful death, and to have someone take that and make it a thing of laughter, of shame—." He turned his palms up helplessly.

Taylor said, "You told me once that you use what is available. That is what I did. Tu is cunning. Treacherous. I do not know if he has killed anyone, but I know he would be happy to see me in his position. I am not, and that is the difference between us. At least he is not crippled."

"Not crippled?" Tho's smile mocked. "His mind is not important?"

"He can form new ideas. He will adjust to his new situation. He would never grow another knee, a new set of knuckles. He will not flinch every time he hears a telephone ring."

Tho looked away. "I apologize. I have made you defend yourself, and I should not. You have done an unpleasant thing that was necessary and you have done it well." He brought his eyes back to Taylor. "I am a cruel man, Major. Not heartless, but determined and cruel. I, too, sometimes scream in the night, nevertheless. I think you would also scream if you worked with another Tu, ten Tus, every day, every week, every year. Men like him—I deal with them constantly. They put bombs in markets, mines under buses, kill people as examples to others. I bring them pain in order to find out who helps them do these things and I am despised, even by you. And yet I could not do what you have done. I wonder why you did it. I see the pain and disgust in your face. It amuses me because it is your people who make heroes of my enemies, even when they are as I am, and I am ashamed to confess I take pleasure in your suffering because I like and respect you. But you are an American."

"How do we ever stop any of it?"

Tho laughed soundlessly, baring his teeth. "There is no way

out, not for men like us. You will leave here, of course, but what has happened will go with you. I will die and my road will end. And we will continue, those who come after you and the ones like me, to kill each other, torture, imprison. The greatest forgiveness left in my country is a quick death. It will be that way until one side or the other dominates."

Taylor slipped into English. "Jesus, it can't be that grim."

"If I were a Christian, I would hope you were praying," Tho said dryly.

"I do not understand." Taylor moved to the window and watched the work party carrying away the sandbags. "Sometimes I really do not understand why you people do not simply quit."

The voice behind him struggled under sudden weariness. "All of us consider it. In the south we have evil and hope. To the north the evil is one great force and the only hope allowed is what that evil approves. Our troubles here will only end if we can find the strength to turn back invasion by that evil. If we lose, you will see the refugees being marched back north and you can watch the joy of your countrymen."

The bitterness in the last sentence seemed to mingle with the sweat on Taylor's spine in a glutinous mass. A shudder failed to dislodge it.

"Duc has gotten almost everything cleaned up outside," he said. "We can go back to the villa now."

Tho headed for the door right away. "Yes, we should leave. I think you have been in this place long enough for one day. But there is one more thing, the continuing interrogation of Tu. I will help you, if you like."

Taylor's glance was transparent in its doubt and Tho smiled. "I will not hurt him. It is not necessary. We must build now, not destroy."

"Amen."

"You are praying again. Wait for us in your jeep. I will instruct the guards and bring Duc."

Taylor went to the machine, the tactile sensations of the familiar seat, the chipped steering wheel, the stiff clutch pedal all marvelously reassuring. He worked the clutch rhythmically while he waited, enjoying the mechanical predictability. Tho and Duc joined him and he lost himself in the concentration of driving.

Winter was writing a letter when he stepped through the open door of the austere office. Looking up, Winter put the pen down and sat erect.

"It's a bitch, buddy," he greeted him.

"Still show that much?"

"Like a lantern in the night. It does something to the set of a man's jaw, like he was trying to eat his own tongue. Incidentally, Tho phoned Loc and told him the essentials and he passed it on to me. Try to forget it for a while. Make your report tomorrow. Get out of here for now."

Taylor smiled wanly.

Winter went on. "I figured you'd be hurting when this day was out, win or lose, so I've got a piece of sunshine for you. I talked to Ly's parents."

A frown pulled at Taylor's features. Winter ignored it.

"I couldn't really lay down any law, but I made them understand we wanted no trouble. They don't like the situation, but they know you won't hurt Ly. And they know it's her decision. Avoid them, though. You're number one on their shit list, so don't aggravate the situation."

"No sweat. Now I have to worry about what happens when I leave."

"You had that to worry about the first time you thought about laying her," Winter said coldly. "I've insured the parents won't make an issue of things. Everything else is between you two. Handle it any way you want, as long as it's quiet."

"Don't shit me. You're just getting your hand in as a marriage counselor for when you retire."

Winter gave him a grotesque wink. "I figure I can mix that with pimping and make my fortune. Unbeatable combination."

Taylor mustered up a smile to show appreciation for the attempt, and once it had served its purpose, said, "You stuck your neck out, coach. I appreciate it."

"Get out of here." Winter flagged at him with both hands. "The sight of you being humble and grateful makes my ass pucker. Why don't you go see her? She's probably at the apartment now, fluttering around with her buddy and that other tomcat, Allen."

Taylor's surprise showed before he could stop it. "You knew?"

"I knew about it almost as soon as he did. She's not a legal wife, and they've been very careful. He's so short now there's little point in moving him out."

"There really aren't any scruples left, are there? There really isn't any place to hide."

Winter's voice softened. "That funny look's back in your jaw. Try to shake it. It doesn't do you much good." He made a face. "Maybe there's a reason for the world to be a cesspool. Meanwhile, if something good comes along, be thankful and grab it."

Taylor was almost to the door when Denby appeared.

"Oh, Taylor. Glad I caught you." He extended a hand that Taylor shook listlessly. "What happened today—Duc was just telling me—it was deplorable, but I think you did it with a minimum of fuss. I was personally pleased to see you accomplish your objective without the brutality we see so much of here. Tu's information will be invaluable. He'll give us good cooperation now. I'll tell you, what you did was psychologically brilliant."

Taylor opened his mouth and Winter's harsh voice cut him off. "I told you I was through talking to you, Major. I told you to get out. Do it."

In the sanctum of the dim hallway Taylor leaned against the wall and swallowed until most of the slimy bile taste was gone. Then he went to the shower.

32

TAYLOR OPENED THE APARTMENT DOOR and shook his head in amusement at the new furniture arrangement. He tried to remember how many arrangements had preceded this one and gave it up. Ly wasn't satisfied to merely busy herself keeping the place attractive but seemed driven to constantly change it, as though the positioning of the objects might create a pentacle to hold out the world.

She came to him and pushed the door shut. "You like it?" she asked, her voice saying she hoped he did. She was wearing

303

her blue *ao dai* and he remembered that this was the evening Hal and Dao were coming for dinner.

He studied the room. "The painting clashes with the sofa and I think the sofa should be against that wall, regardless."

When her face crumpled in shock, he couldn't hold back the laughter. "It's fine, Ly. I don't know how you do it."

She laughed, pummeling his chest. "You frightened me! I worked so hard to make it look nicer and all you can say is 'move the sofa!'"

He said, "I hope you haven't hidden the whiskey," and moved to get it. She stepped forward quickly.

"No, you relax. Let me."

He snapped on the stereo in passing, knowing she'd have a record ready to go. Settling in his chair, he watched her measure the drink, brows together in concentration. At first it pleased him and then a tendril of concern made him duplicate her frown as he considered such intensity exemplified her constant search for perfection in the management of the apartment. He asked himself if it was healthy, knowing it wasn't, knowing she did it because she was trying to build a lifetime of memories for both of them and had less than a year to work with.

When she handed him the glass he pulled her to him and kissed her with a longing tenderness that startled her and then she responded in kind. For a heavy moment afterward they looked into each other's eyes and then she sat on the arm of the chair, leaning against him and they let the music speak for them. He turned his head and nuzzled her breast. She ran her hand across the bristled crew cut.

"Not now, Charles. Later." She rose and he caught her and held her to him.

"We have time. Why not?"

Turning inside the circle of his arms, she leaned her forehead on his chest. "You think I'm silly."

"You're here with me so I know you're silly." He stroked her back. "Later's fine. Don't worry about it."

She lifted her face to look at him. "I *am* silly, and you're no better. I hope you're happy, as I am."

He kissed her forehead. "You know I am."

She hugged him. "I'm glad. I want to be with you and I want you to be happy when you are with me." She squeezed hard, then shoved against him with both hands. "We have guests coming. First you insult my housekeeping and now you'll have me be rude to guests. Shame!"

Taylor walked to the stereo and selected a classical guitar piece for mood. The sound of the TV from the kitchen grated across the more subtle strings and he went to her side, his face drawn into fake anger.

"You're becoming addicted to that thing!"

Her defensive response was immediate and surprising. "I only watch because I have little else to do!"

As quickly as the words were released, she dropped her stirring spoon and reached to take his face in both her hands. "Oh, Charles, I'm sorry. I didn't mean—."

"It's true. I wish we could go home, to *my* home." The sentence broke against the taut set of her jaw.

She turned back to her stove and found her spoon, resuming stirring. "That is how we must live—wishes we know can't come true and everything is pretend. No one is real, we live stories as actors do. Sometimes when I see pictures of the war, it's as unreal as a movie, for just a moment. I catch myself wishing it were so, because then I would know how it ends."

He put an arm across her shoulder and she covered his hand with hers.

There was an urgent pounding on the door that could only mean trouble. He motioned her to stay in the kitchen and moved with cautious speed for his .38 and took a firing stance at an angle from the door. Before he could ask, Allen identified himself.

"It's me! Hal! Tay? Ly? Is anyone in there?"

Ly ran in as Taylor flung open the door and Allen stepped through. He pushed the door shut, pulling the handle from Taylor's hand in his rush.

"I need a drink." He advanced on the bottle. "Do you mind?" He continued without looking for permission.

At the first look, Taylor had pulled Ly to him and now he indicated the sofa. They moved to it, seating themselves and waiting. They continued to wait as his nervous strides hurried him from the cabinet holding the whiskey to the window and back again.

"It's the Colonel. The one that—you know." He practically spat the words at them. "The sonofabitch is here. She got

305

word to me through a friend of hers. I have to wait until she calls me." He stopped pacing long enough to look at Taylor, pleading. Not knowing what else to do, Taylor nodded. It seemed to satisfy Allen and he set himself in motion again. "Why did he have to come now? Three lousy days and I'd have been gone and in another week she'd have been in New York and it would've been all over! Goddam it!"

Taylor tried to sound reassuring. "We don't even know if she's with him, Hal. So he's in town—he could be here for a dozen reasons. And she'd be crazy not to sit tight in the apartment and wait to hear from him."

"She *has* heard from him. He showed up this afternoon with no warning, mad as hell, didn't stay with her five minutes and took off for ARVN headquarters. He knows something's wrong. We're just damned-fool lucky I've moved all my gear out and none was around for him to find. Maybe I ought to get down there, be with her if he comes around."

Ly interrupted, her voice controlled. "Could he know of Dao's plan to leave?"

Allen stopped. "He better not. We've bribed everybody in Saigon to get her cleared out of here."

"What kind of paper is she using?" Taylor asked.

"Her own." He managed a twisted grin at Taylor's surprise. "I thought it'd be safer, in the long run, even if it costs a lot more. Once she's out of the country and the Colonel finds out, all the people I've paid off will be so busy saving their own jobs they'll never cooperate with an investigation. And the big boys will be too embarrassed over the incident to try to call her back. She'll be my wife and a citizen before he can do a damned thing, and then it'll be too late."

Taylor nodded. "I like it better. When you were talking about a Cambodian passport—." He shook his head. "Anyone could have blown the whistle on her and had a legitimate charge to drop on her. This way you've got a lot of people who'll scramble to protect you."

Ly frowned her puzzlement from one to the other. "Cambodian passport? Dao is not Cambodian."

Taylor laughed. "Honey, with a Cambodian passport she could fly away from here and go wherever she wanted, and the damned thing'd only cost one, maybe two hundred bucks. I don't even want to know what a real exit visa costs."

"A lot." Allen grimaced. "I never saw so many open palms in my life."

Ly got up stiffly. "I will make coffee."

"Hey, wait a minute." Taylor hurried along beside her, waving the crestfallen Allen to stay behind. "Hal wasn't criticizing, honey. You know him better than that. He was just saying—."

He paused to grope for the words and she snapped, "You see? You wish to say the same things."

"That's not true. I'm trying to say he and Dao are stuck in a system. If they play by the written rules, they can't accomplish anything, so they do what everyone else does, play by the unwritten rules."

She jerked the percolator off the stove and shoved it under the tap. "And what of you? What rules are yours? Any? None? How long will it take you to forget me?"

He watched silently while she hitched through the business of making the coffee, his own muscles rigid under cold skin. When there was nothing else she could do, she had to face him and she turned swiftly, apprehension and defiance struggling to dominate her actions. He took her shoulders in his hands.

"I could never forget you. I want you with me always. I want you to marry me."

Instead of the reaction he expected, she slipped into the watchfulness of someone painfully aware of personal vulnerability.

"Oh, my Charles." Her words were scarcely more than breath. "What fools we are."

"Not me." He smiled, trying to lighten her mood. "I know what I want."

"And so do I." She remained neutral. "And I know what cannot be." She moved to him, put her arms around him. "I was making a quarrel. I'm sorry. This thing with Hal and Dao. It has me frightened."

"A couple of days. Two and a wake-up, honey. He'll be heading for the States to wait for her. They'll be all right."

"I hope so." She pulled his head down and kissed him quickly, spinning out of his arms and past him. "We have to get back. Hal will wonder."

They both started, wondering if they'd heard the faint knock. The sound of Allen's quick movement toward the door sent them hurrying for the living room. They entered just as he opened the door to the hall and Dao stumbled forward.

Allen caught her, scooping her up in his arms, not before Taylor and Ly saw the swollen discoloration of the side of her face. The left eye was a mere slit on an ugly swelling. Bruised lips drew tight, reflecting pain unseen. Her head lolled as he carried her to the sofa and she made a small coughing sound as he put her down, the good eye blinking shut momentarily. Her dress, dark blue and green, vibrant as always, contradicted her pale features. It clung to her sweat-dampened body.

Ly was by her side before Allen was finished setting her in position, holding her hand in one while the other skipped from point to point, hovering helplessly over swellings and scrapes.

Allen's voice was metal on slate. "He did this, didn't he?"

Ly's shoulders hunched in automatic defense at the menace in the sound. Dao remained silent.

He took the hand Ly was holding in both of his. "Is he still at the apartment? Where is he, Dao?"

She moved her head from side to side, swallowing as if even that effort hurt. On the second try, she strained one word as if through a gravel mesh. "Gone."

"Where?"

She shook her head again, a little stronger. "Gone back outfit. Gone."

He lowered her hand. "I'll catch him."

She strained to sit up, cried out and fell back. He came back to her, standing with his fists thumping his thighs.

A single tear, enormous in its singularity, rolled down her cheek. "You make me cry, make noise," she accused. "He hit me, hit me, try make me tell your name, say you live me. I never tell nothing, never cry. Now you make me do." She twitched from a partially suppressed sob and more tears rushed after the first.

Allen dropped to his knees next to the sofa and dabbed at her face with a jungle-green handkerchief that turned almost black where the moisture soaked in.

"Can we get her to a doctor?" Ly asked.

Taylor said, "Third Field—we'll take your car. Let's get her downstairs, Hal."

Slowly, painfully, Dao rose, warding off their attempts to lift her. "I not baby. I walk." Taylor grinned at her courage

308

and Allen's mute mix of anger and pride as he steadied her. They inched downstairs, Dao leaning more and more heavily on Allen. Still, once in the car, she insisted they wait until she had a scarf and sunglasses properly oriented to cover most of her visible damage.

Later, when the earnest young American doctor suggested a shot to "kill some of the pain," she spat like a cat and heaped scorn on him in broken English that convulsed him and infuriated her further. After being treated, her bandaged exit was as close to flouncing as bound ribs and a limp would allow and Allen's proffered hand was accepted with empress-like largesse.

Taylor and Ly waited until she was out of earshot. "What do you think, Doc?" Taylor asked. "Any internal injuries, anything like that?"

"I didn't see any sign," he said, and frowned. "She wasn't very cooperative. Kept telling me what happened to her was none of my business. Nevertheless, I have to make a report. If the Captain—."

Taylor held up a hand. "No, it wasn't him. I'll level with you, because we need your help. She belongs to a Viet Colonel. I mean, belongs. He found out she's in love with the Captain. If the Colonel finds she's been treated, he'll find out where. Then he'll find out who brought her. There'll be more beatings."

The doctor drew up, stiff and distant. "I don't understand, Major. I saw a lady who'd fallen downstairs, but no one who'd been beaten. Lady named, ah, yes, Nguyen."

Ly smiled at him and the aloofness disappeared. "That help?"

"I owe you one, Doc." Taylor shook his hand.

The doctor said, "Try to keep her out of trouble. She's too pretty for that kind of treatment."

When they rejoined Allen and Dao in the car, she was leaning heavily against him, her breathing deep and regular enough to suggest sleep.

Allen caught Taylor's quizzical look and said, "Reaction, I guess." His own features glistened with strain. Dao greeted them by opening and closing a lackluster eye. Allen continued, "She was running on nerve. As soon as we sat down, she was through."

Dao opened her eye again, working to focus on Ly. She spoke in Vietnamese, the tones stressed and distorted. "The pain in my face is less, but I hurt inside and I am very tired. And ashamed that I have caused you so much trouble. Are you all right?"

Ly's eyes shone with their own tears when she reached to brush a wisp of hair from Dao's forehead. "I am fine. You rest."

Dao's try at a smile was distressing to see, and then the good eyelid slid closed again. Allen lost himself in her face, leaving Taylor and Ly to drive back to the apartment in a silence even the traffic failed to dent.

Despite the previous tension and the shock of Dao's injuries, the car seemed to drift along in a feeling of relief, of mutually shared inner awareness. He stole a chance to look at Ly. She watched the people and machines mill around them with an almost detached air, her apparent disassociation mirroring his feelings.

"Ly?" He waited, watching her readjust her mental focus. "How're you feeling, honey?"

She indicated Allen and Dao with a delicate motion of her head. "I'm fine. I was just thinking about them, and us, everything."

It satisfied him inordinately. Part of his mind ridiculed the words as no answer at all while the other part told him she was thinking his own inarticulate emotions.

He pulled into the apartment parking area and again Dao insisted on making her own way. She accepted help with less disdain, moving with diffidence for muscles beginning to tighten. Awareness of pain in his own temples alerted Taylor to the clenching of his own jaws. In answer to Ly's unspoken question, he indicated for her to go with the others while he finished parking. She was waiting for him when he entered.

"I expected you to stay with Dao."

Ly looked helpless. "She insisted she felt better. I didn't want to force myself in. Hal will take care of her."

Then she was looking at him, expectation clear in her face, and the earlier sensation he'd felt in the car returned like a wave of fullness. He took her in his arms with deliberate tenderness.

"For all our troubles, Ly, I'm happier than I've ever been.

I'm a very lucky man."

Her voice vibrated against him. "We are both lucky. I looked at poor Dao and all I could think of was how much trouble they have. I wondered what my life would have been if you had not come, and it frightened me." She squeezed him very hard. "Could I be as brave as Dao? What would I do if someone beat me?"

"Don't think about it. Don't worry about it. No one can know until it happens and I'll never let it happen to you."

She chuckled and looked up at him, devilment in her eyes. "How do I know you won't do it yourself? I've seen you struggle with your temper. What if you should lose sometime? What then?"

For an instant his eyes went bleak and then he smiled. "I promise you your face will not be damaged." A faint alarm lifted her eyebrows and he warmed to his speech. "It wouldn't give me any pleasure to see your beauty marked, but I've always enjoyed the way you walk. It might be fun to fix it so you can't sit down for a day or two." He dropped a hand down her back. "And the area I have in mind fits my hand perfectly."

Her eyes closed and the quality of the smile altered subtly and she pressed against him, her head on his chest again. The smell of her hair flooded his senses and he tilted her head to kiss her.

At the sound of the doorbell he was suddenly standing alone and Ly was scampering into the bedroom, hands fluttering panic. Taylor shouted at the door that he'd be a minute and twisted at his trousers, trying to convince himself that no one would notice anything unusual about his condition. He swung the door open and tried to hide behind it with a nonchalance that failed but was unnecessary in any event.

Allen was in no mood to observe anything. He stepped past Taylor and said, "I hate to bother you, Tay, but she's asleep and I have to talk. What am I going to do? After I'm gone, what'll happen to her?"

Taylor smiled to himself before answering. The rush of the shower told him Ly had found a way to avoid any sly looks and her own blushes. He sat on an easy chair across from where Allen perched on the edge of the sofa.

"We'll look after her."

"He'll be back," Allen went on, unheeding. "He'll wait until I'm gone and he'll be back, and who's going to protect her?" He laughed suddenly, the sound reminding Taylor of mornings with the taste of bile in his throat. Allen said, "I haven't done much of a job of protecting her, have I?"

"Don't start up," Taylor said. "You might as well be realistic. If you'd been there when the bastard showed, you'd have thumped him and the law would've thumped you. And Dao would have gotten beaten another day. And probably worse. What's important is to figure a way to keep it from happening again."

Allen nodded grudging agreement.

"Has she got any relatives who'll cover for her until she catches her plane?"

"Not that I know of, except some cousins way up in Da Lat."

"Shit. That leaves one place. Here."

Allen objected. "Oh, no. No way." He shook his head. "Forget it."

"The women'll sleep in the bedroom and I'll scrounge up a cot to sleep on out here. The Colonel doesn't know anything about Ly, does he?"

The beginnings of relief carried away some of the lines in Allen's face, and Taylor reflected that it was a face that had aged a great deal today and was now trying to regain lost ground.

Allen said, "No, I'm sure he doesn't. But—."

Taylor moved to grab him by the upper arm and lead him to the front door, ignoring confused protest. "Go on back to her. I'll explain things to Winter. Tomorrow we'll take her out and smuggle her back into the garage in the trunk. She'll tell the apartment guard and some friends she's visiting those cousins in Da Lat and stay in Ly's and my place until the plane leaves. If the Colonel even smells anything wrong, he'll never think to look for her one flight upstairs. Everything'll be fine and I'll put her on the plane myself. Now go on. I'll see you in the morning and if Dao's OK, you can ride back to the villa with me in the jeep."

Allen stopped in the hallway and turned around. "I'll never forget this."

Expressionless, Tayor said, "You may live to curse me."

"Why?"

"Well, she'll be sleeping with Ly, you know, and they'll be talking about men and all that, the way women do, and she's going to find out what it's been like for Ly. Being with a Marine, I mean. I'm not sure you can stand the comparison, to tell the truth."

A strangled "Sonofabitch!" struck at the door as Taylor clicked it shut.

Ly's call interrupted his amusement and he answered as he walked toward the bedroom. She waited until he came in, confusion troubling the face above the wrapped-around towel. "What did you mean, that last thing you said to Hal?"

For a moment he stammered and then noticed the corner of her lip fighting to avoid curling upward and only then did the hidden laughter in her eyes register. He moved toward her. "I'll explain. In detail."

She raised her arms to him, laughing from deep inside. The towel slid away. "I hoped you would," she said.

They said their morning goodbye lingeringly. He held her chin in his hand, admiring her face against the first angry slash of the rising sun and tried to make a joke of it. "I don't know why we make such a production of me leaving. I'm only going to be a few miles away and I'll be back tomorrow evening."

She remained sober. "It's not a question of time or distance. It's because of the past. We have found each other and yet each day is so very—." She caught her lower lip between her teeth, searching for a word. "Our days are so very fragile," she finished.

He went through the mandatory denials, not wanting to spoil the day by starting it with another argument over marriage. It was better to accept the dull pain of silent acknowledgement than to be exposed again to spoken refusal. He kissed her, a utility-clad commuter off to the office. The scene was still playing in his mind after he'd picked up Allen and they were driving from the parking garage onto the street.

The morning traffic was already in full swing, a shade worse than usual this morning by virtue of the three-wheeled passenger jitney stopped dead across the street, its tail-lights winking a puny red warning at the oncoming machines. The driver poked at the engine and his lone passenger sat in the semi-darkness with his unread newspaper on his lap. The headlights splashed them and then the nose of the jeep was on the downramp to the street and they were out of the direct glare. The passenger spoke to the driver and lifted his paper to take advantage of the brief illumination. The driver straightened and looked across at them over his shoulder, then bent under the hood again.

A break in the traffic materialized quickly, a combination of one man deciding to slow down and another deciding to speed up. Of such things are our days made, Taylor thought, and released the clutch. The jeep sprang forward and left, blending in past the three-wheeler. The two men with it were caught by surprise at the unexpected rapidity of the movement, but still managed to bring their weapons up and fire point-blank as the jeep swept by.

The attack numbed Taylor but his instincts drove the gas pedal to the floor. The jeep, still in second, responded with a scandalized leap. Allen's head snapped back and then he rolled forward to a slumped position, his body tucked beneath the plane of the hood. As quickly as the shooting had started, it was over. Taylor shifted to third, moving away from the area as best he could, not troubling to look back. There would be no pursuit by the ambush, and those who did it would have fled. The discordant horns and screeching brakes faded behind them, and still Allen remained doubled over.

"Are you OK?" Taylor shouted.

Allen remained curled and turned a white, agonized face to Taylor. His voice sounded like panting. "I'm hit. My leg. My leg!"

Taylor leaned on the horn. "Third Field!" he shouted unnecessarily loud and unable to do anything about it. "We'll go straight to Third Field! Hang on!"

He asked if it was a bad wound and Allen unbent, eyes fixed on his right knee. Both hands gripped it as though they could fend off the pain. Blood gushed between his fingers and his trousers leg was sodden.

"Get your belt off," Taylor snapped. "Get a tourniquet on the goddam thing!" Allen looked at him dumbly. Pain and confusion and disbelief were pulling him down into shock. Taylor clamped a hand on Allen's bicep and squeezed mercilessly, shaking the other man like a child. "Move, you simple bastard! Get the bleeding stopped!''

Allen grunted with pain, mumbled, and snaked the belt off. He wrapped it around the leg and stopped, looking for something to twist it with. He was looking more alert, but also more frightened.

Taylor said, "Use your fucking weapon." Obediently, Allen twisted the tourniquet tight with his .38. Sweat ran from his face, but the blood slowed to oozing. Then he leaned over the side of the jeep and was sick, roaring heaves that lasted until the jeep slid to a stop in front of the hospital. Taylor pounded on the horn and yelled for a medic.

They came running, wheeling a gurney. Professional eyes accustomed to timing lives noted the tightened belt and the reduced blood flow, saw decent color remaining in Allen's face, and headlong rush slowed to deliberate haste.

The same young doctor who had administered to Dao appeared by Taylor's shoulder and when the Marine turned to him, jammed his hands in the hard white coat pockets and raised his eyebrows in silent question.

Taylor gestured weakly, signalling his helplessness. "Two men," he said. "Nailed us right on the street. We were turning. They only had a shot at him." They set out behind the gurney.

"No one you know?" The doctor spoke quietly, his eyes straight ahead on the form under the blanket.

"Strangers, Doc. Propaganda makers, that's all." He forced the words, each one unaccented.

The gurney disappeared through shining swinging double doors that winked like heliographs. The doctor turned to Taylor. "This is where you stop and I start. I'm sorry your friend got hit. We'll give him our best."

"Never doubted it. What d'you think?"

"All I've seen so far is blood. Check with us in a couple of hours, OK?"

"Yeah. Right." Taylor turned to leave.

The doctor called after him. "Hey, it's not as bad as that. It's hardly lethal. He'll get an R&R out of it. At the very worst, he'll be going home early."

Taylor continued on, not turning, merely raising his voice. "You better hurry, then, 'cause he had one and a wake-up."

"Aw, Jesus." The drawn-out words drifted in the echoing

315

hall and Taylor decided it was as complete a sentiment as any of them could come up with, and probably more than most would get.

Outside, the sun was risen in uncaring beauty. Taylor inspected the jeep, noting the single bullet hole through the hood, marveling that it had knocked out no wires or the carburetor and made them sitting targets. The other seven entry holes were all on the right or right rear of the vehicle. Silver metal, brittle in the morning sun, surrounded the wounds in the gray paint.

He climbed in and started the engine when above that sound and above that of the machines rushing past on Vo Thanh he heard the fly. Fat-bodied, self-important, it sawed past his ear and settled on top of the passenger's back rest. It ducked its head, stroking with hairy legs, then lifted off and buzzed down onto the seat and walked forward to the edge of the gummy scarlet stain just beginning to give up its color. It bent to the wetness and Taylor was suddenly flailing at it with his cover and whispering obscenities until the cloth was soaked and the fly's body was no longer distinguishable.

He threw the mess in the back seat and forced himself to draw in several rib-stretching deep breaths. Even so, it was several minutes before he felt able to get underway.

33

ORDWAY LOOKED AT THE OTHERS AT THE TABLE in the airport terminal and felt some of the joy in his system flow away. It was flattering, he decided, but it wasn't really what he'd rather have. Leaving should include all your friends, and it wasn't going home without having Willy there. The hung-over memories of last night's celebration and today's excuses weren't enough.

Willy and his damned one-man drug crusade.

He thought of Colonel Tho. *It was his fault Willy was off chasing after those people. The big black dude with the pinups would've had their ass by now if Tho hadn't put in backstop at Special Branch.*

That was a bad thing to think about. Even this close to the Freedom Bird, he didn't want to think about having that man come down on him. He concentrated on the others at the table again.

The Major. Naturally, he'd be here. And Kimble. Lucky bastard, him and his fat drop—going home same as me and only did eleven months. And the Old Man and Denby. Never saw two men so full of bullshit in all my life. Poor old Winter —no wonder he looks hurting. No replacements. Unit's going down the fucking tubes, for sure. But I'm getting out. Home. The World. Semper fi, you mothers. I got mine.

He sipped his *Ba Muoi Ba*, Denby's parting gift, idly wondering if it was true they put formaldehyde in it to keep it from spoiling in the heat.

Pa'll shit a brick when he hears that.

The image of his father fixed in his mind's eye.

Pa won't mind me writing to Willy to back up the stuff about importing and all that.

The image shifted in his vision, turned hot eyes on him.

Wasted lies. Be honest with yourself, anyhow. Pa thinks life is a proper furrow and no niggers on the property. If he learns Willy's black he'll have a rag-doll baby. Likely run me off.

Whatever they put in this fucking beer, it makes you sorry the horse suffered so 'fore it died.

Screw it all. I'm going home!

Denby said, "You're quiet today," and it made him jerk his head up. It was a relief to see the squinchy eyes were on Major Taylor and not himself. The Major continued to stare at the sweaty brown bottle without saying anything and Ordway noticed the hubbub in the terminal for the first time. It was strange how the same combination of noises could be good one day and hell the next. He thought back to his arrival and realized that what had scared him then sounded like a carnival today.

"I said, you're quiet today." Denby's fleshy smile hardened with the repetition and Ordway considered kicking Taylor under the table but he looked up before it was necessary.

"Sorry, Colonel. Daydreaming. Being here makes me think about going home, too."

Kimble laughed. "You're not going anywhere, not without Ly."

Taylor accepted the dig with a wry smile. "You're too smart for your own good. And mine."

Denby said, "Speaking of that kind of thing—," and locked his jaws at Winter's fierce glare.

Kimble missed the cue. "Were you thinking about Hal Allen? Have you heard anything about him, Colonel Winter?"

"It's something we shouldn't discuss here." Winter's irritation was abundant. "He's recovering, but the leg's gone from the knee."

"I know, sir. I was wondering about the girl."

"She's with him. Now, goddamit, drop it."

Belated understanding shone from Kimble's eyes. "Oh, I see. I wasn't thinking."

The uneasy silence returned for a few seconds and Denby attacked it, spraying bad jokes about Berkeley students manning antiaircraft guns around Travis to knock down the returning Freedom Birds, about sleeping in until 0600, about civilians who didn't know what 0600 meant, and all the going home routine. Through it all, Kimble grinned awkward delight and Winter's continuing unease grated in subtle discord.

Finally Denby stared at his watch. "Colonel, I hate to remind you, but you've got an appointment with the General, remember."

Ordway watched Taylor closely, pleased to see the Major saw through the act, too.

Officers. As big a pain in the ass for each other as they are for the rest of us. Look at that pig, Denby. Can't make it in the intelligence business, but he can out-bullshit the Old Man seven days a week. The Old Man just don't like ol' Kimble and he just can't hide it. But Denby's so nice it hurts. Slicker'n greased owl shit.

They exchanged brusque, soldierly goodbyes that made Ordway want to laugh out loud until he saw Winter's disappointment.

Kimble looked at Taylor after the others were gone. "You're not leaving with them?"

"I told the General he'd have to wait to see me. Somebody has to keep things in perspective for the old bastard."

The small humor rattled off Kimble's sobriety. He swung his head from Taylor to Ordway and back again as he took off his glasses and polished them and only when they were back on

318

and settled did he say, "And here we are again, the Three Musketeers. We've all got something in common and I was hoping to talk to both of you."

Ordway nodded, uncomfortable. Kimble faced Taylor in time to see him ordering a fresh round, specifying whiskey.

The nervous eyes behind the glasses hardened perceptibly and Taylor willed himself to match the stare. After a pause, Kimble looked away. "I don't know how you knew I needed a stiff drink right now, Major, but I think that's one of the things I dislike about you the most. You have an uncanny knack for determining what other people need. But my need is for more than the drink. I need to know some things about me."

"You'll have to explain that."

"I don't know if I can, dammit." He cocked his body forward, reminding Taylor of the tense anticipation of the first splash into spring's cold waters.

"You know about pressure. I know you don't always react exactly right, and all that shit, but what I mean is, you manage under stress. All my life when things got tough I threw up. I don't understand you. I don't want to be like you, but I'd like to know how you handle your world without coming apart."

The whole thing was half-heard and Taylor felt the mist falling between them, the ice-fog that came and hovered when he was faced with trying to explain to those who hoped the end result of combat was all-encompassing revelation. The cold shielded him, it was his sanctuary against the probing by the ones who truly believed that everything would be solved by understanding. He welcomed it even though he knew it would bring the recurring fear that he was not separated, not distant, but isolated. When the cold and fear intensified beyond a certain point he talked to his hands in his constant need to reassure himself the color wasn't really draining away from them.

"You want me to send you back to the States ready to do battle with the natives?" It was a weary, last effort to deny what he knew was coming.

The ascetic face across the table waggled on the end of its thin neck. "C'mon, Major, don't stroke me with something cute or some Zen-type bullshit. That night—with the jeep—that's the first time in my life I didn't smell trouble coming and get out before it started. I've never stuck around anything long enough to be a coward. I'm an habitual absentee."

"So?"

"Well, shit. Look, I want my baby and there's going to be a fight! You'd just walk in, the way you walk around this goddam place, like you own it. I have to know how to do that, why you're not scared all the time!"

"I *am* scared all the time, but I figured the odds. The only man in Nam who'd burn me for Charlie knows he wouldn't outlive me by more than a few hours, so forget him. Who else? Some nut with a spare grenade or an extra round? Even then, he'll probably miss. It comes down to worrying about an accident and I can't spend my time worrying about accidents or I'd never get anything done."

"I want my daughter." Kimble leaned further forward. "If the man who stole my wife tries to steal my kid, I'll kill him."

Taylor shifted in his chair, raising a hand to brush the stiff crewcut over his ear. Ordway noticed he used his knuckles and it looked like he would throw a punch any instant. He tensed to intercept it and only relaxed when it lowered and the Major went on.

"That's a stupid way to think and a worse thing to say. Do it and you gain nothing. And life's worse for the kid."

"It's what you'd do. You or that cement bastard Winter. You're the one who get things done, to use your phrase. Maybe I wasn't cool when I greased the mother next to the jeep, but I did it, by God, and I can sure do it to get my baby back."

His eyes dilated as he spoke, as though the soul behind them needed the light. His defiance was so alien he was hard pressed to retain it and Taylor played to the uncertainty.

"Is that what you're asking me? To tell you you'll do what's required? OK, if that's how you see it. And if you're wrong, I think you'll learn to live with it, the way everyone learns to live with mistakes. But you know damned well you don't have to kill him to prove who you are."

"I do! It's the only thing this goddam world understands! It's why I'm here and this whole thing happened! If you're hard enough and vicious enough, people leave you alone!"

"You want me to remind you how easy it is to kill a man? So you can do it again? You want to strip the respect off the body

320

and wear it like some kind of fucking pelt? You think finishing that shot-up little VC ennobled you? Think about it!" Taylor was off the chair, leaning into Kimble, forcing him back, their noses almost touching. People looked at them, at the intensity, and looked away.

Ordway felt a strange thrill in being near so much tension, wanting no part of it yet wanting to be in it at any risk. His mind careened, trying to find words for his excitement and there were none. He only knew he wished he was somewhere else and couldn't imagine leaving.

Taylor said, "Remember how he jumped when the first bullet hit him, how he fell? And remember him trying to get up, like a broken animal? He knew he was dead when you put the second round to him, did you realize that? Remember how the wind blew out of him when it hit him? Grunted like a steer in a slaughterhouse, didn't he? Make you proud?"

Behind the glasses Kimble's eyes guttered and mewing leaked through his lips. Taylor backed off, sitting in his chair again. When he spoke, the remnants of what had happened echoed as a tremor in his voice.

"If you can think of a way all that made you a better man, tell me about it."

Kimble's head moved in a sick negative.

"Good. Let's have no more foolishness then. 'Cause we just proved two things." He laughed, and the unexpectedness of it raised Kimble's head.

"First, the way you acted that night ought to give you confidence that you can handle a crisis. The other thing is that what we're talking about is something you can never comprehend. The reason you had to put the second round in that little prick is because he was doing his best to live long enough to get one of us. If he was praying, and he probably was, it was for enough strength to take us with him. You're not like that. Never could be. That doesn't make you any better or any worse, as far as I can tell, only different. But if you try to equate what happened down there to getting your child back from some guy in Philadelphia—." He finished the thought with a careless wave, then continued. "I don't think you really want to kill him and saying you will only creates a kind of obligation. And if you try it and you don't know how to do it and get away with it, you've got trouble. You're not crude enough to shot-gun a man and you're too full of civilization to bomb his car, so why not just drop it? You're boxed."

Coldly, Kimble asked, "How do you survive? Don't your memories trouble you once in a while?"

The futility of trying to explain distracted Taylor momentarily and the fog rushed to cover the exposed part of his mind. At that, he surrendered to the separateness and the faint remaining hope of a genuine connection between them was gone.

"Kimble, I had more in common with that little VC in the sixty seconds of our acquaintance than I'll ever have with you. That's not the point, though. The point is, we're in the same outfit and I simply don't want to see you screw yourself completely out of shape. That's all."

"Not quite." Kimble's eyes were stones, locked to Taylor's. "I want to be honest with you, too. I know you don't respect me much, and that makes it easy for me to tell you I don't care, because I don't like you at all. You play games with living and dying, and that's sick. Look at your idol, Winter. He's going crazy trying to catch one measly little slope and after he catches him, if he ever does, no one in the fucking world will give one shit. And you're right in there with him. You're just like the fucking NVA or the Congs—fanatics, every fucking one of you. You wear the smell of death. I've been telling myself I could be like you if I was threatened enough. May be, but it'd have to be my life that was threatened. You'd kill a man for what you'd call honor or duty or country or to pass the fucking time."

He stopped and stared into his cupped hands on the tabletop and Ordway struggled to catch Taylor's eye discreetly. He was dismayed when the Major spoke to him.

"We've been hammering away pretty rudely, Ordway. I'm sorry. You didn't ask to sit in on this and if you want to shove off or something, go ahead."

"No, sir. No, sir." He swore silently at himself for repeating and unconsciously bowed his neck. "I didn't want in, but I am. I mean, I was there, and I heard all this just now, and I think both of you all are right. You're the way you are, Major, 'cause you've got a job to do. You're a professional in this business. People like the Captain and me, we can do the same things you do, but we're not ready to think it's a business.

What the Captain done that night was live up to what he knew he's supposed to do, same's me. I might could get mad enough to fight a man and kill him. The Captain'd like to, but he don't think he can. That's the difference, Major, and it's why you can't see the thing the way we do. You *know*, sir. You've done it before and I expect you'll do it again and it'll be because you *decided* to do it. I have to tell you, sir, that scares the shit out of me."

At the Major's smile, he wanted to look away, but it was already too late. He'd seen the smile and the eyes and the shift that changed them from mocking cynicism to appreciation.

Then the Major said, "You're a very observant young man, Corporal. And I think far wiser than I've given you credit for. That's my loss." He raised his glass in a silent toast and drained it. Ordway followed suit.

Almost as if neither of them had spoken, Kimble said, "You're right about me, Taylor. I could never be like you. I won't shoot anybody. But I can do something you can't do. I can be finished with this place. You never will be. I don't think you'll make it this time. I think this place is going to get you. I don't know if I'll be sorry about that or not, but right now I think I pity you."

Rising slowly, Taylor's body interrupted a thick bar of sunlight and sent a hugely elongated shadow stretching across the littered floor. A jet screamed into the sky, giving him time to consider and discard several parting messages. In the end he merely gave each man a clipped nod and shook hands. On the way out he was especially pleased to notice his hand was tan and relaxed, the veins standing out in a rich blue. He was whistling to himself by the time he was outside.

Miller sat in the jeep with his eyes closed against the glare and concentrated on a drop of sweat coursing his left arm. It occurred to him it might be a fly and he opened an eye long enough to verify his first impression and closed it again.

For no accountable reason he was seized by nostalgia, so powerful it caught his entire consciousness and pulled it away from the forthcoming confrontation. The feeling faded as quickly as it came and, telling himself he had to trust Tho, he willed himself to remain unmoving. After all, he went on in his mind, a meeting scheduled for mid-morning on a busy street was no place for a hit. Trying to convince himself was hard work and he quit, searching instead for what could have touched off the earlier homesick-like sensation.

There was nothing—the standard scattering of GIs on Tu Do, but the prevailing sound was like nothing that ever happened in Pittsburgh—the cyclos and asthmatic Bluebirds and all the rest—and the sing-song of the whores. He was inhaling, wondering if a smell had been responsible, when it struck him. From one of the bars came the click of pool balls. Larded over that was the muggy day-smell of buildings that only lived at night. He could practically taste the corner hangouts of his boyhood.

"You awake, man?"

Miller opened his eyes slowly, dissecting the greeting for any sign of hostility. He couldn't find any, nor did Mantell's smile appear deceptive, although it bespoke something less than friendliness. The careless drape of his body across the hood showed the name Randolph and sergeant's stripes on worn Air Force fatigues.

"Ready," Miller said. "I got the word you wanted to talk."

"Not a lot." Mantell baited him, enjoying stretching the anxiety. "A friend of mine said I was to give you a message for him." He stopped, and the smile grew.

Miller closed his eyes again and slouched further into the seat. "You get tired fuckin' around, you tell me."

Mantell's voice hardened, full of undisguised resentment. "The rat say you clean. My friend say he'll get to you, but you got to be cool. He be away for a month, maybe two."

"Two months? What kind of shit is this?" Miller sat up straight and turned to glare at Mantell and the small man brightened again.

"Tough shit, big operator. We'll be talkin'." He turned and left.

Miller swore under his breath and started the engine, pulling away. Not until he reached the intersection with Bach Dang and was cruising along the waterfront did he allow himself to think of the bitter lump of fear in the back of his throat. He resolved to think of a proper gift for Tho, suddenly smiling at the thought of a gift in repayment for his life. He'd settle for something symbolic, he decided.

Behind Miller, straddling his motorcycle, sunglasses and

pulled-down hat masking his face, Sergeant Chi decided it was all right to break off his surveillance. He watched Miller make the turn back to the compound and drove past it himself. A few blocks further on he bought a soft drink from a pushcart vendor and relaxed in the shade to enjoy it.

Everything was going as it should, he told himself, swirling the bottle and watching the liquid form a bubbly whirlpool. The black sergeant believed *Trung Ta* Tho was the one who diverted the file clerk in Special Branch. Chi smiled, remembering the sergeant's nervous request for assistance. The smile grew wider as he pictured the expression on that face if he should ever learn that his request never reached Tho and the informant at Special Branch was a Chi nephew. Immediately, however, he was beset by the unwanted picture of *Trung Ta* Tho's face if he should learn the same thing.

He shook his head to chase away such unpleasantness.

After all, Miller had asked him to speak to Tho, and he had convinced Miller that Tho was taking care of the matter and that no mention of their arrangement must ever reach *Dai Ta* Winter or *Dai Ta* Loc. There would be no problems and Miller was protected, free to pursue his single-handed war.

Everything was going as it should.

34

THE INTERROGATION OF Tu had gone on for almost exactly two months and Taylor was so sick of it he dreaded thinking about it. Initially he had called on Tu at all hours of the day and night, keeping him confused and off balance. Further, he let Tu know he was available whenever Tu felt like talking, provided the subject was of interest to his captors. Taylor was accommodating, demanding, dependable, and unpredictable. The result was an emotional dependency on Tu's part, and there grew from it a blighted relationship resembling friendship in the way flood-driven animals are said to co-exist peaceably on high ground. Neither man ever allowed himself to wonder what might happen if the rains stopped.

Or didn't.

For his own part, Taylor entertained the same contempt for Tu as ever. The warm greetings, farewells, and confidences never altered the memory that Tu had hoped to see him gutted on the deck of Trung's apartment. In Taylor's mind, Tu's imprisonment was no more than a muzzle on a rabid dog.

On the other hand, Tu zealously banked the coals of his hatred for Taylor. He despised Taylor's sympathy and cursed himself for discussing his own underground activities, but he did it, because it was the only coin that bought companionship. He told himself the information was too old to be important, laughing to himself at the eager acceptance, then beat his fists on the concrete walls after Taylor had gone. He seized small rewards for being especially cooperative only to revile himself all the more in retrospect.

It was an insane union where hate, scorn, and repugnance were drowned in the juices of the brain and allowed to surface as warmth and welcome. Tu consoled himself that he was a prisoner, hoping against hope that someday he would be free and his superiors would never learn of his breakdown. Taylor consoled himself that every aspect of the technique he was using had been spawned by objectively analytical men in the Lubianka, Pyongyang, and Peking. Occasionally stories filtered through of the treatment afforded the Americans and ARVN prisoners held in the north or by the VC. He avoided thinking of them because when he did he caught himself enjoying each tiny purchase he achieved on Tu's soul. It made him feel like a man enjoying the screams of a rabbit being screwed out of its burrow in the grip of a cleft stick.

Tu had been helpful, his information more timely than he would ever admit. To Taylor's pleasure, Tu now lumped Trung with the profiteers so mutually despised by both sides. He supplied every contact of Trung's and garnished that list with people he suspected. Informants confirmed that Trung's business was faltering and he seemed unwelcome in circles where his popularity once soared. Tu brightened at each revelation Taylor supplied, concentrating his eroded face into an even tighter effort, trying to think of something else damaging. He damned Trung at every opportunity with the joy of a man who has found his personal scapegoat.

Eventually Tu told Taylor that Binh had a wife and daughter living in Saigon.

Winter and Loc bayed like hounds and drove the Unit and every source they could reach to work on finding them. Every imaginable record was checked, double-checked, cross-checked. The woman and her child were sought by scores with the frenzy of conquistadors pursuing El Dorado.

No one turned so much as a name.

Winter reflected the defeat with increasing bitterness, spending ever more time in his office, alone. His bearing remained erect and his manner was as correct as could be asked, but he developed a shortness in his answers and a psychological distance that seemed to increase with every minute spent in his presence.

Harker suffered with him. He watched Winter with steady anticipation, secure that this personality would soon revert to the old one. As the days passed and Winter only became worse, Harker's attitude also changed. The only question in the minds of the remaining men in the Unit was how much of the new Harker was the result of Winter's performance and how much reflected inward anguish over the ambush that had crippled Allen. The two subjects came to dominate his conversation and the others avoided him. To Harker, he was being rejected, and he didn't know why. He became aloof. Most recently he'd taken to volunteering to do the liaison work with the other organizations searching for Binh's wife and child. Reports came back that he was surly, critical, and threw Winter's weight around unbearably.

All those things moved through Taylor's mind as he stood in the hall outside Winter's office, waiting to be called inside. He also thought how uncharacteristic it was of Winter to keep someone waiting, then corrected himself. It used to be uncharacteristic. It was the small incivilities that constituted the major change in Winter.

"Come." The single word rapped command. Taylor entered and assumed a parade rest stance in front of the desk. A manila folder lay on it, red classification stamps and security admonitions glaring like angry scars. Winter acknowledged him with a curt nod, not bothering to look up or offer a seat.

"We haven't heard anything from your work with Tu for a few days," he said. "When'll he give us something we can use?"

"He may never. I'm pushing as hard as I can, sir."

327

"Possibly. I've been thinking." Moving quickly, Winter spun his chair to face the wall and its puffing air-conditioner. "Maybe you've gotten as much out of him as you'll ever get with this buddy-buddy act. A few rounds with Tho and Chi ought to just about wring him dry enough to hang out."

"No way, Colonel. We've got him to the point he's virtually one of us. He needs to talk and we're the only ones he can talk to. If you could see—."

"I know, I know. I get the same shit from Tho, through Loc. I'm still not convinced. I can't believe he doesn't know where the woman's hiding. You say he wants to talk? Good." As quickly as before, the chair spun and Taylor was struck by the bite in Winter's eyes and voice. "Let Tho hook his balls to that telephone generator and I promise you, when Tho rings, Tu answers."

Taylor failed to completely repress a shiver and it aggravated him. His own voice rose. "All that was tried. Well, not all, I admit. Tu's never been tortured. But that's a good thing. I don't think even Tho will agree with you, Colonel."

"He'll do what he's told, Major." The comment hung in the air between them, rotten with implication. Winter looked almost expectant and Taylor wondered, with a cold feeling inside, if Winter was actually hoping he'd respond in anger and lay himself open to a riposte.

He said, "Yes, sir."

The studied neutrality deflated Winter. He dropped his gaze back to the papers on his desk. "See what else you can get from the sonofabitch."

Taylor repeated his answer and was turning to leave when Winter stopped him.

"Sit down, sit down. Stay a minute." The brusque words and gesture were belied by the voice. As Taylor sat on the edge of the sofa, Winter threw him a warped smile.

"I've been letting things get to me," he confessed, lighting one of his heavy cigars. He rolled it around in his mouth before continuing. "To be so near, Tay, so damned close, and come up empty. Do you think Tu's got anything more we can use? Really?"

"I don't think he's holding out on us, Colonel. He may know something he hasn't used. He holds back pieces because he knows that's why we come to see him, but I think if he knew where the woman lives, he'd have said so. On the other hand, he may know something he doesn't know he knows, some little piece of information we can use to lock it all in place. We're working on it."

Winter sighed through the curling smoke and the column shattered in wild swirls. "Well, keep at him. Maybe we get a break." He laughed. "As if it made any difference. Maybe Harker's got the right idea. He was saying last night that he realizes he can't do a thing about Allen's leg but he's determined to put as much hurt on Charlie as he can. Inflicting pain. It seems to be becoming our reason for existence."

Still wary, Taylor restricted his response to a nod.

Winter continued, the cadence of his words much more rapid than usual. "I've let things slide to some degree around here. I want you to know I'm aware of it. From now on, Binh gets first priority, but that's all. He's not the whole show anymore. I'll be paying more attention to Denby's work, for one thing."

"What work?" The scorn popped out before he could stop it and Taylor braced himself.

Instead of anger, genuine amusement broke across the solid features. "'What work,' indeed. He's been very busy, actually, trying to hold back Miller. While Denby's trying to produce the ultimate operation plan, Miller and Minh have produced some respectable drug leads and Miller's pretty close to some of the help and hangers-on at that Major's bar."

Taylor allowed himself to relax a little. "We may be losing our good Sergeant Miller to the crass world of commerce." At Winter's expected surprise, Taylor continued, "He left a letter lying on his desk the other day when he had to answer the phone. I looked down, and there was the letterhead, some import-export business in New Orleans. Probably a connection with Ordway, you know? He was from Louisiana."

"God, I hope he's not thinking of getting out. We've got too few like him."

"A fact. And what about Harker?"

Winter's face clouded. "I can't be sure. I think he intends to make it a career. I'm not sure it's a good idea. I'm not sure at all, anymore."

"I haven't spoken to him much lately, but he seems basically sound. He's just letting this thing with Allen get to him. He'll get over it."

"I hope you're right. We had dinner last night at the My Canh, that floating restaurant. You know what I got for table talk? Him telling me about a guy who used to take a couple of street kids there for dinner every week. Treated a couple different ones to dinner each time. His contribution to something, I don't know. Anyhow, the day Charlie set off the bomb in the place, the guy was there with the kids. One of them was a little girl and she got away from him after the blast and took off across the gangplank for shore, just like Charlie figured. She, and the others, didn't know he'd put a claymore on the bank. When it went, it took her head off, and that's the way the guy found her. Harker says they shipped him home in a week, still talking to himself."

Taylor swallowed. "So he's getting morbid. He's been here too long."

"Morbid? Not morbid, Tay. You didn't hear him. He hates now, truly hates. I want you to keep an eye on him as best you can. Talk to him from time to time."

"I'll try. He's pretty cold to everyone lately."

"I know." With the words, years seemed to fall in on the older man. His head sagged and his hands curled into weak fists on the desk. "Make a try. He's worth the effort."

"For sure." Taylor rose. "Anything else, sir? I'd planned to see Tu today—."

"Do it," Winter interrupted, waving him out. "We've all got work to do."

With Taylor gone, he settled back, drawing on the cigar luxuriously. He let his mind wander, exercising only enough selectivity to confine himself to the past two months. Faces came and went and he reflected with pride that the Unit had accomplished some things while suffering few casualties. Allen's was the worst, by far. The other attrition was administrative. He'd have lost Allen anyway, which was a hell of a way to look at things, but there you were. Then there was Ordway and Kimble. Taylor was getting short, and Harker's extension would be running out. He made a mental note to recommend disapproval if he tried for another extension. Denby was almost through. There'd be a request for early rotation from that one in a few days. Even Miller would be leaving soon, despite his recent interest in extending.

He was going to continue on down the truncated roster, but something about Miller, something no more than a mental hangnail, stopped him.

There was something strange about Miller's attitude and he made another mental mark to find out what had increased the Sergeant's devotion to duty so markedly. Four months ago he'd have died if anyone said extension within his hearing. Perhaps Denby had an idea. Or Taylor.

Small matter. It was winding down. Well, if Nixon was going to pull them out, better to do it and have done. Maybe Harker had a point—take out as many of the opposition as possible and fade out.

The knock on the interoffice door was so weak it was a second before his mind reacted to it. Hurriedly, he said, "Come in, Loc, come in!" He was poised, expectant, when Loc eased into the room. A nervous, sweating Duc followed, grinning and nodding in a welter of uncertainty.

"Sit over there," Loc directed and the unusual directness of the order warned Winter that something was about to break. Loc seated himself on the sofa, across the room from the now clearly frightened Duc. He took a moment to compose himself, using it to inspect creases and the drape of his uniform.

"Major Duc has just revealed some interesting developments. I will let him tell you of them." He fixed Duc with a baleful eye and busied himself with a cigarette as the rotund Major cleared his throat several times and began in careful Vietnamese.

"I am certain you remember the woman, Tuyet, who worked with Trung, Tu, and the man who died when they were captured. Perhaps though you have forgotten, with so much on your mind and she is an insignif—."

Loc hissed.

Without missing a beat, Duc said, "The woman works for us now, but she has been unproductive until recently. She indicated she wished to see me last night and I met her. She has observed a curious thing in the past months."

He paused for breath and Loc's head swung his way. Duc pretended not to notice, but his recital speeded appreciably.

"In the past week or ten days, Trung has had little trouble

331

getting merchandise for his bar. Tuyet was considering quitting work there because his black market connections were failing. He could provide no access to anything and was even short of supplies for the bar. Now there is plenty of everything. She knew the change was important and followed Trung on three afternoons when she knew he was making business calls. On each occasion, he was picked up by a car at his home. Tuyet followed in a cab. I have reimbursed her."

"The important points," Loc suggested.

Still not looking at him, Duc went on. "She was unable to identify the man Trung met, but she learned that the man who picks him up works for an American. Yesterday she followed the driver after he returned Trung to his home. The man went to this address and entered the house." He moved to Winter's desk and placed a typed copy of his report on it, tapping it with a finger.

"The address is that of Mr. Benjamin Barline. Colonel Loc says you know of him."

"Barline?" Winter repeated the name as a whisper, repeating it, louder. "Barline? Are you telling me he is involved with the VC? I cannot believe it! He hates us, but he is not one of them! Has anyone checked? Who have you told?"

"It has not been pursued," Duc answered quickly, "but a records check shows no suggestion of Barline being a communist."

Loc gestured Duc to silence and took over the conversation. "And we have told no one because we are uncertain how to treat the information. But we can draw some very interesting conclusions. While you have been cursing Barline's reports, I have made it a point to analyze what he has written *about*. He is a most industrious man, my friend. And lucky beyond belief. Did you realize that when the Vietnamese workers went on strike against the Morris-Knudsen construction company, Barline reported it would happen before the company was aware of the plan? Two days before the Tet attack, he was in Singapore. He returned in time to file amazingly accurate reports about the start of the operation. In fact, he was in the Cho Lon district only hours before the first VC troops entered and at one time made it back to the center of the city through their lines, within blocks of where another group of journalists was shot down by the same VC. And just about two months ago, when some monks attacked the police around their temple, it was a surprise to the police, but Barline was there, as was a cameraman associated with him.''

Winter gestured wearily. "All right, all right. He's being tipped off. I don't believe he works with the VC.''

"Nor do I," Loc agreed, his voice scalpel sharp, "but I am certain the VC works with him. I believe he is informed and I'm certain he has, quote, antigovernment, unquote, sources.''

"The driver?''

Loc stared at his cigarette. "I don't know, but it seems the only answer." He turned back to Duc. "Repeat what else you discovered.''

Duc stared and Loc nodded slowly. "He must know.''

Sweat blobs suddenly spangled Duc's brow at the hairline and the flesh immediately under his deep-set eyes gleamed a damp satin-finish. He extracted a handkerchief and mopped rapidly. The sweat disappeared, but his face retained a ruddy hue.

"Before the attack on Major Taylor and Captain Allen, Barline and his driver interviewed people at IV Corps HQ, including the Colonel who claims Le Thi Dao as minor wife. The Colonel left there very angry, accompanied by the driver. We cannot account for the driver's movements in Saigon, but we know they left Tan Son Nhut together to return to IV Corps. The next morn—.''

"I know." Winter cut him off. Then, to Loc. "We have already had this argument. Can we link Barline, the driver, or the Colonel to the attack?''

Loc's lips pulled back from his teeth. "I said then, and others agreed, we need no signed confessions or fingerprints. We knew enough then and we know even more now. We *know*.''

The sound of Winter's drumming fingertips told Loc more about the tremendous struggle inside his friend than either of them would have wished.

Winter said, "When you knocked, I was thinking it might be a good idea to eliminate as many of the opposition as possible. Right now. No arrests, no prisoners. Immediately before that I was telling Taylor I knew I'd lost a bit of control lately. I'm trying to be absolutely correct about this problem,

Loc, find some kind of balance. I see the only difference between them shooting Allen down in the street and us doing the same thing to Barline is who squeezes the trigger."

Loc said, "Exactly," in a voice that made Duc blink.

Winter shook his head. "My friend. My old friend. I want to fight our enemies. I don't want to think of myself as a simple murderer. Outright killing, just to be on the safe side—." He stared at the floor.

Once again, a minute gesture from Loc galvanized Duc into action, this time up and off his chair and out of the room almost at a trot. Even after the other office door had clicked shut, Loc continued to watch Winter. Finally he looked away, polished jet eyes fixed on a point far beyond the drab walls.

"This discussion sounds strange to me. If Barline is responsible for the attack on Captain Allen, and I say if he did nothing to prevent it, he is responsible, has he not chosen to side with our enemies? Is he not, then, an enemy? Why should we not treat him exactly as he treats us? We have handled this same problem before."

"But only when we *had* to. We can get this bastard without more killing if we go about it right. We don't have to be thugs or backshooters, like them. Look at us! We're so inured to bloodshed we're starting to talk exclusively of simple-minded execution! Harker's already fallen into the trap. And I'm responsible for that, Loc! I've trained him! I'm not afraid of death or dying or killing. But on a soldier's terms, Loc. We're getting to be more and more like the savages we're up against. We can't do that!"

Loc remained motionless, a detached clarity in him noting a never-before-observed pulse in Winter's throat, a dark blue worm of vein. It swelled and deflated, tale-bearing slave to the unobservable heart. It was almost vibrating.

"I will have to think about what you have said," Loc answered, continuing to study the vein. "If this—this insight —came to you so clearly and so suddenly, it is my responsibility to consider it very carefully and answer as wisely as I can. I will have to think. Will you excuse me?"

Winter tried desperately to explain further as Loc rose with the slowness of pained effort. The unformed words worked his jaw spasmodically until he realized there was nothing more to be said and Loc was waiting with stoic patience.

Finally, Winter closed the conversation, saying, "I would be grateful for your thoughts. I have asked for your help many times and you have never failed me. I am asking again."

Loc let himself out, each movement a deliberate action. He tested himself, observed his control under stress. He tried to force his mind blank, tried to imagine himself suspended in white clouds.

It was impossible. Doubt tore his efforts to shreds and Duc's body wrinkling the upholstery of his best chair refused to disappear behind any white clouds. Accepting a temporary defeat as gracefully as possible, he told Duc, "What you have told Colonel Winter and myself is to be repeated to no one. You will learn more of this driver. You will report only to me and only speech. There will be nothing on paper."

Duc nodded. "We will kill them?"

"Only in a civilized manner." Loc smiled, wanting to shout.

"I don't understand."

"There is a great lack of that," Loc replied and Duc mentally threw up his hands. If Colonel Loc was going to be clever, there was no sense trying to understand him. He was relieved to be waved from the room.

Alone, Loc stared at the point of a pencil, telling himself that Winter's determination to avoid killing was nothing new. In truth, he had always been extremely cautious about such things, insistent on exhausting every possibility before lending his approval to direct action against a specific individual.

He nodded unconscious agreement, remembering other times Winter had attempted to avoid such things and said it was because it was like the VC to behave that way.

It was not an entirely new attitude, then, but he had never stated it so clearly or so strongly.

He had said nothing like it when Taylor dropped the Chinese from the roof.

He had said it so clearly now, for the first time, when the subject was influential, of international importance.

When the target was white.

35

Ly reached across the table to take Taylor's hand, a corner of her mind remaining aloof from her desire to sympathize, holding onto the hope that he, like her, would ignore the unremovable scratches in the cheap veneer. At the touch of her hand, he grasped it in his own with a reflex so quick it startled her. His *barong tagalog* blouse twitched, and there was more than responsive pleasure in his touch. She felt the tension, as she had on other occasions, and even as she wondered that she could know by the touch of his hand that he was troubled, complimentary tension built in her own body. She was glad she had chosen western dress, especially the dark green blouse and skirt. She felt the colors and style gave her an appearance of calm, no matter what her inner attitude. She bit the inside of her lip and wished he wouldn't mention marriage this evening. Not this evening.

His eyes studied hers, expressionless, as though she were a thing to be memorized.

She decided to put an end to the waiting.

"Something is making you unhappy, Charles."

"It's the job." He moved a hand in a tired swing. "It's not exactly boring, but it's not pleasant work. Does that make sense?"

"Certainly." She squeezed his hand. "You're not doing what you should be doing. It would disturb anyone."

Instead of agreement, she received a sharp look and a bitter laugh. Offended, she withdrew her hand.

"What did you think?" she demanded, further angered by the shrill hatefulness of her own voice. "Did you expect to spend your time in an American war film, no real pain, only healthy excitement? Everyone lives happily ever after?"

He surprised her again, smiling that strange way that lifted the right corner of his mouth higher than the left. It made him look like a mischievous child. It was his smile for her and, as always, it banished her temper. He got out of the chair that always creaked relief when he rose and stepped behind her, leaning to press his face to her hair and cross his arms in front of her. His bare arm smelled of soap and the peculiar, almost animal smell of the Occidentals. She closed her eyes, rubbing her cheek on it. All irritation fled, replaced by an amusement with herself. The exotic smell generally repelled her and a room full of them at a party was almost overpowering, but he was different. He was excitement, a delicious feeling of desire and tenderness and—.

She frowned, searching for the word. Belonging. That was it. She took a bite of the arm, gently teasing the taut skin between her teeth, pleased with herself. She knew she felt good because they belonged to each other. She could think of herself with him and didn't have to think of herself as of him.

"I love you, Ly," he said, the words muffled in her thick hair. He dropped his head lower, repeated the words in a whisper by her ear, his breath a cold wave that shivered its way down her back.

She pulled away from him and walked to the sofa where she wedged herself into the corner of the arm and the back, looking at him with a catlike intensity. He followed, planting himself in the easy chair, waiting.

"Are you sure you love me?" she challenged him.

His eyes widened. "I'm almost forty years old, Ly. I think I know that much about myself. Yes, I'm sure."

She slipped off the sofa and paced the small room. She had meant to be so clever, so subtle in her approach to this discussion, and the first question had blurted out with the delicacy of a horse falling through the door. She resolved to be more cunning.

"I asked because I don't always understand you, as Dao didn't always understand Hal and as you both never understand us. And you are not almost forty. You are seven years older than me, that's all, and I will not be called almost thirty."

He ignored the age matter. "You make all four of us sound like not-very-bright children. I can see why you might be upset with our situation, but at least Hal and Dao understood that two people in love should be married."

She whirled on him. "Ah! But who else knows that? In America, will your 'real world' be so real for Dao? Will it accept her?"

"We're a nation of immigrants!" He gestured his difficulty in expressing himself. "Dao'll qualify for citizenship because she'll be married to Hal. She'll be fine. What's that got to do with anything?"

"I know about your people. Your black people are immigrants, too, and there is much trouble. I hear disturbing things about Americans and Oriental people."

"I can't argue that. Some Americans don't like—hell, hate—blacks. Some hate Orientals. Some hate everybody. You've got people exactly like that in Vietnam, goddamit."

"You don't have to swear. There's no reason for you to be angry."

"Yes, there is. I get tired of hearing about our racial problems as if we're responsible for the whole idea. The truth is, we're the only ones who care enough to try to work it out without just killing off the minority."

She drew herself erect to remind him that Vietnam had no such problem and then heard her parents cursing the Chinese as late arrivals and immigrants and money-grubbers, threatening to take over the economy. Then she thought of the Vietnamese record with the original inhabitants of the land. She decided to think about it all in more detail before arguing further in that direction.

"Very well. Dao will be accepted by some and not by others. What of social life? You know what it's like for us now." He darkened and she smiled understanding. "I am grateful for your thought, Charles. But will it be any easier for Dao in America? Can she go to the supermarket without being stared at? Can she go out to dinner with Hal and not be treated rudely by the waiter?"

Taylor had to laugh. "I'd like to see the waiter offend Dao. If she didn't scratch his eyes out, Hal'd pound him in the deck like a tent peg." Concern lingered in her eyes and he grew serious again. "I can guarantee you there'll be times and places where she'll be badly treated, but they'll be very few. She'll be thinking of herself as an American in no time, and when she does, so will everyone else."

"In no time? A woman from this culture?" An out-flung arm encompassed millennia.

"She'll never stop being Vietnamese, for sure. But the point is, no one expects her to. She'll be expected to be Dao Allen, and that's all. But you started all this asking if I was sure I love you. If you think I believe you're asking me about Dao, you're crazy. You're asking about Ly. Have you decided to marry me, after all this time and argument?''

Her heart surged at the quiet, almost apprehensive question, as though he was steeling himself to certain pain. She pressed her hands to her sides, fighting the urge to throw herself into the comforting circle of his arms.

Instead, she stepped to the window and looked down into the street. He waited, patiently silent, while she put thoughts together. A movement at the edge of her vision distracted her and she leaned forward to see a boy, his shirt gleaming white in the light pouring from a store entrance, the young face turned skyward in fierce concentration. Despite her own mental turmoil, her attention was drawn to a point above his head. A massive beetle suddenly hurtled out of the darkness, his path across the slash of light an impossible direct line sideways, altering hardly at all in angle and height. She realized the boy had the beetle tethered to a piece of cotton thread and was flying the insect like a kite, a game played by Vietnamese boys for centuries. For another second she enjoyed the nostalgic diversion, her mind seizing the opportunity to dismiss present tensions for the respite of childhood memories. The boy would play with the insect until he tired of it, she thought to herself, and then free it or kill it. It depended on his whim and his nature.

She had to put her hands on the windowsill to brace herself. The boy and his insect, the cars and other vehicles grunting their way down the street, all wavered, and then she was steady again.

"It's true," she said. "I was thinking of myself, wondering if I could live as an American."

She sensed rather than heard his approach and ached for his embrace, but he stopped, so close his breath stirred her hair when he spoke.

"We can do it, Ly. If anyone can do it, we can. We've lived here almost like hermits. If we can survive that without tearing each other apart, think of the life we'll have when we can be free!"

She reminded herself to be practical. "We have been many places, Charles. To dinner sometimes, to the *cai lung*, even to

339

my cousin's house once.''

"Once! And remember how he looked at me? Talk about discrimination! I thought I'd have to eat out on the sidewalk.''

She giggled. "He is concerned about a woman of his family. You would be the same.''

"That doesn't have anything to do with anything. We're talking about getting married.''

"No.'' She shook her head, more to chase the feeling that his words were hovering around her than to indicate disagreement. "You are discussing marriage. I am talking about a Vietnamese living in America. But I must ask you to answer one question and I will trust you to speak only the truth. Would you marry me because you felt sorry for me?''

He sighed. "I do feel sorry for you. You're crazy. I want to marry you because I love you. And I know you love me.''

Before she was fully aware of what was happening, she had turned and pressed against him, tears burning their way under her eyelids. He was holding her, almost cradling her, and she was crying harder and telling him she did love him, that she always had, and now it was spoiled. Even if she could find the courage to leave with him, he would never believe her again. He acted as if he had not heard, continuing to rock her in his arms, and finally held a handkerchief up to her eyes. She took it and he still said nothing, but continued to hold her, one hand now stroking the length of her hair in slow rhythm.

"You see what I have done?'' Her voice was reedy and she winced, thinking how he must hate it. "If I had told you the truth at first and admitted I loved you, none of this would have happened. I didn't know if I could leave here, be your wife. Now I want nothing else and I'm so afraid!''

The tears came again and she squeezed her eyes shut and hid her face against his chest.

"Afraid of what?''

"That you won't want me, that you won't believe me ever again!''

"Why? Because you said you didn't love me at first? I knew you did, Ly. I wanted it so bad I had to know it was true, had to believe you were lying. So it didn't count. Lies that no one believes don't count. And I'm so happy you're pregnant it makes me want to cry, too.''

She felt her clothes had been torn off. She choked, looked up at him, not believing her ears.

"You know? How could you know? It doesn't show. Not yet. I have only been sure—."

"About two weeks." He grinned down at her.

She nodded, feeling her knees would fail any instant. "About two weeks. How could—?" She stopped, the words a tangled mass in her mouth.

"Little things." He still wore the grin. "Not so much the things you've said as the way you've said them. Caught you looking sideways at yourself in the storefronts. And then to-night, would I marry you because I felt sorry for you? How tricky can you get?"

The warmth of him and the cold dread inside her fought for dominance. "You would not marry me only to have the child? It doesn't change the way you feel about me?"

"Certainly it changes the way I feel."

His smile dropped away and his eyes were the blank glass that said nothing. Her body seemed to melt under her head, a last breath evaporating halfway up her throat.

"I loved you before," he said, "as the woman I desired above all others. Now you carry my child. I love you more than I thought possible."

The tears started again, and this time she didn't care, because she was too happy. She told herself she was being silly until finally he lifted her own hand to her face again and she realized she was still holding the handkerchief crushed in it. She pulled away from him and rushed into the bathroom to repair the damage to her appearance. When she returned to the living room he was waiting in the easy chair. She sat on the arm, leaning against him.

"I was a fool, Charles. Our paths are one. I knew that. Even *Chi* Hong saw what would happen, long ago."

He snorted. "Even *Chi* Hong? Listen, that old woman's smarter than all of us together. And a lot more observant. I'll bet you anything she knew you were pregnant before you did."

A laugh bubbled up from her deepest sense of contentment, a sound that gave her pleasure in itself. The anguish of the past weeks was already a memory. She watched him take her right

341

hand in his and stared down at the crown of his head, so nearly bald with its cropping. She counted the three scars, examining the especially bad one, and again considered asking how he got them and again decided to wait until another time. By tilting her head slightly, she could inspect the first gray flecks at his temple. She touched them gently.

"What are you doing?" He pulled to the side.

"Admiring the gray color." At his quick frown, she couldn't resist adding, "And wondering what you'll look like when you start losing your hair."

"What?" He twisted to look at her. "Who's losing hair? And there's not that much gray, either. One minute you're telling me I'm going to be a father and the next you're telling me I'm growing old."

"I didn't say that," she laughed. "I said you have some gray hair. It's very *distingué.*"

"Let's just forget about my hair, shall we?" He looked away, making her giggle. At the sound he pulled her down into his lap and kissed her fiercely.

"Think about that," he said, "and tell me if that's what you'd expect from an old man."

She put a finger to her lips and pretended to give it serious thought and he roared like a gored bull. When she tried to roll from his lap he held her firmly in place.

"You know," he said, his face squirming to cover a smile, "in all this time, there's one thing about you I've wondered about and never investigated."

A sense of alarm crept through her at the light in his eyes, threatening, but not in the least dangerous. Her heart beat faster.

"What do you mean, investigate?" she demanded. "I am no criminal."

"I don't know if you're ticklish," he said.

The word wasn't familiar but it sounded ominous. She struggled against his grip before sinking back and asking, "Tickle? As to make a child laugh?"

He nodded and she watched in horror as he raised his free hand. She began to thrash, but he held her too tightly.

"I am not ticklish, Charles!" She strained to get some semblance of dignity in her voice. "This is stupid, Charles! I am not a child! Let me go!"

The hand dropped onto her ribs and the last word was an unintelligible screech.

"Don't!" She abandoned pride and begged. "Please don't! I'll scream! The neighbors will hear! They will think you beat me! I will swear to it! Oh, Charles, please!"

He closed his hand and she laughed and yelled at the same time. She managed to gasp. "No more!" and inspiration gripped her. "The baby! The baby, Charles!"

He stopped and his smile turned unsure, skeptical.

She tried to calm her breathing. "I could get over-excited and hurt something. You'd better stop."

He loosened his grip and she snuggled comfortably into his lap. "I promise not to talk about your gray hair anymore." She traced a line down his shirtfront. "I think it looks nice, anyway."

He kissed the top of her head, and she said, "And if you tickle me more, I'll be too nervous to do anything else tonight."

He turned her head to look into her face, his own a blend of concern, desire, and a faint hint of suspicion. "You're sure it's OK? I mean, if the tickling—you know, the baby?"

Another laugh came to her and it felt like a light in her heart. "That's different," she said, stretching to kiss him, feeling the stretch of her muscles, feeling good, knowing that if there was never another happiness in her life, she would be satisfied.

BOOK THREE

36

THE HIGHWAY to Long Binh erupted from the northeast quadrant of Saigon, a four-lane concrete artery connecting MACV with its closest major tactical headquarters. If peace ever came, the road would link the population center with a superior deepwater port. Today machinery streamed in both directions on it in the sweltering afternoon, massive trucks and heavy equipment, buses and bicycles. On its shoulders small businesses struggled for life, constructions ranging from four scrawny poles and a poncho to shade a one-cooler soft-drink stand, to squat stucco monstrosities of functional-modern universality that sold whatever the proprietor had managed to acquire. They all crowded the highway, hunkered down into the red earth with their backsides nervously exposed to the open country behind them.

Duc, discreet in casual civilian clothes, guided his motorcycle around a truck and risked taking his eyes from the green Toyota ahead of him long enough to look at the scenery. From the vantage of the raised road he saw the last of the marsh reeds on his right bow in the wind in random fan patterns. The shape of the land changed again and they were back to gentle curves where pale gray-green scrub grew close to the ground, spreading wide patterns of mottled shade that softened the rusted color of exposed earth.

The Toyota parked beside one of the stands. The owner of the business had tried to bring a festive appearance to his place. Palm branches festooned the roof of a clearly recognizable pyramidal tent, its military markings carelessly painted out. Colored cloth strips dangled in the open spaces where the canvas sides had been rolled up. The multi-hued fringe was

344

hectic in the conflicting breezes from the fields and the high-way. As a crowning touch, a half-dozen large cable-carrying spools were distributed in the sun as tables, each flanked by aluminum-and-plastic chaise longues.

When the car stopped Duc continued toward Long Binh for about two hundred yards and pulled onto the shoulder. When the two men from the car made themselves comfortable at a table, he waited a few more minutes, then executed a U-turn and joined the southbound traffic. Directly across from the stand was a small garage and Duc mentally applauded his good fortune, coasting to a stop in front of the building. A truck rumbled behind him, thundering toward Saigon, its wind-eddies pulling heavy air from the dark interior of the garage. The smell of hot metal, oil, and rubber was a fog and he waded through it to show his ID to the lone mechanic. The grimy, ragged proprietor half-smiled at Duc's explanation of a surveillance and lifted his shirt to display a scar that stitched across his stomach like a lightning bolt. He pointed out a pack-ing case for his guest to sit on and found a practically clean newspaper to protect the neat businessman's trousers. He permitted himself another faint smile as Duc fussily spread the paper. With a quiet wish for good luck, he returned to his work.

Trying to get comfortable, insuring he could see without being seen, Duc massaged painful hams with hands that hurt almost as badly.

Motorcycles! He damned them all. A man had all he needed between his legs and a damned machine there was not only un-natural, it was obscene. Maybe even dangerous. The things were certainly dangerous to life. What else might they do to a person?

He shook his head to dislodge such morbidity, wishing he could hear the conversation across the road.

Failing that, he took some comfort in the observation that Trung was upset by whatever was being said and Barline's driver was in no mood to soften his argument. The latter leaned across the spool-cum-table, his lips moving in short machinegunner bursts. Trung's insect face with its reflective sunglasses remained steadfastly to the front. Even at this dis-tance, Duc could see the gouged frown on his forehead. His occasional movements were agitated.

345

These observations pleased Duc for two reasons. Not only was it good to see Trung in an unpleasant situation, but preoccupation made it all the more unlikely he'd recognize the casual figure following him. Duc adjusted his own dark glasses with a self-congratulatory smile. Not many one-man surveillances were worth the few minutes they lasted. His had lasted much more than a few minutes and had surfaced a positive connection between Barline's driver and Trung. Colonel Loc would be pleased. If there was any justice in the world, possibly even Colonel Winter would be sufficiently pleased to stop growling and swearing for a day. Perhaps two, even.

A change in the driver's position brought Duc to full attention. Something had disturbed him, altered his attitude. A gesturing hand froze in mid-air and he turned away from Trung to lower his head and busy himself with a shoe. Duc searched for the reason and saw nothing untoward, except a young man dressed in the dark trousers and white shirt that was practically uniform for students cruising toward them on a motorcycle. The youth appeared to be looking for someone, and quick excitement stirred in Duc's mind.

At the sight of the green Toyota the young man swerved off the highway. Sudden braking billowed dust and he walked his machine clear of it. He was little more than a boy and his nervousness as he surveyed the customers made Duc think of his eldest son. He forced the thought away and studied the driver and Trung, hungry for their reactions to this development.

Trung paid the scantest interest. The driver remained bent over, still fumbling at his shoe.

The new arrival wallowed in indecision, alternately moving to start the motorcycle or park it. In the middle of his difficulty, the driver gave up his effort to disappear and glared naked rage at him. The youth shied, but gathered himself and strode to that table. The driver rose quickly and snapped a curt phrase at Trung before leading the younger man off to the side. Duc leaned forward, enjoying the spectacle.

After a short dressing down, the young man drew himself erect and spoke furiously to the driver, and to Duc's surprise, the latter listened. In fact, he changed his whole manner, dropping his aggressive, chin-forward posture and becoming pensive. His head bent forward and one hand absently massaged his stomach.

Duc caught himself teetering on the edge of the crate and was reestablishing his balance when another motorcycle growled to a stop in front of the building. The rider stepped inside, nodding nearsightedly to Duc, blinking in the dark. He shuffled across the greasy, littered floor and Duc was mentally dismissing him when a sudden erratic leaping of the shadows spun him around. The customer had his feet entwined in the cord of an extension light. He tripped, put out a hand, and swept a workbench clean. The owner screamed anger and leaped from behind the motorcycle he was repairing. It fell with a grating thump at the same time the light crashed to the floor, contributing its own sharp pop.

For an instant all three men posed in rock-like immobility watching fuel from the downed machine gurgle toward the lamp. Duc moved first, jerking the extension cord just as the gas ignited with a muffled shudder that sent them all flying. Scrambling to his feet, Duc realized he was in the doorway just as the owner appeared, shoving the flaming motorcycle past. It careened away and the owner shot Duc a silent plea before turning back into the acrid, boiling smoke. Calling down curses on the man's idiotic disregard for personal safety, he hurried along behind, pausing to pitch out the hapless customer.

The blaze, for all its smoke, was essentially restricted to the oil-impregnated earthen floor. Scooping up uncontaminated dirt from under benches and out of corners, beating stubborn flames with rags, they smothered it quickly. Duc stumbled into daylight and felt the delicious first breath of clean air solidify in his lungs as he blinked into the startled gaze of Trung. At his startled exclamation, his partners froze beside him. A muttered phrase and the young intruder was trotting for his motorcycle.

Trung whispered more to the driver, a hand at his side twitching erratically. The driver never deigned to look at Duc before moving at a very fast walk toward the car.

The motorcycle was already spewing dirt and grass as the youth wrestled it onto the cement, fighting across traffic to get into the southbound lanes back to Saigon.

Even as that was happening, Duc was moving in pursuit, shoving through the rest of the small crowd, determined to salvage something from the accident.

He told himself, I can always find the driver and Trung is no problem. But the boy was searching for the driver! An obvious breach of security! And news so important the driver had to think about it!

As he roared off down the highway, Duc tried to convince himself that the two Colonels would overlook the aborted surveillance in their pleasure at learning what the young man could tell them.

If he could be caught. Duc gained because of his more powerful machine but the boy was skillful and he was rapidly approaching the city.

Once into that maze—. Duc swore and twisted on the throttle, ramming past a lumbering lowboy. Ahead, the other man dipped in front of a tank truck passing a bus, gaining precious time while Duc had to wait for the olive drab monster to make its way around. He allowed himself to hope someone at the city-entry checkpoint would stop his man, then hastily amended the thought. If anyone there was alert enough to do anything about a fleeting target, their answer would be to shoot him off his motorcycle. Duc prayed the man would survive to be captured.

Unimpeded, he closed the gap between them and then they were flashing past the checkpoint, QCs shouting and waving excitedly. Some rounds cracked overhead a few seconds later when they were intermingled with traffic again, clear of any danger.

Dodging through suicidal gaps, passing on the shoulders, pushing his machine to its limit, the young man managed to keep just ahead of Duc. On one occasion Duc was almost close enough to reach out and touch the rear fender and it occurred to him he had no idea how he was going to make the capture. If his quarry chose not to stop, what could he do?

If I get next to him, he told himself, I can shoot his leg. But if he crashes he'll kill himself. And what if he turns into me? Can I shoot out a rear tire? But that still makes him crash.

He made up his mind to force the man off the road and hope for the best. Colonel Loc would forgive him if the man died, providing he was sufficiently damaged himself. Duc deplored the unsatisfactory compromise.

His eyes were watering severely now and his forearms ached. Still, he was almost on top of his man. They roared past another bus together as if in formation, engines laboring in chorus, and Duc realized they were approaching the bridge leading to the first major built-up area. It was almost too late. He changed his mind, deciding to shoot out a tire.

The young man glanced to his left rear to see how close Duc had gotten and looked directly into the muzzle of the .38. Regardless of the pressure of the wind, his eyes flew as wide as muscles would permit. He leaned away from the threat and raised his hands in terrified surrender. The motorcycle eased toward the right hand bridge railing in a gentle curve that altered rapidly at an increasing angle. Duc tried to shout warning and the wind rushed into his mouth and distended his cheeks, pulled his lower lip down against his chin. He choked and waved the revolver. The other man flinched and dropped his hands across squeezed eyes. Duc braked as hard as he could.

The smaller motorcycle made it over the curb, although the jar unseated the rider. He still had his hands clasped over his face as his feet came up and he tumbled backward. He was in mid-air, horizontal to the road, when the front wheel hit the cement bridge railing. The seat rose, catching him slightly off-center, thrusting him up, out, and in the general direction of the city. The man turned over, his legs still shaped to the long-absent motorcycle, removed his hands, opened his eyes, and had just enough time for a short exclamation of unbelieving dismay before he cannoned into the murky water.

An ancient fisherman in his boat paddled once, languidly, as if this sort of thing happened every afternoon, and was waiting when the youth broke the surface, gagging. With easy efficiency, the fisherman grabbed him by the collar and belt and rolled him aboard. That done, he looked up at the bridge and located Duc, who was arriving at the rail with pistol in hand.

"You are with the government," he declared in a cross tone.

"Yes." Duc had a strange feeling that all was not over yet, and he spoke warily. "That man is my prisoner."

The old man spat. "He was. What I catch in this river belongs to me. I sell what I catch."

"Give him to me. Now," Duc said.

"I sell what I catch," the man repeated, and Duc sighed at the set to the antique jaw. Even the gray whisker bristles looked stiff with defiance.

"Bring him ashore. We will discuss it."

The fisherman nodded and leaned into his paddle.

"What do you mean, by the kilo?" Loc snapped. His eyes narrowed and he spoke in the edged voice of a man whose temper is near boiling. Duc had only seen him this way occasionally. Each instance was burned in his memory.

Before answering, he dabbed sweat from his upper lip. "What could I do? A crowd was gathering. The old man insisted he should be paid for his catch. People were laughing. Some were hostile. It was only a small amount," he finished lamely. Colonel Winter made a noise and Duc looked to see him trying to stifle more laughter behind a hand. Duc smiled his appreciation but Loc's voice snapped his head around.

"Whatever you paid, it is your problem. I authorized no payment. And I never authorized the apprehension of a miserable courier. What waste! The men will be able to tell us nothing and the other two are warned that we have an interest in them. I am disappointed."

"But, Colonel," Duc protested. "Trung only identified me because of the accident. And we know where they both live. I thought the new man might have some information. What he said to Barline's driver impressed him."

Loc made a noise in his throat. "We don't even know if the man is antigovernment. He might have brought news of a family matter." He stopped to look away and when he turned back to Duc the angry eyes were damped to a glow. "Well, we shall see. He is being interrogated now. From the way you describe his actions, I think he will tell us what he can, and soon." He dismissed Duc with a sign.

Embarrassed and hurt, Duc made his way to his office. The sight of Taylor and Harker was at once welcome and disturbing. He knew he would tell them of what happened and they would understand, would help restore his face, but he would still be in trouble with Loc.

The thought of caring about his relationship with Loc brought his attention to a close focus on Harker and for a moment he forgot his own troubles, noting the pinched fold of flesh between the younger man's eyes and the increasing definition of a downward curve to the full lips. Duc felt a prickle between his shoulders at the awareness that Harker's expression was beginning to resemble Tho's. The image ran through his mind as counterpoint while he told them of his adventures.

"He wasn't hurt at all, then?" Harker sounded vaguely disappointed and Taylor flicked a quick glance at him before looking to Duc for an answer.

"Not much. He not even have time swallow much water. You should see face while old man, me bargain how much he worth! He *beaucoup* believe I let old man throw him back if not get good price."

"Not a bad idea," Harker said. "Would've softened him up for Tho."

Taylor said, "You'll have to excuse him. He's feeling especially bloody-minded today. The pressure of his impending promotion to Captain, no doubt." He pushed for a light sound, a failure emphasized by Harker's bleak answering smile.

"He only a scared boy," Duc said. "Better I look away, make like not know them. Maybe Trung tell himself he make mistake."

"The kid's a fucking courier," Harker said. "If he doesn't know anything else, he knows where he picks up his shit and where he takes it."

"Useless already," Taylor said, making no more effort to sound light. "They know Duc grabbed one link in the chain. They've already repaired it with another."

"Then Tho'll find out what else he knows. Who recruited him, who else he knows, what he's been carrying. He'll know something we can use."

"And if that's all he knows, how do you make Tho stop asking questions?" Taylor retorted, and Duc was pleased to see Harker check, then was disappointed again at his answer.

"Why should he stop? The kid's VC. He knows the rules."

"Or the lack thereof." Taylor spoke softly and turned away.

Harker pursued him with his eyes. "All right, then, or the lack thereof. Whose fault is that? You know fucking well they'd do the same to us."

"And you know better than that. 'They do it' is no excuse."

Standing up, Harker said, "No, I don't know better. Ever since I got here I've been hearing people tell me anything Charlie does is OK because he's fighting for a cause. I've got

351

one too, goddamit! If we lose here, they'll throw people like Duc in the slammer and make him eat the key. What do you think would happen to Ly if you had to leave her here and we lost?''

Duc would have sworn the last word was still unspoken before Taylor moved, and yet he heard it choke and somehow Taylor was holding Harker's blouse bunched in the right hand and the left was touching the handle of the .38 on the desk. The sight of the older man's fingers receding from it filled him with a relief that made his bowels feel watery.

Instead of speaking, Taylor swallowed, made a noise like an old woman scolding, and let go of the wad of material in his hand. He made a tentative move at straightening the jacket and stopped short, turning the movement into an awkward wave. Then he was out the door.

Duc sat heavily. He spoke in Vietnamese, too tired to even think in English. ''You make life very difficult for us, you know? You worry about causes and the morality of nations and things you cannot define, like *good* and *bad*. We want peace and we want to live to enjoy it.''

Color still simmered in Harker's cheeks. ''You could get that by surrendering,'' he said, looking at the empty door. He used English and Duc was sorely tempted to make an issue of such inconsideration. He sighed, deciding the man probably had no idea how he was behaving. He kept to English, frowning with the effort.

''No. You right about what happen me if lose. Happen my children, too. That not live enjoy peace. But you have peace your country and I think you little enjoy.''

The bitter anger suddenly washed from Harker's manner and for a moment Duc had the sensation he was looking at a man shedding time. The eyes were those he'd learned to associate with Harker, full of a yearning to understand. In his own mind, Duc had always pictured him as the typical American, a puzzle of complexity and complication, but a man who wanted the best for everyone. The change in the face made him aware how much he missed the other man. At the same time, the new look returned.

''Don't worry about what's going on back in the States now,'' he said. ''We'll outlast those assholes. They've got a lot of support now, but they're still a minority. No matter how much noise they make, it's all they're good for. They sure as hell won't fight. Not unless maybe Canada disappears and they're cornered. They'll parade around and throw shit at cops and fuck each other in the parks, but the first time somebody says they have to fight for their so-called ideals—I mean fight someone who's allowed to blow their fucking heads off—they'll fold. And then we can take care of business."

"And who wants fight them?"

"Nobody. Not yet." Harker moved to the door, shaking off the question. "I've got to go find the Major," he said over his shoulder. "I acted crazy, talking to him that way. If you see him, tell him I'm looking for him, will you, sir?"

Duc stared at the wall.

It was all so confusing. Such a big country, so powerful, so much dissension. Not a paper tiger. No, absolutely not. A drunken tiger, its thoughts twisted and its limbs uncoordinated, but lethal, nevertheless.

He shivered and bent his mind to thinking of dinner and what the children would be telling him about their day. Again, the juxtaposition of his eldest and the youth on the motorcycle crowded his vision and he considered thinking about it but warned himself off. He got up to change into his uniform and thought, instead, of the evening ahead.

He was lacing his boots when the intercom rasped and he winced, thinking how the sound was at its worst at this time of day. He answered and when Loc ordered him up to the office he looked at his watch and groaned. In fifteen minutes he would have been gone.

The sense of cosmic injustice soared as he entered Loc's office. A first view showed not only Loc and Winter, but on their respective flanks, Tho and Denby. He braced himself for what Taylor sometimes called a planet-sized ass chewing. Then he saw the trio sitting prim in their straightbacked chairs against the wall between Loc's office and Winter's. The young man was the one he'd arrested, now dressed in prisoner's shorts and shirt. The frightened eyes sought his, desperate for any familiar contact.

The woman was older, probably in her early thirties. She wore a threadbare *ao dai* and met Duc's eyes with calm dignity. He was unaccountably pleased to see what he thought was defiant pride breaking that surface, like the swift glint of sunlight on rippled water. A child, perhaps four years old, sat in the woman's lap. She was the image of the older woman, staring at Duc with sober calculation.

Anticipation grabbed at his stomach and he faced Loc with his breath locked in his throat.

Loc smiled at him. "Major Duc, I would like to introduce Nguyen Thi Hoa and her daughter, Nguyen Thi Cuc, the family of Nguyen Binh."

37

THE COLORS OF THE EMBROIDERED MANDARIN SLEEVE altered subtly in the changing light intensity Denby created by trailing his hand across the protective glass. He wished he could actually feel the silk without soiling it, then changed his mind, knowing the sensuousness of his imagination was superior to any reality. The truth could never send hues bursting through his fingertips. It was best to leave the material in its frame.

Sitting at his desk, he looked at the mating elephants and found it possible to smile at them, thinking there should be a simile there, a rationale between the massive coupling and patience. Nothing came of it, but he didn't care. He swung the chair in a lazy, repetitious half-circle, looking at the walls but not seeing them, thinking of the reprieve just handed him.

A sense of gratitude toward Duc touched off sympathetic chords of surprise and warmth. He told himself there was no harm in appreciating a successful job. Objective appreciation —that was the trick in getting along with the gooks—accept what few things they did well, try not to go crazy over the fucking mess they made of everything else, and keep away from them as much as possible.

He frowned and stopped the chair.

Winter would have to insist that the American side take charge of the bitch and the child.

His hand moved to tug at an ear lobe. Still, speed was going to be important now. The quicker she spilled her guts, the better. She knew where her husband was and once he was caught the bullshit about other investigations would be forgotten and he could pack his bags and get out. Too bad for her. The way to get the truth quickly would be to give her to Tho. Winter would have to let go of her.

He scuffled for a pad and pen and started compiling a list of arguments for making the interrogation exclusively a South Vietnamese responsibility.

In an hour he was done and sat back to admire what was now a dual list, points for and points against. All favorable arguments were well phrased. The important thing would be to make Winter think he was doing Loc a favor by dumping the woman on him.

The knock on the door broke his concentration and he answered harshly.

Miller marched in and said, "I just heard the Old Man's got Binh's wife and kid."

A whining floor polisher in the hallway seemed to underscore the words. The machine continued to complain through the door after he closed it. The spice smell of the wax remained.

Denby grinned. "How about that? As soon as she opens up, life'll be worth living around here again."

Miller was unimpressed. "I'm thinking about our operation, sir. If you get the plan to him now, he's sure to go along with it. Later, if she comes up with Binh, he might not want to push our show."

A first impulse died in Denby's mouth as he considered the ramifications. He reminded himself that Miller was a fanatic, absolutely out of control on the subject of his damned drugs. This intensity could only mean he felt there was a definite drug presence. And there was no way in hell there was going to be any drug investigation. Not now, not when any need for risk had been eliminated.

He pursed his lips, rolling the words through his mind before speaking. "We're going to have to be patient, Willy. This development is the biggest thing to happen here during my tour. God knows how long it'll take to break the woman, but I'll do everything I can to get our op plan approved as soon as possible. I know how much it means to you."

Miller said, "Colonel, we're getting short. Hell, everybody's short, you, me, Harker, Major Taylor. He's got more time than any of us and he's short. If we don't get something set up quick, it'll be too late. I been thinking. What if I told the Old Man I want to extend to work on it?''

Before he could control it, a wince jerked Denby's features. He gave it full play, turning it into a grimace of concerned disagreement. "I don't think I'd do that just yet," he said, spooning out caution. "He's excited now, and we shouldn't bother him. But you're right, time's short. I'll get a definite program going in the next day or two. Don't worry about it.''

Recognizing dismissal, Miller opened the door and closed it against the keening waxer before giving Denby a parting shot.

"I hope you get to him soon, Colonel. I've done my whole tour without complaining and I've got a free bitch coming. No disrespect, sir, but if he don't give us a go-ahead soon, damned if I won't tell him what I think.''

Denby winked conspiratorially as the door closed on the hard black features and then spun his chair to face the opposite wall and cursed. When he was ready to think again, he lectured himself sternly about excesses. Calmly, he established his principles—neither Miller or Winter must ever learn the investigation op plan was no more than standard format and rough notes in a manila folder. Second, Miller must be prevented from presenting his case to Winter. Lastly, Miller must not be allowed to initiate any action on his own.

He examined the situation, coolly at first, seeing it as exasperating but not particularly threatening. Slowly, however, wisps of apprehension smoked into his thoughts. Why had Miller been so quiet for so long and only now made a threat? And what of Winter's patience? It had been—what, weeks?—with no positive action taken on the investigation. It wasn't like Winter to allow a stall.

Loc.

Loc and Winter.

Facial muscles tightened under fat, giving him a bunched look and he sat up in his chair, alert now, physically and mentally tense.

If Loc and Winter had something going, they might want to keep Miller out of it, either to protect him or because they had something terminal planned for someone and didn't want Miller too close to the action. If that were the case, Winter wouldn't care if his own people never put together an op plan.

That could be it.

Shit, it could be worse. What if Winter was using the phony op plan idea as a set-up, deliberately intending to watch him fail?

Why would any of this happen? Was he borrowing trouble?

He reviewed the start of the whole problem, the news the Major's joint was completely crooked. Now that he thought about it, Winter took that with unusual calm. He was more inclined to shout and roar and so forth. The quiet one was Loc. And what had he done? Shipped the Viet Sergeant who'd gotten his nose into the trough out, into combat, the next day.

He was on his feet without conscious effort, out the door, and standing in front of Winter's office. A spasm wrenched his chest when he realized he'd already knocked, Winter had said "Come!" and he had no idea what he was going to say. He tried to deny the fear—no, the panic—that had gotten him this far, but it twisted in his guts again and he opened the door with gritting teeth, determined to make it work for him.

"Carl. What can I do for you?" Affable Winter. Cheerful Winter. Backstabbing sonofabitch.

"I wanted to talk to you about the investigation on our Major, Colonel." He stepped up to the desk, wondering if Loc had the room bugged, afraid of being overheard, afraid of Winter correctly interpreting his actions.

"I've worked very closely with Sergeant Miller on this thing. After all, he's the one who'll be under the gun, and it occurred to me he's pretty short. What can we do about someone to fill in behind him, sort of a replacement?"

"I wouldn't worry about that." Winter continued to smile. "The important thing is to get the operation underway."

"Yes, sir, but—."

Winter continued smiling, continued talking. It was as if no one else was in the room. "I wouldn't be surprised if Miller hasn't tied in with our counterparts and done a little advance work on his own. I think he'll extend if we get something good going." Suddenly he was laughing, the loudness of it startling. "Poor Miller! He's as crazy as I am. He'll do what he thinks he has to and spend half his time in regret. Haven't you seen him sulking around here? He's already pissed off because we haven't turned him loose."

Denby nodded. "He's a hard-charger. We'll have him working to his heart's content pretty soon."

Winter's smile moved. "I hope so, Carl. I've been doing a lot of feeling sorry for myself and I let this thing hang fire. I'm ashamed of myself for that. Binh's wife may be able to lead us to her husband now. If she can, and we catch him, the scramble in their entire logistic set-up'll look like a four alarm fire in a cat house. If Miller's properly in place, we'll get that fucking Major and everyone around him. I wouldn't want to see us blow that."

"No way!" Denby punched at his glasses. "I'll have the plan ready to go—."

Once more, Winter simply raised his voice and talked over him. "By Friday, Carl. Friday this week. The target leaves here in three weeks, but I'm sure you have those details memorized. I'm not sure we have time to send him home in custody, but I've got time to send him home in a box, if it seems appropriate. I want that plan and I want it to work. We understand each other?"

"As usual, Colonel. I'll have it on your desk by Friday. And maybe a pleasant surprise, as well."

Winter said, "I'll settle for a good op plan, Carl." He lowered his gaze to the papers on his desk and Denby backed outside.

In the safety of his own office he lowered himself gingerly into his chair as if afraid of breaking something. Dull eyes fixed on the wall and he stared, the only movement of his body an irregular blink.

Stupid, egotistical, murderous sonofabitch! You drop the fucking ball and now you threaten to put my ass in a sling for it! "Do we understand each other!" Shit! You knew I didn't have a plan, knew it all along. And you know something about Miller you're not telling me. Double-dealing prick.

His brain shoved the message through that he was staring at the elephants again. A hand flew at them to sweep them from the desk. At the last instant the thick fingers closed, scooping the carving into the air rather than smashing it. He held it while he was uncomfortably extended across the desk with his arm stretched out in front of him and forced himself to remain in that position until the arm was trembling but his breath was steady and regular. He replaced the figurine and sat back.

I'll beat you at your own game, Winter. I ought to let you have the Major killed and then blow the fucking whistle on you, but I'd have to answer too many questions about this past year. I'm going to make you write me a perfect efficiency report. You're not going to threaten me with your idiot Sergeant, either. Whatever you've got going. I'm going to pull the fucking rug right from under you and make you love it.

He closed his eyes and levered the chair back, willing relaxation. The thickened face eased, flowed to a soft mass. The lower lip drooped, damply pink. The features canceled each other out. The face grew unreadable. It was a facsimile.

Miller hiked past the small shops, unaware of the occasional beckoning hand or calling voice. He would have been uncaring had he noticed them. His mind raced, even as his feet moved him through the crowd, shifting, pausing, rushing ahead when the opportunity arose. Once off Tu Do, he could move more easily, but he slowed, not wanting to appear anxious.

Mantell was at his usual table and Miller recognized him even while his eyes were still adjusting to the darkness. He got a perfunctory greeting and no invitation to sit. He pulled a chair out and made himself comfortable.

"I'm tired of fooling, Bobby," he said. "You get to your man, tell him me and my partner have got everything set. We're ready. If you all can't make this deal, we gone."

"Shee-it." Mantell made a sentence of it. "Who you deal with if you don't deal with us? You saw my man. You talked to him. People cross him die, Willy. You ready for that?"

Miller nodded, having no trouble indicating fear. "I give you that. He's a hard sucker, I don't doubt it. But I'm short, Bobby. We don't see some action, quick, I'm gone, not lookin' back, and no hard feelings."

The matter-of-fact attitude seemed to disturb Mantell. He looked away. "You really think you can deal with someone around here and get away with it? You buy one little joint, we know about it before you drop the butt, man."

"We don't need you," Miller said. "This ain't the only place in the world that grows poppies."

Mantell tried to sneer, but he was clearly no longer sure of himself. "You know who's got that part of the world sewed up, man? You think you can deal with *them?* A black? You crazy?"

A rank wave of old sweat masked by perfume struck Miller with almost physical force as Mantell leaned toward him. He swallowed and forced a smile.

"You ever hear of South America, man? A man with ideas, they don't give a rat-fuck what color he is. And the governments there protect friends. It's a business."

"They sell low-grade shit," Mantell defended, "and some of them mother-fuckers is communists. They catch some nigger messin' with dope, they put your ass *under* the jail."

"Not if you make money for them and sell the stuff where they want it sold. And they got more to offer than heroin. They got marijuana by the ton. I mean, by the *ton*. And cocaine like nothin' you ever saw. It's a candy store, baby."

"If it's so fuckin' good, why you even talk to us poor folks?" Mantell sneered. "If you so fuckin' smart, why ain't you rich?"

Miller put his elbows on the table and spoke to the scarred surface, knowing the lowered tone would bring Mantell forward as if on a string. He braced himself against the smell and wished he had a drink.

"Not everybody in the operation is a brother. Might be we could get a piece o' that action, use the muscle from this business to push in. Might be."

In the darkness Mantell's tongue flickered wet as he ran it across his lips. "You talking about runnin' stuff from here and other stuff from there? You sound like the boss. And what about your honky partner?"

Miller raised his head, fastening his eyes on Mantell's. The latter met the stare, held it, and crumbled. He scuffled for a cigarette to hide his discomfort.

"You tell your boss what I told you. He's the one wants to build a fucking empire. All I want is to get rich while he does it. I got to know we got a working deal or I do my thing someplace else. Like I said, man, no hard feelin's, OK?"

Mantell nodded absently and Miller left, breaking into a broad grin only when he'd made the turn back onto Tu Do. Mantell had been so busy dreaming of world conquest he'd forgotten to deny he could reach his boss.

38

TAYLOR SAT ON THE CHAIR opposite the woman and struggled with embarrassment. The cell was a special one, reserved for prisoners of importance, a fact that, in itself, always aggravated him and in this instance gave him an indistinct sensation of decadence. It was clean and neat, with three chairs and a small table and curtains at the window. They were pulled open now, admitting the day, but exposing the bars. He had the feeling that the forthright woman in the cell might have arranged the effect intentionally, determined that you understand she had no need for dissembling.

The institutional smell of the place was unpleasant but hardly overpowering and the sparse furnishings were probably better than any Binh's wife had ever owned. Yet it was a cell, with the feel of a cell that says the walls cannot protect, but, perversely, carry a threat that protection may be begged for and denied.

The woman, correct to the point of anonymity, with her hair pulled back in a tight bun and clothed in black pajama pants and faded blue blouse, gave no hint of being inconvenienced. Her composure rattled his.

Worse, the child stood beside her, bright in her red print skirt. She rested a hand on her mother's thigh and fixed her uncompromising attention on Taylor's face.

"She is a beautiful child," he said, stumbling over the words. His face grew warm.

The woman appeared not to notice and nodded thanks without smiling. "You speak our language well."

He thanked her and she nodded again, asking, "How many children do you have?"

"I have none," he said, thinking this was one hell of a way to run an interrogation, but consoled himself that a rapport might grow from the small talk.

She said, "I have only this one." Her hand reached automatically to the exact height and distance to touch the child's head and pull it to her. "There was a son, older. We lived in a village. The planes came." She looked away from him, cherishing the miniature at her side.

A helicopter hacked its way over the compound. He waited until it was past. "I am sorry."

She looked up sharply. "Why? Did you drop the bombs?"

"No. It was us, however, we who fight your husband. I wish this other thing had not happened."

A door slammed somewhere in the building and her eyes leaped that way, instant tension broadcasting her fear that the sound had significance. When nothing followed she turned back to him.

"It was not your fault. It was not the fault of my husband. In all time, men have killed and called it love or peace or a better plan. It is a madness."

"Have you said this to your husband?"

She smiled and her entire being changed, magically dispelling years and cares. "Do you mean does he know I can be a reactionary female who does not complettely support the will of the Party? How can you know us so well and have to ask me such a question?"

He laughed, stopping short at the child's small-animal expression of alarm. "It was useless. I am sorry. What does he say to you?"

"What can he say?" Her humor burned off at the rhetorical question. Bitterness moved back into her features as if claiming a heritage. "He knows I am right. He knows the killing will never stop. If the people win, they will put the oppressive running dogs in prison and kill them. If the government wins, they will put the liberation fighters in prison and kill them. There is no peace. There never was and never will be. There is only killing."

"Would you believe me if I said I dislike the killing?"

"Of course. None of you like the killing. But you find reasons to continue. If you cannot kill enemies, you turn your friends into enemies so you can kill them."

Disdain curled her lip and she turned away to look out the window. At the edge of his vision, he saw a movement of the hand holding the child to her. It was gently brushing the glistening hair. The sight triggered the anomalous reaction that he had never seen a picture of Ly as a child.

He forced himself to the present.

"You could protect your husband, you know. You know of the Chieu Hoi program. If a man of his importance rallied to the government—."

She shook her head, the movement so fast and so tightly controlled it looked almost like vibration. Continuing to stare out the window, she said, "He will never renounce the revolution. Perhaps you will kill him. Perhaps you will capture him. He will never join you or inform on his comrades."

Her hand might have moved involuntarily, he thought, and started stroking the child to cover it. She could be more wrought up than she shows. His instincts dictated taking a chance.

"You mentioned his comrades. Are they all as loyal to Binh as he is to them?"

"The revolution is his life. Everyone knows that." A vein, dusk-blue against a smooth temple, expanded and commenced a fluttering activity.

"Then why must he hide? What will happen when they find him?"

"His friends in the revolution will protect him." She faced him, haughty.

"They will not protect him from the ones who call him traitor. There will be a People's Court. We both know what that means."

She continued to face him unmoving. He could see no sign of changed posture, but felt the different cast of her body. He wanted to hold his breath, afraid of the fear smell. He pressed ahead.

"Your husband is powerful. He has enemies within the revolution, men who envy his power. They will show him no mercy."

"That is why he must hide!" Her voice rose and the child crowded against her, the solemn eyes never failing in their intent to keep on him.

The woman said, "His friends are preparing the way for his return. The traitors Tu and Trung must be made to tell the truth!"

He ostentatiously stared at the child, letting his gaze wander from her features to the mother's arm, thence to her face. He fastened his eyes to hers, staring through them.

"Trung and Tu will never help your husband on this side of

the grave. I promise you that. And why has not Trung already cleared Nguyen Binh?"

She drew back, watching him from almost a profile attitude. "Trung plays the colonial lackey game." She had difficulty with the words and her hands moved restlessly. "He uses each faction within the revolution against the other for his own gain. He uses you, as well." She drew a deep breath and almost blurted, "If you think he is going to help my husband, you would kill him?"

"Without a thought." He shook his head. "No. That is not true. I said I did not like the killing, and that was not absolutely true. I would kill Trung with pleasure. Some men help the world only by dying. He is one. Your husband is not the same. He would understand."

She interrupted him, laughing. The effect was not the same as it had been earlier. "You speak of my husband understanding as if I would not. Believe me, Major, I understand you both."

Ruefully, he conceded her point. In fact, he suspected, she could give lessons to either of them. He decided to wait for her to speak. For a long time she accepted the pressure with no apparent sign. After a few minutes, she glanced at him irritably before inspecting the room. Once that was done she looked at him even more angrily and turned her head to stare out the window with a determined flair. Taylor was beginning to wonder which of them would break when the child forced the issue by trying to climb into her mother's lap. The woman took the distraction as opportunity and as soon as the child was still, spoke with resignation.

"You are a friend of the one they call Winter?"

He failed to hide his shock. "You know him?"

Her smile was tired. "We know of him. You are friends?"

"He is my commanding officer."

She dropped the smile. "It is not the same thing."

"I am his friend. I believe he is mine."

Her body moved as if she sighed, but her voice was surer. "I am lucky, then." Her weak gesture indicated the cell. "I do not think other people would treat me this way. I thought I would be tortured."

He said, "I promise you no one will hurt you."

She raised her voice. "You cannot promise, so you must

364

not. I know this Winter will try to stop them, but no one can say what will or will not happen to the wife of an official like my husband. But Winter will try and I hoped to reach him."

"You hoped—?" Taylor stammered, not finding words to finish.

Her voice brightened. "My nephew is the first link in a chain that carries messages between my husband and myself. When he was arrested he was asking his uncle how to help me get a message to your Colonel Winter."

"For Christ's sake," Taylor marveled in English, then, "Why?"

The woman dropped her head to kiss the child's head and when she spoke, her lips still brushed the hair. "My husband was afraid his enemies would discover us and force him to come to them."

"Why does he think we will not do the same thing?"

"It is not the way of this Colonel Winter."

"It is not his way. It is not my way. There are others."

Light from the late sun planished her facial structure as she nodded and he consciously admired the deep-set eyes above the molded cheekbones. The child twisted to look up at her, sensing the storm in her mother's body.

"I must hope it does not happen." The words were heavy with fear, and she added, "I swear I do not know where my husband is. I cannot tell you."

They sat in mutual silence until the sun had fallen far enough to stream directly into the window across the woman and child. The child put a chubby hand to the side of her face to shield it while she still looked at Taylor. When she spoke it startled both adults.

"Are you going to hurt us now?"

The question, ripe with the innocent curiosity of a child and spoken with the flat assurance of ingrained knowledge nearly unnerved him. For an instant he feared he would vomit.

"No one will hurt you. No one will hurt your mother." The woman's head jerked and her look at him was a swirl of hope, suspicion, and further warning. He said, "You have my word."

Suspicion won the struggle. "Why do you do this?"

He got to his feet, stretched. "Because I believe you. Because I want to believe you. There is no reason to make you

365

suffer because we cannot find Nguyen Binh."

The answer seemed to enrage her and she shrieked at his back when he opened the door. "Do not think I need your pity! I am as good a soldier as my husband!"

He turned slowly in the opening. "Woman, I know what a soldier you are. Because I am a soldier I will not let you be tortured. Because you, Binh, and me are all soldiers, if we must fight, I will kill you. Think of that, and if you can help me protect him as I will protect you—." The door closed on the unfinished sentence.

He was almost out of the hallway when the guard turned the key in the lock. The echoing rasp caught up to him and raised the hair on the back of his neck.

39

IT WAS DARK by the time Taylor reached the villa. He parked the jeep and sat for a moment, listening to the sounds of the metal cooling, savoring the brief sense of having nothing to do, no matter how false he knew the feeling to be. He closed his eyes, letting the cool night wash him, mind and body, until a sound from the porch distracted him. A figure stirred to the left, outside the glare of the headlights. He turned them off and stepped to the ground as Miller spoke.

"Evening, Major! You're out late tonight. Trouble?" More than curious interest colored the greeting, triggering a warning pull between Taylor's shoulder blades.

He made his way up the steps. Miller fell in beside him, following him inside.

"No trouble," Taylor said. "I was late leaving the interrogation building and got fucked up in the office. Stopped to have some *pho* while it cleared up. Either Loc or the Old Man aboard?"

Miller shook his head. "No, sir."

They went into Taylor's office and Miller waited until the other man was seated before saying bluntly, "Major, my ass is in a sling. Can I talk to you?"

Taylor repressed a sigh. "Sure. You know that. What's wrong?"

Even as he asked, he told himself he should have been expecting this session and should be glad Miller had come to him. Instead, he was wishing there was a way he could weasel out. Miller didn't look well. The confident ease smacked of bravado.

Miller's answer came quickly, well-rehearsed, but still stiff. He'd thought the words too frequently and they fell with the delivery of a bad actor.

"I know I should go to Colonel Winter if I think I have a gripe, sir, but if I do, even if I'm right, I end up with a reputation for bitching, you know? But I do have a gripe, Major."

"Not enough soul food in the rations?" He was pleased to see a residue of relaxation hang on after Miller's fleeting smile.

"Not a personal matter." Miller shook his head. "I'm supposed to be working for Colonel Denby, you know? Major, he don't give a shit if we never do a thing! He just fucks with his papers up there and ever' goddam thing comes down, that's more important than my operation. He just don't give a fuck!"

In his anger, Miller's accent thickened and his hands flailed anger. Finished for the moment, he glared as if daring contradiction.

Taylor said, "I can speak to him. Hint around, not make big waves. But if he doesn't want to push it and the Old Man doesn't want to push him, then there's nothing I can do. And even if you go to the man, you're awful short. Can you get anything done before you rotate?"

Miller leaned heavily against the door jamb. It was obvious he was weighing his answer and Taylor wondered exactly what was opening up in front of him. The suspicion that Miller was selecting what he could tell and what he would not tell was too strong to swallow.

"Listen," he said, cutting off whatever answer was forthcoming, "there's more heat here than I know about, I think. You and Denby are in some kind of love knot and I don't need that. I'll goose him on the op plan, but if you want my advice, you'll take an even strain and let the whole fucking problem slide. Your shot won't win the war. Be reasonable."

Miller smiled. "What if I told you I got a lead'd blow the local scene to shit?"

"Do you? Don't play games with me."

"Yes, sir, I believe I do. I honest-to-God believe if I can get Winter to back me, I can set up a deal that'll hurt the Major and anybody ever sold dope in Vietnam. Maybe in this whole fucking part of the world. But if I make a move without it lookin' like it comes from Denby, they'll all go up my ass for going outside the outfit's rules. It's a ballbuster."

This time Taylor did sigh. "I'll see what I can do. I still think you'd best go to parade rest, but I'll see if we can build a fire under Denby."

Taylor shuffled papers for a second before moving past Miller and into the corridor, headed outside. Miller shouted thanks at his back and he waved without turning. It had been his intention to sprawl on the sack and read for a while and brief Winter in the morning. Now he wanted out of the villa. What with the assumption of authority over Binh's wife and the added confusion surrounding Miller's difficulties, the building was suddenly oppressive.

His spirits rose on the way to BOQ One.

Binh's wife was in custody. That alone would send shock waves rolling through COSVN. They would have to assess what she might know, assume the worst, and move accordingly. There would be immense scuttling in the dark, and for an organization that functioned only so long as it was invisible, even small movements were anathema.

He grinned to himself even as he dodged an apparently homicidal bus driver, turned right and checked in past the gate guard.

At his knock, Winter opened the door and welcomed him with a questioning expression. He wore shorts and sandals and his free hand unconsciously rubbed at the white patch on his chest. Denby sat in the rattan chair, smiling a greeting his eyes denied. Dead white thighs ballooned out of his shorts and a sweat-stained shirt clung where it touched, his excess weight overwhelming the gasping efforts of the air-conditioner.

Winter said, "Still in uniform? What's happening? Trouble interrogating the lady?"

Taylor pulled up a chair, quartering so he could see Denby

368

while he spoke to Winter. "The lady's a tough customer, Colonel. And she doesn't know where her husband is."

Denby made as if to speak and ate it when he caught Winter's frown.

"You're sure?"

— "Certain, Colonel. They corresponded through a courier link Binh set up. The kid Duc caught is her nephew. We can start back-tracking on him, but a dime gets you a dollar he leaves his messages under a rock somewhere for the next guy. And so on, for Christ-knows how many more links."

Winter looked away and Denby said, "How can you be so sure she doesn't know where he is? The whole courier thing could be a lie, or some more stupid VC super-security stuff."

A sardonic look from Winter escaped him and Winter chose to let it go, speaking to Taylor. "Our security should be so stupid. But how *can* you be sure?"

"She told me."

Winter ignored Denby's wordless exclamation, studying Taylor intently. His expression was blank, only the lively eyes moving as they probed. Taylor knew he was being weighed, that everything he'd ever said was being reviewed, that all his decisions and judgements were being re-evaluated and balanced against this last conclusion. He waited, looking at the room, registering the drab walls, and thought how he'd spent his adult life sitting or standing in dull, boring rooms, explaining. He felt very tired and a previously unnoticed ache in his knees clamored for attention.

Still unsatisfied, Winter said, "How did she come to tell you?"

Taylor reviewed the meeting, and at his conclusion, Denby made another snorting sound. Taylor spun to face him.

"Is that a comment, Colonel, or do you have a sinus problem?"

Denby colored. "I can't believe I'm hearing this. The woman showed you her kid and you believe any story she throws."

"She's telling the truth."

"We'll find out." He appealed to Winter. "I said this mess was a Viet problem. Let Tho talk to her for a day or two, him and that ape Chi. She'll tell you where Binh is."

Taylor said, "What's this all about? You're the guy who's

always screaming about sticking our necks out and civilized behavior. What's torturing female civilians? She deserves better. She was on her way in, man!''

"Oh, come on!" Denby scoffed.

"I told you, she knew the Colonel's name! She wants protection for herself and her child. You can't turn your back on that!"

"It's a war, Major."

Taylor was on his feet. "How the fuck would you know? You read about it? Listen, you want her worked over? You do it! Let's see you in the shithole, your nose full of stink and your ears full of sounds and—and—fuck it! Let's see you do your own dirty work, just one time!"

The rattan whined into the bleak silence as Denby shifted his weight to turn away from the threat bent toward him. He looked to Winter.

"I'm willing to overlook that outburst if you are, Colonel. I can understand it. As I was telling you before he came, we have to give her over to them. She's a national. All they have to do is ask for her and we're required to back away, in any case. By voluntarily relinquishing any claim on her, it makes them look good and we're in the clear. If Taylor's right, if they interrogate her their way and she really doesn't know where Binh is, they're the ones who have to do the explaining, not us. We're better off out of it."

Taylor shook his head like a man who's caught himself falling asleep at the wheel and sat back down. When he looked to Winter he was impaled by the burning eyes.

"No more excitement, Tay. Just control yourself. Now, you're telling me I have this woman and she's practically useless to me? I'm no closer to Binh than I was? You're leaving the country in a matter of months and you're telling me the best possible lead I've seen since you arrived is worthless? You want me to believe all that simply because this woman said so and you believe her?"

Taylor felt Denby's triumphant grin, envisioned the glistening face, the pendulous lower lip drawing back under the nervous pink tongue. The pinched eyes would come through the glasses mocking.

"I'm sorry, Colonel. That's the way I see it. But, goddamit, he knows where she is. He told her to get under cover because he's getting pressured. There are people in his own outfit trying to snuff him. He's betting his family's safer with us than with his comrades, and won't that jangle them? If we treat her right, he may walk in. And if we squeeze a little here and there, Charlie's going to dig up every tunnel in the country hunting Binh and he'll have to break cover. And if we damage his family, you can bet he'll die before we ever get our hands on him."

"That's crazy," Denby muttered and when Taylor looked his way he flushed and refused to pull his gaze away from Winter.

Winter said, "Everything's crazy here." He tried to smile at Taylor, the pain in the effort abundant. "I'm going to go along with you. If you believe her, I'll believe her. Loc's going to think I've lost the few marbles I ever had." He paused to chuckle, imagining the scene to come. He sobered, looking to Denby. "Taylor's got a good argument, Carl, and it's no less valid because we didn't think of it. Of course Binh's the locus of a faction struggle. He must feel his friends are losing the debate to some real bastards if he's taking steps to protect his wife."

Denby squirmed and the chair squalled for mercy. His movement stirred air currents of cologne and sweat wrapped around each other in damp embrace.

He said, "Colonel, we've been after Binh, as you said, for our whole tour here. You've been after him even before we got here. Don't let this chance get away. You'll never get this close again."

"I'm going to get him. Not by harming her, though. I want to know everywhere she's lived with him and every place she's ever heard him mention. I mean every piece of ground, every road he's traveled, every village he's slept in and which house. And I want to know where he's met with contacts and who they were. I want to know everything she knows about him. It'll all be history, but if we start shaking the bushes, Binh's friends and enemies'll all be convinced she's breaking and it's only a question of time before we find them. Pressure. More pressure."

He paused, so deep in thought he nodded to himself before continuing.

"Carl, I'm convinced your investigation ties in with this

thing, somewhere. And I know Miller's convinced there's drug money involved. I can tell. I agree with him. Goddamit, it has to be so! It's money in their pockets and casualties for us and Binh's their logistics wizard. We should've been working the connection harder long ago. You know how I feel about the renegade running that bar. Get him."

Taylor was halfway to the door when the pounding started. Surprised, he glanced at Winter, who indicated he should open it. The demanding racket started again before he could reach it. When he flung it open, Harker barely glanced at him before rushing past to Winter.

"That kid Duc brought in yesterday, Colonel? The one with Binh's wife? They greased him, just about a half-hour ago." He ran a hand across his hair and looked around at the others. Winter's face turned to steel.

"Who got him?"

Harker said, "Charlie. There was a call put on him by the MSS and the Interrogation Center was transferring him. They hit some traffic and two guys walked up and zapped the driver and the guard and the kid. The third Charlie dumped a grenade in the back seat to finish anything that might have gotten missed."

"Did they get away?"

Harker grinned, finally coming to a part he liked. "Not this time. There was a truckload of Special Branch right around the corner. They got all three."

Winter clutched the edge of his desk. "Alive?"

"No way, Colonel. You know Special Branch. They made meat out of 'em."

Winter bent as if struck in the stomach and his eyes seemed to retreat in the sockets. Taylor waited for the explosion, but Winter controlled himself, only the whistling of his breath hinting at the unspoken words. Taylor decided a question might defuse things.

"Was there anything on them that could tell us anything about them?"

Harker cut his eyes that way then back to Winter. For the first time, Taylor noticed the younger man was wearing his new Captain's bars.

"I don't know, sir. I just got the word from the MSS liaison. Should I get on it?"

Under firm control, Winter said, "Get all you can on them, the prisoner, and those with him. Find out who at MSS put the call on the boy and why. Get the name of the officer who released him to MSS, the time of release, and the time of the requesting call. Above all, insure no one learned we have Binh's family. Get in with the official Vietnamese investigation. Refer any interference to me."

Harker bared his teeth like an unleashed dog and left. Taylor felt a sharp tear of regret at the sight, thinking how even the promotion had failed to penetrate the new shell. When he faced Winter again, the Colonel was watching him instead of the departing Harker.

"A sorry change, isn't it?" he asked, knowing Taylor would understand.

"Yes, sir. He's a casualty, Colonel. He's not trying to extend again, is he?"

"He's trying."

Denby coughed. "Colonel, if you don't have anything further for me, I'm going to hit the sack. I'm going to be busy tomorrow, putting the finishing touches on that op plan." When there was no objection, he edged toward the door. Winter half-saluted a goodnight.

The two men sat alone, unspeaking, for several minutes. External sounds multiplied in Taylor's consciousness. At first it was only the air-conditioner. Then the rumble of traffic on Plantation Road broke down into separate sounds and he could distinguish trucks from jeeps, cyclos from motorcycles. After that, the sounds in the building became increasingly apparent. Someone in the next room tossed on the bed. A toilet flushed in the distance.

Winter's voice disorganized all of it. "What a mess," he said. His eyes remained fixed on their imaginary point and the words, unaimed, drifted through the room.

Taylor agreed. "And me sitting here's not helping. Ly'll be starting to worry."

Leaning back, Winter shifted his view to the ceiling. "What a lucky bastard you are. You're the only man I know coming out of this slaughterhouse better off than you came in. She's a fine woman. How's she doing?"

Taylor laughed. "Nervous. Acting like a bride. We've got almost all the paperwork out of the way."

"By God, that's right!" Winter was all surprise and consternation. "I forgot, it's not that long before you wicked children make it legal. Have you set a date?"

"There's still a couple of things to get cleared up, but we think we'll be set about thirty days before I rotate."

The earlier tensions drained completely from Winter's features and he smiled. "I'm happy for both of you, really happy. And I hope you'll be happy for the rest of your lives."

"Can't miss," Taylor assured him, moving to leave, "but it's good to know we've got a cheering section."

As he opened the door, Winter called, "Give her my love. Add my apologies for keeping you so busy. Let's get out for dinner one night this week, all right?"

Taylor threw him a thumbs-up and hurried to the jeep to leave for the apartment. He was lifting his hand to pull himself aboard when something stopped him. Ignoring the twisted angles of his pose, Taylor held fast, wanting to be sure he didn't lose the thread of whatever had trailed across his thinking.

And then he had it. It was seared into a corner of his mind, an inescapable image of the child, asking her question. The child who looked like Ly must have when she was that young. The child who would never see him as anything more favorable than the strange looking man who decided not to hurt her.

The thought of her, and her mother, so alone and so coldly considered by everyone around them, turned into an assault and he suddenly needed Ly more than he could remember ever needing or wanting anything.

40

WHEN TAYLOR STEPPED INTO HIS OFFICE the following morning, Harker and Duc waited for him. The Captain rose as Taylor entered, a move Duc watched with carefully hidden amusement. The case of his manner disappeared at Harker's first words.

"We've been waiting to talk to you, Major. I'd like your advice on how to twist some answers out of Barline's driver.''

"Jesus.'' Taylor made his way into his chair. "You really start the day with a smile.''

Harker brushed the comment aside. "The driver's Duong Han and the kid Major Duc caught yesterday's his nephew. The kid wanted Han to find out for Binh's wife how she could turn herself in to Colonel Winter.''

Taylor said, "OK. I hear you. So you think this Han's VC because he knows about the Old Man and he's got enough clout to put Trung back in business. Maybe he is. He's also Barline's pet gopher. How do you think Barline's going to take it if we pick up his man with no more than that to go on?''

Sticking out his chin, Harker said, "I don't want to arrest him. I want to get him off somewhere and ask him questions, that's all.''

Slight movement to the side gave Taylor an excuse to look away from Harker's intensity at the reassurance of Duc's signal of disavowal. Knowing the idea was exclusively Harker's, Taylor forced himself back to the problem, feeling like a man driven from the shade.

Weighing an answer, he caught himself again comparing this Harker with the one who'd awakened him that first evening in the transient BOQ. Association superimposed the face of Miller on his mind and he wanted to tell Harker to forget this thing, to retrieve what he had been.

It happened so often to men like Miller and Harker. Good men, bending under ever-increasing weight, the ideals turning to dogma, means eventually serving as ends. The back of his neck chilled and he feared to go further because he, too, was part of it all.

He used an exaggerated blink to get time to wrench his mind away from that line of thought, slammed mental doors and picked words.

"Han's the same as Trung, involved with the VC at one level or another. Try proving it. And the fact that he knows something about the Old Man is as it should be. Shit, Harker, he works for a reporter—it'd be suspicious if he didn't know about him.''

Harker's lips pulled taut. "If we know he's VC, why should we dick around with him?''

"Listen, one of the assholes mixed up in the riots at

375

Columbia—they asked him something about justifying what they were doing, OK? He said they were doing it because they were right. And they asked how he knew he was right and he said, 'When you're right, you know it.' You're saying the same damned thing."

"If it's good enough for him, it's good enough for me."

"Goddamit, no. Because you've got the muscle doesn't give you the right to stomp on anyone you want, any more than the puke I'm talking about. That's what all this is supposed to be about."

"He is right," Duc said. "You know I hate VC, so you know I think much about men like Trung, Tu, Han—all like that. Be easy kill them, but not good. If not have country with law for all people, be same-same before."

Harker moved to the doorway where he paused to look back. "You're not worried about law or justice. You two think I'll screw it up and get in trouble. I want to hear either one of you tell me you're not thinking the same things I am."

Taylor rose, aware of Duc sliding his chair back. There was another sound and it was a moment before he recognized it as Duc's angered intake of breath.

Taylor said, "I might be. Maybe. You think about that. Look at yourself and your career and then think about me and mine." Harker opened his mouth and he held up a peremptory hand. "I don't want to hear anything else from you for a while."

Stiffly, as if denied a longed-for fight, Harker turned and left. When Taylor started to sit back down, he checked clumsily, caught by the expression on Duc's face. His own blunt "Well?" grated as unnecessarily challenging. He continued his interrupted motion.

Duc spoke in Vietnamese. "You should make things easier for him. You should advise him, not correct him. He expects much from you because he admires you. And maybe he is right about Han. Maybe we should talk to him in a small room."

"I was advising him. He has a good future. Why should he waste it trying to get answers from a man like this Han? If Han identified him for Barline, he would be in terrible trouble."

"I cannot think an American 'wastes' his career fighting the communists beside us."

The words were a mix of hurt and confusion and Taylor

rushed to apologize. "I did not mean the effort would be wrong. My meaning was that any step outside the law could destroy him. You have seen it. To people like Barline, we are the enemy. Whatever Han does or has done, he is already forgiven."

Duc sighed. "I know. I am too easily offended." He ducked his head, almost shy. "Sometimes when you speak of us you speak as of a bad dream that will go away in one year. Even when I remember that your lives are in danger, too, I know the danger will end for you when you go home. I—my family—we have no such home."

"Many times I have wondered how you live with that, and then I have to ask myself what would happen in my country if my people had to face your problems. Would they fight the terrorists or talk about 'inevitable social change' and surrender?"

Duc made a forceful, if transparent, move to change the subject. "Speaking of change, I forgot to tell you I have something that will interest you." He tore through the papers on his desk, sending strays drifting to the floor. He surfaced with a report form.

"In my last meeting with Tuyet—you remember her, from the interro—." He stopped at Taylor's curt wave and started again. "She has been invaluable." Again, he stopped short, this time with an almost furtive air that troubled Taylor. His curiosity faded as Duc pressed ahead.

"A new girl started working at the Friendly Bar almost two months ago. Tuyet says she was the girl friend of a party official for a while and puts on airs, hinting that she knows many secrets. Probably gossip, but she may know something of interest and Tuyet has arranged for me to meet her at a small restaurant this evening."

Taylor sat through it with an occasional move of his head and an infrequent grunt, a facade of polite interest. His mind refused to focus on chatter about a possible new low-level source. Awareness of his lack of attention nipped at his conscience briefly and died.

Images were crowding in on him, more of them this time, the accumulation of his dwindling year. In a few weeks all the faces around him would be new, except for the Vietnamese and Winter and possibly Harker. The thought of Harker was unpleasant. Shock raised his eyebrows as he realized how many of the images were unpleasant—the desperation oozing from Miller, Harker's raw ferocity, Denby's lurking malice. He wondered what his mind would have done with that cast and situation had he not met Ly.

He put a tentative hand to his face, once more wondering if some mystery had happened there that would surprise him the way Harker and Miller had. Duc chose that moment to look up and he dropped the hand quickly.

Even the interruption failed to dispel the mental searching. He asked himself if he would be able to regain his balance the way Winter seemed to have done. That thought was incomplete and it bobbed out of reach like a lost object escaping in a stream. He managed to catch it.

Everyone had altered but Winter. He had bent and come back to standard.

No matter what his mood, he pursued the war with dogged belief and one prime target. What would happen to that when Binh was captured? More than that, what would happen if he were killed instead of captured?

These were inconsequential questions, he decided. The major issue was to understand that they were all changing and to insure that the changes weren't entirely destructive. Ordway was a better man for his experience, surely. Allen had Dao and maybe in time he'd adjust to losing his leg. Hell, yes, he'd adjust. What else? The leg was gone, and that was that.

The unsympathetic finality of his own reaction depressed him, and he could produce nothing sufficiently positive about the rest of them to offset it.

Was that to be the sum total of his year, to carry away as little personal damage as possible? Was that the psychological reward for doing what everyone said was the right thing to do until someone was actually called on to do it?

Duc was asking a question. The words hadn't made it through his own thoughts and the pudgy features were puzzled by the unresponsiveness.

Taylor shook his head and apologized.

"I asked if you know her home, Phu Thuan." Duc apparently attached some significance to the name and he stressed it. "It is hard to imagine a Phu Thuan girl becoming a prostitute like Tuyet, but it is especially sad to learn that she was involved with one of the enemy."

Taylor tried to generate some interest. "Why is this place so special?"

Duc said, "I thought even the Americans all knew about the hamlet of Phu Thuan. For a while, every foreign writer was obliged to write about it, where everyone resists the VC, where the people are so anti-communist the Tet offensive avoided them."

"I remember the name now. One of their girls went wrong, did she?"

"It's more than that. The people are almost one family. They are quiet, keep to themselves. They pay their taxes, send their sons to fight. Because they are who they are, the girl is almost a symbol."

Involved now, and feeling better for it, Taylor said, "You make too much of her, Duc. Her morals are not the concern. What she can tell us is."

"I know that." Duc made a face. "I cannot seem to stop myself. More and more, I look for things, you know? Signs. Symbols. Portents. There has been so much trouble for so long. The French. The Japanese. The French again. And now, ourselves, exceeding anything in the past. I look for a guide, like a man lost."

A compound of frustrations welled in Taylor's throat. Rather than force words that wouldn't say what he wanted, he shrugged and reached for his cigarettes. Duc took the one offered and they smoked a few moments before Duc spoke again. He kept his eyes lowered, protected.

"I sound defeated. I am not. But I am very tired and I feel alone. Without a leader. In our history we have always had leaders. Now we have only figureheads and advisors."

He shifted nervously. "If it were not for the Americans, we would all be part of the northern machine. No one doubts it. But no American seems to understand the price you ask of us. You speak of freedom and we have none."

Taylor felt the flush spread across his face. Without looking, Duc seemed to sense it and rushed on before his friend could argue.

"We are told we must be in your image, and we have tried,

but we do not fit your culture any better than you fit our clothes. Many of us—most of us, I think—would prefer our old mandarins. To westerners, that is alien, so undesirable, but when it was properly administered, that system insured that only the most qualified men were promoted to positions of responsibility."

"When it was properly administered," Taylor repeated with heavy inference.

Due continued to stare at the floor. "Is your own democracy so free of error? And what difference would it make if it was?" He could stand it no longer and he stared into Taylor's face, locking eyes with the other man as if seeking a physical bond. "We are told we must continue to fight the communists in order to be free, and yet we must adopt a form of government that is as foreign as communism in order to get help to remain free. In my heart, I am a small man—a shop-keeper, a minor executive, a civil servant—I want to live in a peaceful place where I can go home to my family, sure they have survived the day. If we did not know what communism means, do you really believe we would resist it only to be blessed by what we have seen of your democracy?"

When Taylor didn't answer, Duc rose to leave. As he passed behind the seated figure he hesitated, his features belying a final thought struggling for expression. After a moment he raised a hand and patted his friend's shoulder and continued out the door.

41

DUC DABBLED AT HIS BOWL OF SOUP absently. His seat in the corner afforded a clear view of the restaurant's kitchen entrance as well as the front door. Through the shop-windows flanking the latter he unobtrusively scanned all passers-by. He noted Corporal Minh across the street in frayed shorts and old cotton shirt, squatting against the wall and looking exactly like what he was, a country boy still uneasy in the big city.

Duc smiled to himself until his eyes fell on his watch.

The stupid woman was almost an hour late. He had told

Tuyet to make it very clear his time was important and he demanded punctuality. Now he'd had to order a second bowl of soup and the waiter was having difficulty hiding his amusement at the impatience of the man in the darkest corner of the restaurant.

The bitch! He pictured her, spreading her legs for some drunken fool while he, Major Duc, aged in this miserable place. The thought heightened his fury for a moment and then he wondered about himself. Did he have the right to be angry with the woman because she was earning a living the only way she could? Was it not worth some of his time to allow her to make a few piasters? He rotated the spoon in the bowl while he examined the question from all angles. No, he decided, it was not worth his time. It was not even worth the time of the Corporal, immobile against his wall. What she was selling to her grunting customer would be the same tomorrow night and the customers were as plentiful as mangoes on a tree. Information could be very fragile. A few miserable piasters, animal release for some stranger who would never recognize her if he saw her again—these things did not count at all against endangering the quality of the information she might provide and the impertinence of willfully keeping two men, and one of them a Major, waiting. He jabbed at the greens in the soup. When she came, she would get a lecture she would never forget.

Perhaps he should beat her a little. Nothing serious, just a few good slaps to impress her. He cupped his chin in his hand and considered that move. A determined memory of Tuyet screaming boiled to the surface of his thoughts and he forced it back. After all, he was not considering torture. More on the order of a fatherly chastisement. Some women needed a man to act like a stern father with them.

He thought of his children, so shamefully spoiled. Stern father, indeed.

He would not strike the woman.

The decision was saddening. A Major engaged in secret work, and one who had certain hopes for continued promotion, should not be so concerned over the feelings of an insignificant whore.

Another glance at his watch brought back his earlier anger. A full hour! After all the warnings about punctuality. The woman had no consideration, that was all that could be said. He summoned the waiter.

"There is something wrong with the soup?" A smirk dusted the waiter's features.

"No worse than I expected." Duc dropped his money on the table carelessly.

The waiter said, "It loses flavor when it grows cold."

"How could it lose what it never had?"

Duc's voice warned that the conversation was over, had gone too far already. The waiter swept up the bowl and other utensils, hurrying into the kitchen. Duc watched him go with the first satisfaction he'd felt since sitting down. Relishing having had the last word, he couldn't resist a last look. He turned as he stepped onto the street and caught the wide grin before the waiter had a chance to pull his head back inside the kitchen entryway. Fury burned Duc's cheeks again.

Corporal Minh watched Duc's solo exit, saw the quick scene with the waiter, noted the rigidity of Duc's back, and groaned. It was bad enough that the meeting had failed, but the added aggravation of the waiter was fuel to a too-hot fire. Minh resigned himself to hearing some hard language before the night was over.

Duc turned the corner and Minh began to count. On one hundred, he stood, scratched his crotch, and ambled off in the other direction. At the intersection he crossed and continued parallel to the street Duc had turned onto. Halfway down that block he stumbled slightly, turning to see what tripped him, and checked back the way he had come. No one was following. At the next intersection he turned right and entered a small shop crammed with food and household items. Duc waited at the end of the single narrow aisle. At Minh's approach, his impatience showed in the way he rubbed forefinger and thumb against each other.

Minh spoke quietly. "No one followed before you turned the corner, *Thieu Ta*."

Duc nodded curtly and led the way back to the street. Once outside, he snapped, "Of course no one followed! Why would anyone follow a man who has spent an hour dawdling over two bowls of tasteless soup? Who would trouble with such a fool?"

Minh hurried to keep pace with Duc's agitated stride. "I do not know, *Thieu Ta*."

"Do not know what?" Duc demanded in a voice full of pre-occupation.

Panic blew through Minh's bowels. What did he answer? Inspired, he said, "I do not know what went wrong, *Thieu Ta*."

"How could you know?" Duc glared at a man on a bicycle, daring him to interfere with his progress through the intersection. Minh dodged behind the protection of the Major's bulk. The man on the bicycle pedaled off, muttering. Duc resumed his angry conversation, unmollified by his minor triumph.

"You are not supposed to know of my arrangements, so how could you know what went wrong? You are supposed to insure that I am not followed, that is all. Farm boys are not entrusted with sensitive situations."

"Yes, *Thieu Ta*."

"Yes, what?"

A drop of sweat trickled through Minh's eyebrow. He wished it was a river and would carry him away.

"Yes, farm boys are not entrusted with sensitive missions."

"See that you remember that. Your job is to help, not interfere."

"Yes, *Thieu Ta*."

A full block passed in grim silence and Minh strained to think of something to establish his eagerness to help.

"Is it possible the woman misunderstood the time of the meeting. *Thieu Ta*?"

Duc stopped as if he'd hit a wall. "Woman?" he said. "What woman? Who said anything about a woman?"

"You did, *Thieu Ta!*" His effort to swallow the tones of indignant protest was successful, but it caused his voice to break like a youth's. He stared at the ground and continued. "You told me to see if the person you were to meet was followed. You said 'she' very clearly. Then you said when 'she' left, you would wait a short while before you came out and I was to see if either of you was followed. I would have done my job, but there was no chance, since she did not come."

He wanted to bite off his tongue.

Duc said, "*I* know she did not come!" He imitated Minh's country accent, throwing in a rendition of the earlier squeak for good measure. "I am the one who made the arrangements. Do not be presumptuous because you remembered one simple face. Did the thought of the woman excite you? Did you sit there in the dark and play with yourself?"

Minh looked Duc directly in the eyes, no longer a Corporal speaking to a Major. He addressed Duc with the dignity of a plain man. "It has been over a year since I saw my wife. I have been with no other woman. If I should touch myself and think of a woman, no one would have to ask."

Duc struggled to maintain his scowl, feeling it crumble. Laughter roiled in his throat and he forced it back, only to have it explode through his nose in a sneeze-like snort. At that, he abandoned all restraint and leaned against a wall and roared, the sound finally dwindling to wheezes and giggles. When he was able, he turned to find Minh still staring at him in reproach. It set him off again for a few moments.

"Corporal Minh," he said at last, "you are a man of character. It is no fault of yours that my meeting was a failure. The woman is the one to blame. You did everything that was asked of you, as you always do."

"Thank you, *Thieu Ta*." Minh's starved lungs sucked air in blessed relief. Trying not to move his shoulders, he wiped his wet palms on his shorts.

Duc checked his watch. "I know where she lives and she does not work at the bar tonight. I will go to her room."

Minh's instant frown caused Duc to explain with chopping hand gestures. "She could be of great value. She has spent much time with Trung and the man who drives for the American, aside from her connection with her VC lover. We may learn much. It is a breach of security and procedure, but I must go."

"You could arrange another meeting, *Thieu Ta*. Going to her home—." He dropped the sentence with a nervous shrug.

"It is wrong. I admit it. But I have the feeling that I am a step away from something very important."

He laughed again and Minh winced, but he only stepped off briskly, so Minh fell into place beside him. He made no attempt to keep step, Duc's mincing cadence far too rapid for his own longer stride.

Minh remembered the embarrassment of finding that even his walk marked him as a villager. He thought to hide his lack of sophistication behind a closed mouth only to have his feet betray him. The city people moved so much more quickly, like the small brown birds that flew up to catch insects and returned to their perch before a man's eyes could focus. The more he watched the city people, the more they reminded him of those birds. For all their flits and twitches, they never went anywhere. Pride surged in him, the awareness that, even if he was an ignorant farmer, he moved steadily in the direction he chose. He wondered if that was a disrespectful thought and decided it couldn't be, because no one would ever know of it.

That was one of the many ways the Americans were different. Was there anything they would not say to each other? He remembered the conversation between *Thieu Ta* Taylor and Ordway at the banquet and his stomach muttered. But Ordway and Taylor had been close, afterward. And now Ordway was gone and *Thieu Ta* Taylor was always just outside everyone's reach.

Duc would have been astounded by the direction of Minh's mental exercise had it occurred to him to consider what Minh might be thinking at all. As it was, he began the last leg of the walk to the jeep by twirling his present problem around in his head. The difficulty was that the more he turned it the more sides it seemed to have and the faster it went until now it was a mass of whirling indecision.

Colonel Loc had been very interested in his initial report about the woman. It was one of the few times Loc ever urged speed in an operation. The pride in that eventually overrode his unease at Loc's insistence that nothing of the woman's association with Han, Barline's driver, should be made known to the Americans. He chewed his lower lip, hopeful he was doing the right thing. Balancing Loc's desire for quick results against his constant demand for secure procedures was a problem that allowed no mental errors. He'd been very lucky in the matter of the youth on the motorcycle. It would be foolish to hope for such luck again. On the other hand, when good fortune was present was the time to act.

They arrived at the compound where he'd parked the jeep for safekeeping and he continued to evaluate the situation as he drove the familiar route to Gia Dinh. The more he thought, the more he wished Taylor was with him, although that would be an even worse security lapse.

In a few minutes they were skirting the passive hulk of the temple at the intersection of Le Van Duyet and Chi Lang. Moonlight filtered through the clouds to be further refined by the meshed leaves above the building. The essence that penetrated to the roof dashed across the tiles like spilled mercury. Duc swung to the right on Chi Lang, then right again a little way on, moving more slowly in a maze of snaking dirt streets and ramshackle buildings, circling back toward the river. He switched off the lights and coasted to a stop at an intersection.

"That house down there—the one with the light in the small window on the ground floor—you see it?"

"Yes, *Thieu Ta*. The light is orange, like there is paper over the glass."

Duc nodded. "Good. The woman lives there in an upstairs room. You wait for me here. I will go to the left, circle the block, and enter as I come back this way. If anyone is watching us now, perhaps they will continue to look in the direction I went, and I will return in the same manner. You understand?"

"I understand. It is a long way to see in the dark, *Thieu Ta*. I will not be sure it is you I see. How long will you be gone?" Minh peered into the gloom, tight-featured with disapproval. "The clouds keep covering the moon. What signal will you give if there is trouble?"

Duc's laugh crackled harshly. "There will be no need for help. Wait here until I return."

Minh moved to the driver's seat as Duc was quickly absorbed into the darker side street. With nothing else to do, he scanned the area, checking windows, challenging each one. They maintained their own vigil, showing nothing more than an occasional fitful chip of moonlight. A dogfight erupted suddenly down the street to his right and Minh realized with shock that he was looking for the sound down his outstretched arm, his pistol trembling at the end of it. He replaced it under his shirt as the snarling and growling changed to retreating yelps. He felt very foolish.

Duc picked his way through the trash and potholes. The buildings ran at an angle to the moon's position, effectively blocking even that light, so his progress was marred by shuffling and near-stumbles. At one point something squashed messily underfoot and a putrid stench immediately asserted its primacy over the general fetid air. He hurried to leave it behind. His stomach heaved and for a few steps he risked the noise to drag the shoe, trying to clean off whatever it was.

In spite of the route, he made good time.

From the front, the building was dark. He climbed the stairs silently and tapped on the door. There were scuffling noises on the other side, as though he'd disturbed small animals. A distant child's voice whined sleep-thick complaint.

"Open the door," Duc said in hushed command. "I want to know why you failed to meet me." It was a careful phrase, serving to identify him for the woman but essentially meaningless to any listening neighbors.

The door swung wide. He stepped inside, into a well of blackness where only the thin line of light under the bedroom door was distinguishable, a glowing gold thread like a struggling dawn.

A sound to his right, a strained exhalation, produced a pure reflex and he whirled, reaching for the gun under his belt. The blow to his stomach felt more like a shove. It knocked his hand away from the pistol and an electric puzzlement at the apparent ineffectiveness of the blow coursed his mind even as he felt himself staggering backwards. The handle of the door gouged the small of his back, another minor disturbance, and then it seemed to be crawling up his spine. He realized he was sliding to the floor and was angry at the odd inability to do anything about it. Confusion and fear seared his brain and he clawed for the gun.

Something kept bumping his forearm. He tried to think what it could be and then he was sitting solidly on the floor, back against the door, and the perverse butt of the weapon was slippery with a mess that defeated his efforts to grasp it.

He dropped his hand, resigning himself to ponderous lassitude and an awesome awareness swept all emotion from him as a wave scours a shore.

He was dying.

A hurried rush of feet intruded on the discovery and the door to the bedroom flew open. Two men rushed across through it, the slower one shoving his partner toward the window in a frenzy.

Duc found their panic faintly amusing. The bloody mass revealed by the wildly swinging light bulb told him the woman on the bed would never bother them and he knew he certainly wouldn't.

The attempt to move sent pain thunder-rolling through his stomach that made him gasp, a contemptible mewing like a starved kitten. He clenched his teeth against a repetition, at the same time wondering why he bothered when no one would ever know.

The sensation of lowering into a welcome rest was undeniable now. He was glad he had not been searched. Colonel Loc would be gratified. He would be equally displeased to learn the operation had been so badly mishandled. While his thoughts floundered he could feel his heart straining to function with a rapidly dwindling supply of material. A secret knowledge said it was racing desperately, and yet the individual beats seemed to come with the plodding thumps of pile-driver blows. Half his mind surrendered to panic for an instant, eliminating conscious thought and replacing it with a swirling smoke of terror and dread. He tried to breathe deeply. The shuddering effort lit pain around the wound that cleared his thoughts.

He wondered about his family, saw the children playing, then gathered around the table for dinner. His wife was there —a good woman. He had been lucky. For all his errors, she truly loved him. The memory gave him respite from the increasing rams of a heart threatening to erupt through his ribs.

A great spasm shot through him. When it had passed, the fear returned. The agonized effort of his heart had changed to a muted fluttering, a sliding sensation in his breast. He pictured bamboo leaves slipping back and forth, shouldering their way through the breeze.

He could hold his head erect no longer. It dropped to rest on his chest. The light was dimming unaccountably, but there was still enough to see the blood from the wound, ebbed to an oozing trickle.

The light failed with increasing speed then, creating undefined irritation. The swaddling blackness reached for him and he folded his hands in his lap with as much dignity as the obscenity protruding from his shirt would permit. After that he deliberately closed his eyes in defiance of the surprised mask he had seen on so many other dead down the years.

A man was entitled to some taste of victory.

42

"YOU ARE CERTAIN YOU HAVE LEFT NOTHING OUT? No one else spoke to the Major all evening? No one else entered the building?"

Although he was the junior man present, Harker's rage had filled the room, demanding attention from the time he entered. As if deferring to a natural force, the others in Loc's office watched him press Corporal Minh for details. Winter moved constantly, brusque activity with no point. Denby sat on the edge of a hardbacked chair, bent forward at the waist. It made him look like a frog poised for a fly. His eyes shattered the image. He was very frightened.

Lieutenant Colonel Tho and Sergeant Chi watched with polite professional interest only slightly marred by rumpled looks that said they'd been sleeping soundly until summoned.

Taylor hoped he appeared as composed as Loc and wondered if the small Vietnamese was having as much trouble accepting Duc's death as the rest of them.

Minh answered Harker through lips that had begun to tremble.

"Dai Uy, I have told you everything and only the truth. No one followed us. There is only a front door and one on the side. I could see both. As soon as I found the Major I looked out the window in the other room because it was the only way in that I could not have watched from the jeep. It is almost three meters to the ground, so no one came in there. Whoever killed the Major was already there and escaped through that window. I picked him up and carried him to the jeep and brought him here."

"Why?" Harker's voice cut.

"It is as I have already said." Resentment surfaced with the words. "I knew if the Major was found there it would mean many questions. I did not want his wife and children to know he died in the room of a whore. I did not think our Colonel would want that. I brought him back here to his office so I could get help from his friends."

There was a bite in the last words and Harker blinked before turning to face the two Colonels. "We can put our hands on the other woman, that hooker, Tuyet. Maybe she can give us a lead—." He broke off at the sight of Winter's shaking head.

"The worst thing we could do. It looks like Duc stumbled in on a murder. We don't know if it had anything to do with her VC connections or if she died because some pimp got overenthusiastic in his work. For now, I think we'll keep the lowest profile possible and see what happens. If we create a stir, everyone in the world's going to want to know why."

"We can't just ignore this thing, Colonel."

Loc's color rose and he interrupted. "It will not be ignored, *Dai Uy*. You have my promise. But Colonel Winter is right. We can learn more by watching. And it is safer."

Taylor flinched as Harker prepared to answer, then relaxed when the strained features turned to the far wall.

Minh looked expectantly to Colonel Loc, who said, "You say you think you were unobserved getting back to the jeep. How did the guard here at the gate react?"

"The Major was leaning against me. I had a poncho over him so you could not see—. He looked drunk. The guard believed me."

Tho spoke up in his flat manner. "If the guard had checked you would have been in great trouble."

Minh's flat answering stare matched the voice and expressed his unconcern for gate guards.

Winter rubbed his hands together. "Colonel Loc, how can we help? I mean with the official version of what happened?"

"I will arrange everything." He turned to Minh. "When you returned with the Major you helped him inside. He was ill, not drunk. He was cutting fruit at his desk when he rose suddenly, in great pain as if from a cramp. He turned, fell with the bayonet. A terrible accident. You will be forced to tell the story many times. You will tell it as I have told you, with no changes or added details."

Minh bobbed his head.

Loc surveyed the rest of the listeners, dwelling on each face before passing to the next. In the silence someone's stomach rumbled, the noise like a bomb. Taylor noticed that each man's eyes moved covertly to identify the source. Loc ignored the disturbance and when he was finished with his inspection, spoke again.

"It is a ludicrous story, so far-fetched it will be unquestioned. We shall not have to account for his activities of the evening."

Chi leaned closer to Tho and they exchanged whispers. Tho spoke to Loc. "There will be investigations. What explains the lack of blood where he is supposed to have died?"

"Everything was cleaned up, of course," Loc said. "There would be no need to maintain the scene, as there was no crime. Merely an accident. Now we must arrange everything and call the Duty Officer. Are you prepared, Corporal?" The black eyes burned at the slight, hunched figure. Minh leaped to attention.

Loc nodded and faced Winter. "It will be done." He gestured at the Americans. "We are grateful for your support."

Winter waved his people toward the interconnecting door before shaking Loc's hand. "I wish there was more we could do. I wish there was no reason to do anything. I know how much you respected Duc. We all did."

A silent nod ended the uncomfortable conversation and Winter entered his own office where the three others stood in an awkward group. Ignoring Taylor and Denby, he addressed Harker.

"We're going to find out who did this. I'll get you your extension if you want to tackle it."

Taylor said, "Bullshit. Duc was my partner." He leaned past Harker, shoving the younger man aside. "You can't take something like this away from me. Duc was a friend. I owe him."

Winter opened his mouth and Taylor pounded the desk. "And no shit about being too involved. You saw Harker go after that kid in there. You call that cool? You want someone

391

to ship over? If that's what it takes to get the mother-fucker who killed Duc, I'm in."

Winter dropped his gaze to the desk top. "I know you're upset. So's Harker. And so, by God, am I!" He looked up, his face mottled, and pointed at the Captain. "You'll observe the investigation of the woman's death with no indication that the Unit has an interest. Now get out of here and get some sleep. Her kid'll be crying and drawing the neighbors and then the police'll be in on it. And now I'd like to speak to Major Taylor alone." His eyes shifted from Harker to stare at Taylor's bunched fists on his desk and Taylor took them back to dangle self-consciously at his sides.

Denby stopped at the door, assuring that Harker was gone before him. He turned back. "Colonel, I wish there was some way I could help. Perhaps if we let my op plan drop, I could take the detail you just gave Harker? I know how you feel, but Duc, and all—." The thought died unexplored.

Winter said, "I've already told you, Carl, your job is that renegade Major. I'll have your answer on how we deal with him by Friday." His lips bent to a tight smile. "With any luck, you and Miller'll still have time to make it work before you rotate." He continued to smile until the door clicked behind Denby, then waved Taylor to a chair.

"Sorry about mouthing off," Taylor said. "It's just that I keep hearing what we're saying as though I wasn't a part of it. Like, there's a baby out there in the same room with its mother, only she's nothing but bloody rags. Minh only mentioned the kid the first time through like he'd say there was a chair in the room, part of the scene, a prop. And now you! All it is to you is something that'll make noise and attract attention. Jesus! The kid's sitting there looking at its *mother*, and we're just letting it happen!"

"I thought about a phone call saying there's been trouble there, but even the Saigon police'll wonder about that and start checking. We don't know who she's told what."

Taylor stood up to pace. "And that's another thing. Us, making up a story about how Duc died. Sitting in that room like buzzards, picking at what's left of him, like he was just another fucking problem instead of one of the best men any of us'll ever know."

"Sometimes you really piss me off." The raw emotion in

Winter's voice snapped Taylor around. "You think you're the only one who has feelings? Listen, before you dragged your ass in here from your cozy little pad, I was in your office looking at what used to be Duc under a poncho. I liked him and respected him and I have to perjure myself telling people he died in a comic strip accident. And if I told them the truth, I'd have to tell them he died because he violated every fucking security rule in the world."

For a moment they stared at each other, the sour taste of mutual embarrassment like shared bad wine. Winter rocked in his chair, his thick hands clamped to the arms. His eyelids shuttered to half-closed.

"Let me think a minute. We both need to cool out and get our wind."

Winter let his eyes close completely, hoping to better isolate himself. For one terrible second he thought he heard scraping noises from the floor below and imagined them moving Duc's body. Half-forgotten images of other limp forms swarmed in his mind and he twisted in the chair.

For some reason he was thinking of Taylor, and he seized the subject as a welcome relief.

Why not send him after Duc's killer? he asked himself. He'd seek him out and kill him ruthlessly.

No, not really. With skill, no remorse, and a sense of justice. He'd probably think of it as ruthless, but the poor bastard didn't know what the word meant. The killing was the easy part. All it wanted was the right psychology, the right frame of mind.

We're the ruthless ones, the ones who sift out the believers —the ones who mean the best—and use them to do the worst. It's like asking the peasants to give up their best for sacrifice, not for their own benefit, but to the greater glory of the priests.

His eyes opened and he stared at the random wave-patterns of the acoustic tile on the ceiling.

Hundreds of men—Jesus, thousands. I've had a hand in teaching thousands of men how to kill and never understood why no more than a dozen had the mental chemistry to be man-hunters, the ones who exercise the dark side of power without becoming overwhelmed by it.

A single line etched his forehead.

But what about that Chinese—what the hell was his name? Eng? Ng? An. That was it, An. He killed him out of plain anger. Well, shit—why not? He thought he had reason and the little idiot tried to cut him, anyhow. The arrest turned into a combat operation, and even if it hadn't, An was an enemy and a nasty order and the world was better off without him.

That was a judgement.

Who had the right to make that kind of judgement?

Nobody.

But if you didn't make it, people made it against you, so you used the cutting edge on them, the men like Taylor, until they'd done their work and then you thought up ways to keep them bright and ready to work again and got them out of the way while the clean hands and trained minds came with their lawbooks to choke anyone left over.

And Harker was lost, falling off to the side. If Taylor had done the wrong thing with the Chinese, he'd done it as a soldier. There was a look to Harker now that said nothing of hard decisions filtered through conscience and weighed against alternatives.

He let the springs of the chair bring him upright and met Taylor's eyes.

"You know we went on borrowed time when we didn't eliminate Trung. The stateside move to cancel our replacements finished us. I'm going to let Harker work with Tho, backtracking to see what they can learn about the woman Duc was to meet. Personally, I'm convinced she was eliminated as a threat to her former lover and Duc blundered in on it. That means Tho's in charge of the investigation and you're not to take things in your own hands. "I'll have your word on it, or you're out."

Taylor managed a half-smile. "You've got my word. But when we get our hands on whoever did it, I won't promise a thing if the deal gets blown again."

"What, blown? What're you telling me?"

"You said it yourself. We let Trung buffalo us and Duc was stirring around in his act and now Duc's dead. I believe the woman was a VC hit, too, and Trung may be in that somewhere. Regardless of who it is, if you can't get him taken down, I'm not promising you I won't do it myself."

"I know how you feel." Winter closed his eyes, and Taylor

wondered if it was to avoid looking at a world where men sat and spoke of hunting other men.

"Know this," he went on. "If you do anything without my approval, you do it with no support. You follow me?"

Taylor's quiet laugh sent heat through Winter's whole body, and he looked away to avoid saying something premature.

The younger man said, "I'm disappointed in the Colonel. I know the difference between murdering and killing."

Winter said, "I know who you are and what you are, Tay, God help us both. I'll be on your side if you'll let me."

After a pause, Taylor said, "Sorry. Again. I've worked with some other people and they looked at things differently."

Winter felt the heat receding and made a mental note to thank Loc for his training, come morning.

He said, "A lot of people see our business in a different light. You may have noticed."

Taylor's laughter was softer this time and what little amusement there was in it conjured pictures of things that had been good and were not to be recaptured.

"I don't know," he said, "sometimes I think there's something really wrong with me. Hell, I know I'm different. But, like the other night, I overheard some aviators talking about lighting off villages and cruising around looking for elephants to strafe. They'll go home with a sack full of Air Medals and if I come unglued and drop the hammer on Trung they'll put me in the brig for good. I'm the heavy in the piece and I'm the one whose blood freezes when I think about naping a bunch of huts and not even knowing who's in them."

Winter said, "Well, we better both get some sleep. Things are going to be rough for a while. In the meantime, you'll let me know whenever you find the answer to whatever your question is, won't you?"

43

LIEUTENANT COLONEL CARL DENBY strode the yellow corridors of MACV Headquarters and marveled to himself how fear makes a man of action of anyone.

If Winter wanted a bust, he'd get his bust.

He introduced himself to Major Rowan, a pleasant looking man of average height, sandy hair and fair coloring, frank blue eyes and a faint crescent scar under his right cheekbone. He looked less like a renegade than anyone Denby had seen all morning.

The Major was quizzically amused by Denby's insistence on privacy, as if he suspected a joke. Denby warmed inside, thinking of the damage his accusations would do to that ingenuous smile. The Major and his score of co-workers labored in a calm office of pastel green plasterboard festooned with charts, graphs, pictures, and carefully tended short-timer calendars. Shooing away a Sergeant, Major Rowan offered his guest the vacated desk chair and prepared himself in his own.

"Now, then, Colonel, what can I do for you? Is this a security clearance interview?"

Denby looked at him from the corner of his eye. "What makes you think there's a security matter involved, Major?"

He disliked Rowan, despite his friendliness. He had the wiry look of a man who'd do physical things with ease and grace. And he wasn't intimidated at all.

He said, "If we're not discussing someone's security clearance, why are we worried about our own security, Colonel? I'm sure I don't handle much classified information on this job." He flipped a hand to indicate the office space.

"I'm not here to talk about military security. Not that kind, at any rate. I'm here to talk about currency violations, black market, drugs—that sort of thing. Do you know anything about those things, Major?"

"Me?" Rowan was at a loss. "Me? I don't understand, Colonel. Are you sure you've got the right man?" He raised his hand to the name sewn on his jacket. "I'm Rowan." He spelled it out.

Denby was certain he was being mocked and he smiled to cover rising anger.

"I'm sure I'm speaking to the right man. In fact, the only reason we haven't talked this over with you before is because we wanted to watch you and learn who your friends are. You're due to go home in less than a week, aren't you? Got a drop, I understand."

"Yes, sir. Leave in three days, to be exact."

Denby's smile broadened. "What if I told you we may have to hold you over for investigation?"

Rowan winced. "I don't think that'd be a good idea, Colonel. After all, if I was doing something illegal and you know all about it, why would you be doing more investigating? And I'm anxious to go home, Colonel. I don't think I'd be willing to stay here beyond my RTD unless I was under arrest. Are you here to arrest me, sir?"

"Not yet!" Denby snapped and immediately wished he hadn't. He tried to compensate by looking superior. "Arresting you would mean bad publicity. It's the Viets we really want. We can make a big issue of breaking up an operation that's been damaging our effort here, hurting our people. I'm here to offer you a chance to get out. Cooperate, and we'll keep you out of it."

Rowan smiled, apologetic. "I'm not in anything, Colonel. I don't know anything about any of this. I haven't sent home a single money order. I don't own anything in Vietnam. If I've done anything wrong, it's messing with the girls out on Plantation Road. I can't believe you investigate everyone who crawls into the wrong sack. And that's another thing, Colonel. You never showed me any identification. Here I've confessed my extra-marital activities and I don't even know where you're from. CID? CI? MPs? What outfit, Colonel? Just for the record."

Denby rose, too furious to try to control the tremor in his voice. "We misjudged you, Major, but that makes us even, because you've misjudged us. We're going to blow this mess away, and you with it. You'll be hearing from us soon. I'll be in touch, you better believe."

Barging past, he nearly struck out at the imperturbable face. He was close enough to smell the man's cologne, a pine scent. His thoughts were already spinning wildly and the aroma switched his mind to the memory of a summer at a Maine resort. The perfume profaned what had been a treasured vacation. It raised a lump in his throat.

It had gone terribly, he conceded as he retreated back the way he had come. The halls stretched interminably, a set from a bad psychodrama. People looked at him as he passed and although they continued on about their business as if he wasn't there, he couldn't dislodge the impression they were all speculating on his future. The closed office doors seemed to speak a particular message to him.

Stepping into the parking lot exposed him to a heat point-blank from the sun. Perspiration sluiced his back and waist-line. There was an energetic volleyball game to his right and it offended him with its careless enjoyment. He practically staggered back into the comfort of the building, resting against the wall to be soothed by the smell of hot sweet grease from the cafeteria down the hall. He wrenched his thoughts from it and walked. Without intent and no idea of time passed, he looked up to discover he was only a few doors from Earl's department.

Earl's first look at Denby brought him to his feet with concern. He took his guest by the elbow and ushered him into his private office. The handsome features grew more troubled as Denby allowed himself to be guided uncaring to a seat.

"Carl, you look like you've caught something. Why are you wandering around here? You should be seeing a doctor!"

Denby clutched the last word, feeling his listlessness fall from him. "It's not me that needs a doctor, it's that madman Winter! He's going to ruin all of us!"

"Ruin? How?"

Denby shook his head and stared out the window. "He's got the idea he can smash the drug traffic here and he's apparently got something to go on. You know what that means. He's like a runaway truck. God knows who'll get trampled before he's done."

"Exactly what's he planning?"

"You know better than that." Denby found a sad smile, lending it reality by thinking how close he was to disaster. "He never tells anyone his plans and if I knew them, it'd be disloyal for me to discuss them. But I can tell you he sent me over here on a wild-goose chase today to talk to some Major he suspects has been hanging out in a place where drugs are sold. God, I was embarrassed! The guy didn't have any idea what I was talking about, and he's only got three days to do! What a going-away present from a grateful command, hey?"

"That's rotten. If he's outside his legal limits again, there could be real trouble. The command's more upset about drugs than anything else. There could be a real hassle if he's interfering with someone else's area of responsibility."

"You think I haven't thought of that? I can see my career hanging by a thread." He looked back out the window and sighed. "I don't know. I'm glad I'm able to retire soon, 'cause he'll see that I'm never promoted."

Earl moved and Denby wanted desperately to see what he was doing but felt obliged to maintain his pose. Then he heard the tattoo of a pencil on the desk. It was such a mundane action, and he'd attached so much significance to what it might be. He asked himself what he expected and had no answers and wondered if his mind was actually being affected by the stress. A muscle twitched in his lower back. The pencil continued to patter, the sound becoming maddening.

He wished he hadn't thought of that word.

Earl said, "I've got some important friends, Carl. Let's not spar now. The thing is, I can help you. People like Winter and the private-army, clandestine-ops mentality are our greatest menace. We're living in a world that needs peace in order for the Third World to develop. His kind'll always fight that, foment trouble, resist any change, any progress. His time's past. The answer today is political. Military confrontation's a last gasp and the nuke's our only possible answer to our only genuine threat. We can't get involved in in-house squabbles like Vietnam. People like us, the officer corps with the political overview, have an obligation to protect the country from the glory hounds. I'm asking you plainly to help me neutralize Winter on this deal. Not to hurt him in any way, but to insure he doesn't get us into another ugly argument with the Vietnamese government over some stupid drug crusade."

It was a wonder to Denby that a heart that knew only desolation a few short minutes ago could withstand such joy. He was saved!

Saved? Christ Almighty, he was *anointed!* If Earl had friends who could trip an old gray eminence like Winter, he

399

had the world by the balls!

He studied his knuckles, hands meshed, hoping Earl would see the white knuckles and glowing red fingertips and recognize the signs of strain. He hoped Earl would assume the strain was the result of conscience and not understand he was seeing a man strangle exhilaration.

When he was sure of his control, Denby said, "I know what you're saying's right, but it's hard to think of him turned out to pasture."

"Not our problem." Earl shook his head in a determined negative and Denby thrilled at the inclusive pronoun. "We're not putting him to pasture or anything else. We're insulating him, making sure he doesn't interfere with things outside his scope. If he makes trouble and it falls back on him, it won't be our doing."

They shook hands, Denby initiating the move. He said, "It takes guts to think out a problem and face the answer. I have to say, I'm unhappy about some of your conclusions, but in the main, you summarized my own idea. I hope we can both work together now and in the future."

Earl settled for a smile and a nod. At the sight of the departing broad body, the vagrant thought came to him that, between personalities like Winter and Denby, he was most attracted to the one he could not attract as an adherent. He brushed dust from his desk and reminded himself that neither personality—nor appearance—was any criteria. Logic was what mattered, the application of cold logic.

Major Rowan stepped off the bus in the BOQ compound and moved indoors with the herd where he idled by the reception desk, watching occupants disperse to rooms. No one paid any particular attention to him, as he expected. Satisfied, he hurried to his own room and changed to civilian clothes and returned to the street. He flagged a Bluebird and after a short ride to check for a surveillance he was certain was nonexistent, he went directly to his bar. Only a couple of the girls were present. They waved and immediately re-established their watch on the door. Four Navy SEALs, already drunk, were the only customers. They leaned toward each other across their table, a human pyramid of mumbling conversation in the rank-smelling darkness. Rowan was glad he'd never felt obliged to drink in the place.

His Vietnamese partner's eyebrows drifted upward when he saw him.

"Not think you come back no more," he greeted him.

"Trouble," Rowan said bluntly. "*Beaucoup* trouble maybe. American Lieutenant Colonel come my office today, say I must tell him about business—money, drugs, all. He know nothing, full of shit, OK? But I think maybe he know Mantell, Mantell boss."

"I not think he know Lenemann. Not many people know."

Rowan shrugged. "I not give one rat-fuck for them. If caught, they talk about sell here, be plenty police. You see they get word somebody talk too much, OK? Then they owe you, me."

The partner winked slyly. "I fix."

Stepping around him, Rowan maneuvered past the battered tables and through the noisome hallway to the back door. He inhaled heavily the evening air that was fresh by comparison and wondered how long it would be before his partner would get up nerve enough to freeze him out. He sighed philosophically. It'd been a good deal while it lasted. He walked away briskly, dismissing that which he couldn't control and turned to debating a filet for dinner or the rib-eye.

A sudden apprehension flooded Sergeant Chi when the phone rang and he stared at it until the second ring snapped him out of his immobility. He answered gruffly, expecting trouble.

Without introduction a voice said, "I am calling about your loan request. The company you wished to invest in is dissatisfied with their newest executive. I remember you were concerned as well. If they let him go, it could affect our position."

Chi's brow ridged. "Loan? Company? What are you talking about?"

The voice was at once suspicious and hesitant. It said, "You have not spoken to us about a loan?"

Chi merely snorted and the voice chilled. "I apologize for bothering you." The connection clicked off.

Lowering the instrument slowly, Chi closed his eyes and

tried to sort things out.

So his cousin had been asked to do a further check on Miller. Had Lenemann found out about Miller and was he now trying to learn how he'd been tricked? If so, not only was Miller in grave danger, but so was the cousin and, inevitably, himself. He balled his fists and hunched his shoulders, wishing the problem had a physical form he could grab.

He asked Tho if he might be excused for a few minutes and when Tho approved, hurried down the stairs and along the hall to Miller's office. He stopped short of the door, his face a caricature of partially hidden confusion.

He had to know more and without revealing his own knowledge. He pounded a leg in frustration, envying Tho's clever, treacherous words that said nothing and made others say anything. He braced himself and entered.

Miller looked up and Chi immediately read the black man's tension. Still, there was a pleased look about him. The earlier apprehension flew from Chi like a released arrow and he reminded himself that a happy subject was a talkative subject.

"Sit down, sit down," Miller said, hands and head combining in animated gestures. "They came to me last night, the one named Mantell? And they want the deal! It's gonna work, Chi! We got 'em, baby!"

Chi smiled back, carefully absorbing the details as they poured from Miller. He was pleasantly surprised to learn Ordway had arranged for real people to fill the roles of the players in the scheme, which would convince Lenemann or his informants in America the plan was genuine until it was too late.

It was doomed though, he told himself with genuine regret. As a plan, it was excellent, but it suffered a flaw they couldn't foresee or correct if it were pointed out.

Trust. The Americans, almost without exception, had an amazing capacity for trusting other people. It was a pity, because a person could grow fond of them and they were always sure to be hurt. It was as bad as having a child whose wits were poor. No matter how much a man loved such a child, he'd never provide support in a father's old age. It was natural to protect him, but when a sacrifice was necessary, a man was obligated to strength. To live in this world you protected yourself and the people who could help you.

Mantell welcomed Miller with a power greeting and they went into the bar together.

Chi, in slacks and sport shirt, gestured to the left and the similarly dressed man on the motorcycle next to his banked across the oncoming traffic and up a side street. Chi followed, pulling up next to him and cutting his engine. The other man stopped, as well.

Chi said, "You will watch from the next corner. If they come out this door, come for me immediately. I will be in the back. Do not look for me. Ride down the street and I will see you and follow. You will identify their vehicle, if they leave that way, and then you will leave. As soon as you are certain I am following the right people, go home. You understand?"

The man said, "I should come with you. I could—."

"I have told you what to do," Chi interrupted. "We will do what we do best, and this time there may be more than watching. No job for a file clerk, cousin. Leave it to me."

Without waiting for further argument, Chi kicked the motorcycle to a roar and sped away. At the next corner he turned out of the storm of lights and machines and the next corner doubled him back on the dark back street paralleling Plantation Road. With his engine barely ticking, he pulled beside one of the houses facing the scabbed back walls of the bars and shops, so different from the garish enticements on the other side. He wheeled the machine around the house, where a boy of about twelve sprang through the back door ahead of a woman's brittle voice.

"Pay the boy now!" A moment later her face appeared in one of the two unglassed windows and although the only light was the glow from the night-action a block away, it showed lined features as hard as her speech.

"Are you so afraid I might die before you get your money?" Chi said, and laughed at the woman's irritated discomfort. He handed the boy the piasters and faced her again. "Has there been any question about us being here? Has it been noticed?"

The woman laughed, barely parting lips that revealed scattered remaining teeth. "Notice? Questions? We are not fools around here."

Chi moved to the side of the building, squatting with his back against one of the concrete block piers holding the small building off the ground. He ignored the passage of time, sure this was the door Miller would come out. His primary question was if he would walk or be carried.

There were distractions. A group of youngsters, the ones the Americans called "cowboys" roared down the street on their motorcycles, nervous in this white man's ghetto, their bravado failing to disguise their hurried passage. After a long period of quiet a young American staggered down the street bawling a song, only to stop and fall heavily against a wall. There was a wedge of illumination at the corner, thrown by a streetlight that seemed to regard the rest of the street as beneath consideration. The boy was at its edge and Chi watched for a while as he tried to empty his stomach. The sounds struck Chi as only slightly less unpleasant than the singing.

The few lights in the neighboring houses had been out for some time when the door across the way opened. Chi shifted gingerly, loosening joints, prepared to move if the need arose. He continued to flex muscles as two men came out and looked over the alley. Chi curled a lip in contempt for people who left a lighted area for a dark one and pretended to search it. Two more men followed, half-dragging a third between them. Chi needed no light to know he was looking at Miller. Two more men followed the trio. One of them spoke, and Chi was trying to decide if it was Mantell's voice when the larger of them answered, and this time he was certain he heard Lenemann.

"I don't give a shit what he said, Bobby, I done made up my mind. This has to be the sumbitch."

Again, the smaller man said something in a voice too quiet for Chi to catch.

"Blow the deal, my fuckin' ass!" Lenemann's anger rang through the darkness, the rest of the group stirring at the volume. "Ain't no deal, asshole! It's a con's what it is. Look, he the only new contact we made, ain't he? And now the heat's comin' down! Use your fuckin' head!"

Miller moved, stood a little straighter. When he spoke, only the pain carried across the street, and that was interrupted by the sound of a fist on flesh. Miller and the two men holding him recoiled.

"You said all I want to hear," Lenemann said, a thickening accent making the words ever more difficult for Chi. The large figure moved toward the door. "Make a example o' his ass. Beat the fucker 'til nothin' left to break an' then dump him in the river to drown. People got to learn not to mess in our shit."

Miller managed a single note of protest that ended in a screech and then he was doubled over and stumbling from one to the other of the men ringed about him. It looked almost playful, like children in a schoolyard game, except for the deep grunts and Miller's weakening cries. Then he fell and was silent and even as Chi thought to himself how his tormenters made up for expertise with sheer force, one of them left the ground in a leap and when he came down, something cracked through the night like a breaking branch. One of the men gagged and walked away, headed toward the house. Chi drew his .45 and aimed carefully. There was another crack from the circle and the man approaching Chi stopped and heaved with earnest, wrenching spasms.

Keeping the automatic firmly pointed at the sick man's middle, Chi was thankful he was making so much noise. Finally the group was quiet, save for the sibilance of labored breathing. Then there was a short command and one man detached to hurry down the street. The rest, including the sick one, rolled Miller against the wall and positioned themselves in front of him.

Chi crept to the back of the house where his motorcycle rested. The boy slept against it. Chi wakened him silently and they muscled the machine away from the house, quartering across a construction site to the street perpendicular to Plantation Road. At that point, Chi dismissed the boy and waited. A darkened car, silver light reflection slipping along its sides, crunched down the street and stopped in front of the waiting group. Straining, Chi was sure he saw only one man get in with the driver while the others threw Miller into the back. He kicked the engine to life and rolled down the street and across Plantation Road, where he turned, parked, and waited again, feeling the muted thunder of the powerful engine under him almost as an extension of his own power as he considered what must be done.

The car followed a few minutes later, turning onto Plantation Road. He allowed some of the now-sparse traffic to fill in and swung in behind. The car proceeded with no precautions, and again Chi was moved to marvel at the ability of the Americans to rely on such things as the spoken word or good luck. He reflected that Sergeant Miller might never do so again if, indeed, he was still capable of doing anything.

The car left the main street and Chi revised his opinion of the driver. Now the narrow streets and lack of traffic would make his following headlight noticeable. It would also lessen their chances of being caught up in curfew endorcement. Further, they were nearing a neighborhood where a body could be thrown from the bank onto the mudflats of one of the minor creeks feeding the Saigon River. The men ahead were not entirely stupid.

Chi did what he could, dropping back and turning off his lights, pulling off to hide, but forced to hold close enough to keep them in sight. When the car stopped, he knew he'd won because the river bank was only meters away from them. He cut his engine and coasted into an alley where he got off quickly and peered around the corner. The car was still, silhouetted heads in the front seat turning from side to side.

Far to the east shots were fired and a flare briefly challenged the starlight, too distant to be more than a thing to draw the eye. As it died, Chi moved forward, slowly, carefully, using the night. He was wedged in a crouch at the base of a tree when the car door opened and he was close enough to hear the click of the latch before it swung wide. A voice from the other side of the car said, "We'll get him out over here." When the driver moved to the side of the car away from him, Chi scuttled across the open space and stopped, his heart pounding, pressed against the chill metal. He heard the slither of Miller's body being pulled from the back seat and moans. He heard Miller's feet hit the ground as they pulled him free of the car and the scream that was a weak squeal.

Mantell said, "Save your breath, mother-fucker. You need it all in the river."

Chi rose and braced his arm on the roof of the car, the extended automatic mere feet from the two men who each held one of Miller's wrists. Mantell said, "Who the fuck—?" before Chi shot him in the face, the impact of the heavy round lifting him clear of the ground in a clumsy backward flight. The other man ducked before Chi could properly aim and the bullet merely hit his shoulder. He spun away, landing on his face, and rolled over on his back. As Chi trotted toward him he covered the wound with his remaining functional hand and dug his heels into the ground to push away like a crippled lizard. He screamed and wriggled, making Chi's aim very difficult and aggravating him because there were already shouts and lights coming from the neighboring homes. The whites of the eyes and gleaming teeth flashed and bobbed and Chi finally shot into the chest, which was an easy target and stilled the motion, and then shot the man in the head.

Hurrying now, sweating a bit, he ran to insure that Mantell was also dead, rolling him over and noting the ruin where the back of his head had been. He wiped his hand on Mantell's shirt and ran to Miller.

The excitement in the background was growing stronger, especially now that the shooting had stopped. Chi muttered to himself when he couldn't find a pulse and smiled when a faint rhythm at last trembled against his fingertips. He ran then, shouting for someone to call the police, started his engine and roared away. After driving for a while, he stopped under a street light and inspected himself carefully for any stray blood.

He cruised easily in the direction of his cousin's house, letting his nerves calm, reviewing each step of the night's activity.

It was all going according to plan. Lenemann would be the first major dealer to pay to continue selling his product. There would be others. Until it became possible to eliminate them. It was all going according to plan.

He let the cool night air carry away more tension, refusing to think of anything except the messages of his senses—the breeze, the vibrations of the machine coursing his body.

A child dodged across the street in front of him and yelled its fright at being paralyzed on the spear from the headlight. Chi swerved, cursing, seeing not the child, but the unwanted memory of Miller being beaten. He regained control and admitted to himself that the plan had not considered Miller or what happened to him. Not originally.

Each man had his fate.

Still, it angered him that they had done that to Miller. It was a rueful admission and he decided he might as well be honest with himself. He wished it had not happened. Worse, he could already feel the urge to make the man Lenemann pay for what had been done.

He picked up speed and made a face into the darkness.

The parking lot was empty, the swimming pool silent, and the few lights in the windows of BOQ One only enhanced the peculiar aloneness weighting Taylor. He climbed aboard the jeep with great care, telling himself that getting busted for drunk driving after curfew would serve as no memorial to Duc.

What would?

Certainly not a bitter six-man wake in a dingy room that ended with the last man out standing by himself asking useless questions of the night.

Memorials?

You went to the funerals and you tried to say a comforting thing to the wives and children and the women thanked you while their eyes hated your life and the children tried to understand and you hated yourself because you were glad to be alive and because there would never be answers for the children.

When it was done, the burying and the words and music and flowers, nothing was changed. Another piece of you was in the ground, waiting for the rest. That was all.

44

TAKING CASUALTIES IS A NATURAL FUNCTION. Peacetime has its training accidents and the root of combat is the sacrifice and exaction of injury or death. The number of men lost by the Records Research Unit was abnormally high for a Saigon-based group, but not to be compared with the abuse taken by any average infantry organization. On the other hand, there is a peculiar psychology involved in group morale in combat circumstances.

A unit may take incredible casualties without any outward effect. On the contrary, not only the survivors but replacements take on a unique hard-bitten quality that eventually defies the enemy, the weather, or bad leadership to do their combined worst.

Headquarters all learn quickly to depend on those units. In the attack they are given the honor of leading, of battering their way through the enemy's defense. They are allowed to execute the brute brawling that leaves only winners and dead in order for other units, blessed with greater élan, to exploit the gap and pursue the defeated.

In defense the rawhide units are never the counterattack force. Again, to them falls the higher honor, the privilege of digging in at the farthest reach, throwing out patrols to determine the numbers, route, and rate of movement of the advancing forces. If the patrols avoid being engulfed they rejoin the unit and participate in absorbing whatever means of destruction the enemy can deliver. If eventually forced to retreat, they hold until softer-skinned rear elements can scurry away.

They share certain universal characteristics. They have an irrational dislike of night operations, not from any fear of the dark or esoteric psychology, but because they know all headquarters personnel forget it takes all day to organize a satisfactory night move and it takes all night to execute it and the people involved ought not to be asked to continue to function the next day as if nothing had happened. They hate listening posts, don't think much of any sort of outpost duty, and vastly prefer combat patrols of reconnaissance patrols, being devoutly convinced that when you find an enemy you don't snoop on him, you kill him.

Occasionally such a unit will pull up, crippled with the inexplicability of an indomitable horse broken down by a minor stumble. The collapse isn't so invariably fatal, but it's sudden and can be generated by something as normal as one casualty. It need not be a glamorous leader, someone popular, or a talisman-figure. One day, one average individual—and almost to a man the unit reviews the myriad honors it has enjoyed and suspects they will never end. The idea grows that these things are no more than a visitation by a God motivated exclusively by caprice and malice.

There is no sorrier lament than the silence of such men.

All those things ran through Taylor's mind as he watched the medical personnel load Miller's white-wrapped broken body into the plane taking him to Japan.

It was absurd to compare this Unit with any kind of combat outfit, he told himself. No matter how many casualties they took, they ate hot food from plates, slept in beds, bathed as often as they wanted—hell, they lived in Oriental splendor. He wondered if his inability to speak was a morbid carryover from an earlier time. It was conceivable that Winter's silence was a result of the same attitude, but how to explain Harker? His long-range patrols couldn't qualify as common infantry work.

They waved one last time and walked back to the jeep. Taylor smiled to himself at the prospect of the Records Research Unit (American Contingent) fitting into a jeep with one seat left over.

Abreast of Two Hundred P Alley he took his eyes from the road long enough to look at Winter in the next seat. "I got the impression Denby didn't want to come today," he said.

Winter kept his eyes straight ahead. "He didn't. He's not very good at goodbyes, you know. And he's got a lot of last-minute stuff before he leaves."

"The sooner the better." Harker's bitterness was enough to make both men flinch perceptibly. "I can't believe Willy was into that shit alone. I think it was a piss-poor operation and he's taking the fall for Denby."

Winter said, "That's prejudice talking, Bill. I've had Carl working on an op plan to nail our slumlord Major. What he came up with is nothing spookier than a financial investigation. His reasoning is that, if we can get him for tax evasion, we can probably squeeze him for everything he knows. And we can do it stateside, where the goddam press won't make a circus out of it. It's a good plan and it means the Army doesn't have to run the investigation. There was nothing in it about infiltrating the drug outfit. Miller told us that, and he was being honest, not noble."

Conversation died again as Taylor pulled up to the gate and started again once they were clear of the guards.

Harker said, "I still say Denby should have had a closer leash on Willy. We all knew he was nuts when it came to drug pushing."

Still conciliatory, Winter said, "The best way isn't necessarily the most popular way. And I'm the man responsible for the decisions, right or wrong. If Colonel Denby was lax in his control, it's as much my fault as his. I happen to think he did

410

everything he was required to do."

Some of the venom faded from Harker's voice. "I'm sorry, Colonel. I know I don't have all the facts and so on. But I saw Willy. Everybody knows that Major was into heroin up to his ass and he's the only American we had a decent lead on and he's been home for almost two weeks. Even Colonel Loc suspects we let him get away clean because he's an American officer. I keep thinking if Denby'd moved faster, been willing to work with Willy, we'd have busted the sucker and taught a lot of people a lesson."

The crunch of gravel underlined the indictment as the jeep coasted to a stop in front of the villa. It seemed a particularly welcome place to Taylor at that moment, a familiar spot where he could relax.

Winter continued the conversation on the way up the stairs. "Maybe you're right, Bill, perhaps I should have pushed harder. But let's assume I did and we pinned the Major to the drug business. Can you see the headlines?" He stopped at the door, his hand on the knob. "And another thing, I don't think we could have put together a legal case. He's too smart, was too well protected here. But we know he's guilty, just as we know things about other people and can't prove them. Would you have had me pass sentence on him? And who would I send after him? Think about it."

Taylor froze his face to a noncommittal stare while Harker flashed an angry glare from one to the other of them.

"If he was selling heroin, he's killed some of our people," he said. "If all you were concerned about is who to send after him, you should've said something. It'd be a pleasure to waste him."

Winter turned away and opened the door. The others followed.

Taylor went eagerly, still thinking sanctuary. The first thing to strike his eye was the refrigerator and the GI can. His imagination brought back Miller's lithe angularity, taut with anticipation as one of his never-ending succession of soft-drink cans arced almost to the ceiling before sloping down to clash among the rest in the trash.

Goddam them for what they did to you, your poor broken legs and arms and the ribs and how many of those white, white teeth did they break off, kick out? The docs said they'd make

411

*you good as new again, Willy, and I pray they do and we catch
the people who did it to you and I can give you their fucking
heads to shoot baskets with.*

He was staring into the hall space when Winter, from halfway to the second floor said, "Come up to the office. It echoes
like a cave down there now."

"I hate it," Harker said, following him. "I was going to ask
if we could move into Denby's office when he's gone."

An infinitesimal move of Winter's head caught Taylor's eye,
either an involuntary movement brought on by Harker's suggestion or a mis-step on the stairs. He opted for the former.
There was a feeling of fluctuation around Winter, like a
cornerback who's lost a step. One day he plays his normal
game and the next he's terrified he's going to get burned and
the only thing he can think of is playing for the interception.
The attitude was a mistake for Winter, but a natural one. He'd
had high plans.

In the office they watched as he puttered with a coffeepot,
the ritual clearly serving to relax him. He was smiling when he
finished and sat at his desk.

"Well, there's no sense in wasting the little time we have
left. As soon as you're gone, Tay, I'm recommending Harker
be transferred to Special Operations Group. He's worked with
them enough to fit right in. In the meantime, I'm detailing you
to police up our records. Select what you think we should pass
on to other agencies and destroy everything else, unless it has
possible historical value. But remember, data concerning the
cover function only."

"Wait a minute." Taylor made no effort to gloss his irritation. "What about the investigation for Duc's killer?"

"Harker's covering that." Winter looked away.

"And Willy? We just duck our heads and let whoever did it
keep on taking care of business? What's going on? A year ago
we'd have been out kicking asses and taking names and we'd
have forced something. What's going on?"

Winter continued to look around the room, eyes swift and
uncatchable as mosquitoes. "A year ago you weren't short.
And there's Ly to think about."

"Think what? Don't try to put this on her. Listen, I'm not
leaving here looking over my shoulder and wondering if I did
my best. Duc and Miller were part of our outfit! I'll be

goddamed if I'll just walk away from them!''

For an instant Winter's eyes stopped and riveted themselves to Taylor's. They gave no clue of the mind behind them.

"I'm aware of the men in my command, Major, and I'm aware of our losses. You were persuaded to join us after you had once decided to something less than your best here.'' His eyes flitted off again. "Why am I mad at you? You haven't enough time to find Duc's killer or prove anything against anyone who was involved in Miller's beating. We can't even guess who killed the two animals with him, for Christ's sake! What're you going to do in the time you've got left? Harker's working on Duc's contacts. There's only enough work for one man. You've turned up nothing. And those files have to be sanitized. It's my decision.''

"So I finish my tour doing exactly what I expected to do here, shoving fucking papers around?''

"That's the way it's going to be.''

An answer died in Taylor's throat at the muffled knock on the door. He recognized the style and turned to watch Denby's entrance. He couldn't understand why he felt pleased to see him until he realized the knock had stopped him from saying something stupid to a friend.

"Well, it's our shortest-timer,'' Winter said, his own gratitude for the interruption apparent. "I was just telling Taylor I want him to go through our files. When can you brief him and sign off on classified?''

Denby had remained posed with just the grinning face showing and now the body followed it in. "Shouldn't take more than a few hours.'' He nodded and the reflected light from his glasses leaped up and down the wall behind Winter.

"Fine, fine,'' Winter smiled for Harker and Taylor. "You two excuse us for a while, will you? I have to talk to Carl about some business.''

Harker was up and gone quickly, clearly glad to leave the stress of the earlier confrontation behind. Taylor left more slowly, reluctant to concede. Harker waited for him in the hall and pushed the door shut as soon as he was clear.

"Hey, man, I'm sorry the Old Man dumped on you. I'll keep you in on the deal, you know? If I get lucky and things start to happen, I'll need all the help I can get. And I don't give a shit how short you are. I'm not taking a chance on getting

413

my ass shot off because you're RTD's up.''

Taylor dropped a hand on the muscular shoulder as they went down the stairs. "You're all heart. But, you know, it's the truth. I'll go nuts if I just sit out these last few weeks." He pulled his hand away and his voice softened. "There was a man in my platoon in Korea, due to go home the next day. We had a patrol going out that night, a nasty one. I scratched his name off the roster and he came to me practically in tears. Said he'd never forgive himself if something happened to one of his buddies, he'd always believe he could've done something if he'd been there.''

"What'd you do?"

"Sent the silly bastard on patrol, what else?"

"He make it?"

"Everybody made it. Lot of the troops thought he brought them good luck.''

"He ought to be here." At Taylor's look, Harker added, "We need some luck. Nothing's happening. I'm beginning to think the Old Man may have said it, maybe Duc ran into a plain murder. I can't find a clue.''

Taylor shook his head, turning off at his office. "I don't think so, and neither does he, but I don't care. I want whoever did it, and never mind their reasons.''

He flopped into his chair without asking Harker in and the younger man took the hint, moving off toward his own work space. He hurried. The echo of each footfall rushed away, sought out an office and fled through the door. Once inside, it was absorbed by dead space. Harker listened to what was going on and it made him uneasy.

Winter listened to Denby's nervous small talk as long as he could, interrupting in the middle of a description of the inefficiency of the household goods packers.

"Carl, are you sure there isn't something you want to tell me?"

Moisture beaded Denby's forehead as if sprayed there. He screwed his face into a complex frown and shook his head. "I can't think—I can't imagine—.''

"Oh, Carl." Winter chided easily. "We know each other too well. You can always think. You can always imagine. I'm very curious to know what you've learned about Miller's free-lance effort. You were going to phone Ordway."

A happy smile swept away the corrugations. "I did. Yes, I did, and I meant to tell you, but I've been so busy—. Have you seen that telephone thing in the basement? Those lights flashing and clocks and God-knows-what? It's like science fiction! They put my call through to that nothing town—."

"I've seen it work," Winter broke in. "What did you learn?"

"Right. Sorry. They had a plan. I had to keep the conversation in general terms, you know, and Ordway understood that, and he was cooperative. They were working together, Ordway making the arrangements in the States and Miller doing the work here. I gathered the idea was to set up a fake buy. Very amateurish."

"I wonder why Miller never mentioned it to you before what happened to him and why he wouldn't talk about it after. Not that he's been able to say much, yet."

"He didn't say anything to me because he knew I'd put a stop to it." Winter shifted and Denby hurriedly added, "I told him I was working on the idea that the Army should avoid this kind of investigation, should get someone else to actually conduct it and we simply cooperate. As I told you, if the investigation works, we look good for being helpful and if it fails the other organization wears the egg on its face. I gave Miller enough to do, told him to maintain a surveillance of the place and a log of all Americans who appeared to be suspicious. I haven't seen any sign of it."

"I remember all that, Carl. You were very eloquent when you brought in your plan and I believe it'll work out as you've said. I still feel we've overlooked something, you and I. You're sure you can't think of something you ought to be telling me? It could be a little thing, as minor as a conversation you've neglected to mention."

"I can't think of any." The chair squeaked derisively as he moved.

"I was wondering. I hope you'll think about it between now and the time you leave. To tell you the truth, when you came up with your plan only the day after Miller was beaten, I hoped you had a real blood-and-thunder epic so we could ar-

415

range for some people to die. I really wanted that."

When he said it, he smiled at Denby as if springing a pleasant surprise. He continued, "As soon as I saw what you'd been leading up to, I changed my mind. Your way's far better. Our Major's fat and happy, certain he's gotten away clean. I've got some good friends in the IRS—retired types. They'll give that bastard special attention. It'll take time, but that's all the better. Think how it'll feel to have them hit him after so long. Christ, it'll gut-shoot him! I have to hand it to you. If he wasn't such scum, I'd say you were being cruel to think of it, Carl, I really would."

One of Denby's pudgy hands crept past his smile and lifted his glasses off. He blinked rapidly while he polished them.

"I'm glad you liked the plan, Colonel," he said, "and I wish I'd been able to convince Miller to play it my way. I couldn't give him all the details, so he must have decided I wasn't doing enough."

"Maybe you'll have a chance to talk to him and explain again. When he gets back to the States, that is. And speaking of that, I'll bet anything that when the Major starts talking he can give us some names and leads that'll take us to the people who worked Miller over. They'll be sure they've gotten away with it by then, too. Oh, yes. The waiting and finally deciding they've made it, and then we *nail* them!"

As he spoke the last words, Winter raised a hand until it was level with his shoulder and drove a clenched fist onto the top of the desk. Even knowing it was coming, Denby jumped and when he went to put his glasses back on he had trouble getting them straight. There were sweaty fingerprints on both lenses by the time he was done. He got to his feet.

"Well, sir, I'm glad you were satisfied. I don't mind telling you, I was afraid you'd be all over me for not planning something more aggressive." The heartiness in his voice improved as he continued until it was like a camouflage job that's been overdone and tends to draw the eye.

"We'll be aggressive, when the time comes." Winter turned on the happy smile again. "Now, you go on getting ready to go home."

Denby spun and hurried from the room. Winter watched the door inch shut, amused that the man would hold to such an insignificant mannerism when he was clearly strung tight as a drumhead.

A few moments later he lowered his head to his extended fingertips, rocking slightly, massaging.

Why couldn't he shake the suspicion that a connection existed between Miller's assault and the practically immediate appearance of Denby's all-bases-covered op plan?

Coincidence?

He made a sound in his throat and closed his eyes in exasperation, thinking how close he was to talking to himself.

There were no coincidences in this business. There was a reason, always. He'd grown old playing with the same marked deck and there were no accidents in it.

He stared at the door as if it could open and release the answers.

Well, he hadn't lied to Denby, and the toady wart was nervous as hell about something. Probably still counting his blessings because his op plan was approved after he'd stalled so long he'd never have a chance to recover if it was turned down. It *did* have cunning and when it worked, it'd go off like a grenade in a straddle-pit.

He decided that was probably the happiest thought he'd manage for this day and determined to put off until tomorrow his opening gambit with the General toward establishing a new organization.

45

TUYET INSPECTED HER FINGERNAILS for what she suspected was the hundredth time and looked away without completing the job, knowing they were as perfect as they had been the ninety-ninth time. She let her gaze sweep the Friendly Bar inhabitants—four girls at the bar, two more working on a couple of soldiers in a booth, and herself, alone.

Alone. The word triggered a sigh. The concept triggered a shudder. She tried to dismiss it with a shake of her head, but the tug of her hair tumbling down her back brought a contrary response and the fear of being alone swept over her more strongly than ever.

She asked herself if she was in love and couldn't answer.

He was a good man, gentle. He knew what she was and said he didn't care. But did he really know? Would he never care? And how would she stand it when he finally decided he didn't want a whore for a wife?

And how could anyone live in America?

Her eyes burned and the tears tried to come again, the ones that always came when she thought about marrying. She could be a good wife, as good as any man could want, but who would let her? There had never been a chance, and now what man would believe her mind rested in a corner and watched while they pushed themselves into her and her body moved and her mouth said things they wanted to hear and she was nowhere near them?

Until now. Until this ordinary man spoke to her and caught her mind as easily as a boy picking a mango.

She walked to the bathroom, careful to look as controlled as ever, grateful for the dark hall where she could let her face relax and the tears flow. She stepped inside and closed the door and dabbed at her eyes, so preoccupied with her puffy image in the mirror she almost missed the sound of the steps approaching. They were a man's steps and they stopped just outside.

"Who is in there?" Trung demanded.

She was still a mess! She backed away from the mirror, careful to make no sound. The door flew open and Trung's angry eyes searched the room. She cowered behind the door, saw him bend down to see that no feet were tucked back out of sight in the stall. He pulled the door shut behind him.

"It's empty," he said. "We'll talk here. No one can come from either direction without being seen."

"Why did you call me here? I could be seen. We have nothing to talk about."

She recognized the voice of Han, the one who drove for the American writer.

"I must disagree." Trung's answer was insistent, but it coaxed, like a persistent beggar's plea. Tuyet wished she had enough nerve to walk out of the room.

Trung went on, "I only want to help us both."

"You think only of yourself!" the other man snapped, having difficulty holding his voice down.

"That is not true." Trung was unoffended. "I am being practical. The same people who had me now have the woman and her child. How long will she be able to resist? How can we know she hasn't already told them what only she knows? And what will the party say of those who have helped keep a suspected traitor hidden all these months?"

Han's scorn was unconvincing. "What woman do you speak of? What traitor? You speak riddles! If you have nothing to say, I must go!"

A sharp click startled Tuyet and she realized she was leaning against the wall to hear better and that someone had just snapped a cigarette lighter on the other side. She put her head to the wall again, very carefully.

"I thought there would be no need for discussion, but I will speak of definite things, if I must. I thought little of the girl from Phu Thuan until it occurred to me that a lover rarely hires someone to do his killing. Once that story seemed odd, I remembered other things, such as you saying you helped build Phu Thuan and you attended classes there. I was still puzzled about how you could do both when there came the matter of three of our comrades surprised at the elimination of your cousin. You didn't appear surprised when that happened. In fact, you seemed relieved."

Tuyet drew back at the boil of incoherent anger on the other side of the wall, but Trung's voice droned untroubled.

"Calm yourself. We are discussing things practically. To get back to your school days, I have investigated. Did you know the first school built in Phu Thuan was built only twelve years ago? The teacher you named was never employed there. But many of the villagers remembered you. One of them said you would always be welcome. That was when I took the chance, my friend. I told them you had asked me to get a message to a mutual acquaintance. I said you were certain the villagers of Phu Thuan would know who I meant and would take care of it."

There was a long pause, so long Tuyet began to tremble, afraid she had made some sound. Finally the other man spoke.

"Very well. He hides near there. What do you intend to do

419

with your knowledge? You know I can have you killed.''

"But you will not, because your own life is no more than a word from ending. No, my friend, we both wish to live. We must work together.''

"What is your proposition? I promise nothing, understand.''

"Of course. To prove my faith, I will confess to you. I am tired of this war, tired of being afraid. And I am tired of being looked down on. And you are as good as dead if the party learns you have contributed to hiding our mutual friend. I think I would like to live in ease in some other place. Hong Kong. Singapore.''

"You would sell him?''

"I have a plan of many rooms. First, we sell your rich American the information that Winter has the woman and child. That way we profit and that bastard is destroyed. Later, if necessary, we reveal the truth about our friend and Phu Thuan. And no more talk of selling him. Has he not bought us? His wife holds your life on the tip of her tongue. Do not look so shocked. It was you who arranged the silencing of your nephew, remember. I suspect you had the girl killed because she spoke too much.''

"Enough! I must think.''

The silence dragged again. This time Tuyet knew it was no fault of hers and she gnawed the inside of her cheek in her impatience for Han's answer.

"The American has influence. Perhaps he can arrange it. I must think more. She is a strong woman. She may not tell them anything. I am not even sure how much she knows.''

Trung laughed, a scratchy sound, as though it was forced through the boards to Tuyet's ears. "I have been in their hands. She will tell them anything she knows.''

There was a sound of footsteps moving away, but Tuyet couldn't be sure if it was one man or two. She twitched in an agony of uncertainty, wanting desperately to get away. The world was being handed to her and she was trapped in a stinking toilet. She bit a knuckle and pushed her forehead against the wall. When she turned to press an ear to the wood her eyes refused to see anything but the doorknob, daring her.

She heard nothing but the muffled sounds of the bar, and

tiptoeing to the door, pulled it back a hair and peered through the slit. The hallway was empty.

Bursting out, she raced to the alley and continued away at a brisk walk, looking over her shoulder at every fifth or sixth step. When she felt safe again, she thought she would drown in relief and hope and happiness.

She turned onto Nguyen Hue, the Street of Flowers, remembering how lovely it was when they filled the broad boulevard with carts full of colorful blossoms that perfumed everything. The discovery that her mind would make room for such thoughts was frightening. She forced herself to turn all her attention to the matter of using her golden information.

The obvious person to talk to would be the American called Harker. There was a disturbing atmosphere around him, but if she was to marry an American, only another one would be able to help with their government regulations. She picked her way through a crowd in front of a sidewalk booth, not really paying attention to the jostling. The man Harker always looked like he was in pain and wished you were, too. Tho was businesslike.

Preoccupied, she stepped off the curb and a car horn bellowed. Brakes howled. She spun, upper arms clamped to her sides and her forearms extended, the fingers splayed. The arrangement registered in her mind even as the sun reflecting from the windshield hit her eyes and blinded her. She staggered one step back and felt the hood of the car rap the ends of her fingers.

She managed a quarter turn away, continuing on across the street, moving clumsily, nodding vacant assurances at spectators. Safely on the opposite side, she sagged against the closest wall and fought to regain her control. It took longer than it should, her brain refusing to stop combining the incident with the clear memory of herself in Tho's chair, hands rigidly extended, lights blinding her.

There was a restaurant a few doors up the street. She hurried there, her step firmer, and slipped into a booth where a bored waiter brought tea. The warm smells and hum of conversation relaxed her further. When the glass was empty, she had her plan in mind. She walked back to Tu Do and turned toward Kennedy Square, exulting in her continued good luck, because

421

today was the day she was to indicate if she had a reason to meet with *Dai Uy* Harker.

Truly, the world had been handed to her.

Harker strolled around the square, studying the towering brick cathedral. In his thoughts, the scene was appropriate. Himself, apparently aimless, camera at the ready. The church, apparently serene, undisturbed by the stresses surrounding it.

Each was lying.

The cathedral was symbol and reality combined for thousands of Vietnamese, a source of solace and a place to meet and indulge in the continual scheming that passed for political dialogue. The church organization was a fountain of leadership that gave purpose to attitudes. When the government became excessively repressive, the hierarchy acted as spokesmen, organized the protests. If the government appeared to be softening toward the aggressors, the black robes quietly drifted into certain ministries and homes and spoke persuasively. The church was, in fact, one of the major components in the pressurized stew that was South Vietnam.

And it was in mortal agony.

The very fabric of the organization was torn. When America turned its sun from Ngo Dinh Diem, few Vietnamese and fewer Americans troubled to ask how it had come to pass. It was unnecessary in either case. The Americans were told Diem was out of touch with the people and his removal from office by any means not only afforded no affront to democratic process but his entire family was unlikable and they all deserved whatever they got. As for the Vietnamese, they were familiar with leaders suddenly stripped of the mandate of heaven. Still, this was an especially difficult morass to fathom.

Thousands of years of recorded experience found the Vietnamese unprepared to deal with a society that sent men to die for ideals while the same ideals were being prostituted by mob leaders preaching of higher commitments that absolved them of all moral restraint. The Vietnamese, proud of survival in the face of a history of virtually uninterrupted internal and external conflict, were not equipped to comprehend a mentality that could organize mass rallies to publicly mourn men killed in combat and later telephone the widows to taunt them.

The ultimately stunning American failure was the inability to grasp success. Only the press openly exulted in Diem's overthrow, and even they immediately turned accusing eyes in all directions save their own. Their attempt at national breast beating struck the Vietnamese as bad taste and worse theater, but what truly galled was the other aspect, the humiliation of seeing their leadership destroyed and the matter treated with the sly evasion of a silent flatulence in a crowded room.

Simple courtesy demanded that the people responsible accept the fruits of their labors with dignity. The honorable next step was to supply the correct leadership implied by the liquidation of the former leader. The people felt they had a right to expect a forthright power grab by someone. Unless, of course, there really was something shameful involved.

The Catholics were hardest hit by the entire performance. Diem was one of theirs, symbolizing a link between east and west and, in himself, the Vietnamese north and south. When he was found wanting and cast down, the Catholics asked themselves what more they could have done. Without a decent answer, thousands began to consider survival as an individual —or family—prospect.

The non-Catholic Vietnamese saw a western power, ostensibly an ally, publicly scourge and destroy its staunchest western-oriented partners and he thought very hard about his own position. For the most part he continued to exist amicably with his Catholic neighbors, increasing the distance between himself and them only so much as prudence dictated. On the other hand, he looked for other supportive alliances. And he began to wonder if it was worthwhile to depend on anyone except himself—or his family, naturally.

Harker paused in his rambling to steady the camera against one of the trees fronting the cathedral. At about knee level, he saw the pinhead, a green one, the kind used to mark maps. His stomach cinched down to a tight ball.

Once a week he walked the square framing the cathedral. His lie was to appear to be doing nothing else. In truth he inspected this same tree on each occasion, hoping to find the green pin and afraid he might. It was Tuyet's signal. Normally, she would wait for him to contact her. Now, however, something had come up, something short of an emergency, but a matter of urgent need.

He would make an appearance at the Ben Thanh market, facing the statue in Dien Hong Square between five and five-thirty that evening. He would remain no longer than three minutes. It was her responsibility to see him. They would not communicate. Ideally, they would never be within a hundred yards of each other. Having seen him, she would know he was agreeing to meet her and would send her instructions.

Snapping the shutter, he stepped away from the tree and cocked the camera again, scanning the area. He saw nothing out of the ordinary and continued his walk, angling toward Thong Nhai Boulevard.

It was a nice day for a walk and if he timed himself carefully, he'd arrive at the market right on time.

He turned left at the corner, drawn to look at the church one last time and was struck by an insane desire to touch it and wish it well.

The next afternoon he walked down an alley and let himself through a gate in a board fence a good two feet taller than his own height. He locked it behind him. Rows of tall plants in containers between the rest of the nursery and the fence provided a concealing tunnel and he wasted no time on the sights or scents, going directly into the potting shed off to his right. Inside, he moved quickly to the door at the opposite end and checked to see if it was locked from the inside. Satisfied with the lock, he peered between two of the boards to see how many legitimate customers were on the property. There was only one and the proprietor had her under control. Using the shed made Harker nervous for that very reason. Even though the clear signal was in the window, there was the time delay in getting from the street and up the alley to the place. It was an added element of chance he accepted with ill grace.

He pulled the single chair to the door and fastened an eye to the crack.

Exactly on time, decorous in print blouse and plain skirt, Tuyet entered the grounds and began to work her way to their meeting.

She was a natural for the business, he mused, and it was not a pleasant thought. Acting of any kind seemed instinctive with her. She examined plants and smiled prettily for the proprietor, all the while insuring she wasn't followed. Her course to the back of the nursery was as erratic and innocent as bird flight. He opened the door for her and resumed his seat.

"I sorry I ask meet you." Facing him, her quietude evaporated and she twisted her fingers together. Harker wondered if it was more acting. "I have see you," she went on. "Got important talk."

"I'm waiting."

She frowned and shook her head. "Need you help. Big favor."

"You're being paid." He moved forward on the chair. "Don't try to hold me up. It's not smart."

"Not hold up! Not smartass!" She shook her head again, growing more defiant. She pointed at herself, jabbing as if to inflict a wound. "I know something much important. I want tell. I got trouble, need help. You promise help, I tell everything."

"First you talk. Then you ask whatever you want. Then we'll see if I can help you."

"Bullshit! I tell you, you give me fuck-all. I not trust you."

"What?" He came up in one move, sending the chair tumbling backwards. Tuyet flinched and held her ground.

"I not care you hit me! I all time hit. One more, ten more—same-same me." She glared and then suddenly she was wheedling. "You help me, please? I tell you important news, make you important. You get Bronze Star, no fucking problem. You promise?"

He busied himself with the chair and sat back down. "I can't promise anything. I'm just a Captain. But you tell me what you've got and I'll see if I can help you."

She turned away, unhappy with the arrangement. After a bit she shrugged and faced him.

"OK. I tell." She took a deep breath before starting, and Harker was dumbfounded to see how much she resembled a frightened child beginning a recitation.

"My boss, Trung, he have talk with other man, I not know him. Trung talk loud, loud." She threw out her chest and postured. "Say he ver' big man, how he going hurt Americans. He say he tell *bao chi*—what you call? American news people—you got the woman and child."

The small shed grew very quiet and Tuyet took an involuntary half-step away from Harker, her hand seeking the surface

425

of the potting table, unmindful of the loam that clung to her soft skin.

Virtually whispering, Harker said, "What woman and child?"

"I not know! They say woman and child. Very important, I think. Trung, he sound off much, much."

Harker looked away. The silence returned, less threatening than before, and Tuyet glanced down at her hand and brushed at the dirt irritably. When Harker got to his feet, she remained firm.

"This is worthless information," he said, and her face fell. "However, you did right to come to me. I am pleased, so tell me what it is you want. I think Trung lies to his friend. You believed him. OK. You tell me, and that is important. I hope I can help you."

"I am sorry." She hung her head. "He make such noise. I think I learn big secret. Make afraid. I think big fucking deal, you know? I make trouble, be horse' ass, I think."

"It's OK," Harker said.

"I want help with American Embassy," she said, looking at the floor. "I want marry. Hard for Vietnamese girl marry American, much argument, fight, bullshit. If somebody big speak, make everything easy, OK?"

"You want go stateside?" Harker bantered.

She made a face. "No, want stay Vietnam, but if marry man, go with him. Be good wife." Only an unbidden flash in her eye spoke the challenge, daring him to cut at her effort to grab this first rung of respectability.

"I will see what I can do. Remember, even for me, it will take a long time."

She touched his arm and pulled the hand back, an almost fearful gesture. "You will try?"

Unsmiling now, he said, "Yes. And now you go. I will contact you."

She smiled even as she inspected the nursery to be sure she could leave safely, turning at the last moment to wave. She moved casually through the plants, touching a leaf here, turning a flower to catch a ray of sunshine at another point.

No one paid any attention to her.

Walking down the street, she happened to notice the last

426

flecks of soil still clinging to a finger. She rubbed it against her thumb and watched the spot come clean and allowed her satisfaction with the meeting to flow unchecked. Her ribs strained at the pressure of the huge inhalation and she let it out carefully, wishing she could use the air to shout.

The *Dai Uy* was a strange man. Looking into his eyes was like seeing several people at once and it was confusing. Perhaps that was why he seemed untrustworthy. But he was no fool and she had seen his reaction to the information about the woman and her child. And he still didn't know Han was involved and he still didn't know someone was hiding near a place called Phu Thuan. Now the game would start in earnest.

If Harker was no help at the embassy she could always go to Han's American boss before Trung did and sell the information about the village and the man hiding there. Influence was more important than money to her now, but money was a very comforting second place.

If the *Dai Uy* didn't help, she would find someone who would.

She checked again to make sure the dirt was gone, but it was a cursory inspection because she was thinking how wonderful a thing the truth could be, especially when it was managed properly.

46

THE UNREALITY OF STEPPING THROUGH THE APARTMENT DOOR and into Ly's arms continually swung at the edges of his consciousness and this was one of the evenings when his credulity balked even as he reached for the handle. She stuck her head out of the tiny kitchen, waved, and disappeared to pop back out with a martini in hand. Taylor exploded into laughter and she looked at him quizzically.

He answered the unspoken question. "It's a crazy world. Crazy, crazy." He flung out one arm and reached for the drink with the other. "For this I get combat pay. Jesus!"

She stepped closer and he kissed her, home from the office.

He wore civilian clothes. Nothing in the room remotely suggested military life until he took the .38 from the belt holster under his shirt and put it on the coffee table.

He slouched on the sofa and pulled her down with him, kissing her more fully. When they parted, she examined him with mock seriousness.

"That's better. When you come in our house, I want you to think only of me, not your crazy world, not even your combat pay."

He kissed her again. "I've spent a couple of very strange hours this evening. Harker's spooky as a cat. Came in with steam coming out his ears. Winter's out of town and won't be back until later and Harker's screaming at the world to find him and tell him to hurry home. He won't tell anyone anything, just keeps saying it's an emergency. I think he's flipped."

"I don't want to hear about it." She tossed her head and rose, moving off toward the kitchen. "I have made *cha gio* tonight. I'm experimenting with a shrimp filling and I want your opinion. And then we're having *thit kho nuoc dua*, the pork in coconut milk, the way you like it. Unless you would rather talk about Harker."

She gave him an arch look over a shoulder and he drained his glass and followed. The *cha gio* was his favorite, paper thin rice flour dough wrapped around mushrooms, onions, beaten egg, bean threads and a meat. Normally Ly used chicken or pork. The spices were the real secret, and the precise deep frying technique. The result was always a succulent finger-length object about the size of a hot dog and sometimes Taylor thought he could eat them until he collapsed. Tonight he was rationed to a mere four, which he dipped in the clear *nuoc mam* before savoring them. The salad was greens with pieces of fruit, apparently Ly's own concoction, and then the pork, steaming on its bed of ever-present rice, redolent of coconuts and herbs.

They discussed the things Ly had seen and done at the market that day and, with the dishes cleared, moved into the living room to watch television. All went well until he declared his boredom and announced he was going to bed to read.

She looked at him sideways and sniffed. "Poor old man and his books."

He stopped in his tracks and turned. "What's that supposed to mean?"

She continued to watch the set. "Nothing. But a younger man would possibly have another reason to go to bed so early. It was only a thought."

When he made no answer she looked to see his face and found him advancing on her. She squealed and leaped from the chair, backing away, deliciously frightened as he maneuvered her into a corner.

"We agreed, no tickling!" Her voice rose as he reached for her. "Don't! I will scream, Charles!" The last word yipped as his hand closed on her side. When he eased the pressure, she fell against him, panting laughter. He folded his arms around her.

"Animal," she mumbled and he tightened his arms, forcing breath out of her in a grunt. She giggled and turned her face up, disengaging a hand to trace his smile.

"You make me happy, like a child," she said. "I love you."

"And I love you." He caressed her back, his hand finally coming to rest on her neck, blanketed by the mass of shining hair. She tilted back against the hand and he kissed her, lingering until her mouth opened and their tongues flicked at each other with silent invitations. She broke away, walking to the television to turn it off. He followed.

"Good for you," he said. "One form of entertainment at a time."

She laughed easily and leaned back against him. He moved his hands across her blouse to cup the outthrust breasts and she arched her back, sighing. After a moment she took one of his hands in hers and lifted it to nibble on his fingertips.

Thousands of words scintillated through his mind, tender, clever, passionate, solemn. He discarded them all, scooping her up in both arms and walking into the bedroom.

Later she lay in the dark and studied his body in the pale light from the window. He was asleep on his back, head lolled to the side, facing her. The angle of the light brought his cheekbones into relief under the darker slash of the shadowed eye sockets. His chest rose and fell in steady tempo, each exhalation a quiet touch on her shoulder. Moving very carefully, she trailed the tips of her fingers across her stomach, the growing child a noticeable bulge now. She moved the hands to

429

a point above her groin and drew them upwards over her body, feeling her face warm as her nipples hardened. She replaced one hand at her side and let the other settle, softly as ash, to his shoulder. She exulted at the pleasure they had known, the delicious sated listlessness that calmed one half of her mind while the other half writhed with lingering eroticism. An alien image wavered into her mind's eye and she couldn't dislodge it. Resignedly, she tried to determine what it was and it dodged. Suddenly it was clear and she had to stifle a cry as she recognized her husband.

He had been a good man. He had taught her the uses of her body which she admitted shamefully she had never appreciated as fully with him as she did with Charles.

She tossed her head to the side, looking at the mirror on the dresser that reflected the dark room in a dream's haze. Was she so wanton, then, to find greater pleasure with her second man than her first? Would she be tempted to encourage a third? A fourth? More? Could there be another man?

As though resenting the question, he exhaled loudly and drew a foot parallel to his other leg, the knee bending until the leg stood poised in an inverted vee. The hairs on the thigh glinted dully and she smiled to herself as she contemplated the disparity between his leg and her own slim one so motionless beside it.

What would it be like to live in a foreign land, waking to find that bulk next to her every day? Her mind drifted to other aspects of his body and she felt her face grow warm again even as the smile spread. Softly, she moved her hand from his shoulder and stroked the hairs on the thigh, so gently they seemed to wave under her touch as water plants bend and sway with the current. The leg grew taut with a spasmodic jerk that startled her, the calf muscle bunching furiously. At the same instant a rumbling explosion tumbled through the night from a distance and the leg trembled, relaxed, and began to unfold back onto the bed. The suddenness of the combination frightened her. She clutched at the descending knee.

He was awake, her arm vised in his hand.

"Ly? What's wrong?" He sat up, searching.

"Nothing, Charles. Something woke me. Charles, my arm."

He relaxed his grip, stroking the area. "I'm sorry. I was out cold." He lay back down, facing her. "What woke you? Are you all right?"

"Yes, everything is fine." It stuck to her tongue. "Fine," she repeated, forcing life into the word. "There was an explosion, I think. Far away."

"Go back to sleep," he said, pillowing her head on his arm. "There's nothing to worry about."

Without any idea why, she found herself rolled over against him, tears burning. Then she heard the explosion in her memory and saw the taut flesh go suddenly flaccid and the tears burst free in the wake of a racking shiver.

"What's wrong, Ly? Don't cry!" He tried to understand what was happening. She burrowed tighter against him, continuing to sob quietly. He cradled her and, confused, could only be solicitous. "It's all right, honey, we're all right. Sleep, baby, sleep."

The pulsing sobs dwindled, stopped. Tears continued to drain down across his bicep, hot as blood.

He settled on the pillow to watch for first light.

One more sunrise. Waiting for God to give me just that one more sunrise. Does He give them as a reward or is each one a new joke? What if dying's the reward and living's a sentence? That's stupid—if it was true, why'd everyone get so damned grim about the trip? I've punched enough tickets, and not a one thanked me.

Sights and sounds foamed behind his eyes and he blinked them away.

Animal. I wonder if she can guess? Stalking. Challenged. Exhilarated. Usually terrified, sometimes assured to the point of contemptuousness. Always wondering if the next one was smarter, quicker, better prepared. Luckier.

The night, cruel as the sea.

He watched out the window and waited.

The knock on the door brought him out of bed in a rolling motion, his hand wrapped around the butt of the pistol waiting on the night stand. Trotting silently into the living room, he crouched at an angle away from the door.

"Who is it?"

"Sergeant Chi, *Thieu Ta*. The Colonels—they say you come." The voice was low, thick with intensity.

Taylor swung the door open, stepping quickly to the side. Chi advanced slowly, watching the pistol with unwavering attentiveness until it sagged.

"It is important. We go villa quick."

Gesturing at a chair with the gun, Taylor hurried to dress. Ly was sitting upright, the tent of the sheet emphasizing her tousled hair, a greater blackness against the dark. The whites of her eyes broadcast fear.

"What is wrong, Charles?"

He was throwing clothes on, the sport shirt and slacks incongruous in the face of the understated urgency in Chi's voice.

"I have to report in. Something's come up."

"It is an attack?"

He kissed her forehead, holstering the gun. "We'd have heard noise by now. Go back to sleep. It's probably a hassle for a list of names. Admin junk."

She grabbed his hand and kissed it. "Be careful."

He laughed. "I'll try not to fall on my pencil. Now go back to sleep." He hated the lie, knowing it was for both of them and not what she deserved. Locking the door with careful deliberation, he trotted after Chi, waiting until they were underway before asking, "What is wrong?"

Chi chose not to look at him. "Colonel tell only come quick. No more."

"Shit! It's two in the morning!"

Chi shifted into Vietnamese. "It is an order."

"There is trouble?"

A quick, sidelong glance from the blank eyes and Chi swerved around a corner. His tongue slid out, glistening in the rush of a streetlight, and traced a path across the upper lip.

"There is trouble, *Thieu Ta*. I say no more."

Taylor growled and slumped. They flew down the deserted streets with only a rare gleam from behind a window to remind them that people still lived in the buildings. The drumming howl of the tires echoed back from imperturbable walls. The pitch rose eerily on the straightaways, crooned down scale at the corners, only to break into a scream slewing around each one. Taylor tried to ignore the sound to review what could cause so much excitement. There were so many possibilities— a tip on a VC operation in the city, a defector wanting to talk, another prisoner to be interrogated.

He inspected Chi and dropped the notion of learning anything from that frowning concentration. They swept to a groaning halt at the compound gate, Chi barking at the guards to hurry.

The tension was infectious. At the Villa, Taylor leaped up the steps and ran to Winter's office. The door was open, light cascading in a bright stain across the hall and up the opposite wall. Taylor went in without knocking.

Winter sat at his desk, Loc in a chair to his right. Harker and Tho shared the sofa. Interrupted argument hung in the air, distorting already sleep-riddled features.

"Sergeant Chi made good time." The approval in Winter's voice labored under self-conscious banality.

"What's coming down?" Taylor asked.

Winter indicated a chair. "I was in a session with a general officer, and when I got to my quarters, Harker was waiting for me. He had a meet with Tuyet today. She overheard Trung telling a third party we have, I quote, the woman and her child, and he's going to the media with the information."

Taylor moved in between Harker and Tho. "He's killing her. How'd he find out?"

"From the one that got away—Han, Barline's driver—in all probability. Who knows?" He shrugged as if the gesture cost him days from his life.

Taylor rose again and moved to look at the papers on Winter's desk. "You're not thinking what I think you're thinking? You want to make sure we don't get blown and Binh's wife doesn't get burned?"

Winter looked away.

Taylor grimaced and moved to the other side of the desk, his hands and eyes moving across the clutter of data. "Nice," he said. "Neighborhood sketch map for getting in and out? Floor plan?" He feigned surprise. "What, no time schedule?"

Loc said, "It must be done quickly, while it is still dark. People will be getting up to work very soon. If we cannot do it in an hour or less the risk becomes too great."

A deep breath turned to a resigned sigh in Taylor's chest. It escaped in a gust and he bent to study the plans more closely. Loc stepped behind him, the prim presence hovering. Tho joined him on the other side, busily sucking a tooth.

After a few minutes, Taylor straightened. Winter looked expectant.

"Let's say I walk from this corner, here, to the side street." Taylor traced the route on the map. "I go in, come out, and continue up the side street and I'm met on the other main street. I'll wear utilities. If I get real lucky, anyone who sees me'll think I'm an ARVN on his way to the base. I want to be picked up by someone on a Honda. No one looks twice at two uniforms on a Honda and we have the darkness going for us."

"Corporal Minh," Loc said and gestured at Tho. "Get him. Tell him he will take *Thieu Ta* Taylor and return with him on his machine. Hurry!"

Tho left at a near run.

Marking the floor plan with a pen, Taylor went on. "The door—a bolt or chain? Is it just a lock?"

Loc shuffled through the papers, pointed at one. "Only a door lock."

"Well, Christ on a crutch." The harshness ripped through the room. "We may get away with this thing after all. At least we don't have to blast our way in or plant a plastic charge on the bedroom wall."

Winter winced but remained silent.

Taylor said, "What about the lock?"

Loc continued to read. "It's American. Yale."

He handed the paper to Taylor who studied it after a sarcastic comment about American locks to protect honest VC from burglars. Replacing the information on the desk with the rest, he asked, "Who collected this information?"

Loc said, "Duc. We thought it might be important one day."

There was a hint of something in Loc's face as he spoke and Taylor froze it in his mind to examine it, knowing it was futile, as it always was. There was no doubt Loc was thinking of several things, but what they might be, no man would guess.

To Winter, Taylor said, "I want a K-54 and a full clip. They're both in an ammo can above the desk in the shop."

Winter tossed keys to Harker. "The one with the blue plastic square on it."

Harker was running as he caught them.

"You intend to leave the pistol?" Winter asked.

"No, sir. Charlie wouldn't do that. The brass will identify the piece and that's all we need. As long as I don't have to use it to get out of that fucking alley, everyone'll connect it with the VC."

"To get out of the alley?" Loc repeated.

Taylor faced him. "No one's going to identify me. No one's going to arrest me."

"Quite so." Loc nodded thoughtfully.

"If that's it, then, I'll go get my utilities on," Taylor said.

Winter stood up. "I'll go with you. Loc, will you think this through again with Tho when he returns, please? See if there's another way or any flaws we can eliminate?"

Taylor smiled wryly on his way out.

Any flaws we can eliminate. That was well told. He thought he'd never seen anything so ragged, so crude. It wasn't so much a plan as a throw of the dice.

A wallet-sized kit in his locker held his lock tools. He examined them carefully, then pulled a clean uniform off the hanger, thankful the Corps didn't require the sewed-on rank insignia the Army used. Darkness would cover the Marine emblem stenciled on his left breast pocket. At least, he amended, he hoped it would, for the sake of anyone who might see it.

The cover. He debated borrowing one from the Army people. "Fuck it," he said aloud, sitting down to pull off his shoes.

Winter broke his own silence. "Meaning what?"

"Meaning this is some dumb shit, coach."

Winter looked unhappy. "We'll give you backup. Any breakdown, if there's any trouble—."

"Hold it, hold it!" Taylor waved clumsily while he continued to undress. "Don't stroke me. If it blows up, I'm in the shit and we both know it. If Trung talks, we've all had it, and the woman's a goner. If I get caught, all I can do is hope I can ditch my tools and claim Trung and I were arguing about the money I lost to him. There was a struggle for the gun. You've probably heard a story like it before. Just don't give me any crap about helping me in any court-martial. It won't make me a bit happier because you couldn't make one fucking word stick."

435

"You're really one cold-blooded bastard," Winter said. He bridled in the chair, huffing like a rodeo bull waiting for the chute to open.

Taylor pulled on a boot. "Sure. You're stroking me again. I'm scared out of my mind. You know goddam well how scared I am." He finished blousing the trousers and rolled his shoulders to settle the shoulder holster in place under the jacket.

A motorcycle snarled to a stop in the parking area and they hurried to Winter's office.

Loc greeted their return, sparing Tho and Minh the slightest nod of acknowledgement as they entered behind them. "A question has come up. What if Trung has a woman with him?"

Winter blanched. Taylor saw it out of the corner of his eye and said, "Hope it's someone you don't know or don't like, Colonel."

Loc said, "If you think it will be necessary, of course."

Harker trotted in and handed the automatic to Taylor, who carefully disassembled the piece and checked each part as he put it back together. Then he inserted the magazine and jacked it clean of rounds. Satisfied, he took the ejected bullets back from Harker and reloaded them, examining each one. Then he worked a round into the chamber and lowered the hammer.

For a moment he was alone and the expressions around him reflected their knowledge of his withdrawal. He held the weapon loosely, studying it, the rugged configuration very similar to the .45 and no prettier. Even the raised black star on the black handgrip was dull. The word funereal came to his mind. He slipped the gun into the shoulder holster as he turned.

"You know what you are to do?" he asked Minh.

Minh's eyes never left Taylor's armpit as he nodded understanding.

Taylor started for the door, hoping his movements didn't look as uncoordinated as they felt.

"Tay!" Winter called. He turned and they each took a hesitant step toward him and stopped. Winter said, "Good luck. And bail out if you think it's best."

The rest nodded, including Tho, who was clearly responding to a cue.

Taylor said, "Don't make me think about it or I'll stay right here." He tried a smile that felt like a thing painted on, and left.

Minh cruised easily through the still-quiet streets. Taylor checked his watch. It was almost 0400. In a little while the cement would be hidden under masses of traffic. Already there were lights in windows that would have been dark only an hour ago. He wanted to clutch at the night, hold it around him until he was done with it, then break clear into sunshine.

The coasting stop terminated introspection. He stepped off the machine and moved directly against the shadowed wall where he remained stationary, looking and listening long after Minh had disappeared around the corner. When he felt it was time, he headed toward the deeper black that was the alley-like side street where Trung's apartment was located. He moved as quickly as possible to the correct door and squatted by the keyhole and suddenly the smell of rancid cooking oil and a barrage of distant wet coughing descended on his senses simultaneously, making his stomach buck. The moment passed. He ran his fingers over the lock face and selected tools from the small leather case. Gently, waiting for resistance before applying gradual pressure, he raked the lock, untroubled by the whispered scrape of metal on metal.

The bolt slid back with a slightly louder rustle and the knob turned silently. The door swung open a few inches and he paused to listen. The throaty sound of deep breathing just short of snoring came from off to his left, where the bedroom was supposed to be.

Duc had died in an apartment with a separate bedroom. It was strange a bar girl could afford that luxury. It had never occurred to him before and he blinked the thought away now.

He pushed the door open far enough to slide through and closed it behind him. The apartment felt even darker than the alley and he strained to pierce the darkness without raising from his deep couch. He concentrated on his breathing, consciously regulating it to steadiness. The sounds from the left continued uninterrupted and he crept in that direction, sweeping the air and floor in front of him with his left hand while he drew the automatic and held it against his chest with his right. A shoulder brushed something and he froze. Gingerly, he tested the object with the sweep hand. It was an easy chair.

The seat cushion lifted off easily.

The breathing was closer now, coming through a doorway that formed a break in the paleness of the facing wall. He covered the last feet to it in quick strides.

A figure lay on the bed, feet pointed vertically and one out-thrust arm above the sheet, fingers curled inward as though holding something. The click of the hammer thumbed back failed to disturb the sleeper.

One pace at a time, setting each foot solidly, Taylor moved to a position directly opposite Trung's head. In repose, his mouth slack and features loose, he seemed to have shed any distinguishing characteristics. He was a man, nothing more or less. In assertion of that fact, he turned his head and exhaled heavily.

Taylor raised the cushion until it was centered in front of the gun muzzle. An uninvited recollection played with the madness at the core of his mind, reminding him of a man who'd been careless with a similar cushion and shot off two of his own fingers. He coordinated the cushion and the pistol intently.

The shots came very close together, two thunderous heart-beats. The second one caught the head bouncing from the impact of the first, driving it back into the pillow. Concussion boomed in Taylor's gut, kneading it into a quivering knot, the way parade bass drums electrify children.

The face on the bed was marred by a black dot just above the line of the eyebrows. A dark trail ran from the right eye to the sheet and formed an irregular blotch.

Taylor hurried out, dropping the cushion and trying to make the gun arm swing naturally. He eased the door open and stepped out into a blessed silence, walking toward the end of the alley, urging his body to move properly.

A voice behind him shouted, "What was that noise?" and another said, "I do not know! Was it a gun? Maybe the soldier knows. Soldier!"

Taylor told himself he must not run.

"Soldier! Did you hear the noise? Who are you?"

A child wailed indignation. Taylor thought he heard a door open somewhere behind him.

It was only a few feet to the sidewalk.

A determined male voice cried, "Wait! You! Come back!"

Taylor was at the corner, turning it, then sprinting for the waiting motorcycle.

Minh roared off as soon as he felt Taylor's body hit his own. The engine drowned any continuing outcry from behind.

They maneuvered through the streets at undistinguished speed, always headed in the general direction of the villa. Finally, Taylor said, "Go up the back alley behind BOQ Two. I'll drop off there and walk it. No one will notice me and you will return through the gate alone."

Minh nodded silently and continued to move on side streets and alleys until they reached their goal. By then there were a few pedestrians and vehicles moving. Taylor slipped off the machine and Minh continued on. A few blocks away he could turn and approach the villa from a different route entirely. No one would connect his arrival with anything of importance.

Taylor wandered into the parking lot, where he clumsily attached the gold leaves to his collar, then lit a cigarette and walked briskly toward the villa.

The gate guards acknowledged him with half-hearted salutes. He kept walking, noticing the time as he climbed the stairs. It was 0432. An eternity gone, another taking its place. The new eternity was thirty-two minutes old, give or take a few minutes. His feet scuffed on the steps, worn-out sounds in the tense dawn. A tick on a clock, a fossil in stone, a mask on a pillowcase—techniques for measuring time.

He counted the steps to the second floor. Duc used to insist it was the first floor.

Winter hurried from behind his desk. "Minh says you were seen but there was no trouble." He steered Taylor to the sofa. "You'll want a drink."

"No, not right now. How about some coffee, please?"

There was a sharp noise that made him jump and he looked, muscles tugging at each other, to see Loc had clapped his hands. Minh leaped into the room.

"Yes, *Dai Ta?*" He forced his eyes to stay away from Taylor.

"Coffee for *Dai Ta* Winter and *Thieu Ta* Taylor," Loc said. "I will have tea. Bring cups for *Trung Ta* Tho, *Dai Uy* Harker, and yourself."

"Me?"

"Only if you choose. You will be here while we review what has happened. Quickly."

Minh practically staggered from the room. Taylor started to light a cigarette, realized he'd just thrown one away outside the room, then lit another one anyhow. They could hear Minh rattling cups and finally padding back down the hall. At Loc's gesture he served Taylor before placing the tray on Winter's desk.

Taylor gulped at his. It burned and it was bitter enough to set his teeth on edge. He decided it might be the best he'd ever tasted and gave his report.

"I don't think I was seen going in. He was asleep and never woke. I fired twice, through a cushion to muffle the noise. The first round hit him between the eyes, the second went into the right eye. I'm sure he's dead." He swallowed another mouthful of coffee and took a huge drag on the cigarette. "The people who noticed the noise called out behind me. I don't see how they could identify me, even distinguish that I'm American. They hollered 'Soldier!' at me in Vietnamese. No one spoke any English. We weren't followed. Minh dropped me off over behind BOQ Two. We came here separately. No one saw enough to make any trouble. Minh did everything exactly as he should have. It's all over."

Loc stood up. "We thank you, Major Taylor. I think even Binh would thank you."

"No thanks involved, Colonel. It needed to be done."

"It did," Loc agreed. "It was you who took the risk. If you had been caught—."

Taylor drained his cup. "Don't remind me. Some day I'll write a book. 'Medals and Courts-Martial I Never Got, And Why I Should or Shouldn't Have.'"

"You'll get a medal for this one," Winter said.

"Hey." Taylor grimaced and replaced his cup on the tray.

"I mean it," Winter insisted. "I'm going to think up something. I know you don't give a shit, but it'll mean something to somebody else one day. And you deserve it."

"Sure. Make it a Legion of Merit. It's pretty and it's got a sort of Buddhist sound to it." He stretched. "I'm washed out, Colonel. I'd like to get me that drink now and fall in the bag."

Winter reached into his desk and drew out a bottle. "I'll

440

buy." He gestured at Corporal Minh and Taylor stopped him.

"I don't need a glass. I don't want to know how much I get." He took the bottle, managing three gurgling slugs before he felt the fiery mass try to bounce. He recapped the bottle and put it back on the desk with a thump.

"Thank you, sir."

They watched him go.

"I think he will sleep," Loc said.

"God, I hope so." Winter poured whiskey in his coffee and sipped at the mixture. "He probably will. If he ever breaks, Loc, he'll fly apart like a grenade."

"I agree. Do you anticipate that?"

"No-o." Winter's hand explored the stubble on his chin as the word extended. "I think he'll hold together long enough. You called him a hunter once. I think there's more to it, as if he thinks he's sifting through a sewer, not even sure there's anything there to find."

"You are disturbed. You become, what is your word? Morbid."

Winter smiled grimly. "That happened ten years ago, my friend. Right now I'm morbid and sleepy. I'll be back in a few hours. See you then."

"I'll leave with you. My car is outside."

They moved down the hall in step. Corporal Minh watched them leave and dragged himself in to police up the cups and tray.

Taylor heard them leave. His blood absorbed warmth from the whiskey pooled in his stomach, distributing it along nerve paths. Muscles relaxed, joints eased. The only thing immune was his brain.

He looked out the window to see the morning was going to be overcast. Rounded clouds in ponderous mass drifted like clusters of grapes, hugely magnified so the eye could discern each subtle variation, each minute individualizing characteristic. The rising sun enameled the undersides with copper and brass.

One more daybreak.

He slept.

47

STEAM TENDRILS SQUIRMED on the undisturbed surface of Loc's morning *pho*. He watched the intermingling columns, trying to follow one through its disappearances and re-emergences.

It was impossible. There was no logic to the movement and everything eventually mingled inextricably.

He wondered if a Buddhist monk in a corner of a temple might be watching the same phenomenon and telling himself that the behavior of the steam wraiths only illustrated the tenet that all things are born to die and be reborn in a different state. Was not man's life a random wisp? Unconsciously, Loc frowned his denial. A man was more than a natural response to physical laws. On the other hand, was not the total man the result of forces that reacted on his body and mind and built a unique product of him, just as the heat, cold, and moisture created the steam from the broth? The frown darkened further, only to disappear as he determined that the key word was unique. The steam fragments were alike, atom to atom, but each man was completely different. So. The analogy was apt, but badly flawed. The monk would have to meditate better than that.

Tasting the soup, he drew back with a start, unready for the fact that it had gone cool.

His mental maundering had cost him the largest part of his breakfast. Irritably, he pushed the bowl aside, following that with a shove for the croissant plate and a more reluctant push of the coffee cup and saucer.

He snapped his fingers and his orderly retrieved the tray. Loc watched him carefully for any reaction to the untouched food and was delighted when the young man showed no sign whatsoever. Loc made a mental note to look into his background further. Perhaps he could be trained for other responsibilities.

With the orderly gone, Loc scrutinized his clothes, realizing it was mere habit, as he'd had no opportunity to spill anything.

Still, like a bird preparing for flight, he preened and rearranged until he was satisfied before snapping his fingers again. The orderly reappeared with the tea caddy and at Loc's nod, spoke over his shoulder. Tho entered and accepted the offer of tea before sitting on one of the chairs. He looked unsure of himself.

"Have you found Han?" Loc made the question unpleasantly blunt.

Tho blinked rapidly. "No, *Dai Ta*. My source at Special Branch says he was seen the day before yesterday in the vicinity of the Friendly Bar. The man who reported said he had only a glimpse of him. But it supports your thought that Trung might have been talking to him about Binh and his family."

Loc pillared his arms on the desk, lowering his head until it rested on fingertips at his temples. He spoke almost to himself. "The more I think about it, the more I am convinced. I am equally convinced the woman Tuyet could tell us more. You will find out if she can."

Tho's agitation had him twisting his fingers in his lap. "What you suggest, *Dai Ta—*." He swallowed. "*Dai Ta* Winter—the other American, Barline—it is very complicated," he finished miserably.

"I wonder." Loc continued to muse. "Get me *Dai Uy* Harker."

Tho seized the opportunity to escape the discussion and departed in such a hurry he was still carrying his glass of tea as he cleared the door. He was empty handed when he returned with Harker and Loc wondered idly when his glass would turn up again. He gestured for them to be seated and spoke to Harker.

"Captain, I must speak to you in confidence. Do I have your word that you will never repeat what I say?"

"Yes, sir. Certainly."

Loc's brow creased. "Think a moment, Captain. Do not be so agreeable. Be sure of yourself before you answer."

Harker shrugged. "I'm sure of you, Colonel. I trust you."

"That could be foolish." Loc looked away from the suddenly wide eyes. "I am Vietnamese. We—you and I—are united against the communists, but there are many things more important to me than American interests."

"I understand that, but until I hear it from you, I won't believe you'd do anything to damage us, so tell me what you

443

want me to hear, sir.''

Loc bit back a sigh. He didn't even have to look at the face of this one. The voice alone screamed sincerity.

Facing him again, Loc asked, "Do you think I respect Colonel Winter?"

"Yes, sir." Harker's sudden wariness showed the conversation had already taken an unpleasant course.

"Then I must tell you I think he is frightened."

Harker froze, and Loc hurried on. "You saw how quickly and forcefully he acted when Trung became a threat?"

Harker nodded, careful now.

Loc said, "Have you ever seen him fail to act in such a way?"

The questions were becoming more to Harker's taste. "Never," he said.

"But we have." Loc again turned away. "The drug-dealing Major was allowed to run home without punishment. We all know the plan to destroy him is questionable. That is all understandable. Still—." He paused, then swung to fix Harker with eyes that stung like whips. "How many men has this Unit eliminated because we knew them to be enemies, *Dai Uy*?"

Before Harker could recover enough to answer, Loc drilled ahead. "Only one other man has ever escaped us when he had so much evidence condemning him."

"One other?"

Loc continued as if unhearing. "I think my friend is already thinking of his new unit, one that will not have the problems we have had."

Harker's lips thinned and he shook his head. "If he didn't move on someone, he had a reason."

"I believe that." Loc's glance was odd, almost hurt. "I am not sure of the reason, however. I think how quickly he moved against Trung and how he failed to move against the others, and I confess I am troubled."

"What others? You only named the Major."

"Only one other," Loc hastened. "And there was only coincidence in his case, so perhaps I am seeing things that are not really there."

"I'm not following you at all, Colonel. Who didn't we go after?"

"It makes no difference," Loc said, then relented in the face of Harker's confusion. "I have trusted you this far. I will say what is on my mind and hope you understand. It starts with Duong Han. I am certain he is the man who told Trung of the family of Nguyen Binh. I believe your source lied. I believe Trung and Han planned together to speak to Barline. If I am correct, there is greater danger than ever, now that Trung is dead. Han will be more afraid."

"But why hasn't Han already told Barline we have Binh's family?"

Loc's shoulders rose and fell in a minute shrug. "Perhaps he is one of the faction who wished to see Binh survive. Perhaps he is a relative. But, again, Han lives in the shadow of one we cannot touch, apparently."

There was a pause before the last word, a vocal hitch that padded it with implication. Harker responded immediately.

"If Colonel Winter thought Barline was actually involved in helping the VC, really protecting them, or something—."

For a long moment Loc studied Harker as if seeing him on display. Then he dryly told of Barline's trip to IV Corps and the talk with the Colonel who kept Dao. When he was finished, Harker's face was flaming.

"If the Colonel knows about that and hasn't moved, then he has reasons," Harker said, defiance replacing conviction in his words.

"That is what I fear most," Loc replied. "I, too, know that my friend will not tolerate a VC. But Barline and the Major are Americans, Captain. and the implications of that fact frighten me."

He stared at Harker again and for a few heartbeats the younger man matched his intensity, only to waver and break the contact to stare at the top of the desk.

Loc dropped his voice. "I tell you this fear so you may help me, Captain. It is only natural that my friend would hesitate to eliminate a countryman. Your civil war is long past and ours is of long standing. If I am right, I only wish to see him protected. I will not criticize and I will allow no one else to, either. But if I am wrong, I must know, in order that I do not misjudge him. It is possible he does not even understand himself that he has shown a—peculiar—hesitation to deal with these men."

Harker visibly winced and as soon as Loc was quiet, rose swiftly. "You have my word, *Dai Ta*, nothing that was said will be repeated. I will help you any way I can." His stiff formality could have been a rebuke.

Loc said, "I thank you. We are lucky you are with us."

Mumbling through goodbyes, Harker left in a haze of conflicting emotions. By the time he reached his office, he knew what he would do. He dialed a number and rapped the desk with a white-knuckled fist while waiting for an answer.

"Hello," he said. "Captain Chavez, please." Then "Chavez? Harker. Not so good, buddy. I need help. Yeah, big trouble. I don't want to talk about it on the phone. Did I see about what? Trung? Yeah, I know him—what about him? No kidding! Who did it? Nine millimeter? That's bad guy ammo. His own buddies must have put it to him, finally. Well, we won't miss the sonofabitch. Who? Earl's blaming *us?* That sucker's crazy, you know? Listen, screw Earl. I got other things to talk about. Can you meet me at the pool at noon? Hey, good. See you."

He hung up and stared at the instrument as if he would smash it, thinking of questions he would put to Tuyet at their next meeting. And how he would put them to her.

He was already stretched out on the pool's edge, drying in the sun when Chavez arrived. He was a swarthy man in bright blue swimming trunks, barrelchested. His arms hung out from his sides, adding to the over-all musclebound look of the short body. The face was pure Indian.

"Be with you in a minute," he said. "I'm going to get in a couple of laps."

Harker waved, unspeaking, unwilling to make an issue of the delay. He watched the heavy body bound into the air and splash mightily. What Chavez lacked in diving skill, he made up for with a surprisingly accomplished stroke that sent him slicing through the water, avoiding other swimmers in the crowded pool with ease.

Harker set himself to be patient and found the shouts and laughter of the crowd strangely relaxing, suggestive of better times and places. The reek of the chlorinated water overwhelmed any alien smells. With his eyes closed, it was just like home. A perverse whim made him open them and the illusion exploded at the intrusion of the white barracks and the view beyond the distant fence. In addition, it was an odd sensation to be sitting level with the water and a good ten feet above the street.

The pool was a huge cement box, above ground. Rumor said they couldn't dig a pool because the engineers hit water and this monstrosity was the only solution. He smiled to himself, remembering how precious the great, ugly thing had seemed to him his last trip up-country. Going off watch, just before sleeping, he'd think of sitting, just like this, on the hot cement and then diving into the cool water to float, face down, as long as he could hold his breath.

Chavez flopped wetly next to him. "Oh, that feels good. Someday I want one just like it. Full of beer."

"And I'll come live at your house," Harker said, but dropped the sociable facade immediately. "Listen, I'm going to pull off something very hot, so don't ask questions that'll screw things up, you dig?"

Chavez rolled his eyes. "Oh-oh. More shit. I have to tell you, buddy, that prick Earl is all over my office now. He chewed one of my people the other day for saying 'Ruff-Puffs.' He says we have to call them Rural Forces and Popular Forces because Ruff-Puffs makes them sound 'like something connected with the U.S. effort.'"

"He's not my problem. What I have to know is who's got an operation going in the next few days, and the sooner the better. Something where they're going to step in shit and they know it."

Chavez squinted. "You really are up to something." He continued to watch Harker as he thought, then looked at his stomach and pushed water drops with a stubby finger.

"Maybe I can help. Over by the border, there's this Viet —a real tiger, part of the Phoenix program. He's got the word on an NVA supply pick-up. Stuff's coming in from Cambodia on barges. He's kept it a secret. Only told me because he knows he's going to need help if his information's accurate."

"Why secret?"

Chavez grunted. "He figures if we hear about it at MACV, they hear about it in Cambodia at about the same time. He may be right."

"Bullshit."

"Maybe. You want in?"

"When's it go down?"

"Night after next."

"Shit! That's no time at all, man!"

Grinning, Chavez flicked more water away. "You said the sooner the better. You said a bad operation. You get what you ask for and then you bitch. Can you lay on your own chopper?"

Harker shook his head. "I want you to come to my boss. Tell him the supplies may be from dumps contaminated in Operation Earthmover. He was in on the planning for that and he'll be curious about any results, so he'll be glad to have me check it out."

"What's Earthmover?"

"It's a Special Operations Group deal we got mixed up with. Just remember the name, Earthmover."

"Got it. I can get over there this afternoon. When do you want to go?"

"Tomorrow morning?"

Chavez gave him a thumbs-up. "Anything else?"

Harker looked him full in the eyes. "We never talked about this. You thought of it this afternoon. You can't remember who mentioned Earthmover to you, but you heard he had some connection with it so you thought of me as an observer. Winter's not to know it's going to be rough and you never told me. Whatever happens, me being near this thing is all a coincidence. Understood?

Chavez whistled. "Very heavy. Ve-r-r-y heavy, old buddy. I'm really curious to see what you're building. But I can dig it." He winked and got to his feet with surprising fluid movement and walked to the pool for another of his wave-making dives. Harker waited until he was at the far end and then walked to the shower room.

He spent the afternoon closeted in his office, hearing the reverberations of other people's conversations roll through the building. Even conversations upstairs were audible, if indistinguishable.

He saw Chavez arrive in a Scout, heard the thumping steps go up and the drone of conversation, then listened to the steps leave and watched the Scout depart. He was waiting for Winter's call but acted properly surprised during their talk. He returned to his office and watched the clock, lurching to his feet when the afternoon was gone and he could carry out his next move.

A cyclo at the gate carried him to within easy walking distance of the nursery. He strolled past the front, pleased to see the three ferns lined up in their vases, indicating all was well. A few minutes later he was in the potting shed again. When Tuyet came into view her movements were less assured, suggesting unusual caution, and the thought brought a tight smile to his face. Her entrance was fearful.

He reached past to help her until the door shut away the world and then his hand snapped to her throat. A thumb and forefinger vised inward directly below her jaw hinge and he lifted until her toes were barely on the ground. His smile still beamed.

"You lied to me," he said.

There was a roaring in her ears, but his words came through clearly. She fought to keep her head despite the noise and the fear and the unremitting pain. She blinked and tears ran down her cheeks. His expression didn't change but he relaxed his grip enough to allow her heels to settle back onto the ground. Hope leaped in her that he was weakening and then she looked into the eyes, unfeeling as a snake's, and in that instant she no longer cared.

Harker felt the sudden loss of resistance as a physical thing, as though energy had transferred itself from her body to his. An eerie ascendancy filled him and he knew he had only to ask and she would respond. The feeling was so awesome that, dropping his hand from her throat, he simply stood and savored while she rubbed at the welts.

It was an effort for him to get to his questions.

"Why didn't you tell me you knew the man with Trung?"

She stared at his shoes. "I think maybe use later."

"Why? I told you I'd try to help you."

"What I hear Americans call insurance. You have. I think good idea I have."

"Well, it was a very bad idea. Now I want to know exactly what they said to each other. And if you leave anything out this time your boyfriend'll be gone before you know it. And he won't be back."

For a moment the hard whore's lines melted to the softer

449

features of the woman who lived behind them. Her eyes came up to his face and drifted away, examined the unpainted boards of the wall as if hoping the calligraphy of the weather-checked wood had a message for her. She spoke in Vietnamese, slowly, repeating phrases she considered important, offering no objection when he demanded greater detail or criticized her recital. When she was finished he asked questions, forcing her to practically re-tell the entire incident. Still her voice remained soft and when it became necessary for her eyes to cross his body to study a different section of the wall, they skimmed across the obstacle with no evidence of acknowledgement.

The exhilaration Harker felt tailed off.

Reverting to English, Tuyet said, "I know I do wrong thing, but I tell you all now. Please, you help me get married permission?"

"You lied to me. Why should I help you?"

Her nod summed up a lifetime of losing. "I think you say that. I go now?"

He gestured and she moved to the door. He hissed a warning and she faced him with a touch of her old flair. "I be careful, not worry. Life maybe shit, but I not ready die yet."

The close of the door behind her cut at him like a knife.

It hurt to lose the moment, the control.

Never before had he felt so completely in command. He knew where to find Binh. He had the man responsible for crippling Allen in the palm of his hand. For several minutes he sat in the half-light with his back to the wall, draining the last pleasure from his success as a man squeezes the last best drops of juice from fruit.

He shivered involuntarily as his consciousness dragged him back to necessities. There was a phone call to arrange.

Outside, the nursery massaged his senses, the faint rustle of the heated breeze in the plants, the scent of rich earth and growth. The air around him felt luminous, alive.

48

BLADES HACKING THROUGH THE MID-MORNING HAZE, the helicopter cleared the red roofs and the dirty white buildings of the city and found the countryside of clear colors basking in unfouled sunlight. Harker felt cleansed as he feasted his eyes on the bitter chocolate of the paddies and the vibrant green of the rice.

He remembered his meeting with Tuyet and realized his thoughts were in terms of highs and rushes and addiction and directed his attention outward again.

They were closing on something white that moved on the surface of the paddy like a strayed cloud. He recognized it as a huge flock of ducks, small boys marching along the dike beside them as their charges dabbled and bobbed. The boys carried long poles and one of them smartly stroked a straggler back into the flock as the other two looked up and waved their sticks, teeth glinting in the sun. The pilot wobbled from side to side in reply.

Small villages rose before them or off to the sides and passed behind. A farmer looked up from behind his water buffalo and his head turned in a steady arc, watching them with complete attention until they were long past.

Harker wondered what could have been going through that mind. Was the farmer seeing again a gunship that shattered his family? Or a force that could relieve him of the burden of supporting a local NVA unit masquerading as rebels? Or was the man simply bored and watching because it was the one thing that would differentiate today from tomorrow?

The pilot interrupted, pointing ahead and down. Rising as far as the seat belt permitted, Harker saw a village off to the left, a mud wall around it highlighted by watchtowers. The pilot and co-pilot searched the area carefully on their approach, maneuvering with professional precision. On the rough landing pad they waited until Harker was barely clear before lifting off again, roaring away tail high, the nose seeming to sniff at the ground while building speed. The pilot held it low for a hundred yards or so and then shot upward, the sound of the machine dwindling as it chuffed off to its next destination.

When Harker turned, a deputation was coming through the gate to greet him, led by a short, slight man in peasant's black pajamas whose confident stride threw his hips into an exaggerated sway. A .45, huge against his small frame, slapped his thigh at every step. The two men trailing him carried M-16s. They, too, wore the traditional black pajamas. Taller than the other man, they moved with more deliberation. Harker knew he was looking at a transplanted city man with two sturdy farm boys as his escort.

The leader introduced himself. "My name Cao." He strained for something else to say in English and Harker answered easily in Vietnamese. "I am *Dai Uy* Harker, a friend of *Dai Uy* Chavez." Pretending not to see the small man's surprise, he went on, "It is important that I speak to you privately. *Dai Uy* Chavez told me of an important matter in your area of responsibility. I think we can help each other."

Cao looked sour and when he answered his voice was pitched low enough to prevent his men hearing his comments. "I am Saigonese, *Dai Uy*, and I have worked with Americans enough to know you treasure directness. Very well. If Chavez has told you what we plan, then you have told someone. By tonight we will either be marching into an ambush or wasting our time."

Harker shook his head. "I hope not, because I will be with you. I do not think I would want these men to think I arranged an ambush for them. If the enemy did not kill me, I am sure they would." He looked past Cao to the two escorts and was shocked to see how young the shorter one was. He was less shocked but less reassured to see his measuring stare.

Cao said, "We have never had an American on one of our operations."

"You have never conducted an operation that was world famous."

"I do not understand."

"That is why we must speak in private."

Cao shrugged and gestured at the gate. "Come inside. Even if we cannot help each other, the people will be heartened to see that one of you is willing to visit us."

Staying an exact half-step in front, Cao led the way. They

passed through a gate breaching the first obstacle in the village's defenses, a double-apron barbed wire fence. Harker noted the precision of the posts and the sharpened punji sticks sown inside the hollow pyramid created by the strung wire. Tin cans dangled from the strands. A few feet behind the geometry of the double apron, coils of concertina wandered in seeming haphazard placement. Looking past them to the wall he saw most of the longer lines were enfiladed from portholes. The last obstacle prior to the wall itself was a moat. They crossed it on a drawbridge and Harker was certain the mud bottom featured more of the bamboo punjis that studded the red earth of the embankment. On entering, he jerked his thumb over his shoulder and said to Cao, "I am very impressed by your defenses, but I saw no mines or claymores. Would you like me to tell Chavez you need more?"

For the first time, Cao smiled. It made him look much younger and, amazingly, much more dangerous.

"We have plenty, thank you. We put them out at night. Always in the dark, always in a different place."

Harker was further impressed.

The children, as always, were the first to shout welcome. Harker answered questions as quickly as he could, enjoying their incredible zest. There was something about the children that always filled him with an anomalous joy and simultaneous melancholy. Their untarnished laughter invariably reminded him of the *sakura*, the Japanese cherry blossoms, treasured for fragile beauty and the fact that their wondrousness could be terminated with terrible swiftness too many ways.

Shy adults edged closer, spoke their greetings and laughed with naive pleasure to hear the tall, blond man answer in their own tongue.

Dignity cloaking every move, Cao led the way into his house-cum-command post. "I live exactly as the people live," he said proudly, indicating his two rooms with a glance. "This is my kitchen and our planning room. I sleep in the other room. We are a poor village, but free. And safe here. Our defenses are good and everything is salvaged, except weapons, ammunition, and our communications."

Harker noted the radio, Cao's link with the government, incongruously technical on a slapdash wooden desk against a mud wall. Even more incongruous was the incredible firepower it commanded. Wryly, Harker thought how the hitch was that the enemy had long since learned to avoid villages like this one and the government couldn't fortify all villages. Even without the government's enemies screaming about coercion, the old strategic hamlet concept was an unbearable strain because the people needed to farm to live and to farm they needed to live near their land and as long as they were on the land and unprotected, the terror came with enough frequency to separate them from the government. Now the country lived in fear while suffering constantly alternating liberations.

Harker dismissed all that and pressed his reason for coming to Cao's village.

"Chavez told me you expect an NVA unit to meet supply barges and unload them tonight and you plan to hit them at first light. Why not report what you know and have a regular unit make the attack while they are busy with the transfer?"

Cao motioned to a chair and settled himself on his cot. "For two reasons. First, as Chavez probably told you, I do not trust Saigon. I told you it is my home? Already I am afraid the operation is useless. But the other reason is the more compelling. The people in this area bring me information. They trust me. The enemy will use local people to move those supplies. If there is an attack before the supplies are safely stored, those people will die along with a few troops. But by waiting until the people are released, I will attack only the enemy. When the main unit hears the fight, they will come running to protect their people and their supplies. *Then* I will call for help."

Harker grinned and leaned forward in his chair. "I think I have found the man I need."

The thirty-man patrol was indistinguishable behind Cao, their black clothes blending into the greater blackness of the night and the shadows of the houses. The slight man glanced Harker's way before signalling his people forward. A shuffling sigh announced the departure of the first element.

Whispering, Cao said, "You see, we go out over the wall, not through the gate. The first men carry mats to cover the wire. The rattling cans are already cleared. The mine party took them down."

"And the mines?"

Cao's teeth flashed in the dark. "Well marked. I hope."

Harker shifted the suddenly heavy M-16 slung on his shoulder. In a few minutes Cao tapped his arm and they were moving up and over the embankment.

It was good to be moving, Harker thought, and his senses expanded in anticipation. The pieces of white cloth on the marked punjis and mines were like light bulbs and when extra effort forced a sound from one of the patrol he heard it with the clarity of trumpet notes.

They crossed the moat on an improvised bridge of lashed bamboo that bent and mourned aloud at their departure.

Going over the wire generated a chorus of scrapes and metallic stresses and he would have sworn he could feel the strands thin out under the hand that braced him.

They moved away on a paddy dike. When the point signalled a stop, each man dropped and knew to cover left or right, ready to react to any trouble.

A sense of kinship grew in Harker as he watched these men perform, bringing with it the double edge of apprehension and the almost euphoric embrace of risk that came with commitment beyond recall. The problems of Saigon were reduced to whining trivialities until he remembered Allen being wheeled out of his sight for the last time.

The man in front of him rose once more and Harker followed suit, first insuring the man behind had seen him do so. Moving along the dike again, there was a different taste in his mouth. The exhilaration was in no way lessened, but the thought of Allen had put a mark on his anticipation and he recognized the fact. It was as if he'd over-sharpened a blade, turning a razor to a wire edge. It would cut once with a wonderful fineness but then fall short until honest steel could be re-established.

Now the patrol moved from the easy going onto a trail that snaked through scrub taller than Harker's head. Several times it skirted yawning pits, anomalous clearings blasted clean of vegetation by the B-29 Rolling Thunder bomb-rains that occasionally rumbled loud enough to be heard in Saigon. The ground grew more irregular and the long line undulated over small hills.

The pace slowed radically in a little while and expectation scented the column as each man scoured the night around him with every sense he could bring to bear. They moved up to the right onto a ridge, carefully avoiding a crest, stuttering to a disjointed stop. A shadow materialized beside Cao and a conversation as muted as insect noises ensued. Then Cao was moving along the line, placing men. He stopped beside Harker.

"The bunker is dug into the face of the hill across the valley on the other side of this ridge. We hope to have a good view when light comes but we dare not try to get closer. I will join you in a few minutes."

No answer was required or expected and Harker crawled the few feet to the top and peered through the vegetation. He could see nothing across the way, strain as he would, until suddenly a light flared, orange-red. A few feet away a man inhaled in a gasp and Harker knew he was thinking that for a cigarette a fool had just marked his comrades.

When Cao rustled into place beside him, Harker told of the incident. Small white teeth flashed briefly in silent amusement.

They waited.

A delicate light stole across the ground into the shallow valley. Voices shouting in command timbre drifted to the men waiting on the ridge.

A line of people appeared on the road from the north, some carrying only burdens, others carrying arms as well. They walked heavily and a sliver of sun splayed wavering shadows through a low pall of dust and out into the rank weeds. Guards flanked the column and although they maintained their positions in relation to the bearers, they appeared to move faster. The column branched off the road and moved to the bunker. The people with loads disappeared inside, emerging empty-handed. The guards peeled off and took up defensive positions. Once everything was off-loaded, the civilians were formed into three ranks and a uniformed figure came out of the bunker and harangued them until the sun was fat on the horizon. When he dismissed them they cheered, a reedy bleat that brought another flash of amusement to Cao's face. He slid down the backside of the ridge as the bearers moved away. Harker looked to see Cao's troops had positioned a 60mm mortar within a few yards of him. He'd heard no sound whatever.

One of the men poised a squat bomb-shaped round over the

mouth of the tube. Cao scuffled back to the ridge line and aimed carefully at one of the men on the other hill. Harker picked a target. He listened to Cao take a deep breath and hold it, did the same, and fired a fraction of a second after the crack of Cao's weapon. Two men tumbled backwards as the bullets hit them and the mortar added its hollow "poomp!" at the same time.

The enemy reacted well as the rest of Cao's people opened fire. They dove for cover and fired back immediately, wasting no time searching for targets, relying on the mere fact of return fire to force down the volume they were receiving. The mortar rounds dropped among them with their peculiar snarling explosions while Cao's men continued their small arms fusillade with steady discipline. A gesticulating figure appeared at the mouth of the bunker and even as he ducked back, bullets chewed at the entry.

A man rose and dashed forward toward the ridge and as quickly as he fell behind some cover, another was up and moving, and then a third. Cao shouted to his right and the next man to rise received the full attention of almost half the patrol. The impact of multiple strikes lifted him clear of the ground and whirled his rifle away from him. The next man never got all the way to his feet before he was smashed back into the weeds. The third survived by surprising everyone and dashing rearward to disappear inside the bunker, barely beating a late reaction.

Cao shouted for his men to cease fire. In the immense silence a moan lifted to the ridge. There was a movement in the brush and a man broke cover and raced for the bunker. When he made it, another man screwed up enough courage to try. With his success, the remaining troops stampeded for the safety of the hole.

Cao's men jeered and laughed. He himself turned a more serious expression on Harker.

"You see the road?" he asked, indicating it with a move of his chin. "We will move to block it where it crosses this ridge. Four men will remain here to keep those people in the bunker. And there is other news. The radioman says District Headquarters knows of this action and has alerted us that a representative from MACV Phoenix office is on his way here."

"Did you get his name?"

"No. Is that trouble?"

"I'm not sure. We will have to see. But it insures adequate support for your men."

"It is something to hope for," Cao said, laughing harshly. He rolled away, shouting to his men. Harker moved with them, sliding off the ridge. The mortar gunners were already waiting. The column moved swiftly back the way it had come and they were in their new positions straddling the road when the first artillery landed near the ridge. For a few minutes the howling rounds systematically marched through the brush. When at last they fell silent one of Cao's four sprayed the bunker entry, the sputter of the small-bore weapon derisive after the impotent roaring of the artillery.

Harker was surprised by the scowl twisting Cao's face. The smaller man read the American's reaction and explained.

"They have better information than we have, *Dai Uy*. They would never risk exposing artillery if they did not know our support will be a long time coming. I think we may be in very deep shit, as I have heard your people say. I think they know they have time to teach us a lesson."

He looked from the American to his men. Harker followed his gaze, seeing the faces clouded with bitter resignation. When Cao ordered digging in, they obeyed, but their attitude confused Harker.

"They act as if they expected this. What is happening?"

Cao plucked a blade of grass and slit it along the central spine with his thumbnail. He continued to make slashes in it as he spoke.

"Many of my men are former VC. At least two are long-time deserters from the NVA, I think. There are some who are deserters from our own army, I am certain. The Division Commander responsible for this area is not fond of combat and he thinks we should all be dead, anyhow."

The radio operator rushed up, heedless of the brush tugging at him. He threw a frightened look at Harker and maneuvered to speak to Cao without being overheard. Cao's face grew bleaker with each word and his knowing look past the radioman into Harker's eyes told the latter all he needed.

"Delays?"

Cao nodded. The radioman was sweating and Harker suddenly realized the man was probably thinking of his family and home a short distance down the road and a vengeful combat force advancing on them. At the sound of helicopter blades the man's eyes were already beaming hope before he turned to look. Seeing only one aircraft, he slumped. Cao barked at him to take off the radio and issued more instructions as the man hurried to comply.

"Go to Hai. Tell him to go to every man on that side of the road and tell them that no one is to speak to anyone who gets out of this helicopter. Speak to no one for any reason. Is that understood? And you tell every man on this side of the road."

The man nodded and trotted off. Cao turned to Harker. "You may not live to see your plan work, even if all goes as you hope. Did you come prepared for that?"

Harker smiled. "I will live long enough to see something work, my friend."

Cao suddenly busied himself with his canteen. "Yes, I see that now. Well, let us get on with it."

The helicopter touched down through its own tornado of red dust and three figures tumbled out. Cao's people stared with rural curiosity at two more Americans and a Vietnamese as they moved clear of the dirt, brushing themselves. A murmur buzzed among the PF personnel at the sight of the taller American and the Vietnamese in civilian clothes.

Harker waved at Chavez and got a wave in return as he got to his feet. To the other American he said, "What brings you out here, Barline?"

Barline continued to whack at his clothes. "A tip. I was told you were out here with these Phoenix people and there's another My Lai going on. Where are the prisoners?"

"We don't have any."

Before Barline could pursue the ambiguous tone of the answer, another artillery round shrieked onto the ridge and one of Cao's men responded with a solitary pop. Barline rounded on Chavez.

"You said the goddam fighting was over! What was that shit?"

Chavez glowered. "I don't control the fucking war. You're the one who beat on the General's desk until he sent me out here with you. If you don't like the service, complain to the cook." He waved an arm in the direction of the artillery.

With no other rounds dropping, Barline turned his attention

back to Harker.

"Don't try to hold out on me, Captain. This isn't your operation. You help me and I'll make a point of remembering it."

"We don't have any prisoners." Harker met Barline's hard gaze and turned away. "We haven't seen a civilian since sunrise. All I can speak for is what's happening where we are right now." He pointed at the bunker. "We chased some NVA troops into that bunker over there. They came from the village to the north. Cao's unit isn't the one doing anything to the civilians in the village. I don't know anything about that and neither does he."

"There's another Popular Force unit up there in the village?"

Harker looked guilty at Chavez before answering. "I didn't say that. I don't know if there is or not. I haven't been near it. Neither has Cao or his people."

"Sure." Barline smiled. "I hear what you're saying. Is there an American with them?"

Chavez made a choking sound and Harker winced. Barline spun on the swarthy man. "You better keep the fuck out of this," he warned, and turned back to Harker. "Well?"

Reluctantly, the words painfully slow, Harker said, "I don't have to tell you anything. I've got my rights, too."

"Really." Barline signalled to Han. "Let's go." Then, to Harker, "Frankly, the idea of you talking about rights makes me want to puke." To Chavez he said, "You're coming with me, Captain."

"Screw that," Chavez said. "You want to see the atrocities? Be my guest. We told you there's nothing for you up there."

Barline hesitated. Without taking his eyes from Chavez, he said, "Han! Ask these people what's going on in the village to the north! Ask about the American running the interrogations!"

Han did as directed, snapping questions at the radio operator. The black-clad PF stared wide-eyed with mute terror at being the man chosen to enforce Cao's edict. In addition, completely baffled by the thrust of the questions, he kept looking nervously to the north as if expecting to find an American leading the NVA unit he knew to be advancing on them. He swallowed audibly and looked to his leader. Cao refused to acknowledge him, glaring at Han. No one spoke.

"Not speak," Han announced. "Maybe something happen they not want tell."

"Bet your ass," Barline growled, breaking off a branch and improvising a white flag with his handerchief. "We'll put a stop to this shit." He shoved Han out onto the road. "You keep hollering, loud. Tell whoever's out there we're friends and—what's the word for press?—*bao chi*. You tell 'em we're *bao chi*."

They moved off down the road. As they started around the first bend, Chavez exhaled gustily. Han's shouted message lost volume, became mere sound. Chavez broke the group's silence.

"You didn't tell me you were going to have someone telephone him and tip this operation. I see what you meant when you said you were setting up something hot. He was in my office at 0400. Had the duty roust me and was talking to a General by the time I got in. He really believes he's got the story of the year."

Harker said, "Believe me, he does."

The manner of the answer cocked Chavez' head. "That sounds funny. What's really going on up there?"

Harker described the morning's action. "Now we've got an NVA force hurrying to stomp on us. I honestly wasn't sure how I was going to handle this Barline deal, but he's running smack at them, and they're burning. It makes that part easy. The hard part is, Cao's called for help and the local General's dragging his feet. I don't care if I get hurt, as long as Barline gets it, but I'm sorry you got dragged in, buddy. It could get hairy."

Chavez winced. "Holy shit! Gimme the radio! Where's it link, District?"

Harker nodded. Chavez grabbed the handset and drew off into the brush, his lips brushing the microphone as he jammed words into it, a mongrel mix of English, Vietnamese, and profanity.

A sudden spackle of small arms fire erupted to the north. It pecked to a stop and only the whir of insects touched the silence. There was another short burst and then another. The silence resumed.

Harker exchanged a look with Chavez, who returned to the radio. A few moments later he handed it back to the operator.

"Special Forces has a liaison at this District. I got him. We'll have a Magic Dragon here in around a half-hour. And the General's found some people. If we can keep from being over-run for a while, the Dragon'll chew 'em up and the ARVNs'll come in behind and clean up what's left."

Harker translated for Cao who shouted his excitement and sent messengers racing with the news.

The first NVA troops scouted the bend in the road, pressing along its flanks, their attention visibly wandering to where Cao's four stakeouts popped an occasional round at the bunker entrance.

The two Americans and Cao watched the advance with grim satisfaction, seeing its intended course designed to sweep up the ridge from the road, rolling up the pesky force that had their supply unit pinned down.

The oncoming *bo doi* moved well, using the ground, never forgetting to check where the next step would take them, as opposed to concentrating on their final goal. It was as professional as could be hoped, good men, well trained and experienced, and the lead elements never had a chance, advancing directly into a hidden, dug-in unit. When the point was no more than fifteen yards away Cao opened fire on him with a long burst that sent him down like rags. The rest of the line opened fire immediately.

From the corner of his eye Harker saw a bright flash from the vicinity of the men still on the ridge, followed by a tremendous explosion from the bunker. He realized the men left behind had been armed with rockets for just that purpose. Ammunition exploded underground and the shock wave rolled across the land and the fighting seemed to recoil, the rattle of small arms insignificant in the face of such force. The respite lasted but a moment, and then the main body of the enemy was coming around the bend in the road, small units advancing in leaps and bounds. The survivors of the lead elements fired to their front, recovering from the surprise that had scythed so many of them. There were cries from Cao's line and somewhere to Harker's right a man began to scream in the mindless way of a destroyed body.

Cao signalled his mortar crew back and sent a runner to pull back his unengaged left wing. The four on the distant ridgeline continued to fire down the valley at the advancing enemy. The troops ignored the long-range sniping, but the artillery managed a few rounds to let them know they were observed. Then it shifted to Cao's line. He signalled again and the extreme right flank took off rearward.

"I will ask you to leave now," he said to Harker and Chavez with almost drunken formality. "I would be embarrassed to have you killed here."

"I'm not wild about it myself," Harker muttered, and punched Chavez' ribs. They both fled down the road at a dead run as the tempo of the enemy firing picked up. A few more yards and they fell in with the PFs on their new, higher line. The Vietnamese paid no attention to their arrival, having already accepted them as partners in the job at hand and too busy to be concerned with differences of any nature.

The two of them joined in the covering fire allowing Cao to pull out the remainder of his men. They broke away as individuals and dodged and darted on their way back, but the enemy shouldered his way onto the ground they'd just left and unleashed a storm of fire after them. Three men dropped outright and the rest dove for anything that suggested cover or concealment. The covering unit's rate of fire increased to hysteric proportions until the artillery resumed its giant's strides among them.

A PF moved off the line, no weapon in his hands. Another called his name and he turned momentarily, only to lower his head at the sound of the next incoming round and run.

Noticing motion to the right, Harker rose a few inches and identified it as troops. They were being outflanked. If they didn't retreat from this position and leave Cao with his men trapped, the entire unit was finished.

Someone down the line shouted and Chavez looked skyward. "It's the Dragon!" he yelled. "I told you it was coming!"

The enemy heard and saw as well. Their fire slacked off immediately. Harker screamed at the PFs to keep the pressure on them, to keep them locked to the ground for the Dragon's guns. The strange, accented voice shouting commands made them pause, and then they reacted with renewed strength. The fire from the men with Cao regained some intensity.

Chavez called the radioman to him and began detailing instructions to the lumbering WWII relic. Propellors droning, it came toward them, roughly paralleling their line and at Chavez' instructions, Harker shouted for the PFs to fire smoke grenades at the enemy, any color. The result was the blossoming of a peculiar bouquet that drew the twin-engined Dragon as to honey.

A new noise struck the battlefield, more frightening than the supply dump explosion, far more soul-searing than normal battle. The airborne Gatling-type guns vomited a virtually solid stream of bullets. The earth danced where they fired, bits of brush, rock, dirt, and unidentifiable things swirling upward like offerings. When the plane stopped firing to bank and return, the enemy didn't even trouble to shoot at it. They ran.

Harker and Chavez watched with relief and satisfaction. The plane made two more passes before Chavez told them they weren't needed any longer. On the horizon there were helicopters settling to the ground.

Cao approached and looked north with them. "They must have found the artillery, I think, and they will soon attack what is left of this unit. Today it is we who give the lesson. It was good you were here to help. We thank you."

"How many casualties?" Harker asked.

"Five dead," Cao said. "Six wounded. One will die. And a deserter, but he will return." He swung his arm in an arc. "Where can he go, poor fool? I will discipline him and we will continue."

They watched the PFs move forward, gleaning the battlefield for weapons and ammunition and information to be turned over to District Headquarters. After a while, they followed, ending up on the original positions they'd held. One of the PFs came toward them from the north, trotting around the bend in the road. He seemed anxious to speak, but hesitated to interrupt. Cao nodded at him.

The man said, "We were getting equipment from the enemy dead, as always. One of them had this in his shirt pocket. I was not robbing him. It was there for anyone to see."

He held out a wallet. Cao glanced inside and handed it to Harker.

The American looked at the papers and spoke to the man. "It belonged to the other American who came here in the helicopter. Have you found him?"

The man shook his head. "We looked for him and for the man with him. We found the white thing they carried. There is blood there." He looked to Cao nervously.

Harker turned to him, also. "Your men are excellent troops. You must be very proud of them."

Cao thanked him and dismissed the other man, who went looking for others to tell what had happened and been said.

They watched him until Cao turned back to them. He looked up at Harker. "You are a mystery to me, *Dai Uy*, you and your friend. I am pleased that I could help you in this matter between you and the other American, whatever the cause. And we owe our lives to your help. You fought with us and you fight very well. I think you are very good soldiers, even though I was unsure of you at first. I think these men who died must have been very bad, because I do not believe you are proud of the way they died."

They stared at each other, digesting the words and the look of the face before them and Harker finally gestured with the wallet. "I'll see this gets turned in back in Saigon."

Chavez reached for the radio again. "I'm calling to get our ass out of here," he said. "I've had all I want for one day, buddy."

Harker didn't hear him. He was watching Cao's PFs remove their wounded. One carried a man piggy-back. There were tourniquets on both of the passenger's legs but blood drizzled from his feet nevertheless. The pattern in the dust looked like ancient writing.

49

WHEN WINTER LED THE WAY into the State Department building the Marine at the desk passed them along with such calculated disinterest Taylor winced. He stole a glance at Harker's face and the locked determination it had shown since he came in from the field to describe Barline's death. For the two days since, he'd been submerged in a silence that created its own gravity, engulfing all communication around him. Even Winter's efforts had failed.

Both Harker and Chavez faced the hurricane of interest generated by the incident with unshakable confidence. They professed no knowledge of information that sent Barline to that particular place, nor had they any explanation for his foolhardy venture forward of the already-threatened line of PFs. The only time either man showed any emotion was Chavez' outburst when he angrily described Cao's insistence on secrecy and the obvious breach that put Barline in the picture at all. Then he apologized for having no more to add.

Harker refused to speak or write beyond the most fundamental facts, made no apologies for his reticence, and seemed to defy anyone to make him say more. At the obligatory press conferences his delivery was stiff and formal and his eyes roved the attendees in a manner later described in various terms, the most popular being "chill" and "hostile."

The interviews had been unqualified disasters, creating more questions than they answered. They left the official MACV explainers at the regular news briefings more exposed than ever to the scorn of their interrogators.

Winter was summoned to Carr's office. Taylor invited himself along on the theory that it might take two minds to think up things to divert Carr from Harker's studied insolence. He had expected to have to argue about it and was uneasy when Winter's quick acceptance revealed his own uncertainty. For the first time since becoming aware of the incident, Taylor had felt afraid.

They stepped out of the elevator into an empty hallway that had the feeling of having been hurriedly cleared. Their steps were heavy sounds, pounding on the carpeting. The secretary in Carr's waiting room rose when they entered, her expression breaking its professional facade long enough to reveal a layer of tension. She asked that the others wait until called, introduced Winter, and left with graceful speed, avoiding eye contact with either Taylor or Harker.

Taylor leaned back and stared at Harker's ear. "Did you set him up?" he asked quietly.

Color rose in Harker's cheek, the only sign he'd heard. Taylor repeated the question, then, "One of us has to know for sure, man—me or the Old Man. We're here to squash it, but it's going to be a lot tougher if you keep asking for trouble."

Harker swung to face him, anger surging. Taylor waved a bored hand. "Don't start on me. You're over-acting and you're getting ready to be a martyr. Tell you the truth, I think you did it."

Again Harker flushed and opened his mouth and Taylor rode over the protest. "Just listen. I don't much care if you got Barline killed or not. He wouldn't weep for me, I don't weep for him. But you've got Winter's ass hung out like a wet pea-coat sleeve, babe, and I'm not in much better shape. We don't need the Unit investigated. We better have our gear in order before we tangle with this guy, Carr. I'm too close to retirement to lose the whole works."

Harker broke the staring match to glance around the room. Taylor watched him and laughed softly.

"Looking for bugs? Forget it. They wouldn't dare. They've got their own problems. While we've got the time, let's hear it all."

It came in nervous bursts, relief becoming more apparent as the details poured free. At the very end, Taylor marked the taut skin around the eyes and the thinned lips of a man laboring under a load even though his strength has long since faded.

He reached out to put a hand on the other man's shoulder. "Hang in," he said, winking. "We can handle it if you don't come unglued, you hear? Nobody'll lay a glove on you if you start behaving right. Stop thinking and acting like you're mixed up in something terrible."

The sullenness returned. "You're the expert, aren't you? You just do it and don't think about it, don't you?"

"I think about it. I try to be objective."

"Is that what you call it?" He snorted before dabbing at sweat on his forehead. "We've all seen you working on your precious objectivity. Or is it only a lack of conscience?"

The muscles in Taylor's jaw wadded and for a second the hand on Harker's shoulder tightened. He closed his eyes in a protracted blink and when he opened them, he put his hand in his lap and spoke comversationally.

"Once, when I was a kid, I was fishing and I fell asleep. I woke up with the damndest feeling I ought to remain absolutely still, so I did, but I moved my eyes and I saw this dog fox with a chipmunk trapped at the base of a tree. The fox'd lunge and the chipmunk'd nail him on the nose every time. A couple of times I thought it was over—the fox got him —but the chipmunk got loose and backed up against his tree again. And pretty soon the fox quit. Dropped his brush, backed off, and went looking for an easier meal. It was a good lesson.''

Harker's impatience swelled his voice. "So you watched an animal save its life. Should I tell everybody Barline threatened me?''

Shaking his head, Taylor said, "I'll bet I've told a hundred people that story and every goddam one of them identifies with the chipmunk. Now, listen to me.'' He tilted forward, eyes hard. "Animals don't have a corner on predation, they're just a whole lot less organized about it than humans. We invented wars, but there's still the occasional one-on-one thing where someone has to die. So I learned from the fox. He knew he could kill the chipmunk, but he knew he could get hurt so badly doing it that his next kill or his next escape might be jeopardized. What I'm saying is, you handled the first half of this deal all wrong. You decided to be the predator, but you got all mixed up with right and wrong and guilt afterwards. You were off base going in, Harker—you didn't back off when you had the reason and the chance to get the hell out, so now we're all sweating. The trick now is to last it out. You break wrong and you take everybody with you.''

Harker mustered a sneer. "I did what I had to do and I'm afraid to take what's coming to me. You've got it all worked out, haven't you? No great victories, no glorious defeats, just a quick, clean kill.''

The chair sighed under Taylor's weight as he sat back and a smell of plastic gushed into the room.

"Forget glory and all that. That was other wars and maybe the next one.'' He rubbed his chin and added, "One more thing. Don't ever give me any more shit about what I've done or how I've done it. I don't plant bombs for civilians. I don't send anybody into a meatgrinder while visions of Presidential Unit Citations dance in my head. I've never once asked for anyone's understanding, but I'll level with you. I expected some from my friends.''

Harker looked down at the figured carpet. "I'm sorry. It's not like I—.'' He twisted his face and gestured helplessly.

"Good.'' Taylor nodded approval, continuing in the face of

Harker's blank confusion, "You stay nervous. And stay puzzled. You haven't done anything, remember. You got caught up in an unfortunate incident. Barline stepped in it all by himself, right? Right. You tried to explain things to him. You've been surly because you keep thinking there was something you might have done to stop him. *He* made the trouble."

The door swung open before Harker could answer and Carr said, "You gentlemen can come in now." There were no clues in his voice and his features were professionally impenetrable.

Surprise almost checked Taylor in the doorway when he looked past Winter and saw Earl's forbidding mask. Harker cleared his throat nervously.

Winter said, "I've been explaining to Mr. Carr that you didn't have any idea Barline was coming to watch the Ruff-Puff operation."

The full import of the speech escaped no one. Carr smiled and Earl's knuckles whitened on the arms of his chair.

Harker said, "That's correct, sir. I said so at the press conferences. If he'd let us know, we'd have arranged for him to go with me. He could have seen anything he wanted. He didn't have to carry on the way he did."

Earl shifted in his chair, then back to his original position, every movement an expression of disbelief.

Taylor caught a change in Harker, an infinitesimal lifting of his chin. "I know what you're thinking, Colonel Earl, and I wish I had an excuse. When Mr. Barline said he was going forward, I told him there could be hostile troops on that road, but he insisted he'd be back before they closed on us. I couldn't stop him."

"The hell you couldn't!" Earl twisted in the chair again. "He was a civilian in a combat area. You knew how close the VC were. I believe you failed completely to warn him of his danger."

"No, sir." Harker looked embarrassed. "I know a lot of people think that because Mr. Barline always acted as if he wanted us to lose this war, but he was entitled to his opinion, sir. And if I'd physically restrained him, Colonel, who'd have defended me if he made a stink about not being allowed to go where he wanted to go? I don't mean to sound impertinent, but are you willing to tell one of these media people he's forbidden to go anywhere, unless it's a classified area?"

"Of course not!" Earl snapped, his color rising. "I wouldn't let him walk directly into a VC attack, either."

Winter said, "Not VC. The unit's positively identified as NVA. We have their track all the way down through Laos into the Cambodian border area."

"So what?" Earl demanded. "The question isn't who killed Barline but how it was allowed to happen. I told you, the Senator is enraged. He wants to know *exactly* what happened out there."

Half-turning, Winter directed his comment to his officers, affecting a gross confidentiality. "Mr. Barline covered the Senator's last re-election campaign. They became good friends. In fact, one of the Senator's opponents—."

Earl made a growling sound as he rose from the chair. "I have to warn you, Colonel, no matter how confidential this conversation's supposed to be, if you continue—."

"Shut up." Winter's command was just loud enough to carry over Earl's speech.

Carr coughed and made as if to speak, but one look from Winter's slitted eyes and he sat back quietly.

Winter said, "I can give warnings, too. If you ever speak to me like that again, I'll have you court-martialed before you can plug in your connections. Secondly, I don't believe a word of the innuendo that was thrown around about your Senator. I'm sure you'd be the first to claim that any accusation has to be backed up by evidence. But that's not slowing you down very much in Harker's case, is it? I think your judgement in this entire issue is clouded by your determination to see it as something where our every move is wrong, just as did Barline. He wrote thousands of words poo-pooing the reports of NVA troops operating out of Cambodia. I find a certain irony in the fact he was butchered by people he's steadfastly maintained don't exist."

It was a long speech, and Taylor was glad it was over. He could feel Earl's frustration as clearly as he could feel the tension headache at the back of his own neck. The whole conversation had gone on long enough. Harker was clearly off the hook. Carr's expression said he was satisfied with their position. Taylor looked at him again to verify and told himself he'd never know if Carr really believed or if he simply acknowledged a good defense.

He was startled to hear Earl speak again.

"Barline's not the only man to die in suspicious circumstances who's had connections with your Unit, Colonel."

The accusation in the statement shot adrenalin through Taylor in a flood, clamping down the pain of the headache, tightening his muscles.

"If you have something to say, get it out," Winter said.

Taylor looked to Carr for help, but the dapper civilian didn't know Winter well enough to recognize the menace in the soft-spoken response. Taylor sighed and leaned back, only to be pulled forward by Earl's next shot.

"There was that man Trung, reportedly shot by the VC as a traitor. I know for a fact he leveled a personal threat at your Major Taylor, there."

Again, very quickly, Winter answered. "So?"

"You arrested Trung. Another man died on that occasion. When Trung was freed, he refused to speak out against his illegal treatment, yet he felt strongly enough about it to threaten this man's life. And now he's dead, slaughtered while he slept."

"You're making an accusation? A charge?"

"You know I'm not. There's no evidence."

"Exactly what I was telling you before. But I'll give you more than you've given me, and assume Trung was killed by American efforts. Was he actively engaged in opposing our war effort? Had his work resulted in the injury of Americans, or their deaths? If those things are true, Trung was a soldier. Why does it become necessary to take him to court? In fact, why does he rate your protection while we don't?"

The normally composed expression cracked momentarily and Earl covered the lapse by looking away. In doing so, his eyes met Carr's and they each held, probing. Taylor watched them, fascinated by the immense power as they sought a clearer view of the inner man. He left them long enough to observe Winter and Harker. They showed no particular interest and it concerned him that he might be reading too much into the staring match. When he checked, however, they were just breaking the contact and Taylor was disappointed no one else had noticed its intensity.

Earl turned back to Winter. "You're questioning my patriotism. You mistake my contempt for an immoral war for

471

a favorable view of the enemy. I'm as philosophically opposed to men like Trung as you are. But he's not the real issue. Do we have the right to interfere in another country's politics? And it is politics, not morality, that got us involved in this war. But it's morality that forces me to challenge your methods. Once your techniques become standard, the differences between Trung's side and our are only external. The rottenness will be universal.''

Carr swiveled his head to Winter, keeping his eyes to the front, the move giving him an automaton mask. Taylor reflected that the man might have been a machine designed to inspect parts produced by another machine.

Winter grinned, a thing with no humor in it. "I don't question the degree of your patriotism. I question its direction. And morality? And techniques? You talk about Trung's death and your suspicions. Haven't you ever been suspicious that two of my men were ambushed by so-called VC within hours after your friend Barline paid a visit to the headquarters of a man who claimed to own a woman one of the men was sleeping with? Tell me about the morality and technique in that.''

The blood drained from Earl's face as if one drop. He remained stock still long enough for color to reappear in his cheeks and then said, "He didn't—," and stopped. His Adam's apple bobbed rapidly.

Winter's face darkened. "He didn't?" he repeated, and waited.

"Your man didn't die for what he did.''

Taylor noticed Earl set his shoulders as he spoke and an apprehensive chill slipped over him, a feeling that another force had entered the room. He searched the faces, Winter's questioning scowl. Earl's returning control, Carr's metallic curiosity. There was nothing to explain the heavy sensation in his head, as if he was being watched. A hint of movement from Harker passed across the periphery of his vision and he half-turned and looked into eyes gone feral underlined by lips drawn to a slash of satisfaction. As unobtrusively as possible, he moved his foot until it was above Harker's boot and lowered it. He was beginning to wonder if the man would ever acknowledge the increasing pressure when Harker started, almost jerking the foot from under. The wild expression changed to fright before settling to bland unconcern.

Taylor looked away to see Carr watching them with interest. Winter broke the spell.

"No, Colonel, my man only lost a leg. But to what purpose? To atone for his sins? Or hers? What of the Colonel's sins? And if Barline was the man who informed the Colonel, can you honestly imagine he was moved by moral considerations? Morality!" The last word came like spit, crude and shocking despite all that had gone before.

Carr said, "Gentlemen, we seem to have strayed far afield of our subject." He nodded in Winter's direction. "I only asked you to bring the Captain here because the Senator requested I speak to you. Frankly, he wanted me to determine if there were grounds for an official investigation." He transferred his gaze to Earl. "I don't see any such grounds. Mr. Barline apparently willfully ignored warnings by Captain Harker and Captain Chavez after insisting on observing a mission he had no legitimate way to be aware of. I'll deny I ever said it, but I'd much rather order an investigation of Mr. Barline's sources."

Earl refused to respond.

Carr went on, "I don't know what's to come of all this. I grew up between the two world wars, you know, always reading how America lost its innocence during the first one. Then I saw the communist empire blossom out of the second, and I wondered why we'd ever gotten involved in either. I came into the Foreign Service because I thought I could help keep us away from such mistakes in the future."

He stopped, seeing back into years of his own. When he remembered the others, he smiled apologetically.

"How comforting it is to find myself in the company of others foolish enough to think they may have a hand in the course of events. Gentlemen, I put it to you that all of us— hawks, doves, tortoises or hares—are damned to spend our lives in a constant struggle that is no more than a waste of time."

Harker flushed. "Sir, you're saying—."

Carr flagged him with a wave. "No, son, I'm not saying we'll lose the struggle with the Russians. Or the Chinese. Or our own fledgling demagogues. But we shall lose, as they shall lose, because none of us are able to build any longer. The present human condition revolves around the concept of destroying in order to build, but we've become Kipling's Bandar-log, incapable of a two-step process."

Various degrees of irritation flickered on the faces of his audience, but Carr was unaware of them. He lowered his gaze to his desk and his lips puckered as if the smooth surface offended him.

Winter shuffled his feet, the scuff of the boots loud in the room. The sound brought Carr from his reverie sharply but he maintained the control that prevented anything like a show of surprise. Taylor thought it would be interesting to match him against Loc.

In his most precise manner, Carr ended the session. "There will be no official statement concerning Captain Harker's or Captain Chavez' involvement in this matter." He looked expectantly at Winter.

"MACV intends to take a similar position, sir. Barline's death was an accident of his own causing. Our people did what they could to stop it."

Carr swung his attention to Earl, every eye following his lead. Earl met no one's eyes steadily, finding the spaces between the other men. There was less surety in his manner, Taylor noticed. Even his slumped posture said he'd lost something since the meeting started.

His answer was made of defiant words in a voice that lacked timbre. "I'll always suspect that any reporter other than Ben Barline would still be alive. Maybe some day we'll know more. Maybe the source who called will come forward."

Harker sat a bit straighter in his chair. "His driver was a source. I wonder if Barline knew he was VC."

"You've never proven that!" Earl exploded, tension spewing as inner dams broke. "The man's dead, unable to defend himself!" He pointed a trembling finger at Harker. Cords strained in his neck like halyards. When he swallowed his chin moved in a thrusting motion.

Carr got to his feet. "It's over, gentlemen. We've all had our say—more than necessary, I should think—and further discussion would clearly be counterproductive. I suggest we all bend our efforts to the business of returning to normal."

Taylor glanced at Harker and without any further cue, they made their way to the door. Winter made the goodbyes. Earl brushed past him, overtaking the other two in the waiting

474

room. He looked at them as if they were completely unknown to him and left, unspeaking.

With Winter's arrival, they retraced their path outside. Taylor moaned at the sight of the traffic build-up. Before anyone could comment further they all froze, listening to the hoarse scream in the distance.

"Rocket," Winter said, managing to get the word in just prior to the explosion. It came to them as a harmless rumble. Taylor looked at the traffic streaming past, watched the people check and saw their faces jerk from apprehension to wary resignation as they set themselves toward home once again. In the distance, sirens howled. The three Americans moved toward their jeep once again.

Harker gestured in the direction of the impact. "That's what we were arguing about up there—whether it's moral or immoral for us to be involved in a war with scummy bastards who shoot rockets into cities. They kill civilians on purpose and it's guerrilla warfare. We bomb a power plant in Hanoi and kill civilians by accident and we're war criminals."

Winter took his eyes from the traffic long enough for a meaningful stare at Harker. "I wouldn't get worked up if I were you. I've had my fill of attitudes. Let's concentrate on doing our job for a while."

Taylor hurried the last few steps to the jeep, anxious to get it started and get back to MACV so he could leave for the apartment and Ly. Discussion had become academic at the sound of the rocket, as it did at any of the war-noises. The explosions in the city were political punctuation marks to Winter and Harker and Earl and Carr, to all of them. Small arms fire was something that underlined a tenet in a textbook. It was something to be read and interpreted.

Not for me, Taylor thought. I have Ly and my child to be born and I know what this is and its not a great politico-intellectual-sociological drama.

It's fear.

It's wondering if the loving woman beside you will live through the night. Wondering if the house will be burned around her during the day. Wondering if a stray bullet will rip that incredible loveliness or if an ethnic purist will destroy her and the life carried in her in the name of a better world populated by people created more in his own image.

Carr's right, only his emphasis is misplaced. It's the incessant yammering that's a waste of time. My child has to grow up free and unafraid and I only know one way for that to happen. If I have to die for it, I know I'm right.

50

CHI HONG OPENED HER EYES with a grave misgiving that vaulted to fright when she realized she had no idea where she was waking. She closed her eyes again, quickly.

Why was the sky above her? There should be the familiar ceiling of her room.

And why was she waking at such an odd hour, and in the midst of such a terrible racket? What *was* all that noise?

When she struggled to sit up her legs wouldn't do what she wanted and her head swam with sudden pain. She blinked, and when she opened her eyes this time there were people running and shouting all around her and for some reason she wasn't surprised. It seemed to be what was right for this time and place.

What time and place?

Shopping. Cho Lon. That was it. She was shopping in Cho Lon and there was the terrible noise and the next thing she was looking at the sky.

She shivered.

There had been an attack! She had been caught in it. That was what all the excitement was about, of course.

It was all coming back. There was a little pain, no worse than a dull headache.

She shifted, her legs still uncooperative, and she looked down, half-afraid, wondering if they were hurt. It was then she saw what pinned them to the sidewalk and screamed.

"Records Research Unit." Taylor reached for a pencil as he answered the phone.

"Is there a Major Taylor there?"

"Speaking."

"Major Charles Alfred Taylor?"

"That's right. Who's this? What's going on?"

"Just verifying, Major. One more question, sir. Are you married?"

'Me? No. What the hell is this? Who are you?"

"Cornelius, Major—clerk here at Third Field?—we got a woman here—two of 'em, one young, one old—and the older one keeps sayin' the young one's your wife, but we don't—"

"She's my wife. Give her anything she needs or wants. Both women. I'll be there in two minutes. You hear?"

"Yes, sir, but the doctor—."

He dropped the phone in the cradle and ran. Harker shouted after him and Taylor threw Ly's name over his shoulder without slowing. Earth and gravel exploded from under the tires as he sped out of the yard and onto the street leading to the gate, where he roared by the angry yells of the guards who had to leap out of his way. He broke across the streaming traffic, sending it into a mad dance of howling brakes, horns, and curses. At the hospital he slewed to a stop and jumped out, landing running, racing into the hospital.

A burly E-5 grabbed him with a hand like a padded vise.

"Whoa, Major, please. Let us help you. It'll be a lot quicker and easier for all of us." He steered Taylor to a bench. "Who is it you want to see, sir?"

"Her name is Ly. Your man Cornelius called me, said she came in with an older woman. I think he meant Hong."

The Sergeant nodded. "Wait here, sir. I'll ask the questions for you."

Reaching the administration desk rapidly, he spoke to the clerk, indicating Taylor. The clerk looked and nodded and Taylor advanced instantly.

The Sergeant turned to meet him, still smooth and easy. "She's one of our patients, sir. Came in with the Hong woman, just as you said. We'll have to speak to Doctor Hall."

"I'll see her, Sergeant. Now."

The man shook his head sorrowfully. "Major, you know it don't work like that. It might not be a good system, but without it, we've got nothing. I'm moving things as fast as I can. Now, please, sit over there until I come back."

Taylor took a step forward and the big Sergeant stood unflinching. "Major, let me put it this way. All you can do is fuck things up and make it worse for the lady."

Taylor felt his head move in an affirmative nod that contra-

477

dicted every impulse in the rest of his body. He forced himself to the bench but sitting in one place was impossible. He walked the few feet to the door and the non-hospital smell outside, unseeing eyes aimed at the unconcern of vehicles passing on Vo Thanh. After an abortive effort at pacing, he leaned against the wall and lit a cigarette, inhaling heavily on the first drag, concentrating his whole being on the impact of the smoke on his lungs.

When he exhaled he was finally able to look around and see. Coherent thoughts emerged from the chaos of shock. He told himself to prepare, be ready for the worst, to be able to console Ly over the loss of the child, if necessary.

Suddenly he thought of her crippled and it was a shaft of pain that struck his chest and radiated in all directions. Other images appeared and sweat poured from him as he strained to shut them out.

He dropped the cigarette and stepped on it with all his weight, turning the ball of his foot with the mindless persistence of a leopard patrolling its cage.

The Sergeant interrupted him. "Good idea, waiting out here in the fresh air, sir. Doctor Hall's waiting. We'll have to hurry."

The last was gratuitous, as Taylor was already abreast of him and moving for the corridor. The Sergeant took a one step lead, calm and purposeful.

Taylor accepted the guidance gratefully, using it to avoid looking at people on beds, people in traction, people passing with their bodies in all descriptions of injury. It was a walk through hell. Every hurt became a thing that could be visited on Ly. The earlier unwanted images swam through his imagination, reinforced by the surrounding misery.

They rounded a corner and a chunky, almost bald man waited. Expressionless eyes bored into him through thick glasses, like sea water held out by ports.

"You're Taylor?"

"Yes, sir. Where's Ly?"

"Thieu Ta! Thieu Ta!" Chi Hong's voice rose from a bed down the ward. "They have taken her from me! Where is my child, *Thieu Ta?* Go to her!" A Vietnamese woman, her head swathed in bandages, hurried through a side door toward the

478

distraught voice, murmuring soothing sounds. Hong's cries subsided to muffled sobbing.

Hall continued to stare at Taylor. "Your wife came in the same ambulance with the older woman. Some kind of servant, I understand. The older one says the younger woman's your wife."

It was a question and Taylor answered it. "Close enough. We're finishing the paperwork now. I want to see her."

Hall wiped clean hands on his white jacket. "It's not important. We—." He stopped, wiped the hands again.

"Major, we did our best, but the damage—." He looked full into Taylor's eyes again and there was pain in his, and then the cold waters claimed it. "You can see her. She may not regain consciousness. We did all we could. I'm sorry."

Taylor felt his knees buckle and kept himself erect only by the strength of the gaze he locked onto the face in front of him.

"Don't tell me that. You can't tell me she's—that there's nothing you can do. We're getting married, for God's sake! She's no part of this!" He heard his voice rise as if an undisciplined stranger abused it. The Sergeant touched his arm and he recoiled. "Me! I'm the one! She's not involved, goddamit, can't you understand that?"

Life stirred behind the glasses again. "Look around you, Major." Each syllable was a whiplash. "There are no soldiers on this ward. Vietnamese females. Aged three, we think, to somewhere around eighty. Don't tell me about involvement. Get a grip on yourself."

Taylor said, "What are her odds? What do I tell her?"

Hall said, "She knows. I don't know how, but as soon as we were done, she looked at me and told me. Comfort her. She deserves that."

When Hall turned to lead the way, Taylor tried to follow but his knees betrayed him again and he stumbled awkwardly. The Sergeant was there as if scheduled, one hand supporting, and as soon as Taylor steadied the hand dropped as if nothing had happened.

He kept pace behind Taylor as they moved through the ward and into a smaller, separate room. The distances between the beds were a little greater. Ly was in the one closest to the door and he was beside her with no conscious movement. When he took her hand in his, it was cool and unresponding. His heart tore at his ribs.

"Ly?"

He thought about the sound itself, to keep the volume down. He imagined his tongue pulling away from his teeth, saw the vowel sound flow across his lip. Her name was always a caress to his mind and he repeated it, trying to make it the same for her.

Slowly, she came to him, progressing from an increased pulse in her throat to the flutter of an eyelid, from open, unseeing eyes to recognition and his name.

"Charles. I knew you would find me." A smile tried her lips and fell away. She said, "Our baby, Charles—I am so sorry. I prayed."

He gripped her hand tighter, amazed at the clarity of her words even as the huge tears welled in her dark, dark eyes to be forced out by closing lids.

"It's OK, honey. It's going to be OK." He hated the insincere rasp of his voice, so crude in contrast to her strength.

Faint pressure said she was trying to squeeze his hand in return. "I will be with our baby." She said it calmly and at his wordless objection, found the strength to open her eyes again.

"It is not use to lie. I know. How could I not know, Charles? This morning I carried life in me. I can feel what is there now. I can be brave, but, please, you must help me. I need you."

"I need you, Ly. I love you. Without you—." He had no words to finish, unable to face the cut of the inference.

Ly said, "You must be strong, too, my Charles," and there was direction in her voice. "I love you so much. All I leave you are memories." Her words caught before she continued. "I want to be remembered by good memories. You must not be sad."

He nodded and felt his face breaking like glass and the tears slid across the fragments.

Suddenly she was exhausted. Her lips parted and the pink tip of her tongue, startlingly vivid against her pallor, licked once and disappeared again. Only as her facial muscles slackened did he realize the will that had maintained her. The sheet moved gently with her breathing and her head lolled toward him, as if she intended to speak again momentarily.

Doctor Hall put his hand on Taylor's shoulder. "I can give you the details, if knowing'll help at all, Major. The simple truth, we're helpless."

Taylor nodded. "I know you did your best. Thank you. I'll stay here with her."

Hall shuffled uncomfortably. "Major, we have visiting hours. We're crowded, and you'll be in the way. Get a good night's sleep and come back in the morn—."

"Forget it." Taylor adjusted a sheet that didn't need it. "You've practically told me there won't be a tomorrow. I'll stay here."

"It's out of the question."

Winter's voice cut across the argument. "We're all staying, Doctor." Taylor turned to see Harker approaching with three chairs. Wordlessly, he placed one for Taylor near Ly's head and, at Winter's gesture, sat the other two in position at the foot. The doctor sputtered confusion. Winter turned eyes on him that matched his own for ancient acceptance.

"Understand, Doctor," he said quietly, "we don't want trouble, but the young woman is different, you see, as is the Major. The world should make exception for the different. And if you think the Captain and I aren't different, try to interfere with us."

In the silence, Hall's face finally worked itself around to grudging agreement. At the last, he nodded, more in understanding than defeat. "She must be very special to you all. If you need anything, let us know." He waved loosely.

Winter turned to face the bed again, bolt upright in his chair, stone featured, arms folded across the broad chest. Harker sat more relaxed, the blond head almost luminous in the increasingly dim room. Night was blanketing the city.

An hour passed. Somewhere an infant cried, the complaint poignant against the steady murmur of coughs and groans and bed-noises that welled through the corridors and wards. Ly stirred and woke, her eyes wide in fright until they found Taylor beside her. Her lips moved in a smile and she lapsed back into unconsciousness.

It was shortly after the baby quieted that she inhaled a particularly deep breath and held it for a moment and expelled it as a soft sigh. Then she was completely still.

"Ly?" He lifted her hand from the bed and leaned over her. At the foot of the bed, Harker was up and running.

Taylor put her hand down to cradle her head on his palm and stroke her hair, continuing to repeat her name in cadence, his voice full of child-like loss.

The doctor arrived with a nurse and Taylor allowed himself to be moved out of the way, never taking his eyes from the figure on the bed. Another nurse hurried in, followed by the steady Sergeant who seemed to be present when needed.

Taylor watched stolidly while the white-clad figures bobbed and shifted around the bed, only his eyes alive. Harker and Winter braced themselves on his flanks, carved temple guards, rock-strong and helpless.

When the doctor turned, one of the nurses was drawing the sheet over Ly's face. Carefully, he worked himself between Taylor and the bed, waiting for Taylor to focus on him. He said, "I'm sorry."

Looking into the man's sincerity, Taylor managed to say, "Thank you." Then he moved to the side for one last moment alone with her and he felt his life distilled to the few hours they had shared. He wanted to speak to her but his throat constricted and he was barely able to pivot and make his way out.

Winter and Harker fell in behind him.

51

"HE'S DRIVING ME OUT OF MY MIND."

Winter shot forward to the edge of his desk chair and continued to watch the door where Taylor had just exited. Harker said nothing. Instead of calming Winter, the additional silence aggravated him further. "He didn't even thank me when I told him he's going home early. I don't think he's said ten words since she died. I wish he'd *do* something. I could understand that, handle it. But he just keeps moving around with that iron mask look. If you didn't know him, you'd think he was perfectly normal. It's horrible."

A nervous gesture earned Harker a hard glare. "You disagree?" Winter challenged.

"No, sir." Harker corrected him quickly, anxious to avoid

another of the sudden temper flare-ups Winter himself had been exhibiting recently. "I'm worried about you, is all. It's been rough around here watching you, too. I told you we could find Binh. I thought you'd be after him like a flash, and you haven't made a move."

"Half right," Winter said. "I passed your information to Loc. He's got people checking the place. You've come up with something really important. Look here."

He was on his feet, animation breaking through the sullenness. Rummaging in his desk, he drew out a map, cleared a place for it and spread it flat. From the same drawer he brought out a tube of clear acetate that unrolled to a sheet the same size as the map. It was marked with red dots. Placed on the map, the dots showed as a spattering of pips surrounding Phu Thuan. Harker moved closer. Spidery numbers printed under each dot indicated dates and times.

"Terrorist action," Winter explained, jabbing a thick finger at one dot after another. "Road mined, grenade in the market, ambushed police patrol. You name it, this area's seen it all. But not Phu Thuan. Never. Make you wonder?"

"They could be too tough." Harker remembered Cao's punji-fanged village and the air of determination about the place.

"Could be," Winter said, "but as far back as Loc's people can find records, there's been nothing. It's not like Charlie to let one go by forfeit. And there's another thing."

Diving into the drawer again, Winter swept aside the first piece of acetate and spread out a second. This one featured two arrows drawn in the red grease-pencil reserved for enemy identification. The heads of the arrows rested on the edge of the map, the shaft of each badly bowed to form a crimson parentheses bracketing Phu Thuan.

"This is where it gets fascinating." Winter bent over the desk and Harker delighted in the increasing animation.

"The Tet offensive in this area. Two columns of VC." His hands described swaths across the contour lines and he recited the names of villages and hamlets in their shadow. "All those places, smashed. Burned. Government personnel hunted down and killed. But not Phu Thuan. An island of tranquility, Phu Thuan." He slapped the hands on the map. "And when the same columns were retreating, escaping the best they could?

483

ARVN forces chasing them had a heavy night battle just here, a few kilometers from the town, when the VC turned and counterattacked. And guess what? The next morning they find dead VC, a few terminally wounded and a fanatic rear guard. The rest? Disappeared.''

"How many?"

Winter made a face. "Probably no more than fifty, maybe a hundred. Fifty good guerrillas could lose themselves in a convent. But what about the wounded? How do you run for cover and disappear with your wounded?"

"You think they ran for Phu Thuan?"

The hands slapped the map again. "I'm sure of it. If we could just be sure. Goddam, think of it! All this time and we may have the bastard!"

"Has Loc been able to tell you anything?"

"Not yet. Maybe that's why I'm letting this thing with Taylor and Ly get to me so much. I don't know." He spun away from the desk and walked stiff-legged to the COSVN chart on the wall. "I don't understand what's happening anymore, if I ever did."

He turned quickly again, the earlier animation now more like erratic fits and starts. "Do you ever hear from Allen anymore?" he asked.

"No, sir."

"And Kimble. You realize we don't know what happened to that poor bastard when he got home? He spent a year with us and left with his life a fucking mess and we never troubled to find out if he's all right and he didn't give enough of a damn about us to let us know."

Harker said, "Hey, Colonel, he was always weird. And Hal's trying to get his act together, that's all."

Winter ignored Harker's defense and turned back to his chart. "And Ordway, that Marine Corporal. The only person he wrote back to was Miller, and that was their own crusade. I wonder if they'll ever bother to see each other again. And Miller. Never a word from him."

"So they don't write letters. Big deal."

"It is. When one of us leaves here, it's like he never existed. The bond isn't taking. Men are brothers here and as soon as they get away, they erase everything from their minds."

"OK, Colonel, what's your point?"

Winter threw him a grim smile. "I'm damned if I know. But it bugs me. I see every man who's served in Vietnam standing in a row, like pigeons on a wire, each one exactly far enough from the person next to him to avoid being pecked. It's a social structure made of very lonely individuals."

"You worry too much. This war and the way things are back in the world won't last forever."

"I hope not." He moved back to his desk, seemingly intent on the map once more, but instead, he said, "You know, that's the trouble. Too much idle bullshit and no solid decisions. We're so introspective and tentative."

"Now, there's something that'll change, for sure. When our people realize how much mealy-mouthed crap—."

Winter gestured it away. "Too much talk, again. Of all the people in the problem, we're the last ones to make more noise. We do the job."

Harker pitched forward, poised like a boxer, chin tucked back so he peered at Winter from under his brows. The young face drew taut but still retained its contoured appearance, like the deflective curvatures of a tank turret. Unaware, Winter continued to study the map.

As Harker relaxed he found it possible to smile when Winter placed the overlays together on the map, first moving a finger from one accusing red dot to another, then tracing the course of the red arrows across the geography.

Harker thought how he looked like a latter-day necromancer weaving his spell over enemies. He wondered if the Round Table knights had ever stood around watching Merlin invoke against dragons. The fancy caught his imagination and he let it run, wishing he had only dragons to contend with, instead of a world that spawned opposition as freely as it created breezes.

The faint knock on the door interrupted them. Before Winter could speak, it swung open to admit Loc, his face split by an unheard of grin. He recognized the map and acetate overlays immediately.

"Very convenient. I have information." His head snapped in a brisk series of nods. "In fact, I have good news."

Moving to the map, he stood beside Winter's looming bulk. He said, "Phu Thuan's destruction will be a major victory." Color rose in his cheeks forming dark oblongs that flowed along the bones. "For years it has been so peaceful we have merely acknowledged its presence. And Phu Thuan is entirely a lie."

Winter looked lost. "A lie?"

Loc reached to lay a deliberate fingertip on the village and Harker had a sense of vengeance lowering. "The ground under Phu Thuan is a maze of tunnels. There are barracks, classrooms, a hospital, and a small munitions factory. It was a staging facility for the Tet offensive. Now it is almost deserted. There is a maintenance force, mostly convalescents in the hospital facility."

Winter pursed his lips and nodded, the composed attitude contradicted by a throbbing vein at his temple. "Binh?" The single syllable brought the tension to a vibrant pitch.

"I think so, *Anh Hai*. I think we have found him."

Winter exhaled and Harker realized from the following rapid inhalation he'd been holding his breath. Only then did he notice the stiffness in his own elbows and move them to work out the pain caused by standing with his fists clenched at his sides.

"How soon can we move?" Winter asked.

Loc smiled again. "Phu Thuan is in the sector of an old friend. I have arranged for a reinforced company. The General has promised helicopters and all other necessary support. We will supply only our personnel and tactical requirements at the pre-attack briefing. I can guarantee surprise when we touch down."

"How soon?"

"The soonest? Tomorrow afternoon, if you like, although the next morning would be better. I have had my men draw up the operation plan. Would you care to see what we have?"

Winter led the way to the door, where he turned to Harker. "I want nothing of this getting to Taylor. Leave him to his problems. We don't need him on this and I'm not sure he could handle anything just yet. You have any questions?"

"One, Colonel. It's not really important." He looked to Loc. "Sir, I just got the word to you and Colonel Winter about Binh a few days ago. How'd you learn all this so quickly?"

Loc's smile turned sly. "As soon as we had your information we arranged for the village chief to be brought here to accept an award for the contributions of Phu Thuan to the government. Colonel Tho and Sergeant Chi made the presentation. The chief will remain our guest until we have inspected his village.''

"I see." He glanced at Winter and saluted. Winter moved his hand in acknowledgement and Loc's office door snicked shut behind them.

Taylor remained on his bunk without moving when Harker's footsteps halted at his open door. He felt no need to speak to anyone. He felt very little of anything. There was a peculiar heaviness in his throat, as if something coarse had wedged there, but no urge to tears.

Was he inured to normal emotions?

It was a frightening thought. He observed it, picturing it blinking on and off in the dark, a red neon sign.

Is Charles Taylor capable of human emotion?

He listened to Harker's receding footsteps, glad to be alone, embarrassed by the self-pity threatening to crush him. He rose from the bunk and stripped for a shower.

The water was warm, warmer than he remembered it from the last time, but it always was. Almost a year in-country and he still couldn't adjust to the idea of hot water on demand. It simply didn't seem right. Nothing did. Everyone was right and everyone was wrong.

He stared at the shower head, erasing thoughts as they came, like one hand writing on a blackboard and the other in pursuit with the eraser. The spray element nestled in its metal holder, a machined multi-eyed cobra's head at the end of flexible tubing. It reflected his face in distortion, huge eyes and nose, the mouth a darker smudge further grotesqued by a drop of water that magnified one corner out of all proportion. It distracted him for the time it took to organize his mind and he planned his words for Ly's mother as he rinsed off and toweled. At his closet he debated civilian clothes or uniform, finally selecting the neutrality of the faded utilities. The bright hues of his civilian shirts offended his eyes.

It never occurred to him to ask for permission to leave the villa. The jeep was clearing the gate when he realized he'd failed to do so. He shrugged the problem aside, uncaring, driving with careless skill. Moving in the relatively light mid-morning traffic was like being adrift on a river and he flowed as the current required. It was a feeling that was further reinforced when he crossed the bridge over the thick pollution of the stream called Rach Thi Nghe. He remembered crossing it when he'd first arrived and passed this way going to Ly's class. The market that had always seemed lively then was hectic now, a mass of noise and confusion. On the other side of the bridge was the familiar alley leading to the Chantareansay Pagoda. Four monks in saffron chanted at the entrance. The words were smothered by machine noise and he could only salvage the sense of supplication in their manner.

Relief mingled with guilt swept through the impression as he thought how he'd be spared having to participate in one of the Vietnamese funerals that frequently wound through the Saigon streets with the ornately carved, gilded, and painted funeral carts that always made him think of circus wagons. It was a shameful reaction and he wished it would go away. With the cars and the musicians and the banners in their violent colors, it was an aspect of Vietnamese culture he'd never adjusted to. The thought that Ly's funeral wouldn't be like that filled him with uncomfortable gratitude. Her people were Catholic. He could handle that. It would tear out his guts but he'd get through it.

He parked in front of the gate and knocked. The guard opened his spy-hole and a sad smile of recognition flitted across his face, replaced instantly by apprehension.

"I can not admit you, *Thieu Ta,*" he said, swallowing hard. "They said you could not come in."

Taylor tried to comprehend the words. "I know they mourn. I only want to learn of the—the funeral arrangements. And to tell them of my sorrow."

"They will not see you." The guard shut the small door.

For a moment Taylor's mind rejected what his eyes saw. His stomach tightened and he feared he would be sick. Then the anger swelled out of control. He corrected his distance and kicked the door. It boomed massively, profundo laughter. He kicked it again, harder, enjoying the shock of the blow traveling from the heel of his boot to the base of his neck. Timing the blows, he set up a steady rhythm.

When it swung open he was in mid-kick and stumbled forward, catching himself on the frame, hanging over the porcelain features of *Ba* Lien. He straightened with as much dignity as possible.

"I apologize for my behavior. There was a mistake. The guard said I was not to be admitted. The tragedy—then this—I am sorry." He gestured at the gate, pleading for her understanding.

She said, "We are having a very private service for my daughter, *Thieu Ta*. Only the immediate family and close friends. We are asking no Americans. I am sure you will understand."

He felt his face flame. "I love her! I do not understand! I will not! Of all people, I—!"

"Stop!" The word flew from the tiny woman like a knife, something that should have been visible in the sunlight, shining malice. "You are not to speak of her! It is because of you and your people she is dead! If you were not in our country she would be alive now! Go home! Leave us our dead and go home!"

She spun on the embarrassed guard and struck him, the sound of her hand on his cheek sharp. "Close the gate! If he makes more trouble, I order you to shoot him!"

The guard reached for the edge of the gate and Taylor pushed the hand aside. Doing so moved him within inches of *Ba* Lien's face and she stared venomously into his eyes without flinching.

He wanted to tell her how cruel she was, wanted to hit her, to somehow hurt her as she was hurting him. Instead, he could only think of one thing to tell her, and suddenly it was paramount that she understand this one thing about Ly and himself.

"I loved her," he said. "I will always love her."

The door thudded shut while he strode to the jeep. He was almost back to the villa before he decided to get drunk. He went to the MACV building where he bought a bottle of Chivas. The clerk took his money and checked his ration card with total disinterest and he wondered if she thought of him as an enemy or a customer or a hand. The idea evaporated before he could come to grips with it, as had all others since the meeting with *Ba* Lien.

He drove back to the villa and carried the whiskey to

Winter's office, where he knocked and entered. Winter's eyes trailed from his face to the package and back again.

"Booze?"

Taylor nodded. "With the Colonel's permission, I'm going to drink myself out of things. I'll be OK by tomorrow." He explained that he was barred from the funeral.

Winter said, "No matter how bad things are, a person like her'll find a way to make it worse. Go ahead and do what you want. Don't worry about tomorrow. Just don't get confused about what that stuff can do for you, OK?" He jerked his chin at the package.

"No problem," Taylor told him. "I'll only sleep sound enough to forget for a few hours. Then I'll be OK."

Winter nodded and Taylor walked down the hall to his room, already opening the bottle and helping himself to a good pull. He had the feeling that Winter was actually relieved to see him taking on a load and couldn't think why that might be, but another swallow of the whiskey chased that idea where so many others had gone that day and he squatted on his bunk, back to the wall, and attacked the bottle determinedly.

52

THERE WAS PAIN ALL AROUND HIM, pain like surf. He was submerged in shallows, but periodically a wave rose and crashed down on him and then the shock was almost enough to make him retch. He tried to get to his feet just as one of the waves struck and he gulped to keep from losing whatever he had left inside.

Wavering, he made his way to the head, wondering what time it was and too busy keeping his balance to look at his watch. Leaning on the edge of the sink, he saw it was 1400, exactly. Unless it was 0200. He looked at the window and saw light and knew it was afternoon. Another look at the watch told him it was, indeed, the day after he'd started drinking.

He soaked his face in the sink, sorry he'd brought so much discomfort onto himself to no purpose. Through the superficial misery of the hangover, the loss of Ly was living flame. Instead of solving anything, he felt degraded. He had denied it

490

to himself while he was getting drunk, but there was no denying it now. The liquor only delayed whatever healing he had to accomplish. It wasn't even a good narcotic.

He shuffled back to his room for hs toilet articles, washed, shaved, brushed his teeth, and began to re-establish his outlook.

The face looking back at him from the mirror seemed no wiser or better equipped to face the world. His eyes stared back, telling him nothing important about the man behind them. He had suffered a loss. He had as much reason to live as before. Maybe more.

Without wanting to, he wondered what the men who fired the rocket must have thought as they sent it on its way. They had to know its ultimate objective was people, just ordinary people. He looked deeper into the eyes and they failed him again and he pounded his fist into the mirror. Glass rang in the sink and blood flowed from small cuts on his hand. He ignored it all, not really aware of it, asking the wild image that squinted from a single daggered shard, "How could they do that? How? *How?*"

Instantly, he was embarrassed. He looked around guiltily while he ransacked his toilet kit for Band-Aids. With the cuts wrapped, he quickly picked the broken mirror pieces from the sink and put them in the GI can.

He stopped on his way out, realizing something was wrong, trying to identify what was missing.

Sound. The building was totally silent. He stepped to the door and looked up and down the hall.

Putting his toilet kit on the shelf, he walked the echoing passageway to knock on Winter's door. There was no response and when he checked, all the other offices were vacant, as well.

The building was deserted. He retreated to his room and put on fresh utilities. On his way out, he checked the offices again. They were as before.

He was moving toward the jeep when it occurred to him that someone might be in the shop. He turned back, welcoming the penetrating cautery of the sun that drew a purifying sweat immediately. When he opened the door to the shop, he startled Tho and Chi.

"Ah, you are awake," Tho said, recovering. "We thought you would sleep much longer."

"It would be better if I did, I think." Taylor grimaced. "It does no good to get drunk. It is only worse when you must stop."

Tho said, "You are fortunate to find that out so quickly. Some men never do."

For the first time, Taylor noticed the radio on the bench in front of Tho. "What is that for?"

Tho ignored Chi's nervous movements and answered easily. "Colonel Loc, Colonel Winter, and Captain Harker are in the field. We are in direct contact."

"What are they doing?"

This time Chi's nervousness was unavoidable and Tho frowned at him before answering.

"They are searching a tunnel network in a village named Phu Thuan."

Taylor's head pounded. "They said nothing of this to me. Why are both Colonels involved?" He closed his eyes and massaged his temples, missing the hasty exchange of glances between the Vietnamese.

Tho said, "They are in the village. They have found many tunnels. They are searching."

The tone of the answer grated on Taylor's ears but he was too preoccupied to push the matter further. He picked a chair to wait with them. A moment later he looked up to find Chi looking down at him, face twisted with indecision.

Caught, Chi said, "I am sorry to stare, *Thieu Ta*, but I do not know how to tell you of my sympathy. I do not know what to say."

Tho turned from the radio. "He speaks for me, as well. I, too, am not sure what is proper to say to an American, except to tell you we share your loss."

The mad contradiction of these two expressing sympathy threatened Taylor's balance, but he managed to explain that what they said was gracious and proper. He thanked them, and even as he did, he was asking himself what he would do to the men who killed Ly if they should fall into his hands. It was a seductive notion. He cherished it, picturing a group watching the first of their number strapped into Tho's massive chair. They'd sweat buckets, waiting their turn. Maybe they'd think about the pain caused by their damned rocket, think of the shattering and the burning.

Another heave rippled through his stomach and a feeling of a thousand needles pricked at the skin between his shoulder blades.

The radio crackled to life and Harker's voice said, "Research Base, this is Research Six. Over."

Tho answered and Harker said, "We have no contact with the target, but have verified identification. The village has been evacuated."

"What the hell does that mean?" Taylor demanded. "Identified what target?"

Tho hunched closer to the radio. "I understand, Research Six."

Taylor moved to stand beside him, positioning himself so Tho would have to look at him.

"What's going on, Colonel? They're onto something. What is it? Binh?"

Tho said, "Yes, it is Binh."

"Why wasn't I told? Why was I left out?" Taylor's accusing look was more violent than the words and Tho's extreme discomfort surfaced in a switch to English.

"It was decided. You were troubled. Colonel Winter, he say not good you go operation so soon you have so much trouble." The language turned Tho's apologetic explanation to petulance and further angered Taylor.

"I'm no child, goddamit. They had no right to treat me like one. I'm going there. What's the name of the place?"

For all the reaction from Tho, the outburst might not have occurred. After a moment he looked up to study Taylor, clearly coming to a decision. Finally he said, "Village Phu Thuan." He pulled a map from the shelf and unrolled it. When he spoke, it was Vietnamese again. "I should not tell you, but I agree with you. You deserve to be there when the animal is forced from its den. This one, in particular, is an example of what—." He stopped so abruptly Taylor thought there must be an external cause, but when he looked, Tho's face was torn by a suffering that was exploding through his defenses as steam ruptures corroded pipe. An inarticulate cry squirmed through clenched teeth, and then he was under control. The previous sentence was left uncompleted, nevertheless. When he resumed conversation, it was in the quieter tones of everyday discussion.

Taylor barely heard him. He felt the information registering like plugs being inserted—map coordinates, unit designations, command personnel, flight times—the part of him responsible for such data was comfortable.

The rest of him was eager hatred. The unknowable view of Tho's inner mind combined with the series of shocks to his own psyche and he knew he was wavering on the edge of madness. He saw himself from a distance, reasonably proud of his intelligence but beset by questions he couldn't hope to answer, never before afraid of death and trembling now with the fear that he might die unrevenged.

The latter brought him up short. Could he bring back Ly and the baby? End the war? Kill all the enemy? There was really nothing he could do. Nothing.

Winter must have felt this way at one time or another, he told himself. And Winter had found his answer. One man. Pick a target and go for him. Subordinate everything else, but don't forget anything. In the midst of complexity, isolate a simple goal.

For lack of a better goal, then, get Binh. After all, who better? One of the gray non-combatants, one of the pro-visioners who made the killing possible. The men who fired the rockets were pawns, like practically everyone else. But some men kept the game alive, and Binh was as close to one of those as he was likely to get. Tho's cry rang in his memory and he applauded the wordless accuracy of it, the hate and the loss. Pain, like everything else, had an ultimate focus, and it was Binh and those like him who lived there, like creatures who'd found a way to shelter in an area too cruel to support other life.

The mechanical voice sputtered from the radio once again, the excited timbre breaking through the matter-of-fact phrasing.

"Research Base, this is Research Six. Over."

Tho barely released the transmission button after his answer before more words tumbled from the set.

"We have contact with the target."

Taylor reached for the microphone and after hesitating, Tho handed it to him.

"What's your situation?" Taylor asked, and all three men tensed. For several seconds the only answer was the hiss of interference. The fluorescent fixtures sealed the listeners and the remnants of Kimble's equipment in an icy tint appropriate to the overall stillness. When the voice came again, it was just as Taylor was pressing the transmission button, garbling the first words.

"—Research Six. Over."

"Research Base. Over."

"We have a stand-off, Base. Target says any further activity from us and they will self-destruct. We are negotiating."

Taylor's fist threatened to crush the microphone. "Shit. Negotiating." He pushed the transmission button again. "What is your evaluation, Research Six?"

The radio crackled, digesting the information before answering.

"Suspect target has an evacuation plan that requires night operation. We are searching for escape routes and talking at the same time."

Taylor stared at the shelves as if answers might be hidden among the litter.

Tho said, "You can be sure Binh has a plan. He will try to escape in the dark, as they fear. If he fails, he will surely kill himself or be killed."

Taylor pulled the microphone back to his lips. "Send a chopper to Tan Son Nhut for me."

The response was immediate. "Negative."

"We have new information that may generate surrender."

The radio resumed its surly hissing and then there was a new voice, Winter's. "Describe the new information."

"Negative, Research Six. This is not a secure net."

Winter's frustration came across as clearly as Harker's earlier triumph. "Report to Tan Son Nhut pad. Helicopter will arrive in approximately one hour. Out."

Taylor checked his watch and pushed the microphone at Tho. As the latter's hand closed on it, Taylor turned to smile at him. Tho remained impassive and Taylor let the smile wither to a faintly hostile look.

"Maybe some debts will be repaid today, Colonel," he said.

Tho said, "With lies? You have no information. You are still ill from drinking. You are making much trouble for yourself."

"No, sir. I have a plan. I have no information, true, but I

can bring news to Binh. It is the same thing."

Tho waved his disapproval. "It is your decision."

"There are no more decisions, only reactions." Taylor turned on his heel and left, the blast of sunlight through the rapidly opening and closing door leaving the two Vietnamese blinking.

Tho looked after Taylor. "He is a man of fire, to cleanse or destroy. And sometimes both. It is impossible to understand him."

Knowing he was expected to answer, Chi said, "Is that not true of all Americans, *Trung Ta?* Sometimes I think they are all insane."

"Insane?" Tho smiled, pointing his chin at the door. "That one, surely. And who can blame him? But he acts carefully. I would not want such a crazy man against me." He laughed and continued, "And now I think I must be crazy. He is a good friend to us, unless he is ever betrayed. Then he would be very dangerous."

Chi turned his back on the door. His upper lip itched and when he rubbed it with a fingertip he was surprised to find it covered with sweat.

The jeep rocked with the sudden stop and Taylor was running for the operations desk before it settled. The huddled woman in the passenger's seat still braced herself with one hand on the dashboard while the other clutched the child to her breast. She drew her shawl more tightly around herself and the child, shrouding their faces despite the fretful complaints from the youngster. The lowering sun was still hot.

When Taylor emerged, he was walking, and the woman relaxed accordingly. She spoke with tentative hopefulness.

"I am afraid. Are you sure we cannot go by road?"

He shook his head, leaning past her to retrieve a bundle. "It will be here in a few minutes. We will wait in front of the building."

The woman allowed herself to be helped out and pretended to accidentally turn away from Taylor's attempt to take the child. Rebuffed, he dropped his hand.

"Try to remain covered well. It is important that no one recognize you," he said.

She nodded, hitching at the shawl again.

He led the way around the building past a clump of decorative bamboo. Long before, someone had planted it at a corner to improve on the sterility of the place, and now it was asserting itself. Macadam bulged upward at its base, peeled back in cracked sheets like punctured metal. The tooth-like projections had taken a toll but the plant was clearly expanding as it chose. The killed outer stalks were forced forward to form a protective bulwark for fresh, green shoots to rise behind.

The woman walked up one side of the root mound and down the other without a glance. They approached a white picket fence and he opened a gate for her. Then they waited, him shifting impatiently and her adjusting the shawl and comforting the child. He identified their helicopter on its approach by its unit markings and as soon as it was on the deck he raced for it, dragging the woman, practically throwing her in with his bundle and leaping aboard himself.

The pilot and co-pilot gesticulated fiercely, pointing at the woman and back at the ground. Their shouts were barely audible, but they made it clear they wanted her out. Taylor fastened seatbelts while he shook his head at them. He leaned forward and the pilot craned back with his helmet off so Taylor could speak directly into his ear.

"We have to take her. I checked with J-2. It's OK."

The pilot shook his head. "We don't carry any Viet civilians. We've got orders."

Taylor shouted into the ear. "If they don't get to Phu Thuan before sundown, the General's going to be pissed. We can go over to MACV and check it out if you want, but it'll make us late. I guarantee he'll have your ass. If your CO wants to make trouble later, that's his problem."

The pilot put his helmet back on and spoke to the co-pilot through the tiny square microphone dangling from it. The co-pilot looked at the passengers and then back at the pilot before grimacing and pointing upward. The pilot busied himself with the controls. As the engine roar increased, the woman bent over. The shawl fluttered in the rotor wind, revealing the child's eyes screwed shut under the precise bangs and a cascade of tears rolling across the round cheeks. The woman's eyes burned at him in a melange of accusation and resignation. He opened his mouth to speak to her, but the engine bellowed even louder, they left the ground, and he shut up to watch.

The pilot turned until they pointed away from the building, then moved forward in the peculiar nosedown configuration that Taylor assumed had something to do with building up air speed. Whatever the reason, he was glad when they leveled and gained altitude. The woman turned away and looked out her side, closing him out.

The city lounged in sprawling shadow, wearing a softness he had never seen before. They flew over the Phu Tho race track and the normally unremarkable flat expanse was a watercolor image, pleasantly diffuse in the waning light. Looking back, he saw the spoked-wheel shape of the Trung Tom Cai Huan, euphemistically the Reeducation Center, but actually a grinding harsh prison. They went into a banking turn, heading more directly to the south. Ahead was the square hulk of the riverbank market, the Cho Binh Toy. A sense of discord in his spirit distracted Taylor and he glanced straight down at the markers of the Quang Dong cemetery, where he'd known it must be. The beauties of the late afternoon disappeared in the bile that burned the back of his throat. He moved his bundle to a more secure position between his feet and leaned back, eyes closed, waiting out the ride.

The woman turned her eyes to their limits in his direction, like a wary animal assuring itself that a watcher slept. His thinned lips twitched and she turned away again.

The attitude change of the descent galvanized Taylor to action. He leaned forward to tap the pilot on the shoulder and motioned to use the co-pilot's microphone. The pilot shrugged approval and Taylor took the helmet.

"I want you to put us down on the opposite side of the village from the two Saigon Colonels running the show down there."

The pilot looked suspicious. "Why?"

"Because the lady's afraid of them. She doesn't really trust them, you know?"

The pilot nodded. "That don't surprise me. What's she got to do with all this?"

"She's the one who's going to get those people out of the ground." He pointed at the village, the search parties clearly visible now, prodding the earth and kicking at brush, eddying outward from a knot of personnel easily identified as the command group.

"I've gone along with you this far," the pilot said. "I'll let you out right over there." He pointed and Taylor gave him a thumbs-up. The co-pilot retrieved his helmet with the aggrieved air of a man imposed upon.

A few moments later the helicopter was whirling in dust, bobbing on the air trapped under the rotors until it forced its way onto the ground. Vietnamese soldiers watched with mild curiosity when Taylor and the woman with her child tumbled out and trotted beyond reach of the blades. Another storm of dust erupted as the pilot lifted off. Taylor peered through it, a hand shielding his eyes. He spotted what he needed quickly and, motioning the woman to remain, hurried toward a trooper carrying a radio. A few words of explanation to the startled Vietnamese Lieutenant and he was using it, in contact with Winter.

"What are you doing on the wrong side of the village?" Winter demanded, scorning radio procedure. "If you've got information, get it over here. Was that a woman got off with you? What the hell are you doing?"

"Finishing this thing. Have you been using a speaker for your negotiations?"

"Affirmative. What's that got to do with you?"

"Checking, Colonel, checking. You used it from where you are now?"

"Yes, goddamit! Time's running out! If you've got something, you get here with it! Now!"

Taylor handed the microphone back to the radioman and faced the Lieutenant. "You are to move your men. Report to the helicopter pad as quickly as possible. It is urgent."

The Lieutenant, fighting the shock of an American fluent in his language, hurried to obey. He shouted orders and noncoms repeated them and in minutes the last of the troops were moving into the gathering dusk at a trot. Impatiently, Taylor waited until they were completely out of sight, then grabbed the woman's shoulder with a muttered apology and hustled her forward toward the village. At the edge of a field, he stopped her. Before them, large-leaved plants almost as tall as his head whispered in the evening breeze, geometric ranks across the ten or fifteen yards to the first houses.

Taylor opened his bundle and extracted a battery-powered loudspeaker. He aimed it across the stroking leaves and spoke, the sound harsh on the gentle night.

"Binh! Nguyen Binh, do you know who I am? My name is Taylor and my wife is dead because of men like you! Do you hear me?"

Across the village Loc's eyes widened in amazement. Winter flinched as if struck. The only one of them to speak was Harker, and he repeated, "Oh, no. Oh, no," until Winter glared him to silence.

"Is he mad?" Loc asked Winter.

"I don't know. I'm afraid—."

Taylor's amplified shouting interrupted him. "Answer me, Binh! Have you already cheated me and blown your rotten head off? I hope not, because I have a surprise for you!"

Binh's answer, muffled and impossible to locate, floated out of the village.

"I have heard of you, Taylor. I did not know of your wife. How could I know anything of your misfortune?"

"Because you made it possible! You did not shoot the rocket, but you planned its shipment, arranged the hiding place, everything!"

Binh's answer dragged like something from a grave. "I have spoken to Colonel Loc and Colonel Winter. They wish me to surrender and I have told them I may. Now you come with curses. What assurance do I have that I will not be killed as soon as you see me?"

Winter spoke into his loudspeaker quickly. "You have my word, Binh. Neither you nor any of your men will be harmed in any way if you surrender now! I promise you that, as does Colonel Loc!"

"And yet your Major screams at me from the other side of the village. I will need time to think."

Winter looked around, seeing the last quarter of the sun above the horizon and felt Binh slipping away the same way. He pounded the horn of the speaker into the palm of the opposite hand. A gust of wind rustled the thatched roofs in dry laughter just as Taylor's voice rose again.

"Binh! Before you crawl back into your hole, there is someone here who has something to say to you!"

Winter looked to Loc. "What's that maniac—?" he managed and then the woman's high singsong filled the air.

"We are here! He says—!" Abruptly, the amplifier was

500

turned off. Without the loudspeaker she was barely audible, a faint shrillness that crept between the empty houses.

"Jesus," Winter breathed, then harshly, to Harker, "Get over there. Take some troops. Stop that crazy bastard. *Move*, goddamit!"

Harker was running, pulling confused Vietnamese in his wake when Taylor started again.

"There's more, Binh, much more. I told you my wife died? She was pregnant, you sonofabitch. Maybe my child would have been a girl. Think of that, Binh, and listen."

Silence washed over the entire village, even Harker and his party stopping in their tracks. A night bird called, a minor note sliding downward in lament. It faded in the dark and then there was the child's cry. One word—"Father!"—and a scream that struck into the brain like opposing electric currents that first numbed and then replaced that small mercy with liquid fire.

Winter was on his speaker as soon as he could make his hand move. "Binh! We have men moving to stop him! Don't do anything! We will stop him now!"

"No!" Taylor's voice cracked, the metallic shriek appalling. "If you send anyone after me, I'll blow them apart, I swear it! And if that bastard does not come out of his hole, he can listen to them die. You hear, Binh? And if you die first, you make their path no better. They will pay for your death. You have ten seconds. Do you want the child to speak again?"

"Do not!" The voice was higher pitched. "Colonel Loc! Colonel Winter! You are soldiers, you cannot let this happen!"

As Winter raised the speaker, Loc placed a hand on the arm. The larger man halted, his lower lip writhing from the action of teeth chewing the inside of it. Loc took the instrument from him. Corporal Minh chose that moment to trot up with flashlights. Loc carefully tested his before switching on the bullhorn.

"Binh." The penetrating voice was a vast change from what had gone before. "We are helpless. We have opposed each other a long time, seen many things. We know we are caught on a river of events. This is a thing we can do nothing about. It is your choice."

A hush unfolded across the village and the personnel

watching it. It spoke falsely of rural peace, but was none the less embraced by all. Unnoticed, darkness had moved in, as well. In the void left by the unspeaking bullhorns, insects broke into tremulous chorus. Then, as if reopening a wound, the child began to cry. The sound seemed not much louder than the buzz of the gnats rising from the brush and it was met by a concurrent taking in of breath by everyone hearing it.

Binh said, "If you will come to the center of the village, I will surrender to you, but first I must see my wife and child."

Pre-empting Winter and Loc, Taylor said, "Impossible. I will bring them close enough for you to see and I will come unarmed, but you will surrender before you speak to them."

Beaten, Binh said, "I agree."

The two Colonels hurried down the dark street, flashlights knifing their way, more in search of Taylor than Binh.

A Vietnamese stepped into the street through the door of a house in the center of the village. Shorter than average, he posed in a wary crouch that accentuated his smallness. The M-16 cradled in the crook of his arm was loosely directed at Loc and Winter. Even as he straightened from the crouch, his final posture was stooped, as if the weight of the weapon hampered him. Lines of exhaustion as telling as fissures in sundried paddy riddled his face.

"I am Binh," he said.

The announcement shocked Winter. He had believed this round-shouldered little man was no more than an advance, sent to test the opposition's integrity, and it was in fact the man he'd sought for years. Now he stood revealed by the merciless flashlights as a picture of uneffectiveness, ragged in filthy khaki shorts, threadbare shirt, and sandals made of tire tread.

Winter's first reaction was irritation. The man who'd eluded him for so long shouldn't look like an incompetent ragpicker. It was demeaning. He searched for something he could respect and when he finally sought the other's features, not as a captor but as one man trying to see another, he found it in Binh's determination to disguise the fear and depression of this moment. Their eyes locked and Winter would have sworn the Vietnamese strained to lift his chin. He was certain he saw something in the return stare of the weary eyes, something that spoke of pride and an intent to forge better days. It made Winter feel much better.

"Where is your Major?" Binh demanded.

"Right here," Taylor answered. He switched on a flashlight and the beams from the others homed on him instantly. Binh inhaled sharply at what they revealed.

Taylor grinned wildly, squinting in the light. He had the child in his arms, left nestling the body, right hand pressed against her head, partially obscuring the face. The hand also held a grenade. The woman hovered behind him, her nervous mincing reminding Winter of a moth pinioned by the accusing light aimed at the man in front of her.

Taylor said, "I cannot see you very well, Binh, but I see the rifle in your hands. You know the pin is pulled on this grenade. Let yourself be searched, call out your men, and give up your rifle. Then I will let these two speak. I do not trust you or them and I have told them if they try to give you a message or if you try to give them one, you will all die right here."

Binh moved the rifle suggestively, but only said, "You are surely the son of all the evil in the world." Without removing his gaze from the girl, he called out over his shoulder.

Men began to file from the building, dirt from the tunnels tumbling from their clothes. Business-like troops collected their weapons as if charging admission to the bright lights that made the prisoners wince and turn away. The speechless responses of the captured to the infrequent curt commands of the captors merely heightened the eerie efficiency of the operation.

The group of six in their elongated formation with Binh in the center concentrated on each other. Taylor's wolf-like mask drew Binh's eyes like a magnet and each time the round-shouldered man looked at it his hands trembled on the weapon he still held.

When the final man was led away Binh gave his rifle to Loc without a word and stood unmoving while a trooper conducted a careful search of his body. At its completion Winter curtly ordered Taylor to free the child.

Slowly, he lowered her, keeping her within the circle of his arms while he replaced the pin in the grenade. He made several efforts to insert it without looking and it was only after Winter grunted impatiently that he was willing to take his eyes from Binh long enough to do the job.

When he pulled his arms away with the now-safe grenade in

503

his hand, the little girl winced at the dazzle of flashlights suddenly striking her face. She raised her hands and cried out, dodging behind Taylor and running for her mother. As the woman was scooping up the child, Winter was past Binh and across the ground separating him from the Marine. He brought his light up and across, the beam disappearing with the solid crunch of the plastic case against Taylor's jaw.

Taylor's cover flew to the side and he staggered back, catching himself on the corner of one of the houses. Harker ran toward them, his light flashing across Taylor's face, picking out the trickle of blood from his cut cheek. Still clutching the grenade, Taylor dabbed with the back of his hand at the stream.

The woman rushed forward as quickly as the burden of the child permitted. "Colonel, Colonel! You must not hit him! We helped him!"

Winter looked dazed and angry. "Helped?" he repeated.

Binh virtually screeched. "You tricked me! That is not my wife and child! This is some bitch you—!" The ranting stopped as Taylor brushed past Winter and moved on him. The beam of Harker's light held fast to the cold face as if the weight of the illumination would arrest him. It merely accentuated the unheeded blood flowing down his right cheek. Loc shook himself into motion, but it was Winter who first reached Taylor's side, holding him by the arm. He spoke rapidly in an insistent voice that carried to the others only as bass vibration.

Taylor acted as a man called from sleep-walking, life coming back to his face in hesitant steps. Binh watched him carefully, understanding exactly what he was seeing and prepared to run if the process changed unfavorably.

The woman advanced, tugging the reluctant child. Taylor heard her, looked back, and when he again looked at Binh, he was smiling. It was a hard smile with the madness gone from the eyes above it.

He said, "Binh, I want to introduce Nguyen Thi Oanh, the widow of Major Nguyen Ngoc Duc. The little girl is their youngest daughter."

Harker's flashlight swiveled to her face and Winter said, "Oh, God," very softly. She stepped up beside Taylor, glaring at Winter before addressing herself to Binh.

"These men have kept your wife and child hidden and protected. Because of them, your family lives.''

Binh's eyes darted around the half-circle facing him. His mouth worked as the implications of the two short statements reached him and in the end he sagged. His sloping shoulders rolled forward, pulling his torso off center and giving him the look of a man hitched to a plow. Just before he dropped his gaze to the ground he glanced at Loc and flat eyes spoke the totality of his collapse.

Loc snapped his fingers and Corporal Minh materialized from somewhere to lead Binh away.

Winter extended a hand to Taylor. "God, I'm sorry," he said. "It was so real, and after—after everything—." He waved the other hand uselessly. "I should have known. I wish I could tell you how sorry I am."

Taylor pulled his hand from the grasp and reached for the cut on his cheekbone. *Ba* Oanh clucked at him and caught the hand, calling sharply into the darkness for bandages. A trooper ran toward them with a first-aid kit. They all watched with quiet amusement as she commandeered the equipment and dismissed its owner before ministering to the wound herself. The child clung to her trousers and watched with rapt attention.

While she worked on him, Taylor said, "It was necessary for you to believe, Colonel. You're not that good an actor. It was what we needed to convince Binh."

Loc said, "Am I the only one who wasn't tricked? I remembered Tu. I only wondered how you had convinced Binh's wife to help save his life. I never thought of *Ba* Oanh. That was very clever."

She sniffed. "That man is one of the enemies my husband fought all his life. When Major Taylor came to me, I was ready." She patted the last strip of tape in place. "There. Now I will leave you to talk."

Minh reappeared, as if on cue. Loc said, "We must wait for morning to leave here. A tent is being put up for you and your daughter and, of course, there will be food. Corporal Minh will show you."

She thanked him and turned to leave and he said, "One more thing, please. I want to tell you you are a very brave woman. Your husband would be very proud."

She blinked rapidly, finding a small smile for answer. Her

daughter watched carefully and, taking her cue from her mother, essayed a smile for Loc, half-turning with shyness. He smiled broadly and then turned away himself. *Ba* Oanh bowed quickly to the others and moved toward the fires where the troopers were already preparing rations.

Loc doused his light, reaching for a cigarette as he did, offering one to Taylor. Harker turned off his light. For a full minute, they all stood in silence.

Winter broke it. "It doesn't seem real. The fact of it hasn't really come through yet." He gently shook Loc's bicep. "We've got him, old friend. He's a prisoner."

They moved toward the troops in step, Loc agreeing as they went. "It's true. Now we must hope he will tell us the things we need to know."

Winter spoke over his shoulder at Taylor and Harker. "We're indebted to you two."

Taylor nodded thanks, leaving the oral performance to Harker. He knew courtesy required words of some kind but he was too spent to think about them. He lost himself in observing the scene around him.

Small groups of soldiers hunched over fires or stood around eating, sipping from canteens, talking and laughing. In the distance, Coleman lanterns burned bright on fresh-cut poles, their harsh glare spilling onto the interrogators at their tables, collecting data from the villagers. Those waiting their turn squatted on their haunches and looked at this new development with the unrevealing watchfulness of thousands of years of practice. In the fire-glow weapons gleamed red and black and young faces lived with heedless vigor. Under harsher lights the administrators harvested what was due them. The people endured. The uniforms and the weapons and the philosophies changed and the people endured.

Winter and Loc stopped by their radio where their cots and sleeping bags were already positioned. Taylor sank to the ground and was wondering if he could scrounge better sleeping arrangements than the bare deck when Harker settled next to him.

He said, "There's something I've got to ask you," and Taylor welcomed the interruption of his own musings.

"What's on your mind?"

Harker plucked at some weeds. "We've been together

almost a year, Tay. I like you and I think you're a damned good soldier. Or Marine, if you want to get picky. I have to tell you that, because I have to ask you something."

Taylor raised a hand. "If it concerns Ly—."

"Hey, man. No." Harker was vehement. "It's this deal tonight. Look, you're leaving damned soon. I've learned a lot from you and Winter and I'm trying to put together some things in my head. It sounds self important to call it a philosophy, but that's what it amounts to. So I have to ask. The bluff about Binh's wife—let's say you didn't have a chance to run it. What then?"

Taylor knew he should be offended, yet felt nothing. He wondered what that signified. He said, "In other words, if it was really Binh's wife, could I have tortured her to get him out? No."

Harker said, "But then you'd be beaten. He only came out because he knew you'd do it."

"He said it himself," Taylor said. "Didn't you hear him? I cheated him, the same as I cheated Tu. Listen, people who tell you there's nothing more important than a human life are full of shit, understand? The things a man believes in, what he loves—if he's not willing to die for them, he's not worth a damn. I took that away from Binh and Tu, I wouldn't let them die for what they believe. I fight them, but I know what makes them tick. We're exactly alike, up to a point. I had to bring *Ba* Oanh out here instead of Binh's wife and I couldn't let Tho keep beating Tu until he died. Both of them know a dream's worth any number of lives. The 'holy life' people? They're easy. They'll always supply their own reason for living. They'll argue and sometimes they'll even fight, but as soon as things get hot, they'll be off somewhere with their reason to live. You want a philosophy? I'll give you one. Learn to love those bastards, buddy, 'cause they're going to get you killed, sooner or later. They'll go on mouthing their noble bullshit and when it's time to make it stick, they'll send in the scum, the fools who believed them, the professionals, and the guys poor enough and dumb enough to get drafted."

Harker waited patiently to see if there was more, a form of nonreaction that surprised Taylor. When the younger man determined there was nothing else forthcoming, he bobbed his head once, as if settling everything he'd heard into place, and turned away. To all outward appearances, he was satisfied. It was an odd performance and Taylor damned him for lifting the latch on such an outburst. Despite having the other man's back to him, Taylor felt exposed. He drew his knees up and wrapped his arms around them.

They were up at dawn to hear the heavy drone of the approaching helicopters. The troops and villagers watched as the star performers in the drama prepared to leave the stage.

It went uneventfully.

Taylor watched Binh's awkward maneuvering to board the machine with his hands bound behind his back. The shoulders twisted for balance and the leg muscles squirmed in ridged patterns to hold the body stable. No one offered to help him.

A movement to his left caught Taylor's eyes and he looked to see Loc assisting *Ba* Oanh and her daughter toward the approaching second helicopter.

As his ride lifted off, he got another glimpse of her and thought of Binh's wife. He thought of Harker's question and asked himself if the idea to use *Ba* Oanh had its root in a genuine desire to hurt Binh and his wife. He scorned the thought as contemptible until the memory of Ly forced itself on him and he had to close his mind to everything.

53

THEY SAT IN THE AIRPORT BAR, listening to the laughter and shouting, drinking *Ba Muoi Ba* in celebration. Winter raised his bottle in toast.

"To your last swallow of this stuff, Tay. We'll meet again some day."

Taylor lifted his glass. "Better times."

Loc and Harker joined in the ritual.

"You will be retiring?" Loc asked, knowing the answer. "What will you do when you are a civilian?"

"Nothing." Taylor answered the questioning looks with a faint smile. "Oh, I'll get a job and all, but from here on, I'm not involved. Never again. I'm going to enjoy what I can and ignore the rest."

"No plans at all?" Winter pressed.

"Nope. It's all gone, Colonel. All the caring, all the commitment, all the worry about 'the right thing.' I'm going my way. *My* way. God help anyone who messes with me."

"Well, that's some relief." Winter worked at levity. "It's good to know you're as hostile as ever."

"For sure." Taylor was unsmiling. "I want to be left entirely alone. I don't think that's asking so much."

Loc said, "It is asking the impossible," tapping ash from his cigarette, "but I hope it comes to you, my friend. You have earned it."

Taylor raised his glass in salute then said to Winter, "And what about you, Colonel? You're short, even shorter than Harker."

Winter said, "Not really. I'm retiring, trying to take it right here. I've got a job offer."

"You're kidding!" Taylor was truly surprised. "When's all this supposed to happen?"

"I'm still working on it. As soon as possible."

Taylor turned to Loc. "I'm sure you knew. Will you be working together at something?"

Loc's near-smile moved across his lips. "Possibly. There are many things that need done. I am not so ready to be a civilian, however. It will be a long time before I am convinced Binh has told us all he can, for instance. However, Colonel Winter and I may be involved in the same project at some time. Who can say?"

Harker laughed. "I'll bet on it. You two won't give poor Charlie any slack at all, will you?"

"I don't really believe we'll have much longer to trouble him," Loc answered. There was apology in his manner and Winter shifted nervously. Without looking directly at him, Loc released the smile for another fleeting moment. He continued to speak to Harker. "My old friend grows uncomfortable. He has heard my song before and finds the melody unpleasant."

Taylor said, "We haven't heard it." He threw out his arm in an exaggerated sweep and ostentatiously scrutinized his watch. "And in thirty minutes I'll be gone and never get the chance to hear it."

Loc pursed his lips before starting. "I think my country is doomed," he said. "Once you have all gone home, I think we will be overrun." Reading the disagreement in their faces, he continued forcefully. "It is not your fault. Certainly not entirely your fault. Your country has tried very hard and honorably to help us become a nation. Many here have abused that effort and the efforts of thousands of our own people. We have taken the worst of your culture and grafted it onto the worst of ours. It is a sickly plant." He looked past them, past the airport, past anything they could see. "I will continue to work for my country, of course, as long as either of us lives."

Winter made a palms-up gesture of helplessness at the other two. "What can I tell you? He's getting to be the most pessimistic old bastard around. Here I'm trying to stay here and he's telling me I won't have any place to stay pretty soon. I think he's trying to get rid of me."

Loc winked at Taylor. "Perhaps there is an empty seat on your plane?"

They all laughed at that, and then Loc sobered again. He faced Harker.

"This is where the real future lies. He is young enough to watch our final chapter and start a new one. We are all used up, as you Americans would say, but here is a man who truly holds the future. What have you to say on this memorable occasion?"

Instead of the deferential smile they each expected, Harker slowly scanned from one to the other until their discomfort was clear. When he spoke, he bent his neck and watched his fingers massage balls of wet paper from the label of his beer bottle.

"I agree with both Colonel Loc and Major Taylor, in a way." He glanced apology at a stern Winter before continuing. "I don't know if Nam'll be overrun or killed from inside, but I don't think it can last with us gone. And when I get back home, I don't want anyone ever telling me again, "The Army should be doing this,' or 'The Army should be doing that.' The Army'll figure out what's best for the Army, if people like me have anything to say about it. We've learned from this mess, too. After this, we'll go to war knowing what's in it for us. If everything's a question of politics, we're going to be right in there. We're being ripped off, our chance to win's being jerked away from us. Those assholes in the States are creating a generation of officers and non-coms who'll never forget that. Guys like Miller and Kimble and Allen—look at what they paid and what they're getting back. For a while, everybody's going to try to forget stuff like that. But you know someday they'll remember how they got here, the lies they ate. The proudest men in the country have been hurt and cheated, and worst of all, they've been shamed. The ones back home hollering 'what if they gave a war and no one came?' should have thought about 'what if we holler for help and there's a price?', 'cause that's where we're at now. They've lost a war and turned loose a new animal. I'm curious as hell to see how it behaves, to tell you the truth.''

Winter was pounding on Taylor's shoulder. "Hey, gyrene, can't you hear? That's your plane they just called! Move out!''

Harker's speech was gone, washed away in the joy of the moment and they laughed and shook hands. The long benches of the waiting room unloaded their impatient cargo and the line was moving forward, the loudspeaker droning about senior officers and women to the head of the line and no one was caring what anyone said. It was an event that precision would never touch and disorganization would never disturb.

They were on their way to The World.

Taylor reached the fence separating the terminal from the field and slapped it as he passed through. Winter thumped him on the back one last time, and the three of them peeled off to watch him load aboard.

Crossing the apron to the plane itself, the line spread out as water running down a window pane will shunt drops off on semi-independent routes only to draw them all to a common meeting place in the end.

Aboard, Taylor exerted himself to get a window seat on the terminal side, knowing his friends would be looking for him. He got one, settling in, smiling at his own haste. That done, he searched until he spotted them. He held a hand to the window, waggled it, and finally pulled his handkerchief free and waved that. At least a dozen people waved back at it, none of them anyone he knew, so he tucked it back in his pocket.

The stewardess began her spiel about oxygen masks and life jackets. Another blond, she could have been the sister of the one he'd seen crying when he got off the plane right here at Tan Son Nhut.

How long ago had that been? Not even a year? Incon-

ceivable. A century. So many things. Ly.

He snapped his head away from blank contemplation of the back of the seat and looked outside for one last glimpse as the first delicate tremble announced their movement.

Suddenly he was looking directly into Harker's eyes and he felt the distance between them shrinking in an elastic retraction that drew them face to face. The blue-lake eyes were calculating and although there was a glow in them, it was only the brittle gleam of crystals that reflect light and never know a warmth of their own. There was purpose there, and dedication, and he admired a myriad attributes even as he mourned their emptiness because look as he would, there was no sign of a soul.

The motion of the plane broke the contact and Taylor's aimless view found the blond stewardess as she finished her lecture. She smiled at him, a lovely, happy smile.